Praise for Karen Kingsbury's Books

Waiting for Morning

"What a talent! I love her work."

Gary Smalley, best-selling author

"Kingsbury not only entertains but goes a step further and confronts readers with situations that are all too common, even for Christians. At the same time, it will remind believers of God's mercy and challenge them to pray for America. The book…reveals God's awesome love and His amazing ability to turn moments of weakness into times of strengthening."

Christian Retailing, Spotlight Review

A Moment of Weakness

"Kingsbury spins a tale of love and loss, lies and betrayal, that sent me breathlessly turning pages."

Liz Curtis Higgs, best-selling author of *Bookends* and *Mixed Signals*

"A gripping love story. *A Moment of Weakness* demonstrates the devastating consequences of wrong choices, and the long shadows deception casts over the lives of God's children. It also shows the even longer reach of God's providence, grace, and forgiveness."

Randy Alcorn, best-selling author

"One message shines clear and strong through Karen Kingsbury's *A Moment of Weakness:* Our loving God is a God of second chances."

Angela Elwell Hunt, best-selling author of *The Immortal*

Halfway to Forever

"*Halfway to Forever* has believable characters you care about. You'll feel their tension, heartbreak, and joy. Karen Kingsbury sweeps readers right in. She really knows how to tell a story!"

RANDY ALCORN, best-selling author of *Deadline* and *The Ishbane Conspiracy*

"Karen Kingsbury's *Halfway to Forever* is an emotionally charged novel of heartache and hope. Keep the tissues handy!"

ROBIN LEE HATCHER, author of *Ribbon of Years* and *The Story Jar*

"Karen's signature style will inspire you and keep you turning pages until the last luscious page."

PATRICIA HICKMAN, award-winning author of *Katrina's Wings* and *Sandpebbles*

Forever Faithful

NOVELS BY KAREN KINGSBURY

Where Yesterday Lives
When Joy Came to Stay
On Every Side
A Time to Dance
A Time to Embrace (sequel to *A Time to Dance*)
One Tuesday Morning
Oceans Apart

THE FOREVER FAITHFUL SERIES

Waiting for Morning
A Moment of Weakness
Halfway to Forever

THE REDEMPTION SERIES

(Co-written with Gary Smalley)
Redemption
Remember
Return
Rejoice
Reunion

THE RED GLOVES CHRISTMAS SERIES

Gideon's Gift
Maggie's Miracle
Sarah's Song

www.karenkingsbury.com

KAREN KINGSBURY

FOREVER FAITHFUL

THE COMPLETE TRILOGY

MULTNOMAH
BOOKS

FOREVER FAITHFUL
PUBLISHED BY MULTNOMAH BOOKS
12265 Oracle Boulevard, Suite 200
Colorado Springs, Colorado 80921

ISBN 978-1-60142-411-2

Wating for Morning and *A Moment of Weakness* are published in association with the literary agency of Arthur Pine Associates Inc. *Halfway to Forever* is published in association with the literary agency of Alive Communications Inc., 7680 Goddard Street, Suite 200, Colorado Springs, CO 80920.

Published in the United States by WaterBrook Multnomah, an imprint of the Crown Publishing Group, a division of Random House Inc., New York.

The Library of Congress cataloged the original editions as follows:
Kingsbury, Karen.
Waiting for morning / Karen Kingsbury.
p. cm.
ISBN: 1-57673-415-3 and 1-59052-020-3
I. Title.
PS3561.I483L66 1999
813'.54—dc21 98-459739

Kingsbury, Karen.
A moment of weakness / Karen Kingbury.
p. cm. — (Multnomah fiction)
ISBN 1-57673-616-4
1. Custody of children—Fiction. I. Title. II. Series.
PS3561.I483 M66 2000
813'.54—dc21 99-050869

Kingsbury, Karen.
Halfway to forever / Karen Kingsbury.
p. cm.
ISBN 157673-899-X (pbk.)
1. Adoption—Fiction. 2. Pregnant Women—Fiction. 3. Brain—Cancer—Patients—Fiction. I. Title.
PS3561.I4873 H35 2002
813'.54—dc21 2001007865

Printed in the United States of America
2011—First Edition

10 9 8 7 6 5 4 3 2 1

BOOK ONE

FOREVER FAITHFUL

Waiting *for* Morning

Dedicated to
my best friend, Donald,
If life's a dance…
then I pray the music keeps playing forever.
Being married to you is the
sweetest song of all.

To Kelsey,
my softhearted little Norm,
I can see in you the beautiful
young woman you are becoming…
especially your eyes,
which so closely resemble your dad's
and your Father's.

To Ty,
my precious son…
whose flowers have given me
the most beautiful bouquet of memories.
I cherish watching you grow
in the image of the daddy you
so clearly emulate.

To Austin,
my greatest miracle…
watching you throw the ball
and make layups
is daily proof of God's unending love
and faithfulness,
even in the darkest days.

And to God Almighty,
Who has—for now—blessed me with these.

Acknowledgments

Writing a novel about the devastating effects of drunk driving was a difficult, emotional journey and one that could not have been taken without borrowing from the pain of others. Searching for that dark place of despair and devastation, I read countless stories of tragic, senseless loss. I pored over the Mothers Against Drunk Drivers Memorial web site and often conducted research through eyes blurred with tears.

For that reason, I wish to thank Mothers Against Drunk Drivers and every person who has ever helped change or tighten a drunk driving law. You may never know this side of heaven all the lives you have saved in the process. I pray you keep on.

Thanks also to the amazing staff at Multnomah Publishers. From sales to marketing to cover design to publicity...please know that God is working through you in ways that will continue to produce books that change lives, especially books like this. Thanks so much for all your help.

Of course, as with my last book, my writing would be nothing without the God-given talents of my editor, Karen Ball. You are a friend and a mentor, and I hope to keep learning from you as long as the Lord allows. Thanks a million times over.

Also thanks to my husband and family for their support and encouragement during what is always an emotional process—the writing of a novel. I am nothing without your collective smiles, cheers, hugs, and endless love throughout the days.

As with other projects, my parents and extended family were again an encouragement that I value deeply. Thanks to you and to the friends in my women's Bible study and other close sisters in Christ who hold me in prayer, asking the Lord to use my writing for his glory.

And finally, a special thanks to my dear friend, Julie Kremer.

One day nearly a decade ago, Julie's husband got a phone call from their teenage daughter. Her friend's car had broken down on the side of the road. Julie's husband did not hesitate but left immediately to help.

While he was out, he was hit and killed by a drunk driver, leaving Julie and two teenage children alone.

I never knew Julie's husband, but I will forever be touched by the way Julie forgave. She brought a Bible to the man who killed her husband, and after that, continued to keep her eyes on the Lord.

Thank you, Julie, for teaching me what it is to forgive…and for giving me a reason to write *Waiting for Morning*.

One

I am in torment within, and in my heart I am disturbed.

LAMENTATIONS 1:20A

Sunday Evening

They were late and that bothered her.

She had been through a list of likely explanations, any one of which was possible. They'd stopped for ice cream; they'd forgotten something back at the campsite; they'd gotten a later start than usual.

Still Hannah Ryan was uneasy. Horrific images, tragic possibilities threatened to take up residence in her mind, and she struggled fiercely to keep them out.

The afternoon was cooling, so she flipped off the air conditioning and opened windows at either end of the house. A hint of jasmine wafted inside and mingled pleasantly with the pungent scent of Pine-Sol and the warm smell of freshly baked chocolate chip cookies.

Minutes passed. Hannah folded two loads of whites, straightened the teal, plaid quilts on both girls' beds again, and wiped down the Formica kitchen countertop for the third time. Determined to fight the fear welling within her, she wrung the worn, pink sponge and angled it against the tiled wall. More air that way, less mildew. She rearranged the cookies on a pretty crystal platter, straightened a stack of floral napkins nearby, and rehearsed once more the plans for dinner.

The house was too quiet.

Praise music. That's what she needed. She sorted through a stack of compact discs until she found one by David Jeremiah.

Good. David Jeremiah would be nice. Calming. Upbeat. Soothing songs that would consume the time, make the waiting more bearable.

She hated it when they were late. Always had. Her family had been gone three days and she missed them, even missed the noise and commotion and constant mess they made.

That was all this was...just a terrible case of missing them.

David Jeremiah's voice filled the house, singing about when the Lord comes and wanting to be there to see it. She drifted back across the living room to the kitchen. *Come on, guys. Get home.*

She stared out the window and willed them back, willed the navy blue Ford Explorer around the corner, where it would move slowly into the driveway, leaking laughter and worn-out teenage girls. Willed her family home where they belonged.

But there was no Explorer, no movement at all save the subtle sway of branches in the aging elm trees that lined the cul-de-sac.

Hannah Ryan sighed, and for just a moment she considered the possibilities. Like all mothers, she was no stranger to the tragedies of others. She had two teenage daughters, after all, and more than once she had read a newspaper article that hit close to home. Once it was a teenager who had, in a moment of silliness, stood in the back of a pickup truck as the driver took off. That unfortunate teen had been catapulted to the roadway, his head shattered, death instant. Another time it was the report of an obsessive boy who stalked some promising young girl and gunned her down in the doorway of her home.

When Hannah's girls were little, other tragedies had jumped off the newspaper pages. The baby in San Diego who found his mother's button and choked to death while she chatted on the phone with her sister. The toddler who wandered out the back gate and was found hours later at the bottom of a neighbor's murky pool.

It was always the same. Hannah would absorb the story,

reading each word intently, and then, for a moment, she would imagine such a thing happening to her family. Better, she thought, to think it through. Play it out so that if she were ever the devastated mother in the sea of heartache that spilled from the morning news, she would be ready. There would be an initial shock, of course, but Hannah usually skimmed past that detail. How could one ever imagine a way to handle such news? But then there would be the reality of a funeral, comforting friends, and ultimately, life would go on. To be absent from the body is to be present with the Lord; wasn't that what they said? She knew this because of her faith.

No, she would not be without hope, no matter the tragedy.

Of course, these thoughts of Hannah's usually happened in less time than it took her to fold the newspaper and toss it in the recycling bin. They were morbid thoughts, she knew. But she was a mother, and there was no getting around the fact that somewhere in the world other mothers were being forced to deal with tragedy.

Other mothers.

That was the key. Eventually, even as she turned from the worn bin of yesterday's news and faced her day, Hannah relished the truth that those tragedies always happened to other mothers. They did not happen to people she knew—and certainly they would not happen to her.

She prayed then, as she did at the end of every such session, thanking God for a devoted, handsome husband with whom she was still very much in love, and for two beautiful daughters strong in their beliefs and on the brink of sweet-sixteen parties and winter dances, graduation and college. She was sorry for those to whom tragedy struck, but at the same time, she was thankful that such things had never happened to her.

Just to be sure, she usually concluded the entire process with a quick and sincere plea, asking God to never let happen to her and hers what had happened to them and theirs.

In that way, Hannah Ryan had been able to live a fairly worry-free life. Tragedy simply did not happen to her. Would not. She had already prayed about it. Scripture taught that the Lord never gave more than one could bear. So Hannah believed God had protected her from tragedy or loss of any kind because he knew she couldn't possibly bear it.

Still, despite all this assurance, tragic thoughts haunted her now as they never had before.

David Jeremiah sang on about holding ground, standing, even when everything in life was falling apart. Hannah listened to the words, and a sudden wave of anxiety caused her heart to skip a beat. She didn't want to stand. She wanted to run into the streets and find them.

She remembered a story her grandmother once told about a day in the early seventies when she was strangely worried about her only son, Hannah's uncle. All day her grandmother had paced and fretted and prayed….

Late that evening she got the call. She knew immediately, of course. Her son had been shot that morning, killed by a Viet Cong bullet. A sixth sense, she called it later. Something only a mother could understand.

Hannah felt that way now, and she hated herself for it. As if by letting herself be anxious she would, in some way, be responsible if something happened to her family.

She reminded herself to breathe. Motionless, hands braced on the edge of the kitchen sink, shoulders tense, she stared out the window. Time slipped away, and David Jeremiah sang out the last of his ten songs. Lyrics floated around her, speaking of the Lord's loving arms and begging him not to let go, not to allow a fall.

Hannah swallowed and noticed her throat was thick and dry. Two minutes passed. The song ended and there was silence. Deafening silence.

The sunlight was changing now, and shadows formed as evening drew near. In all ways that would matter to two teenage girls coming home from a mountain camping trip with their father, it couldn't have been a nicer day in the suburbs of Los Angeles. Bright and warm, a sweet, gentle breeze sifted through the still full trees. Puffy clouds hung suspended in a clear blue sky, ripe with memories of lazy days and starry nights.

It was the last day of a golden summer break.

What could possibly go wrong on a day like this?

Two

How deserted lies the city, once so full of people!

Lamentations 1:1a

Sunday before Dawn

Long before the sun came up, Dr. Tom Ryan stirred from his rumpled sleeping bag and nudged the lumpy forms on either side of him.

"Pssst. Wake up. One hour 'til sunrise."

The sleeping figures buried themselves deeper in the down-filled bags, and one of them groaned.

"Ahhh, Dad. Let's sleep in."

Tom was already on his feet, folding his sleeping bag in a tight, Boy-Scout roll and wrapping it with a nylon cord. He poked his toe first at one form, then the other, tickling them and evoking a giggle from the chief complainer.

"Daaad. Stop!"

"Up and at 'em. We have fish to catch."

Alicia Ryan poked her head out of her bag. "We have enough fish."

Tom was indignant. "Enough fish? Did I hear a Ryan daughter say we have enough fish? *Never* enough fish. That's our creed. Now come on, get up."

More groans, and finally Jenny Ryan's mass of blond curls appeared near the top of her sleeping bag. "Give it up, Alicia. You know how Dad is on the last day."

"That's right." Tom was already pulling a sweater on. "The last day of the Ryan camping trip is famous for being the best day to catch fish."

Alicia sighed and struggled to sit up. She reached for a rubber band and shook her thick brown hair, gathering it into a ponytail. At that hour, Cachuma Lake was cold and damp, and Alicia shivered as she pulled her sleeping bag around her shoulders once more. "What time is it anyway?"

"Not important." Tom unzipped the tent and ducked through the opening. "Time is for the civilized world. Today, there is only us and the fish."

Alicia and Jenny glanced at each other, rolled their eyes, and snickered. "We're coming," Alicia shouted after him. They stretched and climbed into their jeans and sweatshirts.

The annual camping trip was held at Cachuma Lake mostly because it was famous for its fishing. Nestled in the mountains northeast of Santa Barbara off San Marcos pass, the lake was a crystal blue oasis in a canyon that typically experienced temperatures twenty degrees higher than those on the nearby coast. Swimming was not allowed in Cachuma Lake, which supplied all the drinking water to Santa Barbara. For that reason it attracted puritan fishermen, those to whom fishing was a serious venture.

Each year Tom Ryan and his girls spent three days at the lake. Days were devoted to fishing—and occasionally drifting near enough to a secluded cove to watch deer graze unaware. Sometimes they fished in comfortable silence, but many hours were spent with Tom and his teenage girls talking about boys or the importance of a college education or what it meant to live a life that pleased the Lord. There were lighter moments on the water as well, particularly when they recalled embarrassing escapades or memories of other camping trips. Once in a while they laughed so hard they rocked the boat and scared away the fish.

There were afternoon hikes along the narrow shoreline trails, and sometimes they would drive ten minutes to nearby Zaca Lake for a swim or a nap on the beach. Back at the campsite they built a bonfire each evening, cleaned fish, and fried them for dinner. Then in the hours before they turned in, the girls would play cards while their father played his worn acoustic guitar and sang favorite hymns and church choruses.

Campsites were not far from the shore, hidden among gnarled oak trees and without the benefit of running water or modern bathroom facilities. The Ryans brought water in ten-gallon jugs, food in an oversized Coleman cooler, and an old canvas tent that had been in the family for fifteen years. Camping at Cachuma Lake was *roughing it* at its best, and Tom Ryan wouldn't have taken his girls anywhere else.

Jenny stuffed her sleeping bag into its sack and poked her sister in the ribs. "Hey, since it's the last day and all, I just might have to catch more fish than you." She was the youngest, and a friendly competition had always existed between the two.

"Oh, okay." Alicia pretended to be concerned. "I'll try to be worried about it."

Tom kept their aluminum fishing boat docked lakeside while they camped, so there was little to carry as he and the girls waved their flashlights at the trail and made their way to the water.

"It's freezing!" Jenny's loud whisper seemed to echo in the early morning silence. The path was damp and still, awaiting the crest of new-day sunshine to warm it and stir life into the wooded shoreline.

"Remember that feeling this afternoon when we're packing the gear and it's a hundred degrees." Tom grinned.

"I can't believe it's been three days already." Alicia moved close to Jenny so that the girls walked shoulder to shoulder.

"Time flies when you're fishing, that's what I always say." Tom inhaled the air, filled with energy, loving the early hour of the day.

They climbed into the boat and took their seats, adjusting their flashlights so each could see. Tom watched the girls with pride. Like experienced fishermen, they maneuvered about the tackle box and baited their hooks.

"We're off." He flipped the switch on the battery-powered motor, and a deep puttering sound broke the reverie. The sun was climbing quickly, and the girls set aside their flashlights as the boat slipped away from shore.

Four hours later they were back. Jenny was the winner with three catfish, two bass, and a beautiful twelve-inch rainbow trout.

"You guys aren't much competition." She held up her string and sized up her catch. "You were right, Dad, nothing like an early morning run on the lake."

"Oh, be quiet." Tom laughed and shoved his youngest daughter playfully. He and Alicia had caught just five fish between them. "Let's get back to camp. We have a lot to do if we're going to be on the road by two."

Alicia stepped out of the boat and led the way up the trail toward camp. Suddenly Jenny stiffened and pointed at the trail in front of her sister.

"Alicia!" Jenny's scream was shrill and piercing. Tom and Alicia froze, and Tom followed Jenny's pointing finger.... There, coiled two feet from Alicia's muddy hiking boots, was a hissing diamondback rattlesnake.

Tom's heart jumped wildly. "Alicia—" he kept his voice calm, "don't move, honey." He pulled Jenny away and motioned for her to move farther behind him. He had treated snakebites before, but he'd never encountered a snake. This one was already angry and easily within striking distance.

"What should I do, Daddy?" Alicia sounded like a scared little girl.

God, please, protect my girl. And give me wisdom...

"Okay, honey—" he spoke quietly and with more confidence than he felt—"don't let your feet drag in the dirt. Lift them one at a time...very slowly...and walk backward, away from the snake."

Alicia whimpered. "He's staring at me, Daddy. What if he bites me?"

"You'll be all right, sweetheart. That won't happen if you back up slowly." *Please, God, let me be right.* "He doesn't want to bite you."

Alicia nodded. She was an energetic girl, ambitious and rarely given to moments of stillness. But now she moved painstakingly slow, and Tom was proud of her. Right foot, left; right foot, left. Three feet, then four separated her and the hissing snake. Right foot, left…right foot, left.

Tom grabbed her hand and pulled her toward him. Together they backed up even farther to where Jenny waited for them. Alicia crumpled in her father's arms and started to cry.

"Oh, Daddy, I was so scared," she mumbled into his grubby T-shirt.

Tom could feel his pulse returning to normal, and he stroked her hair silently. He could treat snakebites when he was in an emergency room with a vial of antivenin. But here, an hour from urgent care, Alicia might not have made it. "Thank you, God." Then to Alicia, "You did it just right, honey."

Jenny moved in then, wrapping her arms around her father and sister. "I thought you were going to step on him."

Alicia looked at her. "I would've if you hadn't screamed."

Both girls shuddered, and there was a pause while they clung to their father. Fifteen feet away, the snake stopped hissing, uncoiled, and slithered off the path into the shrubbery.

Tom broke the silence. "You know what it was, don't you?"

Alicia sniffled loudly and pulled away from him, running her palms over her jeans. "What?"

"He wanted to see Jenny's catch. Rumors spread quickly along the shoreline in these parts. He had to see for himself."

Alicia and Jenny grinned and wordlessly cued each other so that they ganged up on him and rubbed their knuckles against his head.

"Okay, okay, come on, you monkeys." He took their hands and led them once more toward the campsite. "Let's get the site cleaned up and the car loaded. Mom's waiting for us."

Three

Brian Wesley's body lay contorted, twisted underneath the rear axle of a '93 Honda Civic, while heat from the sweltering Los Angeles pavement radiated through his flesh. He drew breaths in quick, raspy gulps. In the cramped, dark place where he lay, the stench of grease and gasoline was suffocating. His pulse banged loud and fast, the sound of it nearly drowning out the roar of nearby traffic. He had to get air, had to calm the wild beating of his heart, the violent trembling of his hands, and the anxiety that engulfed him.

It had been three weeks since he'd had a drink.

Brian wiped the sweat and grime from his hands onto his worn Levi's and used the last of his remaining strength to steady his fingers. With fierce determination he gripped the torque wrench and made one final turn. There. He tried to breathe more slowly. One Civic rear axle, good as new. Three repairs to go.

If only he could take a few moments to settle his nerves, sip some cool water, maybe chew a piece of mint gum or eat a candy bar. Something, *anything,* before he lost his mind. Every part of him was screaming for a drink. He closed his eyes, and he could feel the fiery liquid sliding over his lips, satisfying the craving that coursed through his veins.

From somewhere near the shop's office, he heard footsteps. They were loud and threatening, making their way toward him.

"Wesley!" The voice barked out over the sound of humming machinery and noisy afternoon traffic.

From underneath the Honda, Brian studied his boss's shoes and struggled to compose himself. He had seen this coming for days. He straightened his legs and used the heels of his worn work boots to push himself out from underneath the car.

"Yeah?" He blinked twice and felt his lip twitch wildly.

Steve Avery, shop manager and owner of Avery Automotive, sized him up like a sack of rotting leftovers. Brian stood and noticed his hands were shaking badly. He forced them into his pockets with a nervous jerk. Avery muttered something about laziness and then turned abruptly.

"Follow me."

I'm finished. Brian swallowed painfully. *Too many guys, not enough work.*

They made their way past several cars in various states of repair and then through a door down a long corridor. Once inside, the roar of the garage died instantly. Avery led the way and made no effort at small talk as they entered a boxy, air-conditioned office.

"Sit down, Wesley." The boss remained standing, sifting through heaps of clutter that covered his imitation oak desk. He did not look at Brian. "I'm laying you off, effective today."

Brian gulped and his heart rate doubled. "Me?"

Avery looked over the rim of his glasses and glowered making Brian feel like a fearful failure of a man. "Yes." Avery spat the word. "Know why?"

Brian shook his head. He couldn't breathe, so talking was out of the question.

"Complaints, Wesley. That Honda was supposed to be done two days ago. These past three weeks you've had more customer complaints than in all your six months combined."

"Well—" Brian tried to steady his voice—"I know business is slow and, uh, with less guys we each have a lot more work and all. So, uh, if you wanna cut my hours some maybe we could, you know, work something out."

Avery stared at him, one eyebrow slightly elevated. "This has nothing to do with slow business. It's you, Wesley. You're the one who's slow. You're lazy and you're making stupid mistakes. There's no discussion here. You're finished."

For an instant Brian thought his anger might actually overcome his anxiety. "Now wait a minute—!" He rose to his feet.

"Sit down!"

Brian's knees buckled as he collapsed back onto the metal folding chair.

"You're not pulling your weight, Wesley. Get your things and leave."

Brian hung his head and rose slowly to his feet. Before the door closed behind him, he felt the distinct blow of one more verbal dagger.

"Too bad you gave up the bottle.... You work better drunk."

Brian stormed around the garage while the others worked quietly, keeping to themselves. He snatched his extra work shirt from the office closet, grabbed his power drill off a dusty shelf, and painstakingly picked up dozens of bits and ratchets, organizing them into his tool chest. Finally, he rolled the ten-drawer red steel container toward his pickup and, with the help of a buddy, heaved it into the bed of his beat-up, white Chevy pickup.

He climbed into the truck, grabbed the wheel with both hands, and dropped his head in defeat.

Brian knew Avery's dig was a lie. He wasn't a better mechanic when he was drinking. Fast maybe, but too sloppy. It was why he'd lost every job he'd ever gotten in the past five years. Customers smelled alcohol on his breath and reported him to the boss, or he'd drink through lunch hour and forget to report back until the next morning.

The drinking had been killing him, destroying him and Carla and everything he'd ever dreamed or desired.

He had tried to quit once three years before. He'd lasted two days. Two lousy days before he woke up in the front seat of his parked car, outside a shady liquor store, at four o'clock in the morning, an empty bottle of Jack Daniels lying on the floor next to him.

After that he'd been a binge drinker for two years. There were five DUIs, two license suspensions, numerous alcohol education classes, and two separate car accidents—once when he rear-ended a neighbor's car and wound up in a head-on collision with a maple tree a block from home, and again when he pulled onto the freeway headed the wrong way. Someone had flashed headlights at him, and he'd turned into a guardrail, narrowly averting a tragedy. No one was really hurt in either accident, and he continued to drink—often waking up with a raging headache and no idea how he'd gotten home.

Carla cried and begged and threatened to leave, but she wasn't serious. Life would always go on as it had—his addiction far more powerful than he.

But all that changed six months earlier when Carla gave birth to their first child, a son, Brian Jr. The boy was a precious reminder of everything Brian had forgotten about life, a tiny living incentive that kindled within him a strong desire to change.

After Brian Jr.'s birth, Brian got the job at Avery Automotive and cut back on his drinking. Finally, three weeks ago, he quit for good. It hadn't been easy. He'd been forced to break ties with Big Al, his drinking partner, and he'd avoided driving by his favorite bars. His hands trembled nonstop, and he had frequent anxiety attacks.

But for the first time in his twenty-eight years, he believed he was a different man. He pictured himself putting in another two years at Avery Automotive and then taking a job with one of the dealers. A high-paying job with medical benefits and a dental plan. He'd buy a new truck and maybe some better tools. Eventually, he and Carla and Brian Jr. could move out of the noisy apartment and rent a small house in a safe neighborhood.

These were big dreams for Brian Wesley, and they had kept

him sober when he didn't think he could last another moment. Now, though, his dreams were good as dead.

He drove out of the shop's parking lot and considered his options. Left turn or right? Left and a mile west on Ventura Boulevard was The Office—a dimly lit sports bar where Brian had drunk away numerous paychecks in the past decade. Right and two miles east was the apartment complex where Carla and Brian Jr. would be spending the afternoon blissfully unaware of Brian's job status.

Right. Turn right. His hands trembled more violently and a thin line of perspiration formed on his upper lip. Panic simmered in his belly, and he gripped the steering wheel harder.

Just one drink, another voice argued. *One drink with the guys, enough to find the courage to face Carla.* He could feel the cool glass, smell the heady scent of forbidden liquor. *One drink. Just one drink.*

He turned his head and stared east. *Carla and Brian Jr.*

Carla would be so disappointed. Especially after he'd struggled to stay clean these past weeks. His arms were shaking now, his knees starting to knock. The drink was calling him, insisting. *One drink...one small drink.*

Three weeks of sobriety had to be worth something, some kind of reward. Besides, if he went home now, he and Carla would have it out, and he'd only wind up out after dark looking for any bottle he could get his hands on. *Do it now*, the voice said. *Just one drink. One drink. Calm your nerves and then go home. She'll never know the difference.*

"I can't...can't let 'em down," he hissed through clenched teeth. He could go home now, tell her the truth, and by tomorrow have a job somewhere else. There were dozens of garage jobs out there. "Just go home." He could feel the anxiety choking his voice, making each breath a struggle. "Come on. You can do it."

He inhaled. It was hard to get enough air. He set his jaw and forced the wheel to the right, toward Carla and Brian Jr.

Then, at the last possible moment, he wrenched the wheel in the other direction, and his pickup swung to the left.

In three minutes he was at The Office. And as he walked inside he could almost feel that first drink sliding smoothly down his throat, washing away his fears and anxiety—and all that remained of his dying dreams.

Nick Crabb was tending bar at The Office that afternoon, straightening bottles and wiping down the counter when a wide-eyed man walked in and stared at him.

"Where's Rod?" The man's feet seemed planted in the entryway.

Rod Jennings was manager at The Office. He worked five days a week and from everything Nick knew about him, he hadn't missed a shift in two years. Rod had a special thing with the regulars, and the guy standing before him had the unmistakable look of someone who had done a great deal of drinking.

Nick dried his hands on a damp towel. "Sick. Food poisoning."

The man blinked and then his shoulders slumped and he sighed. "Figures." He moved toward the bar slowly, hesitating with every step. His hands were shaking, and he glanced over his shoulder nervously.

"Get you a drink?"

The man continued forward in jerky motions until he worked himself onto a stool. "Whiskey on the rocks, straight up." He drummed his fingers anxiously on the bar, his eyes darting from bottle to bottle.

Nick hesitated for a moment. There was something strange about the guy…still he was a customer. Nick grabbed a tumbler, filled it with ice and whiskey, and set it on the bar. "You know Rod?"

"Yeah…old friends, Rod and me." The man's hands trembled

so badly that when he raised his glass he lost a few drops. Then he put the glass to his mouth and the drink disappeared. He set the glass down hard and with more confidence nodded toward the bottle. "Another."

In the other room the opening theme to *Rocky II* began playing. Nick poured a second drink. And a third. And another and another and another.

By the time the sad-looking man at the bar was on his twelfth or thirteenth drink in less than two hours, Nick was beginning to get worried. If only Rod were there. He would know whether the man had passed his limit. As it was, Nick had no idea. He was new at The Office—working to pay tuition at California State University Northridge. He watched the man nervously. He'd never had to cut anyone off before. Besides, the guy was Rod's friend. The last thing he wanted to do was offend the boss's buddy.

Nick wandered into the lounge where *Rocky II* was down to the final fight scene. Over the past two hours, an occasional customer had wandered in for a quick drink, but for the most part it was just the lone customer at the bar. From across the room Nick heard the man tap his glass impatiently.

"Another. Get in here and give me another."

His speech wasn't slurred. But he was getting loud and overbearing. Nick sighed and returned to the bar. "You sure?"

The man narrowed his eyes. "Don't get smart with me."

Nick shrugged and reached for the bottle. "You might want to give it a rest, that's all." He nodded toward the television. "Catch the last part of *Rocky* or something." He splashed house whiskey into a fresh glass of ice, and the man took it roughly. He downed it in three gulps and tossed several ten-dollar bills in Nick's direction. He stood then, somewhat slowly, and reached into his pocket, fumbling for something. Nick was about to offer to help when the man stopped and stared at him, his expression suddenly vulnerable.

"You know—" his voice was low and Nick strained to hear

him— "Rod should have been here."

Nick counted the money and placed it in the cash register. "I told you, he's sick."

The man nodded and began fumbling in his pockets again. This time he found his keys, gripped them tightly in his fingers, and looked up. "Rod would have called her."

Nick cocked his head back and studied the stranger. It almost looked like there were tears in his eyes. "Called who?"

"Carla...and then none of this ever would have happened."

Nick leaned against the bar and crossed his arms. "Who's Carla?"

The man's expression hardened again. "Ah, forget it. You know, there ain't nothing wrong with this world can't be fixed with a drink or two."

Nick studied his customer. "Whatever you say."

The man stared at him through narrow eyes. "What would you know about it? You work back there, looking down at guys like me, guys who drink too much."

"Hey, you okay, man?" Maybe, just maybe, this guy shouldn't be driving. Even if he didn't seem drunk.

The man clutched his keys tightly and shook his head. "Never mind me...get back to work." He turned around and headed for the door.

"Hey, wait a minute. Answer me." Nick came after him. "You okay? To drive, I mean?"

The man stopped and turned around. "Mind your own business."

Suddenly Nick was sure. The man shouldn't be driving. "Hey, buddy, why don't you sit down for a minute. I'll call you a cab. It'll be on me."

"You tryin' to say I can't drive myself home?"

"I'm saying I'll hire you a cab, man. Either that or wait a while before you leave."

A string of expletives split the air. "I'll do whatever I want. And right now I'm going home."

Nick wasn't convinced, but the situation seemed out of his hands. His boss had laid out the definition of a drunk on the first day: if someone could talk fine and walk fine and you were still worried about them, ask. Yeah, well, Nick had asked. There was nothing more he could do.

The man reached for the barroom door handle and missed, grabbing a fistful of air and nearly falling onto the floor in the process. Then with a jolt he threw his body against the door and disappeared into the parking lot.

Nick cringed. Several minutes later he heard the roar of a truck and then the sound of squealing tires as someone pulled out of the parking lot onto Ventura Boulevard.

Tom glanced at the clock and grimaced. They'd gotten on the road later than he'd wanted, but they'd still be home before dinner. He glanced at his daughters and grinned.

They had been driving for nearly two hours, and still the girls had not run out of things to talk about. School was about to start and with the annual camping trip behind them, Jenny and Alicia clearly couldn't wait to see their friends, get their class schedules, catch up on the latest teenage gossip. Tom glanced at them in the rearview mirror of the family's Ford Explorer. Sweet, silly, precious girls.

He sighed and tried to memorize their giggling faces. They were fifteen and thirteen that year, and Tom knew his summers with them were numbered. His little girls were growing up.

Years ago when he and Hannah married, he had assumed they'd have sons. When instead they had Alicia and Jenny, Tom made the most of the situation. The girls went fishing with him every summer from the time they were able to walk. They tossed a football with him and played Little League ball as good as any boys in the neighborhood.

But they also climbed onto his lap at night, melting his heart with their silky lashes and wide-eyed adoration. He was their hero, and they were each his princess. For now he was still the only man in their hearts. He knew that would change soon. Precious little time remained before they would be gone with families of their own, so he treasured this trip even more than the others.

He had never known times like this with his father. His parents divorced when he was ten, and though his father promised to stay close, there was never enough time, and the roadway of his adolescence had been paved with unfulfilled intentions and missed opportunities. One boyhood memory stood clear in his mind. He was in Scouts, twelve years old, and it was the morning of the father-son Pinewood Derby. His father was dating a new woman that month and barely had time for Tom. Still, he promised he would meet him that day.

Tom could still see himself, a skinny, freckle-faced kid watching and waiting expectantly for his father that afternoon. One hour, then two. Other fathers offered to include him but Tom said no. His father would come, he was sure. He waited and waited until finally his friends and their fathers began to leave. As he climbed back onto his ten-speed and headed for home, angry tears trickled down his hot cheeks, and he made a promise to himself. He would never be an absent father. When he had children, he would be there for them.

Tom Ryan smiled softly at the noisy girls in the backseat. He had kept his promise.

He leaned back against the headrest and tuned them out, studying the heavy flow of L.A. traffic on Highway 101 through dark amber Ray Bans. He sighed. He already missed the serenity of the lake.

His mind drifted to Hannah. He'd missed her even more… her smile and her laughter, the way she felt in his arms. Amazing, really. After seventeen years of marriage they were still very much in love. He and Hannah were a rare breed anymore, even among their Christian friends. And to think he had almost married someone else. The idea seemed comical now.

He imagined Hannah's reaction when he told her about Alicia and the rattlesnake. She'd probably go on about how the girl could have been bitten and how they were too far into the wilderness to find help and how maybe the camping trip was too dangerous after all.

He grinned. Hannah wasn't one for camping or threading—*impaling,* she called it—worms on fishhooks or getting her fingernails dirty. She was especially afraid of snakes. But Alicia hadn't really been in that much danger. Besides, he was a doctor, a pediatrician. The snake had only added to their adventure. As their annual camping trip went, this was one he and the girls would remember forever.

He maneuvered the Explorer into the right lane and took the Fallbrook exit. A quick stop at the bottom of the off-ramp, and he turned the vehicle left, under the freeway. Typically there would be a wait at the intersection of Fallbrook and Ventura Boulevard, but this time the light was green.

Good. Tom smiled. *Home in ten minutes.* He pulled into the intersection long before the light turned yellow.

Only Jenny saw it coming. There was no time to scream, no time to warn the others like she had earlier along the path at Cachuma Lake. One moment she was looking at Alicia, asking her about Mrs. Watson's English class, and the next, in a mere fraction of an instant, she saw a white locomotive coming straight at them, inches from Alicia's face.

There was a horrific jolt and the deafening sound of twisting, sparking metal and shattering glass. Jenny screamed, but it was too late. The Explorer took to the air like a child's toy spinning wildly and coming to rest wrapped around a telephone pole a hundred feet away.

Then there was nothing but dark, deadly silence.

Four

How like a widow is she, who once was great among the nations!

LAMENTATIONS 1:1B

Sal's Diner had been in business at the corner of Ventura Boulevard and Fallbrook for twenty-five years, and Rae McDermott had worked the counter faithfully for the last fifteen. That summer afternoon she was thankful the lunch crowd had been light. Another half hour and she could leave early. She needed to get some milk at the market before picking up the baby at the sitter's house. She made a mental shopping list as she ran a worn, bleach-soaked dishrag over the counter.

With a sigh, she stretched, then balled up her fists and pressed them into the small of her back. As she did so she glanced outside at the traffic on Ventura...and frowned. A white pickup truck, headed for the intersection, was speeding. Rae felt a rush of dread. The light was red, but the driver showed no signs of stopping.

She moved across the diner, drawn to the scene, desperately hoping the truck would stop. Suddenly, from south of the boulevard, an Explorer came into view on Fallbrook.

"Dear God..."

The scene seemed to unfold in slow motion, and there was nothing Rae could do to stop it. The two vehicles careened toward the intersection, then collided. The impact was so explosive it was surreal, like something from a violent action movie. The Explorer spun off the ground in a cloud of dust and glass and shredded metal, and Rae watched it sail across the street and wrap around a utility pole a hundred feet away.

"Dear God," she whispered again, and dashed across the diner, grabbed the telephone, and dialed 9-1-1.

Sergeant John Miller of the Los Angeles Police Department was a veteran in handling traffic accidents. He had worked traffic for twenty-three years and had seen hundreds of dead bodies. Most of the victims had never seen the crash coming. They were getting off work or heading home from the market with no idea they were living their final moments. Too often Sgt. Miller had lifted a dead child from the backseat of a car or pulled a dead mother out of a mangled vehicle while her baby cried, unaware of its loss. More times than he could remember, he had watched paramedics perform CPR while someone's father or grandfather or sister or niece bled to death on a grease-covered, trash-strewn piece of roadway.

The temptation was to become callous. Survival, his peers called it. Form a tough veneer, a carefully maintained wall between his emotions and the reality of working traffic in a city like Los Angeles. That's how most of the officers he knew coped with their own vulnerability.

But Miller was different. He was a Christian, a born-again believer who had come to understand mangled vehicles and mutilated bodies as part of a fallen world. Often he reassured himself with Scripture..."I know the number of your days, says the Lord...." "What is your life? You are but a mist that appears for a little while..."

No, he hadn't grown callous, but neither did he fear the dangers that lurked on L.A.'s busy streets. Nothing happened outside God's control, and that was all that mattered.

In fact, he believed his presence at various accidents was often divinely appointed. Sometimes, very quietly, he would pray for—or even with—the victim. Once he had held the hand of a man who was bleeding to death as rescue workers used the jaws-of-life to extricate him from his car.

He'd talked to the man through a hole in the shattered windshield. "Do you believe in Jesus?" He volunteered to keep the victim alert throughout the rescue. He wanted to be sure the man would spend eternity with God.

"I know of him."

Father, give me the words... "He is the Son of God, God in the flesh. He died to give you life, and he wants you to have that salvation now. It's yours for the asking."

The other rescue workers continued their noisy efforts, unaware of the dialogue between him and the dying man. The victim had struggled then, choking on his blood. But his words had been vividly clear. "I want that. Yes, please pray for me."

Sgt. Miller did as the man asked. Rescue efforts had been futile, and the man was listed as DOA at the hospital. But the sergeant knew better. The man was very much alive, and he looked forward to seeing him again in heaven.

The very idea of sharing the grace of Jesus Christ with people in their dying moments made him thankful for his position with the LAPD. He likened it to the parable Jesus told of the workers who worked only a short while yet received an entire day's wage. The sergeant saw himself as the man who introduced Jesus to those who only believed a short while yet shared the same salvation as those who had known Christ all their lives. Physical death was a part of life. Because of his work, Sgt. Miller understood that better than most. All the more reason to cling to Jesus, he figured. Death would not have the final say.

Sgt. Miller received the call at 4:25 that afternoon: Accident with multiple injuries at Ventura and Fallbrook. Two fire engines, three ambulances, and four paramedics were on the way, as were two LAPD squad cars. He grabbed his keys and an accident notebook and moved swiftly through the office, out the back door toward his unmarked car. It was his job to orchestrate the roles of each emergency worker, gather witness information, and make sure protocol was followed perfectly in case an arrest was in order.

As always, he asked God to use him mightily in the next few hours and to comfort the victims and their family members.

"It doesn't matter what task you have for me out there, Lord," he whispered as he flipped on his siren. "Just use me."

Brian Wesley opened his eyes. Was he dreaming?

His head hurt.... He looked around and saw that his windshield was shattered. Shards of glass covered his legs and the seat next to him, and he realized he must have been in some kind of accident. He ran his fingers tentatively over his arms and legs.... Nothing seemed to be broken. He rubbed his eyes and shook his head, trying to clear his vision. It was then that he noticed the front end of his truck was missing.

He gazed across the intersection and saw another vehicle wrapped around a utility pole. People were all around it, working to get inside.

Brian's blood ran cold. This was no dream.

He had gotten drunk and now he'd hit somebody.

"Oh, man, please be okay." His arms and legs shook, racked with the beginning of a raw fear more potent than any he had known before. He tried to get out, but his truck door was jammed. He turned around, kicking it open with his heavy work boots. Eyes wide, heart and head pounding, Brian walked across the intersection.

Today is the first day of the rest of your life...

The cliché floated through his mind—and chilled him to the bone.

Two motorists had stopped and were working alongside a woman in an apron. All were trying to free the people inside the vehicle. As Brian drew closer, he saw them lean inside, then together they lifted the limp, bloodied body of a teenage girl from the backseat and lay her gently on the grassy curbside. The woman with the apron covered the girl's legs with a blanket.

"Oh, no..." It took Brian a second to realize the whining voice was his.

In the distance, sirens grew louder with each passing moment.

Brian tried to swallow, but his throat was so dry it almost choked him. "Hey, man, is she...is she all r-r-r-right?" He was consumed with dread, and he felt his knees start to shake again. The woman in the apron looked up at him, studied him for a moment, and then turned back to the girl. The two men were trying to find her pulse, and one of them began giving her mouth-to-mouth resuscitation.

The sirens were very close now, and Brian could see several emergency vehicles speeding into view. Relief swept him. *Hurry! Hurry! She needs you!* He couldn't take his eyes from the girl lying on the curb. The others continued working on her without acknowledging him. Brian saw the woman in the apron begin to cry and the men sit back on their heels. They were giving up.

"W-w-w-wait...she n-n-n-needs help, man!" He moved toward the girl, but the woman in the apron rose to her feet.

"Get back!" She spat the words at him. "You've done enough!"

One of the men came to put a hand on her arm. "Come on. Let's check the others." They studied Brian for an instant, disgust clear on their faces, then turned to what remained of the Explorer.

Brian saw the girl's face then....It was a pretty face, framed by honey-colored brown hair. But it was a lifeless face. Even he could see that. He sank to his knees ten feet from where the girl lay—ten feet from the body of a girl who would never again hold her mother's hand or kiss her daddy good-night or dance across a living room floor....

A wail erupted from somewhere deep within him. He willed himself dead in her place, willed anything that might breathe life into her once more. Then his wailing became one word, so weighted with regret that he felt it would consume him: *"Noooo!"*

Sgt. Miller arrived at the scene moments after the paramedics and saw both vehicles. The first one, a white pickup truck, had heavy front-end damage. The second vehicle was almost unrecognizable. Miller could see it was a Ford Explorer, one of the safest vehicles on the road, but it might have been made of tinfoil the way it wrapped around the pole. The impact must have been unbelievable, like getting broadsided by a freight train.

Sgt. Miller made his way to where a small crowd gathered near the twisted remains. Immediately an officer filled him in on the situation.

"We have a deceased female, maybe fourteen, fifteen years old; and two additional victims, a male, late thirties, head wounds, massive bleeding."

Miller felt his shoulders slump imperceptibly. A young girl with her whole life ahead of her. He made several notations on the accident report and wondered if she had known the Lord. "Third victim?"

"Female, twelve, maybe thirteen years old, head injury and a broken arm. She has the best chance of making it."

"Identification?"

"We have a home address for the male victim, some pictures. Guy's a doctor. Tom Ryan. Female victims look to be his daughters."

"Next of kin?"

"Nothing yet. Figured we'd do a drive-by when the ambulances leave."

Sgt. Miller nodded. They didn't always do drive-by notification. Quite often family members were notified by a hospital representative. But in accidents this serious, with multiple injuries—perhaps even multiple fatalities—the officers thought it was best to notify the family in person.

"Driver of the pickup?"

"Minor injuries. He's in the squad car, cuffed."

"Drunk?"

"Can't you smell him?"

For a moment, Miller felt defeated. Another family destroyed by a drunk driver. Somehow with all their efforts, they weren't doing enough to stop the problem. He pursed his lips. "You do the test?"

"Preliminary. Failed the straight line. I thought I'd wait for you to get the blood test."

"Witnesses?"

"A lady, Rae McDermott, works in the diner across the street. And a couple of motorists. They're still here."

Sgt. Miller strained to see which of the victims was now laying on a stretcher and receiving attention from two paramedics. It was the young female. "Where's the male victim?"

"They're using the jaws-of-life. He's bleeding pretty bad, trapped in the front seat. I don't think he's going to make it."

The sergeant sighed and closed his notebook. He dismissed the officer and approached the mangled vehicle. Fire department rescue workers were busy on one side of the vehicle, so he walked to the other. Sleeping bags and camping gear had spilled onto the road. An ice chest had opened and dead fish littered the roadway as well. What a way to end a camping trip.

He saw a small passage where the window had been and gingerly stuck his head and upper body inside. The victim's entire left side was pinned beneath layers of metal and draped with fireproof tarps. One paramedic was stationed under the tarp, just outside the driver's door, waiting for the instant he could remove the man and begin treatment. Beyond him, another firefighter used a blowtorch to separate the wreckage while the jaws hummed and screeched, working to peel away the layers of metal.

Miller focused on the victim. There was a gash across the man's forehead, and despite the noise, Miller could hear the man struggling to breathe. Still, he seemed semiconscious. Reaching out, Miller took the man's hand in his own. He raised his voice over the machinery. "Sir, can you hear me?"

The man jerked his head twice and his eyelids began to tremble.

"We're doing everything we can to get you out of here. Can you hear me, sir?"

Suddenly the machines stopped as the separated layers were removed and set aside.

"Let's do it!" It was the paramedic stationed under the tarp. He moved, pressing fingers to the man's neck, feeling for a pulse. Then he shouted to the others. "Come on, *move it!* We're losing him!"

"Can you hear me, sir?" Sgt. Miller asked again. The vehicle was quieter inside now, almost tomblike. This time the man stirred and seemed suddenly frantic, anxious to speak.

Help him, Lord, help him say what he wants to say.

Suddenly the man's lips parted and he worked his mouth silently. Miller strained to hear him.

"The girls…"

This wasn't the time to tell him about the older girl. The man would have to remain calm if the rescue was to have a chance of being successful. He squeezed the man's hand. "Sir, they're already out. We're working on them right now."

The man seemed slightly reassured. A gurgling sound came from his throat, and he sucked in another breath. "Tell Hannah—" the man gulped, clearly fighting unconsciousness—"tell Hannah…the girls…I love them." He opened his eyes, and Miller saw an unmistakable peace there.

"I'll tell them. Now you hang on. We're getting you out of here and you can tell them yourself."

The man gulped again and his eyes rolled back for a moment and then closed. His lids twitched violently and once more his lips moved. Miller squeezed the man's hand another time. "Stay calm now, you're almost out of here."

But the man grew more agitated, his mouth opening and shutting soundlessly. He was slipping away, but he seemed desperate to speak.

Sgt. Miller moved closer. "It's okay, sir.... I'm here. I'm listening."

The gurgling grew louder and the man coughed. Miller held back a grimace. The man was choking on his own blood. He was gasping for each breath, and his words were slurred, but finally they were audible.

Miller strained to understand.

"Tell Hannah...tell her...please, forgive...forgive...."

He said something after that but Sgt. Miller couldn't make it out. "You want Hannah to forgive someone, is that it?"

The man's entire body relaxed, and Sgt. Miller thought he saw him nod.

"We're losing pressure!" The paramedic's voice was angry. "Come on, let's *open* this thing." The machines whirred once more, and finally the man was free. Two paramedics lifted him immediately onto a backboard.

"He's not breathing! Prepare to intubate."

In a blur of commotion the paramedics worked on the man, doing everything they could to stabilize him.

Passersby had gathered, and now a crowd of stricken onlookers gaped at the bloodied man, watching the paramedics work frantically to save him. In less than a minute he was loaded into an ambulance while the EMTs used an oxygen pump and manually compressed the man's chest.

As the ambulance drove off, Miller looked around and knew his work at the scene was finished. He'd talked to the witnesses, each of whom had agreed that the driver of the pickup had sped through a red light and hit the Explorer without ever slowing.

Miller looked at his notes. The other driver was Brian Wesley, age twenty-eight...five prior DUIs. He'd been arrested and taken to the West Valley Division, where he would be booked. He had been given a blood alcohol test—the results of which would not be available from the crime lab for several weeks.

If the results were positive, Wesley would be formally charged with whatever crimes the district attorney's office thought they could prove—anything from driving under the influence to vehicular manslaughter. A plea bargain might be struck, but because of the man's prior record and the severity of the accident, most likely the case would be ordered to trial.

Then months or maybe even a year later, after delays and continuances, when the memory of the accident had faded in the minds of witnesses, a trial date would be set. The trial would drag on for a month or more, and finally Brian Wesley might be convicted. At that point, barring some sort of judicial miracle, Wesley would most likely serve less than a year behind bars for destroying the Ryan family.

Sgt. Miller removed his sunglasses and rubbed his temples. Tow trucks had arrived at the scene and were busy removing the wreckage of the two vehicles. It was late, nearly 5:30, and his worst task lay ahead.

He remembered how the injured man had struggled to speak, how desperately he'd wanted to relay what might be his final message to his family. What was it the man had said? Something about getting mad…or about not getting mad. The sergeant wasn't sure anymore; the past hour had been so chaotic, so tense. Besides, the accident hadn't been Mr. Ryan's fault. No one could be angry at him. Miller shrugged. Best to forget it, whatever it was. For all he knew, the man had mumbled the words out of shock or delirium.

Either way, Miller remembered the most important part of Ryan's message: Tell Hannah and the girls he loved them.

Sgt. Miller sighed. It was time to tell Hannah.

Five

Bitterly she weeps at night, tears are upon her cheeks....
There is none to comfort her.

LAMENTATIONS 1:2A

They drove in silence, Sgt. Miller at the wheel and Officer Rolando Santiago making notations, checking the accident report. Miller noticed that the streets were quiet here, lined with mature shade trees and upper-end homes with large, fenced yards. People who lived in this part of the San Fernando Valley generally safeguarded themselves against the perils of city living by driving sturdy vehicles and protecting their homes with custom alarms.

Pity none of those alarms could have protected the Ryan family against this....

Three turns later the squad car pulled up out front of a well-manicured home on a pretty cul-de-sac.

Sgt. Miller noticed a wooden sign near the front door that read "The Ryans." Under their name was the symbol of a Christian fish.

"Believers."

Santiago looked at him. "What's that?"

He nodded toward the symbol. "The Christian fish. The family must be believers."

Officer Santiago shrugged. "You never know after today."

Miller didn't reply but climbed out of the car and headed somberly up the walkway. Santiago walked in step beside him and glanced at his watch. "Let's get this thing over with. I've got dinner plans."

Sgt. Miller studied his partner a moment, but all he could see was the protective wall. He drew a deep breath. "Let me do the talking."

For two hours Hannah Ryan had fought off an exhausting list of possibilities while staring out her kitchen window, but still there was no sign of her family. She wanted to pray, and even tried a time or two, but she held back. It only made the fear worse.

Dread had begun to consume her, and as the minutes became hours, she stopped looking for ways to keep busy. Instead she was continually drawn to the kitchen window, as if she could somehow make them appear by keeping watch. They should have called by now, and anger joined the emotions warring within her.

When the squad car pulled up, she was no longer fiddling with the pink sponge, wiping and rewiping the sink, but rather she was frozen in place, barely breathing, staring at the dusky cul-de-sac.

A pit formed in her stomach and in that instant, she knew.

She closed her eyes. *Lock the door. Close the blinds. Get the car keys and leave.* Anything but greet the officers who were walking deliberately up the sidewalk. Hannah drew a shaky breath and forced her feet to carry her toward the front door. *Calm, calm. Be calm.* She wiped her trembling palms on her jeans and turned the knob.

"Yes?" She did not attempt a smile and neither did the officers.

"Hannah Ryan?"

"Yes, can I help you?"

The older officer hesitated. "Ma'am, I'm Sgt. John Miller with the Los Angeles Police Department. May we come in for a minute?"

No. Go away. I hate that you're here. Hannah opened the

door and the men stepped into the foyer. She did not invite them to go any further.

"Ma'am, maybe if we moved inside and sat down."

"Listen, what's this all about?" Hannah began shivering. She rubbed her arms, trying to ward off the sudden chill. She did not want to sit down, and she was not in the mood for a slow explanation.

"Is your husband Dr. Tom Ryan?"

O God...please... "Yes, what is it? Has he been hurt?"

Sgt. Miller cleared his throat. "I'm afraid there was a car accident, ma'am. He's suffered serious injuries, and he's been taken to the hospital."

Hannah steadied herself. "What about the girls?"

"Mrs. Ryan, why don't you come with us? We'll take you to the hospital so you can be with them."

"No!" Hannah knew she sounded frantic, but she couldn't stop herself. "I want to know about the girls. Are they okay?"

Sgt. Miller moved closer and placed a hand under Hannah's elbow. "Your oldest daughter suffered serious head injuries. The younger girl has a broken arm and a concussion, but her condition is much less serious."

"No!" She ripped her elbow from Sgt. Miller's hand and leveled menacing eyes at him. "That *can't* be! You're lying to me."

"You need to get to the hospital, Mrs. Ryan. May I help you get your things together?"

Hannah spun toward the desk in the kitchen and froze in place. Black spots danced before her eyes, and she grasped the wall to steady herself.

"Ma'am, you all right?" Sgt. Miller's voice was kind, but Hannah didn't want to hear him. She kept her back to the officers and hung her head.

"Listen," she said firmly. "You've made some kind of mistake."

No, God...no. It wasn't true, it couldn't be. They had the wrong Ryan family, or if there was an accident, then Tom and the girls were probably just bruised and a little cut up. After all, they were driving the Explorer. The officers must have mixed up the information. It wasn't their fault. Anyone could get the facts wrong. Hannah forced herself to relax, and the spots went away. She moved across the kitchen and grabbed her purse from the work desk.

"You can leave now." She turned around to face them, the picture of control. "There's obviously been some sort of mistake. My family has a sports utility truck—it's very safe." She pulled her keys from the purse and glanced at the Lexus outside in the driveway. "I better go, now."

"Ma'am, it's not—"

Hannah cut him off. "What hospital?"

Sgt. Miller sighed. "Humana West Hills. Emergency trauma center. Mrs. Ryan, why don't you let us drive you over there?"

"No, I'm fine. Besides, they'll need a ride home if the Explorer's been damaged."

"Do you have a friend or a pastor, someone we could call who could meet you there?"

Hannah stared at him. "A pastor? I don't need a pastor. I told you, they were in a big vehicle. There must be some kind of mistake."

The sergeant studied her, and Hannah hated the look of pity in his eyes. "All right, we'll follow you."

"That's not necessary." Hannah felt mechanical and oddly void of emotion. She walked past the officers, ushered them outside, then locked the front door behind her. "I appreciate your dropping by. They were camping, you know. Monday's the first day of school."

Hannah knew she was not acting rationally, but as she pulled the Lexus onto Roscoe Boulevard, she refused to believe what the officer had said.

She glanced in her rearview mirror and pressed her lips

together. Why on earth had they insisted on driving behind her? Every time she glanced in the mirror, they were there, a constant reminder of their ridiculous story. Their presence was unnerving. Certainly they must have more important tasks than following her to the hospital.

Then, for just an instant, her mind began running ahead. What if they really had been hit? What if they were hurt…or worse? And suddenly she felt a wave of dread and fear and loss and devastation so great, it was like a monster lurking in the recesses of her mind, threatening to break free. If it did, Hannah knew it would destroy her.

She held the darkness at bay and concentrated instead on the simple facts at hand and not the unknown. At least she knew where Tom and the girls were and why they were late. People were in car accidents all the time. That didn't mean anything really bad had happened. She could picture Tom joking with the doctors, and Alicia and Jenny teasing each other about the story they'd tell at school Monday.

Hannah relaxed a bit. She would get there, make sure the hospital had their health insurance information, and take her family home. Eating at The Red Onion was out of the question, but they could pick up some pizzas. Hannah looked at her watch and saw it was nearly seven o'clock. They were probably starving by now.

Sgt. Miller followed Hannah Ryan with care. He had radioed dispatch and asked them to notify the emergency room that the Ryans' next of kin was on the way, and could they please have the staff minister on hand.

Miller thought again of the symbol of faith on the outside of the Ryans' house. How close was this woman with the Lord? She was striking, probably in her midthirties with a figure she obviously worked to maintain. She had blond hair, clear blue eyes, and her clothing and jewelry were casually elegant.

Certainly she seemed strong, self-assured, and in control.

Still…

If her relationship with God wasn't built on the deepest roots, Sgt. Miller doubted she would ever be the same after today.

At last Hannah arrived at the hospital. She said nothing as she entered the trauma center flanked by the two uniformed officers. She introduced herself, and immediately a nurse ushered her into the patient area. There she was directed to sit in a quiet alcove apart from the hustle of activity.

The monster in her mind moved closer, and Hannah smiled in a vain attempt to keep it at bay. "This isn't necessary." She looked at the nurse. "Really, if you could just show me which room my family is in."

The nurse motioned toward one of the doctors, and he immediately picked up his clipboard and approached her. With him was a man who looked like a minister.

One of the officers—Sgt. Miller, was it?—met him halfway and relayed something in hushed tones. The doctor nodded and made a notation on his clipboard. Sgt. Miller turned back to Hannah and pulled something out of his shirt pocket: his business card.

"Call me if you need anything, if you have any questions at all." His tone was filled with compassion. "I'll be praying for you, Mrs. Ryan."

"Thank you." Hannah took the card, glanced at it, and slipped it into her purse.

Sgt. Miller disappeared down the corridor with the other officer at his side. The man with the doctor seemed to take a cue from that because he pulled up two chairs. He sat beside Hannah while the doctor sat directly in front of her, their knees nearly touching. The doctor cleared his throat and looked into Hannah's eyes.

"Mrs. Ryan, I'm Dr. Cleary and this is Scott O'Haver, our hospital chaplain."

Hannah looked from one man to the other and shook her head, her heart pounding. "This isn't necessary. There's been some kind of mistake. My family was in a big vehicle.... It was safe. I just need you to take me to them so I can—"

"Ma'am—" Dr. Cleary interrupted her—"please...let me continue." He looked like a kind man. Something about him exuded authority and confidence. Reluctantly Hannah settled back in her chair.

"My husband's a doctor, too." Hannah watched Dr. Cleary's reaction carefully.

"Yes, I know. I've checked his medical records. I don't think he and I ever worked together." Dr. Cleary seemed to struggle for a moment. *Oh, no. He's afraid to tell me. No, God...please, no.* "How are you doing, Mrs. Ryan?"

"I'm fine. If you could just take me to them...."

Dr. Cleary checked his notes and drew a single breath. He moved closer and set his hand on Hannah's knee.

No. Don't touch me...don't comfort me. Hannah remained silent as she squirmed and slid her hands underneath her legs.

"Mrs. Ryan, I've been working on your husband and the girls for an hour now," he said. "They were in a serious accident, Mrs. Ryan, hit by a speeding pickup truck. The impact was most severe." He paused and his gaze dropped to the floor for an instant before connecting once again with Hannah's. She looked desperately for some sense of reassurance. There was none. "Jenny sustained a broken arm and a concussion. We are checking her for internal injuries, but her vital signs are strong. She's medicated and very sleepy, but I expect her to show significant improvement by tomorrow."

Hannah sat frozen in place, waiting for the doctor to continue.

"I'm very sorry to have to tell you this, but Alicia didn't fare as well."

Hannah began to rock. *No. No. Not Alicia.... Not Alicia.*

He hesitated. "I'm afraid Alicia received more of the impact and suffered massive head injuries." His words were deliberate and measured. "Paramedics arrived on the scene in minutes, but she was already gone. I'm sorry, Mrs. Ryan. She died quickly and without any pain or fear."

"No." Hannah stood up, shaking—and then she screamed. She tried to push past Dr. Cleary, but he held her gently in place until she eased back into the chair, rocking fiercely and wailing. "No! Not Alicia, no!"

The chaplain circled an arm around her shoulders and leaned toward her. Hannah felt herself losing consciousness, and she crumpled slightly in his embrace.

"Please..." She implored him with every fiber, begging him to be wrong. "She can't be dead, Doctor. I want to see her."

Dr. Cleary drew another breath. "I'm sorry, there's more. About your husband, Mrs. Ryan..."

No...not Tom. It's too much, God. Her heart was racing, banging about in her chest.

"Upon impact your husband hit the steering wheel and suffered blunt trauma to his chest. This caused him to bleed from the aorta, the main artery out of the heart. He was conscious at first while rescue workers tried to help him out of the vehicle. Paramedics were able to intubate him to keep his lungs open, but he was bleeding too badly. He died enroute to the hospital. I'm so sorry, Mrs. Ryan.... They did everything they could."

The only thing that kept Hannah from falling on the floor was Rev. O'Haver. She sagged in his grip, struggling to breathe, to think, to move. But all she could do was say the same thing over and over....

"No. No! Not my Tom.... Not my baby, Alicia. Please, God, *no!*"

The world was spinning out of control, and her heart pounded hard and erratically. She closed her eyes, fighting against the vortex of emotions that threatened to consume her.

She knew she was screaming, could hear it, but it was almost as though it were someone else…someone whose very soul had been ripped from her chest. With a shuddering sigh, she straightened, leaning back against her chair. She clenched her teeth to hold back the screams still clawing at her throat, and noted numbly that her eyes were dry. The greatest shock of her entire life and she hadn't cried.

"I want to see them."

Dr. Cleary nodded. "That's fine. Perhaps you'd like to see Jenny first? I think she'd recognize your voice, and it might help her come around."

Hannah nodded, mute. Rev. O'Haver helped her up, and she followed Dr. Cleary to a room sectioned off by curtains. There lay Jenny, oxygen tubes in her nose, an IV dripping into her left arm. Her right arm was in a cast from the shoulder to her hand.

Hannah ached inside as she studied her little girl. She longed to cradle her close and tell her everything was going to be okay.

But it won't, will it? It will never be okay again.

She moved closer to Jenny and smoothed a wisp of blond bangs off her forehead. There were bruises on the right side of her face, and Hannah had to choke back a sob as she ran her fingers over them. Jenny stirred, moaned twice, and moved her head from side to side.

"Jenny, honey…" Hannah leaned closer to her. "It's me, Mom."

Jenny opened her eyes, and Hannah could see what effort it took for her daughter to focus. "Mom? What happened? Where's Dad and Alicia?"

Dr. Cleary stepped forward and Hannah glanced up at him. He shook his head quickly and mouthed the word, "Later."

Hannah nodded and took Jenny's hand. "Honey, you need your rest now. Why don't you try to sleep and I'll be right here."

Jenny had already closed her eyes, and when Hannah was sure she was asleep, she turned to Dr. Cleary.

"I want to see Tom and Alicia." Her own voice sounded foreign to her, and she wondered again why she still hadn't cried. Was this the denial people talked about after receiving terrible news? She closed her eyes briefly. Maybe…maybe something deep within her knew this was all some kind of terrible joke, that Tom and Alicia were fine, that there was nothing to cry over—

With an impatient shake of her head, she opened her eyes to find Dr. Cleary watching her carefully. "Please, Tom and Alicia…"

He sighed sadly. "This way." He led her down a hallway into another room. And there she saw them, Tom and Alicia, side by side on stretchers. Hannah wouldn't learn until later how Dr. Cleary had directed the nurses to prepare their bodies so they would appear less traumatized. The nurses had wrapped a towel around Alicia's bloodied head and tilted her face so that Hannah would not have to see her battered left side. They had done the same for Tom, removed his blood-covered T-shirt, and wiped his face clean. They covered his head wounds and placed blankets over him so that only his face and arms could be seen. Later, Hannah would forget everything she'd heard after receiving news of the accident.

But she would remember forever the way Tom and Alicia looked as they laid lifeless on those stretchers.

"Dear God…" She clasped her hands, bringing them to her chin. The tears came then, torrents of them.

"It happened very quickly, Mrs. Ryan. They didn't suffer."

The doctor's words rang in her head, but still she couldn't believe what she was seeing. She moved into the narrow space between the two gurneys and stood there, facing Tom and Alicia. Sobs catching in her throat, she stooped and circled an arm around each of them. Loud, wracking sobs seized her, and she was sure this was how it felt to die.

Hannah felt disconnected from her body, as if she were playing a role or watching some other woman deal with the fact that her life had been destroyed. But this was no stage drama, and she was the only woman in the room. There was no mistake.

Her life had been perfect...too perfect. Something had gone terribly wrong, and now Tom and Alicia were dead.

She knew she should pray, but for the first time in her life she couldn't. Didn't even want to. God had let this happen to Tom and Alicia. Why pray to him now? Why ask him to comfort her when he had allowed her very existence to be shattered? She looked from her husband to her child, studying them through her tears, willing them to move or speak or smile at her. When they didn't, she bowed her head and wailed. In one violent instant her family had been destroyed—and there was nothing she could do to bring them back.

When she finally regained her composure, she straightened slowly. Drawing a fortifying breath, she looked at Dr. Cleary and saw him extend his hand. For a moment, standing there in his white coat, he looked just like Tom. Hannah took his hand and let him support her as she struggled to keep from passing out. But she stayed there between Tom and Alicia, unwilling to move from their sides.

"I'm so sorry, Mrs. Ryan." Dr. Cleary seemed to wait until he had her attention before continuing. "There's something I need to tell you. Sgt. Miller was with your husband at the accident scene before he died. He wanted me to give you a message from Tom."

Hannah felt her shoulders drop, and she reached for Tom's hand as naturally as she had for the past twenty years. But now his touch was cool and unresponsive. She shuddered.

Dr. Cleary's voice grew softer. "Before he died...Tom said to tell you and the girls that he loved you."

A single sob caught in Hannah's throat, and she looked down at her husband through a blur of tears. She struggled to speak, and the silence hung awkwardly in the air.

"I want some time with them," she said finally.

"Take as long as you like."

Forever. A lifetime. A chance to celebrate our twentieth anniversary, and our thirtieth and fortieth. Time to grow old together and watch our daughters become young women. Time to see Tom walk Alicia and Jenny down the aisle, time to share grandchildren and retirement and vacations on warm, sunny beaches—

Dr. Cleary interrupted her thoughts. "I need to get back to work, but Rev. O'Haver will be outside in the hallway if you need him."

The men left, and Hannah was finally alone. She studied Tom and sobbed softly. She hadn't had time to say good-bye. If only she had gone on the camping trip this year. Maybe she would have seen the truck…she could have warned Tom. It was all her fault. If she'd been with them, they would have come home earlier, and this never would have happened.

Tom still looked so alive, as if he were sleeping. She still held his hand, but now she turned to Alicia. Beautiful, self-assured Alicia. Her firstborn.

She took the girl's lifeless hand in her free one. "Mommy's here, Alicia." She thought of proms and graduation, college, the wedding her daughter would never have…and she began to weep once more. Alicia's hair stuck out in matted tufts from underneath the bandages. Hannah let go of Tom's still hand and reached over to smooth the silky locks, making her daughter more presentable. Alicia looked so lost on the stretcher, almost as if she were a small child again. Where had the time gone? Hannah remembered being at this very hospital fifteen years earlier for Alicia Marie's birth, celebrating life and the promises it held for their tiny daughter. She was such a sweet baby, such a happy little girl….

Alicia's hand was cold, and Hannah ran her thumb over it, trying to warm it as she'd done when her daughter was a toddler. Alicia always had cold hands. Hannah wanted so badly to pick her up and rock her, to take away the hurt as she'd always been able to do in the past. She sniffled loudly. "Alicia, Mommy loves you, honey." She sobbed twice. "I'm here, baby. I'll always be here. Wherever I am I'll take you with me, sweetheart."

She remembered a week earlier when Alicia had stayed up late talking to her about boys and how she'd know when she met the right one. Now there would be no boys—no future. Alicia was gone, and it grieved Hannah beyond anything she'd ever known.

She turned back to Tom. "Why didn't you come home earlier, you big oaf? You never were on time." She tried to laugh, but it became one more sob, and fresh tears filled her eyes. "If only you hadn't been so late…."

She let the thought hang in the still air, and she squeezed her eyes shut. When she opened them, she struggled to speak. "I guess…if Alicia had to go, it's better you go with her." She gulped loudly, and when she spoke her voice was barely a whisper. "Stay with her, Tom. She's so afraid of being alone."

She stooped and kissed him tenderly on the cheek, his final message echoing in her mind, breaking her heart. "I love you, too, Tom. I've loved you since we were kids. I always have." She sobbed hard. "I always will."

She carefully arranged Tom's hands on his chest, then did the same for Alicia. But she couldn't bear to leave. She bent over and wrapped her arms around them, holding them close and giving in again to the wrenching sobs….

This couldn't be happening….

Finally, when it seemed as if days had passed, she rose and kissed Alicia on the cheek. She smoothed her hair, knowing it was the last time she'd ever do so. "Good-bye…" She turned to Tom and traced his lips with her finger. Then she kissed him tenderly and studied his face one last time.

Finally she turned and, against every instinct in her body, she left.

Rev. O'Haver waited in the hallway outside and cleared his throat as she approached. "Mrs. Ryan, may I speak with you a moment?"

Hannah stopped and waited. She was struggling to find the strength to move, even to breathe, and all she wanted was to be with Jenny. She didn't need some stranger offering pat answers.

"Mrs. Ryan...I understand you and your family are Christians?"

A single huff escaped Hannah's throat, and she wiped her eyes with the tips of her fingers. "Yes, we are." She paused, trying to make sense of her feelings. "A lot of good it did us."

The reverend hesitated. "I can't imagine what you're going through, Mrs. Ryan, but please know it's normal to be angry at God." He paused again. "I'd like to pray with you, if I can."

Hannah nodded reluctantly and sat down beside the man. He took her hands in his and prayed quietly.

Hannah thanked him when he finished. She hadn't paid attention to the prayer, but it was over and she wanted to be polite. She allowed herself to be hugged, and then she stood without saying another word and headed for Jenny's room. Hannah didn't want to be angry with God, but she didn't want to talk to him, either. There were more pressing things to think about. She had to contact family members, make plans for a funeral, and tend to Jenny...

Jenny was all she had left now, a small fragment of a family that only hours earlier had been perfect...complete.

But though Hannah knew she should be thinking about her surviving daughter and the consolation she would need in the days to come, that wasn't what consumed her as she walked down the hall. Rather she found herself focusing on the other driver...the one who ran the red light and killed her family. And as she thought of him, one emotion reigned supreme.

Hatred.

Six

After affliction...she finds no resting place.
All who pursue her have overtaken her in the midst of her distress.

Lamentations 1:3

There was solace in keeping busy.

In her new role as victim, widow, and grieving mother, Hannah learned to keep her grief at bay by burying herself in busyness. And there was a mountain of details to handle.

First she made dozens of phone calls in which she told key people about the accident and asked them to contact others. She notified the girls' schools, Tom's partner, and the insurance company. And she organized the funeral.

There was precious little time to weep, to even think about her loss. And that was fine with Hannah. As long as she was busy, she could avoid thinking about a lifetime without Tom and Alicia.

Now Hannah sat in an oversized vinyl chair next to Jenny's hospital bed and glanced at the clock. Eleven in the morning. Nearly twenty-four hours after the collision. In that time Jenny had only awakened once or twice for a few minutes. They'd moved her to the critical care unit, and at the moment she was sleeping again.

Dr. Cleary had been right—Jenny was no longer in danger. Her blood tests and CAT scan were almost normal, but she was sleepy, coming out of the semiconscious haze caused by the injury. The doctor expected her to wake up soon, and then Hannah would need to tell her the truth.

She studied her notes and tugged absently at a lock of hair.

She had notified Tom's parents, his sister in Ohio…her parents in Washington state. She had no siblings, so there were few people to contact. She had called her pastor, Joel Conner, and he had started a prayer chain at New Hope Christian Church in Agoura Hills, where they had been members for as long as she could remember. Several of the women from her Bible study had come by last night to pray with her and offer assistance. Two had brought meals for Hannah to take home.

Hannah refused them all. She'd considered those women friends once, but that was before the collision…back when she had something in common with them. Now she was in a category all by herself, someone to be pitied. The idea of them sitting around talking about her tragedy in quiet voices made her skin crawl. She neither wanted—nor needed—their charity.

But they wouldn't go away. So rather than appear ungrateful, Hannah allowed one of the women to make plans for a brief reception after the funeral, which was scheduled for Wednesday.

Hannah glanced at Jenny's sleeping form—and was struck suddenly by the thought that it was the first day of school. Hannah's church friends would all be at breakfast—an annual tradition on this day—talking about how quickly children grow up, the merits of their various teachers, and how much time they would all have now that the fall routine was back in place.

Hannah's heart grew heavy and tears filled her eyes. She had cried more since the collision than all the other times in her life combined. She leaned her head back and closed her eyes…but images drifted across her mind of her friends' children greeting classmates, working out the kinks in their schedules, and making plans for weekend get-togethers.

She had called the principal of West Hills High and told him about the accident. He would have told the others, so by now Alicia's friends and fellow cheerleaders would probably be convening in the lunch area, consoling each other and crying over the loss of their friend. Certainly many of them would be at the funeral.

But in time they would get over her absence—life would get in the way, and they would be drawn to the thrill of Friday night football games and weekend dances. They would talk about Alicia on occasion, but she would eventually fade into the recesses of their memories.

Hannah sighed and fiddled with her pencil. She felt as if she had aged ten years overnight—she knew she looked haggard. Her clothing was rumpled from sleeping in the chair by Jenny's bed, and her hair was pulled back into an unruly ponytail. Only her crimson, manicured fingernails gave any indication of her former appearance. She had checked the bathroom mirror earlier that morning, and the person staring back at her with empty red eyes and cheeks ravaged by tears did not look even remotely familiar.

Focus. Concentrate on the matters at hand. That was all that kept her from falling into a bottomless pit of despair—something she could not do because she knew if she ever gave in, there would be no return.

She studied her notes again and pressed her lips together. It was time to contact Sgt. Miller. She wanted to know exactly what happened. The other driver had run a red light. She knew that much. But had he been drinking? Was he on drugs? Hannah had a horrible suspicion that there was something more to the accident story, but until she knew for sure, she tried not to think about it. The hatred she already felt toward the other driver was frightening enough without dwelling on it.

Suddenly Jenny stirred and rolled slowly from one side to the other. Hannah moved next to the bed and took her daughter's hand. A torrent of anxiety and dread consumed her, and she willed herself to stay calm. How would she tell this child, this precious daughter, that her father and sister were dead? She had no idea.

God...she started, but then cut the prayer short. No, she

would not ask. She didn't want to think about God until she had time to examine her feelings. Besides, she didn't know what power her prayers would have. They hadn't kept her family safe.

Jenny moaned and turned toward Hannah. Her eyes opened and she squinted against the sunshine streaming through the hospital window.

"Mom?"

Hannah figured her daughter could make out her face, but Jenny didn't sound sure of herself.

She leaned over the girl's prone body, hugged her, then pulled away slightly and caressed Jenny's forehead with a single finger. There was nothing she could do about the heavy sadness in her voice. "Hi, sweetheart, how do you feel?"

Jenny glanced around the room. "Where…am I?"

Hannah continued to run her fingers gently over Jenny's hair. "You're at the hospital. There was an accident, honey."

Jenny moved her left hand over the cast on her arm. She thought a moment and her eyes grew wide. "The white truck—"

Hannah said nothing.

Jenny seemed to struggle with her memory, then she jolted into a semi-sitting position. Suddenly she looked wide-awake and frightened. "Mom, he was coming right at us…right where Dad and Alicia were sitting!"

Tears filled Hannah's eyes and she pulled Jenny close once more. "I'm so sorry, baby, so sorry you had to see that."

"I wanted to scream, Mom. There wasn't time…I can't… can't remember anything else."

Hannah started to cry and the sound broke the silence. Jenny looked at her, alarm sweeping her young face.

"Mom, what is it? Where are Dad and Alicia?"

Hannah drew back just enough to see her daughter's face. She held her shoulders firmly and looked deep into her eyes. "Honey, the accident was very serious. Alicia and Daddy…they didn't make it, honey. They're gone."

Jenny's eyes filled with horror, and she searched her mother's face. "They're *dead?* Both of them?" She sounded on the verge of hysterics. "Mom? Are you serious?"

Hannah nodded and pulled Jenny close one more time. *"No!"* Jenny moaned softly, burying her face in her mother's shoulder. "No, not both of them."

She did not scream and carry on the way Hannah had done. Rather she sobbed convulsively, clinging to her mother the way a drowning swimmer clings to a life preserver. Hannah could feel her daughter's pain, and she was heartbroken, knowing there was nothing she could do to take it away.

Finally, when Jenny's weeping slowed, she pulled back and studied her mother. Hannah wondered if the girl was going to faint. "Mom," she whispered, her voice stricken. "It's all my fault."

Hannah frowned. "No, dear, of course not. The driver of the other truck ran a red light. Daddy never saw him coming."

Jenny shook her head, her cheeks red and tear stained. "No, not that part. Earlier. We were getting out of the fishing boat, heading back for camp...Alicia nearly stepped on a rattlesnake. She didn't see it but I did. I yelled at her and she stopped....One more step, Mom, and she would have been bitten."

Hannah hesitated. "Sweetheart, I don't understand. You helped your sister by saying something about the snake. That doesn't make the accident your fault."

Jenny drew a deep, shuddering breath. "You don't understand, Mom. If I hadn't said something, Alicia would have been bitten. Dad could have helped her; she would have been okay eventually. But we would have gotten a later start. Maybe an hour later....And we wouldn't have been going through the intersection when that other driver was running the red light. Don't you see, Mom? It's all my fault."

Hannah began to cry softly. "Oh, honey, it's not your fault.

You have to believe that. The only one at fault is the other driver." Even as she said the words, she thought for an instant about the Lord. He could have saved them, but he didn't. Wasn't he at fault? Just a little?

Jenny began weeping harder. "What are we going to do, Mom?" She looked so vulnerable it tore at Hannah's heart, and her hatred toward the other driver grew until she thought it would choke her. "We're going to go home and get you better. Then we're going to make sure the man who did this is punished."

"They're in heaven, right, Mom?" Fresh tears trickled down Jenny's cheeks.

"Yes, honey, they're in heaven. Together."

Jenny nodded and swiped slowly at her tears. She was sobbing so hard it was difficult to understand her. "I want Daddy..."

Hannah held her for twenty minutes, allowing her to cry and grieve the way she, herself, had not yet done. Finally Jenny grew quiet, and after several minutes she leaned her head back and studied Hannah's eyes.

"I'm...I'm glad Alicia isn't alone."

"Oh, Jenny..."

The girl lay back down and buried her head in her pillow. She stayed like that, sobbing quietly, while her mother rubbed her back until she finally drifted off to sleep.

Leaning back in the chair and pulling the bedside telephone over, Hannah clenched her teeth. She glanced at the business card in her hand, then dialed Sgt. John Miller and introduced herself.

"There's something I need to know about the accident." She kept her voice quiet; the last thing she wanted to do was disturb Jenny.

"I have the report right here," Sgt. Miller said. "Go ahead."

"The man who killed my family, was he drunk?"

There was a pause, then, "We think so. He was arrested on

suspicion of drunk driving. The lab tests aren't back yet, but he did fail a field sobriety test."

Hannah felt like she'd been punched in the stomach. With one careless decision that man had ruined her life. She steadied herself and sucked in a steadying breath.

"Where is he now?" She knew the question was angry, but she didn't care.

"He had only minor injuries. He was booked at the station that evening and released on a bail bond. When the results of the sobriety test are in, he'll be formally charged, and then he'll have to enter a plea—guilty or not guilty."

She had one more question. "Was it his first time? Drunk driving I mean?"

"No, ma'am." Sgt. Miller sighed. "His sixth."

The room was suddenly spinning, and Hannah gripped the arm of her chair for support. She reached for the only solid thing she could grab onto—her anger.

"That man had been arrested *five* other times for drunk driving, and he was still on the road? Still drinking and driving? That's *insane!"*

"I know, Mrs. Ryan. I'm sorry...I agree. Maybe this time they'll put him away."

"You mean there's a chance they won't? Listen, Sergeant. I know none of this is your fault, but I will not sit back and watch the courts let this *killer* back on the streets. I'll fight him and the laws and the entire legal system if it costs every cent I have. Even if it kills me."

There was a pause. "The process will be long and drawn out." Sgt. Miller sounded frustrated. "But there are a few things you can do. You've heard of Mothers Against Drunk Drivers?"

"Yes." Hannah was trembling with rage. How could this be happening to her? She didn't want to think about Mothers Against Drunk Drivers. She was supposed to be having breakfast with her church friends, making plans for the school year.

She was supposed to have two, beautiful, healthy daughters

and a husband who loved her.

Sgt. Miller continued. "There's a woman at the West Valley office, Carol Cummins; she's a victim advocate. Why don't you give her a call and see how you can help? Might make a difference when it comes to a possible trial down the road."

"Who is he?

"What?"

"The killer. What's his name?"

"Brian Wesley. He's twenty-eight, married, has a son."

Hannah was furious. "Good for him! Before Saturday afternoon *I* was married with a *daughter.* But he killed them, and I'll do whatever it takes to get him behind bars. When I'm finished with him, he'll wish he'd killed me, too."

"Ma'am..." Sgt. Miller hesitated. "I saw the Christian fish on your door the other day—"

"What of it?"

Another pause. "I'm a believer, too; that's all. I've been praying for you."

"Don't bother." It was all she could do not to spit the words at him. "I have all the prayers I can handle right now."

"Mrs. Ryan, I'm not trying to interfere. It's just that in these situations it's so easy to lose perspective and turn away..."

When she answered, she didn't even try to temper the coldness in her tone. "I'm sure you mean well, Sgt. Miller, but you're just like every other Christian right now. 'It must be God's will.' 'They're home in heaven now.' 'God still loves you.' 'The Lord has a plan—'"

A wave of emotion choked off her words, and she had to swallow hard before she could continue. "I don't want to hear it. Do you understand? Brian Wesley, age twenty-eight, married with one son, just *destroyed* my life! He took *everything* from me and left me with nothing, not even hope. He murdered my husband and daughter, and so help me God, I'll never forgive him as long as I live. Am I being clear? I don't want to hear a list of platitudes or Bible verses right now. I don't want sympathy or textbook answers. I want my family back.…And since I can't have that, I just want Brian Wesley to pay for what he's done."

Jenny lay still, her eyes closed. Her head felt heavy and it was difficult to form thoughts. She knew that the woman she could hear ranting and shouting hateful things was her mother, but when Jenny heard her say those things about not wanting prayers or platitudes, she began to think perhaps the woman was an imposter.

Jenny opened her eyes slowly, waiting for the room to stop spinning. She squinted at the figure by her bed. "Mom?"

Her mother glanced at her. Jenny saw she was on the phone. "Hold on—" she covered the receiver and whispered impatiently—"What is it, Jenny? I'm on a business call."

Jenny stared at her, her mind a blank. Why was Mom angry with her? Dread swept over her as she realized the truth: the accident had been her fault and her mother knew it. "Forget it."

Her mother frowned, her hand still covering the phone. "Don't be like that, Jenny. I'm sorry, okay? This is an important call. I'm talking to the police officer." She sighed impatiently. "Did you need something? A drink? What?"

Jenny felt like a piece of her heart had been sliced off. She squeezed her eyes so her mother wouldn't see her cry. "I said forget it." She rolled over, turning her back to her mother.

Please, please, talk to me…help me…I'm so scared…

But her mother didn't notice. Instead, she resumed her phone conversation. "Okay, I'm back. What I'm trying to say is…"

Tears streamed down Jenny's face as her mother continued to rant at the police officer. What had happened? Why wasn't her mother worried about her, sorry for her? How could a phone call be more important than what she was feeling?

It's because it was Alicia and not me who died. Mom had always loved Alicia more. Jenny wished with all her heart that she could trade places with Alicia. That she could take Alicia's spot in heaven with Daddy and give Alicia back to Mom.

Jenny drew her knees into a fetal position. Then, while her mother continued to yell at the officer, she wept into her pillow, whispering the only words she could think of. "Why, God? Why?...If she doesn't love me, why did you leave me here with her?"

Hannah hung up, her rage so potent it was almost a physical presence. But there was nothing there to vent it on. It seeped through her veins, more powerful than any drug, infusing her heart and soul. She clenched her fists. It was outrageous! How could the courts allow a convicted drunk driver back on the roads to kill Tom and Alicia? She gritted her teeth. She would change the laws—the entire system—if that's what it took.

She ripped a sheet of paper from her pad and began making notations. Her mind raced with plans....She would contact Mothers Against Drunk Drivers....She would attend any court hearing involving Brian Wesley....If she had to, she'd singlehandedly change the drunk driving laws in the state of California. The thought of Brian Wesley fueled her rage, but as her notes began taking form, she found herself strangely comforted.

She had a reason to go on.

Brian Wesley—and his punishment.

The next two days flew by. Consumed with her decision to exact revenge on Brian Wesley, Hannah scarcely took in all that happened. In a blur of events, Jenny was released from the hospital, and she and Hannah attended the double funeral service. Family and friends surrounded Hannah, consoling her.

But every time Hannah looked for Jenny, the girl was alone. She sat in the first pew, her head hung low, her casted arm in a sling.

Hannah felt a quick pang of guilt. She was ignoring Jenny, her only surviving daughter. But on the heels of the feeling came her new resolve. Jenny was young and resilient. Her injuries would heal and she would be fine. They would have time together later. Alicia and Tom, they were the real victims.

And, of course, Hannah. This disaster had happened to her, most of all. She would never recover…never find another man like Tom…never know another daughter so sweet and talented and precious as Alicia…

She had lost the most, and she had no energy for consoling Jenny. She was too desperately in need of consolation herself.

Besides, it hurt too much to talk about the loss, to face the present and the emptiness it held every day. No, it was much safer to spend her time living in one of two places: the angry, uncertain future or the bittersweet past. Her thoughts of the future were directed to one end only: seeing Brian Wesley locked up, knowing he would pay for what he did.

The rest of the time she spent in the past, where Tom and Alicia still lived.

Seven

The roads to Zion mourn, for no one comes to her….
All her gateways are desolate.

LAMENTATIONS 1:4A

It had been two weeks since the accident, and Jenny lay sprawled out on her flannel quilt, her fingers fanned against the cool wall beside her bed…the wall that separated her room from Alicia's. Jenny studied her arms and legs and saw that the bruises were fading. But there were other scars—ones she knew would never disappear.

She studied the wall and drifted back to what seemed like another lifetime, the day they were packing for the camping trip. In her mind she heard three soft thuds coming from the other room: the signal she and Alicia had used for years. One thud meant *Urgent! Come quick! Get in here right away!* Two thuds meant *good night*. And three thuds were a simple three-word message: *I love you.*

Alicia's bed was up against the other side of the wall, and each night whichever of them got in bed first would thud twice. *Good night*. When the other sister responded with two thuds of her own, the first would thud three times. *I love you.* And the other would respond similarly.

The day before the trip, Jenny and Alicia had been in their separate rooms, packing their bags; Amy Grant's "Hearts in Motion" had been blaring from Alicia's tape player. A single thud sounded in Jenny's room. She had dropped her thermal underwear and skittered out the door, around the corner into Alicia's room, where she flopped onto her sister's bed.

"What?" Jenny nosed around inside Alicia's duffel bag, checking the things her sister had packed.

"You bringing your tape player?" Alicia held a fistful of cassette tapes. Amy Grant, Steven Curtis Chapman, Michael W. Smith, Jars of Clay.

"My batteries are dead."

"Mine, too. Can you ask Dad if we can stop and get some on the way out of town?"

Jenny had bounced up. "Sure. Be right back." She bounded down the stairs and in a minute returned and threw herself again on Alicia's bed. "Done."

Amy Grant's voice filled the room, and Jenny watched Alicia dance around, snagging a shirt from her closet and jeans from her dresser drawer. Jenny had wondered if one day she might be as pretty and popular as Alicia. Her older sister's cheerleading uniform lay on the floor near her bed, and Jenny bent down to pick it up.

Alicia was involved in everything. Cheerleading, student council, drama. She had so many friends, and she was good at whatever she tried.

"My room's such a mess." Alicia used her foot to move a pile of clothes against her bed. "I never have enough time."

Jenny considered the floor. "Pretty bad."

"Uuugh. It's a total mess." She stopped for a moment and raised an eyebrow. "Don't tell me *you're* already packed?"

"Yep. Wasn't much. I mean, what can you take on the old, annual camping trip? You know Dad. We'll spend half the time on the lake catching fish."

Alicia froze and glanced back at her duffel bag. "True—" She turned abruptly and began digging in her drawer again. "But I have to have the right shorts...and then if it gets cold, I need my woolly sweatshirt...and at night, you know, around the campfire I like my old jeans..." Her voice drifted as she rummaged through a series of drawers. "If I could just find them."

Jenny stood and stretched. She picked up a shirt from Alicia's floor, turned it right-side out, folded it in half, and set it on her sister's bed. "I hate it when that happens."

She made no mention of the fact that she was cleaning Alicia's mess as she bent down and picked up a rumpled pair of shorts. When the pile of clothes was neatly folded on her sister's bed, Jenny headed for the door. "I just remembered something. My Christy Miller book. I have to bring it."

Alicia straightened and looked around her room. "Jenny! Hey, thanks. You're so nice. You didn't have to clean my room."

Jenny shrugged. "No big deal. That way you'll be done faster. Maybe we can play horse out in the driveway with Dad after dinner."

"You're the best sister in the world." Alicia left the tangled web of clothing spilling from her bottom drawer and came to hug Jenny. Then she grinned. "But I'll still beat you at horse."

Jenny had laughed and returned to her room. A moment passed while she searched for the book, and then she'd heard it. Three soft thuds on the bedroom wall.

Was that just a few weeks ago? It seems like years...like it had happened to someone else.

Jenny's lips trembled and she closed her eyes against the tears. At the sound of footsteps on the stairs she wiped her eyes quickly, then turned to watch her mother enter the room. Mom looked angry again, disappointed. *Is it because I'm the one who lived?* Anxiety threatened to strangle Jenny, as it did every time she asked herself these questions. *Would Mom be so angry all the time if Alicia were still here instead of me?* Alicia had had so much going for her. *If one of us was going to live, it should have been Alicia.* Jenny swallowed and blinked twice as her mother crossed the room and sat on the edge of her bed.

"I've been looking all over for you." Her mother sounded tired, robotic. Jenny tried to remember the last time she'd looked or sounded tender.

She couldn't remember one time since the accident.

She turned away and stared at the wall. "I've been here."

Her mother sighed. "You're always here. Can't you come downstairs and spend some time with—"

"With *whom?*" Jenny turned back toward her mother. "The family? We don't *have* a family anymore, Mom, remember? You keep telling everyone how that drunk driver killed your *family*. So who cares if I stay up here? I'm not your family."

Her mother shrank back, a pinched look around her eyes.

Jenny sat up and forced her face closer to her mother's. "I guess you're right, Mom. Our family is dead. Now there's just you and me, and that's not enough, is it? We'll never be a family by ourselves."

She threw herself back down on the bed and rolled onto her side. She couldn't stand looking at her mother for another second.

"Jenny..."

She flinched at her mother's tentative touch on her shoulder. There was a pause, and when her mom went on, her voice was cold.

"I'm sorry I said what I did about my family being killed. Of course we're a family. But there's a lot to do now, and I can't spend my time sitting up here rubbing your back and helping you get over this. That man, that *drunk driver,* is about to be charged for what he did to your dad and Alicia. When he is, I want to be there. I want to make sure he's locked up for a long, long time. I'm sorry, honey...but I'll probably be very busy these next few months."

Jenny remained silent, unmoving, studying her fingers as they moved slightly, back and forth, across the wall near her bed.

"Honey, what I'm trying to say is I'd like your help in this. We owe it to Daddy and Alicia to make sure that man doesn't ever kill anyone again. It won't help for us to hide away in bed and miss them. Not now, anyway. There's too much to do."

Jenny felt tears burn her eyes and couldn't keep her shoulders from trembling. What was her mother talking about? *I'm just a kid!* she wanted to scream. *How can I possibly do anything that would help send that drunk driver to prison?*

For that matter, what difference could her mother really make? None at all. Besides, who cared, anyway? Alicia and Daddy were gone. Nothing could bring them back now.

"Jenny." Her mother's voice was flat. "Are you listening?"

Jenny rolled over and faced her mother. "If you're asking me to get up, put a smile on, and help you make some kind of plan to lock up drunk drivers, I won't do it."

Her mother's face grew a shade paler. "Why are you lashing out at me?"

Because I hate you. Because you hate me for being alive. "Because. You think you have to get back at that guy. Seek revenge or something."

"Well, Jenny, what do *you* want to do?" Her mother sounded exasperated. "Ask the judge to let him go?"

"I don't *know!*" Jenny's whole body shook, and she couldn't make it stop. "The Bible says to forgive, and you always taught us we should live our lives by what the Bible says, right?" She watched her mother closely. *Please, please, be my mom again. You believed in God...in the Bible....You used to smile and hold me and tell me he would always protect us....*

But there was no smile on her mother's face. She stiffened, and she wouldn't meet Jenny's eyes. "That's different. The man who did this needs to be punished. Don't you think so?"

"I think we should *forget* about him!" Jenny clenched her fists. "Going to court and fighting him won't bring back Daddy and Alicia. I think we should stay home and remember the happy times."

Her mother stood up abruptly, and Jenny suddenly felt so cold she thought she'd shatter into a million pieces. "That won't bring them back either." Her mother's words were like pieces of ice. "Forget I said anything, Jenny. Stay up here as long as you like. And when you're ready to deal with what happened, I'll be downstairs trying to get on with life."

Her mother walked out of the room, and Jenny turned once more toward the wall. Hot tears filled her eyes, and she sobbed softly into her pillow. "Alicia, where are you? I need you so badly."

Through her tears she remembered how they had dressed alike as little girls, walking hand-in-hand to their Sunday school class each week.

"Yes, Jesus loves me," they would sing as they skipped along. "The Bible tells me so."

Oh, Jesus, please help me. I don't want to live without Alicia and Daddy. Mom doesn't understand. She doesn't care about me.

A scene from the funeral flashed in Jenny's mind. A great aunt had come up to her and squeezed her hard, suffocating her in a fog of strong perfume. "Now listen, dear," the fleshy woman had said. "Be a good girl and don't make things harder for your mother than they have to be."

Jenny remembered looking up at the woman, confused.

The great aunt continued. "You must understand she's suffered a great loss here. Now it's up to you to be strong for her."

Jenny had nodded uncertainly. "I'll try."

"You try hard, now, you hear. Your mother needs you."

The woman's words had haunted Jenny several times since then. She squeezed her eyes shut, and another wave of sadness washed over her. *It's my loss, too. Who'll be strong for me?*

"Alicia, come home," she cried softly. "Pleeease, Alicia. I miss you."

Then she raised her hand toward the wall and thudded softly. Three times. And three more.

Over and over and over again.

Eight

In the days of her affliction and wandering
Jerusalem remembers all the treasures that were hers in days of old.

LAMENTATIONS 1:7A

In the haze of grief and anger and bitter rage that consumed her, Hannah realized she was neglecting Jenny. But she felt helpless to do anything about it. She simply did not have the strength to do more than provide for the girl's most basic necessities.

It took all her energy to remember her life as it had been…to remember Tom. She always started back as far as she could remember. That was how it was with Tom. Her catalogue of memories simply did not contain a single day without him.

There had been very few rainy days in Hannah's childhood. An only child, she'd been doted on by both parents. Her grade school years were spent at Cornerstone Christian School where she generally excelled, and each week there was church and Sunday school and dozens of playmates and an entire church family who knew and loved her. What Hannah wanted, she got—and usually with little effort.

She'd grown up surrounded by children from similarly privileged families, where parents stayed together, went to church together, and seldom faced anything more serious than a bad case of tonsillitis or a flat tire on the family van.

Back then it only made sense, though. Hannah was a good girl, and in return, the Lord gave her a life free of speed bumps or bends in the road.

Hannah had many playmates, but her best friend in the

whole world was a boy one year older than she, who lived across the street, three houses down. His parents attended the same church as Hannah's, and the two grew up swinging side by side on the church playground.

His name was Tom Ryan.

On a warm summer day sometime after Hannah's eighth birthday, she rode her bike past Tom's house and skidded on loose gravel. She tumbled over the handlebars and came to a stop on her knees and elbows. Tom, almost ten at the time, dropped his basketball and came running.

"Hannah, are you hurt?" Tom had stooped down and lifted her gently to her feet. He dusted the gravel off her arms and legs and dashed into the house for a wet rag, which he gently swiped over her road burns. "Are you okay?"

"Yeah…thanks." A strange sensation was making its way across Hannah's suddenly flushing cheeks.

Tom found a bandage and carefully applied it to the worst of her cuts. "There, that should do it."

Hannah watched him wide-eyed and knew from that moment on she would marry Tom Ryan one day. She didn't talk about it with Tom, or anyone else for that matter. It was something she took for granted, like the passing of the seasons.

They became even better friends, shooting baskets in his driveway and talking about plans for the future. He wanted to be a doctor; she wanted to have a big family to make up for the siblings she never had. During the school year they did homework together, and in summer they walked to the neighborhood pool and lazed away the afternoons holding diving competitions from the pool's high dive or racing underwater to see who could hold their breath the longest. Hannah hated to lose.

In fact, the only flaw in Hannah's life was her temper. One summer when Hannah was ten, she and Tom were playing basketball when they were joined by a boy who lived two streets down.

After the game, the boy looked at Hannah disdainfully. "You

shoot baskets like a wimpy girl."

Furious, she worked on her shot for weeks after that and refused to speak to the boy again. In her freshman year, Hannah shared a class with the boy and ignored him mercilessly.

"What's with you?" the boy asked her one day.

Hannah sneered at him. "I shoot baskets like a wimpy girl, remember?"

The boy clearly had no idea what she was talking about, but even after he'd apologized, she made a point to avoid him.

"Sure hope you never get mad at *me*, Hannah," Tom had told her once that year. "When you get mad, you don't stop. Ever."

"I think that's why God's so good to me." Hannah had smiled pleasantly. "He knows I'm not good at forgiving."

Through childhood and many of her early teenage years, Hannah was a flat-chested pixie with delicate, cornflower blue eyes, unremarkable features, and gangly arms and skinny legs. The only thing striking about her was her thick, wheat-colored blond hair, which got in the way when she played sports. Hannah thought it was more of an inconvenience than anything.

Tom, however, was a strapping boy with a muscular physique long before he hit his teen years. He had a ruddy complexion, short dark hair, brilliant teasing blue eyes, and a knack for making Hannah laugh out loud. In many ways, Tom was the brother Hannah had always wanted.

They never talked about themselves in any romantic sense, even as they grew older. But Hannah was in no hurry. They had always been together, and they always would be. She wasn't sure how Tom felt, but each night she prayed that when the time was right, Tom would ask her to be his wife. She could not remember a time when God hadn't answered her prayers exactly as she had prayed them, so she had little concern regarding her future with Tom.

When Tom turned sixteen and began dating the majorette from the high school drill team, fourteen-year-old Hannah was not terribly concerned. She was still in middle school, still dressing and acting and looking like one of the boys. She figured her relationship with Tom was bound to change when she turned sixteen and was granted permission to date. That was when she and Tom would fall in love.

Instead, when Hannah turned sixteen, Tom made a decision to attend college at Oregon State University in Corvallis. His father had graduated from OSU, and the family had relatives nearby. Tom would need to leave immediately after graduation because Oregon State had given him a full baseball scholarship, and the team trained all summer.

When she heard the news, Hannah felt as if the bottom had dropped out of her heart. How did this fit into the plans she'd made? She expected Tom to attend college, but she never believed he would leave California and move all the way to Oregon.

She prayed with renewed vigor.

Before he left, his family had a going-away party for him. Hannah was in the early goings of summer league softball that month, but she missed practice the day of Tom's party and went to the mall. There she picked out a sleeveless, rayon dress that danced in the breeze and fell softly on the budding curves of her developing body. She applied a layer of mascara to her fair eyelashes and curled and brushed her hair until it shone and lay in gentle waves around her shoulders. Finally she slipped her tanned feet into a pair of white-heeled sandals that accented her shapely colt-like legs. Before she left, she checked the mirror. Even she was amazed at the transformation—overnight she had become a young woman.

When she arrived at Tom's house, his mother answered the door.

"Why, Hannah...you look so pretty, all grown up." She smiled warmly at Hannah and ushered her inside. "Tom's in the other room. I'm sure he'll be glad to see you."

Hannah held her head high and went into the den. Tom was surrounded by a handful of boys, all seniors at West Hills High, all members of the varsity baseball team.

As she entered the room, each of them stared at her in a way that was just short of rude, but Hannah relished their attention. If Tom were going to leave the state for four years, he would have to remember her as more than the buddy down the block in jeans and a baseball cap.

"Hey, Hannah." Tom looked uncomfortable, and Hannah knew he was registering the change in her appearance. There was a moment of awkward silence before he cleared his throat and said softly, "Nice dress."

Tom stayed by her side the rest of the evening, teasing and making her laugh the way he'd done all their lives. When his teammates tried to have their share of time with Hannah, he found some excuse to take her away or involve her in another conversation.

When she left that evening, he walked her home. They stopped just out of view of her house. Tom leaned casually against the bark of an old shade tree and studied her in the moonlight.

"Kinda feels like the end of childhood, doesn't it?"

Hannah fiddled with a loose curl and nodded. "Yeah. I can't believe you're going to be gone four years."

Tom nodded and angled his head, studying her. "You sure look pretty tonight, Hannah. The guys were going crazy over you."

She shrugged delicately and giggled. "They're just used to seeing me in a uniform with my hair pulled up."

Tom caught her gaze. "Yeah. Me too."

The silence between them grew awkward then, and Hannah made circles in the grass with the toe of her sandal. There was a faint scent of honeysuckle in the early summer air, and she knew she would remember this night as long as she lived.

She smiled. "We had so much fun growing up together… shooting baskets all day and catching crickets at night. Remember that time we had a contest to see who could eat the most watermelon?"

"I won."

"You won and then you got sick all over the front lawn, remember?"

Tom gripped his stomach and grimaced. "I still have a hard time eating watermelon."

"But later, after you felt better, we talked about what we wanted to be when we grew up, remember?'

Tom laughed.

"You always said you wanted to be a doctor."

He nodded. "That much hasn't changed. You always said you wanted to have a big family, lots of kids."

Hannah glanced down, thankful he couldn't see her blushing in the haze of shadows under the shade tree. "I guess I still have some time for that one."

"Hey, Hannah, do me a favor, huh?"

"Sure."

"Pray for me. It's gonna be hard starting over in a place where I don't know anyone and being so far away from home."

She met his gaze head on and smiled. "I always pray for you, Tom. I won't stop now."

He drew a deep breath, and Hannah could tell he was wrestling with his feelings. "Well, I guess I better go. I still have to finish packing."

She was suddenly anxious to keep the conversation going as long as possible. "Will you be back? At break I mean?"

"Yeah. Christmas and summers. Whenever the team isn't conditioning."

"I wish I could see you play."

Tom's eyes lit up. "Hey! You can!…We play at USC and UCLA. You could ride over with my parents. That'd be great!"

"Yeah!"

"And I'll write and tell you all about college life."

"Mmmhhm."

"And you can catch me up on life at school and everything that's happening in the old neighborhood."

"Sure…"

They both fell silent, and Tom glanced back toward his house. "Well, Hannah, come here and give me a hug."

She stepped forward, and they embraced like favorite cousins at a family reunion. When they pulled back, Tom ran his thumb lightly underneath Hannah's neatly curled bangs. "Don't change, Hannah."

She could feel tears welling up, and she smiled uncertainly. "Have a good trip."

"Yeah. See you later."

And with that, life as Hannah had known it changed dramatically. The summer passed uneventfully with only one letter from Tom. She saw him briefly during Christmas break and sat with him and his family at Christmas Eve service. Then she didn't see him until April, when she and his parents went to UCLA to watch his baseball game.

They spotted him before the game and waved, and Hannah felt her face flush at the sight of him. Tom was an outfielder, recruited for his strong arm and high batting average. Though a freshman, he was a starter, and that afternoon he hit a game-winning double. Hannah could barely contain her pride.

But when the game ended, a pretty brunette with a breath-taking figure ran up and threw her arms around Tom's neck. He kissed her lightly on the cheek, and then took her hand in his.

Hannah felt as if she'd been punched in the stomach. She wanted to run back to the car and spare herself this awful moment, but Tom and the girl were approaching fast, and there was nowhere to hide.

"Hey, thanks for coming." Tom was breathless and sweaty, and Hannah thought he looked even more handsome than he had a year ago.

Tom glanced at the girl beside him. “This is Amy.” He looked at the others. “She does stats for the team.” He and Amy shared a smile. “These are my parents, and this is Hannah, my buddy from the old neighborhood.”

“Nice to meet you.” Amy wore heavy makeup; Hannah felt utterly plain beside her. Amy smiled warmly at Tom’s parents and barely paid heed to Hannah.

Hannah gritted her teeth. Plain or not, she would not be outdone. Tom belonged to her not this, this…

“Are you an actress?” Sarcasm dripped from Hannah’s every word, and Tom cast a curious glance her way.

Amy laughed uneasily. “No, do I look like someone famous?”

Hannah volleyed a similar laugh back at Amy. “No, I just thought with all that thick, gray, pancake makeup, maybe you were practicing for a play or something.”

Amy’s face went blank, and there was an awkward silence. Tom looked as if he could have strangled Hannah, but instead he cleared his throat and said, “I met Amy at the beginning of the season.”

“Yes,” Amy purred, squeezing Tom’s hand. Hannah was forgotten as Amy smiled sweetly at Tom’s parents. “Your son is quite an athlete.”

They all chuckled and agreed how wonderful Tom was. And before five minutes had passed, he was pulling Amy by the hand and bidding good-bye to Hannah and his parents. For Hannah, the entire scene seemed to take place in slow-motion, as though it were a horrible dream.

On the ride back to the Valley, Tom’s parents said very little. They seemed to understand that Hannah was hurt. When they pulled up in front of Hannah’s house, Tom’s mother squeezed Hannah’s shoulder. “She won’t be around long. She isn’t Tom’s type.”

Hannah prayed that Tom’s mother was right, but Amy did not go away. She and Tom dated through his sophomore and junior year, while Hannah graduated from West Hills High and began attending California State University Northridge, three miles from home. Tom and Amy were together constantly, even during breaks.

Church was the only place Hannah knew she could see Tom alone. Amy was not a Christian and had no intention of ever becoming one, according to Tom's mother.

"She's a nice girl, but she's all wrong for Tom," his mother would say on occasion when Hannah visited. "He still has medical school ahead, and she's not the waiting type. Besides, Tom needs a nice Christian girl. Someone like you, Hannah."

"Tom doesn't see me like that, Mrs. Ryan."

"One day. Give him time."

But a few weeks before the start of his senior year, Tom and Amy came home with an announcement. They were going to be married in June, right after he graduated.

Hannah was shocked and angry. She had dated occasionally, but her heart resided where it always had—to Tom, even if he didn't know it. She and Tom belonged together. Everyone at home felt the same way, her parents and his, and the kids they'd grown up with.

Everyone but Tom.

The summer passed, and Tom and Amy returned to Corvallis to make plans for their senior year while Hannah was left to ponder her suddenly uncertain future.

That fall Tom wrote Hannah a letter. In it was no admission of love or longing, but rather a rambling of memories of their childhood and the happy times they'd shared. Hannah read the letter five times before tucking it carefully into her top drawer. Why, she wondered, was Tom thinking about her and their past when he should be busy making plans for his future with Amy?

Christmas break came, and Hannah learned that Amy had returned to Walnut Creek in Northern California, where she and her mother had plans to shop for a wedding gown. Tom came home and spent hours hanging out in front of his house, bouncing his old basketball in the mild winter afternoons, his face pensive and troubled. More than a few times, Hannah glanced out her window and saw him gazing toward her house.

Three days before Christmas there was a social at church. Hannah arrived late, and while she was talking with the pastor's wife, she heard a familiar voice.

"Hey, Hannah, what you been up to?" Tom was taller than before, his shoulders broad and full like his father's. Hannah blushed furiously, and then thought of Amy, shopping the boutiques of San Francisco for a wedding gown.

"Oh, hi." Her voice lacked any enthusiasm. "I thought you were back."

Tom studied her, and she knew there was little about her that resembled the rough-and-tumble girl he once shot baskets with.

"Can't believe I'm almost finished up at OSU."

Hannah smiled, her defenses firmly in place. "Then there's the big wedding."

Tom's expression changed and his eyes clouded. "Yeah…the big wedding."

Cheerful chatter filled the hall, and Tom looked around, slightly bothered. "Let's go outside and talk. It's been a long time."

She wondered what the point was, but she nodded. "Okay. I'll follow you."

Outside they found a bench nestled against the church wall facing the parking lot. They sat down, shoulder to shoulder, much as they'd done hundreds of times before. They were silent as they took in the Christmas lights and listened to the hum of conversation in the distance.

"You ever feel like you were about to make a big mistake?" Tom leaned against the side of the bench and faced Hannah.

She pulled her knees up to her chin and wrapped her arms

around her legs. Something about the cool night air and the intimacy of the moment caused her defenses to drop.

"Sometimes."

Tom gazed heavenward. "Amy's not a Christian....She's not..." He looked at Hannah. "She's not a lot of things."

She thought about that for a moment. "You asked her to marry you." Their eyes met, and for the first time since she'd known Tom, it felt as though there was something more between them than just the bond of childhood, something Hannah couldn't quite grasp.

"Yes, I did..."

Hannah felt bold in the darkness. "Why'd you do it, Tom?"

He shrugged. "I don't know. Seemed like the right thing at the time. She sort of orders everything around her, and...I guess her parents were expecting me to propose. I mean, she was talking about our honeymoon and where we'd live when I'm in med school months before I ever asked her."

"Sounds lovely."

Tom stifled a grin. "You don't like her, do you?"

Hannah was silent.

"'Are you an actress?'" Tom mimicked. "Come on, Hannah. You were pretty obvious that day."

She lifted her chin. "I don't have anything against her."

"Oh, okay. If you say so."

"I don't."

"Now, Hannah. You weren't just a little jealous?"

"Of her? *Please*, Tom. Give me some credit."

There was silence again.

Tom sighed. "You know I kinda wish you were jealous."

Hannah ignored that. "What really matters isn't what I think of Amy, it's what you think of her." She waited. "You must love her."

Tom exhaled slowly through pursed lips. "I don't know. I did love her, sometimes I think I still do. But every time I imagine spending my life with her, I end up thinking about..." His voice trailed off and he caught Hannah's gaze. "Did you get my letter last month?"

"Yeah. I didn't know what to write back. It seemed like you were remembering how things used to be."

"Kind of."

She studied him. "Want the truth?"

"Okay."

"After I got that letter, I wondered if you were really happy."

Tom sighed again. "When did you grow up and get so smart, Hannah?" She grinned, and his eyes grew softer. "And so beautiful."

For once, she didn't know what to say.

"Mom tells me every time you have a date. She says you haven't found the right guy yet."

Hannah blushed and glanced down at her trembling hands.

"I don't know, everything seems all mixed up. I'm engaged to a girl who isn't even interested in the Lord, when you're right here, my bestest buddy, all grown up and totally devoted to God. Don't you ever wonder how come you and I didn't get together?"

Hannah's eyes narrowed and a million memories came to mind. "Sometimes."

"How did everything get so twisted?"

She shivered, partly from the night air and partly from the direction their conversation was taking.

"Cold?" Tom looked concerned.

"A little."

He held out his arm. "Come here."

She moved closer and leaned against him. The chill was gone immediately.

He rested his chin on the top of her head. "You know something? These last three years at college I've really missed you."

"Maybe you just miss being a kid."

"We had fun, didn't we?"

She could feel him looking at her, and she knew he was

going to kiss her. Finally, when she could no longer stand it, she looked up into his eyes.

"Hannah," he whispered. Then the moment she'd dreamed of all her life happened. As though it had been destined since before they were born, they came together in a single kiss—one that was slow and filled with every good feeling Hannah had ever known.

When they pulled away, Tom looked startled. "I'm sorry." He was breathless, and she could feel his heart beating wildly against her chest. "I'm so confused right now."

"I'm not a little kid anymore, Tom."

He shook his head, and she thought she saw tears in his eyes. "I know. That's the problem. Ever since you walked into my house that day in that silky dress...you know, at my graduation party." He studied her for a moment. "Ever since then I've wondered about whether we'd..."

"Mhmm." She smiled sadly.

"You, too?"

"Yeah. I've wondered."

"But then I met Amy and..."

"And what?"

"I guess we'll never know."

"*What?*" Hannah jerked away. Of *course* he knew. He'd kissed her, after all!

"Well—" Tom drew back a bit and looked nervous—"I mean...I *am* getting married..."

"I don't see a ring on your finger yet."

"Yeah, but Hannah...everything's all set. I don't know..."

"That's a cop-out, Tom."

"A cop-out?"

"Yes! You're not married yet. Break it off."

He chuckled softly. "You don't know Amy."

She put her hands on Tom's shoulders and shook him. "Listen to you! You don't marry someone because you're afraid of what'll happen if you break up."

He gazed at Hannah thoughtfully and sighed. "I know. There's more to it than that."

She waited a beat and dropped her hands. "So, you do love her." It wasn't a question.

Tom shrugged. "I have a lot to work out, I guess. Come on, let's get back in."

Tears formed in her eyes. "Don't do it, Tom. Don't marry her."

"Hannah..."

She was unashamed of her tears as they spilled onto her cheeks. "Don't marry her."

"Hannah, please." He pulled her close and cradled her head against his chest. "Don't make this harder than it has to be."

He paused, and she knew he could feel her body jerking quietly as she cried.

"Come on, Hannah. What happened to my bestest buddy?"

Hannah pulled away, anger sweeping over her, and met his gaze straight on. "She grew up." With that she wiped her eyes, sniffed once, and stormed back into the church. She didn't talk to Tom again. A month later she heard he was going ahead with the wedding.

Stricken with pain so severe she could hardly breathe when she thought about it, Hannah turned to her best protection—anger. She harbored a grudge against Tom the size of a mountain. How could he make such a horrible decision? Especially after that night at church? She had kissed him, bared her heart to him, and still he had chosen Amy.

As the day of the wedding drew near, Hannah vowed to stay home and avoid Tom whatever the cost. The event was scheduled to take place the first week in June at Knollwood Country Club in Granada Hills, just five miles from the West Valley neighborhood where Tom and Hannah grew up.

In the weeks before the wedding, an invitation arrived at Hannah's house. Her mother responded, stating that all but Hannah would attend. At about the same time, Hannah graduated from Cal State Northridge, and Tom was one of more than a hundred people who attended her graduation party. Hannah felt him watching her from a distance that night, but she ignored him. When he approached to congratulate her, she turned abruptly and began a conversation with someone else.

She had a right to her anger. He had broken her heart, and she would never forgive him.

The day before Tom's wedding, Hannah's parents were at work and she was staging a cleaning frenzy, doing her best not to think about Tom and Amy, when the doorbell rang. She set down the window cleaner and headed for the door.

"Coming!" She stretched and ran her fingers absently through her hair. It was unusually hot and sticky for June, and as she made her way through the house, Hannah thought about driving to the beach that evening. Maybe there she could sort out her feelings.

She opened the door and caught her breath. It was Tom, dressed in worn jeans and a white T-shirt, looking desperately troubled.

Hannah felt her expression go cold, and before he could speak, she slammed the door shut.

He stopped the door with his hand and pushed it open again. "Wait!"

Hannah's hand flew to her hip and she glared at him. "Go away, Tom. I have nothing to say to you."

He sighed. "Hannah, will you stop trying to hate me for one minute. I came here to tell you something."

"Say it. I have things to do."

Tom drew a deep breath and rubbed his palms on his jeans. "May I come in?"

She exhaled dramatically. "I guess." She stepped aside, and he followed her into the foyer.

They stood face to face, studying each other. Finally Tom broke the silence.

"It's off." His voice was breathless, and he looked like he hadn't slept in days.

Hannah frowned. "What?"

"The wedding…I called it off this morning."

Her eyes grew wide. "The day before—?"

He held up a hand. "I know, it's crazy. But it would've been crazier to marry her."

"What did your parents say?" Hannah was so shocked she forgot her anger.

"They were glad I realized it today and not tomorrow."

"What about the…"

"My parents are contacting the guests. Amy and her folks are flying back to San Francisco tonight."

Hannah softened. "She must be furious."

"Yeah, you could say that. She thinks I ruined her life."

"Ooooh boy. I'd never forgive you."

Tom grinned. "Yeah, I know. You haven't talked to me since that night.…Of course, I should have remembered that from when we were kids."

Hannah was afraid to break the silence that followed, but she had to know. "Why'd you change your mind?"

Tom moved closer to Hannah. He raised his hands and framed her face with his fingertips. "I couldn't marry her, Hannah." He hesitated, and she knew if he didn't say something soon her heart would beat out of her chest.

He looked at her intently. "I couldn't. Not when the only girl I've ever really loved—" he moved closer still—"is you. I didn't know it until today, when I realized what would happen after tomorrow. I'd lose you forever.…I couldn't marry Amy after that." His eyes searched hers, looking for her reaction. "Hannah, I love you."

In that instant, she knew her prayers had not been uttered in vain. Indeed, God had seen to it that everything had turned out exactly as she had planned. In his timing, not hers.

Tom stroked her face. "I'm sorry, Hannah. I should have broken it off months ago. Then you wouldn't be so mad at me." He tenderly took her hand in his. "Still hate me?"

Hannah felt tears spring to her eyes. A single laugh escaped, and she pushed at him in mock frustration. "I should hate you forever, you big brat."

"Forever?" Tom grinned.

"Yeah—" Hannah heard the laughter leave her voice—"for waiting to the last minute to realize what I've known all my life."

He caught her around the waist and pulled her close. "I know. But now…can you forgive me, Hannah?"

She paused. "It depends…"

Slowly, he moved his face closer to hers and kissed her as he had so many months ago at the church. A minute passed before he spoke again. "On what?"

She kissed him this time, and when she caught her breath she knew the grudge was gone. "On what you have in mind." She grinned.

He pulled away, and Hannah had never seen him look more serious. "Marriage. Children. Forever." He kissed her again. "I want to spend my life with you."

They were married that summer, and by Christmas, Hannah was pregnant with Alicia. Jenny came along two years later, and Hannah nearly bled to death in childbirth. There was considerable risk that she would not survive another pregnancy, so she and Tom agreed that their family was complete. God had blessed them mightily. They could get on with raising their girls, and then one day they would share a long and happy retirement together.

At least, that was how it was supposed to be.

In the days after Tom's death, when weariness wore her defenses down, Hannah searched for reasons why God had taken Tom and Alicia. What had she ever done to deserve such punishment? Why her? Why, when God had brought her and Tom together in the first place, would he take her husband and leave her so desperately alone?

It was easier to ignore such questions—easier to ignore God, for that matter. She had prayed to him, served him, and loved him all her life. She thought she knew God, but apparently not. He had given her a past filled with sunshine and left her with a future full of darkness. Because of that, Hannah wasn't sure she wanted to know the Lord anymore. She had nothing to say to him. Anything she might ask him for was already gone forever.

In her other life, the one she lived before the collision, Hannah often fell asleep praying. These days she did not find comfort in prayer. How could she? While she passed the time in a blur of tears and rage and vivid memories, Brian Wesley remained free on bail. Three weeks passed from the time of the accident while detectives gathered evidence and criminalists studied the man's blood sample, finally determining that he had been driving with a blood alcohol level of .24—three times the legal limit.

Since Hannah was not praying, she filled her mind the only way she knew how. She remembered. Nights were the worst. She missed Tom so much it threatened to kill her.

She physically ached to touch him once more, to hold him and kiss him and tuck her feet under his legs as she had always done before falling asleep. She would toss and turn in the empty queen-size bed, finding solace only by drifting back to the beginning. Tom at nine years old, shooting baskets in his driveway; she and Tom racing their bikes down the street, the wind in their hair on some endless, golden summer day; Tom alive and young and handsome at his graduation party, seeing her in a dress for the first time; Tom making her heart beat funny every time he was near....

It was the same every night, one memory after another, as if by remembering, she could somehow bring him home to her. Back where he belonged.

Where he had always belonged.

Nine

Her people fell into enemy hands, there was no one to help her.

LAMENTATIONS 1:7B

Drunk driving laws in the state of California were clear. If a person had a blood alcohol level of .08 or higher, he would be charged with drunk driving. What wasn't clear was the punishment exacted for the offense. A drunk driver could face anything from a one hundred dollar fine to several years in prison, depending on a list of variables. That list included whether the person had prior convictions, and especially whether the drunk driver was involved in an accident that resulted in the death or serious injuries of others.

Los Angeles Deputy District Attorney Matthew J. Bronzan was assigned the case against Brian Wesley more than four weeks after the accident that killed Tom and Alicia Ryan. Drunk driving was his specialty, and he had requested this case. Now, on this October morning as he mulled over a stack of documents and crime scene photos, he was beset by a range of conflicting emotions. He grieved for the family who had been shattered by this man's selfish actions. Brian Wesley was a convicted drunk driver, a man with a history of getting behind the wheel and driving intoxicated. This angered the prosecutor greatly. Dealing with the senselessness of drunk driving deaths always did.

But as he sat at his government-issued desk, in his cramped office at the Criminal Courts Building, Matt Bronzan also felt a deep-rooted surge of excitement. This was the case he'd been waiting for. *The People v Brian Wesley* would change California drunk driving laws forever.

There was a knock at the door, and Sgt. John Miller poked his head inside. "Busy?"

"Hmmm. Come on in."

Sgt. Miller pulled up a chair and sat opposite the prosecutor, leaning back so that the chair's front two legs came up off the ground. "Heard you got the Wesley case."

Matt lifted the stack of paperwork on his desk and let it fall down again. "Right here. Got it this morning."

"First time you heard about it?"

"No. Read about it in the papers. I asked for it."

Sgt. Miller crossed his arms and drew a deep breath. "Then there won't be a plea?"

Matt sat back in his chair and leveled his gaze at the sergeant. "Not a chance."

There was silence a moment, then Sgt. Miller stood and paced toward the window. He stood staring through the dirty glass.

"I was there, you know. Saw the dead girl. Watched her sister lifted onto a stretcher and placed in an ambulance. Stayed with their father until they took him to the hospital." Miller remained motionless, his back to Matt. "Mr. Ryan knew he wasn't going to make it, Matt. Made me promise to tell his wife and girls he loved them."

With a sigh, Miller spun around. "I don't want to see Wesley walk."

Matt glanced down and sorted through the photos on his desk. He found one of Alicia taken at the accident scene, her face bloodied, eyes closed. He thought then of the mother who had lost both her husband and oldest daughter in a single instant. "He's not going to walk. I can promise you that."

Sgt. Miller nodded. "I know you're a believer, Matt. And I know it isn't politically correct to talk about such things on the job. But the man's wife, Hannah Ryan, she's a Christian. The other girl, Jenny, is home now, and social services tells me things aren't good. Hannah's turning away help from her church; she's bitter and angry and barely notices Jenny. It's a mess."

Matt sighed and set the picture down. "It always is. Sometimes the anger kills you."

Sgt. Miller looked uncomfortable. "I know you're busy, Matt, but maybe you could give her a call, Hannah Ryan, I mean. Set her up with someone at MADD, give her some direction."

"Sure. I could do that. Her number's here somewhere."

"Good. Well, I gotta run. Let me know if you get a trial on this thing. I'll testify whenever you need me."

Matt thanked him and watched him leave. Then he picked up the photo of the girl and studied her face once more. It was there all right. Something about the nose or the cheek bones, maybe the shape of her face. Victoria Stevens all over again. Beautiful, intelligent Victoria—

Matt stopped the train of thought. He refused to dwell on Victoria. Instead he studied Alicia's picture again and sighed. What would it be like to have a daughter like this? And to lose her? He was forty-one and married to his job, so he'd had no time for relationships. And that sure wouldn't change now. He needed to stay focused.

Because Brian Wesley was about to help him make history.

In the past, prosecutors had taken cases such as the one against Brian Wesley and been fortunate to win a vehicular manslaughter verdict. But recently, other states had upped the ante. In Louisiana and Tennessee, prosecutors had finally convinced juries that this type of drunk driving was not vehicular manslaughter. It wasn't even second-degree murder. If a repeat offender deliberately chose to drink and drive, and in doing so caused a victim to die, it was nothing less than first-degree murder.

Matt nodded. There were only a couple cases he knew of where that charge had stuck, but it *had* been done before. The problem was it had never been done in California.

Until now.

Matt looked at the picture once more and wondered about Hannah Ryan. Who was she? And how was she dealing with the death of her family? How did anyone deal with this type of thing? Matt clenched his jaw. He knew how powerful anger could be…how it could kill.

He set the pictures down carefully, then he bowed his head and prayed. *Lord, if you are willing, let this be the case. Let the standard change, and let the people of this state understand that there will be no more tolerance for drunk driving. And Lord, help Hannah Ryan, wherever she is. Help her forgive, help her go on. Don't let anger win again. Like it did with Victoria.*

He looked up and sifted through his rolodex until he found the number for Mothers Against Drunk Drivers. There was one person who could help Hannah survive.

He picked up the telephone and began to dial.

Ten

Is any suffering like my suffering that was inflicted on me, that the L*ORD brought on me in the day of his fierce anger?*

LAMENTATIONS 1:12B

Hannah was sitting at the kitchen table, reading over a small stack of newspaper articles about the accident and events surrounding the arrest of Brian Wesley.

"Drunk Driving Suspected in Crash that Killed Local Father, Daughter," read the headline of an article that had appeared in the *Los Angeles Times* the day after the accident. A picture of paramedics working around Tom's mangled Explorer accompanied the article.

The story began, "A West Hills man and his daughter were killed Saturday when the vehicle they were riding in was broadsided by a pickup truck driven by a man suspected of drunk driving. Tom Ryan, 41, and his daughter, Alicia Ryan, 15, were killed in the accident. A second daughter, Jenny Ryan, 13, was taken to Humana West Hills Hospital where she was in stable condition."

Hannah's eyes drifted to another article, this one from a few weeks later. "Tests Show Driver in Deadly Accident was Drunk."

She studied the small black-and-white photograph of Brian Wesley. Her enemy. A predator who had taken aim at her family and destroyed it. *I hate you.* She stared hard at the picture. *Whatever it takes to get you locked up, I'll do it.*

A Bible verse slipped through her mind as if she were reading it off the newspaper before her. It was Colossians 3:13:

"Forgive, as the Lord forgave you." Hannah shuddered. *Forgive? Forgive Brian Wesley?* The idea left a rancid taste in her mouth. *Not this time, Lord. No way.*

She blinked away the verse and read the newspaper article. "The driver who rammed his pickup truck into the side of a sports utility vehicle three weeks ago, killing two people and injuring another, was legally drunk at the time of the accident, according to a report released today from the Los Angeles Police Department. The department's crime lab has determined that Brian Wesley, 28, of Woodland Hills, had a blood alcohol level of .24, three times the legal limit, at the time of the crash, which killed Tom Ryan, 41, his daughter Alicia Ryan, 15, and injured a second daughter, Jenny Ryan, 13."

Jenny. She'd grown so silent, so angry these last few weeks....

Hannah shook her head. She couldn't think about Jenny now. She had to get ready for trial. There would be time for Jenny later. She kept reading. "'There will be no plea bargain in this case. We're looking to prosecute this case to the fullest extent of the law,' Deputy District Attorney Matthew J. Bronzan said. 'Maybe even beyond the fullest extent. This might be the case that changes drunk driving laws in the state of California.'"

Hannah considered the prosecutor's words. *"This might be the case that changes drunk driving laws."* She set her jaw. This *would* be the case. She read the prosecutor's name once more: Matthew J. Bronzan. Amidst the horror and shock and grief, she had an ally, a friend. Someone on her side.

She glanced at a sheet of notebook paper beneath the stack of newspaper articles. She'd written Matthew Bronzan's office number and a list of questions she needed to ask him. What did he mean he was looking to prosecute this case beyond the fullest extent of the law? What was she within her rights to do? How could she help? Was there any chance a plea bargain would be struck? The list went on.

She reached for the phone just as it began to ring. Hannah

stared at it, confused for a moment. The phone used to ring constantly. Now, nearly five weeks after the accident, no one called.

Hannah realized she was partly to blame. She had refused help from her church friends, and finally they had stopped calling. The hospital certainly had no reason to call now with Tom gone, and Jenny's friends didn't know what to say so they didn't call. Hannah couldn't remember the last time the phone rang.

"Hello." She no longer recognized her own voice.

"Hannah Ryan?" The woman at the other end sounded pleasant.

"Yes."

"This is Carol Cummins. I work with Mothers Against Drunk Drivers. Matt Bronzan gave me your number."

Matt Bronzan. How did he get my number? "Oh…hello."

"Mr. Bronzan tells me there's a hearing tomorrow. Brian Wesley will be officially charged, and they'll have to decide whether the case will be settled by plea bargain or whether it will be held over for trial."

Hannah picked up the article she had just been reading. "The paper said there wasn't going to be a plea bargain."

"They still have to go through the motions, hear the arguments from Mr. Wesley's attorney, and present arguments of their own."

"But who makes the final decision?" She could hear the panic in her voice.

"Matt Bronzan has the last word. It comes down to what he thinks he can prove in court." Carol paused. "If he sets the charges high, and Mr. Wesley refuses to plead guilty, there will be a trial."

"Good. I'd like to see it go to trial."

The woman paused again. "Sometimes. Sometimes not. It depends on the jury. If they think the charges are unreasonable, there's a chance Mr. Wesley could walk with no punishment at all."

Hannah's rage bubbled closer to the surface. "That could happen?"

"Yes. That's why these cases end in plea bargains so many times. At least that way the drunk driver gets some kind of punishment."

"I can't *believe* that." Hannah's hands trembled with rage.

Carol Cummins sighed. "Unfortunately, that's the way things are in the legal arena of drunk driving cases. Three out of ten jurors identify with the defendant. They listen to the evidence and hear about the violent accidents and needless deaths, and they think, 'There but for the grace of God go I.'"

"Three out of ten?" This was all new to Hannah, and it made her head spin.

"Surveys are done all the time asking people if they've ever driven drunk. Generally thirty percent of Americans have." She paused. "They look at the guy on trial and see themselves. Usually they decide the guilt is punishment enough, and they convict him on a lesser charge or let him go."

Hannah stood up and paced across her dining room floor, the cordless phone cradled against her shoulder as she studied the previous day's article. She focused on the tiny photograph. How could anyone identify with Brian Wesley? Who in their right mind wouldn't want to see a repeat drunk driver locked up? She exhaled loudly. "What do you mean, *lesser charge?*"

"Sometimes a prosecutor will attempt to prove two or three charges at once. If the jury doesn't feel strongly enough to convict on the more serious charge, they can find a defendant guilty of a lesser charge."

Hannah stopped pacing. "But if what you said before is true, that three out of ten will identify with him, the jury's always going to go for the lesser one."

"Exactly."

Hannah closed her eyes, struggling against the wave of rage that pushed at her. She couldn't believe what she was hearing. "What's Mr. Bronzan going to do?"

"I'm not sure. I only talked to him for a few minutes, but he feels very strongly about this one."

"Meaning?"

"There's a chance he'll charge the driver with something very serious and leave it at that."

Hannah considered the possibilities. "But then there's a chance Brian Wesley will get off. Go free. Is that right?"

Carol's voice was quiet. "That's right."

Hannah resumed pacing. "Why hasn't something been done about this?"

"Drunk driving, you mean? We're trying, Mrs. Ryan. That's what Mothers Against Drunk Drivers is all about."

"I want to help." Hannah's heart was fluttering about in her chest. *Whatever it takes.* "Tell me what to do." Hannah paced toward the dining room table and set the articles down.

Carol drew a deep breath. "Well, most of our efforts focus on public awareness. If we can make people more aware of the consequences, we can accomplish several things."

"I'm listening."

"We can reduce drunk driving, for one thing. You've heard of our campaigns. 'Friends don't let friends drive drunk.' 'Be a Designated Driver.' 'Tie one on,' which is our red ribbon program."

"I've seen those. Tied around car antennas, you mean?"

"Right. We pass them out at our office and at various storefronts. People tie them on to show a united force in the war against drunk driving."

"I had no idea…it's so…"

"Organized? Yes, it has to be."

"And the key is public awareness?"

"Right. It stops a percentage of drunk drivers, but it also educates the public."

"The public?"

"Yes. Jurors are chosen from the public."

The words sank in, and Hannah nodded. Of course. She

scribbled the word juror and underlined it several times. "I get it. The more people who understand, the less likely a jury is to let a drunk driving defendant go free."

"Exactly."

Hannah tapped her pen on the notepad. "You say public awareness, and I picture television ads and billboards. I guess I don't see how I can help."

"We have something called a victim impact panel, Mrs. Ryan. Three or four people who've been directly affected by drunk driving travel to schools and local government meetings and make presentations."

Hannah felt tears forming in her eyes, and suddenly her voice was too choked to speak. After a moment of silence, Carol gently continued. "We encourage panel members to bring pictures, their loved one's favorite clothing, anything that will make what has happened more real."

Tears slid down Hannah's cheeks and she sniffed softly. "I could do that, Mrs. Cummins." She paused. "I will do that. When can we meet?"

"Call me Carol. And we can meet soon." The woman's voice was filled with compassion, and Hannah knew she had another ally. "I think we should attend the hearing tomorrow. Are you free?"

Hannah felt an ache in her gut—and a hole in her heart. Tom was gone. Alicia, too. Jenny was back in school, and the two of them barely spoke. Was she free? She shook her head. Her calendar would be open the rest of her life. The only thing that mattered was getting Brian Wesley behind bars. Now… now there was a way to make that happen.

She could tell people what had happened to Tom and Alicia. And maybe, if she worked hard enough, she would do more than put Brian Wesley away. Maybe she would change drunk driving laws forever.

She exhaled sadly. "Yes. I'm open. And please…call me Hannah."

"Okay, Hannah. The hearing is at ten. Judge Rudy Horowitz is presiding. Let's meet outside the courtroom at quarter 'til."

"I'll be there."

"I'll introduce you to Mr. Bronzan. You need to talk to him, see what he wants you to do before you get involved in a victim impact panel."

"All right."

"Oh...and if you could, bring a small photograph of Tom and Alicia. I have a pin with the Mothers Against Drunk Drivers' logo. We'll put their picture inside, and you can wear it anytime there's a hearing."

Hannah was silent, but she couldn't stop the single sob from slipping out.

Carol's voice was compassionate. "I'm sorry, Hannah. I know it's hard. But every bit helps. Sometimes in all the legal maneuvering, the victims are forgotten."

Hannah nodded and gulped back what felt like a torrent of tears. "I'll bring the pictures."

Carol paused. "No one knows your personal pain, Hannah, but that dark place you're in? I've been there."

Hannah's shoulders slumped. She hadn't thought about it before, but it made sense. Carol must have lost someone in a drunk driving accident, too. She closed her eyes tightly, her heart heavier than before. "Thanks, Carol. I'll see you tomorrow."

The conversation ended, and Hannah replaced the phone on its base.

Pictures of Tom and Alicia.

Hannah drew a steadying breath and remained motionless, bracing herself against the kitchen counter as she stared distantly through the living room window into the backyard. They had lived in this house for fifteen years, ever since Tom had finished his residency. The swing set stood where it had since Tom and she assembled it one Christmas back when the girls were four and six.

She studied the swings, and she could see Alicia, her long, honey-colored hair flowing down her back in a single ponytail. As a child, Alicia had spent hours on that swing set. Hannah could remember working in the kitchen, making dinner and passing the time watching her little girl swing back and forth, smiling and singing. She was such a happy little girl.

The image faded, and Hannah padded slowly across the living room to the bookcase and her collection of photo albums. She examined the dates on the side of each until she found the most recent. She took it from the shelf and ran her hand over its cover. Just as she was about to open it, her eyes fell on another album, one from more than a decade ago.

Hannah smiled sadly. She had never been one to toss photographs in a drawer and forget about them. Her album collection was complete, intricately organized.

She removed the older album and opened it, turning the pages reverently. As she did, her breath caught in her throat. On the third page was a picture of Alicia, two years old, sitting in a wagon. The little girl was wearing only a diaper, a lopsided grin, and a white plastic cowboy hat. Alicia's hair had gotten darker as she grew older, but back then her wispy blond locks stuck out from beneath the hat at all angles. Hannah closed her eyes and remembered the moment. She could feel the sun on her shoulders as she snapped the picture…hear Alicia's voice chirping happily, "I'm a little cowpope! Happy little cowpope!"

Hannah laughed out loud, despite her tears. Alicia had been five before she could say *cowpoke* correctly.

Another image came to mind then, and Hannah felt her smile disappear. Alicia, two years old, lying on a hospital bed, deathly white and hooked to IV lines. It had happened a month before Jenny was born. Alicia was taking a nap and Hannah, exhausted from the final days of her pregnancy, decided to slip into her own bedroom and lie down.

She woke to the sound of Alicia choking, gasping for breath. She'd raced to the kitchen to find Alicia curled in a ball, lying on the floor, an open bottle of kitchen cleaner nearby. Hannah had forgotten to put it away.

Dear God, help me! Prayer had been a natural response then.

In the end, as he had always done back then, God came through. Doctors observed Alicia through the night and then sent her home the next morning, singing a merry song about flowers and sunshine as she skipped to the family car.

Hannah shut the photo album, set it aside, and covered her face with her hands. She wept then as she hadn't since the day of the collision. "Why?" she shouted. "*Why,* God?"

She cried out again and again, releasing the anger and frustration and gut-wrenching grief that grew deep within her. Why would God watch over Alicia when she was two, only to walk away from her when she was fifteen? As hard as she tried, Hannah couldn't understand why God had stopped listening to her…why he had turned his back.

"What did—I ever do—to deserve this?" Hannah was sobbing too hard to catch her breath.

Eventually, her sobbing grew quieter, and she stared at the picture of Alicia as her mind drifted. Her favorite hymn came to mind, and Hannah found herself humming along. *"Great is thy faithfulness, great is thy faithfulness, morning by morning new mercies I see. All I have needed thy hand–"*

Hannah jerked, realizing what she was doing, what she was saying. *Stop!* She angrily forced the song from her mind. It was a horrible song, full of lies. The Lord was not faithful; the mornings were without mercy, without any hope or reason for moving beyond the edge of the bed. And everything she had ever needed from God he had taken from her the day Tom and Alicia died.

Hannah's eyes stung with fresh tears. The words of that hymn used to describe the perfect life she and Tom shared. The organist had played it at their wedding. The choir had sung it when Alicia—and then Jenny—was dedicated. If ever there was a hymn Hannah had been able to sing from her heart it was "Great Is Thy Faithfulness." Now the song was nothing more than a painful reminder of how God had let her down. *Great* was *thy faithfulness*.

No matter what else might happen, she would never, ever sing that song again.

She was still sniffling softly, still holding the photo albums, trying to find the strength to search for a picture of Tom and Alicia that she could take to tomorrow's hearing, when she heard the front door open.

"Mom?" It was Jenny.

"In here." Hannah wiped at her tears. She heard her daughter traipse through the house and set her books on the kitchen counter. Then she watched as the girl poked her head into the living room. Poor Jenny. She looked as though she had aged a decade since the accident—and Hannah saw something unspeakably sad in her eyes.

Before Hannah could say anything, Jenny looked intently at her face…then at the photo albums on her lap. Rolling her eyes, Jenny sighed softly. "Never mind." She turned and headed for the stairs.

"Jenny, wait." Hannah stood, too weak from grief to move.

The only reply was the sound of footsteps making their way up the stairs, toward the bedrooms.

"Jenny! I want to talk to you!" New tears filled Hannah's eyes, and she collapsed back onto the floor, her legs curled under her.

You're losing her, too. Hannah closed her eyes against the small voice. *Go. Talk to her before it's too late.*

She shook her head. She wouldn't chase Jenny. The girl was being selfish and insensitive; if she didn't want to talk, then so be it. She grabbed a tissue from the nearby end table and blew her nose. Then she put the older photo album away and pulled the newer one onto her lap.

"Sometimes the victims are forgotten." Hannah clenched her teeth and searched the collection of photos. Tom and Alicia would not be forgotten. Not as long as she had anything to do with the court proceedings.

She drew a deep breath and scanned the photographs until she found a shot of Tom and Alicia. They were grinning into the camera as they worked over the gas grill during a family barbecue at the beginning of summer. It was a close-up and probably the best recent picture of the two of them.

She ran a finger over their faces. Tom had said he didn't know how he'd get through either of his daughter's weddings. Especially after Bob Carlisle's song "Butterfly Kisses" became popular. Any time he heard the piece, Tom would beat his chest once, just above his heart. "Ughh. Kill me with that song. When my girls get married, they're gonna have to pour me out of the church in a bucket. Better buy stock in Kleenex while there's still time."

There was no need now, no weddings to dread, no oldest daughter to walk down the aisle. *Poor Jenny, baby. One day you'll have to make that walk alone.* Hannah worked her fingers under the plastic sleeve and removed the photograph, setting it on the table next to the tissues.

She flipped forward a few pages until her eyes fell on another photo, this one of her and Tom taken that past June. They were atop a pair of rented horses, about to ride through the Santa Monica Mountains. Hannah closed her eyes, and she could feel the cool ocean fog against her skin; her senses were filled with the salty summer air and the sweet smell of horse sweat as it drifted up from beneath the saddle. They had ridden for several hours before returning and driving to Malibu Park, where they had sat side by side on a bench overlooking the deep green canyon and shared peanut butter sandwiches.

Hannah kept her eyes closed. Everything about that moment seemed so real…

Was she still there, sitting beside Tom, waiting for him to tell her it was time to go home? Maybe every devastating thing that had happened since then had only been part of a terrible nightmare.…

She waited—and heaviness settled over her. No. She was

not at Malibu Park. And Tom would never sit beside her again.

In this life…

She shut the reassurance out. There was no comfort in dwelling on thoughts of eternity. If there *was* an eternity. Today was all that mattered.

And today, Tom and Alicia were gone.

She sighed and opened her eyes, allowing her gaze to fall on the picture once again. Tom looked so young and alive, so handsome. He had pulled his horse up to hers and casually draped an arm around her shoulders. Then she'd handed her camera to a stable boy.

"Memories for another day," she'd said and Tom had groaned. He had always teased her about her excessive photo taking.

"Here we go. Dan Rather, capturing the moment for posterity." He raised an eyebrow and met the grinning gaze of the stable boy. "Don't laugh. Your turn will come, boy." Then he grinned at Hannah. "One day I'll have to build us a separate wing just to hold our photo albums. That's how many memories we have for another day."

She looked at the photo, and she could still see the laughter in his eyes. Tears slid down her face again.…Would they ever stop? She shook her head, feeling as though she were falling down a deep, dark well. Would she ever snap another photograph? She couldn't fathom it. Not when the only memories that mattered were those that were already made. She lifted the photo album, clutching it against her chest.

"Oh, Tom…where are you? How can you be gone?" She sniffed and rocked back and forth, cradling the album close. "I'm so alone, Tom."

She squeezed her eyes shut, staying that way a long while, hugging the cold, plastic-covered page against her heart—and with it, all that remained of the man she'd loved since she was a child.

Eleven

He has handed me over to those I cannot withstand.

LAMENTATIONS 1:14B

The meeting took place in a windowless room located on the first floor of the Los Angeles Superior Court Criminal Courts Building. Only two parties were present: Harold Finch, defense attorney for Brian Wesley, and deputy district attorney Matthew Bronzan.

Matt knew his opponent well. Finch was a hard-nosed defender whose primary source of income came from defending drunk drivers. The man's business card sported the image of a martini glass and announced, "Caught having too much fun? Drunk driving arrest got you down? We can help." Matt kept the card tucked into the frame around his desk calendar. A reminder to keep fighting the war, keep battling the cases until the words *fun* and *drunk driving* would never appear in the same paragraph.

Finch referred to himself as "the drunk driver's best friend," and one day Matt did some research to see what made his opponent tick. He was surprised at what he found.

Rumor was that fifteen years earlier, Edward Finch—Harold's older brother—had developed a promising future in law. Common knowledge had it that the two brothers had attended law school together and planned to go into practice one day. Back then, they were hardworking, clean-cut young men; lawyers who dreamed big and planned to change the world by righting wrongs, one case at a time.

Edward never got the chance.

The summer after he graduated law school, he attended a wedding where the air-conditioning broke down during the reception. Hundred-degree temperatures had people sweltering in the ballroom, and Edward spent much of his time camped out at the punch bowl. From everything Matt had heard, Edward Finch had never been a drinker, and he didn't know until the third glass that the punch was spiked. Of course, after that it didn't matter. With all the dancing and mingling, there was only one way to cool down…so Edward drank crystal goblets of punch until he lost count.

Apparently Edward's young wife tried to talk him into calling a cab or getting a room at the hotel, but Edward wouldn't hear of it. So they got in the car. Halfway home there was a police officer pulled off the road, writing someone up for speeding. Drawn by the flashing lights, Edward let his car drift off the road—until he rear-ended the police car, narrowly missing the officer. No one was injured, but the officer took the accident personally. According to court records, the officer later testified that Edward had acted in a "belligerent manner," that he'd been clearly intoxicated and said, "Next time I drive drunk, I'll take better aim."

Edward swore up and down he'd never said anything of the sort, but his trial took place three weeks after a well-publicized incident in which a young mother had been killed by a drunk driver while walking her daughter to school. The jury made an example of Edward Finch, and he received a one-year sentence in county jail.

Midway through the term, his wife left him. When he got out of prison, he was a broken man, a convict with no apartment, no money, no license to practice law, and no chance at his much dreamed-about career. From everything Matt heard, Harold did what he could to help his brother, suggesting odd jobs and encouraging Edward to appeal for reinstatement with the California Bar Association. But depression set in, and Edward began drinking in earnest.

Last anyone had heard, the man roamed the streets in urine-drenched rags, slept under park benches, and was hopelessly addicted to alcohol. A victim of unjust circumstances—at least, that's how Harold saw it.

Matt understood Harold Finch better after finding out all of this, and in some very small way he pitied the man. The knowledge of Finch's past made him human.

Wrong, but human.

In the wake of what had happened to his brother, Harold Finch changed gears and apparently decided that the best wrong he could possibly right was the wrong done to his brother. He would help drunk drivers if it took a lifetime to establish their rights. Early on, so it was said, Finch had been utterly sincere.

"You know the old saying—" Finch was famous for telling jurors as he cocked his head and linked his fingers over his extended belly—"'There but for the grace of God go I.'"

But somewhere along the road of defending DUI offenders—many of whom were responsible for tragic deaths and mayhem—Finch had changed. Gone was the lawyerly attitude and appearance. In their place was the look and demeanor of a pimp, complete with pinstriped suits and vests with shiny gold buttons that strained against the man's sizable gut. Finch also began calling himself Deuce Dog, a play on the slang for DUIs: deuces.

High profile drunk driving cases always seemed to wind up in Finch's hands, and between appointments he strutted through the courthouse, chest puffed out, brimming with confidence and pride.

Matt figured Finch was a case of someone who'd grown callused, hardened to the devastation he defended so well. Bad company had finally corrupted what were, at the beginning, good intentions. The way Matt saw it, Harold's brash and cocky attitude was probably a cover-up for the pain he felt for his brother. Nevertheless, Matt did not want to lose to him.

Not this time.

Matt had gone toe-to-toe with Finch on many cases, and most resulted in plea bargains. Matt hated plea bargains. He'd agreed to dozens of them over the years, but only because he knew the system as well as his opponent did. Sometimes it was better to plea-bargain and send a defendant away with community service obligations, a fine, and a mark on his record. Especially when the alternative was to waste valuable court time prosecuting a case that could very well result in a not-guilty verdict.

Only twice had Matt and Finch battled it out before a jury. Both times Matt had won convictions. The first involved an elderly woman who suffered major head injuries after a drunk driver had run her down while she was carrying a gallon of milk home from the market. Finch's client was convicted of reckless driving and received two hundred hours of community service along with a fifteen hundred dollar fine. Hardly satisfying, considering that the last time Matt had checked, the elderly woman remained in a vegetative state, strapped to a hospital bed at a sour-smelling nursing home.

The second case involved a nineteen-year-old boy who drove his fifteen-year-old cousin home from a party. The nineteen-year-old misjudged the lane boundaries and hit a hundred-year-old maple tree at fifty miles per hour. His cousin had died on impact. Both boys had been legally drunk.

Finch's client was convicted of reckless endangerment, and because it was the boy's first offense, prison time was waived. He, too, received community service and a fine.

Although Matt had won convictions in both cases, clearly Finch had been the victor. His clients were not confined to a nursing home or a graveyard. Their lives went on as they had before, without even a single night in prison to remind them of the consequences of their choice to drink and drive.

Matt gritted his teeth. He'd spent years prosecuting drunk drivers, but still jurors had never connected driving under the influence with intent to kill.

Until now.

Matt's jaw tensed. God willing, he—and the case against Brian Wesley—were about to change that fact.

A blast of cheap cologne filled the room, and he glanced up to find Finch standing there, the ever-present cocky smile on his face.

"Well, well—" Finch tossed his martini business card across the table—"guess we got ourselves another plea to work out, eh, Bronzan?"

Matt met the man's gaze steadily. "Not this time."

Finch's expression changed. "A bit jumpy today, aren't we?" He let loose a tinny chuckle and pulled a document from the stack before him, eyebrows raising a fraction as he studied Matt. "Read it, counselor."

Matt leaned back against the hard wood chair and crossed his arms. "Your client is a repeat drunk driver who caused two previous collisions despite alcohol education. And now he's killed two people. His blood alcohol level was three times the legal limit." He fixed Finch with a hard stare. "There will be no plea…*counselor.*"

Finch paused, and a knowing look danced in his eyes. "Perhaps, *Mr.* Bronzan, you should read the plea before summarily dismissing it."

Matt glanced at his watch and pulled the document closer. "Unless Mr. Wesley plans to admit to murder, we don't have much to talk about."

Finch was silent while Matt scanned the document. He sucked in a deep breath. The plea was brilliant, of course. Matt had expected nothing less from Finch. Dime-store cologne and gold vest buttons aside, the man knew his stuff. Had the plea been for reckless driving or any such minor charge, Matt could have rejected it easily. But Finch had upped the ante. His client was willing to plead guilty to vehicular manslaughter. Even more, he was willing to serve thirty days in jail for the offense.

In all Matt's years of prosecuting, he'd never seen such a

serious crime admitted by way of plea bargain.

There was only one reason his opponent would present such an offer. Matt studied Finch's beady eyes, and what he saw there confirmed his suspicions.

Harold Finch was scared.

Glancing at the document once more, Matt thought of the heartache a trial would cause Hannah Ryan and her surviving daughter. He thought of the many times a jury had refused to convict a drunk driver of even second-degree murder, let alone first-degree. The Ryans would suffer indescribable pain if the jury let Brian Wesley leave the courtroom a free man....

Then he thought of Tom and Alicia...of the family broken apart, destroyed by Brian Wesley's choices. He remembered others like the Ryans who had been dragged through the criminal justice system only to be let down when penalties were inadequate. No, there would be no plea bargain this time. This was the case he'd been waiting for.

Finch looked pleased with himself as he cleared his throat and motioned toward the plea bargain. "Well, Bronzan, do we have a plea?"

Matt slid the document across the table and watched it settle in front of Finch.

"No. We want a trial."

Finch chuckled and looked down the bridge of his fleshy nose at Matt. "Now, I've worked with you for many years, Bronzan. And even though we've been on opposite sides of the courtroom, I've always taken you for a smart lawyer. Clear on the ways of justice. But if I'm not mistaken, I do believe you're losing your edge."

Matt ignored the comment. "Tomorrow this office will officially charge your client with first-degree murder. At that time he can choose to plead guilty or not guilty."

Finch's laughter died abruptly and his gaze hardened. "I don't need a lesson on law, counselor. Look, we're offering prison time here."

"When I'm finished with your client, we won't be talking thirty days jail time, we'll be talking five years in the penitentiary. Maybe more." Matt considered his opponent and how he'd changed over the years. "There won't be a plea, Finch. You can't change my mind."

Finch waited, but when Matt remained silent his eyes narrowed angrily. "Most generous plea I've ever made." He sighed dramatically as he collected the document and stuffed it into his briefcase. "Next time we offer less. Much less."

"There won't be a next time. Not on this case."

Finch arched an eyebrow. "That right? You'll see, counselor. You'll get in court and start talking first-degree murder, start making the vehicle out to be a weapon and Mr. Wesley out to be a killer. Then you'll see the faces on those jurors and you'll panic. A third of the folks in this great nation drink and drive, my friend. And that includes jurors." He studied Matt. "They won't give you first-degree murder. It's drunk driving, after all. Guy goes out, drinks a few beers, has a little fun with the boys, and drives home. The accident was just that. *Any* jail time is out of line as far as I'm concerned." Finch slammed his briefcase shut. "But in this case my client and I have tried to show compassion for the victims. We offered thirty days in good faith."

Matt remained seated, his arms casually crossed. "Thirty days? In exchange for a husband and father, a daughter on the brink of adulthood? Thirty days for two lives?"

"Thirty days is better than nothing, Bronzan. The victims' family would have been happy with that." Finch shrugged. "Now you're going to drag them through a messy court battle. A battle you're going to lose, counselor. And they're going to lose, too."

Matt stood and stretched, and suddenly a mountain of anxiety rose within him. *How can I turn down voluntary jail time? What if Brian Wesley walks?* He released his breath slowly and waited as Finch continued relentlessly.

"Turn down a manslaughter plea and you have nothing left." He shook his head. "First-degree murder? Huh! My client will walk, Bronzan, mark my words."

"The only walking he'll be doing is from his cell to the yard and back."

"You could take the plea and still come out the winner, here, Bronzan. It's not too late."

Matt straightened. "Are you finished?"

Finch shook his head sadly. "You really have lost it, counselor. No way a jury's going to make drunk driving a murder-one issue. Not in the great state of California."

Matt waited, silent, as Finch headed for the door.

"I'll be asking for a delay."

Matt cocked his head. "Just one?"

Finch's eyes grew cold. "One per month until we run out of reasons. By the time this thing takes the floor, the world will have forgotten all about Tom and Alicia Ryan."

Matt thought of the pictures, photos taken at the accident scene. Broken glass and blood and camping gear spilled onto the road. He thought of the young girl laid out on a stretcher, her body stilled forever…so reminiscent of another whose life had been wasted…

He leveled a look at Finch. "Not me. I'll never forget."

The defense attorney studied him as if he were a curious oddity. "You've forgotten the first rule of law, counselor, don't get emotionally involved. First-degree murder?" He scratched his head, his face contorted in disbelief. "You're out of your mind."

Finch left the room and shut the door behind him. Matt stood there, staring after him, his hands in his pockets. *Finch is worried. He's afraid I'm right.* He closed his eyes and sighed deeply. *Please, Lord, let me be right.*

After tomorrow there would be no turning back.

Twelve

This is why I weep and my eyes overflow with tears.
No one is near to comfort me.

LAMENTATIONS 1:16A

Hannah smoothed a hand over her black rayon slacks and straightened her short-sleeved blouse. The hearing was in two hours, and she planned to be early. She walked briskly down the hallway toward the bedroom.

"Jenny? Are you up?"

Silence.

Hannah sighed. Since their disagreement the day before, Jenny had hidden away in her room, even refusing dinner. Hannah strode up to her daughter's bedroom door and knocked twice. No response.

"Jenny, open the door right now!" Hannah shifted her weight and began tapping a steady rhythm with the toe of her shoe. She could hear Jenny moving on the other side of the door and finally it swung open.

"What?" Jenny's eyes were tear stained; her voice sounded thick, as though she were fighting a cold. She was dressed in rumpled pajamas and fuzzy, Dalmatian slippers.

At the sight of her disheveled, clearly miserable little girl, Hannah was pierced with guilt and heartache. She stopped tapping and sighed, her voice sadder than before. "Honey, you haven't said two words to me since yesterday. I need to know your plans. I'm getting ready to leave for the hearing this morning."

Jenny crossed her arms. "What do you want to know?"

"Well, for starters—" Hannah forced herself to sound understanding, even patient—"are you going to school or coming with me?"

Jenny was silent, her eyes glazed with unresolved anger and grief.

Hannah sighed. "Jenny, I think you should come with me today. Carol Cummins called yesterday. She's the woman from Mothers Against Drunk Drivers." Hannah hesitated. "She said sometimes the victims get forgotten in these court proceedings."

Jenny huffed. "No kidding."

Hannah frowned. What on earth did that mean? "I'll ignore that comment. What I'm trying to say is, we need to be there to represent your dad and Alicia. We're the only ones who can do that."

"Dad and Alicia are dead." Jenny turned, plodded across the room, and fell onto her unmade bed. "I'm staying home today."

Hannah's heartbeat quickened and she felt her face grow hot. "That isn't an option. You need to get dressed and make your bed. Then you need to either get yourself to the bus stop or come with me to the hearing."

"I don't feel good."

Hannah's heart sank. Jenny had always been the picture of health. Before the accident, she was routinely recognized for perfect attendance in school. Now she'd missed twelve days since returning to school, and she rarely woke up enthusiastic about anything. "Honey, you've missed too much school already."

Jenny began crying again. "I thought you *wanted* me to miss school! So you can haul me off to court and show me off, so everyone can stare at me like...like I'm some kind of *freak* or something!"

Hannah clenched her fists. *Why can't you understand? Jenny, what's happening to us?* "Never mind. Don't come to the hearing. I just thought you might feel better if you did something constructive."

Jenny sat up, her shoulders hunched wearily. "What's constructive about sitting in a courtroom while people walk around feeling sorry for you?"

"Someone has to represent your dad and Alicia." Hannah heard her voice getting louder, and she struggled to regain control.

"This isn't about Daddy and Alicia. It's about that guy who hit us. You want him locked up and...and you want to use me as some kind of...I don't know, some kind of puppet to make everyone feel sorry for us."

Hannah felt as if she'd been slapped. She reeled, taking a step backward. "That's not fair, Jenny! That man *destroyed* our family. Yes, I want him locked up. So he won't do this to anyone else. If our being there could possibly help get him off the streets, then your dad and Alicia's deaths will not be in vain."

"That's a lousy reason to die, Mom. I need them here. I want them *here*. Besides, I don't care what happens to that guy. I'm not going to court...not today or any other day! It won't bring Dad and Alicia back, and that's the only thing that matters."

Hannah felt the sting of tears. She wanted to go to Jenny, comfort her, and hold her. Take away the hurt. But Hannah's own pain seemed to create an invisible wall between them too high to scale. "Fine. Don't go. But I'll expect you to get dressed and be at the bus on time." Hannah glanced at her watch. "You have forty-five minutes."

"I said I don't feel good."

Hannah's sympathy evaporated. "Listen, Jenny, unless you want to repeat this year, you need to go to school. I don't feel good, either. It's part of life these days."

Jenny was silent again, and Hannah turned to leave. How had this happened? How had she and Jenny grown so distant? If only Tom were here. He would know what to say, how to reach her....

She collected the photograph of Tom and Alicia and placed

it carefully in her day-planner. She had lost so much, and somehow it seemed like the losing had only begun. In the end, when the court proceedings were behind her...would she have lost Jenny, too? Hannah wiped at a single tear, grabbed her car keys, and forced herself to think of the events that lay ahead.

For an instant she considered praying, considered asking God to help Jenny understand. Maybe if she begged him to repair their damaged relationship, he would help them, restore them, so that at least they would have each other. But the thought of praying made Hannah's skin crawl. It was the same creepy feeling she used to get when she and Tom would see a television commercial for the Psychic Hotline.

That was when the idea came to her. She ignored it for a moment, but it wouldn't go away. And for the first time in her life, Hannah considered an unthinkable possibility: Perhaps everything she'd ever learned and believed about God was just fable and fairy tale. Perhaps God didn't really exist at all. At least you could see the Psychic Hotline people, but God...what proof was there?

No God. It was a plausible explanation, and as Hannah tested it in her heart and mind, she felt herself becoming convinced.

Yes, that had to be it. There was no God. No father in heaven who had deserted her, no Lord who had allowed her family to be destroyed. Perhaps all of life was only a random crapshoot.

The idea was strangely comforting, and by the time Hannah climbed into her car and headed for the Criminal Courts Building, she had accepted it as truth.

Brian Wesley sat on a cold wooden chair in a holding room adjacent to Courtroom 201, home of the formidable Judge Rudy Horowitz. He fidgeted with a paper clip, twisting it back and forth until it broke into tiny metal strips. Across the table from him sat his lawyer, Harold Finch.

"You understand the order of events today?" Finch's chest heaved as he tried to catch his breath. The hearing was in fifteen minutes, and Finch had just arrived to court. Late, as usual.

Brian turned in his chair and studied his trembling fingers. "They charge me with murder. I tell 'em I'm not guilty."

"Right." Finch studied him. "Try to sound sure of yourself."

Brian nodded, his eyes downcast.

"You remember what I've told you about Judge Horowitz?"

"No nonsense. Doesn't like drunk drivers."

"Good." Finch breathed easier. "You been off the bottle?"

"Sometimes. I drink a little now and then, but no driving, man. Don't worry."

Finch's face grew red and he frowned. "It's going to take more than that, Mr. Wesley! You need to stop drinking. This case will go to trial, and if the prosecutor can prove you're still drinking, there's a chance you'll be convicted of first-degree murder."

Brian gulped and his palms began to sweat. When he could speak again, his voice was pinched. "You said that wouldn't happen."

"It's never happened in the history of California." Finch set his elbows on the table and leaned closer to Brian. "But jurors are changing. They're only sympathetic to a point. If they think you're going to drink and drive again, maybe hurt *their* families or friends, they just might put you away."

Brian picked up a broken piece of the paper clip and ran his finger over its smooth length. "I'm trying to stop, man."

"How about AA? You connected with a group yet?"

"I went once. Some guy led the thing...kept talking about higher power this, and God that. I couldn't relate, you know?"

Finch waved a hand in dismissal. "The God stuff is part of the deal. No one says you have to believe it, but if you're not in with an AA group, you'll lose the jury's sympathy for sure."

Brian looked down again, and his eyes fell on another paper clip. He reached out and pulled it closer. "So...what? Pretend I'm some kind of Jesus freak?"

"God, Jesus, Buddah, higher power…whatever. Just go along with it. This has nothing to do with your personal belief system. It has to do with keeping your pickled behind out of prison. Understand?"

Brian nodded and bent the paper clip until it was unrecognizable.

Finch summed up Brian, and his face became a mask of doubt. "I plan to win this case, Mr. Wesley. But I am going to need your cooperation."

"Got it."

"All right, that's better. Listen, I have to talk to someone down the hall. I'll be back in ten minutes, and we'll get set up in the courtroom."

Brian did not look up as his attorney left the room. A ripple of terror ran through him like a current of electricity. *How did I get here?* His heart skipped a beat in response. *Wasn't I doing my best work ever, sober for three weeks? How did everything get so messed up?* He closed his eyes and he could see Carla, the devastated look on her face when she picked him up at the county jail the night of the accident.

She had said nothing until they were in her car. Then her voice had been barely more than a whisper. "How could you, Brian?"

He hadn't answered her. He had still been drunk, after all, and there was no point defending himself to Carla. But she'd been relentless, horrified at what had happened. "Brian, do you understand? You *killed* two people!"

He tried to explain that it was an accident…of course he hadn't meant to hurt anyone. But Carla was furious and unforgiving. For days after the accident she stayed away from him, almost as if she were afraid of him. When they spoke, she talked of nothing but the accident, the impending court proceedings—and the biggest issue of all—when Brian was finally going to quit drinking.

A week after the accident Brian could take no more. He moved out and took up residence on the sofa bed at a friend's nearby apartment. Jackson Lamer was a party buddy from Brian's high school days, faithful and true, always ready with a cold one when the chips were down.

"Dude, whatever you need," Jackson had told him after hearing about the accident. He popped the top of an aluminum beer can and handed it to Brian. "Rides to court, AA meetings. Whatever, dude. You're in righteous, big-time trouble, and that's what buds are for, man. Just let me know."

Jackson was a keeper, the kind of friend Brian wished he had more of.

Police had impounded Brian's car, and the few times he had needed a ride in the weeks since, Jackson had come through. Days were difficult, wondering if he should look for a job or wait until the courts were through with him. But evenings were better, he and Jackson would pass the hours sharing a twelve-pack, talking about old times.

Since the accident, only Jackson had been faithful. Everyone else had forsaken him: Avery Automotive, Carla, even the beer. Back in the old days, the drink always made things okay, but ever since the accident, there was no peace—not in drinking or sleeping...and definitely not in thinking. Day or night, whenever he closed his eyes, he was haunted by them. The girl lying lifeless on the side of the road; her father trapped in their family car, his life slowly draining away. A mother and sister left alone, brokenhearted.

He hated himself for what he'd done to them.

He tried to block out their faces, but they pushed their way into his mind anyway. And with them came images of demons, laughing, taunting him, offering him another drink. Brian swallowed hard around the lump in his throat.

The legal proceedings were pointless. Whatever happened in court, he was already trapped in the worst kind of prison.

He looked around, searching for another paper clip, but found none.

A meeting for alcoholics had offered no relief. Finch had

called with the information, explaining that there was a meeting one mile from Jackson's apartment. Brian remembered the evening well. He had stayed clean for the occasion, and that evening Jackson had dropped him off.

"Give it a try, man." He'd shrugged. "Who knows, maybe I'll join you one day."

Brian walked through the double glass doors nervously, signed in, and found a seat. The room was filled with twenty or so men and women ranging in age from early twenties to late fifties. Most of them looked comfortable, like they'd been meeting together for years.

"We have someone new in our group tonight." The leader looked right at him as he spoke. "Mr. Wesley, will you stand and tell us a little about yourself and why you're here?"

Brian wished he could disappear, but he stood, his knees knocking within his worn jeans. "Brian Wesley. I, uh...I was in an accident last week. Uh...my attorney told me about this."

A knowing look came over the leader's face. "Brian—may I call you Brian?"

Brian nodded.

"Brian, was that the accident at Ventura and Fallbrook?"

He looked around the room, suddenly embarrassed. "Yeah."

The leader seemed to wait for him to elaborate. When he stood silent, the man went on. "You were driving under the influence, is that right?"

Brian nodded again and shoved his hands deep inside his pockets.

"Can you tell us about it?"

"Uh...well...no."

The leader nodded. "Okay." He paused. "I'm sure a few of us read about that accident." He looked at the others and his voice filled with compassion. "A father and daughter were killed when Brian, here, drove his truck through a red light at Ventura and Fallbrook. Is that right, Brian?"

Brian's temper flared. "I said I didn't want to talk about it!"

"I understand, but we don't keep secrets in this group. We're here to help you."

Brian wanted to run from the room. "I don't need help. I'm here because of my attorney."

"You're not alone, Brian. A few of those sitting around the room here have been involved in serious accidents. Accidents they caused by driving drunk. But they've found forgiveness in Christ and have accepted his gift of new life."

Brian shook his head. The guy sounded like some kind of religious freak. Who was Christ anyway, and what did new life have to do with drunk driving? What sort of God would want anything to do with him after what he'd done to that family?

His response had been quick. "I don't believe in God, man."

The leader smiled kindly. "That's all right. He believes in you. He wants to meet you right where you are, Brian."

Brian had listened to the man's religious drivel for ten minutes before leaving the meeting early. If there was a God—and he seriously doubted the idea—Brian knew he would have died in that accident. The pretty blond girl and her father would have lived. It was simple as that.

He hadn't gone back to the meetings.

Brian looked at the clock. The hearing would take place soon. He pushed the pieces of broken paper clips with his forefinger until they formed a small letter *s*. He hadn't talked to Carla in three weeks, and he suddenly wondered about Brian Jr. What would the boy think when he realized what his father had done?

He thought of his own father. Red Wesley was a boozer from way back. He floated from job to job, and when Brian was four, he deserted the family and took up with a barmaid across town. Brian's mother got married again, this time to a wealthy, tea-drinking investor. He didn't exactly love Brian, but he bought him whatever he needed, and in his father's absence, material goods weren't all that bad. After a year or so they lost track of Red Wesley. Ten years later his mother was notified that Red had died. Alcohol poisoning.

All his life Brian had been determined to be a better father than Red.

I'm just like him. Brian dug his elbows into his thighs and dropped his head into his hands. *I don't care what they do to me. Lock me up for twenty years. Thirty, even. Then Carla can meet someone, and little Brian can have a different daddy. He deserves better.*

He squeezed his eyes shut and the images returned again. The girl, her blond hair matted with blood…her father moaning from inside the car. The demons, black faces dripping with blood, sneered at him, taunting him.

"Okay, God," his hands shook and his pulse quickened. The dryness in his throat seemed to reach down into his gut. "If you're real then I give up. Take me now. I don't want to live another minute."

Brian waited. Nothing. "I thought so."

He pushed the paper clip pieces around until they formed the shape of a glass. He glanced at the clock once more and wrung his hands together, trying to still their incessant trembling. *Let's get this thing over with so I can go home and have a drink.*

Jenny lay on her bed staring at the ceiling. She still wore the same rumpled pajamas and had barely moved in the two hours since her mother left. It was nearly ten, and the school bus had long since come and gone. Jenny clutched her stomach and rolled onto her side. She hadn't lied to her mother, she really did feel terrible. Her heart pounded and her chest ached…getting air was hard because she couldn't relax long enough to draw a deep breath. Her sinuses throbbed from hours of crying. She had felt this way since the previous afternoon and had passed the night restlessly, desperately trying to sleep.

"Oh, I don't care, Lord!" She rolled onto her side. "Take me.

I don't wanna live anyway."

She grabbed her pillow and shoved it over her face so she couldn't breathe. Seconds passed, and she willed herself to hold firm, keep the pillow in place. Just a few minutes and she would be with Daddy and Alicia. *Take me, Lord. Please.*

Suddenly, when it seemed her lungs would burst, she threw the pillow onto the floor, gasping in great gulps of air.

I can't even do that right. Please take me, Lord.

If only she weren't so weak. She should have held the pillow longer. There had to be another way. Carbon monoxide. Sleeping pills. A razor blade. Something.

Mom doesn't want me. My friends won't talk to me. Please Lord, I want to be with you and Daddy and Alicia.

She tossed and turned, rolling from side to side, gulping in quick, jerky breaths. What was wrong with the air in this room? It was stale, warm. No matter how many times she sucked in, her body screamed for more oxygen. She wove her fingers into her hair, grabbed two fistfuls and pulled as hard as she could. *I hate this, Lord. I want to die. Carbon monoxide. Sleeping pills. A razor.* She ran through the options again and again and again. Until finally she couldn't keep her eyes open a moment longer, and she drifted off to sleep.

Thirteen

The Lord has rejected all the warriors in my midst;
he has summoned an army against me.

LAMENTATIONS 1:15A

Hannah was pacing a short, nervous pattern in front of Judge Horowitz's courtroom when a woman appeared with two large photo buttons pinned to the lapel of her cream-colored jacket. The first held the insignia of Mothers Against Drunk Drivers; the second bore the picture of a kind-looking man in his thirties. The woman was forty-five, maybe forty-eight. Her hair was pulled back, and her eyes held a gentle glow, as though she had found a peace that was rare in a world of suffering.

The woman approached and held out her hand. "Hello. I'm Carol Cummins."

Hannah wondered if Carol could see her heart pounding in her throat. "Hannah Ryan."

"I thought it was you. We're usually the first to arrive and the last to leave." She smiled and motioned toward the courtroom. "Matt Bronzan is probably already setting up inside. Let's go in. I'll introduce you."

Hannah felt her pulse quicken. What would Matt Bronzan think of her? Did she look like a victim? Would she evoke enough sympathy from the people who had the power to put Brian Wesley behind bars? She thought a moment and tried to take on the look of a victim. As she did, she glanced at the photograph in her hand and remembered the truth.

Tom and Alicia were gone. There was no need to pretend.

"I brought the photo."

Carol took it and studied it a moment. "They look very happy." She raised her eyes, and Hannah saw distant pain there.

Hannah looked at the picture once more. "Yes. We all were."

"Well..." Carol drew a deep breath. She took the photo and snapped it carefully into a photo pin, then handed it back to Hannah. "I'd like to hear more about your family some day, Hannah. But right now we had better get inside. The hearing's in just a few minutes."

Hannah pinned the photo of Tom and Alicia to her rayon blouse and nodded. She was ready to meet Matt Bronzan.

Inside the courtroom, Matt straightened a pile of notes and set them down in front of his chair. Adjusting his tie, he glanced at the clock on the back wall. The others would be here any moment. He swallowed hard and rubbed his damp palms together. His decision was made. He was about to go through with it.

He prayed for wisdom and success. It was time. The system had gone along for too many years without recognizing how serious drunk driving and its consequences were. He prayed that this case would change that.

The back door opened, and he turned to see two women walk in. He recognized Carol Cummins from MADD, and he studied the other woman with her. She was striking, despite her swollen eyes and loose clothing. Hannah Ryan. He was sure of it.

"Matt." Carol stopped at the railing separating the spectator section from the rest of the courtroom.

"Good morning, Carol."

She slipped an arm around the other woman's shoulders. "This is Hannah Ryan. The defendant killed her husband and—"

"I know who she is," Matt cut in kindly. His gaze held Hannah's for a moment, then he reached out and took her hand in his. He hesitated. There was so much he wanted to say, but nothing that could help. "I'm...I'm so sorry, Mrs. Ryan."

Hannah nodded, and Matt saw her eyes fill with tears. She seemed unable to speak so Matt continued. "I'm glad you're here today. It does make a difference." He paused. "If you don't mind, I'd like to explain a little bit about what I'm going to do today, what's going to take place."

Carol turned to Matt. "I told Hannah about the first-degree murder possibility."

"Right." Matt still held the woman's hand, and he looked intently at her. "Yesterday I met with the defendant's attorney. They offered a plea bargain."

Anger flare in Hannah's eyes. "A plea bargain?"

"The defendant was willing to plead guilty to incidental vehicular manslaughter. According to their agreement, he would have served thirty days in jail and paid a fine, a thousand dollars I think it was."

Hannah dropped his hand. "You settled?"

"No. I told them we weren't interested."

The woman's face flooded with relief. "So what's the charge?"

Matt paused. "We'll charge him with driving under the influence and causing bodily injury while under the influence for the injuries your daughter Jenny sustained. Those charges don't carry prison time, though."

"What about the rest?"

Matt hesitated. "First-degree murder. All or nothing." He studied Hannah and looked to Carol. "Have you explained any of this to her?"

"Yes. She understands." Carol tightened her grip on Hannah's shoulders. "If the jury doesn't agree with the charges, Mr. Wesley walks away a free man."

Matt drew a deep breath and returned his attention to

Hannah. "My office has been waiting for a case like this, and we believe it's time. The defendant, Brian Wesley, has prior convictions and prior drunk driving accidents. He's had his driver's license suspended, and last year it was revoked. He has participated in alcohol education courses and signed agreements as part of his parole conditions promising never to drink and drive again. At the time of the accident, he had no valid license, and tests showed he had consumed a significant amount of alcohol before driving home." Matt softened his voice. "All of which makes this a very serious situation."

Hannah swallowed hard and stood a bit taller. She hesitated a moment. "Do you think we have a chance?"

Matt smiled. "I think so. First-degree means Mr. Wesley used his vehicle as a weapon and set out deliberately to murder. Premeditated murder, really. It's a tough charge, but there are a few landmark precedents in other states. The question is culpability. To what degree was Mr. Wesley culpable in the deaths of Tom and Alicia."

Hannah's brow wrinkled in a frown of concentration. Matt figured she was trying to makes sense of all he'd told her. "No one's ever been convicted of first-degree murder for driving drunk and killing someone?"

"Not in California, no."

Carol crossed her arms. "We've tried a time or two—" she nodded to Matt—"at least Matt here has. But in the end the jurors simply haven't been ready."

Matt shifted his weight. "We're hoping this case, and the timing, will change that. Thanks to the education from MADD and other organizations, people want drunk drivers off the road. I think they may be ready to do something more drastic than ever before." He met Hannah's watchful look. "I really believe we can get a conviction in this case."

"If you do—" Hannah hesitated. "*When* you do, how many years will Brian Wesley get?"

"The penalty for this charge is twenty-five years to life. It'll depend on the jury's recommendation and the judge."

Carol met Hannah's eyes. "That's one thing we have going for us this time. Judge Horowitz is fairly conservative. He doesn't have much sympathy for people who choose to drink and drive and then kill someone in the process."

"Of course Wesley would never serve twenty-five years." Hannah's eyes narrowed at this, and Matt went on. She needed to know the facts. "He could be out in five, even three years with parole."

"Three years! If he gets sentenced to—"

She broke off when a door opened and Judge Horowitz appeared, his black robe flowing behind him. He climbed effortlessly into his elevated chair and began sifting through documents on his desk.

Another door opened, and Matt watched Harold Finch enter the room. Behind him came the man Matt presumed was Finch's defendant. Trailing the procession was a bailiff. The trio walked past Matt and the two women and found seats at the defense table. Finch whispered something to his client.

Matt turned and found Hannah staring at the men. "That's Harold Finch there on the right," he whispered. "He represents the defendant and typically—"

"Which one is Brian Wesley?"

Matt caught his breath at the anger in Hannah's voice. "I'm not positive, but I assume he's the younger guy on Finch's left."

Hannah was still staring at the man when Matt excused himself.

The hearing was about to begin.

Hannah barely noticed Matt leave or the judge bang his gavel and ask the court to come to order. Her attention was fixed on the man sitting next to Harold Finch.

Somehow she had expected him to be dark and sinister, with the cold eyes of a killer. Instead he was clean-cut with a trim build. He looked like the youth minister at their church. Hannah studied him and felt a wave of nausea wash over her. She clenched her teeth. It didn't matter how he looked. She hated him. *How could you?* She glared at him, boring her eyes in the back of his skull. *How could you kill my family?*

The judge's voice interrupted her thoughts. "In the matter of *The People v Brian Wesley,* I believe the state has a formal charge to file. Is Mr. Wesley present?"

The young man next to Finch nodded. "Yes, sir."

Hannah's gaze remained locked on Wesley as she absently fingered the photo button on her blouse. The nausea intensified. Suddenly the room was spinning, and she had to fight off a wave of lightheadedness. *Don't faint, don't faint, don't faint.* She drew a steadying gulp of hot, courtroom air.

You can do it. She nodded. Yes, she could. This wasn't about how she felt. This was about what she'd lost. And it was about making Brian Wesley pay for his sins. She closed her eyes for a moment and willed herself to be strong. *I'm doing my best, Tom, really I am.*

The judge continued. "Is counsel present for the defendant?"

The man Matt Bronzan had identified as Harold Finch stood. "Yes, your honor."

Judge Horowitz peered down and acknowledged Finch over his oval reading glasses. "Mr. Finch. I assume you will be counsel for the defendant throughout this matter?"

"I will, your honor."

The judge peered at Matt. "Mr. Bronzan."

"Your honor." Matt rose briefly.

"You'll be representing the state in this matter, is that right?"

"Yes, your honor."

"All right then." He glanced at the docket on his desk. "Mr. Bronzan, please would you inform this court as to the official charge against the defendant, Brian Wesley."

"Yes, your honor." Matt stood and stepped back from his

chair. Hannah liked the way he held Judge Horowitz's gaze. "The people of the state of California do hereby officially charge Mr. Brian Wesley with first-degree murder in the drunk driving deaths of Tom Ryan and Alicia Ryan. In addition, we charge Mr. Wesley with driving under the influence and causing bodily harm while driving under the influence for the injuries suffered by Jenny Ryan."

The judge nodded and wrote something on the form in front of him. He looked up. "Are there other charges?"

"No, your honor."

The judge allowed his glasses to slide further down the bridge of his nose so that his squinty eyes could be seen clearly over them. "This is a drunk driving case, is that right?"

"It is, your honor." Matt caught his hands behind his back, and his sleek, dark Italian suit opened enough to expose a crisp, white, button-down, tailored dress shirt and a conservative silk tie. Hannah studied him. He moved with an athletic grace, confident and self-assured. Though she'd only just met him, she trusted him completely. If anyone could put Brian Wesley away for a decade it was Matt Bronzan.

The judge continued. "And you understand, Mr. Bronzan, that by charging the defendant with first-degree murder, you can not later charge him with a lesser crime?"

"Yes, your honor." Matt didn't falter.

"All right then, the charge has been entered." Judge Horowitz turned toward Brian Wesley and his attorney. "Mr. Wesley, the state has charged you with first-degree murder in the deaths of Tom Ryan and Alicia Ryan. The state has also charged you with driving under the influence and causing bodily harm while driving under the influence. Do you understand the charges?"

Hannah's attention flew to Brian. She could only see his back and the side of his face, but his trembling was visible across the courtroom. Good. Hannah didn't feel sorry for him. He was a monster.

Brian rose slowly to his feet and cleared his throat. "Yes, sir. I understand the charges."

"How do you plead?"

Brian glanced down at Finch, and Hannah saw uncertainty on the young man's face. *He deserves this. I hope he's terrified.*

The attorney nodded slightly. "Uh..." Brian faced the judge once more. "I, uh...not guilty, sir. On all counts."

"Very well, then." The judge scribbled something again. "This matter will be handed over to trial. We'll have a preliminary hearing next month and then, presuming there's enough evidence, I imagine it will take several months to get the case scheduled on the docket."

Matt cleared his throat. "Your honor, I'd like to make a request."

The judge nodded. "Go ahead."

"The defendant has been convicted of drunk driving several times. He has caused two other accidents while driving drunk, and he was driving with a suspended license at the time of the accident. We are seriously concerned that he will drink and drive again, and that other innocent people will be put in danger as a result." Matt paced casually back toward his spot at the table. He picked up a piece of paper. "The state would like to file a motion to have Mr. Wesley detained until such time as a trial can be arranged."

Finch immediately leaned over and whispered something to Brian, then rose quickly, tugging his tight vest firmly over his stomach. "Your honor, we strongly disagree with the state's request in this matter. Mr. Wesley is in the process of finding a job. He has a wife and young son who need his income and support. In addition, he is attending Alcoholics Anonymous meetings. His vehicle has been impounded by the state; therefore, we do not feel he represents even the remotest risk to society."

The judge was silent for a moment, and Hannah willed him to side with Matt. *Lock him up! I can't see Tom or Alicia. Why should he get to see his family?*

Finally the judge looked at Matt. "As you know, Mr. Bronzan, it would be highly unusual to jail a drunk driving defendant until the time of trial. As Mr. Finch pointed out, the state has apprehended the defendant's vehicle. I don't believe he will be a danger so long as he stays off the road. I'm afraid I'll have to dismiss your motion."

"Very well, your honor." Matt nodded and returned to his seat. Hannah leaned forward, ready to shout out if she had to. Why had Matt given up so easily?

Harold Finch took the cue and snatched a document from the table. "One more thing, your honor. Mr. Wesley has some medical problems relating to the accident. He's in physical therapy at the present time and will be for several months to come. Should this court find enough evidence at the preliminary to hold Mr. Wesley over for trial, I will be filing a motion for continuance until such time as Mr. Wesley is physically able to aid in his defense."

Hannah was on her feet, about to protest, but Carol gently pulled her back down. "Not now, Hannah. This is part of the game. It doesn't mean anything."

Doesn't mean anything? Hannah glared at Finch. How *dare* he ask for a delay so Brian Wesley could receive physical therapy? Tom and Alicia were *dead,* and now the animal that killed them needed time for healing before he could face his punishment? Hannah could hardly believe it. She narrowed her eyes, fighting the rage that welled up within her and threatened to strangle her.

Judge Horowitz raised a wary eyebrow. "Mr. Finch, I am aware of your reputation and your knack for delaying the inevitable. It is my intent to see that this trial makes it into my courtroom as soon as possible."

"Yes, your honor, but—"

"I am not finished, Mr. Finch." Hannah almost jumped up and applauded at Judge Horowitz's firm tone. She clasped her hands together, listening intently as the judge went on. "I understand that in this case the defendant was involved in a serious car accident and because of that, I will grant your motion. This time. You will need to present this court with documentation within one week stating exactly how much 'physical therapy' Mr. Wesley will need. We will go ahead with a preliminary next month. Then, if the case is handed over for trial, I will review Mr. Wesley's medical records before scheduling a trial date."

"Thank you, your honor." Hannah wanted to slap the smug look off of Finch's face as he sat down.

"Nevertheless—" Hannah's attention jerked back to Judge Horowitz. "You will *not* use the judicial system to file motion upon motion in an effort to delay this trial. I understand how delays might benefit your client, but I simply will not have that game played out in my courtroom. Is that understood?"

Finch smiled agreeably. "Absolutely, your honor."

The judge turned to Matt. "I'll notify you about the preliminary."

Matt nodded, and Hannah marveled at how he maintained his composure. He looked unaffected by Finch's victory. The judge dismissed them, and in a matter of seconds Finch and Brian Wesley disappeared.

Matt met Hannah and Carol at the railing. "No surprises here."

Hannah crossed her arms. *No surprises?* "Then why'd you ask the judge to hold Brian in jail until trial?"

The corners of Matt's mouth raised slightly. "It didn't hurt to ask." He thought a moment. "And maybe it set a tone for the seriousness of this case."

Carol stretched. "I liked it. Definitely took the defense by surprise."

Hannah's head was swimming. She had no idea there were so many innuendoes and subtle nuances involved in prosecuting someone who was so obviously guilty. "What about the delay?" She studied Matt's face and found strength from the confidence she saw there.

"It won't be the last."

Her mouth dropped open. "But the judge said he wasn't playing that game."

"The judge wants Finch to think that. Truth is, if Finch can come up with a good reason for a delay, Judge Horowitz won't really have a choice."

Hannah wanted to scream. "Why?"

Carol put a hand on her arm, and Hannah found the touch comforting. "If the judge refuses a continuance, he gives the defense grounds for appeal."

"In other words if we earn a conviction," Matt added, "Finch can come back later and say his client didn't have a fair trial. He was too rushed to defend his client fairly."

Suddenly Hannah understood and her temper flared again. "That isn't fair."

"We're trying to change that, but we have to play by the rules."

Hannah nodded.

"Listen—" Carol turned toward her—"You're probably drained. Let's go grab some lunch." She looked at Matt. "Join us?"

He shook his head. "I'm afraid I have a full afternoon. But please—" he directed his attention to Hannah once more—"call me anytime if you have questions or concerns."

Hannah would have done anything to help this man win the case against Brian Wesley. "I want him locked up, Mr. Bronzan."

Matt nodded. "We all do." He looked from Hannah to Carol, then back again. "I'll contact you when I have a preliminary date. And certainly if I have any information about the trial."

"Thank you." Hannah fiddled with the photo button once more, and Matt leaned closer.

"Your husband and daughter?"

Carol stood by respectfully as Hannah nodded. "Tom and

Alicia…at a family barbecue last summer."

Matt's expression filled with a mixture of compassion and frustration, and Hannah warmed to him even more. He seemed to understand all she'd lost…

He looked up at her and sighed. "A man like Brian Wesley should never have had the chance to get behind the wheel."

Hannah suddenly had to fight the urge to break down and give way to the tears she'd held off all day. Matt Bronzan was indeed her ally, her friend. He would see this case through and win a conviction. She was sure about it. "I know you'll do everything you can."

He moved to gather his documents. "You have my word."

Hannah watched him leave through the same door she'd seen Finch and Brian exit earlier. Then she turned her attention toward Carol. "Lunch sounds great. I want to get involved as soon as possible." She hesitated, and when she spoke again it was with fierce determination. "I need to get involved."

She and Carol left the courtroom, and Hannah felt herself finding purpose as they talked about the basic structure of the MADD organization, how victim impact panels worked, and what would be the best uses of Hannah's time.

Much later that afternoon Hannah finally drove home and pulled into the driveway.

She turned off the ignition, leaned back in the seat, and gazed at the house. Would she ever be able to do this, come home and walk through the door without being haunted by all she'd lost.

All Jenny had lost.

She felt the heat of shame filling her face. Jenny. Hannah blinked back sudden tears as she realized this was the first time since early that morning she'd even remembered her youngest daughter.

Fourteen

This is why I weep and my eyes overflow with tears.

LAMENTATIONS 1:16A

Carol Cummins had been a member of MADD for nearly ten years. Like others in the organization, her involvement wasn't something she had planned. Rather, she wound up an activist after her husband, Ken, was killed at the hands of a drunk driver.

The man who hit her husband had faced no trial. Instead there was a plea bargain, a backstreet handshake of a deal that resulted in the defendant serving three days in jail and paying a nominal fine. Ken had carried no life insurance, except what was provided by his work, so Carol was left with two fatherless babies and piles of unpaid bills.

Carol and Ken were believers, and the church they attended came through on the bills. Still, there remained a sense of injustice and an anger that no brother or sister in Christ could ease. Frustrated and stricken with grief, Carol turned to Mothers Against Drunk Drivers.

At first, she'd had a vague understanding of the group's purpose. Started by a mother whose daughter had been killed by a drunk driver, MADD's goal was threefold: Educate the public about the dangers of drunk driving, reduce the number of drunk driving accidents that occurred each year, and increase the penalties for those convicted of the crime.

Carol immersed herself in the workings of the organization, passing out literature at schools, organizing press conferences, attending trials of numerous drunk drivers, and gathering signatures to help get tougher laws in California. Her mother lived nearby, so she watched Carol's young children, allowing her to devote her efforts to MADD. She worked tirelessly for more than a year.

Then the breakdown occurred.

She had been speaking at a high school, relating the details of Ken's death and informing the students how just one drink could impair a person's ability to drive.

"Whatever you do," she concluded that morning, "never, ever get into a car with someone who's been drinking."

From the back of the auditorium, a boy stood up and pointed proudly at himself. "That counts me out!" He grinned and looked around for approval. A handful of teens sitting near him giggled, and there was a moment of uncomfortable whispering among the crowd.

"You—" Carol spoke clearly into the microphone, looking at the boy through eyes filled with fury—"You are no better... than the animal who killed my husband."

The giggling stopped abruptly, and the boy slithered lower among his group of friends. Then, aware she had somehow crossed a line, Carol excused herself, gathered her notes and posters and photographs, and left the auditorium.

She drove aimlessly, crying and pounding her fist on the steering wheel. She had made peace with Ken's absence. She had found comfort in her relationship with the Lord. So why was she falling apart? Slowly the truth had dawned...

She had never forgiven the man who killed Ken.

On the heels of that first realization came a second, equally devastating awareness: She did not intend to forgive. Not now, not ever.

She had steered her car toward Malibu Canyon that afternoon and found a quiet spot on the beach where she wrestled with God until sundown. Scripture after Scripture came to mind...*Forgive as you have been forgiven....Unless you forgive, you will not be forgiven.* For every verse that the Lord presented, Carol fought and argued: Too much time had passed since the accident....There was no way to find the man....He didn't deserve to be forgiven.

But in that quiet space of beach, between the pounding of waves on the shore, Carol heard God speak. Forgiveness was not a feeling, it was a choice. And before she returned to her mother's house to collect her children that evening, she surrendered to the One who loved her, and she made that choice. She forgave the man completely.

It was as though she was set free in every area, especially in her efforts for MADD. Everything she did from that point on paid off tremendously. Three years after Ken's death, California tightened its drunk driving laws so that a person with a blood alcohol level of .08 or higher—instead of the former .10—was considered legally intoxicated. Still, as rewarding as that was, it was nothing compared with how it had felt to imagine the face of a drunk driver and forgive him.

It was in this that Carol found meaning in life without her beloved husband.

So when she and Hannah Ryan had gone for lunch a week ago, right after the hearing, Carol had admitted to her new friend that she'd gotten involved with MADD because her husband had been killed by a drunk driver. But because she knew the angry place Hannah was in, she refrained from sharing the rest of her story.

Especially the part about forgiveness.

Now she set a scrapbook of news clippings on her desk and checked her watch. Hannah would be there soon, anxious to exact vengeance on Brian Wesley and anyone else who dared drink and drive.

Carol sighed and looked about her office. Most of the volunteers with MADD shared a workstation or made phone calls from small cubicles. Not Carol. She was full-time and had her own office—small, but private. She glanced at a bumper sticker on the back of her office door: "God is bigger than any problem I have."

She knew it was true, but this time she wondered at the position in which God had placed her. Throughout the court proceedings Carol would stick by Hannah's side, representing MADD and providing a very real reminder of the victims. She would accompany Hannah to trial and comfort her when she fell apart.

And yet…there would be more than that. Carol felt it deep inside. *You brought us together for a reason, Lord.*

She wasn't sure about Hannah. It seemed the woman was blaming the Lord for what had happened to her family, and Carol ached for the loneliness Hannah must be feeling. It was one thing to lose your husband and daughter—Carol could relate to that type of pain. But to lose your sweet fellowship with the Lord, too…

Carol closed her eyes and squeezed back tears. *Help me, Lord. Show me what to say to bring her peace and comfort, maybe even forgiveness.*

She reached into her top drawer and retrieved her worn Bible. Many victims who came to seek or offer help at MADD had no faith. There had been dozens of times when the most Carol could offer was to pray for them. But something about Hannah Ryan was different. Carol had a feeling there were deep roots of faith buried beneath the woman's pain and misery.

There was a knock at her door.

Carol set her Bible back in the drawer. "Come in."

Hannah stepped inside and quickly took the only available chair. She looked painfully thin and frazzled. "I spoke with Mr. Bronzan." Hannah folded her hands over the top of her purse and crossed her legs nervously. "The preliminary hearing is scheduled for next month."

Carol studied Hannah. "How does that set with you?"

"Mr. Bronzan doesn't seem bothered by it. He says it'll give him more time to prepare."

There was a pause, and Carol turned the scrapbook so it

faced Hannah. "Well, I'm glad you could come. These are news clippings we've collected over the years. If you look through them, you'll get an idea of what keeps us busy."

Hannah turned a few pages and looked disinterestedly at the articles. After a few seconds, she stopped abruptly. "Look, Carol…I didn't come here to read clippings. I want to get involved." She hesitated. "Could you tell me about the victim impact panels?"

"We generally wait until after the one-year anniversary of an accident before assigning victims to an impact panel."

"Why?"

"Well, usually victims want to wait." Carol hoped Hannah could see compassion in her eyes. "It's very difficult to get up in front of a crowd and talk about the death of someone you loved."

Hannah shifted impatiently. "It's been almost two months. I'm ready to talk about it now."

The room was silent except for the hum of fluorescent lighting above. Finally Carol drew a deep breath. "Hannah, sometimes it seems we're ready when really we need more time. A lot more time."

"I'm not worried about what *I* need."

Carol waited. Hannah obviously needed to talk.

"What I'm saying is, if I can talk to high school kids or PTA mothers or the rotary club, if I can talk to anyone and tell them what happened to Tom and Alicia, maybe I'll actually reach someone. And maybe that one person will decide not to drink and drive and then—" Hannah's voice caught. "Maybe I can spare someone else the heartache of…of what happened to me."

Carol nodded. "Hannah, I want to talk to you about something off the subject." She fidgeted with a pencil. "At lunch after the hearing you told me you'd known Tom all your life, grew up with him and went to church with him. I began wondering about your faith."

Hannah's expression was suddenly guarded. "My faith is a personal matter."

O Lord, help me…help me reach her. "I know, I'm sorry. It's just…well, I'm a believer, too. I wondered if there was any certain way you'd like me to pray for you?"

"No." Hannah sighed. "I don't see any point, really."

Carol was silent, encouraging Hannah to continue.

"After the accident—" Hannah seemed to steady herself—"I was very mad at God for letting Tom and Alicia die. Now…" She paused. "Now I think I've changed my mind."

"You're not mad at God?" Carol was confused.

"No." Hannah shook her head decidedly. "I don't believe in God."

Carol felt as if she'd been punched in the stomach. *Help me, Lord. What can I say now*? The answer seemed almost audible: *Lamentations. Give her Lamentations*. Carol considered the grief-filled message of that book of the Bible. *No, Lord. Not Lamentations. She needs something more hopeful*.

She cleared her throat. "I think that's normal—to doubt God—after what you've gone through." Carol folded her hands neatly on her organized desk. *Not Lamentations, Lord*. "Maybe if you read the Bible—"

She broke off at the flash of anger on Hannah's face. Hannah's next words chilled the small room.

"I don't need God anymore. And I certainly don't need the Bible. If God does exist, he let me down when I needed him most." Her voice was like industrial steel. "It's easier now just to let go of the whole idea."

Give me something for her, Lord. Please. Again the answer came: *Lamentations. Give her Lamentations*.

"I was thinking maybe Philippians," Carol said. *Certainly not Lamentations*. "Philippians 4, the whole chapter. Maybe that would help you find the Lord's peace and…I don't know, maybe help you remember what's true and good."

Hannah's eyes became even icier. "I appreciate your efforts,

Carol. But I'm not interested. My belief in God died the same day Tom and Alicia did. If I can't have them, I don't want him either."

Carol nodded. She'd said enough. Probably too much. Hannah had clearly reached her limit.

Give her Lamentations.

Carol ignored the urging. "I tell you what, let's go to the video room." She stood and Hannah did the same. "You can watch a tape of one of our recent victim impact panels and get a feel for how it works. Then if you still think you're ready, maybe we could get you started."

Hannah seemed relieved, and Carol wondered if it was because she'd been given the green light for appearing on a victim impact panel or because Carol had stopped talking about the Lord.

The video was powerful—one moving testimony after another poured out of people who had lost loved ones to drunk drivers. Hannah took a tissue from a box at the center of the room. Carol could hear her sniffling softly and saw her dabbing at her eyes every few minutes.

When the film ended, Hannah blew her nose and leveled her gaze at Carol. She hesitated for only a moment. "I'm ready. When can I begin?"

Carol located a folder filled with informational material regarding the impact panels and a questionnaire designed to help victims organize their thoughts before presenting them in a public setting.

"Read through these and give me a call if you're still interested. If you really think you're ready, we could get you on a panel sometime in the next four weeks." Carol paused. "Your goal will be very specific, Hannah. With Matt Bronzan going for a first-degree murder conviction, we need to saturate the public with the idea. Maybe if the notion isn't so foreign, a jury will be more likely to convict."

"I understand." Hannah thanked Carol, gathered her things,

and headed for the front door with Carol close behind. Suddenly Hannah stopped and turned back to her. For the first time that morning, Carol saw vulnerability in the other woman's eyes.

"The preliminary hearing?" Hannah spoke softly.

Carol nodded. "I'll be there." Impulsively she closed the distance between them, hugging Hannah close.

Carol was ten years older than Hannah and decades wiser, but in that instant she felt closer to this broken woman than to anyone she knew. "I'm here for you, Hannah. Call me…if you need anything."

Hannah left and Carol sat down at her desk again. She had lost interest in the day's work, too burdened by Hannah's choice to abandon God. Once more she reached into her top drawer and pulled out her Bible. *Lamentations? What hope was there in that?* She flipped through the pages of the Old Testament until she found the book, then scanned the pages. Her eyes fell on a verse in the second chapter: *"My eyes fail from weeping, I am in torment within, my heart is poured out on the ground because my people are destroyed."*

A chill passed over her. The verse described Hannah perfectly. *But it doesn't offer any hope, Lord. None at all.* She read on.

"He has besieged me and surrounded me with bitterness and hardship. He has made me dwell in darkness like those long dead. He has walled me in so I cannot escape; he has weighed me down with chains."

Carol shook her head helplessly. *I don't understand, Lord. Such a dark word from you. And for what? Why?* She looked down and saw there was more.

"Even when I call out or cry for help, he shuts out my prayer.…Like a bear lying in wait, like a lion hiding, he dragged me from the path and mangled me and left me without help.…He pierced my heart with arrows from his quiver."

Terrible stuff. How could anyone say such things about God? Carol wanted to flip a few hundred pages to the right and read something comforting in Psalms, but she felt compelled to continue.

"I have been deprived of peace; I have forgotten what prosperity is. So I say, 'My splendor is gone and all that I had hoped from the Lord*...."'*

This was going nowhere. Carol blew out a breath of frustration and tried to remember what she had learned about Lamentations. Maybe there was some kind of introduction at the beginning of the book. She flipped back a few pages. Yes, there it was.

"The prophet Jeremiah wept over the awful devastation of Jerusalem and the terrible slaughter of human life that he saw around him." Carol pondered this for a moment. *But how can such a story help Hannah regain her belief in you, Father?*

She read on: *"No book is more intense in expressing grief than this one."*

The introduction continued, outlining the practical significance of Jeremiah's laments—and then what Carol saw made her breath catch in her throat: *"Even though we may begin with lamenting, we must always end with repentance—as Jeremiah does in the book of Lamentations."*

Tears filled her eyes. It was her very own life...word for word.

Carol felt her throat constrict, and gradually she gave way to a torrent of sobs. Suddenly the memory of Ken was so real she could almost touch him. No wonder God had given her Lamentations. She ran the words over again in her mind. *"No book is more intense in expressing grief than this one."*

She had suffered greatly when Ken died; she had lamented in much the same way Jeremiah had over the city of Jerusalem. At first her grieving caused her to have a bitter, hard heart. Anger consumed her, and there had been no peace until she, like Jeremiah, reached a place of repentance, a heart of forgiveness.

Now it made sense! That was why the Lord had wanted her

to share this particular book with Hannah. Carol had passed the way of Jerusalem.

Now it was Hannah's turn.

Fifteen

The Lord is like an enemy…

LAMENTATIONS 2:5A

The MADD questionnaire was harder than Hannah expected.

"Describe loved ones who were killed by a drunk driver." Hannah pictured her husband and daughter, let memories run through her mind, and then began to write. *Tom Ryan, husband, father, memory-maker. Alicia Ryan, daughter, sister, friend to all.*

Hannah squirmed in her seat and reached for a tissue. Her sinuses were clear for a change, and she didn't feel like crying. But tears came anyway, trickling down the side of her face like some kind of permanent leak. She read the next question. "Where were your loved ones going when the accident occurred." Hannah moved the pen across the page. *Home.*

The next section was more difficult. "Describe what you would like people to remember about your loved ones." Hannah sighed and wiped her eyes. Maybe Carol was right. Maybe she wasn't ready for this.

She looked up and saw that the morning had grown cloudy. A gloomy shadow filled the house, bringing a chill over the place where she sat at the dining room table. She picked up the steaming mug beside her and breathed in the smell of apple-cinnamon tea. Carefully she lifted it to her lips and sipped slowly, allowing the hot liquid to soothe her raspy throat.

In the past she might have been listening to David Jeremiah or some other Christian artist as she worked. But she had packed those CDs away a week ago. No point in singing about God if she didn't believe in him.

She reached behind her and flicked on the chandelier lights above the table. Soon the days would grow shorter, and then the holidays would be upon them. The first Thanksgiving without Tom and Alicia. The first Christmas. Hannah tried not to think about it as she studied the questionnaire once more.

When the phone rang, Hannah sighed and set down her pen. Reaching across the table she picked up the cordless phone and pushed the blinking button. "Hello?" Again she was struck by how foreign her voice sounded—dead, toneless, emotionless...like someone who had lost the ability to feel.

"Mrs. Ryan? This is Mary Stelpstra, principal at West Hills Junior High."

Hannah felt her heart sink. Something was wrong with Jenny. "Yes?"

The woman hesitated. "Mrs. Ryan, I think we need to set up a meeting to discuss Jenny."

Not now. "What about her?"

"Well, it isn't something I wish to discuss over the phone. Are you available this morning? Say around eleven?"

Hannah stared at the unfinished questionnaire. Eleven gave her an hour to complete it. "Yes. I can be there."

"Fine. I'll meet you in my office."

Hannah hung up and sighed. When would the nightmare ever end? She returned to the form and saw that it gave her just five lines to write everything she hoped people would remember about Tom and Alicia. *Five lines?*

She moved on to the next question. "What do you think about people who drink and drive." This one was easy. Hannah picked up her pen and scribbled furiously. *Drunk drivers are selfish animals, killers with no regard for human life. They are the worst sort of people on earth.*

She reread her answer and thought of Brian Wesley, sitting nervously beside Harold Finch and hoping for a delay so his injuries could heal before he might have to face a jury.

She clenched her teeth and threw the pen across the room.

The questionnaire wasn't making things better! Even if she *could* reach someone, save someone from drinking and driving, it would never bring back Tom and Alicia. She began to moan and it became a cry that filled the empty rooms of their home. "*Tom!* I can't do it. I can't do this without you!"

She laid her head down on her folded arms, and the tears came hard. She missed Tom and Alicia so badly she thought she might suffocate.

Wiping at her eyes, she glanced at the clock. 10:45. With a start she stood up, blew her nose, and grabbed her car keys. It was time to meet with Mary Stelpstra.

West Hills Junior High sat adjacent to the high school, and neither building was like other stark, stucco-covered Los Angeles schools. Instead these two structures were bright, cream-colored with blue trim, and anchored in a sea of grass. Behind the school were rolling hills and trees and a picturesque football stadium. It looked more like a private university than a public junior high school.

This was where Alicia had earned the right to be head cheerleader and captain of the drama team. Here at West Hills Junior High, Jenny had run track, showing signs of being a promising sprinter. Of course, that was before the accident. As were the times when, after school hours, the Ryans had used the school's expansive green fields for informal Frisbee contests and softball games. It was a beautiful school—and it was filled with too many memories to count.

Hannah ignored all of it.

She strode stiffly toward the principal's office and signed in. In less than a minute, Mary Stelpstra swept into the waiting area and ushered her into her office. She shut the door behind them. "Please, Mrs. Ryan, sit down."

Hannah sat. Ever since the accident it seemed people were forever telling her to sit down. As if whatever news was about to be shared was simply too difficult to hear while standing. Hannah knew she must look terrible, her eyes tear-stained, her makeup smeared…but she was tired, and she didn't care what people thought of her. Right now she cared only for her youngest daughter. "You said there was something you wanted to discuss about Jenny?"

"First let me say on behalf of West Hills Junior High, we are so sorry about your loss, Mrs. Ryan." The principal had the polished sound of a school administrator. She continued. "Our staff, our students, we all loved Alicia very much. We feel her absence sorely."

Tears again. Hannah reached for a tissue and dabbed at the corners of her eyes. She waited for the principal to continue.

"Lately, though, we've spent more time worrying about Jenny. She's missed a lot of school, Mrs. Ryan."

Hannah relaxed slightly. *Was that all? Jenny's attendance?* "She hasn't felt good. I don't think it's anything physical, really…"

Mrs. Stelpstra nodded. "I understand. Actually, her teachers are working with her, helping her with missed assignments. Her absences are to be expected after what she's gone through."

Hannah was relieved, but curious. If they were willing to work with Jenny on her absences, then why the meeting? "I guess I'm not quite following you, Mrs. Stelpstra."

The principal sighed and pulled a folded piece of notebook paper from her desk drawer. "I didn't ask you in because of Jenny's absences." She paused and unfolded the paper, glancing at it and then handing it to Hannah. "I asked you in because of this."

"What is it?"

"Something Jenny wrote in English class yesterday. It's quite alarming, really, Mrs. Ryan. And I wanted to be sure you knew about it."

Hannah felt her stomach turn and noticed her heart had skidded into an unrecognizable beat. She was suddenly terrified as she reached for the paper, her hands trembling. She recognized Jenny's handwriting and read the title scrawled across the top of the page: *"The Best Place to Live."*

Hannah looked at Mrs. Stelpstra curiously. "Was this an assignment?"

"Yes. Jenny's composition teacher asked the class to write an essay on any place in the world where they'd like to live."

Hannah returned her gaze to Jenny's paper and began to read.

"I can really only think of one place where I want to live, and it's not here. Last summer my dad and sister died in a car accident. A bunch of people tried to save them, but they died anyway. Now it's just me and my mom.

"Mom's busy most of the time with court stuff. She wants to make sure the man who hit our car will go to jail for what he did to my dad and sister. I don't know. I don't really care about him. My mom does, though. She doesn't care about anything else. Not even me."

Hannah closed her eyes. *Of course I care about you, Jenny.* She forced herself to keep reading.

"I spend a lot of time in my room now, and I think maybe I'm having anxiety attacks. I read about them once in a book. I get sweaty, and it feels like I can't breathe, like maybe I'm going to die. Sometimes this makes me scared but most of the time it doesn't. I sort of wish it would happen.

"I feel like I'm in some kind of holding place. Kinda like life ended when the accident happened, and now there's just this waiting time. I still believe in God, but my mom doesn't. I heard her telling someone from church the other day that she stopped believing in God when Dad and Alicia died. I don't blame her. I even thought about it. About letting go of my faith. But I can't. I believe Dad and Alicia are in heaven, and I want more than anything in the world to be with them."

Hannah stopped and clutched the paper tightly, closing her eyes against the tears that were coming faster now. *I'm right about there being no God, I know I am.* But she was shocked to learn that Jenny had found out. It was something she should have shared with the girl herself. *This can't be happening. It keeps getting worse, Tom. I can't do this by myself.*

Mrs. Stelpstra handed her another tissue and waited patiently. Hannah wiped her eyes, steadied herself, and continued reading.

"Sometimes that's all I think about. Dying and stuff. How I can get from here to there so we can be together again. Mom wouldn't care. It would be easier for her if I was gone. Then she'd have more time for all her stuff with MADD, and she wouldn't have to wonder why I don't feel good and how come I'm not going to school. I don't know. I've thought about it a lot. The different ways and stuff. But nothing seems easy, and I just roll around in bed at night wondering about it. I can't sleep, that's for sure. I miss Dad and Alicia so much. If there was an easy way to do it, I would. I would in a heartbeat.

"Because of all the places I would like to live, the only one I can think of right now is heaven."

Hannah set the paper down on the principal's desk as if it were contaminated. "I…I don't know what to say. It's like a nightmare that never ends."

The principal nodded. "I understand."

"It keeps getting worse, you know?"

Mrs. Stelpstra's voice was filled with kindness. "We see this kind of thing when one of our students has suffered a severe trauma." She paused. "Have you noticed anything unusual about Jenny's behavior? Anything that would lead you to believe she might…actually consider acting on this?"

Hannah blinked. Surely Mrs. Stelpstra didn't mean…"You mean killing herself?" Hannah couldn't believe she was having this conversation.

"That is what Jenny seems to be alluding to, Mrs. Ryan, don't you think?"

Hannah glanced back at the paper lying on the desk before her. "Yes. I guess so. But Jenny would never really do such a thing, Mrs. Stelpstra. I know my daughter."

"You must remember, Mrs. Ryan, things are completely different now than they were before the accident. Obviously Jenny never would have considered suicide before. She was a very happy, very carefree girl, secure in herself and her place in your family. Now...well, it seems she feels somewhat forgotten."

Hannah's defenses reared. "Wait a minute! I haven't done anything to make Jenny feel this way. We're both suffering... and doing the best we can to get through this...this...."

"I'm not trying to accuse—"

"Then don't!" Hannah drew a slow breath and tried to regain control. "Jenny's right. I've been busy with MADD. I don't want Tom's and Alicia's deaths to be for nothing."

"And Jenny?"

"I spend as much time with her as possible. When she wants to be alone, I let her."

Mrs. Stelpstra paused and retrieved Jenny's paper once more. She glanced over it again in silence. "Some of the letters are smeared...I think maybe she was crying when she wrote it."

Hannah sighed. "We've both been doing a lot of crying. That doesn't mean she's suicidal."

The principal hesitated. "I'm worried about her, Mrs. Ryan."

"I'm worried about her, too, about *both* of us." Hannah leaned forward. Why didn't this woman understand what she was going through? "I'm worried about us finding a way through this pain so we can have a relationship again. I'm worried about whether the drunk driver who did this to us will be locked up or whether he'll walk free." She paused and leveled her gaze at the woman across from her. "But I am *not* worried about Jenny killing herself."

"This paper—"

"That paper is Jenny's way of trying to get attention." Hannah was angry and no longer trying to hide it. "She would never, ever, not in a million years think of killing herself. She knows better than that."

Mrs. Stelpstra set the paper down and leaned back in her

chair. She considered Hannah thoughtfully. "Well, I suppose you know her better than we do."

"Of course I do." Hannah stood, and almost as an afterthought she grabbed Jenny's paper from the desk and folded it, placing it roughly inside her purse. She turned her attention again toward the principal. "Thank you for looking out for my daughter, Mrs. Stelpstra. I even thank you for taking the time to call me in today and share your concerns. But please, don't contact social services or start worrying about needing a suicide counselor." Hannah searched for the right words. "We've suffered the worst ordeal of our lives, and it's nowhere near over. I think we can expect Jenny to be a little upset."

Mrs. Stelpstra nodded and seemed resigned to let the issue go. "I didn't mean to make things worse, Mrs. Ryan. I just thought you should know."

Hannah reached out and shook the woman's hand. "Thank you. Let me know if you have any other reason for concern. But for now I think this needs to be between me and Jenny. I'll talk with her, but again, don't worry about her paper. She doesn't mean anything by it."

Hannah walked from the office, keeping an iron control on the trembling that wanted to overtake her. As she made her way back to the car she faltered. Jenny? Suicidal? Could there possibly be merit to Mary Stelpstra's warning? What if Jenny really didn't want to live? What if she had actually thought about taking her own life?

Impossible. She shook her head firmly and forced herself to keep walking. *Ridiculous.* She knew Jenny too well. They had been through a lot these past months, but Jenny was too stable to consider suicide.

She would talk to Jenny about the paper. But she would not worry about it.

By the time she got home, she had nearly erased the meeting with the principal from her mind. She was focusing again on the questionnaire Carol Cummins had given her. She would finish it this afternoon and get it over to the MADD office. That way she would still have time to read through the other information before dinner. It didn't matter how difficult the material was. She would need every available day to educate the public about the truth....Drunk driving really was murder. If they got the message out now, she was certain Matt Bronzan would win a conviction.

She climbed out of the car and headed for the house. One day she'd have to talk to Jenny about the letter. But not now. Not when there were so many more pressing issues at hand. Jenny's problems would simply have to wait.

Sixteen

The LORD *determined to tear down the wall around the Daughter of Zion.*

LAMENTATIONS 2:8A

On a sunny November morning, an hour before the preliminary hearing in the case of *The People v Brian Wesley,* Jenny arrived at school and headed for the library. She walked inside and peered over a bookshelf. Good. The library was empty except for the librarian, and she was immersed in a magazine. Jenny had only ten minutes before her first class, so she would have to work quickly. She padded quietly toward the computer section.

She had tried to work things out on her own. She had prayed, and in the last few weeks she had even tried talking to her mother. It wasn't her mom's fault. She was just too busy to notice how Jenny was feeling, and Jenny didn't blame her.

She sat down at a row of computer screens and logged on. At least her mother had made some sort of effort recently, asking her questions about how she was doing and whether she was coping. Jenny waited for the welcome screen to appear. Her mother's questions had made her wonder if maybe she had seen the essay, but it didn't really matter. Mom was too busy working for MADD to be worried. Between Carol Cummins, Matt Bronzan, and Brian Wesley, Jenny knew she was the last person on her mother's mind.

The Internet screen popped up, and Jenny clicked the search button. Next she typed three words, "Suicide AND methods AND quick." Glancing nervously over her shoulder, she saw that no one was watching. Then she clicked *OK*.

A list of web pages appeared, and Jenny's eyes grew wide. More than sixteen hundred sites! She scanned the first few and saw that many of them offered advice to troubled people and listed the ways a person could determine if their loved one truly was suicidal. Jenny scrolled past those sites. Her eyes fell on one. "Suicide and Assisted Suicide—It's Nobody's Business if You Do." She clicked it, and a colorful page appeared bearing the same headline. The opening paragraph doubled Jenny's confidence.

"There can be nothing more fundamental concerning individual freedom than this: Our bodies and our lives belong to nobody but ourselves. Our bodies do not belong to our friends, our families, and especially not to the state."

Jenny read on as the web page detailed the ineffectiveness of laws against suicide and then commented on a book that detailed the most successful methods of suicide.

The library was still quiet, but Jenny knew the bell would ring soon, and students would file in. She read quickly.

"With every suicide attempt, there is a chance the effort will fail and the person will wind up a vegetable. For that reason it is better to use fail-safe methods. The problem then, however, is that these methods either hurt—as in hanging or slitting wrists—or they're messy—bullets, jumping off buildings. Sleeping pills are very uncertain because they often cause vomiting before enough of the drug is absorbed into the blood. Therefore, the best technique involves taking the perfect combination of certain pills or inhaling carbon monoxide. When done right, this will lead to a quiet, painless death."

Jenny felt a pit form in her stomach. She hadn't expected the web page to be so graphic. She glanced around quickly and swallowed twice. Her eyes returned to the computer screen and fell on a quotation set apart from the rest of the text. It was a Bible verse. Proverbs 31:6: *"Give strong drink unto him that is ready to perish."*

Jenny sat back in her chair and considered the verse. According to the web page, this proved that God found value in suicide. The idea didn't really match up with what Jenny had been raised to believe...but if God didn't have a problem with suicide, then maybe it really was the best idea.

She felt her confidence grow as she closed the page and scanned the list once more. She found the title of the suicide book from the site and clicked it, but to gain access she had to register for a death service. With a shiver, Jenny closed it and looked for another. Two minutes before the bell rang.

She scrolled past several generic sites until she found one marked, "Untitled." She opened it, and a page appeared with an index of suicide-related topics that people had posted over the past week. She opened one marked, "The Correct Methods." It was written by a paramedic. Jenny began reading:

"I have been a paramedic for seven years, so I have personally responded to many suicides. If you are going to commit suicide, you need to take some things into consideration. First, if you care about your family or whoever you live with, you will do it outside or somewhere easy to clean. Second, if you really want to die, DO NOT call 911. Third, leave a note so they have some idea what made you want to die (it will help the survivors with the grieving process)."

The paramedic went on to discuss specific drug overdoses and other methods and why they would not work. He detailed drugs and drug combinations that would counteract each other, nullifying the intended fatal effect. He also described ways a paramedic could help an unconscious person after a drug overdose so that they would not die. Jenny was spellbound.

"Hanging is a mistake. Every hanging I have been to, the person dropped less than two feet; therefore instead of breaking your neck at the C1-C2 level (cervical vertebrae referred to as a "hangman's fracture"), you strangulate instead. Effective but lots of misery...I know many effective ways, but I am in the job of saving lives so I can't help ya there."

Jenny sighed. She'd thought for sure the article would tell her how she could do it right. Well, at least she knew what not to do. The bell rang, and Jenny clicked the print button. Three pages rolled out of the printer, and Jenny grabbed them, closed down the web page, and signed off the Internet. Some of the information had been good. Jenny ran over it again as she headed for class. *Don't leave a mess, don't call 911, and don't forget to leave a note.*

She felt a rush of relief and for the first time since the accident was filled with something that felt like hope. The Internet was wonderful. Sixteen hundred web pages on suicide. She could get more information tomorrow and the day after that. Pretty soon she would know enough to make a plan, and then maybe next month or the month after that, she would carry it out…finish what should have taken place in the accident.

Before entering her geometry class, Jenny stuffed the printed pages into her notebook. For an instant she remembered how it had felt to be Jenny Ryan before the accident. That Jenny would never have considered killing herself and she shuddered. In some ways the whole notion of suicide scared her. It was crazy. She would have to consider her options carefully.

If only things had gone like they should have…if only she'd died in the accident. Her mother probably wished she had. With all the appointments and lawyers and court dates to deal with, Jenny was only in the way. She replayed the moments before the accident and frowned. How had she survived? Oh, sure, everyone said it was a miracle. Jenny thought it was a curse. She had seen the pictures. She should be dead.

Well, soon she would be, thanks to all that information on the Internet.

And then she and Daddy and Alicia could be together forever. She closed her eyes and pictured it. A never-ending camping trip in the sky.

Brian Wesley rubbed his sweaty palms together and glanced nervously at the courtroom clock. He was early. The preliminary hearing didn't start for thirty minutes.

A bailiff walked up. "You here for *State v Martinez?*"

Brian shook his head and swatted at a stray lock of hair as it fell over his eyes. "No. *State v Wesley.*" The bailiff nodded and walked away.

Life had become a sea of legal maneuverings, and Brian wondered if he'd ever find a way out. If the judge thought they had enough evidence—and Brian's attorney, Harold Finch, thought they did—Brian knew he might serve most of his life in prison. Sweat broke out across his brow. He'd heard about prison once. One of the older guys at the shop did time when he was in his twenties. He'd entertain the technicians with war stories and nuggets of wisdom. Brian remembered some of them. *You don't want to go there, man, but if you do, look out for the soap. If three or more guys come at you, man, just take off running. Oh, and lift something for the belt. Fork, rock, something. Don't go unarmed. Guys die that way all the time. Especially in the shower.*

Brian felt sick to his stomach. How had everything gone so wrong?

The back door opened and Brian turned. A woman entered. She was in her forties, maybe, with a file under one arm and a book in the other. *Too many lawyers in the world.* Brian watched as she scanned the courtroom, locked eyes with his, and then walked toward him.

"I'm not with the Martinez case." Brian fidgeted with his ear lobe. What was she staring at?

"Me neither." She sat down, looking like she had no intention of going anywhere.

"Look, lady, I already have an attorney."

"I'm not an attorney." She turned her body slightly so that she faced him.

Brian sank lower in his seat and fixed his gaze straight ahead. "I gave at the office."

The woman seemed unaffected by his sarcasm. She cleared her throat. "I'm not looking for donations, Mr. Wesley."

He turned to her. "How do you know my name?"

"I know all about you. I know about the accident, about the man and his daughter who were killed. I know about the surviving daughter, and how even though her wounds are healed, a part of her will always be broken because of what you did. I know about the dead man's wife, too."

Brian stared ahead and said nothing.

"You've caused a lot of pain, Mr. Wesley. And whatever is decided here will certainly be what you deserve."

"I don't need to listen to this—" Brian started to stand.

"Wait, Mr. Wesley." The woman reached out and gently took his wrist. He caught her look and paused in surprise. There was nothing condemning in the gaze fixed on him.

Slowly he sat down. "What do you want?"

The woman sighed. "I know your type. You are an alcoholic, so you have driven drunk all of your life. You should have been more responsible, and you deserve punishment."

Brian waited impatiently. "I don't get—"

"Let me finish, Mr. Wesley." She paused a moment. "You have done an awful, devastating thing, but in your heart of hearts I know you did not set out that afternoon to murder two people. You did not intend to destroy that woman's family."

Brian blinked. No. No, he'd never intended that.

"You see, Mr. Wesley, whatever they decide to do with you in this courtroom, you will never truly be free the way you are."

"What's that supposed to mean?"

The woman looked back at the door as though she were waiting for someone to appear. She seemed to be in a hurry when she continued. "Do you know Jesus?"

"Jesus Christ? You mean, like, am I religious or something?"

The woman nodded.

Here we go. "I don't do the church thing, lady."

She smiled again, and he was struck by what he saw in her eyes…calm…*peace.* More peace than Brian had ever seen. Something inside him ached at the sight of it. Why couldn't he feel that? What did it take to look that way…feel that way?

She went on. "I'm not talking about a church thing. I'm talking about a relationship with Jesus Christ. Whether you're in prison or out, you need a savior, Mr. Wesley. And even though you don't do the church thing, Jesus loves you. He loves you, and he's waiting to forgive you."

"I didn't do anything to him." Brian heard the hard edge in his voice.

"Yes, you did." Again, no condemnation. She spoke it like it was a simple fact. "You nailed him to a cross with your sins. He went there to pay the price for what you did that afternoon by choosing to drink and drive, destroy that family."

Brian couldn't think of a comeback.

"Here—" the woman handed Brian a hardcover book—"It's a Bible. Read the gospel of John, and see what you can learn about Jesus."

Brian stared at it. *New International Version Study Bible* was written across the front cover. "Uh…no thanks, lady." He glanced at the courtroom clock. "I need my attorney. Not a Bible."

"Take it. It's yours." She checked the back door once more. "God's given me this job, Mr. Wesley. Jesus loves you. The Bible says so. Read it and see for yourself."

Brian reached for the Bible and felt its heaviness in his hands. "I'm not going to read it."

She smiled sadly. "I'll be praying that you change your mind. Believe me, it won't matter what your punishment is, you'll never be free until you learn the secret of that book."

Brian watched her stand, but before she turned to leave she stopped. "Oh, I'll be checking in on you now and then, Mr. Wesley. Take care."

She moved down the row and disappeared out the back door of the courtroom. Brian glanced down at the Bible in his hand and considered tossing it in the trash can at the back of the courtroom. Instead he opened the front cover and saw writing and a phone number.

"Mr. Wesley…remember, the keys to your prison cell lay between the covers of this book. Call me if you have any questions."

Hannah found a seat in the courtroom ten minutes before the preliminary hearing and noticed Carol Cummins heading toward her.

"Did I miss anything?" Carol gave Hannah's hand a quick squeeze.

"No. Mr. Bronzan is not even here yet." Hannah kept her voice to a whisper.

"Is Jenny coming?"

Hannah scowled. "She had to be at school early for a project or something."

Carol hesitated. "How's she doing?"

"It's hard to tell. She spends a lot of time in her room. Whenever I try to talk to her she gets hard, almost angry at me."

"Have you thought about sending her to a counselor?"

Hannah blinked at the question. A counselor? Of course not. Jenny wasn't sick, for heaven's sake. "No. We never thought much of counselors."

There was a pause. "That's because you had the Wonderful Counselor."

Hannah felt something like a rock in her stomach. "Yeah, well, on that note maybe we *should* look someone up."

Carol's voice softened. "You still have the Wonderful Counselor, Hannah. You just need to go to him."

Hannah sighed. Why couldn't Carol leave this alone? Hadn't she made her feelings clear? "I told you I'm finished with that. Clearly God, if he even exists, did not want to spend a lifetime walking by my side. He left me, remember? From here on out I'm on my own. And so is Jenny."

Carol reached into her notebook and took out a slip of paper. It was covered with scribbled notes. "I wrote these down for you." Carol handed the paper over. "Just some Bible references. I know it sounds crazy, but they're all from Lamentations. I really related to them. Maybe sometime when you have a moment to yourself…"

Hannah took the paper because to refuse would have been rude. She folded it and tucked it into a pocket in her purse, then cocked her head to one side and looked at Carol. Sadness filled her at the sincerity on her friend's face. "I appreciate what you're trying to do, Carol. Really. But it isn't going to work. When I'm alone and nothing makes the hurt go away, I don't go to the Bible. How could I believe anything it says after what happened?" Carol didn't have an answer for that. But then, Hannah hadn't expected one. "I go to my photo albums. Pictures of me and Tom when we were kids, wedding photos, and…and pictures of my little girl—" Hannah's voice broke and she bit her lip. When would the pain stop?

Carol placed a gentle hand on her shoulder. "I'm sorry. I'm not trying to make things worse."

Hannah swallowed, but it took her a moment to speak. "I know. You mean well. But please, no more talking about God and the Bible and how much my old church friends could help. I have you, after all—" she smiled through teary eyes—"and Mr. Bronzan. That's enough for now."

The preliminary hearing was underway.

Matt had given a thorough rundown of the state's evidence, and in response, Harold Finch had tried to convince the judge that his client may not have been legally drunk at the time of the collision. He delivered a long-winded dissertation explaining how it takes so many minutes per drink for alcohol to permeate the bloodstream and how it was possible Brian Wesley's senses had not yet been impaired when the crash occurred.

At first Hannah had been alarmed but from where she and Carol were sitting, she could see the calm in Matt's face, and her concern eased. When Finch finished, the judge ordered a five-minute break, and Hannah watched Matt rise and turn his attention toward her. He smiled and made his way through a small gate in the railing to where she and Carol sat. There was something tender in his eyes, and Hannah had the oddest feeling that somehow this man could relate to her pain.

Carol motioned toward the lobby. "I have to make a few phone calls. I'll be back." She stood up and left as Matt approached and leaned against the back of one of the seats. He nodded a greeting to Hannah. "Glad you could make it."

"I told you, Mr. Bronzan, I'll be here every time there's a hearing." Hannah stared at the back of Brian Wesley's head for a moment and felt her anger rising. "I want him locked up as much as you do."

"Call me Matt."

She met his gaze and smiled a smile that never reached her eyes. "Okay, Matt. Call me Hannah. By the way, you did great up there."

"This is only the beginning. It'll get a lot more heated once we get to trial."

Hannah hesitated. "Then…you're not worried about the… the…"

Matt shook his head. "The argument about Wesley's blood alcohol level? No. I had a feeling we'd get that from Harold Finch. It's a new defense in these cases."

Hannah nodded uncertainly. There was so much involved. She didn't know what she'd do if it weren't for Matt.

The judge returned to his chair, and Matt put a hand on her shoulder. "Carol tells me you're ready to do victim impact panels."

Hannah nodded and closed her eyes. For an instant she saw Tom and Alicia, lifeless, as they'd looked lying on stretchers that day in the hospital. She opened her eyes and the image disappeared. "Yes, we're planning to do one next month. Sometime before Thanksgiving."

"Let's get together before then so we can compare notes. You know, come at this thing from the same angle. It's crucial that everyone who hears you or reads what you say understands about the first-degree murder charge. If we're going to break ground here, we'll need the public's support." He checked his watch. "I've got an appointment right after this hearing, but maybe next week?"

"Absolutely. Whenever you're ready."

"Okay, we'll talk soon." He turned and made his way back to the table.

The judge rapped his gavel once more. "I see that all parties are again present." He gazed about the courtroom. "I've had time to review the preliminary evidence on both sides, and I have determined there is ample evidence to hold the defendant, Brian Wesley, over for trial in each of the charges he faces."

Hannah felt a surge of relief. Matt had been right.

The judge continued. "I've checked the docket and—"

Harold Finch was on his feet. "Your honor, I would like the court to remember that Mr. Wesley is currently undergoing therapy for injuries he received in the accident. We would like—"

"Sit down, Mr. Finch," the judge interrupted. Finch looked surprised as he obeyed the judge's order. The judge glared at him. "You have already informed the court of Mr. Wesley's injuries and his need for therapy. Now, if you'll let me continue—" he faced Matt—"The holidays are fast approaching, and since we must allow time for...Mr. Wesley's *healing* process, I have set a trial date of May 14."

Six months. Hannah hung her head and looked to Matt for his reaction, but as always, he appeared calm and confident. He kept one hand in his pocket, and Hannah was struck by how professional he looked. The jurors were going to love him. "That works fine for the state, your honor."

She glanced at Harold Finch. He was trying to contain a

smile and failing badly. "That should work for my client, as well, your honor. We'll certainly file a motion if Mr. Wesley is still in therapy at that time and needs a continuance."

The judge raised a single eyebrow. "Mr. Finch, let me say something again, in case you have forgotten. This court is well aware of your reputation to delay trials, presumably for the benefit of your clients and to the detriment of the memories of many witnesses. You will not be permitted to play that game in this courtroom. See to it that your client is either healed or transferable by wheel chair. The trial date is May14."

Finch looked as if he might object but changed his mind. "Yes, your honor."

"If that's all, then I'd like to call attention to the next matter on the docket…"

Matt gathered his things, and Hannah watched as Finch and Brian Wesley stood and left the courtroom.

She stared, frowning. What was that tucked into the crook of Brian's arm? Her eyes widened, and fury washed over her as she nudged Carol. "Look at that." She nodded toward the defendant. "It looks like he's carrying a Bible."

Carol looked in the same direction as she stood and swung her purse over her shoulder. "Hard to tell from here. Could be."

Hannah kept her gaze locked on the book in Brian's hands. "I can't believe it! I think it really is." Hannah clenched her teeth, fighting off the powerful urge to throw something at the man. "He probably got it from one of those prison ministry people. Bunch of do-gooders. I wish they'd just leave well enough alone. There's no point witnessing to a man like that. There's no way God—if there *is* a God—would let a worm like Brian Wesley hang around heaven."

Seventeen

Together they wasted away.

LAMENTATIONS 2:8B

Brian got back to Jackson's apartment that afternoon and hid the Bible under his pillow. Wouldn't want Jackson to see it and think he'd freaked out and gone religious or something. The afternoon passed, and that night Jackson brought home a case of Miller, which they shared while talking about the trial.

"Dude, I don't know. I smell trouble this time." Jackson's forehead creased with genuine concern as he crushed an empty aluminum can in his hand and popped open another cold one.

"Tell me about it." Brian turned his can bottom-side-up and guzzled the last bit of beer before grabbing another. "Man, I'm looking at a lot of years behind bars."

Jackson belched loudly. "You've got that expensive dude, what's his name?

Brian laughed, but it sounded hollow even to him. "Finch. Harold Finch."

"That's right. Hey, man, who's paying for that dude?"

"My old man. Called him up in Virginia, and he wired me the bucks. He's loaded."

"Cool." Jackson took several long swigs and set his can down hard. "I thought your old man died."

"Yeah...." Images of Red Wesley, sprawled out drunk on the sofa flashed in his mind. Brian swished a mouthful of the cool, amber liquid around in his mouth and swallowed hard. "Died a long time ago. The money comes from my stepdad, man. He figures I'll stay away if he sends me money. Especially when I'm in trouble."

Jackson thought about that a moment. "That's cool. How loaded is he?"

"Not that loaded. I definitely have to hold a job, man, if that's what you're thinking."

Jackson nodded. "Well, hey, dude, at least you got old Finchman. You might get off yet." He motioned toward the half empty Miller carton. "Hey, man, toss me another, will you? The night's young!"

When Brian opened his eyes the next morning, he had no memory of how or when he finally went to bed. He knew he and Jackson had drunk into the night, but exactly how long, he couldn't say.

He shifted, groaning, and felt something hard beneath him. He tossed and turned and tried to get back to sleep, but there seemed to be a pile of bricks directly under his head.

When he could no longer tolerate the discomfort, he finally reached around near his pillow. His hand found something hard and heavy, and he pulled it out. His eyes widened.

"Oh, man..." The Bible. He'd put it there the day before.

He stared at it and sat up in bed, wincing at the wave of nausea that washed over him. He leaned against the headboard and drew a deep breath. What did he want with a Bible, anyway? He opened the front cover again.

The lady's words were haunting. *"The keys to your prison cell lay between the covers of this book."*

Man. No one talked like that in the bars. Even Carla didn't talk like that. She griped and complained about his drinking. She ragged on him as often as she could. But she never talked about the keys to his prison cell.

Now, through the haze of an incredible hangover, Brian understood the lady's words. She wasn't talking about a cage made of bars and brick. She was talking about drinking. The prison of alcoholism.

As he studied what she'd written, he noticed something else. A few letters and some numbers written underneath her message. It looked strange, like a foreign code of some kind: *Phil. 4:13*. Brian studied it for a moment and then a realization hit. Maybe it was a Bible story or something. Words from the Bible. Yeah, that must be it.

He'd never held a Bible in his hands, let alone read one. But as he lay tangled between the sweat-soaked sheets that morning, his head pounding, he turned the pages gently until he reached the index. He scanned the list of chapters and found dozens of names he'd never heard of.

Then he saw it: *Philippians*. Hey, it was the closest thing to what she'd written. He checked the reference beside it and turned to the corresponding page. Now, what the heck was 4:13? He scanned the text and realized that occasionally there were large numbers that seemed to divide the writing into sections. He found section 4, and noticed that every sentence or two there were other, smaller numbers. His eyes darted past 11 and 12, and finally settled on 13. He read the words slowly: *"I can do everything through him who gives me strength."*

Brian read the words over and over again until his head began to clear and tears filled his eyes. *"I can do everything through him who gives me strength."*

The keys.

Tears spilled onto the delicate pages, and he carefully closed the Bible.

Now if only he could learn how to use them.

Eighteen

The young women of Jerusalem have bowed their heads to the ground.

LAMENTATIONS 2:10B

The call came three weeks later, early one morning, while she was studying the book of Romans. By that time, although she still prayed for Brian Wesley every day, she had decided he was not going to call. He had probably tossed the Bible first chance he had and never gave it another thought. That did not discourage her; she had seen the same rejection from a number of drunk drivers, and she knew she could not change their behavior. God did not ask her to be successful, just faithful. She would continue to pray for change in drunk drivers' hearts as long as she had life.

Her phone rang and she answered on the second ring. "Hello?"

Silence.

"Hello? Is someone there?"

Dimly, she heard the shaky sound of someone either crying or breathing heavy in the background. "Uh…it's…it's me. Brian Wesley. You know from, uh, court the other day."

She closed her eyes. Thank you, Lord. "Yes, Brian, I remember. Have you been reading the Bible?" She hoped her voice sounded compassionate. She could tell this was difficult for him.

"No. Well, I mean, I looked at it or whatever, but…no. I haven't read it. No."

She waited, but he didn't go on. "Is there something I can do for you, Brian. Would you like to pray?"

"No! Nothing like that. Just, well…maybe if you had time…could you, like, you know, meet me somewhere? Just to talk."

The woman considered her schedule. She had planned to meet her daughter for lunch, but she could postpone it. For a moment she considered suggesting a nearby park, but then she caught herself. She didn't know the man, and although she cared deeply for his soul, she did not want to put herself in any danger. "Tell you what, I'm pretty booked today, but why don't you meet me at Church on the Way tomorrow morning?"

"Church where?"

"Church on the Way." She gave him directions. "I'll be sitting in the front row. We can talk in my office."

She listened while Brian drew a deep, shaky breath, then released it slowly. "I guess."

He hung up abruptly, and she replayed the conversation in her mind. There had been so many who had not called after her initial contact.…

Then she hung her head and prayed.

The days were growing colder and Jenny sorted through her sweaters. They were too small. This happened every year, and when it did, she and Alicia would rummage through Alicia's closet. Whatever was too small would be passed on to Jenny.

A chill passed over Jenny, and she rubbed her bare arms. She knew exactly which one of Alicia's sweaters she wanted, and she padded softly into her sister's room.

It had been a week since Jenny had stepped into Alicia's room. It was still exactly as her older sister had left it before the camping trip. Her bed was made and because of Jenny's efforts that day when they'd been packing, the floor was neat. An invitation to a birthday party still stood erect on Alicia's nightstand. A list of scribbled dates and phone numbers lay on a scrap piece of paper beside her phone. Her walls still held poster pictures, one of Amy Grant and another with two cuddly puppies peering over the top of a fallen log. "God help me over the troubles of today," the poster read. Jenny allowed her eyes to linger on the message before turning to Alicia's closet.

A hint of White Shoulders perfume lingered on her sister's clothes, and Jenny closed her eyes. She ached inside for the sound of her sister's voice, for the touch of her hands as they wove her hair into a French braid. All Jenny's life she'd been part of a pair of sisters…without Alicia she felt lost beyond anything she could have imagined. She remembered a time two years ago when Alicia had gone to summer camp with their church. She'd been gone five days, and the afternoon she returned Jenny had waited outside for her to pull up in the church van.

"Jenny!" Alicia had squealed as she jumped from the van, her sleeping bag flying behind her.

Jenny remembered how they'd hugged in the front yard until they were laughing so hard they had fallen in a heap on the grass. "I missed you," Alicia had said when she caught her breath. "Next time you come, too."

Jenny opened her eyes. The sweaters looked much better on Alicia than they did on the hangers. She sorted through the rack twice, but the sweater she wanted was missing. It was a navy pullover with two white horizontal stripes that circled it just above the waist. It had been Alicia's favorite. Mom would know where it was.

"Mom!" Her mother had an appointment at MADD that morning, or maybe with the prosecutor or someone else at the court building. Something. She was always busy these days.

She heard her mother approaching and watched as she peeked into the room.

"What are you doing?" Hannah's hands flew to her hips.

Jenny felt tears sting at her eyes at her mother's mean tone. "I'm looking for a sweater, if that's all right with you."

"In Alicia's closet?" Her mother came a few steps closer and seemed to survey Alicia's clothes, to make sure nothing was missing.

Jenny rolled her eyes. "Yes, mother. In case you forgot, Alicia and I always shared clothes. When she outgrew her stuff, she gave it to me."

Her mother sighed. "I know. I'm sorry. I just thought we should leave things the way they are in here." She tried to pull Jenny into a hug.

Tears spilled onto Jenny's cheeks as she jerked away. "Don't touch me."

"Jenny—"

"No! You don't love me at all, do you?"

"Now, Jenny, that isn't fair. I just don't want—"

"Stop! I know what you want. You want this room to be a shrine. You and I can tiptoe around the house pretending to be alive, but really we're just existing in some kind of…I don't know, some kind of tomb or something."

"It's not like that, Jenny, I—"

"Forget it!" Jenny cut her off, but a whisper of fear ran over her. Was that shrill and trembling voice really hers? "All I wanted was to wear one of Alicia's sweaters. The blue one with the white stripes. I'm cold, okay? Alicia would have wanted me to wear it. But it's…it's missing!" Jenny's tears gave way to sobs, and she felt rooted in place, unable to move as the sobs washed over her.

Hannah slumped back against the poster of the two puppies, stared at the ceiling, and began to cry. "I'm so sorry, Jenny. I do love you. I don't…want you to think just because Alicia's gone…"

"Spare me, Mother, please!" Jenny shook her head. "I don't want to hear it."

Her mother's shoulders shook as she hunched against the wall, her eyes tightly closed. When she opened them, her words were barely a whisper. "The sweater's at Kerry's. Next door."

Jenny hesitated for a moment, wondering if she should thank her mother, or hug her, or say something to mend the distance that continued to grow between them. In the end, she just walked away, wiping her tears as she pushed past her mother.

Kerry and Kim Basil had been friends with Alicia and Jenny most of their lives. Kerry and Alicia were the same age, as were Kim and Jenny. Until the accident, Kim had been one of Jenny's best friends, but now, like so many girls Jenny knew, Kim seemed to be avoiding her.

Jenny knocked on the Basils' front door and waited until the girls' mother answered. She was a heavyset woman who always seemed to have something home-baked in the oven. "Jenny!" The woman wiped her hands on her apron and pulled her into a warm hug. "We've missed seeing you around here."

Jenny savored the feel of a mother's arms around her, but she didn't feel like making small talk, so she pulled away, thankful the woman hadn't noticed her tear-stained face. "Mrs. Basil, Kerry borrowed one of Alicia's sweaters last spring, the blue one with the white stripes. Would you care if I go up and get it?"

"No, dear, go right ahead. The girls are already gone. They take the bus, you know."

Jenny nodded. She used to take the bus, too. Before the accident. Now her mother drove her to school, usually in an uncomfortable silence. Jenny started for the stairs. "Thanks, Mrs. Basil."

"Try the closet shelf," the woman called after her.

"Okay."

Kerry and Kim shared a room, and Jenny had almost never seen it clean. Today was no exception. Jenny glanced around, then headed toward the closet. When they were younger, the four girls had played dress-up and Barbies and a dozen board games in this room. Jenny narrowed her eyes and studied the stacks of sweaters on the closet top shelf. She spotted Alicia's sweater almost immediately and took it gently from where it lay near the bottom of a stack.

She held it up, and she could see Alicia, grinning and challenging her to a foot race at Winter Camp last year. Jenny looked back to see if Mrs. Basil had followed her up. Then she took the arms of the sweater and pulled them around her neck. She held the sweater that way, desperately wishing that Alicia still lived inside it. Her fingers brushed over the soft blue cotton, and she felt the tears again. She folded the sweater gently and tucked it under her arm.

As she turned to leave, Jenny's eyes fell on a folded piece of paper atop Kim's dresser. Kim's name was scrawled across the front, and Jenny recognized the writing. Stacy Carson. Before the accident, the three of them had been inseparable. Jenny, Kim, and Stacy—they'd been a threesome that rarely quarreled, unlike so many other girls who hung out in trios.

Jenny moved closer to the dresser, checking the doorway once more for Mrs. Basil. She studied the paper and saw it was lined. A note. From Stacy to Kim. Curiosity got the better of her, and she lifted it gently from the dresser. She knew what she was doing was wrong, but she couldn't stop herself. The paper unfolded in her hands and she began to read:

"*Hey Kimmie, it's me. Can you believe it? I finished the math test early!!! You should be so lucky. It's not as hard as I thought. Anyway, I talked to Leezer yesterday, and she says she wants me and you over for the sleepover this weekend. Yowwsa! I can't wait. Oh, yeah. She said something about Jenny, but I told her what we talked about. You know, that we feel bad for her and everything—everyone misses Alicia. But Jenny's different now. She's not the same, and the rest of us have to accept it. I told her what we decided. You know, that Jenny really wasn't our friend anymore. She was fine about it. She said she thought Jenny was acting weird, too. She said that happens sometimes. Anyway, Mr. Glintz is staring at me so I better stop. Can't wait for Leezer's party. Love ya! Stace.*"

Jenny felt her blood run cold. These were her best friends.

Writing about a party at Lisa Hanson's house, and she wasn't invited. Was she really that different? She folded the note and set it back on the dresser, then made her way downstairs, outside, and back up to her own bedroom.

She threw herself on the bed and gave way to the flood of tears drowning her heart. Staring at the wall that separated her room from Alicia's, she sobbed loudly, unconcerned about her mother's reaction or the need to be strong for the sake of appearance. Alicia's blue-and-white sweater remained clutched tightly in her arms while the minutes passed. Eventually her weeping stopped.

"Jenny?" It was her mother. Jenny heard the door open.

"What?" She rolled over to face her mother and reached for a tissue.

"It's time to go. I can't be late, honey. I have an appointment at the—"

"I don't care where your appointment is." Jenny thought about staying home, about telling her mother she simply wasn't up to another day at school…another six hours of watching people who once laughed and talked with her now whisper and stare at her in pity…six hours around Kim and Stacy, who were only pretending to be her friends.

No one cared about her anymore. Not her mother, not her friends. No one from youth group had called in weeks. Even God didn't care, at least it didn't seem like it. She sighed and stared at the ceiling.

"Jenny, I won't have one of your temper tantrums today. You need to get out of bed and get ready. We have to leave in five minutes."

Jenny closed her eyes and remembered the Internet. Hope stirred within her at the thought. She needed Daddy and Alicia so badly, and today she had a break after lunch. Maybe she could find out more online information. She stood up slowly, blew her nose and stretched. "You don't need to watch me, Mother. I'll be down in a few minutes."

She moved quickly, suddenly motivated, her mind tracing the electronic paths she would take later that day when she resumed the most important task of her life.

Finding a way to join Daddy and Alicia.

Nineteen

City bus No. 2315 rattled and rumbled east on Vanowen Street, part of a steady flow of morning traffic past Shoup and Topanga Canyon and on into Van Nuys. The bus would take Brian part of the way, and he planned to walk the rest. The brakes screeched as the bus pulled over and Brian got out.

He still couldn't believe he was doing this.

He walked three blocks until he saw it: Church on the Way. *Strange name.* He stood there staring at the building, doubting himself. What was the point in making the journey in the first place?

Brian thought about the man at the AA meeting who'd talked about Christ this and Jesus that. Man! What was he doing here, anyway? He wasn't some religious freak. He didn't need anyone's help. This was *his* problem, *his* mess to figure out. He glanced about and saw a graffiti-covered bench nearby.

What am I doing here?

He turned away from the church, sat down on the bench, and dropped his head into his hands, massaging his temples. Why had she given him the stupid Bible anyway?

The words he'd read came back to him: *"I can do everything through him who gives me strength."* There was something so appealing about the thought. Brian blinked and stared blankly at the traffic whizzing past. He had never been very strong. Not even in high school. His friends could always benchpress more than he.

Somehow he knew the Bible words weren't talking about physical strength, anyway. The more he said the words over in his mind, the more he knew what they meant. Inner strength. The strength to say no when Jackson brought home a sixer of brews. Brian sighed. He'd never had that kind of strength.

The traffic continued, and Brian thought the flow of cars was a lot like his life. The drunken nights and hungover mornings would continue in a never-ending series unless he found the guts to stand up, walk into that church, and stop it. The keys to his prison cell. He gazed over his shoulder, then slowly stood.

With a steadying breath he made his way to the front door and stepped inside. For the first time in his life, in a way that he could not explain and did not feel responsible for, he felt an overwhelming surge of hope.

Hannah climbed out of her car and wandered past a hot dog vendor, down a winding sidewalk shaded by elm trees, and into the back entrance of the Superior Court Building. By now, she moved with confidence. She knew where to go, and she quickly made her way to Matt Bronzan's office. He was expecting her.

His door was open and she peered inside. A subtle hint of men's cologne hung in the air, and Hannah felt herself relax. There was something reassuring about the man, something that went beyond his role as prosecutor.

Matt saw her and returned his sleek, black pen to its upright holder. "Come in." He rose and motioned for her to sit down. "I was just doing busywork."

Hannah settled into the chair and gazed out his window. There was silence for a moment. "It's a beautiful day."

Santa Ana winds had kicked up, and a warm breeze had lifted the veil of smog from the valley. The Santa Monica Mountains were crystal clear, as if all Hannah had to do was reach out the window and she could run her finger over their sharp edges.

Matt followed her gaze. "A last burst of summer."

Hannah nodded and turned her attention back to him.

"Seems funny, with Thanksgiving a week away."

They studied each other and Matt spoke first. "Do you have plans?"

Images of the fight she'd had with Jenny earlier that morning flashed in her mind. "No. Not really."

"It's early, still."

"Yes." Hannah's eyes narrowed and she studied her golden wedding band.

"But you think you're ready for victim impact panels?" Matt spoke slowly and he seemed at ease in her presence.

Hannah nodded. "It'll matter more now than later. Yes…I'm ready."

"Carol's told you about them, how they work?"

"She'll put me with two other victims and assign us to public speaking events. High schools, civic meetings, that sort of thing."

"Right…and you'll have to tell the story, the details about what happened."

Hannah gazed down at her hands again. "I can do that."

"People want to hear about the accident, the loss you've suffered. But then it's up to you to close the discussion with a sales pitch."

Hannah cocked her head. "Sales pitch?"

"Yes. People are drawn by tragedy. They want to know how it happened and why, how they can avoid that sort of thing in their own lives."

Hannah remembered a time when she'd been drawn to such tragedies, too. Back when they only happened to other people.

Matt inhaled deeply. "That's when you talk about first-degree murder."

"Should I say that's what you're seeking in this case?"

Matt nodded. "People will want to know what's happening to the defendant, what penalty he's facing. Tell them he's going to be tried for first-degree murder. Then tell them a little bit about first-degree murder and how it relates to drunk driving."

Matt slid a sheet of paper across the desk to Hannah. "I wrote out some notes for you. Just a description of the charge—murder with the intent to kill—and the reasons some drunk drivers fit the bill."

Hannah glanced over the sheet, noting key phrases: several priors, previous accidents, alcohol training, driving without a license. "These are the same things you said at the preliminary hearing last month."

"Right. It's important that we keep the message short and consistent."

"Because of the audience?"

"Partly. See, the media covers these victim impact panels. Same theory. People are drawn by tragedy, so the papers and news stations send reporters and take your story to the public."

"So we're really reaching more than just the people in the audience?" Hannah thought she was beginning to understand. "We're reaching the people at home, too. Right?"

"We're reaching jurors, Hannah. It's that simple." Matt leaned back and crossed his legs. "You sell the audience on murder-one, you sell the jurors. At least that's the plan."

Hannah sighed and stared out the window again. "Sometimes I can't believe I'm here." She turned to Matt again. "You know, making plans for victim impact panels and discussing murder-one with a prosecutor."

Matt smiled sadly. "Hey, come on, now. We prosecutors aren't all that bad."

Their eyes connected. "I'll never think of you as bad, Matt. You're the good guy…my only hope right now."

Matt shifted in his chair uneasily. "Hannah, don't take this wrong, but aren't you a Christian?"

Oh no, not again. She was growing so weary of this conversation. She folded her arms tightly in front of her. "I was once. A long time ago."

"I thought so." He turned his attention to a small photograph tucked into the frame of his desk calendar. She couldn't quite make out the faces, but she felt her heart constrict when he ran a finger over the image. It must be someone he loved. A girlfriend?

"I'm a believer. Did you know that?"

She shrugged. "I think Carol mentioned something about it." She was no longer enjoying their conversation, and she glanced at her watch. It was time to go.

Matt watched the emotions washing over Hannah's face. This wasn't easy for her. "You don't want to talk about it, do you?"

"No." Hannah fidgeted with her wedding ring. "Ever since the accident…I've had a hard time believing God really exists." She paused. "We went to church, we tithed, gave to the poor, obeyed his word."

"And look where it got you." Matt understood perfectly. Far better than he'd ever wanted to.

"Right." Hannah looked away. "I wouldn't want to serve that kind of God, even if he were real."

Matt nodded. "I remember feeling that way."

Hannah looked up, surprised.

"It was a long time ago."

It was time. Time to tell Hannah why this all meant so much to him. He glanced down at the photo, at the laughing couple smiling up at him…

He removed the photo from the frame on his desk calendar and held it out to her. "This was my best friend Shawn. And his girlfriend Victoria."

Hannah leaned closer and studied the photo. Matt swallowed hard. It hurt to remember his friends when they were young and full of life. Hannah lifted her gaze curiously and waited for him to explain.

Help me, Lord. Help me tell this so she'll understand. He wasn't quite sure why it mattered so much.

He only knew it did.

"Shawn was my best friend growing up. We played ball together and went off to college together. Victoria came into the picture a couple years after that."

Matt gazed at the picture, and then, as though a flood-gate had been removed, Victoria was there before him. And Shawn. He could see the three of them making their way across the campus at Loyola Marymount University, carefree and brimming with enthusiasm, planning study sessions and beach trips, Saturday pizza parties and whatever basketball game was coming up.

Shawn Bottmeiller had been Matt's best friend since high school. They'd both been forwards on the Westlake basketball team. Off the court, Shawn was a slow-moving, handsome dreamer with little drive or ambition, who imagined himself with a career in the NBA. He was lanky with a pretty shot and as much natural basketball talent as anyone who'd ever graced the court at Westlake High.

Matt had been everything Shawn was not. He was a blur of motion, filling out college applications and scholarship forms two years before high school graduation. Matt did not have Shawn's striking looks, but he was fiercely athletic, and hours in the weight room had given him a chiseled body. What he lacked in talent and natural skills, he made up for with hard work and dedication. Matt was a realist, and from the time he could spell his name he'd known he would be a lawyer one day.

"A crummy old lawyer?" Shawn would ask sometimes when they were breathless and sweaty after a game. "Why would ya wanna go and do some fool thing like that. This is the life, man. Hoops, hoops, and more hoops. And girls, of course."

"Someone has to take care of the bad guys," Matt would tell him.

"Oh, I see. You'll be one of those poor, struggling lawyers

who wastes his life getting criminals locked up just to watch 'em get out on some early release program. That oughta be real satisfying, man."

"Okay, how 'bout you, Shawn? Gonna live at home all your life?"

"I—" Shawn paused for effect—"will be playing hoop in the NBA, stopping by your dreary little law office when I'm feeling charitable and giving you free tickets to watch me play."

"Oh, okay. Is there a plan B?"

Shawn looked insulted. "Plan B? Matt, you've lost faith in me, man. I'm still growing, you know. Gonna be six-foot-eight, and then they'll be banging down my door asking me to play for them."

"Do the words 'hard work' mean anything to you? 'Cause that's what it's going to take to get that kind of attention. I for one plan to work my tail off to make state."

"Hoop and work." Shawn looked as if he'd gotten a sudden taste of lemon. "The words don't go together in my book. Hoops are too much fun, man."

Before their junior year, Matt drew up a workout schedule he believed would give them the edge when basketball season came. "Three hundred jump shots a day, two hundred free throws—" Matt was excited as he explained the routine to Shawn—"lifting for an hour, then sprints. And dribbling. We take the ball with us wherever we go. By the time school starts, we'll be better than any forwards in the league. State championship, man. All the way!"

Shawn looked at him, arched one eyebrow, and dropped himself into a beanbag chair. "During summer vacation? You must be missing a screw, my man. Summer is for catching rays and watching babes."

Matt shrugged. "Suit yourself. But don't whine when I make all-state. Then the recruiters will be knocking down *my* door, and you'll find yourself scrambling for a junior college team who'll let you walk on."

"Moi, me, the great one." Shawn laughed. "They'll beg me to play for them, man."

"We'll see."

Matt made time for the beach that summer, but only after he had completed his daily basketball regime. When state playoffs came, Matt led the way averaging thirty-two points per game and eight rebounds. Shawn skated by averaging nine points and three boards, but Matt's prediction had been accurate. He was selected first team all-state, while Shawn received only an honorable mention.

The next year Matt, who had sprouted to six-foot-four, accepted a scholarship to play basketball at Loyola Marymount University. Shawn was forced to attend a junior college. Two years later he transferred to Loyola Marymount, where the closest he got to a basketball court was his seat in the student section. Still, he rarely missed one of Matt's games.

Midway through their junior year, Matt and Shawn took an advanced English comp class and there, sitting in the first row of the large auditorium, was Victoria Stevens.

Being friends for so much of their lives, Matt and Shawn had reached an agreement regarding girls: No girl came between them. Period. They might both find a girl attractive, but if one of them had the opportunity to date her, the other celebrated the victory. There was no room for jealousy in their friendship.

Victoria Stevens was the first girl who threatened that. Everyone on campus knew about her. She was more beautiful than any girl they'd ever seen and utterly unattainable. For the first month, they filed into class early to get a better look at her, but neither of them could figure out a way to meet her.

Then one day they were leaving class after the bell when providence placed Victoria right in front of them. Drawing on his once considerable defensive basketball skills, Shawn slipped his finger under her elbow and dislodged her books. Matt watched the whole thing and saw Victoria's befuddled expression as her books mysteriously tumbled to the ground. Shawn was there at her side as she stopped to pick them up.

"Oh, hey, let me get those for you." He flashed her his famous grin and she met his gaze. Then just as quickly she looked beyond him to Matt, and her eyes lit up.

"Hey, aren't you on the basketball team?"

"Yeah." Matt smiled uncomfortably. Shawn had made the first move. He needed to back off.

Shawn cleared his throat. "Yes, and I taught him everything he knows." He dribbled an imaginary ball, pulled up near Victoria, and shot an invisible three-pointer. He remained motionless for a moment, then raised both hands signifying that the basket was good. "Nothing but net."

Victoria cast a questioning glance at him, but she couldn't hold back her laugh. Shawn and Victoria began dating, and soon they were seeing each other exclusively. On occasion Matt would catch her looking at him longer than she needed, but there was never any reason for him to doubt her affection for Shawn.

One afternoon the three of them were studying when Shawn had to leave for an appointment with his counselor.

"You don't say much, Matt," Victoria said when they were alone.

He shrugged. "We're supposed to be studying."

She tilted her head pensively. "But you work so hard. School, basketball. Don't you ever just want to have fun?"

Matt considered her thoughtfully. "I have fun being the best."

"You and Shawn are so different. He's so, oh, I don't know…goofy, I guess. I wonder what he'll do in life, you know?"

"I think he's going to law school with me." Matt grinned.

Victoria looked surprised. "Really. I didn't know he wanted to be a lawyer."

"I don't know that, either, but he seems to follow me

around." Matt stifled a laugh. He didn't want to get too friendly with Victoria while Shawn was gone.

"Sometimes I wonder what would have happened if *you'd* knocked my books down and not him." She was no longer smiling.

"So you knew about that, huh? He used to do that on the court all the time. Come up behind some poor guy, nudge the ball, and take off without ever looking back." Matt looked down at the textbook and doodled with a single finger.

Victoria lowered her head and caught his eyes again. "Don't you wonder, Matt?"

He drew a breath and released it slowly. "Look, Victoria, you're a beautiful girl, and I'd be lying if I told you I wasn't attracted to you. But you're dating Shawn, and that's about as far as my wondering usually goes."

Victoria nodded once. "Okay. Shawn's a lot of fun and I enjoy dating him. But still..."

Matt looked up once more.

She met his look. "One day...who knows?"

Matt held her gaze a moment longer, then exhaled dramatically, leaned over, and tapped the textbook opened up in front of her.

"So, what is it you're studying anyway?"

Shawn and Victoria continued dating, and her presence in his life seemed to change him. He became more responsible, more aware of the future and its looming reality. While Matt dated occasionally, for the most part he was too busy studying and playing basketball. He spent his free time with Shawn and Victoria, and the threesome became as integral a part of his college life as the school's hardwood gymnasium floor and stuffy locker room.

Before graduation Shawn followed Matt's lead and applied for admission to Pepperdine Law School. His father worked in the movie industry, and money would not be a problem. Funds weren't as easily abundant for Matt's family, but his grades, student involvement, and application essays were such that he received a full scholarship.

Shawn burst into Matt's dormitory when he received the news. "I'm in, man! You and me. Law school. Conquering the bad guys."

Matt stood up and slapped his friend on the back and the two embraced. "Don't worry. It'll be even better than the NBA."

Shawn grinned. "Now, I doubt that, man. Seriously. But hey, this calls for some kind of celebration."

"Yeah, let's plan something. The three of us."

Shawn pulled a small velvet box from his pocket. "I'm seeing Victoria tonight."

Matt glanced from the box to his friend. "What's this?"

Shawn opened it, and there inside lay a glimmering diamond solitaire engagement ring. "Tonight's the night, man."

Matt's momentary disappointment turned quickly to elation for his best friend. "Hey, that's great. She have any idea?"

"Oh, you know the female gender." Shawn flashed his famous grin. "Probably been expecting it for months."

"You sure you're ready?"

Shawn grew suddenly serious. "I've never loved anyone like I love her, man. She's my life."

That night, Shawn and Victoria went to dinner at Gladstones on the beach. They ate steak and lobster and later walked on the sandy strip beneath the restaurant where Shawn got down on one knee and proposed. Matt got the whole story later, all the details—including how Victoria grew teary-eyed and accepted.

The two were walking hand-in-hand along Pacific Coast Highway looking for a less crowded stretch of beach when a Volkswagon careened out of control and struck them from behind. Shawn was knocked onto the shoulder of the roadway, scraped but not seriously hurt; Victoria took the full force of the hit. She flew twenty feet in the air before landing on the pavement, motionless. Shawn scrambled to her side and cradled her broken body, begging her to hang on. He was still holding her that way, sobbing, when paramedics arrived and told him what he already knew. She was dead.

The driver of the Volkswagon had been drunk.

Matt did his best to help Shawn get over her death. They started law school and tried to keep busy. But they were both devastated.

The drunk driver was given ten days in prison and a five hundred dollar fine. He'd been convicted once before, but he was young, and the judge thought he'd be better off taking alcohol education courses than wasting away in a prison. Shawn hated the man, could have gladly killed him given the chance. But none of it would bring back Victoria, and as the one-year anniversary of her death grew near, Shawn dropped two of his classes and spent hours sitting on the grassy Pepperdine hillside overlooking Malibu Beach.

Matt had tried talking to him, tried to help him work through it. But all to no avail. On the one-year anniversary of Victoria's death, Shawn Bottmeiller took a gun from his parents' closet and wrote two letters—one to his parents expressing his love and sorrow for what he was about to do; the other to the man who killed Victoria. In it he expressed his anger and hatred, his inability to forgive the man for what he'd done.

"When you killed her, you killed my dreams. You killed me. Today I'll finish what you tried to do a year ago."

Then he drove to the beach, walked down to the sandy strip where he had proposed to Victoria a year earlier, and shot himself in the head.

Matt, always the realist, always the achiever, doubled his efforts at law school and determined that Victoria's and Shawn's deaths would not be in vain. He finished law school top of his class and took a job at the district attorney's office in Los Angeles. In the process, he met Sgt. John Miller and saw something different about him. When he learned about the man's faith, Matt began attending a Bible-believing Christian church, and a decade after the deaths of Shawn and Victoria, he gave his life to the Lord.

Then, when he had enough experience, he began specializing in one type of case, the only type that really mattered to him.

Cases against drunk drivers.

That had been eighteen years earlier, but now as he watched Hannah Ryan studying the photo of his two friends, it felt as if it had happened yesterday.

Hannah looked from the photo to Matt, and was surprised at the grief she saw on his face.

"Do your friends live here?"

Matt blinked, as though the question startled him, then shook his head slowly. "No." His gaze drifted to the photo, then back to Hannah. "The day Shawn asked Victoria to marry him, she was killed by a drunk driver."

Shock swept over Hannah, and she had to resist the strong urge to go to Matt, to put her arm around him and comfort him. No wonder she'd always felt such understanding from him.

But he wasn't finished.

"One year later, on the anniversary of Victoria's death—" Matt's voice was ragged with sorrow—"Shawn killed himself."

Hannah sat slowly back in her seat. Like her, Matt had lost so much. Because of men like Brian Wesley…the kind of men Matt had worked so long and so hard to prosecute.…

"And so you spend your life prosecuting drunk drivers.…"

"As many as I can."

She could think of nothing to say. This was the compassion she felt from Matt, the understanding. He knew her pain, knew it personally.

Matt drew a deep breath. "After that, I doubted God for a while, too." He lifted his eyes from the picture, and Hannah was struck at the peace she saw in his gaze. "But then I found out the truth. God's ways are not our ways. This world is a fallen place, and bad things do happen to good people. They even happen to Christians. Truth is, I couldn't have made it through without his strength."

Tears stung at Hannah's eyes, but she refused to give in to them. What Matt was saying had the strong ring of truth to it, but she couldn't accept it. Couldn't believe God was real…that he'd done nothing but watch as her family was ripped apart…as Matt's dearest friends were destroyed.…

Matt tucked the photograph back into the frame. "I know you don't believe it, Hannah. But God loves you. Even now."

She didn't reply to that. Instead, she nodded. "It must help…prosecuting them."

But he slowly shook his head. "Not really. The law is still pretty loose where drunk drivers are concerned. That's why this is such a big deal. We'll be making history if we win this one."

Hannah glanced at Matt's left hand and couldn't hold back the question. "You're not married, are you?"

Matt shook his head. "Never had time. I've spent ten years right here, increasing public awareness, waiting for the day when we could get it into the murder-one category."

Good. This was safe ground. This was the kind of conversation she wanted to focus on. "Now here we are."

Matt smiled, and again she saw understanding in his expression. "Not yet. We still have a lot of work to do."

"And that's where the victim impact panels come in."

"Exactly. If we can fill this room with a dozen jurors who are familiar with the idea that killing someone in a drunk driving accident can be murder one…well, that'll make my job that much easier."

Hannah nodded. Her role was clearly defined and she was thankful. She would do this, working for the memories of Tom and Alicia, alongside Matt Bronzan, who had his own memories to fight for. They would win their murder-one conviction and then, in their own ways, they could get on with life.

"Hannah..." Matt's voice interrupted her thoughts. "Do you mind if I pray for you?"

Her heart constricted. "Now?" She desperately wanted to avoid this, but she didn't want to hurt him.

Matt smiled again. "No, not now. But throughout the trial. I don't know..." He paused. "You've lost so much already. I guess I can't imagine losing all that and God, too."

Hannah glanced out the window and waited. After a long while she finally spoke. "You can pray, Matt." She looked at him and felt tears well up in her eyes. "But everything I want, I've already lost."

"I know. I'm not trying to change your feelings. But Hannah, my door's open. Anytime you want to talk, if you need anything, I'm here. And I will be praying."

She believed him, and it gave her a sense of comfort. And hope. She stood up then. "I'd better get going. I have to meet Carol."

Matt rose and reached for her hand. "Thanks for coming." He looked suddenly self-conscious. "I probably told you more than I should have. But I thought you should know where I'm coming from. What I believe, what drives me."

She nodded. She was grateful he had done so...and she felt a closeness to him that warmed her. With a start she realized she was holding his hand a bit too long, so she let go and crossed her arms. "Thank you, Matt. Maybe after the trial we can put this thing behind us—both of us. Unless there's another delay, of course."

"I'm not worried about it." Matt slipped his hands in his pockets. "More time means more days to convince jurors that Brian Wesley is guilty of murder-one."

Hannah tilted her head. "Some people would think that doesn't sound very Christian."

"My obligation to forgive doesn't erase my obligation to provide punishment. Without rules and penalties, this country would have fallen apart decades ago. I like to think that my job is actually quite Christian. Further questions?" He grinned.

Hannah studied him. "You certainly can argue."

"Only when I believe in the cause." He moved around his desk and opened his office door a bit wider. "Let's stay in touch. I want to know how the first victim-impact panel goes, okay?"

Hannah nodded and thanked him again.

As she walked slowly back to her car, she considered Matt and Carol, their strong beliefs, and the role they played in this, her season of grief. She sighed. The world was filled with non-Christians, atheists even. All her life she had shared classrooms and committees and airplanes with them. She drove behind them on freeways, shocked at the boldness of their Darwinian fish and the mockery they made of the Christian world view. They seemed to rule Hollywood, the media, and the voting polls. They had elected Clinton, after all. Millions of them walked the United States.

Yet in this, her darkest hour, when she herself had finally come to join the ranks of nonbelievers, she found herself relying completely on the strengths and abilities of two very devout Christians.

Twenty

My eyes fail from weeping, I am in torment within,
my heart is poured out on the ground
because my people are destroyed.

LAMENTATIONS 2:11A

The sun was sinking slowly behind the mountains, and Hannah wondered if theirs was the only house in America that didn't smell of turkey and gravy and home-baked pumpkin pies. She had asked Jenny about celebrating Thanksgiving and got little response. Now it was four o'clock in the afternoon, and Hannah had just about finished making a small platter of tacos.

"Jenny, time to eat," she called from the kitchen. She wiped her hands on a paper towel and set the tacos on the table.

"I'm not hungry!" Jenny shouted from upstairs.

Hannah sighed. She should have skipped cooking altogether. It wasn't as if making tacos instead of turkey could eliminate fifteen years of Thanksgiving memories. The smell of greasy hamburger made her nauseous. She walked to the foot of the stairs and yelled again. "Jenny, we agreed on tacos for today! I've cooked them and they're ready. Please come down here and eat."

Hannah could hear her daughter padding out of her bedroom toward the stairs. "Mother, I told you I'm not hungry."

"Why didn't you tell me that before? I wouldn't have bothered."

Jenny drifted down a few stairs so that Hannah could see her face. "If I wasn't around—" Jenny was almost snarling—

"you wouldn't have to cook at all. That's what you want, isn't it?"

Hannah stared at her for a moment, then her anger started to build. "I want two things, young lady, and maybe you'd better take notes so you don't forget."

Jenny rolled her eyes, something she never would have done before the accident. Now, she did it constantly. Hannah continued. "First, I want us to stop fighting. It's getting old. We're supposed to be helping each other through this, and instead we're like enemies. It's ridiculous."

Hannah waited, but Jenny remained silent, her arms folded defiantly. "Second, I want you to get down here and eat your tacos."

There was silence again. Finally Jenny released a frustrated burst of air. "Fine. Whatever. You wouldn't know anything about losing your appetite because you don't even miss Daddy and Alicia."

"What?" Hannah's temper rose another notch. "How can you even say that?"

"It's true! All you care about is that guy who hit us—Brian whatever his name is. You want him in prison so badly you've forgotten about Daddy and Alicia."

"That's a lie and you know it, Jennifer Ryan! Everything I'm doing is because I miss Daddy and Alicia, I miss—"

"Then how can you even think about eating *tacos*?" Jenny's eyes blazed. "On Thanksgiving Day? I just don't understand you, Mother."

Hannah fumed silently. "Forget it. Go back upstairs and sit alone in your room. I thought we could start something new, enjoy a dinner together, just the two of us. But forget it."

"Fine." Jenny turned and stomped back upstairs, down the hall, and into her room.

Hannah wandered back to the kitchen table and sat down. She took a single taco from the platter and set it on her stark plate. It was cold, and tiny white flecks of hardened lard had appeared on the fried tortillas. Hannah pushed her chair back from the table, dropped her head into her hands, and closed her eyes.

How had so much changed since last Thanksgiving?

Suddenly she was there again. She could smell the turkey, hear the televised football match between the Cowboys and the Redskins....She could almost see Jenny and Alicia, giggling and darting about the house while Tom and a handful of church friends chuckled in the background.

Each year they had filled the house with a ragtag group of stragglers, friends who had no family in the area. She had never been the greatest cook, and last Thanksgiving was proof. In the seconds before dinner was served, the sweet potato casserole caught fire, setting off smoke alarms throughout the house.

"Just like Dad always says," Alicia had teased. "You know it's dinner at the Ryan house when the smoke alarms go off."

Hannah had been frustrated, but Tom had come up behind her and circled her waist with his arms, whispering in her ear. "Don't worry about it, honey. You can't be good at everything."

Hannah remembered turning around and collapsing against his chest. "Yes, but it's Thanksgiving. I should be able to pull off a meal like this after more than a decade of experience. At least once a year."

"But you're good at so many other things."

Hannah pouted. "Like what?"

Tom put a finger under her chin and lifted it gently as he gazed into her eyes. "Like loving me. Loving our children. God gave me the best woman I could ever hope for. You go ahead and burn the sweet potatoes. Burn the whole meal, for all I care. I could never love another woman like I love you, Hannah Ryan."

She blinked, and the memory faded. The wilting tacos looked even less appetizing now. She could still feel Tom's breath on her neck as he'd whispered those lovely things to her. Tears slid from beneath her closed eyelids, and they fell hot on her cheeks. *Tom, I need you. I can't do this alone.*

With the holidays there would be so many yesterdays to wade through. First Thanksgiving. Then, starting tomorrow, the whole world would be making frenzied preparations for Christmas. The entire holiday season seemed overwhelming.

How could Tom and Alicia be gone? Forever? And when would Jenny stop acting so selfish and try to move ahead, as Hannah was doing?

She stood up, took the plate of tacos, and tossed them in the trash. Tuesday would be her first victim impact panel appearance. She had gone over her notes a dozen times, and she was ready. It was time to start making a difference, time to start reaching the jurors.

Twenty-one

What can I say for you?
With what can I compare you, O Daughter of Jerusalem?
To what can I liken you, that I may comfort you?...
Your wound is as deep as the sea.
Who can heal you?

LAMENTATIONS 2:13

It was days later, and as victim impact panels went, it was an obvious place to start, even if Jenny wasn't excited about the idea.

West Hills High School—where Alicia had been so involved, so popular. If any students would be receptive to a lesson on the evils of drinking and driving, it would be the kids at West Hills. And not just the older students. Hannah would be speaking to the junior high as well, since they, too, had been invited to the assembly.

Hannah slipped into a silk blouse and slim, navy, dress slacks. She had thirty minutes, so makeup would have to be done in a hurry. Leaning forward, she checked herself in the mirror and saw that the dark circles were going away. Sleep was a remarkable cure. Her body had learned to compensate for the nightmare of her waking hours by requiring long stretches of blissful sleep, replete with vivid dreams of happy yesterdays.

Studying her image more closely, Hannah saw it again. There was something different about her eyes, something hard. Before the accident people used to say she had the eyes of a child—eyes that shone with Christ's light. She snorted softly.

Christ's light was nothing of the sort. What people had seen back then was simply a pure, unadulterated joy that came from having her family alive and healthy.

The eyes that stared back at her now looked eighty years old, flat and lifeless. The brightness had been clouded by something Hannah couldn't quite identify, and no matter how she tried, she couldn't will the light back.

Well, not to worry. She knew what it would take—Brian Wesley's conviction. Only then would the cloud lift and the sparkle return.

Jenny entered Hannah's bedroom and stared at her mother with listless eyes. "What time are we leaving?"

Hannah started, studying her daughter for a moment. Why hadn't she seen it before? The light was gone from Jenny's eyes, too. It was all so unfair. She smiled sadly at Jenny. "Let's say in about half an hour."

Jenny exhaled slowly. "Do I have to go, Mom? Couldn't I just hang out in the library and work on my homework?"

Hannah turned to face her daughter. "Jenny, I don't understand you. Do you realize the importance of what's happening today? I get a chance to tell those kids what happens when you drink and drive. I have one hour to explain how wrong that man was who killed your dad and Alicia. Film crews will be there, journalists, reporters. They'll take notes and pictures, and then everyone in Los Angeles will know that Matt Bronzan is seeking a murder-one conviction against Brian Wesley."

Jenny huffed. "I *know,* Mom; you've told me four times since yesterday. But what's that got to do with me?"

Come on, Jenny, you've got to care about this. What's happened to you? "You should be up there beside me, that's what. You're a victim, too, you know. Or am I the only one who's suffering here?"

Jenny looked at her, and Hannah was deeply troubled at how hard the girl's gaze was. Like stone. Or ice. "No, Mom, you're the only one who's *flaunting* it."

At the cold, curt words Hannah opened her mouth, but Jenny cut her off, angry words spewing like molten lava. "You want to take our private misery and lay it out for everyone to see. You cry for the cameras and tell the world how Daddy and Alicia were killed. That way if enough people know, then maybe, if we're *really* lucky, that prosecutor will put Brian Wesley in prison for life."

Jenny paused long enough to take a step toward Hannah. "But, Mom, have you ever asked me what *I* want? No! Because you don't care about me. The only time you want me around is if it works into your agenda."

Hannah swallowed hard. When had her little girl grown so contemptuous of her? "Jenny, please, we've been through this before...."

"I know it and I hate it as much as you do. Why won't you just leave me alone? I don't want to be up there on the panel beside you. I'm not ready to have a question-answer session. I...I don't want to tell someone what it feels like to have your sister killed in the seat beside you." Jenny began weeping then, and Hannah thought the girl looked like she might collapse. "I don't want to do it, Mom. I just don't."

Hannah drew a deep breath and tried to control her temper. She knew she should go to Jenny, hug her and tell her everything was going to be all right one day. But her daughter's temper tantrums had become tiresome, and Hannah sat on the edge of her bed instead. A dozen questions darted through Hannah's mind. *Why don't you care? Why won't you help me? Don't you think I'm hurting, too?*

Hannah released the breath she'd been holding. "Jenny, I can't believe some of the things you say to me anymore. You think I'm only interested in using you, using your pain for publicity? Is that it? Is that what you *really* think?"

Jenny nodded and sniffed.

Hannah wasn't sure how she kept her voice controlled, but she did. "Well, that's a lie, young lady. Nothing could be farther from the truth. I care about you and your future and the way this has changed our lives forever. I love you, Jennifer Ryan, but yes, I am putting my entire life into helping Matt Bronzan convict that killer of first-degree murder. And once he's locked up, once he's punished for what he did to us, we can start fresh, learn to live again. Because this is all we have left. Me and you."

Jenny stared at her mother as if nothing she'd said made any sense. "You think everything's going to be okay just because some guy goes to prison? It doesn't work that way, Mom."

Hannah was tired of fighting. "Finish getting dressed. I'll take you to school. After that it's up to you. Come to the assembly with your class or stay away. Don't sit on the panel with me unless you want to."

Jenny walked away without another word.

The silence continued the entire trip to school. When they pulled up, Hannah reached out and tried to take Jenny's hand, but Jenny opened the car door and quickly stepped out.

Hannah leaned over in the seat, craning her neck to see her daughter. "Jenny, I hope I'll—"

The car door slammed shut.

Hannah entered the auditorium and saw that the media had already arrived and set up. *Oh, good. Thank you—*"

Hannah froze. *Thank who?*

The question stumped her for a moment, but she shook it off. Thank good fortune, thank the media, thank no one in particular.

She made her way across the wood floor, over a maze of heavy black electrical cords lining the back of the auditorium, where two of the three major networks had cameras stationed. Reporters milled about with notepads, interviewing students who wandered past. Hannah notched the minor victory—

Carol had said there was always a chance the media wouldn't show.

She studied the stage. Five desks for the five panel members, each sporting a microphone. Hannah felt her hands growing cold, and she thought about Carol's warning: "Sometimes just before you take the stage, you're nearly overcome with nerves." Carol had several suggestions on how to combat this, but only one that Hannah thought applied to her.

Remember Tom and Alicia.

She reached up and felt the photo pin and knew she would be all right. She wore the pin anytime she went out, anymore. Jurors were everywhere.

Hannah approached the stage, greeted the others, and took her seat between one of the MADD representatives and a highway patrol officer. She glanced over her notes and then at her wristwatch. They were scheduled to begin in five minutes.

The room was filling with giggling teenagers, and Hannah found herself staring anxiously at the entryways. Would Jenny come? Training her eyes on the double doors, Hannah studied the stream of kids still pouring in and spotted her daughter's class. Her heart raced when she spotted Jenny at last. She was the last one in the group to enter the building, and she sat a ways off from the others, alone.

Hannah stared at her, willing her to look up. *Watch me, Jenny.* But the girl kept her eyes downward. *Come on, Jenny, I need you up here. Look at me!* A chill passed over Hannah's arms and she shuddered. Her daughter had become little more than a stranger.

The others had already spoken, and finally it was Hannah's turn. She introduced herself, and a wave of whispers washed over the teenage crowd. Hannah caught some of what they were saying…"That lady up there is Alicia's mom." "Oh, my gosh, this is actually Alicia's mom!" Hannah waited until the whispers died down, taking the opportunity to glance again at Jenny. Her eyes were still on the floor.

Hannah cleared her throat and began. Sparing no details, she explained how Brian Wesley had plowed his car into her family's Explorer, killing both Alicia and her father, Dr. Ryan. The students sat spellbound as Hannah described Alicia's head injuries and Tom's internal bleeding.

"Alicia's sister Jenny was spared, thankfully." Hannah hesitated and for a moment she caught Jenny's gaze across the auditorium. She smiled, hoping Jenny would know it was just for her, but the girl seemed suddenly busy with her shoelaces. Hannah scanned the faces before her. "Even though Jenny lived, she will never, ever be the same again. All because someone made a choice to drink and drive. A choice to kill."

Hannah segued into a list of increasing penalties and tougher prosecution where drunk driving was concerned. Jenny's expression was indifferent as Hannah talked about Matt Bronzan and his quest to reduce the number of drunk driving accidents each year. Hannah explained that if a person chose to drink and drive despite prior convictions and alcohol awareness classes, the stakes were higher than ever before.

"The man who killed my husband and oldest daughter is being charged with first-degree murder." She let that sink in a moment. "First-degree murder. That's usually reserved for people with guns and knives, but now it's been used a few times across the country to convict drunk drivers. The prosecutor believes he can win a murder-one conviction. He believes the time has come to let people know just how serious this is."

Hannah paused then, drawing a breath. This was the hard part. "You know, Alicia should be out there today, sitting with you, joking with you." She looked at Alicia's cheerleader friends. "Cheering with you. She should be here. But she's not, and it's all because someone chose to drink and drive."

She waited, studying the faces in the crowd, some crying, many who had been over to the house to visit Alicia and Jenny in years past. Her eyes narrowed, and she forgot about the television cameras for the moment. "Alicia is gone. Her father is gone. Nothing we say or do here today will bring them back."

She shot a glance at Jenny—the girl's head was bent down nearly to her knees. *If only she would listen.* "We can't bring them back, but we can make a difference. We can make it so that their deaths were not in vain."

There was silence while the students waited. Hannah had the feeling that at this point they would do whatever they could in Alicia's memory.

"If you cared about Alicia, then please, take a stand against drunk driving. Go out from here and say enough, already. No more!" She met the somber gazes directed at her. "Spread the news about what's going to happen to Brian Wesley. Get the truth out: you choose to drink and drive, knowing the risks involved, then you're going down for first-degree murder. Murder one! Please. If you loved Alicia, do this one last thing for her. Thank you."

The students remained motionless, and the muted sound of crying and sniffling filled the room. Hannah glanced at the cameras and saw one directed at Alicia's three cheerleader friends who were crying, clinging to each other.

"Thank you, Mrs. Ryan." Betty Broderick from MADD nodded in Hannah's direction, then turned to the students. "Now, if you have any questions..."

Hannah knew she had reached these kids, and she felt a sense of accomplishment, elation even. She had notched a victory for MADD that day, a victory for Tom and Alicia. The news would broadcast what she'd said, or at least parts of it, and by tomorrow people across Los Angeles would be aware that drunk driving might lead to a first-degree murder conviction.

Hannah felt a ray of hope for the first time in weeks. She couldn't help it. Four months of this and Brian Wesley wouldn't stand a chance.

She could hardly wait to speak to other groups.

She looked out at the students and saw a handful of arms raised. As Betty Broderick started responding to their questions, Hannah sighed. She had gotten through it. Jenny must be so proud of her! She glanced to the spot where her daughter had been sitting—and sudden tears welled up in her eyes.

Jenny was gone.

Twenty-two

The visions of your prophets were false and worthless;
they did not. . . ward off your captivity.

LAMENTATIONS 2:14A

Christmas was fourteen days away, but Brian Wesley wasn't waiting for December 25. The celebration was now. He'd been forming the plan for days, and he was finally ready to carry it out.

Brian smiled at himself in the mirror. He had a reason to be excited as he got ready that morning. He had been sober again for three weeks.

At first he had credited his sobriety to the strange Bible words, as if somehow that code, that Phil. 4:13 or whatever, had made a difference. As if maybe Christ, if there was such a person, really had given him strength. Or in case that lady had prayed for him like she promised, and his staying clean was some kind of answer.

He knew better now. Staying sober had nothing to do with God or prayer or Bible words. It was merely a matter of deciding not to drink.

He wasn't even sure why he'd called the lady in the first place. Probably because he was fairly freaked out about the trial, worried about spending life—or any time, for that matter—behind bars. Maybe it had something to do with that bit about the keys to his prison cell. The trial would be here before long, and prison was looking more and more likely. Freedom was bound to interest him.

Still, when he thought back to that day at Church on the

Way, how he'd poured his heart out to some strange woman, he decided he must have been losing it. Imagine, going to church and talking with some middle-aged religious freak about the Bible. Crazy. He was embarrassed about it now, to think he had actually considered turning religious or seeking some kind of revelation or conversion.

There was an explanation, of course. The drinking had made him crazy enough to visit her. Finch had told him he didn't stand a chance in court if he couldn't lay off the bottle. The woman and her "prison keys" had merely been in the right place at the right time, when he was feeling particularly vulnerable.

Brian straightened the covers on the bed in the spare room of Jackson's apartment and considered his heritage. He came from a long line of religious scoffers. He chuckled out loud. Imagine him—Red Wesley's son—falling into some Jesus cult or something. Brian shuddered at how close he'd come.

Christianity was for losers. Being sober helped him see that.

Brian made breakfast and tossed an empty egg carton in the trash. The can was full of Jackson's empty beer cans. He and Jackson had finally made a rule: no beer in the common areas. All drinking was to be done in private. That way if Brian wanted to stay clean, he didn't have to watch Jackson get oiled every night. Jackson had stuck with the rule. Good old Jackson.

Brian dressed in a clean pair of Levi's and a knit pullover. Today was the day. He paced about the apartment wondering how best to go about it. He stared at the telephone. His money was almost gone, and he considered calling his old man and asking for more. As stepfathers went, Hank Robbins was good that way. Brian stopped pacing and sat down. He hadn't thought about his stepfather—or his mother, for that matter—for years. *I wonder how they're doing...?* Brian knew now, of course, how his stepfather felt about him. He held none of the illusions he'd had as a young boy, back when a new bicycle or an ATV or a Ford Mustang on his sixteenth birthday felt like love. The man had only put up with him because of his mother.

He remembered when he first learned the truth.

He'd been seventeen and out with friends...and he'd come home early. Unlocking the front door he heard Hank talking. The old man never raised his voice. If he had a difference of opinion with someone, he would walk outside, wait a while, and then work things out when he came back inside. He was a cool one, old Hank.

But that night as Brian entered the house Hank was shouting....

"I don't *care* what you want! It's completely unreasonable. I will not have that boy live here a moment longer than necessary!"

"You wish it were tomorrow, don't you?" His mother sounded like she was crying, and Brian strained to hear. "He's my son, Hank. Doesn't that mean anything to you?"

Hank's voice grew softer. "Yes...but he's also the son of a no-good, alcoholic loser. You know I've done everything in my power to provide for that boy. I promised you that when I married you, and I've kept that promise. At least give me that."

His mother sniffed. "I know. Brian's never wanted for anything. I just wish...I wish you loved him."

"Caring for Brian has nothing to do with love." Brian remained frozen as the words ripped at his heart. Hank's voice became softer, kinder. "It doesn't matter, really, does it, honey? I love you....I've always loved you. But when that boy turns eighteen, he's on his own."

His mother was quiet, as though considering Hank's words. Then she sighed loudly. "I guess you're right. I just hate to think of him out there by himself. He's still so young."

"Sooner he learns the ways of the world, the sooner he'll become a man." Hank hesitated. "Don't worry, dear. I'll help him out a little."

The money. Brian felt a pit form in his stomach.

His mother spoke again. "You always do, Hank. Brian is

lucky he has you." There was silence for a moment. "I just thought maybe he could stay a few more years..."

Hank's voice grew loud again. "No! The subject is closed. Now let's not have anymore nonsense about this. The boy is trouble, darling. Pure trouble. He'll be lucky if he graduates from high school. He's a drinker and a partier. He's just like his father."

"Don't say that!"

"It's true! The writing's on the wall."

"Oh, Hank, I don't want him to grow up like Red. I want the best for him." His mother sounded sad again.

"I can afford to help him. And then we can get on with life and all the..."

Brian couldn't listen to any more. He sneaked out the front door and jogged out to his Mustang. Tears blinded his eyes as he drove off, and eventually he wound up at the beach, sitting on the hood of his car, gazing at the cold, stormy-gray surf long after sunset.

"The boy is trouble, pure trouble.... He'll be lucky if he graduates from high school.... The writing's on the wall.... He's just like his father...just like his father...just like his father."

After that Brian stayed away from home as much as possible. Then, right after he graduated, he told Hank he needed his space, wanted freedom. The old man willingly shelled out a thousand dollars so Brian could set up an apartment. Brian was doing mechanic work at a shop a few miles away, and the payments weren't a problem.

But late at night, when his party buddies had gone home and the silence was deafening, Brian wondered what his life was worth. His father had left him; his mother had chosen Hank; and Hank...well, the old man had been nothing but a phony from the get-go.

It was during those long nights, when daylight seemed forever away, that Brian began drinking in earnest. He had always been able to party, but those awful, lonely nights had nothing to do with celebrating. He needed an escape, and Budweiser became his best friend. Constant, reliable, and always able to put him at ease.

By the time Brian thought twice about his nighttime beer consumption, he was an alcoholic, a willing slave to the demons of drink. That year, with so many hungover mornings, Brian's work ethic began to slip until he was on the verge of losing his job. He knew what he needed to do, but nothing worked. He and the Buds were, well, buds. There was no separating them. Not until one night a year later.

The night he met Carla Kimball.

Carla was a pretty girl with the most beautiful hair Brian had ever seen. Thick and wavy, it shimmered down her back and caught the attention of every man in the place.

She was oblivious. She sat alone at the end of the bar gazing into a glass of straight orange juice. She was barely five feet tall, no more than a hundred pounds including her hair. She looked like a little girl playing grownup—one without a care in the world.

The moment Brian saw her he set his beer down and leaned toward his buddy. "Now there's a catch."

Brian wasn't exactly a lady's man, but he held his own. When he saw a girl he wanted to know better, he generally approached her and introduced himself. But as he watched Carla from across the bar that night, he couldn't get up enough courage even to stand.

Finally, just before closing time, the girl stood up and sauntered toward the juke box. She considered the selections and then seemed to changed her mind.

"Looks like she's getting ready to leave," Brian's buddy said.

Brian swallowed and decided he needed to make his move or lose the chance forever. He walked up to her, and, standing nearly a foot taller, he smiled down at her and told her his name. If he lived a hundred years, he would never forget the way she grinned at him that night.

"Took you long enough." Her eyes danced playfully.

"What?"

"I've been watching you. You've been trying to get the guts up to talk to me all night."

Brian glanced at the stool where she'd been sitting. "Is that right? What? You got eyes in the back of your head?"

She had giggled again, her laughter ringing like wind chimes on a pleasant summer morning. "Maybe."

They sat down, and Brian learned her name and why she was drinking straight orange juice.

"My mother was an alcoholic. She died last year before I could get her help."

Brian digested that information. "Same with my dad." It had sounded strange to hear himself call Red *Dad*. "He left when I was a little kid. Died of alcohol poisoning."

"I guess we're kind of like…kindred orphans, then." The smile disappeared and sadness filled Carla's face. "Nothing good comes from alcohol."

Brian checked their surroundings. "Might be a stupid question, but if you hate the drink, what're you doing in a bar?"

Carla's laughter rang out again. "I like people. And people hang out in bars. Besides, I'm the designated driver. My friend's counting on me."

Brian had been ready to order another Budweiser, but in light of Carla's comments he refrained. Besides, the bar was closing and it was time to make his move.

"Your friend…" He hesitated. "Is it, uh…you know…is he…"

"You mean is it a guy?" She laughed. "No. My friend, Shelly." Carla glanced across the bar at a girl and guy kissing in the corner. "But the way things look, she won't be needing me after all."

"Meaning?"

"Meaning I think she found someone else to go home with."

"I see."

"There's just one problem."

"What's that?" Brian drew closer to her, flirting for all he was worth.

"It's her car. If she goes with him, I'm stuck."

From across the bar, Carla's roommate approached them. "Hey, Carla, give me the keys."

Carla looked at her drunken friend suspiciously. "Who's driving?"

"He is. Now come on, give 'em to me."

"What about me?" Despite her question, Carla did not look terribly bothered. Was this a common routine with these two?

Carla's friend glanced at Brian. "You'll find some way home. You always do."

Well, that answered that.

As her friend walked away, Carla shook her head. "She'll be sorry in the morning and I'll forgive her. Happens all the time."

Brian stretched. "It's getting late…"

"We have time." She shrugged, and again Brian thought she looked like a little girl.

"Hey how old are you, anyway?"

"You first."

"Okay." He sat up proudly. "Nineteen. Of course you'd never know it by looking at my driver's license." He winked.

Carla's face fell. "So you're a big-time drinker? Fake ID. Nights at the bar, the works."

"Now wait a minute, I like meeting people, that's all. Just like you." Brian hoped his breath didn't smell too badly of beer. "Besides, you must have a fake ID. Otherwise you wouldn't be here."

Carla huffed. "I'll have you know I'm twenty-one, a very sophisticated and mature woman by your standards."

The bartender had finished cleaning. "Let's go you two, last ones out."

They stood and strolled toward the door, and Brian grinned down at her. "You may be sophisticated and mature, and I may be little more than a school boy, but you, my dear, are without a ride. And this immature guy with the fake ID would like to give you a lift home."

Carla studied him closely, her face inches from his. "All right." She paused. "But let's get one thing straight before we start something here."

Brian waited anxiously. He was already making plans for Carla to spend the night. If not now, then next week or the week after that. It would happen, he was sure.

Carla's eyes grew serious, the laughter gone. "I don't date drinkers, Brian. You drink, I'm outta here."

He raised a solemn hand and struggled to appear as serious as she did. Whatever it took. This was one girl he didn't want to lose. "You have my word on it, Miss Carla Kimball."

Brian couldn't remember how long he kept his promise. He and Carla went home together that night and never looked back. She had shared an apartment with an aunt and had been looking to get out. A week later, Brian helped her move in with him, and they grew deeply attached, more so than anything Brian had ever experienced. For a while he didn't even miss the beer.

"I love you, Brian," Carla would tell him.

He'd respond with a nuzzle or a kiss, anything to avoid saying the words. Brian didn't want to love anyone, not after what his mother and Hank had done to him. Need was something he could relate to. Love...well, that was something altogether different. Carla had told him if he ever became a drinker, she'd leave him. Brian wasn't sure, but he thought there was a chance that at some point he might drink again. Just one or two beers, nothing serious. But if Carla left because of that, there was no point loving her now.

Two years later Brian did start drinking again. One or two beers quickly became a sixer, and then half a case. He'd come home late and lie about where he'd been. It took Carla a month to learn the truth, and when she did, she stared at him sadly.

"I loved you, Brian." The expression in her little-girl eyes tore at Brian's heart. "But I can't stay with you if you keep drinking."

He apologized and made a handful of lofty promises. Twenty-four hours later he was drinking again, and a month after that, Carla packed her things and said good-bye. She moved in with a friend and refused his phone calls.

That's when Brian knew the truth. He loved Carla more than life itself.

He found her at her friend's apartment a week after she moved out, and he confessed his feelings. "I should have told you sooner." There were tears in his eyes as he spoke. "I love you. I've never loved anyone like you, and I'll never love anyone this way again. Please…work with me. Help me get past this thing."

Despite her strong convictions, Carla had loved Brian too much to stay away. She moved back in and agreed to help him. They got married in a simple civil ceremony, and he stayed sober for nearly a year.

The next time Brian began drinking, Carla didn't threaten to leave. There was no point. She was in for the long haul, and the certainty of her commitment gave him no reason to let up. Not long after, he had his first drunk driving arrest, and then another, and three more after that. There were the accidents and alcohol-training courses. When little Brian Jr. came along, Brian renewed his determination to stop drinking. But that, too, had been short-lived.

Carla stayed, but her laughter stopped sounding like wind chimes on a summer morning. Instead it sounded hollow, as though she were only pretending to be happy. Worst of all, she didn't look like a little girl anymore.

She looked like a woman who'd been through a war.

Brian glanced at the clock on the wall and saw that an hour had passed. He didn't like remembering Carla that way. It was nicer to think of her as she'd been the night they first met, when she sat alone drinking orange juice at the end of the bar. Before she cared whether he drank or not.

He sighed and stood up, tugging his stiff jeans into place. He was through drinking now, through for good. And it was time Carla knew about it.

He sorted through a pile of rumpled one-dollar bills and two folded tens. Thirty-two dollars. All the money he had left at this point. He thought about the gift. Thirty-two dollars should be enough for what he had in mind.

He went downstairs and waited at the bus stop. He was getting used to buses now. They were cheap. On the ride to the mall he wondered how Carla was doing, whether she missed him or not. They hadn't talked since the preliminary hearing. Brian had started drinking pretty much nonstop after that—right up until the day he'd met that lady at church.

He shook his head. He didn't want to think about the lady or the booze. Drinking was in the past now. He got off the bus and strode into the side entrance of the mall. Frenzied shoppers crowded the aisles, searching for the perfect Christmas present.

Brian moved quickly in and out of the crowd until he saw the store he was looking for. Spencer's Gifts. They had the best jewelry, and they didn't charge a month's wages for something simple.

Brian had bought Carla's wedding band here.

He walked in and found the jewelry case. There they were: gold-plated hoop earrings. Brian could picture the look on Carla's face when she opened them. He pointed at the pair, nestled in a cardboard box.

"Can you giftwrap 'em, man?"

The clerk—a teenage boy with blue hair and a tiny hoop that pierced his lower lip—stared at him blankly. "You mean, like, with Christmas paper?"

"Yeah. Giftwrap."

The kid laughed. "Dude, that's for, like, the big-time jewelry stores. But hey, I'll give you the box."

"Right. Okay. How much is it?"

The blue-haired boy rang up the sale. "Eighteen twenty-five."

Brian gulped. He counted out the ten-dollar bill and eight ones. Then he fished in his pocket for a quarter and took the package. He darted across the corridor, found a giftbag for two dollars, then took a piece of scrap paper from the cashier and began writing.

"Carla, I know I've said it before. But this time I'm serious. I'm done drinking for good. I bought you two hoops because I'm twice as sorry, twice as serious. My promise, like these earrings, will go on and on. True as gold. I need you, babe. Help me through this trial. Stay by me. Merry Christmas. I love you. Brian."

He left the mall, boarded the bus, and half an hour later he stood outside the apartment where Carla and Brian Jr. lived without him. He was almost as nervous as he'd been that first night in the bar, but finally, clutching the small gift in his left hand, he made his way to the front door and knocked.

Seconds passed, and Brian wondered where she could be. It was the middle of the day, and Brian Jr. should have been napping. Carla was always home for Brian Jr.'s nap.

He knocked again and waited. Finally he heard the click of the lock and the door opened a few inches. Carla stepped out, closing the door behind her.

"Brian..." She looked nervous and he felt a wave of fear. Carla never looked nervous. Angry, sad, frustrated. But not nervous.

"Carla, honey, I have good news..." He stood straighter and smiled tentatively. "I stopped drinking. For good this time."

With one hand still on the door handle, she sighed. "Really, Brian...you came all the way here to tell me that?"

He felt another wave of fear. "I need you, baby. I brought you something for—"

"No, Brian. I don't want anything from you. We're finished." She glanced back at the door, clearly anxious.

Brian sucked in a deep breath. "Carla, I know I've let you down before. The kid, too. But—"

"Brian, stop! This is crazy. You're…you're on trial for murder. *First-degree* murder. You're going to spend the rest of your life in prison. We're finished, Brian. Now go home."

He tried to move past her but she held her ground. "Come on, Carla, let me in. I have a present I want to give you. Then you can see for yourself that I'm serious this time."

"Brian," Carla hissed. "Go home! I don't want your—"

At that instant, the door behind her opened and a man appeared. He was wearing boxer shorts and a T-shirt. His hair was wet…he looked as though he'd just taken a shower.

"What the—" Brian took a step toward the man, but Carla put her hand on his chest and stopped him.

"Brian…don't. I'm…I'm seeing someone else now."

The stranger put his arm protectively around Carla and glared at Brian. "I believe the lady asked you to leave."

He stared at Carla, and then at the strange man beside her. He felt lightheaded, sick to his stomach. For one horrible moment he thought he would faint there on the doorstep—or possibly die of a heart attack.

Once more he looked at Carla, and he could see the pain in her eyes. She spoke in a voice that was little more than a whisper. "I'm sorry…"

Without saying another word, Brian turned and walked away. At the end of the row of apartments, he passed a smelly dumpster. He stopped and stared at the package in his hand, then tossed it angrily over the side of the bin and kept walking.

He wandered out onto Ventura Boulevard and headed east, away from the intersection where everything in life had changed four months earlier. A block away he saw a liquor store. Before he knew it, he was inside. He found their least expensive bottle of whiskey and handed over what was left of his money.

He gave a sick chuckle. "You gift wrap?"

The old man behind the counter twisted his face. "What's that, boy?"

"Aww, never mind. Private joke." Brian took the bag and twisted it tightly around the neck of the bottle. Then he boarded the bus and went back to Jackson's apartment. Drinking had to be done in private, those were the rules. Brian took his bottle to his room, tore off the cap, and began swallowing fast.

"It's finished, Brian.... It's finished. I'm dating someone else now."

He hadn't even gotten to see Brian Jr. He'd been gone only a few months and already he'd been replaced. Brian was too shocked to be angry. Anger would come later.

He raised the bottle, and the liquid burned his throat as he took three long gulps. The walls were flexing, in and out, back and forth. He looked around and the entire room was in motion. He sank slowly to the floor. Suddenly they were all staring at him, crowding the room so that it was hard to breathe.

There was Red Wesley, laid out flat on a sofa while his mother sobbed at the kitchen table. Hank announced in a loud voice, *"He's just like his father...can't you see it? He's just like his father."* Carla was there, too, and the stranger with his arm around her shoulder. *"It's over, Brian. I'm dating someone new...someone new...someone new."*

He took another long swig from the bottle and closed his eyes. He didn't care anymore. He only wanted to be alone. Forget about Carla and promises and gold hoop earrings.

The bottle was more than half gone, and Brian felt himself losing consciousness. The room was spinning faster, and he closed his eyes. Suddenly a loud noise pulled him from his stupor. This time when he opened his eyes, he saw something that sent a surge of bile into his throat.

Right in front of him was the blond girl and her father, their car wrapped around the utility pole. Only now the girl was crying, and Carla was standing over her, trying to help her breathe. Suddenly they all turned on him, glaring at him, hating him.

"Go away!" Carla shouted and she ripped the gold hoops from her ears. *"You're a murderer and a liar and a loser! I hope you rot in prison."*

As quickly as they'd come, they faded away, and he could see more clearly. There was still something left in the bottle. He raised it to his mouth, missing wildly at first and then finally finding the mark. Nausea welled up, but still he drank, swigging down what was left until the bottle was empty. There was a strange noise, like air leaking from a rubber tire. He tossed the bottle aside and looked up.

Demons filled the room before him.

Dripping blood and spewing venomous taunts and accusations, they crowded in around his face. He swung at them, shouted at them to stay away, but they drew nearer still, hissing and smelling of death and sulfur. They were carrying something, and Brian saw that it was a rusted, black chain. Before he could get up or run away or close his eyes, the demons bound his wrists and wrapped his arms tightly against his body.

He was utterly trapped, and the demons began hissing one word, over and over. Brian's heart beat wildly and he struggled to break free. *What was the word? What were they saying?* The noise grew louder, each word a hate-filled hiss.

Finally Brian understood.

Forever. Forever, forever, forever.

He was trapped. The demons had him and they would hold him forever.

He wanted to break free, to scream for help and chase the demons away before they killed him. But instead he felt his insides heave. Once, twice, and then a third time, until it seemed his stomach was in a state of permanent convulsion.

And then all he wanted was to die.

Brian woke up, face down in a puddle of pasty vomit, his entire body shaking violently from fear and alcohol poisoning.

The room smelled like rotten, undigested food and urine. He noticed his pants were wet, and he realized he must have soiled them. His head throbbed, and he recoiled as he touched his hand to his hair. It was matted with crusted vomit. Suddenly he remembered the hissing creatures. Using only his eyes, he glanced from side to side.

The demons were gone.

But this brought no relief. They would be back. He knew with every fiber in his being that it was so. He struggled to his feet, wiped the vomit from his eyes and nose so he could breathe better, and staggered toward the phone.

It was time to call the Bible lady.

Twenty-three

The hearts of the people cry out to the Lord.
O wall of the Daughter of Zion, let your tears flow like a river
day and night; give yourself no relief, your eyes no rest.

LAMENTATIONS 2:18

In the end, they skipped the tree and presents and agreed to go out to dinner on Christmas Eve. Hannah thought that even that was a stretch since neither she nor Jenny wanted to be reminded that the rest of the world was celebrating Christmas. The "Silent Night"s and "O Come, All Ye Faithful"s were not a reminder to fall and worship at baby Jesus' manger—they were a reminder of his broken promises.

Jenny might still believe, but Hannah knew better.

December 25 would be merely another day to prepare for the trial, another chance to work on victim impact panel information and clip newspaper articles dealing with drunk driving.

The restaurant was packed, and their Christmas Eve dinner was filled with long periods of silence and uncomfortable conversation. Hannah set her napkin down and leaned her forearms on the table.

"Jenny, what do I have to do?"

Jenny stared at her, her eyes listless and empty. "What?"

"To make things right again. Between us."

Jenny doodled a circular design in the Alfredo sauce on her dinner plate and said nothing.

Hannah hung her head for a moment. What would it take to reach the girl? She looked up again. "See? You don't talk to me...you won't even look at me."

"There's nothing to say, Mother."

Jenny sounded so tired that it pierced Hannah's heart. But she pushed the feeling away. If Jenny was tired, it was her own fault. Hannah had tried everything she knew to help her daughter! "That's great, Jenny. We've lost everything that matters to us; our lives have changed forever, and you tell me there's nothing to say? Well, here are some suggestions. Tell me how you're doing, how you're feeling...ask me how we're going to make it. How about that, huh?" Hannah knew she didn't sound sympathetic, but she didn't care. She'd had it with Jenny's self-pity. "Maybe then we'd find something to talk about."

Jenny leveled her gaze at Hannah. "I think it's a little late to be asking."

Late for what? Jenny wasn't making sense. "Meaning...?"

Jenny stared at her plate and resumed doodling. "Meaning maybe you should have asked me those questions when... when...oh, never mind."

A cord of concern rang on the keyboard of Hannah's mind. Jenny was no longer angry, and that was a relief. But now she wasn't speaking or making eye contact, either. She wasn't anything—except completely detached.

Hannah closed her eyes briefly. *All I want is my family back...the way it used to be! Is that so terrible?* When she spoke once more, it was with the weight of more burdens than she thought she could carry. "I love you, Jenny. I'm sorry if I've been busy."

Jenny shrugged. "It's okay."

The conversation stalled again as the waitress cleared their plates. The silence as Hannah paid the check and they walked to the car was oppressive.

Back at home, Jenny immediately excused herself and disappeared to her room. Hannah watched her go and felt like an utter failure. Jenny was free-falling away from her, and Hannah was helpless to do anything about it. *Don't look too deeply at this. It'll all be okay after the trial.* She wandered through the quiet house and sighed, studying the framed photographs.

They had smiled so easily back then. She couldn't remember Jenny smiling even once since they'd lost Tom and Alicia. Maybe this was how it was going to be from now on. No holidays. No smiles. No communication.

Tomorrow there would be a garden of golden memories to be walked through, but Hannah didn't want to go there now, not yet. She didn't want to stroll through yesterday and savor the fragrance of all they had once been. She would rather work on her drunk driving speeches. She didn't want to think about any of it, and she certainly didn't want to think about Jenny, alone in her room, besieged with her own thoughts of Christmases past, probably crying herself to sleep.

The truth was suddenly unbearable.

Hannah turned off the downstairs lights and padded slowly up to bed. The world was a heavy place, especially when it rested squarely on your own shoulders.

That night, somewhere between lying awake and falling asleep, Hannah moved her leg and in the process slid her foot under a section of the covers that was weighted down with a heavy book she'd tossed there earlier. Still, for an instant the weight wasn't a book at all. It was Tom, his leg, comfortably stretched across the sheets just inches from her own. Hannah stirred, and the weight remained. She enjoyed the feeling of Tom's leg on hers, heavy and warm. Suddenly a realization pulled at her. If his leg was here, that meant—

"Tom?" She sat straight up in bed and breathlessly peered through the darkness. Then slowly, as she had at least ten times before, she realized who she was and where she was and what her life had become.

She was a woman alone who had lost everything.

And tomorrow was Christmas.

Since his father died four years earlier, Matt Bronzan usually spent holidays with his mother. She lived two hours north and he enjoyed the drive. But that year his sister had flown their mother to Phoenix so she could be with her grandchildren for Christmas.

Matt didn't mind being alone. He lived in a four-bedroom ranch home in an elite subdivision in Woodland Hills and had come to appreciate the house's solitude when he needed a break from court. In the week leading up to Christmas, his housekeeper had set up a twenty-four-inch decorated tree on an end table and purchased a four-pack of cinnamon buns at the mall.

When Christmas morning dawned, Matt heated the buns and brewed a pot of Starbucks Holiday-blend coffee. He sat down at his glass-topped dining room table, savoring the rich aroma as he ate. When he was finished he did something he did every morning. He opened his burgundy leather Bible and began reading.

He was in Romans 12 that morning and he savored the words, searching for every morsel of truth therein: *"Love must be sincere. Hate what is evil; cling to what is good. Be devoted to one another in brotherly love.... Practice hospitality...."* The words jumped off the page and landed squarely on Matt's conscience.

"Be devoted to one another...brotherly love...practice hospitality."

Images of Hannah Ryan came to mind, and suddenly he saw her not as a woman to be pitied for losing her husband and daughter but a woman to be pitied for turning her back on the Lord. He'd done everything he could to help her with the trial, but what had he done to help her in her faith struggle? According to Carol Cummins, Hannah had refused all contact with her church friends, and she had few, if any, relatives in the area. He pictured Hannah and her daughter sitting at home alone....He remembered how difficult Christmas had been for him after Victoria's and Shawn's deaths. He bowed his head then, overcome with gratitude that God had drawn him out of his own doubt and depression so many years ago. *Give me wisdom, Father. Use me...*

Drawing a deep breath, he reached for the telephone.

Hannah answered on the third ring. "Hello?"

"Hannah…it's Matt Bronzan."

She hesitated, and Matt wondered if he was making a mistake. "Hi, Matt. Don't tell me you're working on Christmas day?"

Matt chuckled. "No. I'm hard on myself, but even workaholics take off December 25."

"Yeah, I guess."

He thought a moment. "You don't sound too good."

She waited too long to answer. She'd been crying. He'd be willing to bet on it. He drew a steadying breath and jumped in with both feet. "Listen, why don't I swing by and get you and Jenny? The three of us can drive out to Santa Monica and walk along the pier."

"You mean…right now?"

"Right now. It's a beautiful day. We can talk about whatever you want. And we'll buy Jenny some cotton candy or something."

Hannah hesitated again. "Why, Matt?"

"Because…I've been there, remember? And I wish someone had kidnapped me for the first three or four holidays after my friends died. Believe me, anything will be better than staying alone in an empty house filled with memories."

He wanted to tell her that God had used Scripture to impress the idea on him, but he knew better. Hannah Ryan didn't need a list of Bible verses. She needed brotherly love and hospitality….

"Okay." Hannah didn't sound sure. "I guess. Be here in an hour."

She gave him directions and the conversation ended. Matt slipped a sweatshirt over his head and felt a sudden prompting to pray for Jenny. The whole time he was getting ready, constant prayers were in his mind, prayers for the sweet girl who had refused to attend any hearings, the girl who Hannah said had become more withdrawn with each passing week. Something was about to happen to Jenny, Matt could feel it, and he prayed for her as if his life depended on it.

Hannah was sitting in a living room chair studying a tree in the front yard when Jenny walked by.

"Honey, we're going to the beach with Mr. Bronzan." Hannah realized she didn't sound very enthusiastic.

Jenny stopped in her tracks and stared at her mother. "Mr. Bronzan?"

Hannah met her gaze. "Yes. The prosecutor, remember?"

"I know who he is. Why are we going to the beach with him? Today? On Christmas?"

Hannah shrugged. "He asked."

"Oh, I get it. That way we can spend the day plotting how to ruin Brian Wesley's life. Is that it?"

For the first time in days Jenny sounded angry, and Hannah almost enjoyed it. Anything was better than the indifference that had come over her lately.

"He said we can walk along the pier and talk."

"About what?" Jenny put a hand on her hip.

"I don't know. Maybe about how lousy it is that drunk drivers get to celebrate Christmas and the ones they kill never will again."

Jenny rolled her eyes. "Like he would know."

Hannah turned to face Jenny. "I will not have you talking that way about Mr. Bronzan. He's the one who can take away the pain we're in. He's on our side. And yes—" she swallowed—"he would know. He had a close friend killed by a drunk driver many years ago. It's not something you forget."

Jenny considered that for a moment, and hope sparked in Hannah's heart. Then her daughter shrugged. "I'm not going."

Hannah wanted to cry, but she felt as though there were no tears left. She sighed and reached her arms out to Jenny. "Come here, Jenny. Please."

Jenny took one step backward. "No. I don't want a hug, Mom. Just leave me alone. I'll be fine."

Hannah struggled to her feet as if every movement was an effort. She closed the gap that separated her from Jenny and reached for her shoulders. "Come with me, Jenny. It'll do us both good."

Jenny pulled away. "No! I won't. I'll be fine..." She turned and headed for the stairs.

"Jenny, please...you're making this so much worse."

Jenny stopped on the fourth stair and spun back around. "Mom, there's nothing *I* could do that would make this worse than it already is."

"You are not an adult, and if I tell you to come, you'll come." Hannah followed her daughter toward the stairs.

"I'm not going, Mother. I don't want to be with Mr. Bronzan. I want to be with Daddy and Alicia. If I can't do that, I want to stay home. I wish I never had to leave this house again!" She turned and ran the rest of the way up the stairs.

Hannah realized she would have to call Matt. She had no right spending Christmas Day with him while her daughter lay alone on her bed. She reached for the telephone and stopped. Maybe Jenny needed to be alone. Maybe that would give her time to sort out her feelings. Besides, she and Matt needed to talk about the trial.

She leaned into the stairwell and spoke loud enough for Jenny to hear. "Since you're not willing to go, you can stay home. Don't leave the house, though, is that understood?"

Silence.

"Jenny?"

"Yes, I understand." The cool indifference was back.

"Jenny, try and use this time to think about your attitude. You've changed so much since the accident."

"Yes, Mother."

"We both lost when that man killed Daddy and Alicia. Maybe you could think about that and stop taking it out on me."

"Yes, Mother."

Hannah sighed. She was rambling, and Jenny wasn't listening to a word. She heard a car pull up, and Hannah glanced out the living room window to see Matt climb out and make his way up the front walk. "Jenny, Mr. Bronzan is here. I'll be home in a couple hours."

"Enjoy your *date,* Mother."

The word was like a sharp slap, and Hannah froze. How could Jenny say such a horrible thing? Hannah felt tears sting at her eyes. *She pushes and pushes...* She shook her head. *Maybe we'll never get beyond this...*

"Enjoy your date." Jenny's words echoed in Hannah's mind, accusing her, pulling her down. Oh, why had she ever agreed to go with Matt in the first place?

He was a business acquaintance, a friend. Nothing more. There couldn't be more because she was still in love with Tom.

She would always be in love with Tom.

As her mother slammed the door shut, Jenny skittered across her bedroom floor and gazed out the window. How *dare* that man take her mother to the beach on Christmas Day. Her dad had only been dead four months. Jenny watched the way he opened the door for her mother and slid into the seat beside her. The high and mighty Matt Bronzan could tell her mother whatever he wanted. Jenny could see the writing on the wall.

She slumped back across the room and locked her bedroom door. Maybe Mr. Bronzan was a blessing in disguise. Maybe he would move into her mother's life and make it whole again. But where did that leave her? Jenny thought about the answer and realized it was a simple one. If her mother was preoccupied with Mr. Bronzan, then maybe the time had come.

She reached under her bed, pulled out a small plastic bag of pills, and dumped them on her bedspread. Her mother would be home in two hours, maybe three. She stared at the heap of pills and ran a finger through them. If she took them now, she would be unconscious in fifteen minutes, but death would take a while longer. Maybe an hour, maybe more.

Jenny knew how long it took her to die depended on the number of pills and how quickly her metabolism worked. Factors she couldn't control. If she did it now, she might even be dead before her mother came home. But if not, she needed to have the door locked so she could buy a little more time. That way, though her mother might find a way to break into the room, she wouldn't have enough time to save Jenny's life.

The pills were multicolored, coated with a gelatin for easy swallowing and digestion. Sleeping pills and some outdated pain medication she'd found in her father's medical bag. The Internet had taught her that there was little mess with pills. That meant her mother wouldn't have a lot of trauma.

Jenny hesitated. She was so close, so desperate to be with Alicia and Daddy. Suddenly she heard the voice. It spoke to her often these days and it always said the same thing: *Take the pills. Take the pills. Do it, Jenny. Take the pills.*

If she did it now they could be together in one hour. She drew a deep breath. *God, give me the strength.*

The pills looked ominous, dozens of them heaped up in the center of her bedspread. Jenny picked up a small handful and rolled them around in her palm. *Don't be mad at me, Lord.... You know I love you.*

Suddenly there was a soft thudding sound. Then another and another. Three thuds, coming from Alicia's room. Jenny dropped the pills and stared at the wall. Three thuds. The signal she and Alicia had used all their lives.

I love you.

Jenny's hands began to tremble and then her arms, until finally her scalp was tingling. There was no one in the next room. The sounds echoed in her mind, and she wondered if she had heard them or only imagined them.

Jenny willed herself back to last Christmas when she and

Alicia were in their rooms, racing to clean them before dinner. But it wasn't Christmas past. It was Christmas present.

"Alicia…" Tears spilled from her eyes and she squeezed them shut. "I love you too."

Jenny wasn't sure how long she sat that way. Eventually she fell asleep, huddled against a mound of pillows, her hand resting on the wall that separated her room and Alicia's.

The beach was empty that afternoon, and Hannah figured it was because most people had better things to do. She and Matt walked along the pier slowly, gazing out to sea. The day was cool and overcast, not quite seventy degrees, and a breeze blew off the Pacific Ocean. Hannah was glad for her bulky sweatshirt.

Matt was so easy to be around. During the drive he'd talked about a few other cases he was working on, and the time had passed quickly. Now, as they studied the succession of waves hitting the shore, a comfortable silence fell between them.

"Your case is coming along." They stopped walking and Matt leaned against the white wood railing. "I wasn't sure if you wanted to talk about it."

Hannah nodded. "Is it looking strong?" She folded her arms and studied him, making sure that several feet separated them.

He gazed back out to sea. "I keep looking for a loophole, a weakness, some way the defense will be able to convince the jury this wasn't murder one."

"And?"

"I don't see one." He turned toward her, and his eyes held a wealth of sincerity. "It's a strong case, Hannah. I really think we can do it."

She gazed through the slats of wood that made up the pier, looking down to the water below. When she was a little girl she'd always been afraid of the slats, afraid she'd fall into the ocean and drown. The slats didn't bother her now. She was in way too far over her head to worry about drowning. She lifted her eyes to Matt's. "I've got four victim impact panels lined up for January and February."

"They're making a difference. I've seen you on TV a couple times now."

Hannah glanced up, eyes wide. She'd been on TV? "You have?"

"Yes. You look determined—and beautiful, in a tragic way. And very angry."

He thinks I'm beautiful. Hannah's gaze fell, and she chided herself for enjoying the thought.

"People watch that kind of thing, they read it in the paper, and pretty soon they start to see drunk driving a little differently. After hearing your story, some of them will be fed up. Once the public takes on that sentiment, murder one is only a matter of time."

An ocean breeze blew Hannah's hair back, and a chill ran down her neck. She gritted her teeth. "Good." She pictured Brian Wesley locked in a solitary, rat-infested cell. "I wish they still did hangings in the public square."

Matt raised his eyebrows and his voice grew soft. "Is that what this is all about?"

"What?" Hannah snapped. "I hate Brian Wesley. Surely you of all people understand that."

"I understand." Matt's gaze fell for a moment and then found her eyes again. "But I don't like what I hear in your voice."

"Oh, please." Hannah didn't have patience for this. "Brian Wesley is the reason we're doing this. You know that."

Matt thought for a moment. "I want to see Brian locked up, but only because that's the punishment he deserves. He's not the reason we're pushing for murder one."

"He's *my* reason."

Matt shook his head. "He's just one drunk driver, Hannah. We want to change the way people look at drunk driving on the whole. Then maybe we can prevent the kind of thing that happened to your family."

Hannah paused. Matt was right, of course. That should be the reason. Still, that wasn't what motivated her to get up before a crowd and bare her heart about the collision.

Picturing Brian Wesley in prison was what motivated her. Nothing more, nothing less.

"Hannah—" Matt interrupted her thoughts. He rubbed his hands together to keep them warm. "Is everything okay with Jenny?"

She shrugged and began walking again. She could feel the hard, angry lines creasing the skin around her eyes, and she pressed her lips together. *I bet I don't look beautiful now.* She shook the thought away. There was no point worrying about how she looked. Smiles came from the heart. Her face was a direct reflection of her feelings.

She thought about Jenny. "At first…after the accident, Jenny was mad at me. Not Brian Wesley. She doesn't hate him like I do. She never has. She hated me, and we fought all the time." Hannah's heart ached as she remembered how quickly her relationship with Jenny deteriorated after Tom and Alicia's deaths. Hannah searched for the words. "But now, I don't know…it's like she's given up. She's thirteen years old and she acts like she's finished living."

Matt's expression changed. "You don't think—"

Hannah caught the look in his eyes and shook her head. "No, nothing like that." Hannah didn't mention the school principal and her concerns that Jenny might be thinking about suicide. "Jenny's a very stable girl. But she and Alicia were so close and now…it doesn't seem like she knows how to go on."

Matt nodded as he walked alongside her. They were approaching the end of the pier. "I had this strange feeling earlier that I was supposed to pray for her."

"Really?" Hannah felt a twinge of anger. She didn't want to talk about prayer this Christmas day. That life was behind her.

But Matt nodded and went on. "I prayed while I was getting ready and the whole time I felt that something bad was about to happen to her."

Hannah rolled her eyes. "Great. Figures that'd be the kind of thought you'd get about Jenny. When God is against you, he doesn't pull any punches does he?"

Matt was quiet and they walked the last few yards to the end of the pier. A seal splashed near the pilings below, and they watched him for a few moments. "God isn't against you, Hannah." Matt's voice was quiet, and she had the distinct impression he was trying not to start an argument.

She braced herself against the white railing and stared up at the cold, gray sky. "It doesn't matter. I don't believe there is a God anymore. Not after what happened."

"It's a fallen world. People get hurt. Injustice happens." Matt rested his back against the railing and faced Hannah. "That's because of mankind, not God."

She wanted to scream at him, to push him away. How dare he tell her it wasn't God's fault? "He could stop it. If he's really a great and mighty God, then he could have caused Tom to be ten seconds slower that afternoon. Or made Brian drive ten seconds faster. Something. But he didn't keep it from happening and that's—that's why I stopped believing."

"Sometimes he has a different plan."

Hannah sighed and moved forward, leaning her body on the railing and gazing down at the churning sea below. "I never *wanted* a different plan. Only Tom and Alicia…all of us—" Her voice caught, and she sank down on a nearby bench. Tears spilled from her eyes and she wiped them dry.

Matt knelt on one knee next to her and ran a hand soothingly over her shoulder. "It's okay. You can cry. The Lord understands…"

She tried to shut out the words. She had heard enough about the Lord. "Please, Matt…"

"I know, I know. You're not ready."

Matt's voice was like an anchor in what seemed to be the greatest storm she'd ever faced. Still she disagreed with what he was saying. "I'll never be ready. God abandoned me, and that's not the kind of God I used to believe in."

"Hannah, the Lord never—"

"No!"

"Give me a chance. The Lord does understand. John 11:35 says—"

"I don't want to hear it!" She buried her face in her hands, shutting out both the sound and sight of Matt Bronzan. "Please, Matt."

There was silence, and when Hannah opened her eyes, Matt was standing again, leaning against the railing, studying her. "Okay. No talk about God. But don't let yourself drift too far away. You might not be able to find your way back."

As though I'd want to…

She wiped the tears off her cheeks. She'd been gone long enough. She wanted to get home, back to Jenny and the miserable existence that was their life these days.

Matt seemed to sense her thoughts. He stuck his hands deep into his pockets and straightened. Hannah pictured Tom and remembered how he had moved so similarly, with the same athletic grace.

He reached out his hand. "Come on, let's get you back home and see how Jenny's doing."

The sound of the front door opening brought Jenny instantly awake. She glanced around the room and felt her arms. She was alive, but she couldn't remember why. Then she saw the pills scattered on her bedspread and her heart sank.

She had fallen asleep.

Now her mother was home and it was too late.

She gathered the capsules and quickly dropped them in the plastic bag. She could hear her mother's footsteps making their way closer to her room. Leaning over her bed she tossed the bag of pills far underneath. She didn't know what had made her fall asleep, but she wasn't going to worry about it. There would be other opportunities.

And when they presented themselves, she would be ready.

Twenty-four

He has besieged me and surrounded me with bitterness and hardship. He has made me dwell in darkness like those long dead.

LAMENTATIONS 3:5–6

January blended into February and then into March while Hannah kept herself too busy to worry about Jenny or the impending trial or anything but the victim-impact panels. The media ate it up, reveling in the story for all its human interest elements and ground-breaking possibilities. Before the end of March, Hannah appeared on two local television talk shows and *Good Morning America.* They showed pictures of Tom and Alicia and talked in reverent tones about Hannah's strength, her determination to see that justice prevailed.

"A day is coming," Hannah would tell them, "when I will finally be at peace. That will be the day Brian Wesley is convicted of first-degree murder."

Sometimes Hannah wondered about Brian, where he was, what he was doing. Once she asked Carol about it over lunch, but the woman didn't seem the least bit worried.

She shook her head. "It isn't healthy for you to worry about this." Carol hesitated. "Remember back a few months ago…I asked you to read Lamentations? Have you done it?"

Hannah sighed and set down her club sandwich. "No. And I don't plan to. If I remember, Lamentations is in the Bible, and I'm not interested in reading the Bible anymore."

"Hannah—"

"Please, Carol. Between you and Matt, I'm beginning to

think there's a conspiracy. 'Poor Hannah, throwing away her faith when she needs it most.' I don't want to be your project, Carol. If there is a God, then he might as well take the stand right next to Brian Wesley. Because when it comes right down to it, God allowed this. He could have stopped it. So why in the world would I want to read Lamentations, or anything else God has to say?"

Carol seemed flustered. She sipped her apple juice, as though giving herself time to gather her thoughts. "I…well, I've been praying about it. I feel there's a message for you there, Hannah. Every time I ask the Lord…when I don't know what to say to help you…Lamentations comes to mind."

Hannah picked up her sandwich and brought it to her mouth. "Let it stay there, Carol. I'm through with Scripture." She took an angry bite, chomped it, and swallowed. "Now what I really want to know is what's happening with Brian Wesley?"

Carol glanced down at her plate and poked at the remainder of her sandwich. "I don't know."

Hannah continued. "I keep thinking of that day in court when he had a Bible under his arm. If it was a Bible. I mean, it's possible he's going around thinking he's some kind of Christian or something."

Carol looked up and spoke in a quiet voice. "Would that bother you?"

Hannah's face grew hot and her heartbeat quickened. "Yes, it would bother me!"

"I think you spend too much time worrying about Brian Wesley. It isn't healthy. Really. You have enough going on. Leave Brian to our friend Matt."

They changed the subject, but in the weeks that followed, when Hannah was preparing a speech or talking before TV cameras or clipping newspaper articles, she couldn't stop wondering about Brian. The thought of him carrying a Bible repulsed her, and she wasn't sure why. Especially in light of her conviction that God wasn't real anyway.

But if he was, it would be just like God to save the man who killed her family. Forget about Tom and Alicia. But Brian Wesley? *He* would be a man worthy of God's time and attention. That great, merciful God.

Hannah's sarcasm ran deep, and she fed it regularly with bitter thoughts. Just let God try and save Brian Wesley. She hadn't been pouring herself into the victim impact panels for nothing. God couldn't save Brian Wesley from prison. Wesley—and God—were about to go down in flames.

The trial was only weeks away.

But troubling thoughts of Brian Wesley weren't all that distracted Hannah from her mission. Jenny continued to withdraw. The principal contacted Hannah two more times—once in January and again in February—worried that Jenny was slipping through their fingers. Both times Hannah had a conference with the woman.

"I think she needs to see a counselor, someone with experience in grief." The principal eyed Hannah, who politely thanked the woman and left without discussing the matter further. The second time, the principal's warnings got to her.

When she left the school office that afternoon, she went straight to the local bookstore. Moving quickly through the aisles she located the self-help section, picked out a book on teenage depression, and thumbed to the section labeled, "Recognizing the Symptoms."

Hannah read them carefully. "*Change in behavior…change in conversational patterns…change in eating habits…sense of withdrawal…change in appearance…talk of suicide.*" Any of these, the book said, could signal deep depression or even suicidal tendencies.

A chill ran through Hannah, and then she chided herself. *You're overreacting. This is ridiculous. People from families like ours don't suffer from depression. They get upset; they get over it. They become fighters; they change public opinion about drunk driving;*

they fight for a murder-one conviction.

What they didn't do was kill themselves.

She shut the book and returned it to the shelf. When she walked out of the bookstore that day, she promised herself never to consider such an absurd thing again.

Jenny was going through a hard time, that was all. But she would be fine. She was only putting on an act because she was angry at Hannah for being so involved in MADD. When the trial was over, Hannah would lessen her involvement, take some time so she and Jenny could rebuild what they'd lost.

Yes, when the trial was over, life would fall back into place.

April arrived and with it a motion from the defense. Matt called and explained it to her over the telephone. Brian Wesley was still suffering back pain, still needed medical attention and wouldn't be able to assist in his defense until July 14 at the earliest. The motion would go before the judge in a few days.

Hannah had expected the delay, but still she cried for two hours when she heard the news. The idea of Brian running free for another three months nearly suffocated her. Carol attended the hearing with her, and they sat together, watching as Matt went to work, handling himself with his usual poise and professionalism. The judge listened to both sides and called a recess. They had their answer before the lunch break.

"I've decided to grant the delay." Judge Horowitz's voice did nothing to hide his ill feelings toward the defense. "But I'm through playing games with you, Mr. Finch." He scrutinized Finch from his high place in the courtroom. "It is not my idea of 'fair and speedy' when reasons are concocted to delay the inevitable. Your client will face trial, and he will do so July 14. Not a day after." The judge waved his hand in dismissal. "Be gone from my courtroom."

Hannah left court that day convinced that the delay would help the prosecution, that it would buy time for her to continue with the victim impact panels and give Brian Wesley one less reason to appeal the case.

Still, when she arrived home she felt drained and defeated. She sank into the old leather recliner. She would be speaking later that week to a hundred local attorneys, and yet the very idea of it left her cold. It was hard to get excited about changing laws when the process moved so interminably slowly.

She was pondering this when Jenny walked past carrying a glass of milk, heading back upstairs. The girl was still missing a lot of school, and even when she did go, she came home and spent her afternoons upstairs. Hannah was tired of it.

"Hello, Jenny."

She continued toward the stairs.

"Aren't you going to say hi?" Hannah heard the lack of enthusiasm in her own voice. There was no warmth, no love…nothing but emptiness.

Jenny paused and turned, and Hannah fully expected her daughter to ignore her question.

Instead, she gave one simple response. "Hi." The word was monotone, spoken in obligation.

Hannah sighed. "You missed a hearing today."

Jenny stared at her.

Hannah was sick of her daughter's silence. "'Oh, really, Mom, what hearing did I miss?'" Hannah mimicked the response she had hoped to hear from Jenny, and this time she did not give the girl time to respond. "I'll tell you. They delayed the trial. Not April anymore, but July. July 14."

Jenny shrugged. "So?"

"*So?* Jenny, what's *wrong* with you?" Hannah surged to her feet, her voice loud and shrill.

"Nothing." She turned toward the stairs.

"Wait!" Hannah stomped her foot. "Why don't you care about this? Don't you see? The man who killed your father and Alicia is having his way with us!"

Jenny took two angry steps toward Hannah. "I could ask

you the same thing, Mother." The girl was shouting now, and Hannah realized again that she preferred an angry Jenny over an indifferent one.

Her daughter's eyes suddenly filled with tears. "Why don't you care about *me?* Daddy and Alicia are gone, but I'm here, right here in front of you. And all you care about is that man who killed them."

"That's not true and you know it!" Tears slid down Hannah's face as her voice rang through the house. "I do care! It's *you* who doesn't care, Jennifer Ryan. We're both victims here. I want you beside me at these hearings."

"Well, I want a mother who spends her time with me instead of trying to convince a bunch of strangers all over the city why Brian Wesley is such a bad guy."

"You don't understand, do you?" Hannah tried to lower her voice. "The victim impact panels are making a difference. They're changing the way people view drunk driving. And one day they'll be responsible for saving lives."

Jenny screamed at her then. "What about *my* life, Mother? What about saving me?" The words were no sooner out than Jenny stopped, a horrified look on her face. She covered her mouth with a trembling hand, drew back several steps, then turned and ran toward the stairs.

"That's another thing!" Hannah followed her retreating daughter. "I'm tired of all your threats and little ploys for attention. *Everyone's* tired of it. I love you, and I want things to be right between us. The sooner you realize that, the better."

Jenny stopped and turned back toward Hannah once more, her mouth open. "Ploy? Is that what you think?" Hannah caught her breath at the hatred in her daughter's eyes. "You'll see, Mother." Jenny turned and ran up the stairs, shouting once more as she disappeared up the stairwell. "You'll see!"

Hannah shouted louder than before. "Stop threatening me, Jenny! I do love you, but you'll never know it acting like that."

"Shut up, Mother!" Hannah heard a door slam shut.

"Shut up, Mother…" The words hit Hannah like a slap in the face, and she reeled backwards, sinking once more into the recliner. A picture filled her mind of their family walking into church one sunny, Sunday morning. She and Tom had held hands while Alicia and Jenny, maybe twelve and nine years old, skipped along in front of them.

She closed her eyes and savored the memory. As she did, she could almost hear their voices.

"Love you, Daddy. Love you, Mommy." The girls waved as they reached the door of their Sunday school classroom.

Tom crouched down and met them at their level. "Okay, one last time. What's your memory verse?"

"'Blessed are those who hunger and thirst for righteousness, for they will be filled. Matthew 5:6.'" The girls rattled off in sweet, singsong voices.

Hannah held the image, studying them a while longer, remembering them….she was surprised how quickly the girls' memory verse came to mind after all these years.

Maybe that was the problem. Maybe teaching the girls those Bible verses had been a bad thing. Now that God had proven himself to be a fraud—or at least not the good God everyone thought him to be—maybe the Scripture verses were actually harmful.

Hannah thought about the fight she and Jenny had just had. *"Shut up, Mother. Shut up, Mother."* She couldn't get Jenny's words out of her mind. Finally she stood up and grabbed her car keys. She needed to make a visit, needed to be close to someone who loved her.

Jenny heard her mother drive away and sighed in frustration. She glanced about her room. She was angrier than she'd let on about the trial being delayed. She'd had it all worked out and now this meant waiting.

Unnecessary waiting.

Her mother thought getting a first-degree murder verdict was the most important thing in life. Well, Jenny would show her. She had the pills ready, the note written.

The day of the verdict, that was the day she had chosen.

While her mother was waiting for the big decision, she would finally join Daddy and Alicia. Later that day, when the trial was over and the last cameraman had gone home, her mother would truly be free. She would be finished with everything that held her back—the trial, the victim impact panels... and Jenny. After the verdict, her mother would never need to worry about how to make things right between them.

She'd been so close. Now she would have to wait until after July 14. Verdict day would probably come a few weeks after that.

She flopped on her bed and lay on her stomach, her arms wrapped around the pillow. Maybe she should just do it now and get it over with. She could still hear the voice, whispering to her, telling her to go ahead and be done with it.

She rolled onto her side, restless, agitated. She didn't want to attend the trial. She'd told her mother at least a hundred times, but still she pushed. *She never listens to me. No wonder we fight so much. What does she expect?*

In the fog of confusion that filled her mind, Jenny wished she and her mother could be at peace with one another before the big day. Suicide was forever. There would be no turning back, no time for regrets.

For a moment she was assailed with doubts. Maybe there was another way. If only things were like they used to be between her and her mother. Jenny felt tears sting at her eyes again.

Alicia had always been their parents' favorite, but before the accident Jenny had at least felt loved, appreciated. She would give anything to have that feeling again. If she felt her mother truly loved her—instead of just saying she did—then Jenny would attend the trial and maybe even throw away the pills.

Yes, if she could be sure of her mother's love, she might be able to live her life out and then join Daddy and Alicia whenever the time came.

"I have come that they may have life and have it to the full...."

The Scripture filled Jenny's mind and she sat up, hugging her knees to her chest. That had been happening a lot lately. The strange voice would whisper to her, telling her to take the pills...and then she'd hear another voice, one that was clearer, filled with love, speaking Scripture she'd memorized years ago. But the Bible verses made her nervous....They were always about life and living...and that made her wonder. Maybe God didn't believe in suicide, maybe he didn't want her to take her life, after all.

The problem was her mother didn't love her like she used to. And Daddy was busy loving Alicia in heaven.

She leaned over her bed and reached for the shoebox. Setting it on her bedspread, she lifted the lid and examined the contents: a bag with dozens of colorful pills, a water bottle, and an envelope containing a good-bye letter.

Jenny pulled the letter out, opened it gently, and began to read.

"Dear Mom..." She closed her eyes for a moment and tried to imagine what her mother would be feeling when she read the letter for the first time. She opened her eyes and continued. *"First let me say I'm sorry. I never planned to hurt you with this; it was just something I had to do. Ever since the accident, you've been too busy with your speaking things to spend time with me. Too angry to notice me, even when you're home. It's okay. I understand, really. You lost everything that matters to you. Daddy and you have been together a long time, and I know you miss him a lot. Alicia, too. She was your first child, and I know she's always been a little more special.*

"Then there's me. Ever since the accident, you and I haven't been the same. We fight all the time and finally I decided it was time to go. I'm just in the way here anyway. Still there's a few things I want

you to know. I enjoyed being part of this family, at least before the accident. You were always a good mom, so don't think this is because of you. It's not.

"Also, you can do whatever you want with my scrapbooks and things. Give the clothes to someone who needs them. Maybe since it'll be just you now, you can sell this house and get on with your life. If I'd stayed, I would have wanted to sell it. You can only walk around a museum of memories for so long, Mom.

"Anyway, that's all. I just wanted you to know this isn't your fault and that I'm sorry. I wanted to be with Daddy and Alicia and Jesus. You don't want me talking about Jesus anymore, and sometimes I think I miss him as much as I miss Daddy and Alicia. This is the only way I know to make things right. Love forever, Jenny."

Two tears fell from Jenny's eyes and splattered on the sheet of paper. She brushed them off, folded the note once more, and returned it to the shoebox.

She was ready.

Now it was only a matter of waiting.

The cemetery looked like something from a postcard as Hannah pulled up and parked in the visitor lot. The setting sun cast a glow over the rolling green hills and elm trees, causing the leaves to shimmer in the gentle breeze. Rosebushes lined the roadway throughout the grounds, lending a sweet smell to the springtime air.

Hannah drew a deep breath and leveled her gaze eastward, toward the plot where Tom and Alicia lay buried. Then she checked her appearance in the rearview mirror.

She was still beautiful, she supposed, but not in the way Tom had always liked. He had always loved her eyes most of all, and since the accident her eyes had changed. They looked almost as if they belonged to someone else. Each morning she saw them—hollow, hard, hateful eyes with none of the beauty Tom had loved.

It's all Brian Wesley's fault.

The eyes looking back at her grew harder, angrier. Brian had stolen everything from her, even the way her eyes had once made the man she'd loved weak in the knees.

She tried to will the bright-eyed innocence back into her eyes—after all, she was going to visit Tom, and if in some inexplicable way he was able to see her, she didn't want him seeing her eyes like this.

She tried thinking about happier times, about Tom, their childhood, the way he'd shown up on her doorstep the day before marrying someone else. She thought about their wedding and Alicia's birth and Jenny's.

But her eyes remained empty.

Brian isn't the only one; it's God's fault, too.

You don't believe in God anymore, remember? So it can hardly be his fault.

She ignored the thought. Maybe there was a God, and he didn't like her. Maybe this was his way of showing that.

There was nothing she could do about her eyes. Not until she heard a guilty verdict. Then they would light up again.

She climbed out and stretched, gazing at the blue sky. *Tom? Are you there? Are you looking down on me?*

The temperature was cooling, and Hannah didn't want her visit cut short, so she strode across the grassy knoll, weaving her way around various plots and tombstones until she found them—two simple, granite grave markers and a section of earth covered with new grass.

She sat gingerly on the edge of Tom's stone and ran her fingers over his name. *Dr. Thomas J. Ryan.* The insanity of it all struck her. Tom Ryan, the man she'd loved all her life, dead...buried beneath mounds of dirt while she spent her days trying to change public opinion, trying to figure out how to make a life for herself and Jenny.

It wasn't possible.

She traced the *T* in Tom's name and felt the tears. She'd only come to the cemetery three times since the accident. She would have come more often, but she was simply too busy fighting the war against drunk drivers.

Or rather, the war against Brian Wesley.

"They got a delay." Her whispered words sounded strange in the silence. She traced the *H,* and a single tear fell onto the grass. Maybe that was why cemetery grass was so green—it was watered by the tears of the living. She tried to swallow a sob, but it remained lodged in her throat. "No trial until July 14."

Her finger moved slowly around the *O*. "But…Matt says it'll be okay. He's the prosecutor, you know. The one I told you about before." She placed her finger in the groove at the base of the *M* and began tracing.

"I'm still getting the word out, talking to whoever will listen. Matt says it looks good. First-degree murder for a drunk driver, Tom. It'll be the first time in California."

Her finger moved along the upward slant of the *A*. "Things aren't…they aren't too good with Jenny."

A sob escaped then and several tears fell. She wiped her eyes, and for a moment a torrent of sobs convulsed her chest in an attempt to break free. She sighed, struggling to control herself. Slowly, her finger wound lazily down the *S*. "I don't know what to do about her, Tom. She…she hates me."

Hannah squeezed her eyes shut, and more tears ran down her face. Could Tom see her, hear her? She thought for a moment and then opened her eyes. Slowly she traced the *J*. The only way Tom could see her now was if he was in heaven. And if he was in heaven, then God was real after all.

But if God was real, what were Tom and Alicia doing six feet under? What was she doing talking to a gravestone in the middle of a lonely cemetery on a beautiful spring evening? Hannah sighed and her finger found the *R*. "Tom…I miss you, honey. I miss you so much."

People said the ache she felt from not having him to hold—

from not having his hand in hers and his body in bed with her at night—would fade. But it hadn't. It was stronger than ever. She traced the *Y* and moved on to the *A*. "Tom, I can't do this without you. Where are you? Can you hear me?"

She finished tracing the *N* and buried her head in her hands, giving in to her sobs and allowing the grief. There had been so much involved in planning for the trial that she had rarely taken time to cry in the last few months. Now, with the trial moved to July and Jenny refusing to talk to her, there was finally time. Hannah cried until the cool breeze against her arm reminded her of the late hour. It would be dark soon.

Slowly she lifted her head and let her eyes fall on Alicia's stone. Sliding herself over, she perched on the edge of the granite square and gazed at the name written there. *Alicia Marie Ryan.*

She began tracing the *A*. "Oh, Alicia...Alicia, baby, Mommy's here."

A mother's instinct, strong and palpable, swept over Hannah. Alicia was in trouble. Hannah was consumed by a suffocating fear. The girl was trapped down there, underground where it was cold and dark and frightening.

"Alicia! Mommy loves you."

She nuzzled her face against the cool gravestone, her tears mixing with the loose dirt. "Alicia! I'm here, baby!"

For a single moment, Hannah considered clawing away the dirt, tunneling her way to the casket and prying it open so she could hold Alicia close. Just one more time.

Even if all that was left of her were bones.

Twenty-five

He has walled me in so I cannot escape;
he has weighed me down with chains.

LAMENTATIONS 3:7

Three months passed and finally the day of the trial arrived. In the warm early morning of July 14, four hours before jury selection, Carol Cummins read the final chapter in the book of Lamentations. *"Restore us to yourself, O* LORD, *that we may return; renew our days as of old..."* She finished the chapter, closed the leather cover of her Bible, and stared out her dining room window.

She had read Lamentations twice through since suggesting it to Hannah. She'd read about Jeremiah and how he and his people had felt deserted by the Lord. *"The Lord is like an enemy..."* Hannah might as well have written the words herself.

Carol had read Jeremiah's feelings of abandonment and intentional persecution. It had struck her how, like a single light in a dark place, Jeremiah had declared amidst death and destruction that indeed, God's mercies are new every morning, that his faithfulness truly is great.

She remembered the day she'd come to that realization herself, on the first anniversary of her husband's death.

In the end, Jeremiah's lament had turned from dark despair to a powerful desire for restoration with the Lord. If only Hannah could grasp that truth.

Hannah was poring over a scrapbook she'd made of newspaper clippings and of photographs of Tom and Alicia. When it came her turn to speak, she would be ready, complete with visual aids to show the jury the extent of her loss.

It was hard to believe it had all come to this. All the victim impact panels, all the interviews, all the effort at changing public opinion. In the end it came down to what happened over these next few weeks.

Jury selection would take two or three days. Hannah flipped a page and gazed at a photo of Alicia at her kindergarten graduation.

Matt wanted to stay away from singles. They would have the mentality a prosecutor feared most of all: "*There but for the grace of God, go I...*"

She turned another page and caught the image of Tom, grinning widely as he held a string of rainbow trout on one of his summer camping trips with the girls.

Retired people could be trouble, too. Most of them would be old enough to be Brian's parents. They would sympathize with his youth and be hard-pressed to convict him of first-degree murder when he had so much of life ahead.

Hannah sighed and shut the scrapbook, staring absently at the wedding band that still adorned her finger.

Women jurors would be good, much better than men. Matt had explained the law of averages: a man was more likely to drink and drive. Therefore, men would empathize more with Wesley. They would look at him and see themselves, and that was something Matt wanted to avoid.

Hannah knew Matt intended to play the averages. She ran her hand over the leather binding of the scrapbook. "Wish me luck, Tom."

She felt the sting of tears but willed them away. There was no time for grieving now.

It was eight o'clock and jury selection would begin in two hours.

In the end, it took Matt and Finch two days to choose a jury of seven women and five men. One of the women was single, a redhead in her early twenties. One of them was retired, a volunteer librarian quickly approaching seventy. The men included three who were married, two of whom were parents. One man was single and in his thirties; another in his fifties was divorced after two failed marriages. The alternates were a man and woman, both in their forties, both married.

Twelve ordinary people...representatives of society, the combined voice of justice. Hannah watched them carefully. Did they know the power they held now that they'd been chosen?

It was Friday morning. Opening statements were minutes away, and Hannah was the first to arrive in the courtroom. She found a seat in the front row, directly behind the prosecutor's table. At this point, she had worked so hard she almost felt like part of the team, one of Matt's assistants, battling for justice in a system that rarely seemed just.

Matt entered the courtroom through one of the side doors and found her immediately. "Hannah, how're you doing?" He spoke in hushed tones.

"I'm ready. I have a good feeling about this."

"Have you prayed about it?" Matt stared deep into her eyes, and she felt a connection there, something she couldn't define.

Reluctantly she looked away. If only she could say what he wanted to hear. But she couldn't. "You know I haven't."

"Pray, will you, Hannah? For me. I need all the help I can get."

Hannah nodded, but she could tell by his expression that he didn't believe she would do it. She pushed away the guilt tugging at her.

Carol moved in beside her, took her hand, and squeezed it once. "Here we go."

Hannah leaned over and hugged her. She wouldn't have survived the past year if it hadn't been for Carol. The two had spent nearly every day together at MADD's office, and many times Carol had taken Hannah to lunch to talk about her feelings. Sometimes just knowing Carol had made it through this dark valley was enough to keep Hannah going. She searched Carol's face now. "I feel good about it. How 'bout you?"

Carol nodded and whispered. "The way Matt works, I think we're about to make history."

Matt was up first. He stood, and his dark, tailored suit hung gracefully on his lanky frame. He looked youthful as he approached the jury and nodded a greeting, thanking them for serving as jurors. For fifteen minutes he talked about the details of the case. Then he turned his attention to Hannah.

She knew what he was about to do, and she watched him amble slowly toward where she sat. When he was inches away, he greeted her. Then in a voice loud enough for the jury to hear, he asked if he could borrow the photo button she was wearing. Hannah took it off and handed it to him.

Matt studied the photograph as he made his way back to the jury box. Holding it up for them to see. "This is Dr. Tom Ryan and his little girl, Alicia." He moved slowly in front of the panel so that each member could see the photo. Hannah watched them strain to get a closer look, and she knew Matt had been right. They needed to be familiar with Tom and Alicia, not just with the cold facts of the case.

"Tom Ryan was a family man, active in his church, involved in the lives of his daughters. Each summer he and the girls took a camping trip, sort of a summer's end hurrah. They would fish and hike and boat, but those trips weren't about the number of trout they caught. They were about building love and relationships. Something at which Tom Ryan was brilliant."

Matt looked at the photo once more. "Alicia was just fifteen when she died at Brian Wesley's hands. She was on the verge of everything wonderful in life. She was active in student government, a cheerleader whose smile made an impact on everyone around her."

Hannah shifted her gaze to the defense attorney. He was busy making notations on a pad of legal paper. Probably trying to appear disinterested in Matt's statement.

Matt continued. "Dr. Ryan left behind his other daughter, Jenny, a twelve-year-old who has had trouble smiling since the accident. A young girl who will never know the security of having Daddy waiting at home when she goes on a date. A girl whose dad will not be there to walk her down the aisle when she gets married. A very sad, very troubled girl who once was the picture of carefree innocence."

Hannah could see tears sparkling in the eyes of two female jurors. Matt turned his attention back to Hannah as he crossed the courtroom and passed the photo button back to her. He kept his focus on her as he continued. "And of course there is Hannah Ryan. Tom and Hannah were childhood sweethearts." He smiled sadly. "In all her life, there has never been—" Matt looked deeper into Hannah's eyes, and again she felt a connection she couldn't explain—"probably never will be anyone for her but Tom Ryan."

"Hannah lost her husband and her best friend, her confidante, the father of her children. The man around whom she had built her life." Hannah felt a strange tugging at her heart, and she directed her gaze at her wedding ring. Matt was right. There could never be anyone else.

Matt looked at the jurors and strolled toward them again. "I am here to prove to each of you that what happened to the Ryan family was not—absolutely *not*—an accident."

Matt put one hand on the railing in front of the jury, the other in his pants pocket. He leaned forward, facing the jurors squarely. Then his gaze traveled to Brian Wesley, who sat, white-faced, his hands on the table before him. When Matt finally spoke, his voice rang with sincerity. "Don't let Mr. Wesley, or anyone else who chooses to drink and drive, get away with murder." Matt straightened, nodding to the jury. "Set a standard that other prosecutors can follow. A penalty that will save lives."

He nodded toward them politely. "Thank you."

Hannah caught only fragments of Harold Finch's opening statement. Something about being deeply troubled at the thought of drunk driving being a murder-one offense and how anyone might make such a mistake. She wasn't really listening. Her thoughts were still swimming from all that Matt had said.

She realized Finch was winding up and sat up straighter in her seat, determined to pay attention. "Mr. Wesley had suffered through a bad morning. He'd been laid off from his job and didn't know how to tell his wife." Finch hesitated. "What happened? What happens to a lot of people when they get bad news? He wound up at the bar. He had a few drinks, thought about his troubles, and set out for home."

Finch stood up straighter and hiked his suit pants back into place. "What happened between the bar and his front door was not something Mr. Wesley intended. So what was it?" He paused. "It was an accident. An *accident.*" Finch's expression was one of great regret. He shook his head sadly. "Yes, Mr. Wesley made poor decisions. And yes, as a result, there was an accident."

Finch scratched his forehead absently, as though momentarily lost in thought. His hand fell back to his side and he stared at the jurors. "If you decide that drunk driving is akin to first-degree murder, you must understand that the next person involved in such an accident might be you, or the guy next to you. It might be the PTA mother out with the girls, or maybe the hardworking father sharing a few drinks with his buddies over an afternoon football game."

Carol shook her head angrily and leaned toward Hannah. "Like that would make it okay?"

Before Hannah could agree, anger filled Finch's voice. "You and I know the truth, don't we? *We* don't need three weeks of evidence. Lumping someone who makes a mistake, someone who drinks and then drives, into the same category as gun-wielding bank robbers and vicious gang members is ludicrous. Utterly ludicrous."

Tears filled Hannah's eyes and she hung her head. She could see Tom and Alicia and Jenny as they'd loaded the Explorer with sleeping bags and coolers and fishing poles. They'd been so happy, laughing and teasing each other about who was the best fisherman. She remembered hugging them, feeling them in her arms before they pulled away, one at a time, and began the journey that would destroy their family forever.

Brian Wesley *was* an intentional killer, and Hannah wanted to tell that to the jurors before they forgot everything Matt had already said.

Unable to bear it, she wept softly, covering her face with her hands. As Harold Finch took his seat, Carol placed an arm around Hannah and rubbed her back gently. Distantly Hannah heard the judge dismiss the court until later that afternoon. Then before she could collect herself, Hannah heard Matt's voice…felt his tender hand on her shoulder.

"Hannah…"

She looked up and accepted a tissue from Carol. "I'm sorry. I didn't mean to break down."

"You have nothing to apologize for." Matt removed his hand and stooped down to her level. "Don't worry, Hannah. Finch didn't say anything I didn't expect." Hannah sighed and adjusted the photo button on her lapel. "Did they get a good look at Tom and Alicia?"

Matt nodded and Hannah saw the sadness in his eyes. "They did." He hesitated. "Come on. Let's get a bite to eat. I need to get back in an hour to meet with the first few witnesses."

As she rose to follow Matt and Carol from the courtroom, Hannah thought about calling Jenny…but there wasn't time.

Her closest friends in this, her new world, were waiting for her; and so, anchored by their support, she walked past the pay phone without a backward glance.

Twenty-six

Even when I call out or cry for help he shuts out my prayer. He has barred my way with blocks of stone; he has made my paths crooked. Like a bear lying in wait, like a lion in hiding, he dragged me from the path and mangled me and left me without help.

LAMENTATIONS 3:8–10

Court resumed at 2 P.M. and Matt called his first witness.

Rae McDermott, the waitress from Sal's Diner, took the stand. She related the events that led up to the accident. She told the court how she was getting ready to leave for the day when she spotted a white truck speeding east along Ventura Boulevard, approaching Fallbrook.

"From where you stood, were you able to see the traffic signal, Ms. McDermott?" Matt spoke from a place midway between the jury box and the witness stand. He looked down, apparently checking his notes.

"Yes, I could see the traffic signal clearly."

He nodded. "What color was it?"

"Red. It was a red light." Rae glanced disdainfully at Wesley. Hannah could have hugged her.

"So...you watched the defendant, Mr. Wesley, drive his white truck through a red light, is that right?"

Finch was on his feet. "Objection, your honor. Prosecutor is leading the witness. She said the light was red when she looked out, not when the defendant passed through the intersection."

Judge Horowitz looked bored by the interruption. Hannah could have hugged him, too. "Overruled. Continue Mr. Bronzan."

"Thank you, your honor." Matt glanced back at the witness. "What color was the light when the defendant drove his truck through the intersection, Ms. McDermott?"

She jutted her chin out and spoke in a clear, condemning tone. "The light was *red.* It was red as he approached, red when he drove through, and red when he barreled into the Explorer. It was red the whole time."

She shot Harold Finch a glare, and Hannah almost burst into applause.

"And after the impact?" Matt asked.

"I hurried toward the Explorer and began working with two other motorists to help the victims." She shook her head, clucking sadly. "That poor little girl—"

"Objection, your honor!" Finch bellowed. "Please ask the witness to confine her answers to the questions asked!"

The judge nodded and looked at Rae kindly. "The witness will please answer the questions and refrain from elaborating."

Rae smiled up at the judge. "Whatever you say, your honor, sir." Then she shot another glare at Finch.

Matt stared down at his notes again, and Hannah thought she caught a glimpse of a smile. But when he looked up, he was all business. "At some point did the defendant exit his white truck and make his way toward you and the two motorists?"

"Yes."

"Did anything about the defendant suggest to you that he'd been drinking?"

Finch jumped up. "Objection! The defendant had just been involved in a severe traffic accident. It would be impossible for a bystander to know whether the defendant had been drinking or whether he was merely injured in the accident."

Judge Horowitz considered that. "Sustained. Rephrase the question, Mr. Bronzan."

Matt moved closer to the woman on the stand. "What do you remember about the defendant when he approached you after the collision that afternoon?"

"He stunk."

Rae's answer brought a few muffled giggles from the jurors. Hannah glanced at the panel. *Good.* They liked Rae McDermott. Matt waited for the court to be silent again. "He...stunk? Can you elaborate for the court, please?"

"Sure." She flipped her hair back. "I work at a diner, serve drinks to half the people all day long. Heck, done so all my life. The defendant—" she cast another contemptuous glance at Brian—"smelled like booze."

"*Booze* as in alcoholic beverages? Wine...? Beer...? That kind of thing?"

She nodded firmly. "He smelled like beer. In fact, if I were a bettin' woman, I'd say he'd had himself a case of beer before getting in that truck."

"*Objection!* Your honor, there's no way this witness can possibly know how much alcohol, if any, the defendant consumed before getting in his truck."

Judge Horowitz looked slightly amused. "Sustained. The jury will disregard the last part of the witness's answer."

Hannah drew a deep breath and felt a wave of exhilaration. The judge's warning was too late. The jury already had the image in their minds—Brian Wesley stumbling out of his car, reeking of alcohol. There was nothing a judge could say to undo the mental picture.

Matt continued. "Ms. McDermott, can you identify the man you saw that day, the man who drove through the red light, crashed into the Explorer, exited his truck, and then made his way toward you and the two motorists. The man who smelled like beer."

"Sure thing." Rae pointed toward Brian Wesley. "He's sitting right over there."

"Thank you, no further questions."

When Finch was through cross-examining, it was four o'clock, and Judge Horowitz dismissed court until Monday. Hannah stood—and suddenly she was surrounded by members of the media, many whom she recognized from her work with victim impact panels. A chorus of voices vied for her attention.

"Hannah, was there anything that surprised you about the opening statements?"

"Do you have any comments on Harold Finch's suggestion that a guilty verdict would set a dangerous precedent?"

"Are you happy with the prosecutor's approach?"

"Do you have any predictions about a verdict?"

She had become a media darling, and she handled their questions like a professional, understanding why they were drawn to her. The media saw her as the beautiful, angry widow with a cause. They liked her, and they played her point of view perfectly in the press. She took time with them gladly and left only when Matt appeared in the distance and motioned for her.

He smiled at her. "Do you have a few minutes?"

She was breathless from speaking before the television cameras, rocked with feelings that ranged from anxious anticipation over the trial, bitter hatred toward Finch and Brian Wesley, and a cavernous sense of loss.

What she should do was go home. Spend time resting… time with Jenny. Still…

Spending time with Matt was extremely appealing. He was safe and kind and on her side. He didn't fault her for her involvement with victim impact panels, and he didn't badger her to read Scripture. He was her friend, and now—in the wake of a flood of emotion—she wanted nothing more than to find a quiet place and talk with him.

She glanced at her watch. "I've got time, why?"

"I thought we could talk, brainstorm about how the trial might go and how things went today." He began walking down the corridor, and she fell into step beside him.

"Okay. Let's go outside though. It's stuffy in here."

Matt nodded. "You're right. We'll spend enough time inside over the next few weeks."

They headed for the stairs, and as she had earlier, for a

moment Hannah considered Jenny, home alone, despondent. A nagging voice reminded her that she should go home and try to make amends in their relationship, but she had no patience for Jenny's self-pity. She was tired of trying and too busy fighting the war for justice. The trial would be over soon enough. There would be time then for mending the bond between them.

"Thinking about Jenny?" Matt gazed down at her as they moved out into the courtyard.

How could a man who barely knew her be so perceptive. *He's a Christian.* The thought came before she could stop it. *He's an attorney*, she silently retorted. "Yeah. She should be here."

"You're angry with her, aren't you?" Matt lowered himself onto a graffiti-smattered cement bench, leaving plenty of space for Hannah. She sat at the other end and turned to face him.

"Sometimes I think I'm mad at everybody." She studied him. "Everyone but you and Carol. I wouldn't have made it this far without you two."

"Jenny's pulling for you, too."

Hannah huffed softly. "She has a fine way of showing it."

"May I say something?"

Hannah sighed. "What?"

"Be careful. Don't let her think this trial…anything…is more important than she is to you."

"It's not that. She has to understand—"

"Hannah." Matt's interruption was gentle. "Long after this trial is over, whether we win a conviction or not, there will be you and Jenny. Don't lose sight of that."

"We *will* win a conviction." Hannah crossed her arms.

"If it isn't God's will, it won't happen."

Hannah sighed and looked skyward. "Please. Don't start talking about God's will. If it was his will to allow Tom and Alicia to die, then certainly it would be his will to allow Brian Wesley to go to prison for the rest of his life."

"Not necessarily."

A pang of doubt hit Hannah. "Matt…is there something you're not telling me?"

He shook his head. "No, nothing like that. I feel confident about winning a conviction." His gentle eyes scanned her face. "I just don't want us to put all our hope in that. The true hope comes from knowing that you and Jenny will be all right, that God has a plan for your life long after this trial is over and forgotten."

She bit her tongue to hold back the bitter retorts she could have said. Matt was her friend and he didn't deserve her anger. Instead, she directed the conversation back to the trial, asking Matt how he thought the day had gone and what they could expect in the weeks to come.

He answered her questions, but she could see in his eyes that he knew what she was doing. And she was grateful to him for letting her get away with it.

The day had gone too well. She simply couldn't bear to have it—or her time with Matt—ruined by talk of a God Hannah could no longer trust.

By the time Hannah got home it was dark, and the lights in the house were out. She tiptoed up to Jenny's room and opened the door. The girl was asleep in bed.

Jenny doesn't need me.

Hannah was hit by a sudden, powerful urge to kiss her little girl, to brush her blond bangs off her forehead and pray over her as she had done all her life before the collision. But everything had changed now. Jenny didn't want to be kissed, didn't like her mother touching her forehead. And Hannah knew better than to pray.

She sighed, shut the door, and made her way to her bedroom. Jenny didn't need anyone. She had survived one of the worst traffic collisions in the history of the San Fernando Valley. Certainly she would survive another few weeks without

Hannah's undivided attention.

Before turning off the light, Hannah spotted Tom's old, leather Bible, still sitting atop his dresser. Nearly a year had gone by, and Hannah had packed away most of Tom's and Alicia's belongings. But Tom's Bible had been so dear to him, his faithful companion each morning in the early hours, long before Hannah or the girls were awake. Other than photographs, Tom's Bible was the only reminder that he once had lived there, once had shared a room and a life with Hannah.

The worn Bible called to her at times like this, times when the echoes of another endless, lonely night ricocheted off her bedroom wall making it nearly impossible to sleep.

Back in the days when she could sing "Great is Thy Faithfulness" and mean every word, back when she and Tom shared and lived their beliefs, she would occasionally pick up his Bible and scan the pages, enjoying the notations he'd written in the margins.

But Scripture held no hope for Hannah now. She turned her back so that the Bible was out of view, and fell asleep dreaming of the way things used to be.

Twenty-seven

He drew his bow and made me the target for his arrows.

LAMENTATIONS 3:12

After her mother left for court Monday morning, Jenny dressed, pulled her mountain bike from the garage, and set out for the cemetery. It was four miles away, but Jenny knew a shortcut. With school out and the verdict still two weeks away, she knew exactly what she wanted to do. She hopped on her bike and set out.

Twenty minutes later she pulled up to the spot where Dad's and Alicia's tombstones lay on a grassy knoll. Jenny climbed off her bike and dropped down crosslegged next to the stones.

"Hi, Dad. Hi, Lecia." She wrapped her arms around her knees. A warm, summer breeze drifted through the nearby trees, and Jenny wondered if she should have worn sunscreen. She planned to be here all day.

"I can't believe it's been almost a year. Gosh…if you guys only knew how much I miss you."

A pair of swallows sang out from opposite trees, but otherwise there was silence.

"Mom is so freaked out. All she cares about is the guy who hit us and getting him into prison. She spends all her time on it."

Jenny examined the tombstones closely. "I'll be with you guys pretty soon…I'm waiting for the verdict. That way Mom will be finished with everything all at once. The trial, the guy who hit us, and me. I'm only in the way."

With no other visitors around to bother her, Jenny began to

cry. Her chest convulsed, and she sobbed like she hadn't done in weeks. Not for her father and sister because she would see them again soon. She cried for her family, for the way they had been before...the way they would never be again. When her sobs slowed, she stretched out along the ground, closed her eyes, and placed one hand on her father's stone, the other on Alicia's. She fell asleep that way, tears still drying on her cheeks, reaching out to the only people she knew loved her.

Across town at the Criminal Courts Building, Hannah watched Matt speak with a bailiff and then head toward her. He appeared upbeat and full of energy.

"I've reviewed the list of witnesses." He smiled. "Depending on cross-examination, I should be finished by the end of the week. Finch doesn't have much. If everything goes right, he'll be done Wednesday. That could mean a verdict as early as Friday or the following Monday."

A swarm of butterflies invaded Hannah's stomach. "That soon?"

Matt nodded and gently squeezed her hand. "In a case like this, the sooner we make our argument the better. Juries get bored with statistics and redundant testimony. Two weeks is perfect."

She nodded and spoke in a choked whisper. "Go get 'em, Matt."

The first witness of the day was Sgt. John Miller. He testified about the accident scene, how everything had appeared when he arrived, how badly the Explorer was damaged, and how Brian Wesley had failed two field sobriety tests.

The next witness was Dr. Larry Keeting, head of the crime lab and the person responsible for the results of the blood alcohol test.

Matt immediately took the offensive on the issue of timing and how quickly alcohol absorbs into the bloodstream.

Hannah kept her eyes trained on him, trying to see the scene through the eyes of the jurors.

Dr. Keeting was very clear. Although a person's blood alcohol level can continue to rise for an hour or more after the beverages are consumed, in Brian Wesley's case this would not have changed the facts.

"So you're telling us that it is possible that Mr. Wesley's blood alcohol level was lower than .24 at the time of the collision?"

"Perhaps. Based on progressive absorption, it is possible his blood alcohol might have been as low as .18 at the time of impact." Dr. Keeting was dressed in a three-piece suit and spoke with a great deal of authority. Hannah added him to the list of people she would later thank.

Matt turned slightly toward the jury. "So what you're saying is that even if Mr. Wesley's blood alcohol level was lower than what it was while taken at the station, the lowest it could have been was .18, or more than twice the legal limit, is that right?"

"Yes." Dr. Keeting paused. "Of course, there is great possibility that the defendant's blood alcohol was actually higher at the time of impact. Absorption reaches a certain peak sometime within an hour after consumption. After that, the level begins to decline."

Matt looked surprised, and Hannah stifled a smile. "So, if that were the case, what would Mr. Wesley's highest possible blood alcohol level have been, Dr. Keeting?"

The doctor checked a stack of notes in front of him on the witness stand. "According to our projections, the defendant might have had a blood alcohol level as high as .28."

Finch spent nearly an hour cross-examining Dr. Keeting, but it was like trying to poke holes in a brick wall. Later that afternoon when court adjourned, Matt assured Hannah the testimony had been better than he'd hoped.

"The best is yet to come." Matt smiled as he and Hannah strolled alongside Carol Cummins toward the elevator.

Hannah looked at him. "The bartender?"

He nodded. "Found something out yesterday that will help a great deal."

"Good. He's the last witness, isn't he?" Hannah pushed the elevator button as they waited with a handful of people.

"Right. Wait 'til you hear him. He's great." Matt leaned closer to Hannah and Carol, speaking in a whisper. "Answered prayer."

Carol nodded.

Oh, brother. Hannah looked away. "Come on, Matt. Give credit where credit's due."

She waited for a retort but it didn't come.

Matt gained more points the next day. Brian Wesley's coworkers and former bosses testified about Brian's alcohol problem and how well he hid it. Next came three people who ran state-sponsored alcohol awareness classes. Each provided the jury with proof that Brian Wesley was indeed aware of his problem and that he'd been counseled about the dangers of drunk driving.

A representative from the state's parole board brought in documentation signed by Brian stating that he understood that if he drank and drove again someone could very well die. The department of motor vehicles showed proof that Brian was driving without a license at the time of the collision.

The week wore on, and Hannah sometimes found herself tuning the testimony out while she focused on Brian Wesley. What kind of animal was he, anyway? What had he seen in those final moments before driving his truck into her family? She seethed as she stared at him. He was loathsome and worthless, and he deserved life in prison. Now that he was days away from getting it, her hatred toward him was so intense it left her drained, empty, incapable of any other emotion.

Harold Finch, meanwhile, remained relatively quiet. He

objected occasionally, but not nearly as often as he had at first. Hannah figured he probably didn't want to alienate the jury.

Matt's final witness was Nick Crabb, the bartender from The Office. In brief and succinct testimony, the bartender told the jury that he'd been bothered by the defendant's drinking. He had asked him if he'd needed a ride home, but despite the fact that he'd seen Brian drink large quantities of beer and whiskey, it was difficult to determine if the man was dangerously drunk or not.

"Think back, Mr. Crabb." Matt settled his hands in his pants pocket and gazed thoughtfully at the witness. "Do you remember how many drinks the defendant consumed that afternoon?"

Nick squirmed in his seat nervously. "Well, uh, it's been almost a year now, and we have a lot of people sit at the bar."

Matt nodded. "I realize that, Mr. Crabb. I'm asking—to the best of your knowledge—if you can tell this court how many drinks the defendant had?"

Nick nodded. "Okay. Well, after the accident I wrote some notes."

Finch leaped up. "*Objection*, your honor. We have no way of knowing when the witness actually wrote those notes."

Hannah's pulse raced when Judge Horowitz looked intrigued. He turned to the witness. "Did you date your notes, Mr. Crabb?"

"Yes, your honor. I'm a business student at Cal State Northridge...and, well, I guess I write the date on just about everything."

Judge Horowitz smiled. "And you are willing to testify under oath that you wrote those notes immediately after the accident?"

"Yes, your honor."

"Very well. Objection overruled."

Hannah turned briefly toward Carol, and the two shared a quick grin. This was why Matt had been looking forward to the bartender's testimony. The man kept notes!

Matt cleared his throat and continued. "Let me see if I understand this. After the accident, you wrote down the date and some details about the defendant, is that right?"

"Yes, I have it right here." Nick held up a piece of notebook paper.

"I see." Matt moved closer to the witness stand and peered at it. "And what prompted you to write these notes?"

Nick swallowed and glanced nervously at Brian Wesley. "I, uh…I read about the accident in the newspaper, and I knew the guy'd been drinking at The Office. I served him. I figured I might have to talk about it one day in court, so I jotted down some details."

Matt smiled. "Thank you, Mr. Crabb. That was very conscientious of you."

Hannah saw Harold Finch whisper something to Brian Wesley.

Matt continued. "Now, did you note anywhere on that sheet how many drinks Mr. Wesley consumed on the afternoon in question?"

"Yes…it's, uh, right here." Nick studied the piece of paper. "I served Mr. Wesley about six shots of whiskey and eight beers."

A murmur ran through the courtroom, and Hannah shut her eyes. Fourteen drinks. No wonder Tom and Alicia hadn't lived long enough to say good-bye.

Matt waited for the crowd to still. "So fourteen drinks altogether, is that right?"

"I'm estimating, but I think so. It could have been more."

Matt raised an eyebrow, and Hannah saw him glance briefly at the jury. She followed his gaze and saw that they looked stunned. They might drink, they might know someone who drank…but *fourteen* drinks? "Now, Mr. Crabb, did you make any notations about how long Mr. Wesley had been drinking?"

Nick glanced down at his notes again and gulped. "Yes. He came in after lunch sometime, maybe one, one-thirty. And he left after three."

Harold Finch looked restless but he remained in his seat.

Matt nodded. "Is there any way you can be certain about those times, Mr. Crabb?"

Hannah willed the bartender to say the right thing. *Please…please…*

"Well, there was a movie running on the bar TV, *Rocky II.* Mr. Wesley arrived just as I was putting it in, and it was over by the time he left." Nick glanced at his notes once more. "I figured that had to be at least two hours."

"Fine. So he drank for two hours—fourteen drinks, maybe more—is that right?"

"Yes, sir." Hannah watched the young bartender expectantly. She knew what was coming.

Matt stood squarely in front of the witness stand. "At some point Mr. Wesley decided to leave, is that right?"

"Yes."

"Were you concerned that he might be too drunk to drive home?" Matt kept his tone matter-of-fact. This wasn't the time to point fingers at the bartender.

Nick Crabb sighed, and Hannah saw the burden he carried. He'd been the final line of defense, the only one who could have stopped Wesley from getting into the truck and barreling down Ventura Boulevard. He'd had the chance and he'd missed it.

Nick drew a deep breath. "Yes. Just before he left I decided he was too drunk to drive."

Murmurs rose across the courtroom, and Matt waited a moment. He raised his voice slightly, and the jurors strained to hear. "Did you act on that decision?"

Nick nodded. "Yes. I asked him if he was okay to drive."

Hannah felt her heart sink. She followed Matt as he paced slowly toward the jury. "Do you remember what Mr. Wesley told you?"

Nick sighed again. "Yes. He told me to mind my own business."

Across the courtroom Finch leaned over and whispered

something else to Brian. Hannah glared at them and turned her attention back to Matt.

"Then what happened?"

"I...I told him to sit down a minute...told him I'd call a cab so...so he wouldn't have to drive home." Nick hung his head.

"What next, Mr. Crabb?"

"He got mad."

Matt raised an eyebrow. "Could you explain your answer, Mr. Crabb."

The bartender straightened, and for a moment his eyes connected with Hannah's. He was sorry. Hannah could see that, and she wasn't sure how she felt. This man's testimony would help put Brian Wesley away for a very long time. Then again, if only he'd said something different, done something... physically contained Brian, anything...perhaps they wouldn't be here today. Perhaps they would all be home living life the way they were supposed to. Happily ever after.

Nick was silent, and Matt tried again. "Mr. Crabb, please explain to the jury what you meant when you said that the defendant got mad when you offered to call a cab."

"Well, he told me he could drive home if he wanted to. Then he cussed at me a few times. He told me he was leaving, and he turned around and left."

"Do you have some sort of test, some way of determining whether a person who has been drinking should or shouldn't drive?" Matt slipped his hands in his pockets and leaned slightly against the railing.

"Yes. My boss had told me to watch how customers talk, how they walk. Mr. Wesley seemed okay that way, but he'd had a lot of drinks in a short time, and I was worried. So I did what the boss said to do in that situation. I offered him a cab. When he refused, I thought I was out of options. There was nothing more I could do."

"Okay, now let's see if I have this straight. The defendant, Brian Wesley, spent two hours drinking at least fourteen alcoholic beverages, then refused your offer of a cab and left the bar despite your warnings. Is that right, Mr. Crabb?"

The bartender swallowed, struggling to find his voice. "Yes."

"No more quest—"

"There's something else."

Matt looked at Nick in surprise, and the young man met Hannah's eyes once more.

"If I had to do it over again, I'd tackle him to the floor, tie his hands, anything. The only way out would be over my dead body." His voice was barely a whisper, his eyes were still on Hannah's. "I'm sorry."

Tears spilled onto Hannah's cheeks. She nodded and hung her head. It was easy to hate Brian Wesley, easy to hate any attorney who would defend him. But this man, this college student, was not her enemy. They had both lost that day and clearly he, like Hannah, still suffered.

Finch bounded to his feet, his face red. "*Objection!* The witness's statement went beyond the scope of the question, your Honor."

Hannah looked at the judge and saw him nod sternly. "Sustained. The jury will disregard the last statement."

Matt paused a moment, and Hannah knew he was allowing the jurors time to soak in what had just happened. Nick Crabb had apologized to her. Finally Matt looked up from his notes and thanked the witness, turning him over to the defense.

Harold Finch whispered something else to Brian and then stood up. Hannah thought he looked like a snake. A boa constrictor. She wondered if the jury saw him the same way.

"Mr. Crabb, has the defendant ever done anything to personally wrong you?" Finch's voice was sharp, full of accusation.

Nick blinked twice. "No. I don't know what you mean."

Finch shook his head and cast a knowing look at the jury. "Listen, here, Mr. Crabb. Isn't it true that you were hired by the prosecution, instructed to write those notes, and paid to appear here today in order to ruin the defendant's chances at an acquittal?"

Matt was not typically quick to object, but this time he was on his feet and doing so forcefully. "I object, your honor. Mr. Finch is badgering the witness about something that was not brought up in the direct. If it isn't brought up in the direct—"

"Yes." Judge Horowitz peered over the rim of his glasses at Harold Finch. "If it isn't brought up in the direct, it cannot be brought up in the cross. You should know that Mr. Finch. Objection sustained."

Finch continued to question the bartender for more than an hour, always stopping just short of harassment. Finally he tried to cast doubt on whether Nick Crabb had even tended bar the afternoon of the accident. In response, Nick produced another sheet of paper.

"What's that?" Finch's tone was filled with mockery. "More notes?"

"No, sir." Nick held the single sheet of paper higher so that Finch could see it. "It's a copy of my time card from that day. I asked the owner for a copy of it after the accident, when I figured I might need to testify in court at some point."

Hannah wanted to laugh out loud. Finch had been caught at his own game. Had he avoided this line of questioning, the jury would never have seen the meticulous care Nick Crabb took to present accurate details. Now the idea of the defendant consuming fourteen drinks looked like the gospel truth.

Hannah caught Matt's expression, and he winked. This one was theirs.

She could have kissed him!

Matt had another chance with Nick on redirect, and he used the opportunity to establish the specifics of the photocopied time card. Nick had indeed worked that afternoon. He had started at 11:00 A.M. and clocked out at 3:30 P.M. The details were perfectly in keeping with Nick's testimony. When Matt was finished with the bartender, he turned to the judge and nodded. "The state rests, your honor."

"Very well." Judge Horowitz scanned the courtroom. "It's

nearly three o'clock, so we'll adjourn until tomorrow at which time we will hear from the witnesses for the defense. Court dismissed."

Hannah closed her eyes and said a silent thanks to Matt Bronzan. They were halfway there, and because of Matt, Brian Wesley's days of freedom were disappearing fast.

Carol leaned toward her. "I need to get going. See you tomorrow."

As Carol left, Hannah was engulfed by a sea of reporters. When she had answered each of their questions, her eyes searched the front of the courtroom for Matt. Twenty minutes had passed, and Hannah figured he would be gone, but she found him leaning against the prosecution's table, his arms and ankles crossed, staring at her. Their eyes met, and the air seemed charged...alive...between them.

She waited while he gathered his files.

The trial was half over. Hannah could barely contain the sense of joy and victory she felt. When Matt stood and their eyes met again, she didn't hesitate. She went toward him, into his open arms, laying her head against his broad chest, letting her tears of gratitude fall on his shirt.

His arms wrapped around her back and held her close. And for the first time in decades, Hannah found herself being held by a man other than Tom Ryan.

Twenty-eight

He pierced my heart with arrows from his quiver.

LAMENTATIONS 3:13

Brian Wesley showered earlier than usual the next morning and paid particular attention to his appearance. He would be the first witness to take the stand in his defense, and he wanted to be clean and neat. If he really was a changed man—and he believed he was—then he needed to look the part.

Hot water pounded his shoulders, and steam filled the bathroom of Jackson's boxy apartment. *Lord, I'm gonna need your help today. I can't do it alone.*

Brian closed his eyes. The next few days would be the hardest in his life. First he would testify, talk about his past failures and how he'd become a changed man in the process. Then, at some point, Harold Finch would call Carla as a witness. She would testify that Brian never actually intended to kill another person.

Finch had been square with him. He would serve time in prison regardless of the verdict. Worst-case scenario, driving under the influence held a penalty of several years. And if the jury didn't convict him of first-degree murder, they would certainly give him the maximum for driving drunk. Ten years, maybe more.

Brian's heart began beating fast, and he recognized the beginnings of an anxiety attack. Times like this he could still taste the alcohol, still feel his body reaching for the drink that would destroy him.

"Do not be anxious about anything, but in everything, by prayer

and petition, with thanksgiving, present your requests to God. And the peace of God, which transcends all understanding, will guard your hearts and your minds in Christ Jesus. Do not be anxious about anything, but in..."

Over and over he repeated the verse from Philippians 4. It was a weapon, a demon slayer, and he used it every time they came back. Funny thing, too. Because as long as he could remember, relief from anxiety had always been something that came in whiskey bottles and beer cans. But this...this Scripture thing—having God's word memorized, ready to wield like a weapon anytime the beast of anxiety appeared—this was really something.

Better than the bottle ever was.

That Bible lady had explained it best: Scripture words were alive and active. They worked every time. They never lost their power like some dime-store battery. Brian stepped out of the shower. *"Do not be anxious about anything, but in everything..."* One thing was sure. This Bible thing was truth.

And it was his last hope.

He toweled off and dressed in his best new jeans and a button-down flannel shirt. A bit hot for July, but they were the nicest clothes he had.

He thought about Finch's advice: *"Make the jury love you or it's all over. Don't let 'em smell your fear. Let 'em see a sad man, someone ruined by the bottle, but don't let 'em see a killer. Make promises, even if you don't plan to keep them."*

He planned to make promises. What Finch didn't understand was that he planned to keep them, too.

Brian sighed and pulled a clean, white sock onto his bare foot. He wasn't sure about Finch anymore. The man was a good enough attorney, worth the money. But he didn't play fair, and that bothered Brian. Ever since meeting that woman down at Church on the Way, a lot of things about his old life bothered him.

For a moment he could see the young girl, lying dead on

the shoulder of the road, hear her father several feet away moaning for help, dying, trapped in his car.

Brian swallowed hard. *"Do not be anxious about anything, but in everything, by prayer and petition..."*

The image faded. He finished dressing and then checked his appearance in the Budweiser mirror that hung on Jackson's apartment wall.

He stared at his reflection. "Gonna need your help today, Lord."

For a moment he studied the man in the glass. He didn't look the same. Something different...something in the eyes maybe. He grabbed a fistful of change for the bus and studied himself once more. Yes, that was it. Something gentler in the eyes.

He wondered if Carla would notice.

An air of expectation hung over Judge Horowitz's courtroom that next Tuesday morning. Harold Finch was there early, and Hannah thought he was wearing a new suit for the occasion. It fit a bit more loosely, but its loud pinstripes, satin cuffs, and gold-plated buttons still gave him the look of a mob boss rather than a lawyer.

Matt looked relaxed as he read a stack of documents and jotted down notes.

Hannah's eyes fell on Brian Wesley. He looked freshly bathed, neatly dressed. His hair was shorter than before...and there was something different about his face.

Hannah wanted to shake him. How could he put on a front, act like someone society could live with when he was a cold-blooded killer? He'd deliberately chosen to kill Tom and Alicia. He would do it again if this jury gave him a chance. He might pretend for a while, but nothing, no one—not God himself—could ever change Brian Wesley.

Is anything too hard for God?

Hannah blinked back the Scripture and huffed out loud. Some things apparently were. Like keeping Tom and Alicia alive.

The proceedings began, and Finch was on his feet calling his first witness. Brian Wesley. Parading about the front of the courtroom, Finch established Brian's background as a faithful worker and husband, as a man troubled by a continual drinking problem. He worked his way up to the point of the collision, highlighting the fact that Brian had been sober for three weeks prior to August 28.

"Now, on the afternoon of the accident, what transpired prior to your visit to the bar?"

Brian frowned slightly. "You mean, why did I decide to drink again?"

Finch waved his hand, shaking his head. "Okay, fine, why did you decide to drink again?"

"Well, I got laid off."

"And were you depressed?"

"Yes."

Hannah held her breath, her blood all but boiling. She'd like to give both of them something to be depressed about.

Finch strutted farther from the witness stand so that he was adjacent to the jurors. His stance, his expression, it all gave the jurors the impression he was one of them…the thirteenth juror.

"So you went to the bar and had a few drinks, something to lighten your spirits, is that right?" Finch's tone was hostile and Hannah struggled to understand. Weren't they supposed to be on the same team?

Brian stared at his attorney with a strange expression, almost as if he were angry with the man. "It was a stupid thing to do. I'd been clean for three weeks, and if only I'd just gone home to Carla—"

"Just answer the question, please, Mr. Wesley." Finch didn't look pleased.…Sighing and exchanging a long-suffering look with several jurors, Finch continued. "Why did you go to the bar, Mr. Wesley? Did you go there planning to kill someone?"

Brian's face twitched slightly. "No, of course not."

"Did you go intending to hurt someone, perhaps destroy someone's vehicle in a traffic accident?"

Brian shook his head.

"Answer out loud for the court, please," Judge Horowitz said. He looked interested in the testimony for the first time that day.

"No, I didn't intend to hurt anyone."

"Fine, then let's go a little further. You sat at the bar for a certain amount of time. Do you know how long you sat there, Mr. Wesley?"

Brian shrugged. "I didn't take notes or nothing."

"Answer the question to the best of your knowledge."

"I don't know. My memory's a little hazy on it, you know?"

Finch's jaw dropped half an inch, and Hannah caught Matt's suddenly alert look. Certainly this wasn't the line of testimony Finch and Brian Wesley had practiced.

Finch cleared his throat. "I am not asking for a vivid account. I am asking you to tell this court, as best you can remember, how long you sat at the bar on the afternoon of August 28."

"Okay." Brian looked determined to come up with an answer. "I think that guy was probably right, that bartender guy. Two hours maybe."

Finch looked about to swallow his tongue. "Fine. At the end of that time, when you left the bar, did you think you were drunk?"

Hannah expected Finch to ask Brian how many drinks he'd consumed in that time. When he didn't, she figured he was starting to fear Brian's answers. She couldn't blame him. Brian's testimony was strangely unsettling.... Of course, it was favorable for the prosecution, but why on earth was he making statements that might harm his case?

Finch was waiting for an answer. "Do you understand the question, Mr. Wesley?"

Brian nodded and then caught himself. "Yes. I understand. I don't know that I really thought about it, to be honest. I drank a lot, and I wanted to get home."

"So you didn't think you were drunk, correct?"

Matt leaned forward slightly, as though he were about to object, but he waited, poised on the edge of his seat.

Brian's face grew red. "Listen, man, don't put words in my mouth."

A hush fell over the courtroom, and Finch stared at Brian, clearly stunned. In a strained voice he requested a moment alone with his client.

The jury was ushered out, and for ten minutes Brian and his attorney talked in hushed but heated tones. Hannah sat stone-still as she watched them reach some kind of apparent agreement.

"Your honor, we're ready for the jury again." Finch wiped a layer of perspiration off his forehead and shot a glare at Brian.

Hannah's head was spinning. What was happening? Why was Brian suddenly fighting with his own attorney? Then it struck her, and she leaned toward Carol. "It's an act!"

Carol considered her. "Maybe."

"Carol, come on! Don't you see it? They make it look like Finch is the bad guy, the slimy defense attorney. Brian's the guy who's trying to come clean, trying to be straight with the jury. The jury sympathizes with him, and we lose the conviction. It's all an act!"

Carol looked from Brian to Finch and back to Hannah. "Let's watch and see what happens."

The jury was back in place, and Finch's friendliness seemed forced as he phrased his next question. "Were you drunk when you left the bar that afternoon, Mr. Wesley?"

Brian leaned back in the witness stand. "I might have been. I didn't think about it."

"Okay." Finch stayed near the stand. His hands twitched at his sides, and Hannah thought he looked like he might strangle Brian if he gave anymore unexpected answers. "Did you plan to leave the bar that afternoon—*maybe* drunk—and drive your car through a red light on Ventura Boulevard?"

"No." The sadness on Brian's face pierced Hannah. It was an image that didn't fit into the category of behaviors she had assigned him. He was an animal. Animals didn't look sad.

"Did you plan to kill Tom and Alicia Ryan on the afternoon of August 28?"

"No..." Brian's voice dropped off, and when he spoke again Hannah watched everyone in the courtroom strain to hear him. "It was an accident."

Finch shot a satisfied look at the jury, dabbed at another layer of perspiration, and then turned to Judge Horowitz. "No further questions, your honor."

Matt rose slowly to his feet and studied Brian for a moment. "Did you know that drinking shots of whiskey and glasses of beer would affect your blood alcohol level, Mr. Wesley?"

"Yes."

Matt nodded and moved slowly toward the jury. He turned back to Brian. "Did you know it was against the law to drive a vehicle with an elevated blood alcohol level?"

"Yes." Brian seemed defeated and Hannah felt smugly glad. *This is just the beginning, buddy*.

"Did you sign a statement promising to never drink and drive and agreeing with the fact that to do so was to risk the lives of innocent motorists?" Matt's voice was calm, matter-of-fact.

"Yeah, I knew it."

Matt nodded again. "And you chose to do it anyway, is that right?"

"Yes. It was a stupid mistake."

"Just stick to the question, Mr. Wesley. Did you choose to do those things regardless of the consequences, yes or no?"

"Yes."

"Mr. Wesley, *Webster's Dictionary* defines *accident* as a tragic event that does not involve fault. Do you understand that definition?"

"I think so…yes."

What in the world was going on? Brian was clearly not fighting his own cause on the stand. Hannah shifted uneasily in her seat.

"Based on that definition—a tragic event that does not involve fault—can you honestly tell us that what happened on the afternoon of August 28 was an accident?"

Brian paused for a moment, and Hannah could see that he was wrestling with his answer. "No."

At the quiet admission, Hannah's mouth went dry, and her heart beat so hard she thought it might explode. Had Brian Wesley just said what she thought he'd said?

He met Matt's gaze without flinching. "Based on that definition, I can't…I can't call it an accident."

Reporters stationed along the back of the courtroom began scribbling furiously as a hum of discussion broke out among those in attendance.

"Order!" Judge Horowitz glared at the gallery. "I will not have you disrupt this court." He looked at Matt. "Continue."

"No further questions, your honor." Matt shot an amazed look at Hannah, and then returned to his spot at the table.

Finch worked the rest of the day trying to undo the damage done by Brian's admission that the crash hadn't been an accident, but it was useless. Hannah didn't know what kind of act they were playing, but whatever it was it had backfired.

If the trial ended now, Hannah felt certain they'd win their conviction.

The week dragged on with a physicist testifying that Brian's blood alcohol may have been lower than the police test showed because of the rate of alcohol absorption into the bloodstream. On cross-examination, the witness admitted that

Brian's blood alcohol may have been higher, as well.

"A waste," Matt told Hannah when court was adjourned for the day. "Nothing that'll hurt the case."

"So things still look good?" Hannah felt stronger in Matt's presence, as if being near him brought her closer to a point of healing.

"Yes." Matt patted her hand and then hesitated. "Hannah... how's Jenny?"

She started and stared at him. Jenny? She hadn't thought of Jenny in days. Weeks...

She shrugged. "I'm not really sure. Still moping, still riding her bike aimlessly around town, pretending she's a loner."

Matt sighed. "Be careful, Hannah. She's still a little girl. She needs you."

I need her, too. She blocked out the thought. "You don't understand. She's different than...than before the...than before. I can't reach her anymore."

"Okay." Matt looked troubled. "I don't mean to meddle. I'm worried, that's all." He was silent a moment. "I'm still praying for her."

Hannah resisted any overt show of doubt. She looked deep into Matt's eyes trying to understand how he could maintain his faith in light of the pain all around him. "Whatever makes you feel better, Matt."

On Thursday morning, Finch called his last witness, Carla Wesley. Hannah studied the young woman through critical eyes. Brian Wesley's wife had a good figure, but was otherwise hard and unattractive, with dark circles under her eyes.

White trash. Hannah glared at Carla as she took the stand and hated her for choosing to love a man like Brian Wesley. *Judge not, lest you be judged....* Hannah pushed the Scripture from her mind. How long would it take before Bible verses no longer flashed at her?

Finch established who the woman was and that she and Brian were no longer living together. Carla testified that she had been aware of Brian's drinking problem. Then Finch moved to the heart of the issue.

"Was Brian a violent man, Mrs. Wesley?" Finch leaned against the jury box.

"No."

"I'm sorry, I couldn't quite hear you. Could you repeat the answer?"

Carla fidgeted in her seat and glanced at Brian, who kept his gaze downward. "No. He was not a violent man."

"Was he an angry man?" Finch appeared confused, as if he were trying to solve a difficult riddle.

"No. He wasn't angry."

Finch nodded, still puzzled. "Then he must have had tendencies toward murder, is that it, Mrs. Wesley?"

Carla shook her head quickly. "No, of course not. Brian was always…" She glanced at her husband, and for an instant Hannah saw their eyes meet. "He was always a gentleman."

Hannah huffed softly. *Gentleman.* Brian and his wife were equally worthless as far as she was concerned.

Finch scratched his head. "The prosecution is trying to convict your husband of intentionally killing two people, Mrs. Wesley. You've known him many, many years. Certainly you would know if he had ever planned to kill someone. Would you say you know Mr. Wesley very well?"

Carla's eyes filled with tears, and a smudge of mascara appeared under her right eye. Her voice was choked when she answered. "Yes. I know Brian very well."

"So you would know if he had homicidal tendencies, the desire or intention to kill someone?"

Matt had been observing the proceedings passively, but now he rose to his feet. "Your honor, I object to the last question. Mrs. Wesley cannot testify as to the intentions of her husband. Mr. Finch knows that. The witness needs to stick with what she personally observed or heard him say."

Judge Horowitz nodded. "Objection sustained. Disregard the last question."

Finch paced for a moment and wound up a bit closer to Carla than before. "Mrs. Wesley, did you ever hear your husband say he intended to kill those people?"

Carla batted at an errant tear making its way down her cheek. She sniffed and shot another look at Brian. "No. Brian had a drinking problem, but he never wanted to kill anyone."

For an instant, Hannah felt a pang of empathy for Carla Wesley. Both women had lost, and neither of their lives had turned out the way they'd planned. Hannah swallowed hard and her compassion dissolved. Still, that woman had chosen to marry a creep like Brian. It was difficult to feel sorry for her.

Finch made his way back to the table. "No further questions, your honor."

Matt rose once more and nodded politely at Carla Wesley. His tone was kind. "Mrs. Wesley, did you ever warn your husband about his drinking problem?"

Carla gulped and stared at her hands for a moment. "Yes. Lots of times." She looked up at Matt again. "But he was an alcoholic. He couldn't stop drinking—" she glanced at Brian—"not even for me."

Matt nodded. "Very well. And did you ever warn your husband that if he didn't stop drinking and driving, he was going to kill someone?"

Hannah held her breath.

Carla paused, clearly unwilling to answer.

"Answer the question, please, Mrs. Wesley." Judge Horowitz sounded impatient, ready to see the testimony finished.

Carla sighed and her shoulders slumped. "Yes. I warned him."

"You warned your husband many times that he had a drinking problem, and you warned him that if he didn't stop drinking and driving he was going to kill someone. Is that right, Mrs. Wesley?"

Carla refused to look at Brian as she nodded. "Yes." Another tear fell onto her cheek. "I warned him."

Hannah shot a look at the jury and saw they were caught up in the implications of Carla's testimony. Matt cleared his throat and continued. "You warned him, but he did it anyway, is that right?"

"Yes, obviously." Carla pursed her lips and sat up straighter in the witness stand. Hannah wondered about Carla Wesley's mother. Where had she gone wrong in raising Carla to marry a man like Brian Wesley. *What about your own daughter?* Hannah was startled by the sudden question that rattled through her mind. *Jenny is fine. We'll have time together after the trial.* The voice vanished as quickly as it had come.

Matt nodded again. "Thank you, Mrs. Wesley. No further questions, your honor."

"Call your next witness." Judge Horowitz waved a hand toward Finch.

Finch rose, pausing momentarily, then, "The defense rests, your honor."

Hannah exhaled slowly. It was over. No more surprises, no more questioning. It was finally over.

"Very well then." Judge Horowitz adjusted his glasses, drew a deep breath, and directed his gaze first at Finch and then at Matt. "We will take a brief break until 2 P.M. At that time we will hear closing arguments." He banged his gavel and left through a door behind his chair.

Hannah watched as Matt sorted through a stack of documents, and Finch and Brian whispered in some sort of consultation.

"Well, this is it." Carol turned to Hannah.

Hannah massaged her temples. "I can't believe it's finally over."

Carol nodded, her eyes distant. "I remember this part." She looked sadly at Hannah. "Be careful."

"What's that supposed to mean?"

"You've convinced yourself that a conviction will bring you peace, it'll release the anger that's tearing you up. It's the answer to all the problems left behind when Tom and Alicia died."

"It's all I want." Hannah felt the beginning of tears.

"I know. That's all I wanted, too. But it took me a long time before I found the secret to having peace in my life again."

What was she talking about? Didn't she know how much Hannah's head was pounding? How confused she was already? Hannah didn't need this. "It's no secret, Carol. When that animal is locked up, Tom's and Alicia's deaths won't be in vain."

"But there won't be peace."

Hannah was silent.

Carol reached out and took Hannah's hand in hers. "And even a conviction won't bring Tom and Alicia back."

"Don't you think I know that?" She had fought the front line of this battle, and now they had almost reached a victory. There would always be sadness, but a guilty verdict would bring Hannah peace no matter what Carol said. Immediate, perfect peace.

Carol's eyes were so sad Hannah wanted to weep. "Okay. But if you still feel empty when it's all over, I'll be here."

"The only way I'll feel empty is if Brian Wesley walks out of this courtroom a free man. And personally, I don't think that's going to happen. Now let's change the subject before you ruin my day."

Twenty-nine

They mock me in song all day long.

LAMENTATIONS 3:14B

Closing arguments were about to begin, and for the first time all week the jury looked wide-eyed and attentive. An air of excitement buzzed through the courtroom as reporters speculated and spectators recounted evidence in the case. If history were going to be made in Judge Horowitz's courtroom, they wanted to remember every detail. Especially the lawyers in attendance. Someday it would make for great storytelling: the case that changed California drunk driving laws forever.

Matt spoke first, reminding the jurors of Brian's history of drinking and driving. He moved quickly to the day of the accident. "No one wants to get news from the boss that he's been laid off." He walked slowly back and forth in front of the jurors, meeting their intent gazes. "Mr. Wesley packed up his things, loaded his truck, and headed for the road. That's when he made his first choice. He could have gone home. Instead he went to the bar."

Matt stopped and leaned against the railing. He walked the jurors through Brian's every movement that afternoon, emphasizing the choices Brian had made: the choice to go to the bar, the choice to drink, the choice to get drunk, the choice to drive home, the choice to ignore warnings from Carla, the state, and finally the bartender.

"Brian Wesley made deadly choice after deadly choice. Regardless of his history." Matt stared at Brian for a moment, and Hannah watched the jurors do the same. Matt faced them again. "Brian Wesley signed a document agreeing that to make those very choices was to risk life. He knew his choices were deadly." Matt paused. "He told you so himself."

He told you so himself. Hannah closed her eyes, and suddenly she was sucked back to a moment, decades earlier…it was Tom's mother saying those words, days after he proposed to her.

Hannah had been fretful that afternoon. "I don't know, Mrs. Ryan, he spent so long loving that other girl…"

Tom's mother had set a plate of warm cookies on the table and motioned for Hannah to sit. "Oh, no, dear. He never loved her like he loves you, not for a moment."

"But how can I know he really loves me?"

"Hannah, dear, you know he loves you. He told you so himself."

Told you so himself…told you so…told you so…

If there had been a way back—a river to swim, a bridge to cross, an ocean to sail—she would have taken it. She would go back to that warm, Southern California afternoon when she and Tom's mother were speculating about the future, and she would start over again. Relive every day, every minute with Tom. And Alicia. And Jenny. The way everything was before. And when it came to that terrible day last August, she would stop time.

If there was a way.

Hannah felt the sting of tears, and she opened her eyes reluctantly. Matt was still speaking, and she chastised herself. She had to pay attention. It was Brian Wesley's final hour. After this she would have peace. Finally.

Matt's voice was deliberate and intense. "I want you to close your eyes for a moment. Go ahead, close them." He waited until the jurors did as he asked. "Okay now. I want you to imagine three people you love dearly are in a vehicle…coming home from a summer camping trip." Matt waited. "Can you see them? See their smiles? Hear their laughter, hear the fish tales and the retelling of campfire stories? Can you see them?"

Matt walked silently across the courtroom and stopped in front of Hannah. He held out his hand wordlessly. She nodded, reaching into a bag she'd brought for this moment. Inside were two photos. One of the Ryan family, taken the Christmas before the collision. The other of Tom and Alicia. She handed them over to Matt and watched him carry them carefully back to the jury.

"Keep your eyes closed, please." He began pacing again, this time staring at the photos of Hannah's family. "Coming the other direction is Brian Wesley. A man with so many drunk driving arrests the system's nearly lost count. A man who by drinking and driving has already caused two traffic collisions. A man who has signed a statement—signed a legal document—agreeing that for him to drink and drive again could very likely result in death. His or someone else's. A man who has been warned, over and over again. A man who knows that the gun he's wielding is loaded."

The courtroom was so quiet Hannah wondered if everyone could hear her beating heart.

Matt continued, his voice softer still. "Can you see him? Guzzling fourteen drinks over a two-hour span, stumbling out of the bar and heading toward his pickup truck? Can you hear Nick Crabb asking him to wait for a cab? Listen, now. Hear him swear at this young, inexperienced bartender. Can you see him storm out of the bar? Hear his tires squealing as he peels out onto Ventura Boulevard?"

Matt stopped and stared at the jurors, who sat with their eyes still closed. "This is a man who has chosen to drink and drive despite the risks, despite the potential for death. Can you see him behind the wheel, eyes barely open?"

Matt's words came faster now, louder, his tone more urgent. "Now picture your loved ones again, getting off the freeway, their car loaded with camping gear, almost home. They head for the intersection—the same intersection Brian Wesley is about to plow through. Your loved ones move through that intersection at the exact same instant—" Matt stopped, and when he spoke again, his voice was heavy with sorrow. "And in that moment, those three people you love so much are obliterated by an impact as severe as a freight train. One of your loved ones is dead before she ever knew what happened. Another is dead minutes later. The third, alive…but forever devastated."

Hannah was barely aware of the tears sliding down her cheeks. She watched as Matt drew close and leaned against the railing so that he was only inches from her. "You can open your eyes."

The jurors did so but instead of looking at Matt, they stared at Hannah.

"You have not met Hannah Ryan. She has nothing to add to the testimony in this case. But if those had been your loved ones killed by Brian Wesley's speeding truck, if that were you sitting there—" he gestured toward her—"where Hannah's sitting, would you think it was an accident? No. You'd think it was intentional murder. First-degree murder."

Finch squirmed in his seat.

Matt held up the pictures and stared at the faces of Hannah's family once more. Then he looked back at the jury. "It's up to you."

The jury strained to see the photos, and Matt moved closer, positioning them so each of the twelve could study the smiling faces, frozen in a moment that was gone forever.

"It's up to you to open the door. Pave the road to a new California, a place where people will think twice before drinking and driving. A place where people like Brian Wesley won't have a chance to load up and shoot because they'll be behind bars.

"You hold the keys, and I ask you—" Matt turned the photos so he could see them once more—"I beseech you on behalf of Tom and Alicia Ryan, on behalf of young Jenny Ryan and her mother, Hannah. I beg you on behalf of your own loved ones who deserve safer streets. Please...return a guilty verdict. What Brian Wesley did to Hannah Ryan's family was not an accident. Let's stop calling it one. Thank you."

Finch wasted no time. He struggled to his feet, coughed, adjusted the buttons on his vest, cleared his throat. Papers rustled in his hands. Hannah realized he was doing everything he could to break the mood Matt had masterfully created.

He smiled at the jurors and gestured toward them as if they were family gathered for a summer reunion.

"Now you folks are a lot smarter than the district attorney might think." He smiled broadly, dabbing quickly at the perspiration on his forehead. "The good D.A. asks you to close your eyes and imagine. I never heard of anything so ridiculous in all my life." Finch shook his head disdainfully and leaned his belly over the railing, propping himself up on both elbows and looking hard at the jurors. "How dare the district attorney ask you to close your eyes in this case? I will ask you to open your eyes. Open them wide. Look at the defendant."

Twelve pairs of eyes shifted toward Brian Wesley. Hannah scowled at him through narrow eyes, hating the way he hung his head. Only a worthless human being would try to look humble now. She gritted her teeth. He was detestable. Certainly the jury could see that much.

Finch smiled at Brian, and when it was obvious there would be no eye contact between attorney and client, Finch turned back to the jury. "He's not a killer." The attorney searched the faces of the jurors. "You needn't fear him in dark alleys like some hardened criminal. Mr. Wesley is an alcoholic. He needs help. Your help."

Finch paused and raised an eyebrow. "You know, what happened to Brian Wesley could have happened to you. Drink a few too many, wind up in a tragic accident." He straightened his arms, rising several feet above the jurors. "But that doesn't make you a killer, anymore than it makes Mr. Wesley one. He made a series of poor choices. But Brian Wesley did not set out on the afternoon of August 28 to kill two people. The prosecution has not proven that in this courtroom. They have not proven that Brian Wesley chose to kill that day. No. He didn't set out to kill. He just wanted to get home."

Finch moved away from the railing and adjusted his vest buttons. "He was a guy down on his luck who drank a few too many, a guy who wanted to get home. It was an accident, folks. We feel for the family, the victims. But that doesn't change the facts. Brian Wesley never intended for anyone to die. And murder one means a person must intend to kill. Please, folks—" Finch gripped the railing with both hands and once more leaned toward the jury, his voice filled with passion—"Vote with your heads and not your hearts this time. You convict Brian Wesley of murder one in this case, and the next person serving a life sentence for drunk driving might be someone you love. It might even be you."

Finch was finished, and it was time for Matt's final rebuttal.

"What we are talking about here is the repeat drunk driver." He stopped and faced the jury, clearly concerned. "You don't have to worry about serving life for drunk driving unless you're a repeat drunk driver, careening headlong toward a fatal collision."

He waited and Hannah held her breath. "But there is something you and your loved ones do need to worry about. And I ask you today, as you begin wading through the details of this case, please, worry about it. Worry about leaving here and getting on the streets in a state that allows a man with a string of drunk driving arrests and revoked licenses and alcohol-related traffic collisions—a state that allows a man like Brian Wesley—to be on the road when he should be behind bars."

Matt moved closer to the jury box. "And something else. Mr. Finch told you Brian Wesley was not a man to fear." Matt glanced at Hannah, and the jury followed the direction of his gaze. "To tell you the truth, men like Brian Wesley scare me more than convicted felons. I can avoid the places a convict might hang out. But Brian Wesley? I might be coming home from a fishing trip, chatting with my family, and boom! The people I love most are dead." Matt raised an eyebrow and shook his head. "Laws being what they are today, I can't avoid a man like Brian Wesley. And *that* scares me."

Matt leaned against the railing and folded his arms. "Mr. Finch wants you to think of Brian Wesley as someone down on his luck, just trying to get home. Well, that's all the Ryan family was trying to do. Three days in the mountains, end of summer, school's about to begin. They were coming home."

He faced the jury squarely and slid his hands into his pockets. His voice was strong, but Hannah thought his eyes looked damp as he continued. "What happened to Hannah Ryan could happen to me—" he met their eyes—"or you. Any day. Anytime. Anywhere. Remember, there are two reasons why Brian Wesley should be convicted of first-degree murder. The first is to punish him. He took a weapon, in this case a pickup truck, and made a choice to use it under the influence of alcohol. That's intentional murder, and it must be punished as such.

"But the second reason is just as valid. The second reason is to protect people like Hannah Ryan. People like you. It's time, friends, please. Find Brian Wesley guilty of first-degree murder, and let's put an end to this madness now. Before it's too late."

The judge finished giving instructions, and the case was handed over to the jury. After just two hours the foreman notified the clerk.

They had reached a decision.

Thirty

He has broken my teeth with gravel; he has trampled me in the dust.

LAMENTATIONS 3:16

Because of the late afternoon hour, Judge Horowitz determined that the verdict would be read at 10 A.M. the next day. The moment Matt heard the news, he was on the phone to Hannah. A quick verdict wasn't good.

"So fast? What does it mean?" Hannah sounded frantic, and Matt's heart went out to her.

"It could go either way." He wanted to be honest. "But usually...quick verdicts wind up in favor of the defense."

Hannah was silent for several seconds. "*What?* That's impossible!" Matt could see the fury that would be in Hannah's eyes as clearly as if he were standing in front of her. It made him wish he'd told her the news in person so he could take her in his arms and comfort her.

"Remember, Hannah, we had the burden of proof. Brian is innocent until proven guilty, and usually it takes longer to study the evidence and determine guilt. Usually."

"Then we'll have to appeal, find a loophole. Something. He has to pay for this, Matt. He can't just—"

"Hannah, I didn't say he was acquitted. I just wanted to warn you. There's a chance. A good chance. We took a gamble in this case and didn't leave the jury much choice. All or nothing."

Hannah made no response, and Matt could hear her quietly sobbing.

"Hannah? Are you all right? I can be there in five minutes if you need me." Matt almost hoped she'd say yes.

"No." She gave two quick, jerky breaths and steadied her voice. "I'm okay. I have to talk to Jenny. She's…she's been in her room all evening."

Matt felt Hannah's heartache as though it were his own. He had to resist the urge to ask once more if she needed him. He wanted to be there. Wanted to help her. But he didn't ask it. He didn't want her to mistake his intentions. Not now. He changed topics instead. "I'm still worried about her."

"Jenny?" Hannah drew a weary breath. "I think she'll be okay. She's just hiding out until the trial's over. When I have peace, she will, too."

Matt sighed. "Hannah…what if the verdict…" He couldn't bring himself to finish the sentence.

"Don't, Matt. Please. I simply can't imagine the what-ifs. It's late and it's been the longest week of my life. My daughter hates me, and after tomorrow I have to put this behind me and get on with making a life for the two of us. Right now I have no choice but to believe that tomorrow you will win your conviction, and finally—" her voice broke once more, and she sounded beyond tired. "Finally, I can have peace."

Matt tapped a pencil on his dining room table and searched frantically for the right words. She wouldn't have peace. He knew she wouldn't. But there was no point trying to convince her. Not right now. "Get some sleep, Hannah."

She laughed, but there was no hint of humor in her voice. "Are you kidding? With Jenny upstairs pouting and the verdict sitting in some sealed envelope down at the courthouse? *You* sleep, Matt. I'll see you tomorrow."

"Okay, but if you're going to be awake anyway, at least pray, Hannah. Please. Jenny needs your prayers."

"She doesn't need prayers, Matt; she needs her daddy and her big sister." Hannah sighed and the emotion drained from her voice. "And not even your God can give her that."

Matt cringed. *Lord, give me the words. Hannah's your child. Jenny, too. Help them, Lord.*

When he remained silent, Hannah drew another deep breath. "I'm sorry, Matt. I don't mean to take it out on you. You've been wonderful through this whole thing. I could never have climbed into that legal ring and duked it out with Finch like you've done. You were my only weapon in the biggest fight of my life."

"That's why God brought me into the case."

Hannah paused. "God has nothing to do with it. He checked out months ago. August 28, I think it was."

Matt could almost see the bitter root strangling everything beautiful in Hannah Ryan. But there was nothing he could say. "Enough. Good night, Hannah."

"Night, Matt." She hesitated. "See you tomorrow."

He clicked the off button on his cordless telephone and set it on the kitchen counter. Hannah Ryan. He wandered to the cupboard, pulled out a glass and filled it with ice water. What would become of her after tomorrow, when she learned that peace wasn't something one could buy with revenge? Win or lose, tomorrow night Hannah would be as unsettled as today. Maybe more so.

The glass was cool against his hands. He wandered into the living room and settled into a leather recliner. He pressed the drink to his face. Hot, hazy, summer days. Why had the Lord put Hannah in his life, anyway? And what would happen if they lost this case?

He surveyed his empty house. Normally after a day in court the solitude brought him peace. Today, for some reason, it made him feel lonely and old. Television didn't help, so Matt turned in early and pulled out his newest copy of the Bible—a clothbound, men's edition. Matt did not keep a well-worn copy of the Bible in his house. He liked reading the Bible through, marking it up as much as possible, and then starting fresh with another copy.

He fell asleep reading Philippians 4, somewhere between the peace that passes understanding and doing all things through Christ who gives strength. But he didn't dream of Paul and his profound letter.

He dreamed of Hannah Ryan.

Hannah studied her bedroom as she hung up the telephone. It had been nearly a year, and Tom's Bible was now packed away with his other things. Only a picture of them taken on their tenth anniversary remained on the dresser. The clutter Tom had always tossed there had long since been cleared. There were none of the keys and coins and receipts that had collected there each week while they were married.

Tom was gone. The room was proof.

She stood and stretched. Her bones were tired, but she wasn't particularly interested in sleep. Besides, the last few nights she'd woken at all hours with the most frightening nightmares. Hannah shuddered. There was no point dwelling on the dreams now. She had business to take care of.

Tiptoeing upstairs, Hannah tried to work up her courage. Anymore it was an amazing feat to get two words out of Jenny, and nights like this Hannah was almost too worn out to try. She knocked at the door.

"What?"

The girl didn't sound angry. She didn't sound anything. After tomorrow they could start working on their tattered relationship, but how long would it take? Months? Years? "Can I come in?"

Silence.

"Jenny? I want to talk to you." Hannah allowed the wall to hold her up as she closed her eyes. "Open the door, Jenny."

Footsteps, then Hannah heard a click. Jenny opened the door a crack, but by the time Hannah looked inside, she was already back on her bed, staring at the ceiling, eyes hollow.

Hannah pulled up a chair and sat down, facing the girl. For a single moment she remembered their old life, when she would climb into the girls' beds with them, snuggling and giggling and making girl-talk long after bedtime prayers. Now there was only awkwardness between them, forcing Hannah to keep her distance. She settled into the chair and tried not to think about it.

"The trial ended today." Hannah waited and for an instant there was a flicker of something in Jenny's eyes. Concern? Interest? Whatever it was, Hannah knew she had caught the girl's attention.

When Jenny said nothing, Hannah felt her frustration begin to grow. "Did you hear me?"

Jenny didn't roll her eyes or sigh as she had done so often lately. Instead she leveled her gaze at Hannah. "Yes, Mother. I heard you."

There was no point waiting for Jenny to ask questions. She wouldn't. Hannah set her chin. "It went well, I think. Matt did a great job presenting the case. But there's still a chance Brian Wesley will be acquitted. We'll know tomorrow."

Jenny stared at her mother blankly.

"I thought you'd like to come. Tomorrow, I mean. I know you haven't wanted to be there before. But it is the verdict, after all. If we win, I want you to be there."

Jenny's face twisted. "If we *win?* Mother, listen to yourself! No one's going to win tomorrow."

"If Brian Wesley goes to prison, we will win. It's that simple."

Jenny sat up in bed. "No, it's not that simple...." She looked like she was about to say something else, but apparently changed her mind. Shoulders slumped, she began picking at her bedspread. "Never mind."

Hannah leaned forward, trying to get up the courage to touch her daughter, to pull her into a hug. Anything to bridge the distance between them. "Things will be different after tomorrow." Silence. "You have to understand, Jenny. After Daddy and Alicia were killed, I didn't know what else to do. I had to fight. Tomorrow Brian Wesley will be taken into custody.

Where he's belonged since he did this awful thing to us."

Jenny looked up, and Hannah was shocked to see that her little girl had the eyes of an old woman. "You honestly think a guilty verdict will make things different? Between us?"

"I know they will, honey. The battle's almost over." She hesitated. "Just this once, could you come to the trial with me? Please, Jenny."

Jenny shook her head quickly. "No. I won't go. I told you that." Her voice was panicky, and Hannah drew back.

"Okay, forget it. I just thought…after all this time…oh, never mind." Hannah stood up and headed for the door. Her heart felt like a dead weight within her.

"Mom…"

Hannah spun around. In that instant, in that one single word she heard the Jenny she'd lost, the one she hadn't heard since they'd said good-bye in the driveway the day they left for the camping trip. The one that never made it home. Hannah searched her daughter's eyes, but she wasn't there. When Jenny spoke again whatever Hannah had heard was gone. The indifference was back.

"Nothing."

"Tell me, honey."

"It's nothing, Mom."

"Jenny…it's been so long since we've talked. Really talked." Hannah hated the awkwardness between them. She paused, desperately trying to think of the right words. "I'm here. Let me know when you're ready."

Jenny's eyes were blank and she didn't nod. Instead she lay down, turned her back to her mother, and faced the wall.

The rejection was more than Hannah could bear. "Fine. Turn away."

"Get out, Mother. I'm done talking."

If that's the way you want it, Jenny… Hannah stared at her, and in a voice so frigid it was foreign even to her, she spat one final sentence at her daughter: "Thanks a lot, Jenny, and oh, yeah, I love you, too." Hannah stormed out of the room, her heart pounding, her eyes dry.

That night as Hannah fell asleep, she realized she had no one to love, no one who loved her. Somehow she had died without anyone noticing. Her corpse was still breathing, but she was dead. As she tossed and turned, battling relentless, unseen, torturous demons, she wondered how it was, someone could love God most of her life and still wind up in hell.

Sgt. Jon Miller was having trouble falling asleep, but not because of unseen demons. Lately he'd been bothered by the accident…the one from a year ago. He had convinced himself it was the testimony. Acting as a witness for the prosecution had brought up memories he'd almost forgotten. The young teenage girls, one dead when he arrived on the scene…and the man, Dr. Tom Ryan. And especially that scene in the car when the man was trying to speak his final words.

He couldn't for the life of him understand why that particular memory kept making its way into his mind. He had done as the man asked, passed on his final message for his surviving family. Sgt. Miller turned in bed and saw that his wife was sleeping soundly. He sighed. His eyes were open, but all he could see was Dr. Tom Ryan, trying to speak, struggling to form those final words.

Tell Hannah and the girls he loved them. That was it, wasn't it?

Miller rolled over onto his other side and shut his eyes. Maybe he should get up and read his Bible. God's promises always helped him fall asleep. He flipped so that he was flat on his back. He was about to pray when he heard the voice.

Remember the rest.

Miller's eyes flew open and he sat up straight in bed. Had he imagined that or had someone actually spoken? He glanced about the room, but nothing had changed. He released the air from his lungs slowly. Sinking back into the pillows he felt his heart race. Must have been a dream. Maybe he was falling asleep after all. He closed his eyes. *Lord, thank you for letting—*

Remember the rest.

His eyes flew open and he shot up once more. His eyes sought his wife, but she was snoring. He propped his pillows and leaned back, heart racing, searching the room for the source of the message. *Remember the rest?* The image appeared again, Dr. Tom Ryan, bleeding to death, trying to gurgle out the last part of a farewell.

Could that be it? Was there something more to his message?

Suddenly the image cleared, and a realization came over Sgt. Miller so strong that he could feel his nerves calming, his heart rate returning to normal.

Dr. Ryan had said *two* things, not one. Tell Hannah and the girls he loved them and…and something else. Something that hadn't seemed very important at the time.

Now if only he could remember what.

Thirty-one

I have been deprived of peace; I have forgotten what prosperity is.

LAMENTATIONS 3:17

They met in a thicket of trees just outside the courthouse some two hours before the verdict. Neither of them wanted to be seen together. Especially praying together.

Heads bowed, voices soft, they lifted their direst concerns to the Lord. Finally, they thanked him for whatever he was about to do. It was getting late, and there were people moving in and out of the courthouse. They sat on opposite sides of the bench, silent.

"Are you nervous?" She studied him. This might be their last conversation outside prison walls.

He shrugged. "It was a quick verdict. Could mean an acquittal." His eyes stayed down and he picked nervously at the rough skin around his fingernails.

"You don't look happy."

He shot her a quick glance. "I'm not."

She nodded. That was understandable. A person could be spirit-filled and still be unhappy.

"In some ways I wanna serve time." He drew a shaky breath. "If they let me walk…I'll never be able to face her."

"You're not in control here, Brian."

"I know, I know. We've been talking about it, me and the Lord."

"Just do what's right. God will take care of the rest."

He looked at his watch. "I have to meet my lawyer."

She stood and gathered her purse. "I'll be praying."

Jenny's hands trembled as she sat at the breakfast table. It was verdict day—for Brian Wesley and for her. She stared at the soggy cornflakes in front of her, but she could see her mother, darting about the kitchen, grabbing gulps of black coffee. She was reading something, probably newspaper articles about the accident and the victim impact panels. Her life's passion.

"What are you doing today?" Her mother set her coffee cup in the sink and glanced at Jenny.

Mom was obviously still mad about last night, and suddenly Jenny was sorry she'd been rude. It would have been nice to be at peace on their last morning together.

She took another bite of cornflakes. "Nothing."

Her mother waited, impatient to leave. "Fine. I'll tell you how it went when I get home. Not that you care."

Jenny watched her grab the car keys from the counter and head for the garage. No kiss. No good-bye. She listened as her mother drove off, and then she trudged upstairs, shoulders heavy, heart empty.

It was time.

After all the planning, it was finally time. She pulled the box from beneath her bed and examined the contents once more. Pills. Water. Good-bye note.

Not that you care.... Not that you care.... Her mother's words haunted her, but she shook them off. She did care. Not about the trial, but about Daddy and Alicia. It would only be a few hours now until they were together. If only she'd hugged her mother or said good-bye. Two lonely tears slipped from her eyes and landed on her bedspread.

Sniffing loudly, she dried her eyes and sat up straighter. There was no time for regrets now.

She had to get busy.

It was almost time. Hannah felt as if she'd waited her entire life for this moment. The courtroom was filled with people spilling into the hallways, straining to get a view of what was about to happen. Hannah took in the scene as it unfolded. Brian and Finch huddled at one end of the table; Matt and his assistants at the other.

Matt had met her downstairs earlier and assured her that if Brian was acquitted on first-degree murder charges, the state would see that he served the maximum time for drunk driving. It was the least they could do.

"Don't talk like that," Hannah said. They stood against a wall, facing each other in a quiet corridor near his office. Their voices had been hushed and inches separated them.

"Hannah, you have to be realistic. What if they come back with not guilty?"

She didn't hesitate. "I'll kill him myself."

"Hannah…"

"I'm serious."

He had sighed and pulled her into a quick hug. "Let's go. It's time."

That was an hour ago.

Carol Cummins leaned over and whispered to her. "If anyone can pull this off, it's Matt Bronzan."

Hannah nodded. "He's worried."

Carol studied Matt for a moment. "You'd never know it."

A hush fell over the courtroom as Judge Horowitz entered and took his seat. The moment of the verdict had arrived.

The judge glanced around. "I see that there are a great number of people interested in the outcome of this trial. I warn you, matters will be conducted in a quiet manner. I will not allow my courtroom to become a media circus." He banged his gavel. "Court is in session. Will the bailiff please bring in the jury."

The bailiff moved toward a door on the side of the courtroom, disappeared for a moment, then returned with the jurors in single file procession behind him. The jurors took their seats.

The pills were calling her, beckoning her to a better place where she and Alicia and Daddy could spend eternity together. She opened the water and picked up three orange capsules. *Please, God, let this work.* She slipped the pills into her mouth and took a swig of water. For a moment Jenny thought she was going to gag, but then she took another swig and felt the pills go down.

There were dozens of pills on her bedspread. She picked up three more capsules, and this time they went down easier. She reached down and found three more. Swallow. Three red. Swallow. It was easier than she'd thought. Before she knew it, the pile was gone. She had done it.

Now all she had to do was wait.

Matt watched the jury file in and take their places.

The judge looked at them. "Has the jury reached a decision?" Matt glanced at Hannah and saw that her eyes were closed, her hands clenched tightly. His heart constricted. *Father, I'd do anything to give Hannah the peace she so desperately seeks. Help her, please.*

The jury foreman stood up. "Yes, your honor."

"Very well. Please hand the verdict to the bailiff."

The foreman did as he was told, and the bailiff carried it to Judge Horowitz. He read it silently, his expression unchanging. He leaned over and handed it back to the court clerk. The judge looked about the courtroom. "The clerk will now read the verdict."

A petite brunette in her late fifties stood, her mouth near

the microphone. She unfolded the verdict and cleared her throat.

A strange feeling was working its way through Jenny's body. She felt her heart beat erratically. Her hands shook…then her arms…finally every part of her was trembling violently.

Was this it? Was this death?

The room started spinning and all the edges blurred together.

"I have come that they may have life…I have come that they may have life…I have come…"

Scripture filled her mind—bringing doubt with it.

Suicide was murder. Wasn't that one of the Ten Commandments? *"Thou shalt not kill.…I have come that they may have life…"*

Jesus didn't want her to take her life. Daddy, either.

She needed to get to the bathroom. Someone online had told her if she took the pills then changed her mind, her only hope was to vomit. *Get up!* But her legs would not obey. She stuck her finger down her throat and gagged, but nothing came up.

Jenny beat her stomach with her fists, willing her body to reject the pills, but they sat like a ball of poison in her belly. It was getting harder to breathe. She had tricked herself into thinking this was the answer when it was really no answer at all.

It was a lie straight from the devil. And now it was too late.

The court clerk was reading and Hannah hung on every word.

"We, the jury, find the defendant, Brian Wesley, guilty of the crime of drunk driving." She paused and prepared to read the second verdict. "We, the jury, find the defendant, Brian Wesley, guilty of the crime of first degree-murder against Tom Ryan and Alicia Ryan."

Tears flooded Hannah's eyes, and her hands flew to her face, providing the only privacy in a room where suddenly all attention was focused on her.

They'd done it! They'd won the verdict. Brian Wesley would spend the rest of his life in prison. Matt had been brilliant. The evidence had been glaringly obvious. That's why the verdict had come so quickly.

We won! We won! Guilty! We won…we won. The words ran through her mind, over and over. Every panel, every hour of research, every meeting with Carol, all of Matt's hard work…it all had paid off. It was the victory she'd waited for all year, and now it was time to celebrate. Brian Wesley was going to prison. Murder one. History-making murder one.

Her hands remained spread across her face, and she heard herself weeping now, louder and louder. She felt Carol's arm come around her shoulders, and she struggled to gain control. Dimly she heard Judge Horowitz banging his gavel, calling for order.

She had pictured this moment a hundred times. She'd imagined she would jump up and congratulate Matt, look at the jurors and silently thank them for making the right choice, then proceed to the cameras for a series of interviews.

Instead, she was consumed by the greatest heartache she had ever known.

It was her grandest moment—the moment of justice and peace—but not one of the people she loved was there to share it with her.

If this is peace, how will I ever tolerate a lifetime of it?

Jenny was dizzy. She lay back on her bed and began to cry, but she only heard the deep, raspy sound of her body gasping for breath.

No! Please, no! Her mind screamed the words, but her mouth no longer worked. Suddenly she remembered something from one of the Internet sites. You know it's working if your fingernail beds begin to turn blue. She held up her hands, steadying them, straining to see them as the images blurred. It was impossible to tell, but she thought she saw the deadly blue there.

She gasped once more, but black spots blocked her vision. Suddenly all she wanted to do was sleep.

Please, God. I want to live. I want...

Her thoughts faded. She could no longer feel herself trying to breathe.

Two seconds later, she was unconscious.

Matt released the air from his lungs slowly. "Thank you, God." He turned to face Hannah.

The entire courtroom had erupted into conversation, but his eyes were fixed on her alone. She was hunched over, head buried in her hands, weeping. She needed him, and in that instant he felt an attraction for her that went far beyond the scope of the trial. He chided himself for the feeling. *Must be the intensity of the moment.* He started to rise from his seat, then remembered the proceedings were not officially finished. He sat back down, his neck craned, his eyes still on her.

Poor Hannah. He had won, but not her. She had lost everything. Not even this verdict could change that.

The judge banged his gavel. "Order! Order in the court."

Gradually the people who filled the room and much of the corridor outside fell silent once more. Judge Horowitz gave each of the jurors the opportunity to affirm their verdict. Then he continued with final instructions.

"The bailiff will take the defendant into custody until such time as his sentencing hearing, which will take place two weeks from today in this courtroom at ten in the morning. At that time—" he looked at Brian Wesley—"the defendant and the victims will have an opportunity to speak. That is all for today. Court dismissed."

He banged his gavel one final time, and Brian Wesley stood to face the bailiff. Cameras captured the moment as handcuffs were snapped onto Brian's wrists, and he was led away.

It was the first time Matt had been able to look into Brian's eyes since his testimony days earlier, and what he saw there was surprisingly familiar. Peace. Brian looked content, ready to take his punishment. Matt stared, stunned, and suddenly he knew Hannah's concerns had been warranted.

Brian Wesley had the eyes of a believer.

Matt turned toward Hannah and saw that she was still sobbing. He watched her hands drop, saw her eyes follow Brian as he was led away. He didn't want her to stay around the courtroom. She needed to be home with Jenny. *Get her home. Now!* The urging impelled him from his seat.

"Matt..." She stood up and hugged him, gripping his neck and burying her head in his shoulder.

"Shhh...it's all right. It's over now." He knew the cameras were on them and he pulled away, studying her face. The hatred was still there. And the bitterness and a dozen other emotions with the exception of one: peace.

A reporter made his way over and stood between them. "What's your reaction to the verdict, Mrs. Ryan?"

She straightened and wiped her cheeks with her fingertips. "I think it's wonderful. The streets will be safer when we can be confident about convicting repeat drunk drivers of first-degree murder."

"And what about Mr. Wesley? Do you think he deserves the full sentence, life in prison?"

Matt watched Hannah's eyes narrow, and he cringed at what was coming.

"Yes. He deserves a life sentence. And then he deserves to rot in hell."

Hannah was barely aware of her surroundings as she drove home. She had expected to feel something...elation, excitement, the thrill of victory. *Something*. But as she turned into her driveway she felt strangely numb. Exactly the way she'd felt before the verdict. She glanced in her rearview mirror and saw Matt pull in behind her. He had talked her into going for lunch, but he thought they should tell Jenny the news first.

Together they walked up to the house.

Matt waited while Hannah turned the key. "She can come with us if she wants."

Hannah huffed as she opened the door. "Good luck. Jenny doesn't do anything that involves me these days." She headed for the stairs. "Jenny?"

No answer.

"She must be sleeping. Wait here, I'll wake her and tell her the news." Hannah trudged up the stairs. She had a throbbing headache and couldn't wait for the day to end. She entered the hallway and headed for her daughter's room.

"Jenny, I'm home." Again, no response. She was wasting her time. Jenny wouldn't care, anyway. She turned the doorknob to the room, but it was locked.

Hannah sighed impatiently. "Jenny, it's me. Wake up."

Nothing. Hannah banged on the door.

"Jenny, come on." She was shouting now, angry because she knew her daughter was ignoring her.

"Jenny...open the door this instant! Do you understand me?"

Silence.

Suddenly Hannah heard voices from the corner of her memory....The principal...*"I don't know, Mrs. Ryan, under normal circumstances a girl like Jenny would never consider suicide...but now..."* Then Matt...*"I'm worried about her...you don't think she'd try anything crazy, do you?"*

Terror seized her and she grabbed the door, rattling it frantically. "Jenny, open up!"

Twisting the knob roughly, she pushed her shoulder into the door, but it held. *God, no. Please…*

"Matt!"

He was at her side in seconds. "What—"

"Jenny's locked in there! She won't answer. Open it, Matt. Whatever it takes, just get it open!"

"Jenny, this is Matt Bronzan! Open the door, okay?"

When there was no response, he gently pushed Hannah aside. Then in a single, quick motion he jammed his shoulder against the door, and it flew open. Hannah followed him into the room, and they saw her. Sprawled out on her bed, her skin gray, pills scattered on the floor beside her. At the foot of the bed lay a box with a note on top of it. Matt picked it up, read two lines and dropped it. Instantly he grabbed Jenny's wrist.

"What's wrong with her?" Hannah screamed. She bent over Jenny, shaking her.

"I can't find a pulse!" Matt grabbed Hannah's shoulders. "My God, Hannah, call an ambulance!"

Thirty-two

So I say, "My splendor is gone and all that I had hoped from the Lord.*" I remember my affliction...the bitterness and the gall. I well remember them, and my soul is downcast within me. Yet this I call to mind and therefore I have hope: Because of the Lord's great love we are not consumed.*

Lamentations 3:18-22

Sometime between watching Matt perform fifteen agonizing minutes of mouth-to-mouth resuscitation on Jenny, and hearing paramedics radio the hospital to inform them a suicide-attempt was coming in; sometime between reading Jenny's suicide note in the ambulance, and authorizing doctors at the emergency room to pump her daughter's stomach, Hannah began doing something she hadn't done in nearly a year.

She prayed.

Not that she'd had some deep realization that God was real or that his promises were true. Rather she had simply reached the end of herself, of everything she knew about coping.

Her prayers were pure, desperate instinct.

An hour after arriving at the emergency room, Hannah was still uttering the same silent prayer as she sat in the waiting room on a cold, vinyl sofa, Matt at her side. *Please, Lord, please let her live. Don't let her die, God, please.*

Thirty minutes passed before Hannah heard purposeful footsteps.

"Mrs. Ryan? We need to talk about your daughter."

Hannah lifted her head, stared at the doctor, and gasped.

Dr. Cleary. The same doctor who had told her the news about Tom and Alicia.

She screamed then. *"No!* Not again! Get away!" She bolted up from the sofa and pushed the doctor out of her way. "Not Jenny! *No!* No more!"

She was screaming, struggling to make it to the doorway, when she felt two firm hands on her shoulders.

"Let me go!"

"Hannah—"

"Nooooo!" People were watching, getting up and moving their small children away, but Hannah didn't care. She would not hear the same news about Jenny that she'd already heard about Tom and Alicia. She needed space, needed air, needed out. Anywhere else. She struggled to break free, but now the arms eased firmly around her waist, holding her fast.

"Go away, Doctor! Let me g—" She spun around, and suddenly the fight was gone.

It was Matt. "Matt…"

"Shhh. It's okay. Calm down."

She sagged against him, gasping for air. No matter how many breaths she drew in, she couldn't get enough oxygen. Her words came in short, choppy spurts. "Tell…the doctor…to go…away!"

"Hannah, blow the air out." Matt pulled a few inches back and spoke to her gently, slowly. "Come on…do it."

Something deep within Hannah knew she needed to obey him. She pursed her lips and blew out a puff of air that wouldn't have flickered a birthday candle.

"Again…several times…come on, Hannah, sweetheart." She sank into him, exhaling three times without taking a breath. *Please God…*

Matt met her gaze. "There…better?"

She nodded, but tears filled her eyes as she looked up at him. "Stay with me?"

He nodded and gently led her back to where Dr. Cleary was

waiting. Matt's arm was wrapped tightly around her shoulders, supporting her.

"Let's go in another room." Dr. Cleary started to turn.

"Wait!" Hannah was frozen in place. For an instant her eyes connected with Dr. Cleary's. She had to know. "She's dead, isn't she?"

Dr. Cleary reached out and touched the side of her arm. "No, Mrs. Ryan, she's not dead." He looked about the waiting room and saw that they were alone. "Tell you what, let's sit down right here."

Matt and Hannah sat back on the sofa, and Dr. Cleary sat across from them. His eyes narrowed with concern. "Mrs. Ryan, Jenny's in a coma. She was very nearly successful in her attempt to take her life, and we know she was without oxygen for some period of time." He hesitated and looked at Matt. "Are you the one who performed CPR on her?"

He nodded.

"It saved her life." His gaze came back to Hannah. "But she's still in critical condition. Things could go either way."

Hannah gulped two quick breaths. "What…what does that mean?"

"Breathe out," Matt whispered, and she obeyed.

"Comas are unpredictable." Dr. Cleary shook his head slightly. "She could come out of it today, or not for twenty years. Also there's a chance she may have suffered some brain damage."

Hannah couldn't breathe. She gulped huge breaths of air, but it didn't matter. Matt was telling her something, but she couldn't hear him. She was growing faint…"No…can't be…Not Jenny…It's all my…all my…all my fault…"

Matt caught her as she fell, then she passed out.

Hannah slowly opened her eyes. She was lying on a narrow cot with bright lights glaring at her. She felt woozy, her eyelids heavy…and she wanted to close them. She glanced around.

Where was she?

Sterile bandages were stacked on a nearby counter, and there was a chart on the wall detailing various views of the human ankle before and after injury.

Then it came back in a rush. She was in the emergency room, and Jenny was somewhere lying in a drug-induced coma. Fear gripped her.

God…please, no! She sat up too quickly and rubbed the back of her neck. This can't be happening. Tom and Alicia, dead. Jenny lying in a coma from a drug overdose. She needed to find Jenny and wake her up. She thought of the girl's suicide note. *You've been too busy….You lost everything that matters….I'm just in the way….You can only walk around a museum of memories for so long….You don't want me talking about Jesus….Sometimes I think I miss him as much as I miss Daddy and Alicia….This is the only way…*

A powerful desire swept Hannah then. She wanted to be on her knees, in a chapel. She didn't understand it, didn't question it. Just felt the sense as it filled her to overflowing. She looked around. She needed a chapel.

Before she could get her feet on the ground, Dr. Cleary appeared. "Hannah, how're you feeling?" He came alongside her and took her pulse.

"I need to go—"

"That's fine. Your vitals are good."

"How's Jenny?" Tears filled her eyes and spilled onto her cheeks.

"The same."

"Matt? Mr. Bronzan…did he go home?"

"No. He's upstairs with Jenny. Sitting by her bed. He told me about the verdict. I've been following it in the papers. I know it must have been very hard for you." Dr. Cleary paused. "We're doing our best to make sure the media doesn't find out about this."

Hannah nodded, tears blurring her vision as she stared down at her leather heels. She was still dressed in the same skirt and blouse she'd worn for court. Had the verdict been only that morning?

Dr. Cleary interrupted her thoughts. "It was the right verdict."

She nodded again, silent.

"Listen, Mrs. Ryan, I've asked the hospital social worker to stop in if you'd like to talk. You've got a lot to deal with…"

Hannah shook her head, but she made sure her tone was kind. "I already have a counselor, Doctor, if you'll give me permission to go talk to him."

"Here, at the hospital?" He looked confused.

"Yes." Hannah's head was clearing quickly. She sat up straighter, determined. "May I go?"

"Is he expecting you?"

Hannah nodded. "Yes. Can you tell me how to get to the chapel?"

With every step she took, Hannah knew with increasing certainty that God was, indeed, expecting her. She knew it because he was speaking to her.

He'd done so before; she knew it. But she'd closed her mind, her heart. Now…now her heart was shattered, decimated on the rocks of her rebellion and anger. Now her defenses were gone, and all that was left was brokenness…contrition…

"I have loved you with an everlasting love…"

Yes. Oh, yes…I know…

Still, a hundred thoughts battled for position in her mind, both accusing the Lord and assaulting him with questions. *Why? Why if you loved me? Why if you loved them? Why us? Why when so much of life lay ahead? Why, Lord?*

The questions came as steadily as the click of her heels on the hard linoleum floor. She was still angry with God, but by the time she reached the chapel, she was absolutely certain that he knew that. God was listening. He had never stopped. He was as real as the nightmare that had become her life.

"Come, let us reason together..."

I'm coming, Father, I'm coming...

She pushed opened the chapel door and crept inside. Twelve empty, cushioned pews filled the room, and gentle lights shone on a single object at the front. Hannah moved slowly down the center aisle, her eyes fixed straight ahead.

It was not an ordinary cross, but a life-size one of two rough-hewn wooden beams roped together in the center. It stood there, a challenge to anyone who doubted the depth and height and breadth of Christ's love.

A challenge to Hannah.

Tears flooded her eyes, and she took two steps closer.

She had forgotten about the cross. Oh, it was there on the gold chains people wore at the grocery store, emblazoned across an occasional bumper sticker or novelty T-shirt. But this cross—this symbol of pain and suffering, this weapon of splintered wood and iron stakes slicing into the Lord's back, ripping through the flesh in his wrists and feet, this reminder of how the Savior gasped for air and asked the Father to forgive his killers—this cross would forever show the world what Hannah had forgotten until now.

Jesus loved her.

She stopped in front of the cross.

"He was...a man of sorrows...familiar with suffering....He...carried our sorrows...the punishment that brought us peace was upon him, and by his wounds we are healed."

She closed her eyes, not even trying to stop the tears. Peace. She'd sought it for so long and so hard, and it had been here all along.

"We all, like sheep, have gone astray, each of us has turned to his own way; and the Lord has laid on him the iniquity of us all..."

Reaching out, Hannah ran her fingertips over the splintery

surface of the cross. Anyone who would die that kind of death for her, had to love her. That truth struck her to the core.

Hannah's knees went weak with the force of the sorrow that washed over her. She had suffered much this past year, but it had been worse because she had exchanged the truth about God for a lie. She had rejected any comfort or solace or hope that the Lord would have offered, choosing instead to fight her battles alone. By doing so, she had built an icy fortress of self-pity around her heart, shutting out God and Jenny and anything but her desire for revenge.

The cross towered above her, the beams as thick around as her waist.

She stared up and imagined the Lord looking down at her, forgiving her for walking away. And finally, in that moment, the sorrow was more than she could take. She wrapped her arms around the cross and wept, loud, inconsolable cries for forgiveness. Slowly, humbled by the weight of her sin against God, her arms slid down the rough, wooden beam until she lay in a heap at the foot of the cross.

Jesus had not stopped loving her when Tom and Alicia were killed. Life took place on the enemy's ground. And the enemy would always allow drunk driving and senseless murder and evildoers like Brian Wesley.

But there was more to the battle, and for a season Hannah had forgotten. Yes, this world was Satan's domain, but God had already won the war. The enemy was no longer a threat to Tom and Alicia, for they were celebrating in the very presence of the living God. Tom and Alicia had only been on loan in a place that was never meant to last forever.

Our citizenship is in heaven.... The words were a physical comfort to Hannah as one after another Scriptures filled her mind. She was only passing through, a foreigner in a strange land. Like all who followed Christ, whether she walked this planet eight years or eighty, it was only a journey. She wouldn't ever really be home until she reached heaven's doorsteps.

She wept then, remembering the times she had rejected Jenny this past year and how she had allowed the girl to stumble through the most difficult time in her life with neither her support nor God's.

"I'm sorry, so sorry, Father. Please, don't punish her for my sin..."

When her weeping finally eased, she prayed—and it was as if she'd never stopped, as though there'd never been a distance between her and God.

She was restored. By God's grace and mercy, she'd been restored.

Lord, I'm sorry. I don't deserve her. But please, if it be your will, please...please let her live. She sniffed loudly and ran her fingers underneath her eyes. *Come, Holy Spirit. Please come to me. And whatever happens, Father...Thy will be done....*

Suddenly she had an overwhelming desire to read Scripture. She let go of the cross and rose to her feet, then made her way into one of the pews and opened a Bible. She fanned past the Old Testament, through Matthew and the gospels and on into Revelation.

What did one read after being away from Scripture for an entire year? *Lamentations.* It was as though Carol Cummins was sitting beside her, whispering in her ear. *Read Lamentations.*

Nodding, she flipped back into the Old Testament until she found the book written by the prophet Jeremiah. All year Hannah had resisted Carol's advice to read this book. Now she devoured the words.

Her eyes filled with tears once more when she reached the second chapter. *"The Lord is like an enemy...my eyes fail from weeping, I am in torment within, my heart poured out on the ground because my people are destroyed...you summoned against me terrors on every side...he has turned his hand against me again and again...he has made my skin and my flesh grow old...*

Hannah thought of how her eyes had changed, how her features had grown hard and sour, how even the guilty verdict had not brought her peace. She bowed her head.

"I can't take anymore, God...Please...let her live."

"Hannah."

The voice came from behind her, and Hannah spun around, wiping at her tears.

"Matt...what is it?" She grabbed the Bible and moved to meet him in the aisle.

He took her hands in his. "It's okay. It's Jenny." His eyes shone with joy, and Hannah's heart leapt. "She's awake, Hannah. She's calling for you."

"Oh, dear God, thank you!" Hannah hung her head and cried. How was it possible for one person to produce so many tears?

Matt pulled her close and stroked her hair. "It's okay, Hannah. Come on...Jenny's waiting."

She nodded, her face against his shirt. Then, the Bible still clutched to her heart, she walked with Matt back to her daughter.

Jenny looked tired but alert, and Hannah rushed to her side, gently setting the Bible down near the girl's feet. "Jenny, honey, are you all right?"

Matt stood on the other side of the bed, his voice kind and concerned. "She hasn't said much. Just 'Mom.' Dr. Cleary said that was normal."

Hannah lowered her face so it was closer to Jenny's. "Oh, Jenny, I'm so sorry, honey. I've been awful...it's all my fault."

Jenny swallowed and cleared her throat. "No."

"Honey, don't try to talk. You need your rest." Hannah stared into her daughter's eyes and smoothed a wisp of bangs back off her forehead. "I love you, Jenny. Things are going to be different. I'm so sorry. I want us—"

"Mom..." Jenny's voice was hoarse. "Not your fault..."

Hannah wanted to tell Jenny to rest, to sleep, but she could see the girl had more to say.

"I wanted…to be with Daddy…and Alicia."

"I know, sweetheart, I know." She rested her head on Jenny's chest, holding the girl close. "I'm so sorry, honey…"

They stayed that way a long time, until finally Hannah straightened and once again stroked Jenny's blond bangs. "I understand, sweetheart, really. We'll get help. For both of us. Things are going to be different."

Jenny nodded and her eyelids lowered. "At the end…I prayed. I wanted to live, Mom. Really. I love you."

Hannah wrapped her arms around the girl and held her close, whispering into her hair. "Thank God…thank God you're alive."

Jenny's eyes opened again, and her gaze was questioning. "God?"

Across the room Matt grinned at Hannah. "God?"

Hannah's eyes glistened with old and new tears. "Thank God Almighty. I told you things were going to be different."

Jenny's eyes filled with light, as if God, himself, had breathed new life in them. "Mr. Bronzan says you won."

Hannah looked deep into her daughter's eyes. "Not really. Not 'til about an hour ago."

Jenny nodded. "I'm glad he's guilty." She glanced at Matt and then back to Hannah. "I'd like to go to the sentencing…if that's okay with you."

Hannah felt her heart soar. Not because Jenny wanted to attend the sentencing, but because the girl was alive. And because after all that had happened, her daughter still loved her.

Two hours later, Matt had gone home and Jenny was sleeping. Dr. Cleary had evaluated Jenny and determined that her recovery had been utterly miraculous. Judging by her vocabulary and clarity of thought, the girl was in the process of making a complete recovery.

It was late, nearly ten o'clock, and the nurses had prepared a reclining chair where Hannah could spend the night. Now, with the lights dim and the hum of machinery confirming the fact that Jenny was alive and well, Hannah returned to Lamentations.

Chapter 3 showed the prophet's change of heart. He was no longer lashing out at God, accusing him. She read, curious—and suddenly her eyes stumbled onto something that made her catch her breath.

"I remember my affliction...and my soul is downcast within me.... Yet this I call to mind and therefore I have hope:...Because of the Lord's great love we are not consumed, for his compassions never fail....They are new every morning; great is your faithfulness."

It was her hymn. She'd known it came from the Bible, but until now she hadn't realized where. No wonder God had placed this book on Carol's heart, knowing that therein lay the words to Hannah's favorite song.

The melody ran through Hannah's mind, and she wept anew. Jenny was here, alive and well. They had their entire future ahead of them, and Brian Wesley was about to spend the rest of his life in prison. Indeed, God's compassion would never fail her, his mercies were new every morning. Especially today.

Hannah found even more hope at the end of the third chapter: *"You have seen, O Lord, the wrong done to me. Uphold my cause!...Pay them back what they deserve, O Lord, for what their hands have done...."*

Hannah closed her eyes. God loved her and forgave her. He was going to help her. Brian Wesley was the enemy, the one who had wronged her. Now God would uphold her cause and see that Brian Wesley paid.

She closed the Bible and stared at the ceiling. She could hardly wait for the sentencing.

Thirty-three

You have seen, O LORD, the wrong done to me.
Uphold my cause!…Pay them back what they deserve,
O LORD.…And may your curse be on them!

LAMENTATIONS 3:59,64–65

It happened on the twenty-second straight night of dreaming about the accident.

At four-thirty in the morning, hours before the sentencing of Brian Wesley, Sgt. Miller finally remembered.

The moment he did, the sergeant's mind was released from what had seemed to be a holy vice grip. Like a modern-day Jonah, he had a message to relay to Hannah Ryan—and the sooner he did so, the sooner he could get on with his life.

He climbed out of bed, showered, and found his place at the dining room table. He wrote the note quickly, making sure to capture every detail.

Then, for the first time in three weeks, he drank his morning coffee in peace.

The cameras were back in full force for the sentencing.

History had been made in the state of California, as evidenced by the articles and editorials that had filled the newspapers every day since the verdict. The facts were in place. Now it was time to capture the feelings.

Hannah and Jenny sat in the first row beside Carol Cummins. Hannah surveyed the front of the courtroom, watching for Brian Wesley. Fourteen months had passed since he had mowed down her family, taken Tom and Alicia from her—finally she would look in his face and tell him how she felt about his actions that day. Her scrapbook sat in a bag at her feet.

From what she'd read in Lamentations, Hannah was sure God would fight this battle for her. She had a right to her anger. If the prophet Jeremiah could rail against a wrongdoer without showing forgiveness, then so could she.

Jenny slipped her hand into Hannah's and squeezed. "Love you, Mom."

Hannah's eyes locked onto Jenny's, and she pulled her daughter close, gently kissing the side of her head. "Love you, too, sweetheart. Thanks for coming. You didn't have to."

Jenny nodded and shifted uncomfortably. "I know. I wanted to."

Hannah hugged her again and remembered earlier that morning. They had awakened at six o'clock, dressed in shorts and T-shirts, and headed for the middle school track where they walked three miles. It was a routine they'd started when Jenny got home from the hospital, and Hannah treasured every step they took together. That morning, Jenny talked about the collision and finally admitted to Hannah that she felt guilty.

"Alicia had so much going for her, Mom," Jenny said as they powered around the track. "It should have been me who died."

"The truth is…you *both* should have died." Hannah was breathless, but she wanted to make a point. "Jenny…the only reason you lived…is because God has great plans for you. You're a miracle, honey."

They walked in silence for a length, and then Jenny surprised her. "It's good to hear you talking about God again."

Back at home, they shared breakfast and spoke little about the hearing. Hannah could sense Jenny's uneasiness, and several times she assured her daughter that she didn't have to go. Hannah could hardly believe she had berated Jenny so badly for not attending the earlier hearings. It was one of many areas the Lord had shed light on since Jenny's suicide attempt.

Hannah would be grateful as long as she drew breath for this second chance with her daughter.

Judge Horowitz entered the courtroom, drawing Hannah's attention back. She sat up straighter and wondered again why she still didn't feel complete peace. She frowned. She could understand why the verdict hadn't brought her peace…but neither had her restored relationship with the Lord.

She felt a gentle prodding. *Hannah, listen to me…*

She recognized his voice, the same sweet calling she'd relied on all her life before the accident. *What is it, Lord? What else can I do?*

Maybe God wanted her to listen closely to the hearing. Maybe after Brian was sentenced she would finally realize that perfect peace—the peace that passes understanding.

After all, this was her chance to face Brian Wesley before the court. She would tell him about Tom and Alicia. Then, when he was hauled off to prison fully aware of how much he'd taken from her…then she would have peace. Wasn't that the message of Lamentations?

Jenny glanced over and smiled weakly. "It's almost time."

Hannah's eyes locked onto the back of Brian Wesley's head. "It's something I have to do." She turned to Jenny. "You understand, right?"

Jenny hesitated, and Hannah saw how much she'd aged in the past year. She was not the carefree girl she had been when they pulled out of the driveway that summer day so long ago. Brian Wesley had taken that, too.

"Yes, Mom. I understand. I'll be praying for you."

The judge banged his gavel twice. "Come to order." He hesitated a moment, glancing at the docket before him. "We will proceed with the sentencing of Brian Wesley, who has been found guilty of the crime of first-degree murder in the deaths of Tom and Alicia Ryan.

"First, I want to state for the record that I have received a pre-sentence probation report on the defendant. Because of his history of alcoholism and driving under the influence, the probation department is recommending the maximum sentence, to be served concurrently with alcohol rehabilitation. The department advises that at such a time as Mr. Wesley should be deemed cured of his alcoholism—"the judge raised his eyebrows skeptically, then cleared his throat and continued—"At that time the department suggests Mr. Wesley should be released at the soonest, most reasonable opportunity."

Hannah tried to make sense of that and glanced at Matt. His eyes told her it was okay, and that was enough.

"Also, I have a letter from—" the judge sorted through a stack of papers until he found what he was looking for—"the defendant's ex-wife. She asked that I read it for the record and I will do so now."

He held the sheet and read:

> *"'Dear Judge, My name is Carla, and I was married to Brian Wesley for many years. I am raising his son. I saw Brian drink a lot in our marriage, but he never raised a hand to me or our boy. He was not a bad man, even though he drank. I know what he done is wrong and he should be punished. But I would appreciate it if you would be kind and give him the least many years in prison as you can. Things are over between us. Little Brian won't never know his Daddy.'"*

Hannah watched Brian hang his head. She huffed lightly and angry thoughts fought for position. *Good. Grieve. I hope the boy forgets you ever existed. You deserve every moment of heartache.*

She couldn't wait to tell him so.

Hannah, listen to me….

What? I don't understand, Lord. I'm listening as hard as I can.

The judge finished reading and paused. "Under the California Victim's Rights Act, I will now allow any victims who are present to speak."

Matt rose to his feet. "Mrs. Hannah Ryan would like an opportunity, your honor."

"Very well, let the record reflect that Mrs. Ryan, a victim, will be speaking next."

Hannah wanted to ask the Lord for strength, but it felt strange. She frowned at the odd feeling and instead squeezed Jenny's hand and met Carol's eyes. Then she reached for the scrapbook, headed for the witness stand, and took her seat.

She stared at Brian and realized it was the first time she'd seen his face during the proceedings. Her eyes narrowed, and she saw Brian struggle beneath her gaze. A movement caught her eye, and she saw Matt cross his arms and study something on the floor.

Hannah adjusted the microphone and stared at three pages of typed notes. Her anger was so intense it might well have been a visible shield about her.

Careful, Hannah. The warning seemed strangely out of place, and she ignored it.

She drew a thin breath. Her hands trembled, and she steadied the letter before her. "More than a year ago my husband, Tom, and my two daughters, Alicia and Jenny…left home for their annual camping trip. It was something they did every year at the end of summer. They were coming home on that August day when—"

Suddenly a sob lodged in Hannah's throat, and she lifted her eyes to meet Brian's. For a moment all she wanted to do was spit at him or slap him or knock him down. She wanted to hurt him physically the way he'd hurt her. She caught a tear on her fingertip and continued. "They were coming home when you killed them. You didn't care about who they were or where they were going when you killed them. So now I'll tell you who they were. Because I think you need to know.

"Tom was…" This was harder than she'd thought. She gulped and swiped at more tears. "He was the love of my life. We grew up side by side and thought we'd be…together forever."

Hannah glanced up; Brian was staring at his hands.

"Look at me!" She leaned forward, clutching the stand. She wanted to cross the distance between them and—and—

Her heart pounded as she recognized the truth. Her anger was about to explode into a fit of rage. She had to gain control, to say these things with dignity. She released a single breath and relaxed back into her seat, regaining composure as quickly as she had lost it. When she spoke again the anger was there, but it was contained once more. "I asked you to look at me, Mr. Wesley. You owe me at least that."

When he met her eyes, she paused, then flipped through her scrapbook and held up a photo of Tom. She spoke, not in a voice of sorrow, but of seething, carefully managed fury. The tears came in streams now, and she gave up fighting them. "Tom was all I ever wanted in a man. He was…he was my best friend."

She turned to another page and held up a portrait of Alicia. "You killed my little girl, too. My precious firstborn." She looked up and met Brian's gaze. "You wouldn't know anything about someone like Alicia—" Hannah glanced toward Jenny—"Or my other daughter…Jenny. Because people like you, selfish alcoholics who think nothing of taking a life…people like you don't have anything in common with people like my girls." She looked down at her notes and then back at Brian. "Alicia was beautiful, inside and out. She would have done anything for anyone and usually she did. You killed her and…"

That was as far as she got. She began sobbing. Unable to hold back the sorrow, she put head down in her hands.

She didn't know how long she sat there, weeping, but when she felt someone at her elbow, she lifted her head and saw Matt with a box of tissues. He placed a supportive hand on her shoulder and squeezed gently. Hannah met his eyes and nodded.

Sitting straighter, she sniffed and blew her nose. There were things she needed to say, and she had to say them now, to Brian Wesley's face, or she would spend the rest of her life angry at missing the opportunity.

Peace. After this I'll have peace. She glanced at the judge. "I'm sorry."

Judge Horowitz nodded, his eyes compassionate. "That's all right, Mrs. Ryan. Please continue."

Hannah nodded and swallowed. Then she caught Brian Wesley's eyes once more and finished. "You killed Alicia, and any children she may have borne. You killed her family… because of—of your selfish choice. You killed her future." She shuffled pages until she was staring at the third page. "I no longer have a husband. I no longer have my oldest daughter. And my youngest daughter, Jenny—" tears coursed down her face but she continued—"Jenny has suffered severely because of this. She will not have her sister to share the future with.…She will not have a father to walk her down the aisle when she gets married."

Hannah looked up and found she still had Brian's attention. "For a long time I hated God because of what you did. Now I know I was wrong about that. This wasn't God's fault, it was yours." She was nearing the end, and she leaned forward again, spewing hatred with every word. "You…you are a despicable human being. Worthless…hopeless…heartless…without any concern for the lives of those around you."

Hannah, Hannah, Hannah…

What was the Lord trying to tell her? Why now? Hannah pushed the thoughts away. Whatever it was, she would have to worry about it later.

When she continued, her voice was slightly more controlled. "Today, before this courtroom, I am asking Judge Horowitz to hand down the stiffest, most severe punishment he can legally assign. You are an animal, a ruthless, cold-blooded killer who will kill again and again until someone locks you up."

She drew a trembling breath, and when she spoke again her voice was a snakelike hiss, each word pronounced with increasing rage. "I hope you rot in hell, Mr. Wesley. Because I will never…"

Hannah!

"—ever…forgive you for what you took from me."

Brian hung his head. Hannah collected her scrapbook and excused herself from the witness stand. *There.* She had done it. But instead of the peace she had hoped to feel, she felt choked by the same emotion that had strangled her since the accident: merciless, bitter hatred.

Thirty-four

Moreover, our eyes failed, looking in vain for help;
from our towers we watched for a nation that could not save us.

LAMENTATIONS 4:17

When Hannah said she wanted Brian Wesley to rot in hell, Matt linked his hands and lowered his head until it was resting on his fingertips. *Lord, this can't be what you want from Hannah. Help her, please. The anger is going to kill her.*

He let go a heavy sigh and leaned back in his chair, knowing there was more to come.

"Are there any other victims who wish to speak?" Judge Horowitz looked to Matt, and then Hannah.

"No, your Honor." Matt rose briefly and then sat back down. Brian Wesley was next, and Matt had a sudden urge to join Hannah, to put an arm around her and steady her. He couldn't explain it, but he was sure she wasn't going to like what Brian Wesley was about to say.

"Very well." The judge turned to Finch. "Would the defendant like to speak on his behalf?"

"Yes, your Honor." Brian Wesley made his way slowly to the witness stand. He hung his head and didn't look up until he'd been sitting for several seconds. He had no notes.

Dressed in jailhouse orange, his hair poorly cut, his body bent and rail thin, Matt thought the man looked the part Hannah had assigned him. A cold-blooded killer. A criminal who didn't care who he hurt. But there was something in Brian Wesley's eyes....

Brian lifted his head and searched the courtroom until he

found Hannah, and Matt held his breath as Brian began to speak.

"Mrs. Ryan, I agree with everything you just said. You're right. It was all my fault, and I deserve my punishment."

Matt glanced once more at Hannah; she looked like a human fortress, arms crossed, body back against her chair, eyebrows lowered suspiciously.

Please, Lord...

Brian continued. "I am worthless, despicable, and untrustworthy on the streets of this city. But there is one thing I'm not. And that's hopeless." His gaze didn't waver. "What I did was terrible and wrong, and before these witnesses today I want you to know I'm sorry. I'm sorry, Mrs. Ryan, really—" his voice broke—"if I could change it, I would. If I could go back..."

As Matt watched and listened, he had the surest sense that Brian Wesley's remorse was genuine. He looked at Hannah... did she see it, too? No, one side of her upper lip lifted, and she laughed without the slightest trace of humor.

Brian went on, undaunted. "I can't go back, Mrs. Ryan. But I am sorry. I'll be sorry every day, the rest of my life. But I do have hope because of someone I met after my arrest...someone who's here today. She told me about Jesus and how his blood had already paid the price for my horrible sins. I gave my life to him, Mrs. Ryan."

Hannah's face lost all its color, and she looked frozen in icy shock.

"That woman told me Jesus loved me even though I killed your husband and daughter. But she told me something else. She told me it was right for me to serve time here, now. In this life. I done the crime, and now I need to do the time. She's been the best friend I could ever have hoped for. You know her. Carol Cummins."

Matt watched helplessly as Hannah was cut by the truth. After today Carol would be on Hannah's hate list as well—and it would take all Hannah's time, all her energy, and what was left of her beauty to tend to the bitter root that was even now spreading through her heart. His eyes shifted and fell on Jenny. She, too, looked stunned as she hung on to her mother's arm.

Brian rattled on about the virtues of Carol and how she had brought him a Bible and led him to the Lord, but Hannah was barely listening. *Carol Cummins?* The woman she had confided in nearly every day since the collision? Carol was…the enemy? Hannah turned in her seat and glared at Carol.

Carol sighed and spoke in a whisper. "I'm sorry, Hannah. I wanted to tell you—"

"Don't talk to me!"

The same sense of shock she'd felt when she first learned of the collision hit her again. Her entire world was suddenly upside down, and she wanted to grab Jenny's hand and run from the courtroom.

Brian Wesley was talking to her again.

"I may be in prison for the rest of my days, Mrs. Ryan, and it serves me right. But believe me, I am a new man because God used Mrs. Cummins to change my life forever." He paused and kept his eyes on Hannah's. "I am sorry, Mrs. Ryan. I'll be sorry for the rest of my life. And I don't blame you if you never forgive me."

Brian finished, and Hannah had a hard time making her mouth work as she whispered to Jenny, "I'll be in the hall." The judge dismissed them for a fifteen-minute break, but Hannah was out of the courtroom before he finished speaking.

Matt watched Hannah go. The moment he was free, he left the courtroom and found her staring out a dusty window, her arms crossed.

"Hannah—"

She spun around. "Were you in on this, too? This…this

betrayal with Brian Wesley?"

Matt wanted to pull her close and soothe away the shock, but not with reporters lurking nearby. He held her gaze and shook his head. "I knew nothing about it."

She wrapped her arms around herself and turned back toward the window. Her voice was a strangled whisper. "How could she?"

He had an answer, but not one Hannah was ready to hear. "Come on, let's get back. It's been almost fifteen minutes."

When they returned, Matt saw that Carol was gone. He wondered if the two women would ever speak again.

They took their seats and waited.

Less than a minute later, Judge Horowitz returned and shuffled through a slight stack of papers. "I have reached a decision—" he looked up and met Brian Wesley's gaze—"young man, you have made some very poor choices in your life, and they resulted in a first-degree murder conviction. It is up to me to decide whether you should serve twenty-five years or longer for your crimes.

"I considered the letters for and against you, listened to arguments in which people asked for the minimum sentence and the maximum. Before I read the sentence, I want you to know that I based my decision primarily on your history of drinking and driving. I believe you cannot be trusted with standard alcohol treatment programs or promises to stay away from the wheel of a car. I believe you are a dangerous and very real risk to this community. Because of that, I hereby sentence you to serve fifty years in the state penitentiary."

There was a rustling throughout the courtroom as the news sank in. Judge Horowitz had made legal history; he'd sentenced Brian Wesley to the longest prison term ever handed down for deaths by driving under the influence.

Matt glanced at Hannah and saw she and Jenny hugging. He could tell by the way Hannah's shoulders shook that she was crying. It was everything she had hoped for. A murder-one verdict and a record-breaking prison sentence. And yet…

Hannah looked more heartbroken than ever. *Please, God, help her…*

"Order…" The judge frowned at the crowd. "Order! Immediately!" He returned his gaze to Brian. "With time off for good behavior, it is possible you will be up for parole in fifteen years, but not sooner. That is all. Court dismissed."

Hannah knew the reporters were waiting. This was her big moment, the chance to tell the world thank you. She had won in every possible way except the one that really mattered.

Tom and Alicia were still gone.

And now there was something new that grieved her nearly as much as the loss of her family. If Brian Wesley was telling the truth, if Carol had indeed betrayed her and led him to the Lord, then no prison could contain him now. If he was a Christian, then he was saved by the blood of Christ, heaven-bound and free indeed. He might live a season behind bars, but he would spend eternity in a mansion. Worst of all, one day when Hannah was reunited with Tom and Alicia…Brian Wesley, the man she'd come to hate with a driving passion, would be there, too.

It was the greatest injustice of all, and more than she could stomach. Carol's betrayal felt like a javelin piercing her midsection. Jenny had to be feeling the same, but she hadn't spoken a word. Maybe she didn't understand the implications of what Brian had said.

The courtroom buzzed with activity, and Jenny leaned against Hannah. "You did good, Mom. He won't hurt anyone else."

Hannah squeezed her daughter's hand and dabbed at her tears. She kept her eyes forward and watched while the bailiff came for Brian and led him away. This was it. The moment of peace.

But it didn't come.

Instead Hannah felt strangled and angry and tired and betrayed.

Brian wasn't in prison. She was.

She led Jenny into the hallway and answered a handful of questions from the media. Then she caught a glimpse of Carol leaving the courtroom. She must have sneaked back in before the sentencing, and now she was trying to get away without speaking to Hannah.

She thanked the reporters and turned to Jenny. "Honey, I need to talk to someone. Why don't you go wait over there with Mr. Bronzan." She pointed to where Matt stood in the doorway of the courtroom, talking with several spectators.

Jenny nodded and moved toward Matt. Ever since learning how he had saved her life, Jenny had opened herself to him. Now, just two weeks later, the two were fast friends.

Once Jenny was safely in a conversation with Matt, Hannah raced down the hallway. Carol was about to board an elevator. "Wait!"

Hannah expected Carol to be embarrassed, ashamed of what she'd done. Instead when Carol turned, her expression held no apologies. She waited while Hannah quickly closed the distance between them.

They stood face to face, and Hannah felt her eyes fill with tears. "Is it true?"

Carol did not blink. She nodded solemnly. "I had to, Hannah."

Hannah had fought so long and so hard she had little energy left for this battle, but somehow she summoned anger from the shards of her broken heart. She did not scream or rant, but there was venom in her voice. "You were *supposed* to be my friend."

"This isn't the time…" Carol started to turn back toward the elevator.

"Wait a minute! Don't tell me this isn't the time. You're the one who broke my trust."

Carol sighed. "I don't expect you to understand, Hannah. Not now, anyway."

Hannah's hands flew to her hips. "I'll *never* understand. I poured my heart out to you. I thought you were on my side."

Carol stared at Hannah, clearly puzzled. "Are you so far gone, Hannah, that you don't remember the very basic truths of the faith?"

She stared at Carol. What on earth was she talking about? "Don't give me a sermon—" she waved her hand toward the window—"there are a million people out there looking for a savior, Carol. And you had to give the good news to Brian Wesley? *Brian Wesley?*"

"I gave it to the person God asked me to give it to." Carol hesitated. "After my husband died, I gave a Bible to the man who killed him. It was the only way I could finally let go and forgive. I've been giving Bibles to drunk drivers ever since."

Hannah was stunned. "From your office at MADD?"

"No. From my office at Church on the Way. I head up the prison ministry there."

Carol might as well have punched her in the stomach. "Well, maybe you should have told me sooner so I could be prepared. Hearing Brian Wesley give you credit for his *conversion*—" Hannah spat the word—"was like getting news that Tom and Alicia had been killed all over again."

Carol sighed. "I'm sorry you feel that way. All I can tell you is my concern for you was, and is, genuine. Usually I don't get involved with victims, but Sgt. Miller thought…oh, never mind. I never meant to do anything that would hurt you."

Hannah was speechless. "How did you think I'd react? Surely you didn't expect me to fall facedown in the courtroom and praise God over one sinner repenting of his way. That man killed Tom and Alicia. He is a worthless human being."

Carol's reply was so soft Hannah barely heard it. "Not to Jesus."

She clenched her teeth. "I have nothing else to say to you.

You...You betrayed me. You're on his side, not mine." She leveled bitter eyes at Carol. "I hope heaven is a big place because I want to live eternity without ever seeing you or Brian Wesley."

Hannah didn't wait for a reply as she left Carol standing there. She found Jenny and bid Matt good-bye.

Matt looked concerned. "You okay? Want me to come with you?" Hannah smiled through her tears. At least he was genuine. He was the only friend she had, he and Jenny.

"That's all right." The reporters were gone, and she leaned toward him, wrapping her arms around his neck and resting her head on his chest. They had been through so much over the past year, she almost felt like she'd known him a decade or more. "Thank you, Matt. I'll never be able to repay you for what you've done."

He pulled away and searched her eyes. "Would it be okay if I took you and Jenny out for dinner? It'd be a shame to stop spending time together now. Besides...I want to talk to you about Carol."

Hannah laughed bitterly. "After the past month I'd say we better make it dinner once a week." She thought of Jenny and her voice grew serious. "I don't know what I would have done without you."

Jenny moved closer and hugged Matt's waist. "Me, too, Mr. Bronzan. After I took the pills I prayed God would save me and he did. He sent you."

When she and her daughter left the courthouse minutes later, Hannah had a strong feeling something was missing. She checked her purse and found her car keys and her sunglasses. Then it hit her. She had expected to feel a sense of relief, to walk out of the courthouse that day a different woman. And in that light something was indeed missing. Hannah felt fresh tears as she realized what it was.

It was peace.

Thirty-five

Restore us to yourself, O LORD, that we may return;
renew our days as of old unless you have utterly rejected us
and are angry with us beyond measure.

LAMENTATIONS 5:21–22

The plain white envelope lay on her front doorstep, tucked neatly under the welcome mat. Jenny had already gone upstairs to change clothes when Hannah spotted it and sighed. She didn't know if she had the energy to pick it up. The day had been long, and she felt strangely defeated. The sense of victory and accomplishment had never come, and the peace she had so desperately sought had turned out to be as elusive as justice was.

She stared at the envelope. *Advertising.*

Yet as she moved into the house, something made her stop and pick it up. She slit it open and gently removed the letter. It was simple, less than a page. Hannah began to read.

"Dear Mrs. Ryan, My name is Sgt. John Miller. I worked the accident scene the day your husband and daughter were killed. I came to your house with the news that day, and later I talked with you at the hospital. You may not remember me, but I remember you. For the past several months I've been thinking about the accident almost as if God wanted me to remember something."

Hannah's heart beat faster. *What was this? Why now?*

"This morning, I remembered what it was. I was with your husband in the minutes before he died, and he wanted me to give you a message. He wanted you to know he loved you and the girls—"

Hannah closed her eyes and remembered Dr. Cleary telling

her Tom's final words. Tears stung her eyes and she read on.

"—but there was something else. And that's what I finally remembered this morning. At the time it didn't make sense, and I figured he must have been hallucinating or suffering the effects of blood loss. But now I am convinced that I need to deliver his message to you in its entirety.

"Tom told me to tell you to forgive, Mrs. Ryan. He wanted you to forgive."

Hannah's eyes locked on the word, hearing it as Tom had spoken it years ago when Hannah was mad at the boy who beat her at basketball…and again years later when Tom reminded her there was no victory in holding a grudge against the girl he nearly married, no gain in hating her.…

"Forgive her, Hannah…let it go." She heard it as clearly as if Tom was saying it to her.

Then, like a parade in her mind, Hannah recalled a dozen times Tom had told her that over the years. She closed her eyes, choking back a sob. And now…even after he'd been gone for so many months…he was telling her again.

Her eyes ran over the sentence until it was seared in her heart. *"Tom told me to tell you to forgive, Mrs. Ryan."*

Forgive. Forgive. He wanted you to forgive.

She moved outside and sank into the porch swing along the side of the house. It was a private spot bordered by jasmine. Hannah knew Jenny wouldn't come looking for her yet, and she was grateful. Her entire body was numb from the shock.

Tom had known.

He had laid there in the middle of the twisted wreckage of the Explorer, aware his minutes were numbered, and he had thought of her. The collision hadn't been his fault, and he knew that someday, somehow, Hannah was going to hold his death against someone. He better than anyone knew what would happen then. And so his final words had been for her: *Forgive, Hannah. Please forgive.*

"I can't, Tom, it's not fair. I have a right to this…" Her voice was a tortured whisper as trails of tears made their way down her face. "He did it on purpose."

But Tom's words, his final message, remained.

Forgive, Hannah…forgive.

She wept, imagining her dying husband worrying about the condition of her heart. Did he know her that well? Did he know she would turn her back on God? That her unforgiving heart would force her to forfeit a relationship with the savior?

Hannah's answer came from deep within.

Yes. Tom had known.

And God had placed it on Sgt. Miller's heart until finally he remembered Tom's words and brought them to her now.

She wept and prayed and fought the message. She did not want to forgive Brian Wesley. Indeed she would rather die than do such a vile thing. Eventually she crept back into the house and found Jenny napping on the sofa. Hannah found her Bible on the end table and carried it back outside.

Maybe there was something else in Lamentations, something she'd missed. After all, if Jeremiah had felt it was all right to be angry with his enemies, didn't she have the same right? She had been in Scripture many times since the night in Jenny's hospital room…but she had never finished Lamentations. She opened it now and began chapter 4 again, reaffirming her reasons for asking God to pay back Brian Wesley and curse him.

Then she read chapter 5. At first the lament sounded familiar, similar to the rest of the book. Then her eyes fell on something that caused her heart to skip a beat.

"Joy is gone from our hearts; our dancing has turned to mourning. The crown has fallen from our head. Woe to us, for we have sinned!…Restore us to yourself, O LORD, that we may return; renew our days as of old unless you have utterly rejected us and are angry with us beyond measure."

Hannah stared at the words as the reality hit. *We have sinned…restore us… angry with us.* Jeremiah and his people had suffered great loss. They had been victims in every possible way, yet at the end of the book of Lamentations Jeremiah was confessing sin. Repenting. Apologizing. Asking God to restore him and his people and hoping God would not be too angry with them.

Hannah searched her heart and tried to imagine what she had done wrong, what sin she had committed that could possibly require repentance. She had made things right with Jenny. What else was there?

Again, as though Tom were standing before her, she heard the words: *Forgive, Hannah…forgive.*

Tom's words pierced her heart. She was guilty after all.

With a heart so troubled she thought she might die from the pain, she began to pray, wondering, like Jeremiah, if it was too late, if she had made God too angry.

Scripture memorized years ago came rushing back.

"Forgive and you will be forgiven…If you forgive men when they sin against you, your heavenly Father will also forgive you. But if you do not forgive men their sins, your Father will not forgive your sins…forgive as the Lord forgave you."

Hannah closed her eyes and let the truth wash over her. As it did, she read Sgt. Miller's letter once more, hearing Tom's voice as he spoke his words of love to her. She sighed heavily, folded the letter, and stood on wobbly legs.

She knew what she had to do…and she was fairly certain it would kill her. But it was what Tom wanted. What God wanted. It was just a matter of doing it.

Making her way to the kitchen telephone, Hannah lifted the receiver and took the first step.

A woman answered on the second ring. "Hello?"

Hannah paused. "Carol, it's Hannah. I have something to tell you…"

Thirty-six

Because of the LORD's great love we are not consumed,
for his compassions never fail.
They are new every morning; great is your faithfulness.

LAMENTATIONS 3:22–23

A warm breeze picked up speed across a dirty, vacant field and brushed over Jenny and the tall man sitting beside her. Bits of trash and dirty cigarette butts mixed within the weeds that grew from cracks in the asphalt, and Jenny wondered what it was like inside. She was quiet, hands folded in her lap as she turned once more to watch the visitor entrance.

"How long do you think it'll take?" She looked at Matt Bronzan. He'd had so many of the answers they'd needed over the last year...she was sure he had this one, too.

He turned toward her and leaned over, resting his forearms on his thighs. "Takes a while to get through security."

Jenny nodded. There were dozens of strange characters scattered throughout the outdoor waiting area. Occasionally someone would come from inside with a small bag of belongings and wander off toward a dirty, graffiti-covered bus stop. The freeway was only a hundred yards away, and the grime and pollution of inner-city life filled the air.

None of it mattered, though, with Matt beside her. She moved closer to him and sighed. "Sometimes I miss Daddy and Alicia so much...."

Matt nodded. "There'll always be times."

There was an easy silence between them.

"Matt..." Jenny studied his eyes intently. She'd wanted to

ask this question for the last three months, ever since she saw him hug her mother…well, in *that* way. "Can I ask you a question?"

"Sure." Matt smiled at her.

"Do you love my Mom?"

His expression changed and he sat straighter. His eyes looked suddenly bright, and she saw the hint of a smile on his lips. "Well, young lady, where did that come from?"

Jenny shrugged. "I don't know. You're here, aren't you?"

Matt nodded and stroked his chin with his thumb. "You have a point there."

Jenny giggled. "It's okay. I like you being here."

Matt leaned closer, and a pang went through her. His eyes were so full of wisdom. Just like her dad's eyes had been.…

"Let's make it our secret for now, okay?"

She grinned. "So I'm right? You do love her?"

Matt shook a playful finger at her. "Oh, no you don't. I'm the lawyer, remember?"

Jenny laughed again. It felt so good to laugh. "Okay, you win. I won't say anything."

"You're a good girl, Jenny Ryan."

She met his eyes again. "But you *do* love her—"

"Jenny…"

She felt her grin widen at the teasing threat in his tone. This was going to be fun. She hugged herself, then her smile faded. Biting her lip, she glanced up at him. "I know it's too soon to tell the future…but Matt, please don't ever go away."

He stared at her, and she felt the warmth of his love—of Christ's love— surround her.

"I'm not going anywhere, Jenny. You can count on that."

"Promise?" She felt like a little girl, clinging to all she had left in the world.

Matt put an arm around her and pulled her close. She snuggled against him, smiling as his answer washed over her. "Promise."

Hannah had moved through several levels of security and now she was in a holding chamber, waiting for the signal. She thumbed through her Bible and found the letter from Sgt. Miller. She had made the appointment six weeks ago, now she had to follow through. And yet she still felt like she wore shackles on her feet, chains around her wrists....

She wanted to forgive, really. But she was having trouble seeing Brian Wesley as worthy. Even now. Forgiveness was Tom's gift, not hers.

A heavy steel door opened and a uniformed officer stepped into the waiting room. "Mrs. Ryan?"

Hannah stood. "Yes?"

"We're ready for you." He looked at her Bible. "You'll have to leave all your belongings with me."

Hannah nodded and did as she was told.

"Right this way."

She followed, feeling as if she were being led to the executioner's block.

The deputy stopped at a door with barred windows and opened it with a key. He stared at the prisoner shackled to a chair inside then turned to Hannah. "Ten minutes."

Hannah stepped inside, refusing to look at him. Not yet. She stared at the floor and found a seat at the simple, pressed wood table. She could see his feet, just across from her. *Help me, God. I still want to choke him, hit him, make him suffer for what he did.*

Forgive...forgive, Hannah.

She squeezed her eyes shut and felt two tears slither down her cheeks. She swallowed. *Please, God. Give me strength.* It was now or never. She had just ten minutes.

He interrupted her thoughts. "You...you wanted to see me?"

Hannah lifted her head and met his eyes—and gasped softly. In that moment she didn't see the eyes of an alcoholic, of a killer. She saw Tom Ryan's eyes…gentle, spirit-filled eyes.

The unmistakable eyes of a godly man.

In the face of those eyes, Hannah did the only thing she could do: she broke down and wept.

Brian shifted uncomfortably, clearly unsure what to say.

The minutes were getting by, and Hannah knew it was time. She fought for control over her tears and wiped her eyes. "You told me…at the sentencing that you were sorry."

He hung his head, and an errant tear slipped onto the table. "I am sorry, Mrs. Ryan. Every day…every minute."

Hannah nodded. Her stomach was in knots and she swallowed hard. And now she knew why she'd felt shackled. She had been locked in a prison of bitterness and hate, and only Tom's dying words had reminded her of God's truth: "You shall know the truth, and the truth shall set you free…"

Free. She longed to be free. At peace.

She had lived in the dark prison of hate for too long. The way out was right in front of her. She took a deep breath.

"I forgive you, Brian." Fresh tears filled her eyes. "It is what my husband wanted…what God wants. And now, it's what I want, too."

The words were no sooner past her lips than she felt it…a rush of peace so real, so sweet and comforting, that it took her breath away. It coursed through her entire body, and she felt like a wind-up toy whose workings had been fully released.…

She settled back into her chair, the tension she'd felt earlier completely gone.

This was what she'd waited months to feel, and she chuckled softly. How ironic that it was here, locked in a boxy room face to face with Brian Wesley, that she felt more peace than at any time since her life had been ravaged by the accident. Her smile broadened. How pleased Tom would be if he could see this. A second wave of peace washed over her.

He could.

Brian's mouth hung open, and he looked from side to side,

as though this might all be some kind of joke. Fumbling with his fingers, he began speaking in quick jerky sentences. "You don't...you don't have to forgive me, Mrs. Ryan. Really...It was my fault. All my fault....You don't need to forgive me. I don't deserve it. I don't—"

Hannah held up a hand, and he fell silent. "None of us deserves it, Brian. This wasn't a decision I made lightly. I understand now that no matter what you did, Carol was right. Jesus loves you, and...he wants me to forgive you. For your sake. And for mine."

Hannah felt God urging her to go one step further, and she did so without hesitation. "I believe you mean what you say, that you're sorry and you never want to hurt anyone else the way you hurt me." She paused, amazed at how easily the next words were coming. "I want to pray with you, Brian."

His eyes grew wide. "Carol told me crazy things would happen if I gave my life to the Lord, but I never...not *this* crazy—"

Hannah smiled, wanting to weep all over again. How much time she'd wasted...."We serve an amazing God. I've had to learn that the hard way." She reached toward him and held out her hands, palms up. Slowly, almost reverently, he placed his shackled hands in hers. She closed her fingers around them, the hands that had slapped money down on a bar fourteen months ago, hands that had raised one drink after another to his lips until he was too drunk even to walk a straight line, hands that turned a key in the ignition and steered a truck through a red light into the side of her family's Explorer.

They were the hands of a killer, but Hannah held them warmly. As she did, she felt only freedom, and her heart soared with hope. She bowed her head.

"Lord, thank you for this meeting, for bringing me to this point in my life." There were tears in her eyes and she swallowed hard. "You know what I've been through...what has led me to this decision. And you know that I am sincere when I say I forgive Brian.

"Please be with him now, Lord. He has a long time to spend in prison and...and I pray you use him to touch the lives of others around him." She paused as a sob caught in her throat. "Help him forgive himself, Lord. In Jesus' name, amen."

There was a knock on the door, and the deputy walked in. "Time's up."

Hannah squeezed Brian's hands, and he looked deep into her eyes. "Thank you, Mrs. Ryan."

She pointed heavenward and nodded as she stood to leave.

Without looking back she followed the deputy down the hallway. Her battle against drunk driving was not over. She had her priorities straight now, but she knew, as long as she drew breath, she would stay involved in the fight for tougher laws and greater awareness.

Ahead sunlight flooded the jail, and Hannah was overcome with the need to be back outside, where her future waited. She peered through the double glass doors, and among the sea of people waiting in the lobby, she saw them looking for her. Matt had a protective arm around Jenny. She ached knowing that Tom would never again be there to protect their daughter. But the fact remained that there would be times when the girl needed protecting. This was one of those times....Matt was here and he was real. As she made her way to them, she thanked God for his presence in their lives.

They both saw her at the same instant, and another sob caught in Hannah's throat once they were all together. There were tears in both Matt's and Jenny's eyes as they looked at her expectantly.

"Well?" Jenny took a step closer and hugged her gently, laying her head on Hannah's chest.

Hannah nodded. "I did it—" Her voice broke, and she hung her head as Matt put his arms around both her and Jenny in an embrace that needed no words.

It felt as though a horrible chapter in her life was finally over. As freeing as it had been to go to Brian, to forgive him, the reality of what had just transpired left her drained.

They held each other for a while, connected in every way that mattered, until finally Hannah stopped crying and caught her breath. "I have a crazy thing I want us to do." She looked from Jenny to Matt.

"What?" Jenny wiped her cheeks with her sweater sleeves and looked confused. "I thought you'd wanna talk about Brian and whatever happened in there."

Matt raised a curious eyebrow, and Hannah caught his gaze and held it. "Later. I promise. But right now I want you to sing with me. Please. Both of you."

"Sing?" Matt still had one arm around Hannah, one around Jenny.

Hannah nodded. "My song. 'Great Is Thy Faithfulness.'"

A look of understanding filled Matt's eyes, and he bowed his head. Then in a voice that was both quiet and strong, he began to sing.

And there, in the midst of bedraggled prisoners struggling with their first moments of freedom and hollow-eyed parents waiting and wondering where they went wrong, the song began to build.

Three voices rang as one, reaching the end of the first verse and launching into the chorus: "Great is thy faithfulness, great is thy faithfulness..."

The defeated and desperate around them lifted their eyes and listened until a worn-out woman in the corner stood on shaky legs and joined in. Hannah smiled at her and watched as a white-haired man farther down the bench rose to his feet and added his voice.

Another and another stood until there were ten people standing amidst fifty. Ten hapless, harried souls who, in that moment, found hope in the message. Finally even the hardest eyes around them grew noticeably softer.

"Morning by morning new mercies I see..." Hannah continued to sing, studying the strangers whose voices joined hers.

She saw pain there, suffering...and something deep within her told her they knew what it was to walk away from a loving God when life didn't turn out like it was supposed to. They knew what it was to struggle with pain and anger, waiting for morning.

If she could, she would take each one and tell them they didn't have to give up, that in Christ there really was hope. It might take months or even years but one day, as sure as every one of God's promises was true, morning would come.

She held tighter to Matt and Jenny, warmth filling her heart. She was going to survive. God's love had filled her future with bright possibilities.

Her voice grew stronger.

This was her song. It would always be her song. And some far-off day she would sing it in the presence of her mighty and loving Lord, with Tom and Alicia at her side.

She closed her eyes and with a full heart lifted her hands toward heaven, singing to an audience of One.

"All I have needed, thy hand hath provided. Great is thy faithfulness, great is thy faithfulness, great is thy faithfulness, Lord unto me."

I hope you have gained much by traveling with Hannah Ryan through the truths of Lamentations. There were times—in the early stages of writing this book—when I thought about scrapping the idea, writing something simpler and easier to produce than a story about a family devastated by a drunk driver. Especially a faith-filled family like the Ryans. But I believe God has allowed me this time and place to produce fiction for a reason. People of faith have struggles, too. They hurt and die and are tempted. The characters in my books will likely always be dealing with more than a jilted love. They will be real people, dealing with real issues. And I hope, because of that, they will help you, the reader, grow in your faith.

I pray that the underlying message in *Waiting for Morning* was clear: bad things do happen to good people. And not all Christians respond to tragedy by falling on their knees and reaching for their Bibles. Sometimes we travel a long, dark night waiting for morning.

It's like Jesus said when he assured his disciples, "I have told you these things so that in me you may have peace. In this world you will have trouble, but take heart! I have overcome the world" (John 16:33).

What assurance! What perfect peace! What a glorious morning awaits those who, like Hannah, learn to take their burdens to the foot of the cross.

If you have ever faced such a journey, it is my prayer that after reading *Waiting for Morning* you know you are not alone. Whatever you are facing today, God sees you, he loves you, and he has already won the battle for those whose faith is in him.

I've heard it said that all of us are either coming out of a trial, heading into a trial, or living through a trial. Drunk driving, car accidents, illness, financial struggles, relational breaks, marital unfaithfulness…these are things that happen to everyone. The difference is how we choose to respond, where we find our strength.

Many of you reading this book already have that sweet fellowship with our Lord. For you I offer encouragement and ask you to pass this book on to someone who feels alone in his or her trial.

But for you who have not made a commitment to Jesus Christ, there is no better time than now. Accept his free gift of grace, buy a Bible, find a Bible-believing church. Otherwise when the trials come, you will have no morning to wait for.

May God bless you and keep you in his care and may his face shine like the dawn even in the darkest of days. Until next time…

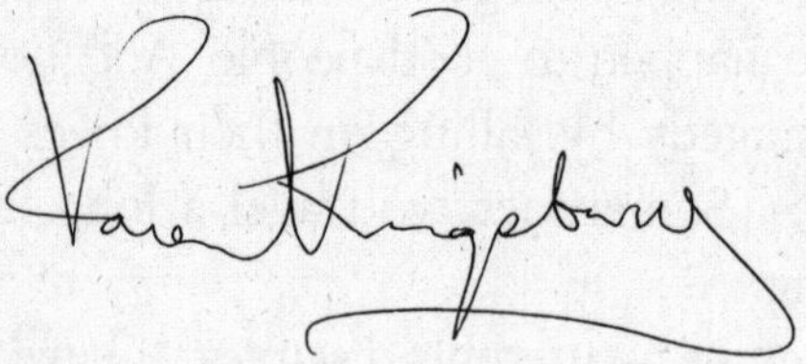

Discussion Questions

1. Was there a time in your life when you felt you were "waiting for morning"? Describe that time?

2. What did you do to survive? What would you do differently based on what you know today?

3. In what ways did you see God's hand at work during that time? What good has come from it?

4. Which character in Waiting for Morning could you most identify with? Which character could you least identify with? Why or why not?

5. List as many ways as you can remember where God showed His mercy to Hannah in her darkest days. How has God shown His mercy to you in yours?

6. Read Lamentations 3:22–23. What are the promises these verses deliver? Which one is most precious to you at this point in your life? Describe a time in your life when these promises could have helped or did help you.

7. Jenny thought the answer to her problems was to end her life. What led her to believe that? When has the enemy of your soul whispered wrong solutions to you? What were the consequences?

8. Which character(s) represented for Hannah God's promise that He will never leave nor forsake us? How did those character(s) deal with Hannah's anger toward God? How do you deal with the anger of hurting people?

9. Ultimately the lesson in Waiting for Morning is one of forgiveness. Describe a time when you had trouble forgiving someone. How did you act toward that person, inwardly and outwardly? How did that make you feel? At what point did you, like Hannah, find peace in this situation?

10. Oftentimes God uses outward situations or other people to help us get unstuck from a bad place, whether we need to forgive or obey or draw closer to Him. For Hannah, God used the police officer's delayed message from Tom. What has it been for you? What was/is God trying to tell you about your life? Are you listening?

BOOK TWO

FOREVER FAITHFUL

A Moment *of* Weakness

Dedicated to...

Donald,
My love song, my heart's mirror image, my best friend—
Who once upon a yesterday looked to God alone during our own
Moments of weakness...
And whose faith is today still my greatest strength...
Life with you is good; it's all good.
And since I can't slow the passing of time I am doing my very best
To savor it.

Kelsey...
My sweet girl, my most priceless treasure...
Your music is in my heart,
The voice of one whose love is the very definition
Of pure and whole and right.
Little Norm, can it truly be that you've reached double-digits?
And that your little-girl time with us...
Is more than half over?

Tyler...
My handsome, lanky sunbeam...
You continue to give me bouquets of
Laughter and sunshine-filled memories...
I love everything about you, Ty.
No matter how tall you grow you'll always be
My little boy.

Austin…
Who races and rolls and rough-houses through our home…
Even the toughest athletes take timeouts…
And when you take yours and those sticky, baby arms make their way
Around my neck…
I think of the miracle you are…And I am grateful.
Grateful beyond words.
Whenever I wonder how much God loves me, I never have to look further than you.

And to God Almighty, who has—for now—
blessed me with these.

Acknowledgments

My novels are not written without drawing on the research and true-life events that happen around me. For that reason, I'd like to thank several people for the help they have sometimes unwittingly provided me during the writing of *A Moment of Weakness.*

First, I'd like to thank the American Center for Law and Justice (ACLJ) for their tireless work in fighting for religious freedom in the United States. One day while listening to an ACLJ broadcast, I heard a woman call in because she was being sued by her husband for complete custody of her child. The reason? The woman was a Christian. And in that moment the story line for *A Moment of Weakness* was born.

Also, I'd like to thank my friend, Sherri Reed, aka Evil Buster. In the small town where she lives, Sherri started a campaign against Channel One—a real U.S. Department of Education program, which offered free televisions to public school classrooms as long as the students watch a fifteen-minute program each day. The program—which did not require parental approval—included government-chosen documentaries on topics that are at best questionable. Five minutes of the programming is commercial spots geared directly to school children. Over the course of a year, Sherri led a parent group that convinced the local school board to cancel the programming and give the television sets back to the government. I drew heavily from Sherri's experience in writing certain sections of *A Moment of Weakness.*

My medical scenes—no matter the book—are always written based on the expertise of my close friend and brother in Christ, Dr. Cleary. I am humbly indebted to him for allowing me, a would-be, self-appointed medical expert of the Verde

Valley, to pick his brain at all hours of the day and night.

A very heartfelt thanks goes to my amazing editor, Karen Ball, whose God-given talent is responsible for making my fiction what it is today. And also to the entire staff at Multnomah, from Don Jacobson and Ken Ruettgers to the sales and marketing and publicity teams, to cover design, and editing. I am amazed at what God is doing at Multnomah and humbly blessed to be part of it. Thank you for believing in my work.

As with each of my books, I could not have written this one without the help of those who care for my precious children during crunch time. For that reason I'd like to thank Christy and Jeff Blake (and Butter for making Austin's naptime a bit cozier). And also my dear, sweet friend, Heidi, for making Tyler part of your family on so many occasions.

A special thanks to my parents who have believed in my writing since I was old enough to hold a pencil and to my extended family for their love and support.

Also thanks to my church family and friends, especially Christine Wessel, who knows my heart and has held me up in prayer on so many occasions; Michelle Stokes, who has a house with her name on it next door to mine; Lisa Alexander, who has been there from the beginning and always will be; and Heidi Cleary, who will take a piece of my heart with her when she moves away this summer. I love you all.

Oh, and thanks to the Skyview basketball team—you fiery, slam-dunking, hard-working, amazing guys who have given me so many reasons to cheer, even on deadline! Each of you and your families feel like a part of mine, and I cherish the fleeting moments we have together!

Finally, thanks to Grandma Polly Russell, who went to be with the Lord during the writing of this book. Thank you for teaching me what it truly is to love.

Part I

"For I know the plans I have for you," declares the Lord,
"plans to prosper you and not to harm you,
plans to give you hope and a future.
Then you will call upon me and come and pray to me,
and I will listen to you."

JEREMIAH 29:11–12

One

May 1977

THE OLD BIDDIES SAT IN A CIRCLE, THEIR TIGHTLY KNOTTED HEADS turning this way and that like vultures eyeing a kill. Only this time the carcass was the Conner family, and no one was quite dead yet.

Hap Eastman watched from a corner of the Williamsburg Community Church fellowship hall. He'd done his part. Started the coffee, laid out the pastries, set up the chairs. It was something he did every Saturday morning for the Women's Aid Society, and every time it was the same. The old girls started with a list of needs and prayer requests and ended with a full-blown gossip session.

Hap's wife, Doris, was president, and at forty-five the youngest of the group. So Hap hung around tinkering with fix-it jobs in the kitchen or perched on a cold metal folding chair in the corner, a cup of fresh brewed French Roast in one hand and a Louis L'Amour novel in the other. Four days a week he was a jurist laden with a heavy workload and weighty decision making. Saturdays were his day to relax.

Hap had already heard the story from Doris and generally when the birds got going, he tried not to listen. But days like this it was nearly impossible.

"I don't care what anyone says. We need to talk about it." Geraldine Rivers had the floor, and Hap eyed her suspiciously from a distance. Geraldine was a talker from way back and in charge of the social committee. Generally when the gossip got going, Doris and Geraldine fanned the fires and battled for position. Especially in the heated sessions, and Hap figured this was about as hot as they'd ever get.

"We haven't read the minutes yet." Louella tilted her face in Geraldine's direction. The minutes were still tucked in her unopened Bible, so her comment was more for appearances than anything else.

"Minutes mean nothing at a time like this!" Geraldine nodded toward Doris. "Tell us what you know, will you, Dorie? Several of the ladies here haven't heard what happened."

The vultures nodded in unison, and Doris took her cue.

"It's really very tragic, very sundry. I almost hate to talk about it at church." She paused for effect, smoothing the wrinkles in her polyester dress. "You all know the Conner family, Angela and her husband, Buddy—"

"Buddy's been drinking alcohol at the tavern lately. Louella's husband saw his truck there last week, isn't that true?" Geraldine knew this to be true but enjoyed her own voice too much to be silent for long.

Doris frowned. "Right. He's become a regular drunkard. Now, Angela...well, she's another story. A flirtatious type, not given to things of the Lord." She looked around the circle. "Nearly everyone in Williamsburg has suspected her of cheating on Buddy."

The old birds nodded again.

"Well, yesterday I got a call from Betty Jean Stevens...you've probably noticed she's not here today." Doris's face bunched up like it did when Hap forgot to take out the trash. "Seems all those rumors were true. Betty Jean found out last week that her husband's been seeing Angela Conner on the side. And I don't mean at the Piggly Wiggly."

A collective gasp rose from the circle, and six of the girls started talking at once.

"Bill Stevens and that loose woman?"

"Why, that hypocrite!"

"A deacon at Williamsburg Community has committed adultery?"

"He'll need to make a public apology before I forgive him!"

"I knew something was happening between those two!"

The cacophony of accusations grew until Geraldine rapped her fist on the table. "Quiet, all of you! Quiet!"

They had obviously forgotten about Hap and his novel, and he gazed at them over the top of his book. The biddies fell silent again, and Geraldine lowered her gaze, trying to look appropriately indignant. "There's more...."

Doris brought her hands together in a neat fold. "Yes." She drew a deep breath. "For the past few weeks Bill's been...taking a motel room with the Conner woman. Apparently she set about trying to seduce him for some time. And...well..."

"There's a temptress in every town!" Geraldine obviously intended to maintain her presence even if it was Doris's story.

"Betty Jean says Bill tried to ward off her advances. But last month...he gave in."

"I do declare, Angela Conner's a harlot. She's always been a whore!" Geraldine snapped at a lemon pastry and dabbed fiercely at the filling it left on her lips.

"Yes, I believe she is." Doris looked glad that Geraldine had said it first. Hap sighed. "But the worst part happened last night."

The birds were nodding their interest, waiting breathlessly for the rest of the story.

Doris sipped her coffee, and Hap knew she was enjoying the way she held her audience captive. "Last night...Bill

Stevens ran off with her. The two of them. Just like that, they up and left town."

Several of the women were on their feet firing questions.

"Where did they go?"

"Does anyone else know?"

Doris kept her back stiff, her nose in the air. Hap hated it when she got uppity, and this was one of those times. She answered their questions with all the condemnation she could muster.

"D.C."

"The capital?"

"Yes. Betty Jean says Bill sat her down last night and told her they were through. Told her he's in love with Angela, and they're starting a new life in Washington, D.C."

"Dear heaven, how's Betty Jean handling it?"

"She's ashamed, broken. But she saw it coming. About a year ago, Bill began meeting with Angela to talk about a business venture."

"Business venture?"

"I guess we all know what type *business*—" Geraldine spat the word the way boys spit watermelon seeds on a summer day—"that was, don't we?"

Doris hesitated. "Betty Jean's just thankful the children are grown and out of the house."

"Angela Conner was bad blood from the get-go. Last year, I think she was seeing that attorney in town. You know, the divorce lawyer."

"I'm sure you're right. Everyone this side of Richmond knows the Conner woman and how she was always sniffing around for a man to bed."

Hap raised an eyebrow. *A man to bed?*

"What about Buddy?" Again Geraldine was determined to keep the discussion alive.

"Buddy's disgraced, as well he should be. Any man who can't keep his wife at home *should* be ashamed of himself." Doris looked at Geraldine for approval. "And I have it on good word that he won't be back to Williamsburg Community Church."

"I certainly hope not." Geraldine finished the pastry and wadded her napkin into a tight ball of crumbs and sticky paper. "The man's a drunkard."

There were several nods of approval, then one of the vultures gasped. "Oh, dear heaven. What's going to happen to little Jade?"

Jade. Hap felt his heart sink. He'd forgotten about the sweet ten-year-old, Buddy and Angela's only child.

Geraldine did nothing to hide her righteous indignation. "Isn't she the one who pals around with your Tanner?"

A deep crimson fanned across Doris's face. "The Conners live in our neighborhood, in Buddy's mother's house. Tanner is about the same age as the Conner girl, so it's only natural that the two play together. It doesn't happen often."

Doris wasn't telling the entire story, and Hap knew why. The reason was an ugly one. He and Dorie had two boys: Harry was twenty and worked for the city dump—a detail Dorie never told the girls at the Women's Aid Society. Then there was Tanner. Even at twelve years old, Tanner was everything Harry hadn't been. He was bright and handsome and the finest athlete in primary school. Doris thought he was going to be president of the United States one day. How would it look if he had already made the social mistake of befriending the child of a woman like Angela Conner?

Of course, there were other reasons Doris detested the children's friendship. More complicated reasons. But Hap didn't want to think about those on a sunny Saturday in May when he was supposed to be relaxing. He shifted positions, but the biddies were too caught up to notice him.

"Didn't you say something about Buddy leaving town?" Geraldine was working on another Danish.

Doris lowered her voice. "Buddy's moving. Taking the child and getting as far away from Virginia as he can."

"He must've been planning it," one of the girls chimed in.

"Certainly he saw it coming."

Doris nodded. "I assume. Either way, Angela and Bill are gone, and by next week, Buddy and the girl will be gone, too."

"I feel sorry for the child." Louella fingered the pages of her Bible and the minutes, which remained unread.

Doris huffed. "Daughter of a woman like that! I say good riddance to bad rubbish...."

Hap knew his wife was thinking about their son. He and Jade were more than casual neighborhood pals. They were best friends, and for the past year, Tanner had insisted he was going to marry Jade when they grew up.

Doris was wagging her finger. "You know what the Bible says. Bad company corrupts good character."

Geraldine raised an eyebrow. "Tanner?"

Doris nodded, her cheeks flushed again. "My boy doesn't need a girl like Jade around to tempt him. He'll wind up a father before he's sixteen."

"Doris!" Louella seemed genuinely shocked.

"Well, it's true. I'm glad they're leaving. Especially after what they did to Betty Jean. She's my best friend, after all."

Geraldine clucked her tongue against the roof of her mouth. "Doris is right. Williamsburg is a place filled with old money, old family ties, and old-fashioned values. The Conners are trouble, pure and simple. The girl is sweet now, but with a mother like hers we all know how she'll wind up. Where are they moving?"

Doris cleared her throat. "Washington state somewhere. Buddy has a brother in a small town.... Kelso, I think it is."

"Pity the good folks of Kelso, Washington, when a family like the Conners moves to town." Geraldine nodded her head decisively.

"Now, now..." Doris's tone was friendly again, and Hap saw she was making an effort to look the part of a righteous Christian leader. "Let's not be vicious. We need to concern ourselves with Betty Jean. After all, the Conners will be gone soon, out of our lives for good."

Hap knew Doris's last comment was more for his benefit than for anyone else's, and as she said it she looked right at him. None of the biddies knew the real reason Doris felt so strongly about Angela Conner, but Hap did. Her comment hit its mark, and Hap lowered his gaze back to his novel. What had happened between him and Angela Conner was decades old, but that didn't matter. No matter how many years passed, there was one thing Doris Eastman would never forget.

The sins of Angela Conner.

The children rode their bicycles into Tanner's driveway, laid them on the pavement and flopped down on a grassy spot in the center of his neatly manicured front lawn. The discussion had been going on for several minutes.

"I still don't get it. Where'd she go?" Tanner plucked a blade of grass and meticulously tore it into tiny sections.

Jade shrugged and gazed across the street toward the two-story house where she had lived for the past three years. "Daddy says she's gonna meet us in Washington. That's all I know."

Tanner chewed on that for a moment. The whole thing

sounded fishy to him. Mamas didn't leave for no reason. And people didn't move without making plans first. "Do you think she's mad at you?"

"Of course she's not mad. She loves me. I know it." Jade tossed her dark head, and her eyes flashed light green. Tanner had never seen eyes like Jade's. Green like the water of Chesapeake Bay.

"Why doesn't she just come back? Then you wouldn't have to move."

"I told you, they already decided. We're moving to Washington. Mama went on ahead of us, and Daddy says she'll meet us there."

"In Washington?"

"Yes, Tanner. I told you she didn't *leave* me. She just needed some time alone."

Tanner plucked another piece of grass and twisted it between his thumb and forefinger. "But she didn't say good-bye, right?"

Jade sighed, and Tanner saw tears form in her eyes. "I *told* you, Tanner. She left early in the morning. Daddy said she probably knew I would be sad so she left before I woke up. 'Cause she loves me."

"Did she leave a note or anything?"

"Daddy said he didn't need a note." Jade swiped at a tear, and her voice was angrier than before. "He knows where she's going, and that's why we have to move. We need to get there so we can be with Mama again. She would never wanna be alone that long."

Tanner still didn't understand, but he saw that his questions were bothering Jade. He sat up and crossed his legs, studying her curiously. The only time he'd ever seen her cry was two years ago when she jumped a curb on her bike and flew over the handlebars. But that was different. Now Tanner wasn't sure what to do. He decided to change the subject. "How far away is Washington?"

"Daddy says"—she leaned back on her elbows and stared at the cloudless sky—"it's about as far away as heaven is from hell."

Tanner thought about that for a moment. "But you're coming back, right?"

Jade nodded. "Of course. We'll meet up with Mama, and then Daddy's gotta do a job there. He said it could take all summer. After that we'll come home."

Tanner relaxed. That sounded all right. Even if the whole thing still seemed kind of weird.

"I gotta go." Jade rose and climbed back on her bike. "Daddy needs help packing."

Tanner stood and pushed his hands deep into the worn pockets of his jeans. "You leavin' tomorrow?"

She nodded and worked her toe in tiny circles on the pavement. For a moment Tanner thought she was going to hug him, then at the last second she pushed him in the arm like she always did when she didn't know what to say.

Tanner pushed her back, but not hard enough to move her. "Hey, I'm still going to marry you."

Jade huffed. "Shut up, Tanner. You're a smelly old boy and I'm not going to marry anyone."

"One day you'll think I'm Prince Charming," Tanner teased.

Jade couldn't keep a straight face, and she began giggling. "Oh, okay. Right. Sure...whatever you say." She shook her head dramatically. "I would never marry you, Tanner. Sometimes I think you're crazy."

"Got you smiling, though, didn't I?"

They grinned at each other for a beat and then Jade's smile faded. "I'll see ya later."

Tanner kicked at a patch of grass and sighed. "You better come back when summer's over."

Jade's eyes got watery again. "I *said* I'll be back." She began pedaling down his driveway. Halfway home she turned once and waved. Tanner raised one of his palms toward her. He'd heard his parents whispering about Jade and her daddy the other day. Tanner didn't catch all the details, but it was obvious his mother didn't think the Conner family was ever coming back.

It was good to know she was wrong.

As Jade disappeared into her house, Tanner felt a subtle reassurance that somehow, someday soon, the two of them would be together again.

Two

June, 1988

DORIS EASTMAN WATCHED THE 727 ANGLE ACROSS THE COLUMBIA River and make its final approach toward the runway. Seated somewhere inside the plane, Tanner would be waiting, excited to see her, anxious to be back in the Northwest.

The thought frustrated her. She would have done anything to keep him at Princeton where he belonged.

Hap must have been crazy to move here in the first place, and now that he was gone, Doris had every intention of getting back to Virginia. Poor old Hap. Retired from the bar two years earlier with dreams of being a lawyer again in Portland. For a tennis shoe company of all things. And despite his history of heart problems.

No matter how many times she thought about his decision, she'd never understand. They had had plenty of money in Virginia and a reputation Hap had earned after twenty years of serving as a superior court judge. Countless social invitations, the best seats at their favorite restaurants, season tickets to the opera…they'd had everything they'd ever wanted. And of course, in Virginia they were closer to Tanner.

Hap hadn't been concerned with any of that. His buddy Mark Westfall, another attorney, had moved to Portland three years before. Mark had played professional basketball after college and eventually took a job in the legal department of the shoe company. It wasn't long until Mark had convinced Hap that Portland was the place to retire. No snow, no heat, no smog. Only beautiful greenery and endless opportunities.

Doris watched the plane taxi toward the gate and sighed. Good old Mark had forgotten that greenery comes at a price. The rain had been incessant and besides, what kind of retirement was it to take on a second career? And with Hap nearly sixty years old? She'd seen the heart attack coming, even if Hap hadn't. Too many fast-food lunches and too little exercise all heaped on a workload that seemed to grow every month.

They'd moved to Portland in November—to beat the cold Virginia winter, Hap had said. That year Williamsburg hadn't had an inch of snow all season. Oregon, meanwhile, had record-breaking rain.

Even now, with June already here, the cursed Northwest was shrouded in clouds and drizzle. Who could jog or even walk in such a dreadful place? Hap tried it for a while, jogging in the rain. But that lasted only a month. His heart attack came just after Easter.

Now she was still in the process of settling the estate, handling Hap's affairs and packing up the condominium. She planned to be back in Williamsburg by fall, and if she'd had anything to do with it, Tanner could have waited and seen her then. For the life of her, Doris couldn't imagine why her son would want to spend a summer in the Northwest.

He'd explained it a dozen times. Some sort of internship program with the Kelso board of supervisors. If it were anywhere else, Doris would have been pleased with the assignment. But Kelso? Of all the places in the world, her son had chosen to take an internship in Kelso, Washington?

Of course, Kelso was still big enough that the odds of them running into each other were slim. Even if they did, Doris doubted they'd recognize each other. Jade had moved away eleven years ago, after all.

Still...it worried her.

She remembered talking with Tanner about it last week. "Son, I don't understand. Why Kelso?" Doris was not about to mention the fact that Jade might still live there. Tanner hadn't brought up the girl's name in years; certainly he had no idea that she had moved to Kelso way back when.

"I told you, Mom. I want to spend weekends with you, going through Dad's stuff, helping you pack for the move. The board of supervisors had an internship available in Kelso. It's near Portland. I had all the qualifications. Seemed like a perfect match to me."

Doris tried to detect anything false in her son's voice, but there was nothing. He didn't remember Jade; wouldn't look her up. The whole thing was just a coincidence.

She moved closer to the window and wondered again why she was so worried. There were thousands of loose girls prowling about for a man like Tanner—and Jade Conner would certainly be a loose girl. Just like her dreadful mother. Poor Betty Jean had never been the same after Angela Conner ran off with Bill.

But Doris had her own reasons for hating the Conner woman. Reasons no one knew anything about. Doris felt the sting of angry tears, and she banished the memories from her mind.

She would hate Angela Conner until the day she died.

Five years ago Doris got word from one of the women at the Aid's Society that Buddy and Jade were still living in Kelso. Someone knew someone whose brother maintained contact with the family. Apparently Buddy was an unemployed drunkard, and Jade ran the streets. If that were true—and Doris was sure it was—then there was no need to worry about Tanner. He'd never be interested in a girl who ran the streets, a girl who probably slept around, a girl with a scandalous past.

A girl whose mother had very nearly ruined their lives.

The college girls Tanner dated were virginal types, clean-cut and wholesome. Even then there had never been anyone serious. His faith wouldn't allow it.

That was another irksome thing. Tanner's incessant faith.

She and Hap had brought him up in the church and left it at that. A modest faith could have been an asset to his political future. Instead he'd taken to reading the Bible and quoting Scripture. He attended some crazy nondenominational church on campus and talked about God's will this and God's will that.

Doris hoped it was only a stage, something he'd outgrow. There was no room in public office for religious fanaticism. Especially in one who leaned as heavily to the right as Tanner did.

His obsession with religion would pass, Doris was certain about it. Just like his fascination with Jade. For three years after she moved he had asked about her and when she was coming back. Doris remembered the time when Tanner was nearly fifteen and he'd wandered into the backyard where she was weeding.

"Mama, tell me the truth. Jade isn't coming back, is she? Not ever." Tanner was gangly in those days, all knobby knees and giant blue eyes.

Doris had leaned back on her heels and shook the soil from her work gloves. "Why must you persist in asking such questions, Tanner? What is it about Jade? She's been gone nearly three years."

"I'm going to marry her one day, Mama. How can I marry her if she doesn't come back?"

Doris remembered feeling lightheaded at the suggestion of Tanner and Jade wedded in matrimony. She had forced herself to take deep breaths. The daughter of a harlot? Doris had to stifle the anger that rose within her. "Son, you're too young to know who you want to marry."

"I'm not too young, Mama. I know what I want, and I want to marry Jade Conner. I decided a long time ago."

Doris wanted to tell him the girl was worthless, trash. A weed in a garden chock full of roses. Instead she smiled warmly at the boy before her. "Well, dear, first she'll have to move back to Virginia. And honestly I don't see that happening."

"I can't remember where she moved. Where was it, Mama? Was it Washington, D.C.? Maybe I can get her address and write to her."

Doris stopped herself before spurting out the city and state. "I'm not really sure, actually. Out west somewhere, I think." She had resumed her gardening, loosening a weed and then pulling it out from the root.

Tanner had crossed his arms angrily. "I'm going to marry her one day, Mama. Even if I have to search the whole country and find her myself."

An attendant announced the arrival of Tanner's flight, and Doris blinked back her son's words, shuddering at the memory. If anything had been an act of God, it was the fact that Jade Conner never came back to Williamsburg, Virginia.

Doris folded her hands and noticed her palms were sweaty. Her fears about the girl were irrational, weren't they? Tanner couldn't possibly know Jade lived in Kelso. It was coincidence, pure and simple. What could go wrong when he would only be in town a single summer? The weeks would dissolve in an instant, and then he'd fly back to New Jersey, back to Princeton where he could prepare for his senior year.

Doris didn't know what his first assignment would be when he graduated, but she knew it would be political in nature. He had been groomed for public office since he was a small boy. Every friendship, every activity, every article of clothing, every class, each student government office, even his role as an award-winning athlete was a line on what had become a stellar resume. She'd designed a packet on Tanner's accomplishments midway through his junior year and touted it to all the Ivy League schools. Scholarship offers had been plentiful.

He and Hap had complained for a while, thinking Tanner would be better off at a West Coast school where he could play sports. But finally she'd convinced them. A Princeton education would be priceless. Besides, the time had come to stop playing games. Tanner had a brilliant future at hand and not a moment to waste. Now he was nearly ready. He would graduate next summer, and the climb would begin, one rung at a time.

People were streaming through the gate with that bewildered look travelers wore. She moved closer, and there at the back of the pack she saw him. He was nearly a head taller than the masses, and he drew the stares of several women in the crowd. People had always noticed Tanner. He had a magnetic quality that couldn't be taught or trained. It was more of a birthright. As he drew closer, she saw his skin had lost the paleness of three months ago when he'd flown out for Hap's memorial service. He had some color now, and he was taking on a more pronounced jawline. *Perfect. The public loves a good-looking politician with a strong jawline.*

He was going to look wonderful in the White House.

"Mother, you look lovely as always." Tanner strode toward her, wrapped her in a hug, and grinned.

They made small talk, and he kept one arm around her

shoulders as they headed toward the baggage department. After a few minutes, Tanner's tone grew serious. "How are you, Mom, really? Dad's been gone a while now. I've been praying for you."

Doris squeezed him tighter. "Thanks, honey. I miss him. But we had a wonderful life. I'm glad he didn't suffer."

"It's good you're moving back to Virginia. I think you've had about as much of the Northwest as you can stand." Tanner's eyes danced as he nodded toward a wall of windows and the thick, gray sky outside. "You'll feel better when you get back to sunny Virginia."

"Yes..." She paused. *The sooner the better.*

Tanner was telling her something about the internship and the projects at hand, but she wasn't really listening. She was wracked by thoughts of Jade and Tanner and Kelso, Washington...and the memory of a fifteen-year-old boy with earnest eyes insisting that one day he'd marry the girl.

Even if he had to search the whole country and find her himself.

Three

Midday at Kelso General Hospital was typically a quiet time, especially in the children's unit. Most of the younger patients napped or watched afternoon cartoons; others were too sick to sit up, and they slept, usually until dinner.

But that Monday, the fourth of June, Jade Conner was at the nurse's station reading a book for her science class at Kelso Junior College when she heard whimpering. She worked three afternoons a week as a nurse's assistant in the children's unit, and she could hardly wait to finish her education and begin nursing. The children needed her. They were frightened, unsure of why they were sick and wondering whether everything was going to turn out all right.

The whimpering grew louder.

"Wanna check her, Jade?" The head nurse was buried in paperwork, and Jade nodded. She stood up, tucking a strand of short dark hair back behind her ear.

"Coming, little one. I'm coming." She worked her way across the hallway to Room 403. Shaunie Ellersby. Four years old. Recurrent kidney infections. Doctors were running tests, but there was a strong suspicion that the child's kidneys were failing. Shaunie had been in the hospital off and on for the past six months. This time she'd been in for more than a week, and her mother had finally taken to staying home between meals to tend to Shaunie's two younger sisters.

"Sweetie, I'm here. What's wrong, baby doll?" Jade cozied

up next to the child and gently stroked her forehead. She knew she was Shaunie's favorite nurse, and the two had been fast friends since the girl first got sick.

"I miss my mommy." The little girl squeezed out the words between stifled sobs.

"Ah, it's okay, sweetie. She'll be here later, I promise." Jade kissed the child's forehead. "Want something to drink?"

Shaunie nodded, and Jade saw her sadness fade. "Apple juice."

"What's the magic word?"

"Please?"

Jade smiled. "Okay. Be back in a minute."

When she returned with the drink, she took her spot once more on the hospital bed beside the little girl. Shaunie took several long sips from the straw. After the third mouthful she smiled up at her. "Thanks, Jade."

"Sure, sweetie. Hey, what say we talk for a little bit?"

Shaunie nodded. "Guess what? Mommy painted my bedroom."

"She did?"

"Yep. Pink and white with little flowers."

"Oh, I wish I had a room like that. Your Mommy sure is nice."

Shaunie nodded and finished her juice. "Jade, do you live here?"

She grinned and tousled the child's hair. "Here? At the hospital? Of course not, silly."

"Then where do you live?"

"At home, like everyone else?"

"With your mommy and daddy?"

A twinge of sorrow seized Jade. The answer never came easily. "No, sweetie. Just with my daddy."

Shaunie's face scrunched up. "What about your Mommy?"

Jade felt the sting of tears and blinked them back. "I don't have a mommy."

Shaunie's eyes grew wide. "Why not? Did she die?"

The child's innocent questions rattled around in her heart like pebbles in an empty tin can. "She lives far, far away, baby doll. We never see each other anymore."

Sadness filled the child's face. "That's too bad. How 'bout your daddy. Does he paint your room sometimes?"

Jade thought of her father, passed out in his easy chair, beer bottles littering the living room floor. "No, sweetie, he doesn't. But think what a lucky little girl you are to have a brand new room waiting for you when you get home."

Shaunie considered that for a minute, and Jade ran her fingertips over the child's forehead. The little girl's skin had a yellow cast, and her eyes still looked tired from the infection that ravaged her body. The doctors had done more tests that week, and Jade hoped they wouldn't find anything seriously wrong with her.

"My mommy and daddy don't live too far away from me, do they, Jade?"

"Well, honey, no. But you don't live here, you live with your mommy and daddy."

"Sometimes I live here." Shaunie didn't seem distraught by the fact.

"That's true, I guess. But Mommy and Daddy are very, very close. They can visit all the time."

For now, anyway. Unless the county voted to shut down the children's unit. A stab of fear set free a batch of butterflies in Jade's gut. There had been talk about closing the unit for months. Budget cuts were needed, and someone had designed a plan to eliminate the children's ward at Kelso General. If that happened, sick children like Shaunie would have to go an hour south to Portland for care. An hour that meant the difference between a child getting to see her parents several times a day or being left alone in a hospital with infrequent visits at best.

The city was going to discuss the idea at a meeting that afternoon. The plan made Jade furious.

"Yes, honey, you can see your mommy and daddy any time you want."

Shaunie nodded and wriggled about, an anxious look on her face. "I have to go potty."

Jade helped her out of bed, careful not to tangle her IV lines. When the ordeal was through, she eased the child back under the blankets.

"You're pretty." Shaunie yawned.

Jade smiled and kissed the little girl on the tip of her nose. "Thanks. You, too, princess."

"My mommy says you look like Meg Ryan with dark hair."

"Does she now?" Jade laughed.

"Who's Meg Ryan?"

"Oh, she's someone in the movies."

"I think you're prettier than her." Shaunie laid her head back on the pillow and rubbed her eyes. "I need to take a nap-time now."

"Okay, baby doll. You do that. I won't be here when you wake up, but I'll see you tomorrow."

"Where will you go, Jade? Home to see your daddy?"

She hugged the little girl close. *Only when I absolutely have to, honey.* "No, sweetie. I have to go to a meeting."

"Okay." Shaunie yawned again and her eyelids fluttered. "Night-night, Jade."

"G'night, honey."

Rarely had anything mattered this much to Jade. She slept

in the house where her father lived, but the hospital was her home. She had volunteered in the children's unit since she was sixteen. Now that she worked there, she would fight the county with everything she had so Shaunie and Kelso's other sick kids would never have to be shuttled away to a hospital in Portland.

Jade returned to the nurse's station and glanced at the clock. It was nearly three. The meeting was at four and was expected to draw a hundred people.

Jade pushed aside her science book and began scribbling on the back of a blank admitting form. If she had a chance, she intended to talk about the kids at Kelso Hospital. Shaunie had given her an idea. She began putting her feelings on paper until she'd filled an entire page with notes.

The thought of Shaunie being separated from her parents made her throat constrict. *Help me, God. Let them see how badly we need this place.*

Jade was not religious—she didn't attend a church or read a Bible—but ever since she was a little girl she had talked to God, especially when she was alone. And she was alone often.

She thought about the townspeople who would attend the meeting and wondered whether they, too, wanted to keep the unit open. Jade would know many of them, she was sure, and she hoped her words would persuade them to join the fight. While the people of Kelso who knew her did not go out of their way to be friendly to Jade, most of them didn't seem to hold her father's alcoholism against her. Jade didn't care if they did. She didn't need anyone's approval. She didn't need anything at all.

Except the children's unit at Kelso General.

A unit whose fate was entirely in the hands of the county's board of supervisors.

Four

THE OFFICES OF THE COWLITZ COUNTY BOARD OF SUPERVISORS for the city of Kelso, Washington, were located above city hall and adjacent to an auditorium where town meetings had been held for the past fifty years. Tanner had spent the morning in meetings and used his lunch hour to unpack his files, reference books, and rearrange his office.

Tanner surveyed the worn-out cubicle that would serve as his workspace for the summer. His mother would have been appalled. Nothing but cherry wood and inlaid carpets for Tanner Eastman. A politician on the rise needed the right type of office even if it meant having his mother come down and make over the place herself.

He ambled toward the last of his things, a stack of legal books that would barely fit on his desk. These were treasured books, and whether he'd need them or not during the internship, he intended to read them: *Religious Freedom Fading Fast*, *Whatever Happened to God in America?*, *One Nation Under God?*

He stood the books where he could see them, wondering what his mother would say if she knew what really interested him. Hogwash, no doubt. A waste of time. Silly notions. Extremism. Tanner smiled. The books were a secret, but they were nothing compared with the secret he harbored in his heart. The secret of what he really wanted to do with his life.

Fred Lang, one of the younger supervisors, peered around the pressed board that made up the east wall of Tanner's new office. "You 'bout ready?"

"I think so." Tanner reached for a folder.

"You did read the file we sent, correct?"

"Four times." He handed Lang the folder. "I put together a few pages in summary, stating the board's reasoning, highlighting the profit and loss statement for Kelso General's children's wing. It's all in there."

Lang took the folder and glanced through it. "Impressive." He looked up at Tanner. "This is a hot one. Town's pretty riled up about it, what with a closure affecting sick kids and all." He hesitated. "What would you think about presenting your summary at the public meeting today? Since the townspeople don't know you yet."

Tanner shrugged. "Fine with me."

Lang's shoulders relaxed and the lines on his forehead were replaced with a broad smile. "Okay, great. We'll introduce you, tell them you're working with the board for the summer. Then hand you the floor. We'll handle the questions when you're done."

Tanner shot a glance at his watch. "The meeting's at four, right?"

"Right. We need to be there half an hour early to compare notes."

"One question."

Lang leaned against the particleboard but straightened again when it threatened to topple. "Shoot."

"The file wasn't real clear on the alternatives, other ways the county could cut the budget besides closing the children's unit."

Lang sighed. "To tell you the truth, there really hasn't been time. Elections are coming up this fall, we've got the police staff about to go on strike. Budget cuts are a reality, and this was an easy choice."

"Maybe not to the townsfolk." Tanner wasn't trying to be difficult, but if he was going to be on the front line, he needed to know how to respond to the fire.

"Don't worry, we'll take the heat. You just give 'em your presentation. Maybe then they'll stop thinking we have something against their kids."

"Small town syndrome?"

"Too small. Everyone on the board knows someone who's taking this thing personally. The town thinks we're a bunch of ogres who have it out for them."

Tanner wondered. "Nothing personal involved?"

"No. Just the simplest cut we could make. The one that took the least time to figure out and helped us make ends meet."

Tanner nodded. "Is there a Plan B?"

"Plan B?"

"The town's coming out for the meeting, right? What if there's more outrage than you're counting on? It's election year, after all. You said so yourself. Maybe we should have a Plan B."

"Such as?"

"Such as taking the summer and seeing if we can find somewhere else to cut the budget."

Lang gripped his chin with his thumb and forefinger and nodded slowly. "Not a bad idea." He let his hand drop. "But don't tell the people that."

Tanner folded his arms. "First rule of sticky politics: Work like you have a Plan B, talk like you wouldn't consider it."

Lang smiled. "I like that. But it wouldn't be us finding somewhere else to cut the budget. It would be you."

Tanner chuckled. "I figured as much."

Lang patted Tanner roughly on the shoulder. "Welcome to summer internships, my friend. We'll keep you so busy you'll look forward to final exams."

"I don't doubt it."

Lang had lightened up considerably in the past five minutes and seemed ready to make small talk. Tanner didn't mind that he'd been made chief scapegoat on the issue. He didn't know a soul in the state of Washington, and it wouldn't hurt to have a friend in Lang.

The man shot a look around Tanner's cubicle. "Public office, right? That's the goal?"

"How'd you guess?"

"Princeton degree in poli-sci, political internships, get elected to councilman or congressman. Maybe the big time, state senator, or even the White House." Lang huffed and a grin appeared on his face. "I've worked with you dreamers before."

"Yep." Tanner studied the stack of books he'd unpacked moments earlier. He suddenly felt like a load of bricks had been dumped on his shoulders. "That's always been the big dream. Public office. An elected servant of the people. It's something I've…" he searched for the right words, "known I'd do…as far back as I can remember."

The ten-member board of supervisors had finished its private meeting and now sat along a panel at the front of the auditorium. The room was filling fast, and Tanner could feel the tension. Scattered about were clusters of townspeople, whispering and gesturing and casting disdainful looks toward the board.

This wasn't going to be a discussion. It was going to be a lynching. They didn't want to lose the children's unit at Kelso General, and they appeared ready to demand the heads of the people who did.

Tanner scanned the room. Mostly older people, longtime residents, probably, and several serious-looking couples.

Parents of sick kids, no doubt. He continued searching the room…and his breath caught in his throat.

She was in the back row, sitting by herself. She couldn't have been much more than twenty, slim and athletic looking with short, windblown hair the color of roasted walnuts. She was studying a pile of notes on her lap, and Tanner realized she was wearing a nurse's uniform. *Great. Another voice against us.* Despite the scowl on her face she was breathtaking. The girl glanced up and met his gaze, and for a moment a look of recognition flashed in her eyes. Then she looked quickly away.

For a moment, Tanner's political poise wavered, and he considered going to her. There was something familiar about her, though Tanner couldn't decide what it was. He watched her for another few seconds, then returned to his notes. The girl didn't matter.

If she worked with the children at Kelso General, then they were about to become enemies.

The meeting was underway, and several minor matters of business had been taken care of. Now Lang had the floor, and he was reading from Tanner's resume.

"We have a young intern with us for the summer. He's from Princeton University and—" he shot Tanner a look—"will probably become a household name one day in political circles. This afternoon he's going to brief all of you on the budget status and the intended closure of the children's unit at Kelso General Hospital." A chorus of grumblings began to build, and Lang was forced to raise his voice. "If you'll please give him your attention. Mr. Tanner Ghormsley."

Tanner hesitated for a moment. *Ghormsley?* Some great start he'd made in becoming a household name if his boss couldn't even remember what to call him. He didn't bother making a correction. He stood and felt a sense of serenity. Crowds did not make him nervous.

"Ladies and gentlemen, first let me thank you for coming. I understand that many of you have serious concerns about the closure of the children's unit at Kelso General." He paused, guessing that nearly two hundred people had packed the auditorium. Not one of them was smiling. His eyes found the girl in the back, but she was looking at her notes again.

He cleared his throat and began explaining in succinct detail the condition of the county's budget. When it was apparent how desperately cuts were in order, he began talking about the children's unit. The numbers told the story. Kelso General was owned by the county and simply was not making enough money to warrant a children's ward.

"Children's units are more costly because equipment must be adjusted on nearly every level. Smaller beds, smaller machinery, smaller needles and tubing and testing devices." He looked for a softening among the crowd and saw none.

He went on to tell them how other units at the hospital were essential and that children could still be treated in the emergency room once the children's unit was closed.

"Children who need hospitalization will be transported to Portland's Doernbecher Children's Hospital. Of course that facility is one of the finest in the nation."

Finally, Tanner dealt with the most difficult truth of all. "The fact is, Kelso General is costing this county a lot of money. While none of you wants to see the children's unit closed, it would be far worse to see the entire hospital shut down."

He cited towns that had lost hospitals because of the drain on county funds. "The board of supervisors feels very strongly that this town does need a hospital. Kelso General has a tremendous reputation in the medical community, and the staff there has played a part in saving the lives of hundreds of Kelso residents. You may know someone who is alive today because of Kelso General. Perhaps you, yourself, are here because you had the privilege of living near a top-notch medical facility."

Tanner scanned the faces before him, relieved to feel the tension easing. "We all want to keep the children's unit. But if it means the difference between losing Kelso General or keeping it up and running in this great town, is there any question what the board should do? Thank you."

So much for Plan B.

Tanner sat down and watched as the clusters of people who had been frowning and grumbling quietly considered what he'd said. He could almost read their minds. Children were wonderful and all, but no hospital? Nowhere to go when chest pains struck in the middle of the night? Longview's St. John's Hospital was ten miles away and a far cry from Kelso General. Several elderly citizens in the back of the room stood and headed for the exit.

Tanner turned and looked at Lang. There was relief in the man's eyes, and Tanner silently thanked God. There was no doubt about one thing: The Lord had given him a gift of persuasion. The children's unit was as good as gone. Maybe his mother was right after all. Maybe he would love being a politician.

Lang stood up. "Are there any questions?" Another batch of townsfolk stood and headed for the door. "All right then, at this point we'd like to—"

"Wait!" It was the girl from the back. She was on her feet staring at the people who were leaving. "Don't go! You can't give up that easily." She motioned toward Tanner. "He doesn't live here; it's not his hospital."

Lang coughed once. "Uhhh, Miss…Conner, is it? Do you have a comment you'd like to address to the board?"

The girl spun toward Lang. "Yes, sir, I do."

Tanner sensed that for some reason the crowd didn't like Miss Conner, whoever she was. Still, the citizens who had started for the door were turning around and making their way back to their seats.

"I believe we've already shared with you the fact that we don't want to cut the children's unit. We simply don't have a choice." Lang sighed impatiently. "But go ahead. Make your comments known."

The girl clenched her fists tightly and stood straighter, her eyes blazing. As she met the eyes of her fellow townsfolk, the look on her face softened. "Don't be fooled by some…some stranger who doesn't know us. The board of supervisors would never close down Kelso General. Not in a million years. That hospital is a source of pride and strength in this town…every one of you knows that."

She glared at Tanner, and he was struck by the color of her eyes. There was something hauntingly familiar about her, like the strains of a long-ago song that had once played over and over in his mind. *Have I seen her somewhere before? Do I know her?* He banished the thought. It was impossible; he'd never been to Kelso before in his life. He glanced down at his notes, preferring them to the penetrating anger in the girl's eyes.

Her voice was ringing with sincerity. "The county budget covers hundreds of items. Certainly the board can make their cuts somewhere else. And if the hospital isn't making money—" she waved her hand toward the board members—"well, then, maybe we need a new board of supervisors. A facility like Kelso General should be making money, or there must be something wrong with the people responsible for it."

A quick glance at the crowd told the story. Outrage was back in the people's eyes, and Tanner summoned his strength. Maybe Plan B wasn't dead after all.

The young woman reached down and picked up a snapshot of a blond child, four, maybe five, years old. "This is Shaunie. She has kidney disease." Her voice remained strong, but Tanner could see tears in the young woman's eyes…those green, gorgeous eyes. "She's spent most of the past six months at Kelso General's children's unit." The girl paused. "Today, Shaunie said something to me that I want you to hear. She told me she was glad her mommy and daddy lived so close."

Tanner shifted his gaze and saw a few women in the crowd with tears running down their faces. *Wonderful.* Apparently everyone in town knew little Shaunie.

"I held her in my arms and told her that her parents lived *with* her, not close by somewhere else. But Shaunie shook her head and told me as sweetly as she could that sometimes she lived at the hospital. And when she did, she was glad her mommy and daddy were close."

Handkerchiefs were yanked from purses and several women dabbed at their eyes. The sound of stifled sniffles filled the auditorium, and the citizens strained to hear the young nurse. "Medical research has proven that children heal more quickly, more thoroughly when they are happy. When they're not afraid."

She pointed to Tanner again, and he wished he could disappear. The girl was stunning, and he could feel the fight leaving him. What was he doing arguing with her, anyway? *It's not my budget, lady. You can keep your children's unit…and anything else you want with eyes like—*

"That…that *man* wants to move Shaunie to Portland, more than an hour away. How well do you think she'll recover from kidney disease when her mommy and daddy don't live close by."

Her attention was back on the people. "Please. Don't let them close the children's unit without a fight. We need to stick together and tell this board that we won't reelect them this fall if they don't find some other way to cut the budget."

Tanner caught several of the board members exchanging glances. Obviously "reelect" was the buzzword. He could almost feel them implementing Plan B. The beautiful nurse was finishing her plea. "Let's take a vote. Please. Everyone who wants to keep our children's unit open, raise your hand."

Hands filled the auditorium, and Tanner watched as his persuasive presentation dissolved like sand in a stormy ocean wave. If he wanted, he could take her on, go head-to-head with her in debate, sway the people back to his way of thinking. But then, he wasn't up for reelection this fall. Besides, he'd angered the nurse enough already.

Lang looked to the other board members for approval, and Tanner saw several of them nodding. Leaning forward, Lang smiled politely at the townsfolk and spoke into the microphone. "If there are no other comments, the board wants all of you to know we appreciate your interest in coming to the meeting today. We also want to thank our new intern for his presentation. Although he has done his homework and made a strong case for closing the children's unit, the board wants to assure you that this matter is far from decided."

Tanner grimaced. Nice. Make it sound like the whole thing had been his idea. He'd be lucky if he got out of the building alive.

Lang was rhapsodizing about being a servant of the people and doing only that which was best for everyone, but the crowd was growing tired and more frustrated. Eventually Lang caught on. He smiled in Tanner's direction. "We have therefore decided to postpone any decision on this matter until the first week of September."

Tanner wasn't surprised. That was long enough for him to spend the summer researching a better way to balance the budget and save the children's unit, and late enough that the supervisors could take credit for it. *Ah, the life of a political intern.*

The meeting was over, and the atmosphere had done a one-eighty. The clusters of townspeople stood in bunches, congratulating each other. They had a lofty air about them now, as though they were far superior to the board of supervisors.

Tanner watched as several of them approached the girl who had championed the children's unit so well. Again he had the feeling he'd seen her somewhere before. What had Lang called her? The citizens talked to her in a manner that seemed far friendlier than their earlier reception. She remained aloof, an ice queen. But still there was something about her…

Lang approached him. "Tanner, great job up there. We almost had 'em."

"Eastman." Tanner's eyes were trained on the girl.

Lang's face went blank. "What?"

"My name. Tanner Eastman."

A beat. "What did I call you?"

"Tanner Ghormsley. As in Professor John Ghormsley. The man who arranged my internship."

Lang shrugged. "Oh well, they don't know who you are."

"Yeah, well, after what happened here today maybe I should thank you." Tanner collected his file, but his eyes still followed the girl. Every move she made reminded him of something he'd seen before, someone he'd known before.

Lang followed Tanner's gaze and huffed. "She sure did us in.

She's worked the children's unit for years. Obviously a bleeding heart—"

"Wait a minute!" Tanner's eyes widened and his heart pounded in his chest. It couldn't be, but then...Where had she moved? Wasn't it somewhere out west? Maybe even somewhere in Washington? Tanner's mouth went dry as he stared at her, still standing there across the room. "What did you say her name was?"

"Who?" Lang looked around, trying to make sense of Tanner's question.

The young nurse was gathering her things, making her move to leave, and Tanner was filled with a frantic sense of urgency. "The girl, the nurse. What's her name?"

Tanner knew he couldn't wait another moment. He had to know if he was right. He began pulling away, heading toward her, and for a single moment he focused his gaze on Lang, desperate for his answer. "Come *on,* what's her name? You said it earlier."

"Oh, her." Lang nodded toward the girl. "Conner. What's this all about? The meeting's over, Tanner."

"I have to talk to her. What's her first name?"

"Ummm, I'm not sure. Wait a minute, I'll think of it." Lang concentrated and then pursed his lips, tapping a single finger on his chin. "Let's see. Jean, was it? No, not Jean...."

Tanner thought his heart might burst. Lang was still concentrating. "Jane...no, that's not it."

"Think, Lang. I have to know." The girl was leaving, and he absolutely had to know her name, had to find out if it could possibly be her after all these—

Suddenly a knowing look crossed Lang's face. "I've got it. Unusual name. Jade, I think it is." Lang nodded. "Yes, that's it. Jade. Miss Jade Conner."

Five

TANNER STARED AT LANG AND FELT THE BLOOD DRAIN FROM HIS face. For a moment he stood frozen in place. Jade Conner? The girl who'd fought so eloquently against him was Jade Conner?

Tanner shoved his papers at Lang. "I'll see you at the office." Lang took the documents, a bewildered look on his face, as Tanner ran toward the door where he had last seen Jade.

He scanned the area in both directions, and then he saw her, fitting a key into a newly washed Honda.

"Jade!" He wore Italian dress pants and a starched white button-down with the finest tie his mother's money could buy. But he dodged the mingling citizens like a wide receiver eluding tacklers. He was at her side in seconds.

She turned around and scowled at him. "What do you want?"

Tanner gulped. Where should he begin? His heart was pounding as he searched her face, her emerald eyes. It was Jade. Eyes as green as the water in Chesapeake Bay. No wonder she'd seemed familiar. "Yes, I…well, you're—"

"How did you know my name?"

Her question caught him off guard, and when he hesitated she pounced. "Listen, I don't care who you are or where you're from or what lofty Ivy League school you attend. You have no right coming to our town and trying to convince those people it's okay to close down the children's unit. That's our hospital, not yours, and personally I don't care if you have some kind of agenda to work out…"

She railed on him for nearly a minute, which gave Tanner enough time to catch his breath. He relaxed and studied her. She was beautiful. Much more so than his memory of her could have imagined. He watched her eyes flash the way they had back when they were children, and he felt himself smile.

Tanner soaked in the sight of her. Jade Conner. He'd actually found her after all these years.

She released a heavy sigh. "You know, you are an arrogant, wicked man." Her jaw was clenched, and Tanner felt a twinge of remorse for causing her such grief. "Kelso General is filled with sick children, children you care nothing about, and all you can do is walk in here, give your professional speech, and then stand there *smiling at* me. I wish you'd turn around and go back to wherever you came from." She spun around to her car and opened the door. "I have nothing more to say to you, Mr. Ghormsley."

Tanner paused. *Don't you recognize me, Jade?*

"Eastman..." He waited while the word hit its mark. "Tanner Eastman."

It took her a few seconds. Then slowly she turned around and faced him once more, only this time she leaned against her car for support. Some of the color had faded from her face, and her voice trembled when she spoke. "Your name is Tanner Ghormsley."

"No." Tanner took a step closer. "Mr. Lang got it wrong."

They stood there for what felt like an eternity, searching each other's eyes. Tanner saw her expression soften and then fill with disbelief. Finally her eyes grew wet and she shook her head. "No. It can't be..."

"Jade, it's me. Tanner."

Tears spilled onto her cheeks, and he circled his arms around her, drawing her close as she did the same. All those years as childhood friends and they'd never hugged like this. But now, with the evening traffic whizzing by and the last of the stragglers from the meeting still filing past them, it felt like the most natural thing Tanner had ever done.

He pulled back, his arms still around her waist. She wiped her nose with the back of her hand and then pushed her fists into his chest like a petulant child. "So tell me, what do you have against our children's unit, huh?" Her tone was completely different now, almost teasing, but Tanner could tell she was bothered…and wanting to understand.

His voice was little more than a whisper. "I have nothing against your hospital, Jade. I'm an intern. They sent me a file and I wrote a brief. When I reported in this morning, they told me I was in charge of the presentation."

Jade released a shaky sigh and then, for the first time that afternoon, she gave a short laugh. "I should have known. Those snakes on the board used you as their scapegoat."

Tanner watched her, a dozen questions filling his mind. He ran a thumb along her cheek and allowed himself to get lost in the memories her face evoked. As he did, he felt his eyes brimming with unshed tears. "You never came back."

Jade could manage only a slight shake of her head as her eyes grew watery again.

He thought back to that afternoon on his front lawn, the day Jade said good-bye. It was all coming clearer now. "You were going to meet your mama in Kelso." He was transfixed, trapped in her gaze, carried back to the spring of his twelfth year. "You were supposed to come back when summer ended."

A wall went up in Jade's eyes and she stiffened. "We ended up staying."

"But why? What happened?"

She stared at her hands, and he had the strong sense that

she was wrestling with something. Finally she sighed. "Mama never came back."

"She didn't?" Tanner frowned. "Where did she—"

"I don't know. Daddy still won't talk about it." Jade kept her eyes trained on her hands, and Tanner saw they were trembling. "I used to think she got killed in a car accident somewhere between Virginia and Washington."

"And now?"

"I found a letter from her a year after we moved, postmarked D.C." Jade's expression was hard and Tanner realized the years must have been difficult for her. "She told Daddy to tell me she was sorry. That kind of thing."

The truth about what she was saying hit Tanner like a truck. Jade's mother had walked out on her with no intention whatsoever of coming back. No wonder Jade never moved back to Virginia. His heart broke for her, and he pulled her close again, stroking the back of her head as if she were still the ten-year-old girl he had grown up with. "I'm sorry, Jade."

She remained stiff and although she allowed him to comfort her, Tanner could tell she wasn't crying.

"Have you heard from her since then?"

"No. It doesn't matter. She's dead as far as I'm concerned."

Tanner got the point. The topic was closed. He pulled away again, this time completely. He had so much to tell her, so many years to make up for, but he didn't want her to feel like he was prying. He leaned back against her car so they were standing side by side.

"How old are you, anyway, Jade? Twenty, twenty-one?"

She smiled, and Tanner could see she was glad he'd changed the subject. "Twenty-one. And you're twenty-three." She studied him for a moment. "So...if you're an intern I guess you're staying in town?"

"Rented an apartment for the summer. Furnished. And one of the supervisors lent me a car. The internship lasts through August."

Jade cocked her head. "Where's Princeton, anyway?"

"New Jersey."

"Hmm." Jade hugged herself and looked away. "You like it?"

"It's all right." Tanner didn't want to talk about Princeton and politics and his well-planned future. "So what's it been? Twelve years?"

"Eleven, I think. A lot's happened since then."

Tanner gazed at the treetops behind city hall for a moment then back at Jade. "I thought about you all the time after you left, wondering what happened to you."

Jade hugged herself tighter. "The minute I saw you I thought...I thought you looked like my old friend, Tanner. The way I imagined you might look grown up."

Tanner watched her, how she brushed her hair back from her face and tilted her head just so. He was mesmerized by her, taken aback by the fact that his long lost friend wasn't a little girl anymore. She was the most beautiful woman he'd ever laid eyes on.

"Let's go somewhere. Talk, catch up." Tanner reached for her hand, but she pulled it back and again her eyes found something on the ground. He searched her face, but her troubled expression did nothing to explain her actions. Then it dawned on him..."I'm sorry...I didn't even ask. Are you married, Jade? Is there someone waiting for you?"

She viewed him through cautious eyes. "No. I just...people will talk. I like to keep my distance."

Tanner hesitated. "Okay. Sorry about the hand thing."

A slight grin appeared, and some of the caution in Jade's eyes faded. "Forgiven." She stared at him a moment. "I'm sorry for overreacting."

"No problem." Tanner was surprised at how he ached to take her in his arms and kiss her. From the time he was in high school he could have had his pick of beautiful women. They left notes on his car, messages at his dorm, and propositioned him to his face. He wasn't interested. He trusted God's plan for his life, and part of that plan was being sexually pure until he was married. Despite the women who sought after him, holding to that conviction had never been a struggle.

Yet none of them had ever made him feel the way he felt now, standing on a city sidewalk, Jade Conner filling his senses.

Tanner had a feeling that whatever wounds Jade's mother had inflicted on her daughter's heart, they had left her scarred. He would have to move slowly if they were going to be friends again. "Wanna get something to eat?"

She nodded. "I know a great hamburger place."

He patted her car. "You driving?"

Her eyes twinkled. "If you trust a girl who can beat you in a bike race."

Tanner didn't smile. The emotions she stirred in him were too deep to make light of. "The question isn't whether I trust you..." His voice was softer, his face less than a foot from hers. "It's whether you trust me."

Jade said nothing, just considered his statement, meeting his gaze while a dozen emotions danced in her eyes. Finally she caught his neck with the crook of her arm and hugged him close. His arms circled her again, and he clung to her the way a brother might cling to a long lost sister.

He held her that way for nearly a minute all the while praying that she wouldn't see the truth. How the feelings that assaulted him now were far from brotherly.

Six

IF TRAIN TRACKS HAD RUN THROUGH THE TOWN OF KELSO, THE house where Jade and her father lived would have been on the wrong side.

Their two-bedroom rental was sandwiched between a cluster of miscellaneous mobile homes and a weed-infested trailer park on Stark Street. The city dump was within eyesight, and a bitter stench drifted down the roadway whenever a breeze kicked up. What with the rusted washing machines and broken-down automobiles cluttering the yards up and down Stark, it was difficult to tell where the dump ended and the neighborhood began.

Crime had never been much of an issue in Kelso. A sleepy town that survived on industry along the Columbia and Cowlitz rivers, most of the people who lived there had done so all their lives. Still, when there was a domestic incident or a drug bust, inevitably it was on or near Stark Street.

Jade was used to her neighborhood. That night when she pulled into her driveway and stepped around broken engine parts and a Mustang that had died five years earlier, she didn't give a second thought to the condition of her home.

She had found Tanner Eastman. After ten years of sorrow and struggle she had come face to face with the one who had been a single ray of light in an otherwise cavernously dark past. Somehow, someway, despite the years gone by, he had found her, and she desperately needed to talk to someone about what she was feeling.

Jade opened the front door. "Dad?" It was Monday night, and if there'd been enough work at the garage to keep him past noon, he would have worked the whole day. In that case, he would probably still be sober enough to talk.

There was a crash in the kitchen, and Jade followed the sound. The cracked kitchen countertop was covered with a dozen empty beer bottles, the mangled remains of five fried chicken parts, and congealed pools of spilled gravy. Her father was leaning against the refrigerator, swaying slightly and standing in a pool of beer and broken glass.

He saw Jade and scowled. "Don't jus' stan' there!" He glared at her with bloodshot eyes. "Clean it up!"

Jade sighed. "Daddy, why do you have to do this?" She set down her purse and stooped to pick up the larger pieces of glass. "Did you cut your foot?"

"Footz fine. Hurry up. You think I like bein' stuck here?"

For as long as they'd lived in Kelso, Jade had had two fathers. One, a quiet, hard-working man who was humbly apologetic to her for his ineptitude at knowing what it took to raise a little girl. The other…the other stood before her now. A belligerent, drunken, miserable man who took out his frustration with life on Jade because she was the only one around.

Mornings were the best. He would wake up groggy and pained from the hangover, and his voice, his eyes, his entire countenance would be different.

"Jade, baby, could you be a doll and pick up some milk when you're out today?" he would say on his way out the door. Sometimes he'd search for her and hug her. Occasionally he would apologize for the night before. Always he wore regret in his eyes and the haunting shades of failure.

Jade took a rag and began cleaning the floor as her father stepped unsteadily around her and wiped his wet feet on the threadbare carpet. She was still picking up broken glass as he shuffled to his easy chair. She would never understand how he managed to hold a job at the garage, fixing cars and making enough money to get by, when he went to work each day ravaged by the effects of another hard-drinking night.

She could hear him pop the top on another bottle. "Where ya been?" He didn't talk when he was drunk, he barked. His voice was abrasive, short tempered, and full of accusation.

The glass was cleaned up, and Jade ran the cloth once more over the floor, hating the way it made her hands smell like beer. "I ran into an old friend, someone from Virginia."

Her father was used to holding conversations in a drunken state. He thought over Jade's comment and then bellowed. "What friend?"

Jade wiped her hands on a towel and took a spot on the sofa across from her father. "Tanner Eastman. Remember him?"

Her father belched loudly. "Eastman...Eastman. Oh, yeah. Snobby folks across the street."

Jade noticed the gravy stains on her father's undershirt and the chicken crumbs scattered on the floor around him. She wondered what he would think come morning if he could see how he looked now. "Tanner wasn't a snob. He and I used to play together."

"You did?"

"Yes." Where had her father thought she was all those hours she spent away from home? *He didn't care then, and he doesn't care now.*

"I don't remember it."

"It's true, Dad. Until we moved he was my best friend."

"Whas he doin' here?"

"An internship for the university he attends."

Her father scowled. "Told ya he was a snob." He raised his

bottle and took a long swig. "Ahhhh. What about ol' Jim Rudolph? Whatever happened to him?"

"I'm not talking about Jim, Daddy."

Her father raised part way out of his chair in a threatening motion. "Don' get smart with me, y'ng lady. You might be grown up but you still haffa show a little respect."

Jade stared at her hands. Why did she bother?

Her father plopped back into his chair. "Don't get your hopes up, Jade."

"What?"

"That Eastman's a snob. 'S too good for trash like you an' me."

Jade stood to leave. She'd had enough of her father's encouragement for one night. "Tanner's my friend. We had a nice dinner and caught up on our lives." She paused and felt the sting of tears. "And don't worry, I don't have any hopes about him."

"That's good. Jim Rudolph wouldn't like it if you took up with 'nother man."

A pit formed in Jade's stomach. Why must her father persist with talk about Jim? Hadn't she made herself clear?

"Daddy, I don't love Jim. I don't even like him. He asked me to marry him, and I turned him down, remember?"

Her father scratched his armpit and stared at a wrestling match on TV. "You're an idiot, Jade."

Her heart deflated like a two-week-old balloon. "I am not an idiot." There was no point carrying on a conversation with her father when he had been drinking, but sometimes Jade couldn't help herself. Most nights, these were the only conversations they had.

He faced her again and raised his voice another notch. "You're an idiot! Jim comes from good, hard-workin' family.

He's gonna be a teacher, and you turned him down. I said it before and I'll say it again—" he took another swig and finished the bottle—"Jim Rudolph's the bes' thing ever happened to you, Jade." He tried to focus on her, but his head bobbed unsteadily, and he finally gave up and turned back to the match. "You shoulda married him. No one else'll ever want you."

Jade felt her shoulders slump. Every time she let herself get sucked into a discussion like this one she wondered the same thing: Was it the beer, or did her father really hate her?

He belched again. "Get me 'nother beer, will ya?"

Jade stared at her father. Most of the time she did as he asked, but this time he could get it himself. Maybe break another bottle in the process. She needed fresh air before she let go and threw something at him.

She exhaled through tightly clenched teeth and spun around. She was already outside when she heard him stumbling toward the kitchen. Apparently he'd forgotten about her. Jade breathed a heavy sigh. The air was warm and damp, hovering like a blanket against Jade's skin.

The covered porch was the best part of the house. It ran along the entire front and was deep enough to find shelter even when wind drove the Northwest rain sideways. Jade had read hundreds of books on this porch, spent years here dreaming about a different life.

When she was a little girl, she had considered running away, moving in with somebody else's family where there would be a mom and a dad and dinner hours and laughter. But over time she had learned to fend for herself, avoiding her father when he was drinking and escaping to imaginary worlds on the front porch.

Jade wandered across the creaking boards. The porch was

cluttered, of course, like everything else about their house. Jade would have loved to clean it up, to throw out the junk. But her father had collected most of it from his years as a mechanic. Parts that could be fixed and sold if he ever found the time, engines he could repair and use again if only he'd had a sober evening in which to work.

She spotted a cardboard box marked Starters and Ignition Switches. It had been there for at least five years, and Jade had used it as a chair so often it felt almost normal to do so. She pushed it out so she could see the dusky sky. Her heart felt bruised from her father's comments, and Jade thought about the irony. Men were easily struck by her looks, but the most important part, the place where her heart and soul lived, was battered beyond recognition. Her father was right. Why would anyone else want her?

Especially someone like Tanner Eastman.

Jade sighed and stared into the dimly lit sky. It was nine and night would settle within the hour. Maybe she should throw on a pair of sweats and jog. Her mind was racing far too quickly to think about sleep. Jade felt as if she'd drifted downstream in time and was being sucked into a whirlpool of memories. Memories she'd almost forgotten.

She smiled. Who would have thought after all this time…? What if she hadn't gone to the meeting? What if he'd chosen an internship somewhere else?

Seeing him again made her ache for the little girl she'd been and the way she had missed him so desperately the summer after she and her father had moved to Kelso. For three years, they'd been best friends. His parents were busy and so were hers. Together they found time for each other, a world where they chased butterflies and jumped rope and played house. He was the father and she was the mother. Or she was the sister and he was the brother. Sometimes they would stay in character all day long.

Tanner's mother didn't like him going to other kids' houses, so most of the time they played at his. His backyard was the stage for a hundred games of make believe and mysterious monsters and unrivaled challenges and story lines.

Jade remembered one of Tanner's favorite games. She leaned her head back, and she could see them as they were more than a decade ago.

"Okay, Jade, close your eyes." Tanner would take her hand and lead her to the corner of the yard. "See how much you trust me."

"Not this again!"

"Come on, you love this one." Tanner had been persuasive back then, too.

"Okay." Once her eyes were closed he would lead her on an obstacle course through the yard. "Come on, Jade. Trust me; don't open your eyes."

"I won't! I promise."

And she hadn't. Her trust in Tanner had been absolute.

The sky was growing black, and a handful of stars poked their way through the darkness. Even now those days with Tanner stood out as the happiest time in her life. The years since then had been wracked with disappointment and insecurity. Everyone who mattered had let her down. Everyone but Tanner. He was the only person she'd ever truly trusted.

Back then she'd been certain she would marry him one day. Other kids teased them about it, but secretly in her little girl heart, she knew it wasn't a joke. How could she marry anyone else?

A lump formed in Jade's throat and she swallowed hard. Everything had changed since then. Jade knew more about marriage now, how it could make a person crazy.

She sighed. Every moment with Tanner tonight had been magical. They'd grown up in two completely different worlds, yet still they shared a bond that had not faded.

Tanner's words from earlier that night echoed in her mind now.

"I want to see you tomorrow and the next day, and the next..." He'd stared deep into her eyes. "I want to know what you're about now that you've grown up."

Jade wanted to see him, too. She wanted to bare her heart to him the way she had as a child. But while the bond between them hadn't seemed to change, their circumstances had. There was no way to bridge their worlds now. Tanner would never be interested in her. Besides his internship only lasted through the summer.

Still there was something about the way he had looked at her earlier that night that made her heart sing. If she hadn't known him better, she would have said he looked at her the same way Jim Rudolph did.

And Jim Rudolph's intentions were obvious.

Jade had met Jim when she was a freshman in high school. He was a senior that year, quarterback of the Kelso football team, a tall, stocky boy with a baby face. Most of the girls at Kelso dreamed of dating him, but Jade hadn't been interested. Throughout high school she enjoyed dozens of acquaintances, but no lasting friendships. Close friends would eventually want to come over and meet her parents. And Jade was not willing to share that part of her life with anyone.

So she remained aloof. Girls envied her; boys found her a challenge, but she was never concerned with any of them. She found comfort in running and biking and reading mysteries. In the controlled world she had created for herself there was no room for relationships of any kind.

But Jim Rudolph simply would not take no for an answer.

In Jade's freshman year he followed her around campus between classes and asked her to every one of the school dances. Jade always told him no, but eventually she allowed herself to make small talk with him. It was harmless. Jim wasn't a threat to her isolation.

After all, he could never love anyone the way he loved himself.

Still he persisted. Long after he moved to Corvallis and took a dormitory room on campus at Oregon State University, he continued his pursuit of her. He would stop by her house when he was home on break, chat with her father and wait for her to come home from school.

Jade made sure she never encouraged his attention, but he continued pursuing her all the same.

"I could have any girl I want, do you know that, Jade."

"I'm so impressed, Jim." She remembered busying herself in a magazine, staunchly ignoring his advances.

"Come on, Jade. You like me. Admit it."

She had been bored with the conversation. "No, Jim. I don't like you. I tolerate you."

Jim had laughed like that was the funniest thing he'd ever heard. "Do you know how many girls would die to be in your shoes right now?"

Jade had glanced down at her bare feet and sighed impatiently. "I'm not wearing shoes, Jim."

"You know what I mean."

"Not really."

He had studied her. "You play a better game of hard-to-get than any girl I know. You know what else?"

Jade was certain she hadn't looked up. She rarely gave Jim

the privilege of eye contact. "What?"

"You're not so bad looking for a girl who plays it cool."

"Change the subject, Jim."

"Why?"

"Because I'm not interested. If you must come around and talk to me, then please stop pretending I'm your girlfriend. I'm not."

He'd seemed indifferent. "You seeing someone else?"

"No. I'm not seeing anyone. I don't *want* to see anyone. How much clearer can I be?"

"Fine. One day you'll wise up and come to your senses." Jim puffed out his chest. "But you better hurry. I won't be free forever."

Jade had a hundred memories of conversations like that one. Then, last summer, when Jim graduated from college, he did the craziest thing of all. She was working at a sporting goods store in town when he came in wearing a wide grin. He motioned for her and she followed him outside.

"Jade, I know this is a strange place to ask you..." He pulled a tiny velvety box from his pants pocket.

She remembered feeling deeply alarmed and then trapped, like she might suffocate. She knew what was coming, and she was helpless to stop it.

He opened the box and therein lay a smallish diamond ring. "I already asked your father.... What I'm trying to say is, I can't wait around forever, Jade. I want to offer you the chance of a lifetime. Your daddy said so himself." Jim had grinned and Jade thought she might hyperventilate. "What do you say? Marry me and let's stop playing games with each other."

She cringed now remembering her reaction. She had pushed the ring away and cried loudly. "Jim are you out of your *mind?* I don't want to marry you. I don't want to date you. I never have."

He had stared at her blankly, then methodically closed the tiny box and hid it back in his pocket again. "You don't get it, do you?"

"No, *you* don't get it! You've hung around long enough that I consider you a friend. Not a great friend. Not even a good friend. But I have never given you the impression that what we have is more than a casual friendship."

Jim's face reflected the pain her words had caused him. But almost instantly his expression had changed and a wicked grin broke across his face. His eyes boldly roamed the length of her. "Don't you see, Jade? You're nothing. Nobody. Your father's an alcoholic; you have no friends. What're you going to do? Live alone for the rest of your life?" He shrugged as if she'd done little more than turn down an offer of dinner and a movie. "Have it your way. But one day you'll come to your senses. I'm the best thing that ever happened to you, Jade Conner. And don't you forget it. Give me a call when you change your mind."

Jim still called now and then, but Jade had the feeling he was giving up on her. He wasn't a bad guy, really. Just shallow and self-centered, and the thought of being married to him made Jade nauseous.

She stretched and forced Jim's face from her mind.

No, Tanner hadn't looked at her the way Jim Rudolph had. Tanner saw straight into her soul. But he was also attending one of the finest universities in the country with plans to be elected to public office. He had a wonderful family, more money than she would ever see, and a future brimming with possibilities.

Whatever came of them this summer, it would not amount to more than friendship. Tanner deserved someone like himself.

And she...well, maybe her father was right. Maybe she

deserved someone like...like Jim.

If that were true, Jim had been right that day in the sporting goods store. Because she would rather live alone till the day she died than marry Jim Rudolph.

Seven

It started with evening walks along the Cowlitz River and up the trails through Tam O'Ashanter Park and quickly progressed to dinner every night that week. They ordered pizza and watched a baseball game at Tanner's apartment. Another time they ate at a Chinese restaurant and flew kites on a bluff overlooking the banks of the Cowlitz River.

By the end of that first week, Jade hoped the summer would never end.

Most couples spending this kind of time together would have considered themselves dating. But Tanner had not looked at her again the way he had that first night, after the town meeting. He did phone her every day when he was finished at the office and seemed happy to spend time with her. But then, she was the only person in town he knew. Nothing in his manner or words gave her any indication that he desired more than friendship from her. He didn't seem to think of her in a romantic sense, and Jade was glad. What could possibly come of it?

They lived in worlds separated by three thousand miles and a chasm of time too great to bridge.

Even so, Jade was enjoying herself immensely. She was surprised at how freeing it felt to spend evenings away from home. By the time she got home each night, her father was asleep, and she would creep to her room unnoticed. No yelling or threatening or accusations.

No one telling her she was an idiot.

It was Friday evening, and again Jade and Tanner had plans to be together after work. They met in front of his apartment just after six. Tanner greeted her with a hug and a bag of sub sandwiches. "Joe's Deli?"

"Mmm. Good choice."

"The supervisors said I couldn't go wrong at Joe's."

Jade followed him inside. "The supervisors…ah, yes. My favorite people. At least they're good for something."

He flipped on a light, pulled out two paper plates, and set them on the table. "How's Shaunie?"

Jade wasn't used to someone asking about her day. Three days ago the question would have made her suspicious, but now she smiled as she sat down at the table. "The infection's gone. So far her tests look good. She might be able to go home tomorrow."

Tanner sat down across from her and peeled the wrappers off two subs. "Pray?"

Jade nodded and quickly bowed her head. Tanner had prayed often that week—over every meal and sometimes after spending an evening talking. Just to let God in on the conversation, he'd told her.

When he was done, he caught her gaze. "You care about her, don't you?"

"Shaunie?" It was wonderful talking with someone who so easily read her mind. "Yes…like she was my own daughter."

Tanner took a bite. "Think you'll have a daughter one day? Kids?"

"I don't know." She glanced down at her plate where the sandwich looked suddenly wilted.

Tanner set his food down and leaned back in his chair. He studied her in silence for a moment then tilted his head. "Every time I bring up relationships you shut down." His voice was soft, and Jade could hear how much he cared for her, how much he wanted her to open up to him. But how could he understand what her life had been like? How it felt to have your mother leave and be raised by an alcoholic father?

She sighed. "I'm sorry."

Tanner pushed his plate aside and rested his forearms on the table. He leaned toward her when he spoke. "No, *I'm* sorry. I don't mean to make you uncomfortable. I just want to know you, Jade…what you're thinking behind those beautiful eyes."

Her heart skipped a beat, and she wanted to bolt from the table, escape back to the private solitude of her cluttered home and stuffy bedroom. She forced herself to remain seated, studying her plate.

"It's about your mama, isn't it?" Tanner inched his chair near hers, then reached out with gentle fingers to take her hand in his. "I'm here. If you want to talk about it."

Jade had hidden her feelings about her mother for so long, she'd become expert at it. But being around Tanner that week had weakened more walls than she cared to admit. Right now, with Tanner stroking her hand and questions about her mother dangling in the air like so many skeletons, Jade felt the dam breaking.

She still hadn't looked up, and as the tears gathered they spilled freely onto her plate.

Tanner must have seen them. He moved closer still, put an arm around her shoulders and hugged her close. "It's okay, Jade. I'm here."

She had never cried about her mother's leaving, preferring denial at first and anger after that. But here, with Tanner's breath against her face and her father miles away, she no longer had the desire to fight the pain that welled within her. Instead she slumped against Tanner's shoulder and gave in to a torrent of grief. He stroked her hair and turned so that his other arm embraced her also. In hushed tones he uttered caring words, calming words until her sobbing eased.

"I'm so sorry." Tanner was still stroking her hair and her back, comforting a place in Jade where the child still lived. A child who had spent too many years alone.

Tanner pulled away, found a tissue, and handed it to her. "It must have been awful."

Jade blew her nose and leaned back, settling her gaze on his. She stayed that way a while, and Tanner waited, letting her decide when she was ready to talk. Like the tears, there had never been any place for words regarding her mother. Now finally she was ready. Tanner cared how she felt, what had happened to her after she moved from Williamsburg.

Jade drew a shaky, deep breath. "She never even said goodbye."

Tanner kept his eyes trained on her.

"I still don't know exactly what happened. Something... someone must have caught her attention. Whatever it was, she left and never looked back."

"Did you ever ask your dad?"

Jade closed her eyes. "A hundred times. The answer was always the same. 'Your mother's a whore. Don't bring her up again in this house.'" Jade's voice echoed with anger as she recalled her father's words. When it came to the disappearance of her mother, anger was the only emotion Jade's father had ever displayed.

"So you still don't know what happened?"

She shook her head, then hesitated. Tanner eased closer again, his arm around her shoulders once more. She struggled to find the right words. "There must have been some other man. Otherwise Daddy wouldn't have called her a whore."

Tanner stroked her arm, and Jade pulled slightly away so she could see his eyes. "You asked me if I want a daughter someday." She blinked back fresh tears. "Probably not. Because that would mean getting married, and I've seen what marriage does to people." A picture of her father passed out in his vomit came to mind, and she dismissed it. "I would only want a child if I could provide her the home I never had. A mom and a dad and security. A place where she would be loved."

Tanner stroked her cheek again. Still he remained silent, and Jade knew he was giving her the space to say everything she'd never said. She sighed. "What kind of mother leaves her child and never looks back? She never called me or visited me or remembered my birthday. Didn't she love me, Tanner? Didn't she care about what I might feel when I was old enough to realize what she'd done? To realize she didn't want me?"

She began crying again and through her tears her voice rose. She hated her mother for what she'd done, and it felt good to be able to finally say so. "Other little girls talked about their mamas…how they baked or shopped for them, how they curled their hair or helped them with their homework.

"Every time someone asked me about my mother I felt like a piece of my heart was being strangled."

Jade relaxed against Tanner's chest and stared at a picture on the wall. The image of Tanner and his parents outside their home in Virginia smiled back at her. She closed her eyes. How could Tanner relate to this sorry picture of her adolescence?

Jade clung to Tanner. It didn't matter if he couldn't relate. She felt utterly safe and cared for, and now that she had begun, she wanted him to know everything.

"I was thirteen when I got my period. We'd seen the film in school, but I wasn't ready. When I saw how much I was bleeding, I hid in my backyard behind a trash pile. I cried and cried, scared about what was happening to me."

She craned her head and found his eyes again. "Do you know what I thought? I thought I was dying, Tanner. Because I didn't have a mother to tell me…I had to sneak into my dad's wallet and steal five dollars so I could buy pads at the corner store. I wasn't even sure how to use them or where the blood was coming from."

The memory churned in her stomach. She faced Tanner. "I could never, ever in a million years do that to a child. If I had a child I'd want him to have two parents, so he would know he was loved by a mother and a father."

Tanner was silent, listening, watching her. Jade felt more tears and she blinked them back. "I'd cherish everything about him. The baby years, the toddler years. Kindergarten and grade school. I'd volunteer in his classroom and take him with me on walks. I'd make scrapbooks of his life so he could see where he came from and know where he was going. I would be his closest friend in the world, and we'd love each other forever." Jade paused. "Maybe that's why I feel so strongly about the children's unit at Kelso General."

Tanner placed his finger under her chin and Jade could see in his eyes that he understood. When he spoke his voice was filled with compassion. "Those are your children. You don't want me or the board or anyone else taking them away from you."

Jade nodded. "I can't tell you how many times my dad has told me I'm nothing, a nobody without a future…. But when I'm with those sick babies, I know what I'm supposed to do with my life. That's why I was so mad that day at the meeting."

Tanner still cupped her face with his hand, tracing her jaw and staring deeply into her eyes. "Your father says that to you?"

He was clearly horrified, obviously unable to fathom a

father like hers, and again Jade felt their differences. "All the time."

"You don't need that, Jade. The man isn't good enough for a daughter like you. You should leave home. Get a place of your own."

Jade nodded. "I will. As soon as I finish my nurse's training."

Tanner stood then and moved across the room. When he returned, he held what looked like a Bible. "I want to show you something."

"In the Bible?" What did this have to do with her sordid life? Jade watched as Tanner flipped his way through the pages. She noticed highlighted areas throughout and tiny scribbling in the margins. Apparently Tanner was a man who took the Bible seriously. He quickly found what he was looking for.

"Here it is. In Jeremiah. God was reassuring the people through the prophet Jeremiah that if they turned their hearts toward him, he would be faithful with them for all times."

Jade nodded, still not sure what this had to do with her.

"I want to read you something from Jeremiah twenty-nine." He put his finger on the section of text, and Jade saw it was already highlighted. "'I know the plans I have for you,' declares the LORD, 'plans to prosper you and not to harm you, plans to give you hope and a future.'"

Tanner passed the Bible to Jade. "Here, read it again."

Jade read it to herself and then looked at him. "What does it mean?"

He angled his head back thoughtfully and considered her question. As he did, a feeling, a hot sensation spread across her cheeks, and again their differences seemed glaringly obvious. "I uh…well…we didn't read the Bible much."

There was nothing condescending in Tanner's expression,

but Jade had the sense he could see into her soul, as if he knew her heart long before she was willing to frame her thoughts with words. She hung her head slightly. "Okay, never...We, well, we weren't exactly church-goers." She hesitated. "I talk to God sometimes, though. When there's no one else to talk to."

Tanner's eyes lit up. "Good. That's all this is, really. God's way of talking back to us." He pointed to the verse in Jeremiah again. "So what you see there is a promise that applies to anyone who puts their trust in the Lord, just like it applied to God's people back then. Because that's how God feels about those who love him." Tanner ran his finger under the words again. "I know the plans I have for you...plans to give you hope and a future."

It sounded nice, Jade had to admit. But had she ever put her trust in the Lord? She didn't think so, but she wasn't willing to discuss it with Tanner. Not now. She tried to imagine how different her life might be if the Bible verse were true. Almighty God? A plan for her life? She didn't think so, but it was comforting to think about. "Thanks, Tanner."

"Do you believe it?"

She shrugged. "Hasn't happened so far."

Tanner's shoulders dropped. "That's why it's so important that you accept him as your..." Something in his eyes withdrew. "Never mind...I'm not trying to confuse you, Jade. But you've got to believe God loves you. Your life's just beginning. Don't you see?"

"I see that our sandwiches are wilting."

He eyed the partially eaten subs and smiled. "I get the point. Topic closed."

They finished eating and watched the movie—a comedy Jade had seen twice before. But watching it with Tanner made every line new, and she laughed until she could barely breathe.

When it was over, they sat facing each other on his rented sofa.

"I have an idea." Tanner laid his arm across the back of the sofa so that it was nearly touching Jade's shoulder.

"I'm listening."

"Come with me Sunday to Portland. I've been so busy I haven't called my mother in days. I promised I'd see her this weekend—" he leaned closer and his eyes clouded with doubt, as though he was sure she'd say no before he finished asking— "we could go to church in the morning and spend the afternoon with my mom. Have dinner at her house, something like that."

Panic coursed through Jade's veins. She'd barely known Tanner's mother back when they were children. Even though she hung out at his house, his mother rarely made herself available or went out of her way to be kind to Jade. "Do you think she'd want me to come?"

Tanner moved closer so that his arm rested against her, and there was a flicker of something deeply intimate in his eyes. Once more he drew nearer to her, then—as though he'd changed his mind—he stood and leaned casually against the wall. He looked down at her, and for an instant his eyes darted along the length of her. Then just as quickly they connected with her eyes again. What was that look on his face? Almost as if she could see a piece of his soul, a piece she couldn't quite read. Was he nervous? Afraid of saying something wrong? Whatever it was, he was trying to hide it.

"Of course she would. You're a familiar face from the old neighborhood. She'll be thrilled that we ran into each other again after all these years."

Jade imagined dinner with a cultured woman like Doris Eastman. She was proper, a regular churchgoer—and Jade was terrified at the thought of trying to meet the woman's approval.

But it might be nice...spending a day at church with Tanner, then the two of us being with his mother....

Tanner was waiting for her answer. "Do it, Jade. It'll be great. I know this amazing church ten minutes from my mom's house. Crossroads. Lots of people, great music, incredible preaching. You'll love it."

Jade drew a deep breath. "Promise she'll like me?"

He laughed. "My mother? Be serious. What in the world's not to like?"

"Okay. Want the truth?"

Tanner nodded.

"The church thing has me interested."

"Good." He broke into a grin. " I'll call Mom tomorrow and let her know."

Jade stood and moved closer to him. "I should get going. I've got to be at the hospital early—"

She paused when he shifted away from her. Confused, she looked at him—and frowned. There it was again. The strange fear thing in his eyes. Like she'd caught him thinking something he wasn't supposed to be thinking. He moved away abruptly and crossed the room to get a drink of water. When she followed, he moved with his glass to a lone chair in the corner of the room.

Stopping in her tracks, Jade planted her hands on her hips and shook her head at him. "Are you trying to avoid me?" She was teasing, not sure what to make of his nervous behavior.

For a moment, Tanner opened his mouth but no words came out. Then he smiled the smile that Jade was sure would one day win him thousands of votes in public office. "Yes, in fact I am." He waved his hand near his face and wrinkled his nose. "Onion breath. I don't want to knock you over. I should have known better than to order onions on the subs."

Jade laughed and collected her purse and car keys. "Mine can't be much better. Hey, thanks again for dinner." She grinned, still caught up in the laughter. "Especially the onions."

Tanner walked her to the door and watched her go. When she was halfway down the sidewalk he yelled out to her, "Talk to you tomorrow."

Her car was parked just outside his front door, and he watched her until she had climbed inside and drove off. As she made her way through town toward the city dump, she had the unusual feeling that all was right with her world. She had laughed more that night than the past five years combined.

It was Tanner, of course. He made her heart feel light as the summer breeze dancing over the Cowlitz River, as though she were normal for the first time in her life. As though she didn't have a mother who'd abandoned her and an alcoholic father at home.

As though the only friend she had in the world weren't only passing through her life for one golden summer.

Tanner watched her drive away. Then he closed the door, sank against it, and blew out the air that had been collecting in his lungs all night. His voice was a frustrated moan. "Jade... You're killing me."

Onion breath. That was believable enough. He sure couldn't tell her the truth: that every time she got close, his flesh was being assaulted by incredible feelings he'd never imagined existed. He could hardly tell her that after the movie, with the two of them so close on the sofa, all he'd wanted to do was take her in his arms and...and...

He closed his eyes. *Lord, I'm struggling here. Why does she make me feel this way? I can't even be near her without wanting to kiss her, to hold her, to...Lord help me. What I really want is for Jade to come to know you. I should be leading her to you, not...well, you know."*

It was a feeble prayer, but it was all he could manage.

No temptation has seized you except that which is common to man....

The words echoed deep in his soul, and he felt a wave of reassurance. God was with him. He heard Tanner's prayers and he understood. Tanner recalled the rest of the Scripture and knew that God would not let him be tempted beyond what he could bear. And that when he was tempted, the Lord himself would provide a way out.

Tonight, without a doubt, God had done exactly that.

Eight

It wasn't that Jade had ever suffered a bad experience in church. Rather it was simply that her father hated the place. He insisted it was some church back in Virginia that had forced them out of town, across the country to Kelso.

"Church folk are hypocrites," her father would say when Sunday rolled around each week. "They like pointing fingers at ya. They'd recognize you as the daughter of a whore and make you leave the building."

Jade had heard that a hundred times, and as she drove with Tanner south on I-5 she heard it again and again in her mind.

"What are you thinking about?" They passed Ridgefield and were heading toward Vancouver. According to Tanner's calculations they'd be at Crossroads Church in fifteen minutes.

Jade stared out her side window. The rain of the week before had disappeared, and the past few days had been brilliantly sunny. With the blue sky as a backdrop, the layered brush and trees along the freeway looked vibrantly green. She turned to Tanner. "Whether they'll like me."

"Jade, they won't even know you. Crossroads is a big church. We'll just be two more people sitting in the pews."

Still she had the feeling someone would know. Someone would spot her and recognize her for what she was and ask her to leave the building, just like her father had always said.

The parking lot was full, and traffic attendants directed the flow of cars leaving the earlier service as well as those arriving for the next one. Jade had never seen this kind of crowd at any church gathering. The thought of being among so large a sea of people made her relax. Maybe she'd be safe after all.

Tanner walked alongside her, and for an instant Jade wished he would take her hand. He'd been careful not to since she'd pulled away that first day after the meeting. Of course, he'd held her hand that night at his apartment when she told him about her mother. But that was only for comfort. Now, even though it would never be true, she wished he'd hold her hand for different reasons: to show the world she belonged to him.

The church was filling up quickly, and they found seats near the back. Jade saw how comfortable Tanner was, reading the bulletin, filling in the blanks on the sermon outline form inside. She clutched her papers tightly and sat low in her seat. People greeted each other, hugging and smiling, and Jade took in all of it. In one of the pews, a cluster of people bent their heads together in what Jade assumed was prayer. She couldn't hear what they were saying, only that they were saying it quietly, out loud.

Okay, God, I'm here. I'm finally in a church. Help me last through the hour without getting kicked out.

Jade's conversations with God were always very simple and to the point. She talked to him like she would a friend, as if he was always with her ready to hear what she had to say. This other prayer, this thing these people were doing, was not something she understood. She sat stone still, uncomfortable around so many good people.

The music started, and Jade was struck at how it filled the building. Full and professional sounding, the band up front included a piano, several guitars, drums, and a keyboard. The music filled Jade's heart with peace, and again she felt the tension ease from her body.

She had figured church music would be like she'd heard it on television. Somber, sullen, sung in soprano with little emotion. The music at Crossroads was vastly different. The worship leader played the piano like no one Jade had ever heard. She listened carefully to the words. It was a song about how the Lord had torn down the walls around the hearts of his people and loved them through every step of their lives. And it was a commitment in turn to walk beside God and speak his truth as long as breath could be drawn.

The music built to a crescendo, and Jade was taken aback by what was happening around her. Scattered throughout the church, a number of people were closing their eyes, raising their hands while they sang. *What is this, God? What are they doing?* She glanced at the bulletin, somehow embarrassed by their strange actions. Near the printed words to the music was an invitation to join in the singing—*worship* they called it. There it also said that occasionally people might raise their hands while worshiping. It went on to explain that this was merely a spontaneous act of love toward God.

The band was repeating the song, and this time Jade felt herself humming along. The tune was catchy, the music enjoyable, and the words...Jade felt like she could have written them herself. They filled her heart to overflowing.

From you, Lord, I won't part.... You've torn down walls around my heart....

It was that part, the walls around the heart part, that sent chills down Jade's arms and caused tears to well up in her eyes. *Is that what I've done, God? Put walls around my heart?* She closed her eyes. *Tear them down, God. I can't breathe inside these walls.*

The third time through, she sang along and meant every word. She caught Tanner smiling at her and smiled back. And somewhere inside her heart she felt a rush of fresh air. There were two more songs, and they, too, seemed to be written for Jade alone. But it was the fourth song that made her tears spill onto the bulletin in her hands. It talked about having a father who knew his children by name, one who was proud to call them his own, one who would never leave her no matter what.

One who didn't think she was an idiot.

Jade sat, unmoving, ignoring the tears. Was this what it felt like to have walls torn down? Walls that had stood around her heart for more than ten years?

The music was over and a man stood to talk. Tanner had told her that the pastor, Bill Ritchie, could be heard on the radio across the country and that his sermons were powerful. Jade wasn't sure what Tanner meant.

All she knew was that she wasn't looking forward to the message.

This would be the part where he would get in their faces, condemn them and criticize them. He would shout and tell them they were terrible sinners and warn them about hell fire and brimstone. Then would come the part where he would demand they give money otherwise God couldn't possibly have mercy on their souls.

Instead, Pastor Ritchie smiled. "Isn't it a glorious day in the Lord? Let's rise and give him thanks."

The crowd was on its feet, and Pastor Ritchie was reading something from the Bible. It had a poetic ring to it, something about how God had known them from the beginning, how he had formed them in their mother's wombs, and how all of their days were planned from the beginning.

Was it true, God? Had he really formed her in her mother's womb with plans for her from the start? Jade made a note to ask Tanner later where the Bible really said that.

For the next half hour the pastor talked about choices that

face all people at one time or another. The first choice, he told them, was whether or not to believe God's claims about himself and his son, Jesus Christ. Rather than a lecture, Pastor Ritchie's sermon was more like a fireside chat. He strolled from one side of the stage to the other, making eye contact with individuals and holding the audience captive in the process. Occasionally he'd chuckle out loud or smile fondly when giving examples about how people often worked all their lives to keep God out, only to give in when crisis hit.

"And let's face it, folks," Pastor Ritchie said. "We're all going to have to deal with crisis at some point."

Jade listened intently. The second choice, the pastor said, was whether people were willing to give their lives to the Lord and let him do with them what he wished. He talked about the futility of holding tightly to a life lived without Christ when there was such freedom in living alongside him.

The time flew by, and soon the pastor was winding up. Jade was mesmerized, spellbound by the way the man's words made sense. She hadn't glanced at Tanner once through the pastor's sermon. She hadn't looked anywhere but straight ahead, soaking in what the man was saying, amazed at how completely it applied to her.

Pastor Ritchie paused and studied the group of people before him. "The thing is, folks—" he held his arm up and pretended to stage an arm wrestling contest with an invisible opponent—"God won't wrestle with you forever." He let his arm fall forward. "Eventually he'll let you have your way." He hesitated again. "Let's not let that happen. If you've never made a decision for Christ, isn't it time? Shall we pray?"

Jade closed her eyes and felt the tears again. She had talked to God, but never tried to live for him. Tanner's words from that night in her apartment came back to her—*the promises are for anyone who loves the Lord, anyone who has given their life to God.* She'd kept him at arm's length, not wanting to get close to him any more than she'd wanted to get close to anyone else. He wasn't her Lord—he was another of her many acquaintances.

Pastor Ritchie was praying. "Father God, I know there are some here today who've never made you Lord, never given their lives completely to you. You brought them here today so they could finally make the right choice, take advantage of this opportunity so that not another day would go by without their names being written in the Lamb's book of life.

"Oh, maybe they think they're here because it was something to do on a Sunday morning, maybe a friend asked them here and that's why they came—"

Jade wondered if someone had told him. How come everything he said seemed to apply directly to her? Had Tanner planned this? The pastor was finishing the prayer. "Of course we know the truth, Lord. You brought them here today so you could meet them where they are." He paused and it was as though Jade could physically feel the walls around her heart crumbling. "With everyone in prayer, eyes closed, if you are one who wants to make Jesus the Lord of your life right here, right now, raise your hand, would you? Raise it high so I can see it."

Jade squirmed in her seat, tears streaming down her face. She was tired of fighting through life on her own. And though she had no solid reason to believe the things Pastor Ritchie had said that morning, somehow she was desperate to do so. More than she'd ever wanted anything.

The pastor's voice was kind, beckoning. "Anyone else. Please, don't let another day go by. Believe me, there's nothing outside those doors that matters more than meeting Jesus

Christ for the first time right here, right now, before another minute goes by...anyone else?"

And in that moment, as though her arm had a mind of its own, Jade's hand was up.

It was true. She wanted to give her life completely to the savior that Pastor Ritchie had shared about, and she wanted to do it now, before another minute passed.

Eyes still closed, hand raised, Jade heard the pastor finishing his prayer, thanking God for those who had taken that first step of faith. The pastor paused. "Now, will those of you with hands raised please stand up. Come on, stand up. No one's watching."

Terror ran through Jade. She couldn't stand up! Not here, among this sea of churchgoers. They would know she was different and ask her to leave. No, she wanted only to fade into the pew and treasure this decision quietly in her heart.

Stand, my daughter.

She heard the voice deep within her soul and recognized it the way a child recognizes the voice of her daddy. God wanted her to stand, and with that knowledge she did so without hesitating.

Pastor Ritchie continued. "All right, now will those of you who are standing please make your way up here to the front. We have guys and gals who want to pray with you, help you nail down what a new life in Christ really looks like. It is absolutely essential that you do this. Come on, right up here."

Jade leaned down and whispered to Tanner. "Come with me?"

He opened his eyes and she saw his unshed tears. Somehow he must have known the way God had been calling her. Maybe he had even prayed for her. He rose and walked with her toward the front of the church. From upstairs and other areas, a handful of people—most of them with tearstained faces—were also making their way to the front where two men with kind eyes stood waiting.

"Let's praise the Lord for what he has done here today among us," he said. And then the pews of churchgoers, the people Jade had feared since she was a young girl, did something that nearly brought Jade to her knees.

They applauded.

Her father was wrong. They hadn't looked on her with disdain, hadn't asked her to leave. Instead they had shown her what it was to worship the Lord in song, they had listened alongside her to Pastor Ritchie's amazing message.

And now…now they were clapping because of her decision.

Nine

TANNER HELD HER HAND AS THEY WALKED ACROSS THE CHURCH parking lot, and she enjoyed the feel of his fingers intertwined with hers. Her soul felt remarkably light, and she was filled with an overwhelming sense of hope. Once they climbed inside Tanner's car, he turned to her, his eyes glistening.

"Is it what you really want, Jade?"

She studied his face and remembered that he had always been like this—concerned for her. She drew a deep breath. "All my life something has been missing. Now I know what it was."

"I remember when I gave my life to the Lord…." Tanner leaned against the car door, facing her. He was in no hurry to leave and Jade was glad. They hadn't been able to talk yet, and she still had so many questions.

"When was that?"

Tanner's gaze shifted to the distant mountains and the shimmering white peak of Mt. Hood. "I was in high school. A bunch of us went to a Young Life gathering, and for the first time I realized God wasn't a program or a club or a part of my heritage. He was a living God, waiting for me to turn my heart to him."

"Exactly." Jade leaned forward, remembering the meeting they'd just had with one of the associate pastors in the church prayer room. "That's how I felt in there. Like God was waiting for me to make a decision for him."

Tanner nodded. "Back then our family attended Williamsburg Community Church. Same as your folks, I think."

Jade nodded, and for a moment she started to hear her father's bitter words. *You're nothing but the daughter of a –*

She shut them out and focused her attention on Tanner instead.

"Anyway, I'd never thought about having a personal relationship with God. That night I opened my heart and asked Jesus inside. I studied the Bible daily over the next few weeks, and at the end of the month I got baptized."

Jade sighed. "Yeah, that's another thing. I think I want to do that, too, but what is it?"

Tanner smiled and focused on her. As he did he leaned closer, taking her hands in his. "Baptism is part of giving your life to Christ." His eyes lit up. "Hey, I have an idea. I have a beginner's Bible study. I keep the notes written in the back of my Bible. We could go over it together. Tomorrow, maybe."

Jade watched him, and her heart soared. She'd never allowed herself to feel so deeply about anyone, but something about Tanner was unquestionably safe. Despite all the reasons a relationship between them couldn't possibly work, she felt herself falling hard. "I'd like that."

Jade had once heard love described by one of her nine-year-old patients. *It's like an avalanche,* he'd said. *When it happens to you, the best thing to do is run for your life.* Jade thought about that and knew it was too late. She was already in over her head.

Tanner's eyes remained locked on hers. "You're going to love getting to know God better, Jade. No matter what else happens in life, you'll always have Jesus with you." He paused. "I can't imagine life any other way."

She drew a deep breath, and her grip on Tanner's hands tightened slightly. It was time to bring the walls down all the way. "Remember that first day after the meeting? You asked me if I trusted you...."

A knowing look filled Tanner's eyes, but he stayed quiet.

Help me open up to him, Lord. She closed her eyes for a moment and when she opened them again she felt a new strength she hadn't had before. "You told me the question wasn't whether you trusted my driving or not. It was whether I trusted you."

Tanner's voice was quiet. "You never answered me."

Jade leaned closer and placed one of her hands on Tanner's upper arm. "I trust you, Tanner. I always have. I trust you now more than ever." She felt her eyes fill with tears and saw that he was listening intently to every word she said. Her hand fell back to her side. "That's all...I just wanted you to know."

His borrowed car wasn't very large—a four-door sedan in which Tanner was already close. But as she finished speaking, he moved closer still and took her face in his hands. "Now it's my turn...."

Jade searched his eyes, wondering what he was going to say. Whatever it was, she had a strong sense that it would change things between them forever. He raised his hand gently as she waited, tracing her cheekbones with his fingertips. When he finally spoke it caused feelings in her that were almost more than she could bear.

"I love you, Jade." His voice was mesmerizing, and she felt herself sucked into his gaze. She might live a hundred years, but the memory of this single moment, this day, would remain alive forever. "As long as I live, I'll never love anyone the way I love you right now."

Tears blurred Jade's vision, and she blinked them back as Tanner pulled her into an embrace. She didn't cry because she doubted Tanner's words or feared them. Rather, she cried because she believed them with all her heart. And though she couldn't quite yet voice the words back to him, she felt the same way. She loved him; truly she did.

Even if they only had this summer, she knew one thing for certain: She would never love any man like she loved Tanner Eastman.

Ten

DORIS LOOKED AT HER WATCH AND TAPPED HER FOOT NERVOUSLY. One-fifteen. They had four o'clock reservations at Beaches—a steak house on the river. That would give them plenty of time to talk first.

Something about Tanner's elusiveness bothered her. He had called and made plans to spend the afternoon with her, but when she asked him why he hadn't called much, he hesitated and blamed it on work. But how much work could a summer intern have the first week on the job? Certainly not so much that he couldn't find time to call. Then Tanner had done the strangest thing. He'd told her he wanted to bring a friend.

"A friend?"

"Yes, mother. I'm not a social outcast. I do make friends on occasion."

"I know that, dear." Who could he possibly want to bring to meet her? Who could matter so much to him in such a short time? "Definitely. I think it'd be lovely if you brought a friend."

Doris had been too taken aback to ask further questions, too afraid of his answer. It couldn't be the girl. There was no way he would have run into her so quickly. Probably someone on the board of supervisors, a fellow intern, maybe.

But why hadn't he said that?

She glanced about, satisfied that the condominium was impeccable as always. The cleaning woman came twice a week, and now that Hap was gone it wasn't much of a cleanup. Doris heard a car door outside and walked to the front window.

There was Tanner and a girl, a beautiful, brown-haired girl. Doris couldn't quite make out her face….

She gasped out loud, filled with sudden, desperate panic. *It was her*. It couldn't be, but it was. Doris was positive. The girl was older, taller, more womanly. But the resemblance to her mother at that age was uncanny. The couple moved closer, and Doris saw the girl's emerald eyes. Yes, indeed. *Same seductive eyes as her mother.*

Doris wanted to lock the door, pretend that she'd gone out for the day and forgotten their visit. But it was too late. Tanner had spotted her and he waved in her direction. That's when Doris saw something that made her stomach turn.

Tanner and the girl were holding hands.

She drew two deep breaths and steadied herself. This was no time to faint. She would have to put on a good show for Tanner's sake. He would never understand her feelings about Jade Conner, and the last thing Doris wanted to do was turn her own son against her.

Calm. Be calm. She exhaled slowly as she reached for the doorknob. There was nothing to get worked up about. Jade was not the type of girl Tanner would be serious about. Besides, he would go home at the end of the summer. Eleven more weeks. Then he'd forget about her.

"Hello, Tanner." She stood stiffly, waiting for him to approach her. When he did, he pulled her into a loose hug, gently kissing her on the cheek.

"Good afternoon, Mother." He turned to the girl who stood beside him. How was it possible? *Wretched girl.* It was all Doris could do to maintain her composure. She hated Jade for trying to look shy and demure, like a blushing virgin. *Exactly the way her mother had looked so many years ago when Hap—*

"Mother, I'd like you to meet an old friend of mine." He put a protective arm around Jade, and Doris had to fight the bile that rose in her throat. "This is Jade Conner; remember her mother? From Williamsburg."

Tanner searched his mother's face, obviously looking for her reaction. Doris summoned all the theatrical ability she could muster. "My goodness, you don't mean little Jade, the pixie from across the street, do you?"

"How do you do, ma'am?" Jade looked nervous, and Doris wondered what she had to hide. *Are they already sleeping together?*

She banished the thought and nodded politely toward Jade. "Well, you certainly have grown up since last I saw you." Doris forced a smile. "You're a mirror image of your mother, Jade."

Doris searched the girl's face for a reaction, and sure enough, her slim shoulders fell slightly and her smile faded. Tanner seemed to sense an awkwardness between them, and he took the initiative, his hand still firmly clasping Jade's. "Let's go inside. Mom, maybe you can whip up some of your famous iced tea."

"I've got a pitcher chilling in the refrigerator." Doris trailed behind them. *This can't be happening.* This couldn't be Jade Conner walking into Doris's very own living room, holding Tanner's hand, and having the nerve of looking exactly like her temptress mother? Doris steadied herself as she made her way to the kitchen and poured three glasses of tea.

It's just for the summer. She served the drinks and took a seat across from Tanner and Jade. She hated how they looked so comfortable together. Jade had obviously wasted no time getting close to Tanner. *Like mother, like daughter.*

"So tell me, Jade, how ever did the two of you meet up again after such a long time?" Doris hated having to play friendly with the girl, but Tanner was watching her, so she had no choice. She refused to let the girl come between her and her son.

"I live in Kelso, ma'am. Lived there since we left Williamsburg."

Tanner smiled fondly at Jade, and Doris felt as if someone had kicked her in the stomach. Why was he looking at Jade that way? What had gone on this past week? Doris forced herself to listen to what her son was saying.

"Jade works in the children's unit at the hospital. The board of supervisors had a meeting Monday night to discuss the possibility of closing that wing." He nudged Jade playfully with his elbow. "I had the good folks of Kelso just about convinced until Jade, here, took over. Next thing we knew the idea was tabled, and Jade was sounding more like a legal intern than a nurse."

Jade smiled shyly but said nothing. Rather than validate anything about the girl, Doris changed the subject.

"So, Tanner, you must have been busy with work this week. I thought I'd hear from you more often." She was prying, hoping to find out how close the two had become.

Tanner looked at Jade again and the two exchanged a look that terrified Doris. It was the look of two people in love.

"The work's been okay. Mostly I've been with Jade. May I tell her?" He looked at Jade, and Doris saw the girl nod her approval. *Dear heaven, what is this? What terrible announcement are they going to make?* For a moment, Doris felt her heart stop. *Don't tell me they're considering...*

Tanner beamed as he spoke. "Jade gave her life to the Lord today at church."

Doris's heart resumed beating. So that was all. Tanner had spent a week with the girl and already he had converted her. *Naturally.* Doris resisted the urge to roll her eyes in the wake of Tanner's announcement. *Whatever happened to old-fashioned denominational Christianity? The kind you didn't wear on your sleeves or try to spread among your friends?* "I suppose I should say congratulations." Doris nodded a brief smile in Jade's direction.

Tanner was apparently too excited to notice Doris's lack of enthusiasm. "We went to Crossroads…that church I like over in Vancouver. At the end of the service Jade made a decision for Christ." Tanner turned to his mother, and she was hurt by the joy she saw there. It wasn't right that a girl like Jade Conner could make her son feel so happy. *Get away from him before I—*

"Isn't that great, Mom?"

Doris paused. What could she say? "Didn't you have a faith before, Jade?" She knew she sounded abrupt, and she hoped Tanner wouldn't think she was being rude. She wanted to tear the girl apart, ask her about her background and how many young men had fallen prey to her the way…well, the way young men had fallen prey to her mother so many years ago.

Jade's voice was barely audible. "No, ma'am. We weren't churchgoing folk."

Doris nodded once. This was her opportunity. "Ah, yes. Now I remember. Your mama ran off, didn't she? With the Stevens man, wasn't it? Back before you and your daddy moved away."

A crimson blush spread across Jade's face. *Good. You deserve to suffer embarrassment. It's a small enough price compared to what Tanner will suffer if he stays with you for long.*

Jade struggled for a moment as though she wasn't sure what to say. "Uh, yes, ma'am…I…I'm sorry. Which way is the restroom?" The girl's face was filled with alarm, and Doris thought she almost looked shocked. As though this were new information to her….

Jade stood and Doris pointed down the hall.

When the young woman was out of earshot, Tanner hissed at her. "Mother! That was completely uncalled for."

Doris remained calm. "What, dear?"

"That bit about her mother running off. Don't you think that's hard enough on her without you bringing it up now? When we've only been here five minutes?"

Doris waved a hand at her strapping son. "Tanner, don't be silly. A girl like Jade isn't bothered by hearing the truth about her mother. After all, she's lived with it all her life."

"What do you mean, 'a girl like Jade'?" Tanner was getting angrier by the moment, and Doris searched for a way to defuse the situation.

"I mean nothing by it, dear. Don't get excited."

Tanner's eyes narrowed as he set his jaw. "Listen, Mother, don't bring it up again. It's not an easy thing for her." His voice was still a whisper. "She's my guest, and I want you to make her feel comfortable—not force her out of the room."

Doris rose and patted her son on the shoulder. "Fine, I won't let it happen again. I didn't know your friend was so sensitive."

"Don't you like her, mother? I mean, you could have said something nice. She just gave her life to the Lord an hour ago."

"Of course I like her, Tanner. I meant no ill will by what I said." She leaned down and kissed her son on the top of his head. "Forgive me?"

Tanner sighed. "Yes. But please be more careful. I care a lot about her."

Doris smiled, hiding her alarm as she strode into the kitchen to refill their glasses. There was no place in Tanner's life for a girl like Jade Conner. He was going to be a senator, a congressman. He was headed for the Oval Office, and he would need a wife as cultured and well bred as he.

Doris considered the exchange she'd just had with Jade. She had come close, but she hadn't quite crossed the line, and she congratulated herself for making the comment seem like an innocent mistake. After all, it was the single detail from Jade's past that Williamsburg people would obviously remember about her.

And the reality was that Doris had struck first blood. If there was going to be a battle for Tanner, she hoped Jade would remember this moment.

Because she wasn't going to lose him to the daughter of a harlot without a fight.

Eleven

SCRIPTURE WAS LIKE A MIRACLE SALVE ON WOUNDS JADE HAD long since thought would never heal. As the days of summer wore on, she and Tanner spent as much time in God's Word as they did sharing walks along the shores of the river and late-night conversations on his apartment patio.

She was falling in love, but not just with Tanner—with life itself and most of all with God's promises.

Tanner was incredible, a walking encyclopedia of Scripture references. No matter what the conversation, he was always ready with a verse.

If she grew sad over his impending departure: *All things work to the good for those who love God....*

When they discussed how a long-distance relationship might work: *Nothing is impossible with God....*

The times when she fretted over the children's unit at the hospital: *Cast your cares on him for he cares for you....*

If she got ahead of herself and wondered who would take care of her father once she moved out: *Do not worry about tomorrow for tomorrow will take care of itself....*

And of course her favorite: *I know the plans I have for you...plans to give you hope and a future.*

Scripture really was alive and active. It worked in her heart and changed her perspective so that every day was bursting with hope and promise. She and Tanner had found a church in Kelso where the Bible was preached and people seemed to care about each other the way they had at Crossroads.

By July, the two of them were regulars and had joined a Bible study class. The second Sunday of that month, Jade was baptized—like the preacher had quoted from Scripture, "for the forgiveness of her sins and the gift of the Holy Spirit."

Each day she listened to praise music while she got ready for school. The words spoke of the wealth of feelings that filled her heart. One evening in late July while she was humming a song about how nothing could compare to the love she had in Christ, her father shoved open her bedroom door and scowled at her.

"What's that garbage you're listenin' to?"

Jade turned down the music and silently uttered a prayer for her father. "Christian praise music. Was it too loud?"

Her father rubbed his temples, muttered a string of expletives, and squinted. "No. It's too religious. God this and God that. Since when did you start believing all that trash?"

"Tanner and I bought it at church a few weeks ago. I'm sorry you don't like it, Daddy." Jade took a step closer, studying her father's eyes and wondering how he became such a miserable man. "Anyway, I like it. I'll turn it down so you can't hear—"

"Tanner?" Her father bellowed. "You're still seeing that snobby kid?"

Jade sighed. "He's a man, Daddy. And yes, I'm still seeing him."

"He's using you, Jade. You know that, right? His kind don't associate with our kind but for one reason only."

"Daddy! It's not like that!" Tears filled Jade's eyes, and she smelled stale alcohol on her father's breath. *Why can't he be happy for me? Just this once.*

Her father studied the CD cover in her hands. "This Tanner

guy's got you converted, is that it?"

Jade felt her face grow hot. Her father would never understand her precious faith. But still, maybe this was an opportunity to share some of the gospel with him. "Yes, Daddy. But it isn't Tanner's doing. It's God's. He'd been calling me for a long time. I finally listened, that's all." She paused. "He's calling you, too, Daddy."

"Shut up!" Her father all but snarled, his eyes angry. "You might be a holy roller, but don't go preaching to your old man. I know all about church people and if you're one of them now, maybe you better pack your things."

Later that night she related the encounter to Tanner as they sat side by side on his sofa, listening to Steven Curtis Chapman.

"It scares me, Tanner." They held hands and sat close enough so the bare skin on their arms was touching. "I have two more years before I finish nurse's training. If he kicks me out—"

"Shhh..." Tanner held a finger up to her lips and gently brushed a lock of hair off her forehead. "Keep your focus, Jade. God has a plan, even if you wind up on your own."

She was quiet for a moment as they studied each other. Every day she felt more comfortable with him, and even though they hadn't done more than hold hands, something deep inside her had started to stir whenever he was near. She knew by the look in his eyes that he felt the same way, but...

"What are you thinking?" His voice was tender, patient.

She let go of his hand and drew her knees up to her chest. "How weird I am."

Tanner grinned. "But then, we already knew that."

Jade's heart was heavy and she didn't return his smile. "I'm serious, Tanner. I'm the strangest girl in the world."

"How so?"

Maybe it was time. She'd never talked about this part of her life, but she couldn't hide behind her aloofness forever, pretending she didn't have an aversion to attachment. At some point she would need to talk about why she never allowed herself to get closer to him. "Okay. But I've never told this to anyone before. It might take a while."

Tanner took her hand in his, leaned back against the sofa and waited.

Should I be telling him this, Lord? She heard no answer and finally she steadied herself. Now that she'd started she would have to finish. She only hoped he would understand. "I know there are times when you want to…to kiss me." She paused. "Right?"

His eyes softened and he nodded slowly. "But I can tell you don't want to. So I've kept my distance."

Jade drew a shaky breath, her eyes locked on his. "It isn't that I don't want to. I care about you." She was struggling, searching for the strength to continue. "It's just…well, I've never kissed anyone before. I've always thought it was repulsive."

Tanner raised an eyebrow. "Kissing?"

Jade's eyes filled, and she could barely make him out through the cloud of tears. "That's where it gets complicated. It was something that happened a long time ago. I was eleven or twelve, I think…"

Tanner's eyes filled with concern, but he held his silence. Still, she saw the alarm in his eyes and knew what he was thinking. She shook her head. "I wasn't raped or anything. But still…"

He tightened his grip on her hand. "Tell me."

"Okay." She hated thinking about that night, but maybe

talking about it would help. "Well, that night my dad had been drinking, only instead of coming home by himself he brought a friend."

"A guy?"

"Yes. Just as drunk as he was." Jade pulled her hand from Tanner and hugged her knees again. She stared at her feet and saw that even they were trembling. Why couldn't she have had a normal childhood like Tanner? As if he could read her mind, Tanner put his hand on her arm and massaged it. If only he could rub away the memories of her past. *Lord, give me strength, please.*

She drew a shaky breath. "Anyway, I was in the living room, watching television when I heard them. The guy made some comment about me, and then I heard my dad laugh. He told the guy to give me a try if he wanted. Daddy told him I was probably loose like my mother so it didn't matter to him what the guy did."

Tanner slumped forward like he'd been hit. "He said that?"

Jade nodded.

"What happened?"

"I tried to leave, but they heard me and blocked my way." Jade hung her head. How could Tanner care for her after hearing this? "My dad was laughing, and the guy, his friend, came toward me and grabbed my hair."

She looked up and saw that Tanner's eyes were moist as he silently encouraged her to continue.

"He smashed his face against mine and…and kissed me." She felt tears running down her face, and she desperately wanted to finish the story, to move past it. She forced herself to regain composure. "After that he and my dad left. They were both laughing like it was the funniest thing they'd ever seen." She hesitated and looked at Tanner, searching his eyes. "That's the only time I've ever been kissed."

Tanner released the hold he had on her arm and angrily combed his fingers through his hair. Slowly he blew the air from his lungs. "That man is no father, Jade. Why didn't you tell me?"

Her voice was choked with emotion. "I—I couldn't."

Tanner groaned and leaned toward her, taking her in his arms and stroking her back. "I'm so sorry, Jade. I wish..."

The tears came again, and she collapsed willingly into Tanner's comforting arms. She felt safe and loved there. *What was this? Why did Tanner make her feel like she never wanted to be anywhere but in his arms?* "It's okay." She muttered the words against his chest. "It could have been worse."

"But look how it's hurt you. No wonder you've kept your distance."

Jade pulled back and uttered a short laugh. "You've kept your distance, too. Remember the onions?"

A strange expression crossed Tanner's face, almost as though there was something he wanted to tell her but couldn't quite bring himself to do it.

"What are you thinking?" Jade wanted to know. She wanted to know everything about him.

The curious look disappeared from his eyes. He pulled back slightly and put his hands on either side of her face. "Nothing. You're right. I've prayed a lot about you...us. I haven't wanted to make you uncomfortable. It's okay that we haven't kissed."

"I've prayed about it, too." Jade rested her hands on his shoulders as she studied him, savoring the closeness of their faces, his sweet breath and day-old cologne. They stayed that way a while until finally she whispered. "I'm not repulsed now."

Tanner searched her eyes, clearly questioning the intent of

her statement. In response, she moved closer, her gaze unwavering. He ran his fingers down her neck and traced her collarbone. When he spoke, it felt like his words were aimed directly at her heart.

"A kiss…between two people who care about each other…should be something beautiful…something you remember."

Jade nodded. For the first time in her life, she wasn't afraid of love. She loved Tanner with everything she was about, even if she hadn't been willing to tell him. And now…now all she wanted was…

She could feel his fingers trembling as he slowly traced her lips. "Jade, would it be all right—" he moved closer—"if I kissed you?" His voice was barely audible, his eyes still locked on hers.

She swallowed and nodded. As she did, he lowered his face the remaining distance to hers and tenderly kissed her jaw, her chin, her cheek, until finally his lips found hers. Jade heard him moan softly as she returned his kiss and her fingers worked their way up his neck to his face.

The feelings that ravaged her body in that moment were so great she feared she might die of pure pleasure. But they did something else. They brought about a strange aching that caused her upper body to move more closely against him. Their kiss continued, and Tanner parted his lips ever so slightly. As he did, the feeling in Jade grew stronger, almost urgent.

Tanner pulled away first, breathless, his eyes searching Jade's. His body was on fire with desire so strong it had been all he could do to tear himself from her.

Lord, what have I done? Douse the fires that rage within me, please! He felt his body relax. Jade was watching him, and he didn't want her to feel guilty in any way.

He framed her face with his fingertips once more. "That's the way a kiss is supposed to be."

Jade's eyes grew troubled. "Is it wrong? In God's eyes, I mean?"

Tanner drew a deep breath. How could anything that felt so right be wrong? *Okay, God, help me on this one.* He steadied himself. "Did you feel anything? While we were kissing, I mean?" They had gotten close enough over the summer that he felt comfortable asking.

Jade nodded and a pretty blush crossed her face. "I felt..." Her gaze dropped to her hands. "I didn't want to stop."

Tanner leaned forward and set his forearms on his knees, close to Jade but not touching her. "Me, too."

"And that's bad?" Jade's question was genuine, and Tanner was struck at how inexperienced she was. In many ways she was like an orphan who'd never had the chance to grow up.

Woe to anyone who causes one of these little ones to sin....

The Scripture sent a wave of alarm through Tanner, and he stared at his shoes. Jade was waiting for an answer. *Help me, Lord.* He looked up and met her gaze. "Well, those feelings are kind of like a warning. You know where they lead, right?"

Jade nodded. "I knew girls in school who slept with their boyfriends. It was so foreign to me, though, I guess I never really understood what the big deal was." She looked at him, her soul laid bare before him. "Until now."

"It's a big deal to God. Sometimes a kiss like..." he let his eyes drop briefly to her lips..."a kiss like that one takes people to a place where they can't stop. Do you understand?"

"I think so..." Her voice trailed off and Tanner saw she was struggling with something. "Have you ever...you know?" The blush on her cheeks darkened.

"Slept with a woman?" Tanner was glad for their conversation, glad to be honest with his feelings after hiding them for so many weeks. "No. I've done some dating, some kissing. But God's Word is really clear on the issue."

"What's it say?"

Tanner reached over and grabbed his Bible from the end-table. He flipped to Galatians and found the verse he was looking for. With the Scriptures in his hands, he felt his body cooling, but still there was a tremble in his voice. "It says here that the sexually immoral will not inherit the kingdom of God. There's other verses about sex outside marriage being sinful."

"So that's why you've never done it?"

"I believe God has a plan for me." He studied her eyes, wondering if she could see how badly he wanted her to be part of that plan. "A plan for you, too, Jade."

"Like that first Scripture you showed me, the one from Jeremiah?"

"Right. I don't want to mess up that plan by acting outside God's will. Make sense?"

He set the Bible down and took her hands in his. She still looked puzzled. "So is…is kissing like that a sin, too?"

Tanner sighed. *It couldn't be, could it, Lord?*

He didn't wait for a response. Instead he leaned toward her, wove his fingers firmly through her hair, and kissed her again. Immediately the fire returned, and Tanner forced himself to come up for air.

Desire, once it's conceived, leads to sin, and sin when it's full-grown leads to—

The answer was clear. But Tanner shook his head. "No. Kissing like that isn't a sin…" They'd done nothing wrong. A kiss, after all, was only a kiss. His eyes were trained on hers, and he kissed her more slowly this time, speaking to her only when he needed to breathe. "It's what…it leads to…"

He felt her nod, and the fire in him raged hotter when she brought her lips to his. After a while she tipped her head so she could see his eyes. "We can't let it go further."

"I know." He raked both hands through her hair, angling her face, kissing her closer. "We'll have to…be very careful…."

Jade closed her eyes, her lips moving on his. When she pulled away she stared at him, her face shadowed by concern. "Promise?"

Tanner pulled her close and kissed her again. She was addicting…. But there was no harm in this. He would never let it go further. No matter how his body screamed for more, he could never hurt Jade that way. Never hurt his Lord that way.

Finally, breathlessly, between kisses that grew more and more urgent, Tanner whispered the one word he meant with all his heart.

"Promise…."

Twelve

The heavenly, hot days of August raced by with Jade and Tanner spending as much time together as their schedules would allow. Tanner had taken his promise to her seriously, and they spent more time outside and in public than before. When they wound up at his apartment, she set herself a curfew and went home by ten o'clock.

Tanner's work with the board of supervisors had turned out to be productive. Although there was still a chance the board might close the children's unit at Kelso General, Tanner had found a dozen alternatives that would balance the budget and keep the unit open.

Jade loved hearing about his work. He was bright and articulate, and she knew he would make a brilliant politician one day. She had long since given up her earlier efforts to maintain some emotional distance with Tanner. He had worked his way into the very core of her heart, and no matter what their futures held his presence there would remain.

Although there were more questions than answers, they often sat in folding chairs on his apartment patio and talked about the future.

"Move to the East Coast, Jade. You could finish school there, do your nursing just like you planned." Tanner would take her hand and squeeze it gently, his eyes imploring her to agree.

But Jade knew that wasn't the answer. Tanner still had a

year of school left, and then he could take an entry level political position anywhere in the country. It didn't make sense for her to relocate. Not yet. Besides, Tanner had talked about marriage, but he hadn't asked her to marry him. Jade wanted to know his intentions before she made any life-changing decisions.

"I'm going to miss you, Tanner...." She wasn't afraid to say it, and although she'd never told him she loved him, she was convinced he knew.

"I'll be back.... I promise." Tanner told her that nearly every time they were together. "On breaks and three-day weekends. I'll fly out, and we'll figure out what we're going to do."

Jade would study him, wondering what the future really held for them.

"I let you go once, Jade Conner. But I won't let you go again. I want to marry you one day."

Many times, when there were no answers in the discussion about their future, they talked about religious freedom and the fact that many of the privileges Americans had long taken for granted were being undermined by liberal political groups. Tanner was strongly opinionated on the topic.

"We need a group who'll fight for the rest of us. Someone who can step in and take charge when a student is told he can't bring his Bible to school, or a child is forbidden to talk about the nativity at Christmas."

Jade was impressed with how well read he was on the topic. He was familiar with landmark cases and had a very clear grasp on what he considered the eroding of religious rights in America.

She couldn't help but be struck by the fact that he lacked that energy when he talked about becoming a politician. But when she would pry further, he would change the subject.

Often they talked about her spiritual growth and how hungrily she sought God's word for every situation. And many times she asked about his mother, how she was doing and whether she was making progress in packing up her condominium.

She and Tanner had been back to visit his mother twice, and, in Jade's dreams, she imagined staying in close contact with the woman after Tanner returned to school. Although Mrs. Eastman was never quite warm, Jade could picture getting phone calls from her and spending Sunday afternoons with her until the woman moved back to Williamsburg.

Then, several weeks ago, Tanner had stopped taking Jade along when he visited his mother. It had seemed odd to Jade, but she hadn't wanted to bring it up, hadn't wanted to ask why he no longer included her. She was afraid of what Tanner would say if she did.

One day, a week before Tanner's internship was up, they were on his patio, side by side soaking in the steady summer sun and talking about the memories they'd made those past months when there was a break in the conversation.

"I'm going to spend Saturday at my mother's."

Tanner looked uncomfortable as he spoke, and Jade understood. If they talked about the weekend, they would have to acknowledge that Tanner was going back to school. "So you'll leave Saturday."

Tanner nodded. "We can be together Friday night, but Mom wants me to help her go through a few more things before I leave."

Jade was quiet. She felt the sting of tears but she refused to cry. Not yet. "What time's your flight?"

"Three-forty-five Saturday afternoon."

Why didn't he ask her to come with him to Portland? She could drive her own car and make her way back without him.

Why was Tanner's mother so off-limits lately? In the quiet, Jade found the courage to voice the question. "She doesn't like me, does she?"

"Who?" Tanner's blank expression made Jade wonder if maybe she was only imagining his mother's dislike.

"Your mother. I get the feeling she doesn't approve of me."

A momentary sadness appeared in Tanner's eyes; then he hooked her neck playfully in the crook of his arm and drew her near, kissing her tenderly on her forehead. "Of course she likes you. She's just…stiff, I guess."

Jade pondered the thought. *Is that really all it is?* "I don't know."

"No, really, Jade. She's told me herself. She thinks you're great."

"Then why haven't you invited me to Portland with you lately?"

Tanner looked frustrated. "My mother asked me to come alone. She said she felt more comfortable talking about my father when I was by myself."

Jade thought about that for a moment and decided it was a plausible explanation. Still…

"Have you told her about us?" Jade leaned toward him and kissed him on the mouth, a kiss that lasted longer than she intended. She finally pulled away and eyed Tanner. "Have you told her how we are now? How…serious we are?" She was trying to sound lighthearted, teasing even. But deep inside she wondered. If he were proud of her, wouldn't he want his mother to know how serious they'd become?

Tanner squirmed uncomfortably. "Not exactly."

Jade withdrew her arms from Tanner's neck and sighed. "Why not?"

For the first time, Tanner sounded impatient with her. "You

don't know what it's like to have a mother like mine."

The moment he said it, regret flashed in his eyes. Jade looked away. *No, Tanner. I don't know what it's like to have any sort of mother at all.*

He sighed. "I'm sorry. It's just...ever since I was a kid my mother has planned my life for me."

Jade knew that. This past summer there had been many times when Tanner shared the ways his mother had organized his childhood so that when he went to college he would study politics and one day be ready for a position in public office. She exhaled slowly and placed her hand on his knee. "I know. I just wish you'd tell her."

"I will eventually. See—" he hung his head and stared at his feet for a moment before looking up again—"she has this idea that I should finish college, take a position in government somewhere, and then get married once I'm established. She's told me a hundred times how a girl can be the undoing of a man. Especially a man who might one day find himself in the White House."

Jade stood, pacing the patio area with her arms crossed firmly in front of her. "And you believe that? That I might be your undoing?" She was angry and didn't try to hide it.

"No, of course not." He rose and was at her side instantly. "Jade...you can't think that. It's just—"

"What?" Jade felt the tears well up, but she didn't care. Let them spill over onto her face. Tanner was making it sound like he was ashamed of her, and for an instant she could hear her father.

"You're a waste, an idiot, Jade. Jim Rudolph is the best thing that ever happened to you."

She turned her back to Tanner and tried to work through her anger. He was at her side instantly, putting his hands on her shoulders and holding her close, but she remained stiff in his arms. "Why do I feel like you're embarrassed about us?"

He gently turned her so she faced him, and she saw nothing but sincerity in his eyes. "You have to trust me, Jade. It isn't the right time. She'll think I'm throwing away my political chances."

"Is that what you think?"

"Of course not."

"Then why are you so afraid of her?"

Tanner was silent. He stuffed his hands into his shorts pockets.

Jade quietly fumed. *Stand up for me, Tanner.* She positioned herself so she could make eye contact with him. When she spoke she was careful to hide her frustration. "Your mother is a good woman, but she can't run your life forever."

"She expects so much of me." He seemed to be speaking to himself as much as to Jade. "She wants me to be the president, for heaven's sake. Do you know what kind of pressure that is?"

Tanner moved back to his chair. He sat down, set his head in his hands, and stared at the cement beneath him. Jade waited a moment then moved nearer, crouching on the ground beside him, her hand on his knee as she searched his face. "What about you? What do *you* want?"

Tanner shook his head. "I don't know anymore."

Jade considered what she was about to say. She'd wanted to say it many times before, whenever he got excited about religious freedom, but she hadn't wanted to seem pushy. Now she felt she had no choice. "You don't really want to be a politician, do you?"

Tanner kept his eyes trained on the ground, but Jade saw them fill with tears. For a long while he stayed that way, considering her words, silently mulling over them. Then finally he shook his head again. "No."

Jade sighed and rose to her knees, circling her arms around his neck. They stayed that way as Tanner drew a deep breath.

"I have the gift for it, the total package like my mother's always said. She's probably right. One day I could wind up in the White House if God were willing."

"I'd vote for you." Jade felt Tanner chuckle at her soft comment.

"Thanks." He pulled away and met her eyes straight on. "I must be crazy."

Jade smiled, allowing herself to get lost in his eyes. "How come?"

"I'm about to leave the only woman I've ever loved to finish an education I'm not sure I care about that will lead me into a job I know I don't want to do. It doesn't make sense."

She ran a finger over his brow. It felt so good to hear him being honest with himself.

"You know what I'd really like to do?" Tanner's expression was somber. Their arms were still locked around each other, their faces inches apart.

"Kiss me?" She smiled. He was leaving too soon for them to be so serious. She wanted to enjoy these last days.

He tousled her hair and grinned. "That, too. But besides that—" his smile faded—"when I think of spending the rest of my life in a job, there's only one thing I'd really love to do." He paused. "Fight for—"

"—religious freedom." She finished his sentence and saw his eyes widen in surprise.

"How did you know?"

"I've been with you every day lately, remember?"

Tanner was quiet, and Jade knew he was thinking of his mother again.

"She'd think I'd flipped for sure."

"Does it matter what she thinks? God gave you this desire for a reason, Tanner."

"I don't know, I can't change directions over night when I've been planning my life one way all these years."

"Why not?" His mother would understand eventually, even if she didn't right now. "You're young, Tanner. At least think about it. Pray about it. Please?"

He nodded. "Okay." He drew her nearer still and lowered his face to hers. Jade's body responded to his closeness, and she was thankful they were outside in broad daylight. He kissed her neck and whispered in her ear. "Now, about that other thing I'd like to do…"

Jade had gone home, but Tanner was still feeling the effects of her presence. They had kept their promise, limiting their physical contact to kisses only. But some of the kisses they shared…It was a good thing they'd taken to ending their evenings in prayer. Talking to God had a way of dousing inappropriate desire in an instant.

Tanner moved into his bedroom and flopped onto the comforter. *Lord, I don't want to be president of the United States. I want to marry Jade and stay here with her forever. Help me know what I'm supposed to do.*

He thought about their conversation earlier, and Jade's words challenged him. Why was he studying to be a politician if that wasn't where he felt God was leading him? And how in the world would he break the news to his mother?

He stood up and wandered toward a desk in his bedroom. Immediately his eyes fell on the file he sought and he pulled it out, thumbing through it until he found what he was looking for. It was a flyer announcing a trip that would take place in mid-September—just three weeks away. The trip was to Hungary and would be led by Youth with a Mission. Tanner's eyes scanned the information until he found the line that mattered most: "Trip objective: To study religious freedom and the consequences of what happens when those freedoms are taken away."

Do this, my son.

The voice was clear and Tanner closed his eyes. *Lord, is this what you want? Is this where you're leading me?*

It would mean taking extra courses in the summer so he could still graduate with his class, but suddenly it was the single thing he wanted most in life. Jade was right. He could see religious freedom being stripped away all around him, and now he was being called to do something about it. He would take the trip, graduate, and marry Jade. Then he would enroll in law school and after that, he'd open shop. He would take on the liberal special interest groups bent on destroying religious freedom, and he would rely on the Lord's strength every step of the way.

He would make the phone call in the morning.

His mother would simply have to understand.

Thirteen

THE DAYS DISSOLVED LIKE SO MANY HOURS UNTIL FINALLY IT WAS Friday. Their last day together.

Tanner presented Lang and the others on the board with a stack of briefs detailing the conclusions he'd reached on the budget issue and several other items he'd been involved with. Good-byes were exchanged and Lang patted him firmly on the back.

"I expect to see your name on a ballot one day, my boy."

Tanner smiled. The two had enjoyed a friendship that complimented their working relationship. But a twinge of guilt tugged at Tanner's conscience. His name would never be on a ballot if things went as he hoped they would. He thought about the phone calls he'd made that week—everything was in order, but he had yet to tell anyone about his decision. Not Lang, not his mother. Not even Jade. He would do that tonight when they were together.

He nodded to Lang as he finished packing up his cubicle. "You never know. Maybe it'll be the other way around."

They made small talk until finally Tanner heaved his box of belongings into his arms and left. On the way home he picked up a Hawaiian pizza with olives—something he and Jade had shared every Friday night since they had run into each other back in June.

She was waiting outside his apartment for him, and when he approached her he could see she'd been crying. "Jade…" He set the pizza box down on the roof of her car and drew her into a full embrace. They remained that way until he felt the flames of desire begin to dart through his body.

Be careful, my son....

Yes, tonight especially. Tanner knew he would have to be especially cautious if this was the way his body was going to react to a sympathetic hug.

Jade pulled away and sniffed, wiping a hand under one eye. "I don't want to talk about it. Not yet. I can't."

Tanner understood. It would be hard enough to say good-bye without starting the process now. He held the pizza against his body with one hand and took her arm with the other. They were both tired of looking for ways to spend time together in public. Tonight they had given themselves permission to visit at his apartment. Just the two of them for the last time in what might be months.

Neither of them was hungry, so they talked about work and school and church news—anything but the fact that in twenty-four hours he'd be gone. They watched a sitcom, and when it was over they turned off the television and played three games of backgammon, all the while pretending summer would stretch on forever and that this wasn't the last night they'd have together.

Finally, sometime after nine o'clock, Tanner heated up the pizza, and they sat down to eat. The mood between them had changed and neither was willing to make small talk. The night was drawing to a close, and sooner or later they would have to find a way to say good-bye.

They ate their pizza in silence, allowing a somberness to fall over the meal despite Tanner's intention to avoid the sadness until the last possible moment. Finally, Jade pushed her half-eaten pizza aside and turned toward him.

He contorted his face into different shapes as he ate, trying desperately to make her smile. "All right, come on. You'd better smile or I'll have to call in the tickle police."

Jade shook her head and her eyes filled with tears. "I'm sorry, Tanner. I can't."

He sighed and set the rest of his pizza back on his plate. Her eyes were so green when she was sad. He ran his thumb over her left brow and smoothed her hair back behind her ear. It was hard to believe that by the following night, three thousand miles would separate them. "I won't be gone forever.... I told you I'll visit."

She nodded and blinked, sending two tears spiraling down her cheeks. "It won't be the same. I want you to stay...."

"Me, too. But I can't."

"I know." She blew a loose strand of hair off her forehead. Her eyes grew distant and her tone hard. "Your political career awaits you."

It was time to tell her. No point in making her wait until the end of the evening to know what he'd done, how she had caused him to change the direction of his entire life's plan. He lifted her chin so that their eyes met again. "I have something to tell you."

Jade did not look enthused. "What?"

"Ah, come on, Jade. You can sound more excited than that." He grinned at her, but still the sorrow on her face remained, and Jade said nothing.

"All right, then. Time to call in the tickle police." He wiggled his fingers up into her armpits and jabbed twice at her ribs.

"Don't!" Jade laughed, and the sound of it made Tanner's heart soar. He continued, poking her, tickling her mercilessly until she leapt from the chair and placed it between them. "Stay back!"

Tanner tried a few more jabs but she kept her distance. "Here I come." He stood up and started for her as she uttered a short scream.

"Stop!"

"Okay, okay, relax." He raised his hands in surrender and grinned breathlessly. "I'm done. No more tickling."

She waited, and when Tanner kept his promise, she pushed away the chair that separated them and placed her hands on her hips. "That's better. Now, what news were you going to tell me?"

"News?" He was having trouble thinking with her standing so near, breathing hard from being tickled. He pulled her to him instead and kissed her. "I love your smile, Jade. Don't stop smiling just because summer's over."

She kissed him back and then whispered, "Okay."

He found her mouth again and moved his lips over hers, massaging her jaw gently with his thumb. "Remember what Scripture says in Jeremiah. 'I know the plans I have for you…'"

"'…plans to give you hope and a future.'" Her voice was barely audible, and they remained in each other's arms, their eyes locked. "Now…what were you going to tell me?"

Tanner struggled to control the feelings that welled up inside him. There was no end to the longing her nearness caused him. Reluctantly he pulled away. "Okay…come on. I'll show you."

She looked around. "What?" Her eyes scanned the room.

"Come on, it's back here." He motioned for her to follow. He had planned on leaving her in the living room. He'd go get what he was after and bring it back to show her. But he didn't want to miss a moment with her.

Be careful, my son…be careful.

Don't worry, I will. He wasn't a fool. He had no intention of letting things get out of hand tonight with Jade. There was no reason to worry, just because the flyer and the gifts he had for Jade were in his bedroom. It was merely a matter of convenience.

She followed him through the living room, then hesitated. He turned around and laughed. "Come on, don't worry. I won't bite."

She raised a doubtful eyebrow, but he laughed again. "Jade, you have to trust me.... Come on, silly. This'll just take a minute. Besides, it's almost time for your curfew."

Sadness fell over her face at the thought, but she followed him in silence. When they were in his bedroom, he directed her to sit on the foot of the bed.

"What's going on?"

"You'll see." He went to the desk, opened a drawer, and pulled out a single long-stem red rose, an envelope, and the flyer regarding the trip to Hungary. Then he turned around and joined her on the foot of the bed. "Here. These are for you."

Tears filled her eyes again and she tilted her head, looking from him to the rose and back again. She was clearly too choked up to speak.

"Read it." Tanner leaned toward her and braced an arm behind her so their sides were touching.

Jade dabbed at a tear as she opened the envelope and pulled out a greeting card with a picture of a breathtaking rainbow across the front. She opened it, and over her shoulder Tanner read the words he'd written earlier that day. "My sweetest Jade...from beginning to end, this has been the summer of my dreams. God has used you in so many ways to draw me closer to him, closer to everything he has wanted for me. One day soon I want to marry you. But not yet. I have some planning to do first. In the meantime, know that I am thinking of you always, wherever I am, whatever I'm doing. I love you, Jade. Thank you for opening my eyes. All my love, all the time, Tanner."

Scribbled underneath he had written the verse that had come to represent everything they shared. The verse he had spoken to her only minutes earlier. "I know the plans I have for you…plans to give you hope and a future."

Jade finished reading and closed the card. Her arms moved slowly around his neck, and as she held him, he could feel her beginning to sob.

He ran his hand softly down the back of her head. "It's okay, Jade, honey. I love you. I'm not going away for good. Hey—" he pulled back—"there's something else I have to show you."

She drew three quick, convulsive breaths, and Tanner could see she was trying to compose herself, trying to keep a flood of tears from letting go. She waited while he presented her with the flyer. "What's…what's this?"

"Open it." Tanner grinned and watched as Jade unfolded the paper. A moment passed as she read over the details, and when she looked up at him, her eyes were filled with questions. "I don't get it."

"I found that flyer almost a year ago. Think about it, Jade…what better place than Hungary to study what happens when religious freedom is taken away?"

"Hungary?" Her voice was quiet.

"Yes. I picked up the flyer and carried it with me because I wanted so badly to go." He hesitated. "Only there was no way I ever would. Not as long as my goal was public office. But after our talk the other day I knew I had to go. I wouldn't be happy unless I did."

"But…what about your classes?" She ran a trembling hand through her hair.

"I called the university and made arrangements, then I contacted Youth with a Mission. They had room for me so I paid in full. I leave in two weeks for Hungary."

"How long will you be gone?" Jade searched the flyer.

"Two months." Tanner grinned, proud of himself for finally making this decision. "But I'll write."

"Two months in Hungary?" Jade looked bewildered, almost fearful. "What about…"

Suddenly Tanner understood her fears. She thought he was cutting her out of the picture, and he rushed to explain himself. "Don't you see, Jade? I'll take the trip, work extra hard to graduate in May, and then next summer I want us to get married. After that I'll be going to law school for a few years, and when I'm finished, I'll take my place in the fight for religious freedom. It's my life and I'm going to do what I want with it, what God has planned for me."

Jade scanned the flyer again. "Wow. I can't believe it."

Tanner studied her and a sliver of doubt pierced his heart. Why wasn't she excited about his plans? *She loves me, doesn't she, God?* He believed her feelings for him were sincere, and yet she'd never said the words. Never declared her love. He took her hands in his. It was time to find out.

"Jade, you know how much I love you…." She nodded, a faint smile curving the corners of her lips. He paused. "But…but you've never told me if you feel the same way." He kissed her once, tenderly. "You've never told me you loved me."

Tears came to her eyes again, and he forced himself to continue. "Do you?"

She circled her arms around his neck once more and hugged him, resting her face against his chest. When she spoke, she pulled away and looked into his soul. "You're the only one I've ever loved."

"Really?"

She nodded and traced his lips with her finger. "I used to imagine I'd marry you one day, even back when we were kids."

He was flooded with relief. "Me, too."

"I think I loved you even back then, Tanner."

He moved his lips against hers as he ran his hands along her back and the sides of her neck. "I love you, Jade. Marry me...."

She was crying openly now, and when he kissed her again he tasted her tears. Her sobs made it difficult to hear her answer but he heard it all the same. "Yes. Yes, I'll marry you, Tanner."

His mouth covered hers and he held her closer.

Get out of the bedroom!

The warning sounded clearly in his mind, but he brushed it off. What difference did it make what room they were in? It was their last night together, after all. Tanner stroked the back of her head and drew her to him again. "God brought us together...and when I leave tomorrow, I'll take you with me in here." He touched the area over his heart. Then he placed his hands on her shoulders and searched her eyes. "We'll be together again, Jade. I promise." Their kiss was longer this time. "I'll never, ever leave you."

He took her hands in his and felt a strong reaction to the contact. But this time he didn't hear any warnings. Instead, he pulled her close, nestling her against him. Softly, near her ear, he whispered the truth: "I never could have done this if it hadn't been for you." He drew back and saw that Jade's eyes glistened with happy tears.

"Does your mother know?"

"I'll tell her tomorrow."

Their kiss was more urgent this time, and after a few minutes he felt her stiffen in his arms. She pulled away and caught her breath. "I should go. You have to get up early."

"Okay, soon." Tanner studied her eyes, memorizing her. He would never forget how she looked, sitting beside him in her sleeveless denim shirt and cutoffs. Eyes as green as they'd been back when she was a child. She would always be the most beautiful woman he'd ever seen.

He knew he should let her go, walk her out and tell her good-bye. But in that instant he couldn't bear the thought. His lips moved up her cheekbone toward her earlobe. His body shook from the flames that shot through him, and he wondered if she could sense the depth of his passion. "Jade..." The word came out low and breathless. "Oh, Jade, what you do to me."

He lowered his lips to hers, savoring their closeness, savoring her.

Leave the bedroom! Go! Flee!

The warnings were distant, easily dismissed. God would not let him be tempted beyond what he could bear. He wasn't really losing control; his body only felt that way. He ran his fingers lightly down the length of her bare arms and felt her skin chill under his touch.

"Tanner..."

"It's okay." He pressed his lips to hers, stopping her questions before she could ask them. Ignoring the dim warnings, he moved his lips down the curve of her neck.

She moaned softly, and reaction jolted through him. Was this how it felt to lose control? To be so drawn in that there was no human way out? He banished the thought. He could stop if he wanted to. They were just saying good-bye, sharing a memory that would help them endure their long separation. His breathing came faster, and he gave himself permission to kiss her shoulders, her throat. Permission to continue.

Finally, Tanner knew he'd gone too far. Desire drove him, and it was far more powerful than he'd ever imagined. He couldn't stop it.

In that instant, despite everything he knew to be true and right, regardless of the promises and plans of a mighty God, Tanner knew something else.

He no longer wanted to.

Warnings echoed loudly in Jade's mind as well, rattling her heart and making it difficult to breathe. Verses about the sexually immoral and adultery and desire leading to death. But Tanner knew what he was doing, didn't he? He wouldn't let things go too far. He would stop before it was too late

She could trust him.

Flee, my daughter. Flee!

She heard the silent voice and was filled with alarm at the heat coursing through her. *Come on, Tanner, stop.* She needed to leave, needed to be anywhere but in his bedroom, kissing him, wrapped in his arms on the foot of his bed.

He'll be gone tomorrow. We're just kissing. Can't we have this one moment to say good-bye? Eventually the warnings grew dim.

Tanner moved his mouth down her neck toward the hollow of her throat, and she tipped her head back, shocked to hear herself moan. Her body ached with a need she knew could be met only one way.

Never, Lord. We'll stop. I promise. This is only because he's leaving. Help us, Lord.

Flee!

She closed her eyes and refused. Things were under control. They were two grown adults, after all. Slowly she drew closer to Tanner until her mouth was on his neck, tasting the saltiness of his skin, the stubble of his day-old shave. She gripped his arms and felt him flex beneath her fingers. He was strong and good and right. His very presence felt like a dream come true.

Gently, tenderly, ever so slowly they fell back onto the bed, still locked together, their kisses hungrier than before.

Tanner moved so that his chest lay partially over hers, and his kisses became longer, deeper. Another wave of alarm washed over her. "Tanner…we can't…"

For a moment he stopped, breathless, and held a finger to her lips. "It's okay…." He brushed back her hair with tender fingers. "Don't worry, Jade." Another kiss. "Just relax…. We'll stop in a minute…."

Her body blazed with desire, and she knew deep in her heart that Tanner was wrong. God would not be okay with this. But, then, they were still only kissing, weren't they? Certainly he would forgive them for being together like this longer than usual. Just this once.

Jade ran her hands over the muscles in his lower back, pulling him closer to her. "We have to stop. We have to…"

Tanner moved his mouth along her throat again and brought his knee over hers. "We will." He looked at her then, and she saw he was trembling, his eyes filled with wanting her. "We won't be together again for so long." His lips traveled up her neck as he made his way to her mouth. "We'll stop…. Don't worry."

Ten minutes passed and then twenty. All the while she assured herself they could stop, they would stop. She was safe here in Tanner's arms, a princess being loved by her one and only prince.

But as the evening grew later they kept on, trapped in a

moment of weakness stronger than anything either of them had ever known. And sometime after midnight, when they dressed in silence and Tanner walked Jade to her car to kiss her good-bye, she was no longer a princess.

She was a whore, just like her mother.

Fourteen

SHE WAS TIRED ALMOST IMMEDIATELY, AND ON THE TWELFTH DAY the nausea kicked in. That night, Jade clutched her sides as she lay on her bed, weeping. Over and over she told herself it was nothing more than the obvious. She hadn't been eating well since Tanner left for Portland, and her father seemed to be shouting at her constantly.

Most of all, she had become shameful in the sight of God.

A sick stomach was understandable.

It was two days before Tanner would leave for Hungary, and she was an emotional basket case. Since Tanner had gone back to school, she'd done her best to avoid her father, choosing instead to spend the hours locked in her bedroom. Penance, she told herself. For committing the unpardonable sin.

Summer classes were over, and the fall schedule would begin at the end of the month. She increased her hours at Kelso General, thinking she might somehow show God the sincerity of her sorrow, how much she wanted him to think her good again.

She brought her knees up nearly to her chin, curled up under the covers, sobbing alone in the night. *I'm sorry, Lord. Forgive me. What have I done? Why did we go against your plan?*

She heard no response. As though the Lord had utterly and completely abandoned her.

Maybe her constant weeping could explain the tiredness and this strange nausea that had come upon her. That had to be the reason. It had to be. She shut her eyes, forced out her fears, and focused on surviving.

"I miss you, Tanner." She whispered into her pillow. Almost as though he'd somehow heard her, the telephone rang. Jade answered it quickly so her father wouldn't pick it up in the other room.

"Jade, it's me...." Tanner's voice sounded tinny and hollow. *A payphone,* she thought. And instantly he felt a million miles away.

She tried to speak but a single sob escaped before she could say anything.

"Jade, you're crying...talk to me...." She heard people laughing in the background.

"Where...where are you?" Her voice was thick with tears. She knew Tanner wouldn't want her crying, but she couldn't change how she felt.

"Cafeteria. The pay phones in the dorm were busy." Tanner sounded rushed, and Jade was having trouble feeling close to him. Everything about their conversation felt strained, and the realization brought another wave of tears.

"Jade, baby, stop crying. Everything's going to be okay." He sounded so far away, and in two days he would be thousands of miles farther. Once he left for Hungary, there would be no contact between them for two months. He had told her he'd write, but mail delivery could take two weeks or longer. Since his group would move from place to place, there was no way she could write to him. Their contact—however limited—would be completely one-sided.

A minute had passed and still Jade quietly cried, unable to answer.

"Jade, what's wrong with you? Why won't you talk to me?"

She sought desperately for something to say, but there was nothing.

Tanner's voice grew impatient. "I feel bad, too, you know. I never meant for…oh, you know what I mean."

She stifled her sobs. "I know."

"I'm sorry. How many times do I have to tell you."

She choked out her response. "I told you…I'm not mad at you. I just feel bad. Like we blew it."

"I know." He lowered his voice. "I said I'm sorry. What else can I say?"

She continued weeping, struggling to speak. Nothing felt right anymore. "It…it feels like things are different between us."

"Come on, Jade. That's your imagination. Satan wants you to be buried under guilt so you'll never be happy again."

"I should have stopped it, Tanner. I had a choice and I didn't." She tried to compose herself. "Besides, we haven't come to the Lord together and asked for forgiveness."

He fell silent, and Jade wondered why. Didn't his heart seek repentance over this? Didn't he think they should come before the Lord as a couple? Maybe his faith wasn't what it had seemed to be all summer. Jade felt even more sick at the thought.

When he finally answered, the impatience was back. "Listen, I have to get going. I have a lot to do before I leave. I didn't call to hear you cry for thirty minutes. I already got that earlier when I talked to my mother. Naturally she thinks I'm crazy, throwing away my future and all." He paused. "I was kind of hoping you might be able to cheer me up."

Jade stared at the phone, open mouthed. *Is it so easy for him to dismiss what we've done, how it's changed things between us?* "I'm sorry. I don't feel very cheery."

"What *do* you feel, Jade? Do you still love me?"

She felt her anger rising. "Of *course* I love you. But I feel all messed up inside. Like we've turned God against us and like...no matter what we do now our plans won't succeed." She wept more loudly. "Right now I feel too ashamed to even talk to you, and you want me to be cheery?"

He sighed slowly, and she could hear more voices in the background. He was obviously in a busy part of the cafeteria, and it gave her the feeling he wasn't paying attention. "Okay, we were wrong. *I've* said that. *You've* said that. I'm sure we've both admitted it to God. We're both sorry. Now we pick up the pieces and go on. You can't let what happened change things between us."

She was silent for a moment, trying desperately to fight off the nausea that passed over her. "It's too late." She drew a deep, steadying breath.

"What's too late?" He sounded tired.

"Things have changed already."

"Well, then maybe you and I have some thinking to do over the next two months."

Fear ripped through Jade's heart. *What are you saying, Tanner? Are you breaking up with me?* "I'm not sure what you mean by that...but I love you, Tanner. I just can't pretend things are the same."

Tanner paused. "Fine. Listen, I gotta go, Jade. I love you. I'll be praying for you. Just because we made a mistake doesn't mean God's forgotten about us. Jeremiah 29:11 is still true. Okay?"

His words sounded hollow, forced...and Jade swallowed the lump in her throat. "Okay. 'Bye...I'll miss you."

"I'll miss you, too. And I'll write."

They hung up, and Jade flopped onto her stomach, sobbing as if her heart would break. *Two months.* There would be no conversation between them for two months. He hadn't been gone two weeks, and already their relationship was strained. *What'll happen in two months?*

She turned onto her side. A collage of Kelso General's sick children hung on the wall, and she stared at it. When was her last period, anyway? She calculated the dates as she'd done a dozen times since August thirty-first....

What she and Tanner did hadn't been planned, so they hadn't used birth control. And now she realized that she'd been smack in the middle of her cycle. Her period was due tomorrow: September fourteenth. Ever since she was thirteen they'd come every twenty-eight days without fail. As predictable as her father's drinking.

God, what'll I do? What if I'm pregnant?

But instead of the Savior's kind prompting, she heard unholy voices, voices that had haunted her since that Friday night at Tanner's apartment.

Whore! Your father was right! You should have run off with Jim Rudolph. Tanner deserves better than a piece of trash like you.

She closed her eyes, trying desperately to shut out the voices. For a moment she glanced at her Bible and considered looking through it for help. But she hadn't been able to open it since Tanner left. She felt too dirty, too much a hypocrite to hold God's perfect word in her filthy hands.

Her period did not come the next day or the next, and by Friday, three weeks after that night at Tanner's apartment, Jade did not need a pregnancy kit to tell her she was with child. Nevertheless it was time to take the test. Otherwise she might never really accept the truth.

A few days later she drove to a remote part of town and found a drug store she'd never been to before. There she paid for a test that promised accurate results just one day after a missed period. She took the test home and performed it in the bathroom, careful to hide the packaging in a brown paper bag. Three minutes later two pink lines appeared in the test-tube window, and she had her answer.

She was pregnant.

The next day she skipped classes and stayed in bed, suffocating beneath her warring emotions. At times she wept, thrashing about under her covers, wondering what had gone so wrong in their plans and why they'd been so weak that final night together.

Other times she was overcome with fear. What would she do? Where would she live? How quickly could she get word to Tanner? What kind of mother would she be?

The last question was easy. She would be everything her mother hadn't been. Nothing and no one would ever separate her from the infant she carried. Regardless of the cost—and she was sure their choice that night would cost them much—she would love her child unconditionally as long as she drew breath.

If this were two years from now, Tanner and I would be celebrating. Nothing could have contained what she knew would be their mutual excitement. And even in the midst of her turmoil, the reality of what had happened to her filled her with awe. Tanner's child was within her…a baby created out of their love for each other. *Only we didn't wait for God's perfect plan, and now everything is wrong.*

She wanted desperately to talk to Tanner, get his reaction. He'd been in Hungary for a week and she had hoped to receive a letter from him but so far there had been nothing, no word at all. Would he want her to move out to New Jersey and marry him immediately? Would he send her away, sickened by the sight of her? She thought she knew the answer, but she wasn't sure anymore. Everything had changed.

Should she tell her father? She would have to let him know eventually. But how would he take the news? What names would he call her? Jade wept again because she knew the answer. The weeping and wondering and wishing she could go back in time continued until late in the evening, when finally she arrived at a plan. She would call and see if Tanner's mother knew a way to get a message to him. He had explained to Jade that the group leaders allowed only emergency phone calls back to the U.S. Surely this would qualify. After all, it was his baby, too. Between the two of them, they could figure out what to do.

She made the call the next morning and waited. Tanner's mother answered on the second ring.

"Hello, Mrs. Eastman, this is Jade." She waited but there was no happy greeting, no words of acknowledgment. Jade started to tremble, and a wave of nausea forced her to sit down. "Mrs. Eastman? Are you there?"

"Jade..." the woman sounded as though she were trying to place her, almost as if they'd never met. *How come she doesn't know who I am?* Hadn't Tanner been talking about her during his visits? An alarm rang deep within her.

"Ma'am, this is Jade Conner...Tanner's friend from Williamsburg. Remember? We visited your house together a few times back in June?"

"Oh! That Jade. Yes, I'm sorry. Forgive me. I must have been distracted." Mrs. Eastman sounded friendlier, and Jade breathed a sigh of relief. "How are you, dear?"

"Uh...fine, thanks. And you?"

"Well, I must admit my arthritis has been acting up. But otherwise I'm just fine. Getting ready for the move back to Williamsburg and missing Tanner, of course. But otherwise good."

"That's what I'm calling about." Jade waited a beat and then plunged ahead. "I was wondering if you knew some way to get a message to Tanner?" She crossed her arms against her stomach and closed her eyes. She felt like she was going to throw up but now was not the time. She held a piece of notepaper in her hand and prepared to jot down whatever numbers Tanner's mother might give her.

"In Hungary?"

Jade exhaled slowly and breathed in again, forcing herself to continue the conversation. "Yes. I thought you might know who to call."

"Why, dear, surely you know he can't receive calls. He's on a missionary trip." The woman sounded pleased with her son, and Jade wondered if she'd had a change of heart. Tanner had said his mother had been furious when she learned of his intentions to change career paths and spend two months in Hungary.

"Yes, ma'am, I know he can't. This...well, this is kind of an emergency. I really need to talk to him."

"An emergency? Why, Jade, are you okay?" The woman's voice was filled with warmth and concern, and Jade felt tears sting at her eyes. If only her own mother had been there to comfort her and give her direction.

She swallowed hard. "I'm fine. It's...well, it's very important that I talk to him."

"I'm sorry, dear. I'm fairly certain I don't have any numbers." The woman sounded worried for Jade. "Of course, we could always call Youth with a Mission. They might know how to reach him." She hesitated. "If you don't mind, Jade, what's the emergency?"

Jade almost wanted to tell her. Maybe Tanner's mother would know what to do next, maybe even find the right words to assure her everything would be okay. "It's…personal, ma'am."

Mrs. Eastman hesitated. "Personal?"

Jade paused. "Yes. I really don't want to talk about it until I've had a chance to speak to Tanner."

For several moments Mrs. Eastman said nothing, and Jade assumed she was searching for numbers. She was completely unprepared for the serenity in the woman's voice—or for what she said next. "Are you pregnant, Jade?"

Jade's vision grew blurred and she thought she would faint. What was this? How had Tanner's mother known? Jade blinked and tried to focus on her surroundings. Maybe she hadn't heard the woman correctly. "Excuse me?"

"I'm sorry if I'm prying, but…Tanner told me what happened. That the two of you slept together. He was quite honest about it."

Jade's head swam in a sea of unanswered questions. Why had Tanner told his mother? He'd been afraid to tell her they were dating, but now he'd told her they'd slept together? She gulped and searched for something to say. "He…he told you that?"

"Why yes, dear. He tells me everything. We're quite close, you know."

"I…I know. I just didn't think…"

"Well, dear, are you pregnant?"

Jade began crying. "Yes…I am." She struggled to speak. "That's why Tanner and I have to talk. I don't know what to do, Mrs. Eastman. Please…help me."

The woman's voice was soothing and reassuring. "Tomorrow is Sunday. Why don't you drive down, and we'll spend the afternoon together. I'm sure we can figure something out."

"Okay." She thought about attending Crossroads on the way down, but then changed her mind. They hadn't recognized the fact that she came from tainted parents, but surely they would recognize what she had become since then. She would avoid church until she had a plan and knew what to do. "Would two o'clock be fine?"

"Yes, dear. I'll look for you then. Drive safely."

Jade's heart soared with hope as she hung up. Tanner's mother liked her! She had been warm and kind and understanding in the wake of what had to have been the most shocking news she'd ever received. Maybe Tanner had told his mother about his intentions to marry her.

Jade lay back on her bed, her mind racing ahead to a host of possibilities. Maybe Mrs. Eastman would ask her to come around more often, offer to attend doctor appointments with her. Perhaps she would be the mother Jade had always wanted and everything would fall in place.

If Mrs. Eastman could love her, then life was suddenly filled with promise. Maybe things really would turn out all right.

She ignored her father that evening, skipped dinner, and for the first time since Tanner left, she slept soundly. The morning couldn't come soon enough, and when it did she hummed happily to herself as she got ready. Whether they figured out a way to contact Tanner or not, Jade knew that with Mrs. Eastman on her side everything was going to be okay. The plans she and Tanner had made were shaky, but they were still intact. God had forgiven her.

And he had blessed her with a friend like Mrs. Eastman in the process.

Fifteen

Doris Eastman paced the plush carpet of her uptown condominium, fuming. She had been right, of course. On every account. Jade Conner was a loose, good-for-nothing seductress just like her mother.

The nerve of the girl, calling her for information about how to reach Tanner.

Doris replayed the conversation over and over. The moment Jade mentioned that there was an emergency, bells began sounding in her mind. She knew what kind of girl Jade was. The emergency could be one thing only.

When Jade mentioned it was personal, Doris had taken a chance. Tanner hadn't told her anything about his relationship with Jade. Through July and August she'd asked him to stop bringing the girl to her house and he'd agreed. He hadn't even put up a fight. How important could the girl be to him, really?

Doris considered herself a Christian woman, but she'd had no trouble lying to Jade earlier. Nor would she hesitate to do what she planned when Jade arrived. She would lie a hundred times if it meant protecting Tanner from a girl like Jade. Besides, if she hadn't lied, Jade would never have opened up to her in the first place, never planned to visit that afternoon. Doris wondered what other dark secrets she could extract from the girl.

Not that it mattered.

Doris planned to do most of the talking. She tapped her

foot anxiously and looked at her watch. Her plan was perfect, and she congratulated herself for being so cunning in her old age.

Woe to you, woman…remember the height from which you have fallen….

The thought interrupted her plotting, and she scowled. Where had *that* come from? She hadn't read a Bible in twenty years. For a moment she thought of Tanner and the hours he'd spent preaching to her, warning her to get right with God again. Huh! What a hypocrite he turned out to be.

Perhaps she should have told him long ago what had happened with his father. How during her engagement to Hap, that Conner woman had shown up on his doorstep one night…how she'd wormed her way inside, just like the women in Proverbs. And how she'd…

Doris couldn't bear the thought.

But at least if she'd told Tanner, he might have made better choices that summer. She considered her son's decisions over the past months and shook her head angrily. The boy was crazy. First he'd given up his political future. Then he'd decided to spend two months on a missionary trip to God-forsaken Hungary. And finally he'd bedded the daughter of a…a woman like Angela Conner. Obviously Tanner had suffered some sort of mental breakdown or emotional collapse over the summer. Perhaps a delayed reaction to his father's death.

Whatever it was, it was all Jade's fault.

She looked at her watch again.

Hurry up, Jade. She smiled. *The web's ready and the spider's waiting.*

Jade parked her car outside the Eastman condominium, grabbed the bouquet of fall flowers from the front seat, and headed up the sidewalk. She had eaten a few saltine crackers on the drive over to stave off any nausea. Although pregnancy was completely foreign to her, she thought it must have been early to be experiencing so strong an upset stomach. Maybe Tanner's mother would help her know what to do, and what to expect in the coming weeks and months.

She hoped Mrs. Eastman would enjoy the flowers. She was filled with peace at the thought of knowing she could talk about her pregnancy and that Tanner's mother truly cared about what happened to her. She rang the doorbell and waited.

Doris Eastman was always dressed impeccably and today was no exception. She wore an eggshell knit skirt, a sweater with a pearl snap, and handsome, low-healed shoes. She welcomed Jade with a warm smile and ushered her inside. "Come in, Jade. You look well."

They moved into the front room, and Mrs. Eastman directed her to a comfortable oversized sofa chair. "Make yourself at home.... I'll get us something to drink."

"Thank you, ma'am." A sense of warmth came over her at the woman's words, and Jade played them again in her mind. *Make yourself at home...at home...at home.*

Tanner's mother returned with two glasses of water. When they were both situated, Doris cocked her head, her eyes filled with concern. "Now, dear. Tell me what happened?"

Jade drew a deep breath and pressed her hand to her flat stomach. "I can't really believe it myself."

"You're sure though? You took a test?"

Jade nodded. "I'm already feeling sick. It'll probably be a strong baby."

Tanner's mother slipped one leg daintily over the other. "Have you told anyone else?"

Jade took a sip of water and shook her head. "Just you." She let loose a brief laugh. "Never in a million years did I think Tanner would have told you about us."

Mrs. Eastman smiled. "Tanner and I talk about everything." She paused and dabbed her lips with a napkin. "Whenever he gets in trouble, I'm the first person he turns to."

What a wonderful mother she is. Jade relaxed back into the chair and noticed that her nausea was gone. She was perfectly at ease in Mrs. Eastman's home, struck again by her gracious concern and kindness. Why had she ever doubted this woman's intentions? She was gentle and serene and warm as the recent Indian summer days. Jade imagined her offering support every time Tanner…

Every time he got into trouble? She hesitated. "That can't have been too often, knowing Tanner. His getting in trouble, I mean." She grinned, enjoying the easy banter of their conversation.

Mrs. Eastman leaned slightly forward and took another sip of water. "Not as a boy, no. But ever since the girls discovered him—" the woman made a face that indicated the severity of the problem—"he's gotten in trouble more times than I care to count."

Tanner? In trouble with girls? The pointed blade of alarm stabbed at Jade, and she felt the smile fade from her face. "Is that right?"

The woman looked surprised. "Oh, didn't he tell you, dear?"

Jade had the strange sensation that something bad was about to happen. "Tell me what?"

"Tanner has two children on the East Coast." Mrs. Eastman folded her hands comfortably. "Of course, he doesn't talk about them often. I send their mothers a check every month, and that's about the extent of it."

Jade's vision grew blurred again and her head was swimming. What was this woman saying? Tanner had no other children. He'd never even been with a…"I…I didn't know."

Doris angled her head sadly. "I'm sorry, dear. I thought you knew." She spanned the distance between them and reached for Jade's hand. "Tanner can be an awfully convincing storyteller, I'm afraid."

"How…how old are the children?" Jade felt like she was having an out-of-body experience. She was talking, desperate to know the truth about the man she thought she loved. But her breathing seemed to have stopped, and she was certain she was going to faint.

"Amy is three. Tanner met her mother his senior year in high school. They were very physical, very fast, but Tanner never cared for her. He offered to pay for an abortion, but the girl wouldn't hear of it. Now she gets her monthly check like clockwork."

The nausea was back with a vengeance, and Jade knew she needed a bathroom. She forced herself to wait, to hear the sickening news. "The other child?"

"Justin. Almost two." Mrs. Eastman paused. "Tanner had three women between the mothers of the children. Two of them took him up on his offer and had abortions. The other one must have gotten smart and used birth control. There's been at least five women that I know of. What I mean is, this certainly isn't the first time I've helped him out of trouble." Mrs. Eastman's eyes softened, and she gently squeezed Jade's hand. "I guess you're number six."

"Will you excuse me?" Jade rushed out of the room and barely reached the bathroom in time. There she vomited until there was nothing left inside her.

Until her stomach was as empty as her breaking heart.

It couldn't be true! It was a nightmare, and any moment she was going to wake up and start the day over again. Her stomach convulsed again and nothing came up. *Dear God, is it true? Was everything he told me a lie?* Had he manipulated their time together that summer so that she'd sleep with him? Her heart raced and once more her stomach convulsed, as if her body were trying to rid itself of everything about Tanner Eastman.

When she was finally finished, she stood and wiped her face. Her legs were wobbly and her head pounded. It couldn't be true, could it? Tanner loved her. He had wanted to marry her, to wait until then before they…She made her way slowly back to the living room and sat down.

"Are you all right, dear? You look pale." Tanner's mother extended her hand and Jade took it. After all, it wasn't her fault Tanner had lied.

"I'll be okay."

The woman paused and presented two separate snapshots. "I found these while you were gone. This is Amy and this… …is Justin."

Jade stared at the photographs, and she was blindsided by another wave of nausea. There was no mistaking the resemblance. The children had Tanner's piercing blue eyes, his strong jawline. They were gorgeous—and very much without a father.

The shock was wearing off. The pictures were proof—no question about it. Tanner had lied to her from the beginning. And like numerous other women before her, she had believed him willingly.

Anger began to replace her shock. "He doesn't stay in touch with them?"

Mrs. Eastman shook her head sadly. "I'm afraid not. He isn't very fatherly, actually. Doesn't even send presents on their birthdays."

Jade felt whatever color remained drain from her face, and again Tanner's mother leaned closer. "You don't look well, dear. Can I get you anything?"

"I'm sorry…I feel faint, I guess. This is all such a shock. He…he never told me any of it."

The woman huffed in frustration. "I really thought he'd outgrown this irresponsible behavior. Especially what with his decision to work for the governor's office next year."

Jade's head spun faster. "What?"

"Certainly he told you that much."

Jade shook her head. "He's going to law school. He wants to fight for religious freedom."

Mrs. Eastman released a sad laugh. "He loves to talk about religious freedom. That was something his father and I always wanted for Tanner. That he might pursue a career in law, fighting for his faith. Despite his failings, he's still a very religious young man, you know. But last week he accepted an entry-level position in the governor's office. The governor of Virginia."

Jade drew three quick breaths. She felt sick again, and her body shook uncontrollably. No matter how hard she tried she couldn't get warm, couldn't stop the trembling. "What about Hungary?"

"Tanner's such a thrill seeker, he just couldn't resist the challenge. It will look good on his resume, of course, that he spent a semester helping the people of Hungary restore their rights. And you can be sure that's how it'll appear on his resume."

"I'm sorry, I…" Jade spread her knees and hung her head, desperately trying to stave off the fainting spell that had suddenly engulfed her.

"Here, dear. Have some water." Mrs. Eastman was by her side, offering the drink.

Jade took two sips and then slowly returned to an upright position. There was something she wanted to know. "Tell me one thing, Mrs. Eastman...."

"Yes?" The woman returned to her chair and smiled sympathetically.

"Did Tanner love any of those other women? Did he talk about marrying them?"

"Tanner has a double standard that way. He considers marrying a girl until she gives in to his advances. Once a girl has slept with him, he has no further interest. Wouldn't look good on his political resume."

Jade thought about Hungary. Was it true what Tanner's mother said? Was Tanner not at all interested in fighting for religious freedom? Had he lied about that, too? Her body was seized with cramps, and she shook from the overload of shock. "But he told me politics were *your* idea."

For a moment the woman's eyes hardened, but then almost instantly they were kind again. "No, no, dear. Tanner's wanted to be a politician as far back as I can remember. Oh, his father and I would have loved him to be a lawyer, helping the religious among us. But Tanner is very single-minded. When he wants something, he gets it...when he doesn't, well..."

Jade thought of little Amy and Justin. He hadn't wanted them or their mothers, and now he lived his life completely separate from them. It was the same thing he'd do to her.

Mrs. Eastman was watching her, and Jade was overcome with a sense of loss. How could she have been so wrong about Tanner? After being his best friend so many years earlier....

"Jade, dear, I'm afraid Tanner can be very irresponsible. But he's my son and I love him. One day the whole world will love him."

Jade's eyes filled with tears. Shock and anger were giving

way to repulsion. She had been used and made to feel like a whore at the hands of a man who had lied about everything. Certainly he had lied about his love for her. No wonder he sounded so short-tempered during their last telephone conversation.

"Here, dear—" Mrs. Eastman handed Jade a tissue—"I see you're upset. Should we see if we can find an emergency number for Tanner?"

Jade clenched her jaw and gritted her teeth. "No, thank you. I have no interest in calling him now."

"Oh, dear, I'm so sorry. I shouldn't have said anything."

Jade felt the steady stream of tears on her cheeks, but she was not filled with grief. No, what filled her to overflowing was much more direct, more simple. Hatred. That's what she felt. If she hadn't seen the pictures of the children, she wouldn't have believed a word of it. She had thought she knew Tanner better than she even knew herself. But now… "No, Mrs. Eastman. I'm glad you told me. You spared me from making a fool out of myself."

"Now, now, child. How could you have known?" The woman reached for her purse, opened it, and pulled something out. "You're planning to keep the baby, is that right?"

Jade nodded fiercely. "Definitely."

"Well, I'll treat your child the same way I treat Amy and Justin. But there are a few stipulations I'd like to discuss."

Stipulations? What in the world was she talking about? This wasn't a business transaction. Jade stared at Tanner's mother and noticed something she hadn't before: The kindness was gone.

Mrs. Eastman cleared her throat and continued. "You will not put Tanner's name on the birth certificate. He'll not want anything to do with the child anyway, and it will only complicate things. Also, you will not mention the identity of the baby's father to anyone." The woman crossed her legs again and smiled through hard eyes. "Tanner will be a household name one day, and he and I will deny to the death that he ever had anything to do with you. Is that understood?"

"I thought…you seemed like you wanted to help. Like you wanted to be a part of my baby's life. You've been so…"

"Friendly? Do I have a choice?" Mrs. Eastman cast her a look of disdain. "As long as Tanner keeps getting girls like you pregnant, it'll be up to me to cover his tracks. There will be no room for scandal in the White House. Tanner will be remembered for his high standards, his moral character. I've told the same thing to the other women."

"So you're in charge of cleaning up after him, is that it?" Jade forced herself to breathe, to remain seated even though everything in her wanted to walk over and choke this woman. How dare she place demands on Jade and her unborn child? "What if I don't agree? What if I choose to put his name on the birth certificate anyway?"

The woman made an exaggerated shrug of her shoulders while her eyes shot daggers at Jade. "That will be your choice. But the moment you do, you will be cut off from any financial assistance I might otherwise give. Also, I will hire a batch of attorneys to sue you for child endangerment and complete custody of that brat you're carrying. And then you'll lose the child for good." Mrs. Eastman uttered a short, mocking laugh. "Girls like you would never win a court battle against the Eastman estate. If you know what's good for you, and you want to be a mother to that baby, you'll take the money I'm about to offer and any other money I send you, and once in a while you'll send me a photograph." Mrs. Eastman smiled wickedly. "I like to be kept apprised of my grandchildren."

Jade was on her feet, grabbing her purse and keys. "I don't

want your money." She glared at the woman, sickened at how hateful and evil she was. Just like her son. "You and Tanner don't have to worry. My baby won't have anybody's name but mine." She paused. "And I'll never tell a soul as long as I live who the baby's father is."

Tanner's mother settled back in her chair. "I thought you'd see it my way." She held out what looked like a check. "It's a cashier's check. I never send Tanner's children money any other way. Wouldn't want it to be traced, you know."

Jade stared at the woman in shock. She was every bit as good a liar as Tanner. To think she had spent nearly an hour believing the woman cared about her! A sickening shudder coursed through her veins. She needed air. "Keep your money. I said I don't want it."

Mrs. Eastman raised an eyebrow and continued to hold the check in Jade's direction. "Are you sure? It's ten thousand dollars."

Jade's eyes widened and she hesitated. She was about to set out on the world pregnant, single, and penniless. She could live with her father for a while, but once he found out about the baby...

Anxiety wrapped its arms around her, and even her teeth chattered from the shock. How could this be happening? Her body trembled with rage, furious at the way Tanner had tricked her, betrayed her. Maybe he did owe her something after all. It wasn't much. It wouldn't replace the fact that her child would be without a father, but it would help. It would mean that her baby wouldn't starve while she figured out how to find a job.

"I'm not sending you pictures." Jade held her ground, too angry and proud to approach the woman.

Mrs. Eastman nodded. "Very well, then I won't be sending you monthly support."

Jade hesitated. She desperately wanted to take the check and rip it in half. But the truth was, she had no other means of existence. She had to think of the baby. "So you give me ten thousand dollars and that's it? Neither of us ever looks back?"

"I told you, Jade, I like you." The woman's eyes were hateful as she came near, the check clutched in her outstretched hand. "Consider the money a gift."

Everything in Jade was repulsed at the thought of taking this woman's check. *Think of the baby. Tanner should be responsible for something.* Jade snapped the check from the woman's hand. "One thing..."

Mrs. Eastman waited.

"Don't tell Tanner." She had made up her mind in the last few minutes. If he hadn't been a father to the other children, he'd never be one to this baby either.

The woman's mouth curled into a smile that looked practically evil. "Very well, dear. You have my promise. I'll not mention a word of your...this situation...to anyone. Not even Tanner."

Jade's heart fell at what she'd just done. Tanner would never know about the baby now, never know what had become of Jade and the child she bore. She wanted to spit at Tanner's mother for being so obviously glad about the fact. "I'm leaving now, Mrs. Eastman. You'll never hear from me again."

"Very well." Tanner's mother ushered her to the front door and glanced anxiously at her watch. "You'd best get going."

Jade's head was spinning, and she thought she might need a bathroom again. None of it mattered. She had to get away from this woman, had to find a place to get her bearings. Feeling unsteady on her feet, Jade moved as quickly as she could down the sidewalk toward her car. Mrs. Eastman raised her voice so Jade could hear her. "I'm sorry things didn't work out like you thought they would. You know, I think Tanner really liked you, Jade."

She spun around. *He loved me! Even if he lied, he loved me!* She wanted to tell Tanner's mother how great her son's feelings had been, but it was too late. Mrs. Eastman saw Jade's hesitation and cast one final dagger her way.

"But you weren't the marrying type, were you? Just a tramp like all the rest."

With that, Tanner's mother disappeared behind her door.

Inside the house, Doris Eastman peered through the window and watched until Jade's car disappeared from sight. *It worked! That stupid girl believed everything I said.*

It had been the pictures, of course. Jade was having trouble believing the lies about Tanner until she saw the pictures of Amy and Justin. Doris felt utterly satisfied with herself as she moved into the living room and found the framed photographs of the children on the coffee table where she'd left them.

Her oldest son had never been much of a business man, never gifted with the social graces and heady future that awaited Tanner. But Doris would say this for him: He always remembered to send pictures of his children.

Jade felt like she'd been trampled by a herd of wild horses.

As she pulled away from Doris Eastman's home, she tucked the cashier's check into her glove box and started the engine. Three blocks down the road, she pulled over, and for the next hour she wept until she thought she would die from the pain.

Tanner had loved her, hadn't he? She sobbed and struck the steering wheel with her fists. He had told her the Lord had plans for her, that she was a precious child of God, and that next summer he would marry her. Jade shook from the weight of it all. So many lies. No wonder he hadn't written to her since he left. He was finished with her.

She thought about all the ways Tanner had fooled her. Pictures of little Amy and Justin came to mind again, and she felt another wave of nausea. What kind of man would call himself a Christian and turn his back on his own children? If she'd had any doubts about the awful things Mrs. Eastman had told her, the pictures of Amy and Justin dissolved them. Those were Tanner's children. She had no doubt whatsoever.

After an hour, she pulled back onto the road. She needed to get home and face her father. *Help me, God. I can't do this alone.* The prayer seemed to bring a sense of peace in her heart. She would survive. She had her baby to think about now. As she headed north on I-5, she was struck by the fact that only two things had been true about that summer.

First, she had become a Christian. She might be the very worst one of all, but the fact remained that God had called her his own. No litany of lies from Tanner could mean her salvation wasn't true. She had a long way to go before things were right with the Lord, but one day they would be good again. He was her everlasting father, and nothing could change that.

Second, as long as she lived she would never, ever love any man the way she had allowed herself to love Tanner Eastman. All the earthly love she had to give from now on would be showered on one alone.

Her unborn child.

Sixteen

After decades of oppression and government bans on Bibles, the Hungarians were hungry for God's Word. Knowledge of that fact kept Tanner going even on days when he missed Jade so badly he felt physically ill.

The trip had been a whirlwind such that had there been the opportunity for phone calls back home there certainly would not have been the time. Since the trip was equally devoted to research and outreach, Tanner and seventeen college seniors from the East Coast spent their mornings going from school to school with a local translator.

The truths they were allowed to share to public school children would have sent the ACLU into a tailspin of lawsuits and outrage.

They kept their message simple. God was creator of all, sovereign and eternal, compassionate and full of love. His son, Jesus Christ, had come to the world, laid down his life for the sins of all so that any who believed in him might live forever. His word was truth. Period. And faith in him was the only hope for the world.

When Tanner wasn't speaking, he watched in amazement as the wide-eyed Hungarian children eagerly—almost desperately—soaked in the gospel message. Even more stunning were the public school administrators who welcomed Tanner's group and their message with open arms.

Back home students were not allowed to mention Jesus' name, even during the week before Christmas. Easter break had become spring break, and prayer was often forbidden at graduation ceremonies. Schools permitted rock lyrics with a message of hatred, but a student dare not sing a song of praise to God. Children with the freedom to purchase guns opened fire in schools, killing their classmates, particularly Christian classmates. And the ACLU defended those same students' right to brandish symbols of death, swastikas, and hate slogans on their notebooks and T-shirts.

Tanner wondered how long it would be before the United States government banned Bibles? Before Christians were hunted down and thrown into jail for being 'conspirators against the government'? Tanner feared the answer, and it motivated him to learn all he could during his time in Hungary.

From before sunup to late in the night, Tanner was absorbed in the process. He and his peers studied archives, interviewed former government officials, taught children, and made home visits to the families of school children who had requested additional information. Everyone wanted a Bible, and by the ninth day the Youth with a Mission leader had run out and wired back to the states for additional supplies.

They heard horrendous stories from the recent past, stories of people being jailed, tormented, and beheaded for their faith. Early in the trip, Tanner met a teenage boy named Peter. He was a ward of the state, and when Tanner brought the gospel message to the boy's classroom, he began filling in details for his classmates, quoting Scripture in the process.

Tanner asked the boy how he knew the Bible so well.

"My parents were Christians," Peter said through the translator. The boy's faith shone through strong eyes. "They taught us the Scriptures late at night, when police could not hear. We all committed to memory books of the Bible. Letters from St. Paul about suffering for the faith."

Peter hesitated. "Before the change in government, police found out what my parents were doing. They came one night, broke into the house, and shot my parents in the head. My parents were holding their Bibles when they died."

Tanner learned from Peter that he and his two sisters were forced to watch their parents' execution. Afterward, they were separated and sent to different parts of the nation to be raised as wards of the state. Peter had not heard from his sisters since.

After more than a week of hearing similar stories, Tanner was motivated like never before. The United States would not go the way of Hungary if he had anything to do with it. And God had showed Tanner that he would, indeed, have much to do with it.

In the quiet moments—moments scheduled for devotion, reflection, and Bible study—Tanner was more certain than ever that this was his calling. He would be a warrior for religious freedom in a country desperate for someone to take on the cause.

He memorized Romans 10:14–15, repeating it to himself when he became discouraged. *How, then, can they call on the one they have not believed in? And how can they believe in the one of whom they have not heard? And how can they hear without someone preaching to them? And how can they preach unless they are sent?*

He would carry the message back home where God would use him to expose the ways religious freedom was fading in America. He prayed God might use him in an amazing way so that no American child would ever be ripped away from his parents because of his or her faith.

No, he would never forget Peter or the people of Hungary.

His determination drove him to continue even when he missed Jade so much he couldn't sleep, couldn't eat. With her half a world away, he realized for the first time how long a week could be—or a day. Or, for that matter, even an hour.

Tanner's bed was a worn-out, government-issued cot, and he shared a room in a decaying school dormitory with three students from East Coast universities. On the first day of the fourth week, Tanner lay awake, wishing he could toss and turn, but knowing he would fall on the floor if he did.

I miss her, Lord. Let her know how much.

He shifted slightly and winced. The foam rubber mattress was supported by bars that dug into his ribs whenever he moved.

Sleep did not come easily in Hungary, but the quiet hours allowed him to reflect on his summer with Jade, especially the days before his trip. He had been impatient with her, and he wished desperately for the chance to call and apologize. If only Jade weren't so deeply depressed about the way they'd fallen that night.

Tanner flipped onto his back and gazed out the dusty, double-paned window. What he and Jade had done was wrong. He would give anything to go back in time and heed the Lord's warning that night. But there was no going back. The way they'd gone against God was something they could never undo, and Tanner realized they would suffer consequences as a result.

One of which was the way Jade had felt worthless about herself since that night.

Before leaving, Tanner had assured her several times that God still loved her, still had her name in the Book of Life. He promised her they would set more stringent boundaries next time they were together. He would not make the same mistake twice.

But at some point, Tanner believed they needed to move on,

and he'd shared that thought in their final phone conversation.

Tanner's eyes adjusted to the dark, and he could see his roommates sleeping soundly. He sighed, lifted his head, and turned his pillow over. Of course they were sleeping. None of them had let God down in the weeks before taking this trip. None of them had a troubled fiancée a million miles away. He lifted his head again and folded the pillow in half.

He thought of the Scripture about temptation and God providing a way out. No doubt, God had given him ways of escape that night. Tanner had simply ignored the warnings.

He sighed and tried to think of something else. It wasn't always a good thing to dwell too long on Jade. Feelings of repentance tended to give way to feelings far less pure.

He was counting down the days until next summer. Two-hundred and seventy-two, come morning. As far as he was concerned, the school year couldn't go by quickly enough, because then Jade would be his wife. Once that happened, the feelings that plagued him now would be a blessing.

On the first day of the trip, he had written her a lengthy letter apologizing for being impatient with her when they last talked. He missed her, loved her, couldn't wait to see her, couldn't wait for the day—not far off—when he could marry her. His letters since then spoke everything he felt in his heart;...he hoped she had received them by now.

Tanner prayed for Jade often and thought of her throughout the day. But as he turned onto his side again, in the early morning hours of his tenth day in the field, he couldn't get the image of her out of his mind. It wasn't desire he felt, but concern, alarm.

Tanner flipped onto his stomach and stared out the dirty windowpane to the swaying silhouette of maple trees outside. *What is this, God? What's wrong? Why is she so heavily on my heart?*

Jade's in trouble, my son. Pray. Pray quickly.

He heard the urging in his heart and felt a sense of terrifying alarm. Without hesitation he closed his eyes, bowed his head and for the next hour—sometimes in tears—he prayed for the woman he loved with all his heart.

The rains had started again, helping to wash away the memories of summer that haunted Jade. It was Monday afternoon, and she sat on the familiar box under the covered front porch praying for wisdom and waiting for her father to come home. She had to tell him soon; her health coverage was provided through her father's job at the garage. But how would he ever understand? What would he do to her once he found out? And how was it that forty-eight hours earlier everything had seemed like it was going to work out?

No matter how the facts shouted the truth, she still found herself wanting to believe Tanner. If she thought it might change the truth, she would have called Mrs. Eastman and told her how badly mistaken she must have been about Tanner, how Tanner had never been with any woman before and how he would always love her more than life itself.

But every time she reached for the telephone, she remembered the photographs. And the fact that she'd still not received even a single letter from Tanner. Then the reality—as impossible as it was—would set in.

There was a rumbling at the end of the street, and Jade knew it was her father's pickup. She glanced at her watch. Four o'clock. That meant he'd run out of work early and spent the hours since lunch at the bar. Jade clenched her jaw. *Lord, give me the words. Help him understand.*

She watched her father swing the pickup into the driveway

and squarely hit a rain-filled rut before jerking the truck to a stop. He staggered out of the truck, and Jade was seized with a fear she'd felt hundreds of time. *Dad...you're going to kill someone driving like that.*

He walked slowly, tripping over his feet and very nearly falling on the porch steps before he stopped, lurched slightly, and spotted her.

"Whatcha doin' home? Aren't ya supposed ta be with them sick kids?"

Jade's heart pounded. Maybe she should wait and tell him some other time, when he hadn't been drinking. She swallowed and stepped toward him, and the alcohol on his breath assaulted her sense. If she waited until he was sober, she might never have the chance. It was now or never.

"I'm not working today, Daddy." There was disgust on his face as he studied her. Then he shrugged and turned away. She took another step in his direction. "I have something to tell you."

Her father spun slowly back around and scowled in a way that made Jade's insides shrivel. He waited a moment and then shouted at her. "Well...spit it out!"

"Daddy, let's go inside."

Her father did not look happy, but he moved into the house and flung himself into his recliner. Jade followed and sat on the sofa across from him. She picked at the foam rubber sticking out from holes in the cushion. *Help me, God. Please.*

"Daddy, something's happened and you need to know. I want you to know."

A strange, angry look filled her father's eyes, and he pushed himself up straighter in his chair as he glared at Jade. "What'd you do?"

Her response came quickly. "Nothing...I mean..." She was

filled with shame. "Tanner and I..." She paused. "Daddy, I'm pregnant. I have to see a doctor."

Her father leaned back slowly in his chair, his mouth twisted into a sneer. "So, I was right all these years. You turned into a slut jus' like your dear old mother."

"Daddy, I'm not a—"

"Ah, shut up!" Her father narrowed his eyes, his face flushed. Jade wondered how much he'd had to drink, and she was suddenly afraid of him. He snarled when he spoke again. "You don't need a doctor for an abortion. Clinics do that kinda thing."

Jade shook her head. "No, Daddy, I'm not getting an abortion. I want this baby. But I need to see a doctor."

Her father eyed her as if she were worthless. "Where's the won'erful neighbor boy who got the goods from you? If you're havin' his baby, why don't you go live with him?"

"He's gone. He's...he's not in the picture anymore."

Her father came out of his chair so suddenly that Jade gasped. In seconds he was towering over her, glaring at her. "He's not in the picture because you're a no-good whore—" he raised his hand over her—"like your *mother.*" As he said the last word, his hand came down and slapped her, hard, across the face.

The stinging force took Jade by surprise, and she cried out as her head rocked back from the impact. She brought her arms up, cowering behind them in an effort to stave off any more blows.

Her father's hand was still raised, but he lowered it slowly. He looked less angry and more shocked at what he had done, but his eyes still glistened with contempt. "I always told you Jim Rudolph was the best thing that ever happened to you. He'd a married you. But now that you're knocked up he won't want you, either. No one'll want you."

Jade tried desperately to stop the tears, but they came anyway. *What can I say to make him understand?* "Daddy, I'm an adult now. I'll get a place of my own, and I won't be in your way. But I need your help. I can't go through this alone."

Her father sneered at her. "You'll get no help from me. You made your bed...now you can lay in it. Just like a pig in its slop. I won't be respo'sible for your brat."

Jade stared at her father, stunned. She had expected him to be angry, but this...There was no way around what he was telling her now. He wanted nothing to do with her. "Daddy, I'll—"

"Get out! Get your things and leave. You've got yourself in grown-up trouble, Jade." Her father was shouting, shaking in anger, and Jade feared he might hit her again. "Now be a grown-up and get out!"

Jade considered ignoring her father's command, writing it off as something crazy spoken in a moment of intoxication. But then her father's eyes locked onto hers, and in them she saw that no amount of time or circumstances could change the truth. He didn't love her.

But I love you, my child. I know the plans I have for you....

Jade blinked back the voice. If God loved her, he had a strange way of showing it. As for his plans...they had disappeared weeks ago in Tanner Eastman's bedroom.

Her father took a step toward her, his fist raised again. "Get out!"

Jade wondered how she had lived with him this long. If he wanted her out, then she would leave. And whatever happened, she would not look back. Not ever.

She turned and went to her bedroom. In an hour she had stuffed all her worldly possessions into three pillowcases and an old suitcase. There wasn't much. She hadn't saved scrapbooks from high school or photo albums of days gone by. There were a dozen mystery novels, a photograph of her in her mother's arms when she was two, and a dozen journals and diaries. She had barely enough clothes and shoes to fill the suitcase. A few posters and knickknacks.

Everything Tanner had given her she placed in a small box. A dried rose, several cards including the one he'd given her their last night together. Two teddy bears, a gold bracelet, and a framed photograph of the two of them taken by a passerby one afternoon when they were at the river.

She looked over the collection and thought ahead fifteen years to a time when her child might treasure them—the only reminder of a father who never existed. But then she pictured Mrs. Eastman and her sickly sweet smile threatening to steal her child with a team of powerful lawyers if she dared tell the truth about who the baby's father was.

She wasn't afraid of her child's eventual questions, but she was terrified of Mrs. Eastman's threats and the hatred behind them. No one would ever find out Tanner was this baby's father, even if she had to eradicate all signs of him from her life. Trash day was tomorrow. Folding the container so the contents would stay put, she carried it outside and pushed it deep inside the trash can.

Exactly where her box of dreams—and everything associated with Tanner Eastman—belonged.

When she was finished packing and loading her car, she found her father snoring on the sofa, two empty beer cans lying on the carpet below him. She studied him for a long moment and wondered if she should wake him and tell him good-bye. This would, in all likelihood, be the last time she stood in this living room, the last time she saw him.

But she was strangely unaffected.

She studied him one final time, his undershirt riding up on his belly, his workpants covered with week-old grease stains. She could hear his accusations as clearly as if he were still shouting at her. *You're an idiot, Jade...worthless, just like your mother....*

Jade felt no connection whatsoever to the man lying before her. *He never loved me. Even in his sober moments.* He had felt guilt and remorse and inadequacy. But never love, Jade was sure of it. And she would not tell him good-bye. If this was how it felt to have a father, she was thankful her child would be spared.

Jade turned and without looking back she left, walking away from the house where she'd spent eleven years, and leaving all the sordid, sad memories that went along with it.

Later that evening, Buddy Conner woke up, belched loudly and rubbed his bare belly. *Stupid undershirt never stayed put.* He stood, moved his tongue along the inside of his pasty mouth, and tried to remember if there were any beers left in the refrigerator.

"Jade, get me a beer." He waited but there was no response. "Jade!"

Then he remembered. She was pregnant and he'd told her to leave. He hadn't really meant it. The girl could live here for a while, anyway. She was his daughter, after all. And he hadn't exactly been surprised by her announcement; he'd always known she would wind up like her mother. He raised his voice. "Jade, get in here."

His words echoed through the house, but there was no response. Buddy scratched his armpit and shuffled down the hall to Jade's room. Posters were gone from the walls, and her closet was empty.

He shrugged. She was gone, but she'd be back when she figured out how hard it was living on the streets with a baby on the way. They could live with him, but if Jade thought he was going to raise the kid, she was in for a rude awakening. *No, sir, not Buddy Conner.* He was a busy man, and he had no intentions of raising some fatherless brat.

He huffed as he moved back down the hallway. He was a generous man, but he had to draw a line somewhere. The effects of a perpetual hangover pulsed at Buddy's temples and he thought about getting a drink. But there was something he had to do first. Now that he was sober enough to concentrate and Jade wasn't around.

He lumbered into his bedroom, pulled out his top dresser drawer and took out a bundle of three envelopes. Letters from that snobby neighbor boy, postmarked Hungary. Buddy carried the letters into the kitchen and ripped them into a dozen pieces. He may not have been a very good father—he may not have been a lot of things—but at least he'd kept these letters from Jade. Uppity kid like Tanner Eastman wanted one thing and only one thing from a girl like Jade. Well, he'd gotten what he wanted, but he wasn't getting anymore. Buddy simply wasn't going to stand by and watch the guy break his little girl's heart.

He wadded up the torn pieces of the boy's letters and tossed them in the kitchen trashcan where they settled unceremoniously on a pile of rotting spaghetti and beer-soaked cigarette ashes.

Jade would never know the difference.

Seventeen

DRIVING SEEMED TO BE THE ANSWER AT FIRST. SHE HEADED TOWARD I-5. "Where do I go, Lord? Where would you have me set up a home for this child? How can I ever make it alone?"

Tears streamed down her face as she drove, making it difficult to see. The windshield wipers swished out a rhythm, and the rhythm became taunting words in her head: *Whore, whore, whore, whore…*

Every movement was another reminder. Jade blinked back her tears so she could see the road more clearly, but they continued to come. She had lost everything except the one thing no one would ever take away from her.

Jade placed her hand over her abdomen and massaged the area gently. *Stay safe, little one. Mommy's here. Mommy'll never, ever leave you, baby.* She realized that she would have to withdraw from fall classes at the college. She had more to think about than school. On her way out of town she stopped at Kelso General, and when she had collected herself, she went inside and informed the head nurse on the children's unit that she was going to be gone for a while.

"Everything okay, Jade?" The woman looked concerned. "You look like you've been crying."

For a moment she wanted to tell the old nurse everything, but then she stopped herself. There was no point making the staff at Kelso General think poorly of her. They would know soon enough. "I'll be all right. I'll let you know when I can come back."

Before she left, she checked on Shaunie, who was back in the hospital with more kidney problems. But the child had been discharged earlier that day. It was fitting. There wasn't anything keeping her in Kelso anymore.

She drove to the freeway, heading south toward Portland. Without realizing her plan, she exited west Highway 26, and two hours later she was at the beach. The rain came down in heavy sheets, and she pulled into the parking lot of a motel with a neon-lit sign that promised color TV and vacancies. The paint was peeling on the office door. She paid forty-two dollars cash and took her room.

A small table and chair sat by a narrow glass door overlooking a deserted highway and beyond that the ocean. She was too frightened to cry, too painfully aware of the truth. She was twenty years old, pregnant, without a friend in the world or medical benefits, and with barely enough money to get her through her pregnancy. What would she do then?

She thought about praying but changed her mind. It hadn't helped her so far. If anything, it had brought her bad luck. Jade chastised herself for thinking that way. It wasn't bad luck, just a lack of connection with the Lord. God had saved her, but like her earthly father, he no longer seemed to want anything to do with her.

For I know the plans I have for you....

Jade disregarded the thought. No, if she was going to find hope and a future out of this problem, she was going to have to find it herself. She sat back in the chair, motionless, allowing herself to sort through the possibilities. There were relatively few, really, and each of them involved single parenting, full-time daycare, state-provided medical treatment, welfare, and low-income housing. There were children who managed to do well under such circumstances.

Jade began to shiver. *Not my baby.*

The sun disappeared beyond the water and hours passed. Ten o'clock. Ten-thirty. Eleven. Still Jade sat, unmoving, desperately trying to think of a solution.

Then, just after midnight, the answer came. It was so obvious she didn't know why she hadn't thought about it before. As soon as she formulated the plan, she began to cry, her heart sinking like sand in an hourglass. *Is this it, Lord? My hope and future?*

She didn't wait for a response. *I don't care; I'm doing this. It's the only choice I have.*

The cost will be high.

Jade squeezed her eyes shut, willing away the holy whispers that ricocheted about in the corners of her mind. *It's my life.*

You were bought with a price.

Jade's crying grew harder, and she felt herself losing control. This time she answered out loud. "Stop! I have no choice…."

No, my daughter, you do have a choice. I know the plans I have for you…plans to give you hope and a future.

Jade covered her ears with her hands. *I have no hope, no future. She* wrapped her arms around her midsection. *I have to do this. Now, leave me alone!*

Silence.

Jade waited, but the voice had stopped. God may not have wanted her to do the thing she was about to do. But he hadn't provided any alternative, either. She thought about the plan and realized it was true, the cost would be high. Nothing less than her heart and soul. But if it meant protecting her child, it was a price she was willing to pay.

In return, her baby would never lack anything. There would be food and a warm bed and a mommy and daddy. What more could a child need? She fell asleep then, dreaming of the infant inside her and whether he or she would have Tanner's eyes or his tall, athletic frame.

The next day she checked out of the motel, drove to Portland, and got the directions she needed. At five o'clock she stood on the porch of a man she had never intended to track down.

"Well, well, well…" Jim Rudolph allowed his eyes to wander lazily over the length of Jade. "What a pleasant surprise. I always knew you'd come to your senses one day." He leaned against the doorframe. "Tell me…have you changed your mind about my offer?"

Jade wanted to turn and run back to her car. *There's no choice now. Think of the baby.* The voice didn't seem like God's, but it was the only one she could hear. She closed her eyes briefly. "Yes. May I come in?"

Jim opened the door wider, and without hesitation Jade walked inside. She would do anything for the child she carried. Even this. It didn't matter. What she was about to do would never involve her heart. She would be kind, dutiful, pleasant. Grateful she had someplace to turn.

In exchange, Jade knew Jim would provide for her, shower her with attention, and treat her well. He would give her child a home and a name. Yes, Jim lacked the depth of character to ever love her the way Tanner had seemed to love her. No, she would never love this man. But she would be indebted to him forever.

That Saturday the two of them stood before a justice of the peace. And in ten minutes, Jade Conner became Jade Rudolph.

Eighteen

The Virginia sky stretched like blue canvas over the Richmond Airport as Doris Eastman waited for her son to return from Hungary. She had missed Tanner. He was such a good, idealistic, young man, just what the country needed, perfect for public office. The way Doris saw it, she was willing to forgive him and move forward. Tanner had sowed his wild oats—first with the Conner girl and then with this trip to Hungary. There was still time between now and graduation to line up a political job. Still time for Tanner to come to his senses.

His connecting flight from New York was scheduled to arrive in five minutes, and Doris had to admit she was nervous. The issue with Jade would have to be handled delicately; Tanner must never know that his mother lied to protect him. Even so, Doris was worried about how Tanner would react when he heard the news about Jade.

Thoughts of the girl and her sudden wedding brought a smile to Doris's face. When she'd first learned about it, she'd been unable to contain her elation. At least she didn't have to lie to Tanner. Jade had taken care of the problem herself.

To think she had almost avoided making the phone call.

It had been two weeks after Jade's visit, and Doris was bothered by the girl's anger. What if she tried to find out the truth about Tanner's background? Doris was plagued by such questions. She knew she'd done a brilliant job of lying that day;

Tanner's older brother's children looked just like their uncle. Jade had believed every word.

Still, Doris had been uneasy and so she called.

An airplane taxied slowly up to the gate, and Doris breathed a sigh of relief. She hated Tanner being in the air. Too uncertain. Too many risks. Now he was here and he was safe—safer than he knew now that Jade was out of his life.

She remembered the phone call like it was yesterday.

A man Doris assumed was Jade's father answered and spoke in short, gruff sentences.

"What do you want?"

Doris had been taken aback. "Well…I need to speak to Jade, please."

"Jade don't live here no more."

A flicker of concern had rattled through Doris's bones. "Is that right? Well, would you have a forwarding number for her?"

"I ain't plannin' on keeping in touch with her."

Doris struggled to think of the right questions. "All right, then. Could you tell me where she moved? Maybe I can look her up myself."

"Listen, I don't know who you are, lady, but I'll tell you why Jade left. She got herself pregnant, and now she's run off and got herself married. They live in Portland somewhere, I think."

Doris had been stunned by the man's revelation. Jade…married? With Tanner in Hungary? Then there had been someone else the whole time. Instantly, Doris regretted giving the girl the money. The brat probably wasn't even Tanner's. "Did you say she was married?"

"What'sa matter, lady? Ya deaf?" *Rude, belligerent clod.* Doris felt tarnished for even speaking with him.

"I'm surprised, that's all. I thought…I didn't know Jade had planned to marry."

"Listen, lady, she's married, okay? She's knocked up and she's married. Married a guy named Rudolph. Jim Rudolph, okay? Listen, who are you, anyway?"

Jim Rudoloph. Doris had never heard the name before. "Uh…never mind. I'll try to contact her another way."

The man had hung up on her, and in disbelief Doris marveled at her good fortune. She had planned to tell Tanner a lie. Something about how Jade had never really loved him and how she'd disappeared without a trace while he was gone.

Doris hadn't perfected the story and was working frantically on making it sound truthful until she'd placed the call to Jade's home. After the conversation with the girl's father, Doris's problems felt as if they'd disappeared completely.

In the weeks that followed, Doris moved back to Virginia, set up house in a retirement condominium in Williamsburg, and made time for old friends. She was no longer worried about what she'd tell Tanner when he got home. The story was simple. Jade had gotten pregnant and married a man while Tanner was off witnessing to the Hungarian people about God's love. There was nothing more to say. Once Tanner was able to grasp the truth about the girl he assumed he loved, he would disregard her as a bad seed and be thankful he hadn't wasted more time on her.

She stood and stretched and watched the stream of people until she spotted Tanner.

God, help me sound believable.

It had been a while since she'd prayed, and the silent words felt strange in her heart—stranger still when they were not followed by any measure of peace or assurance. It didn't matter. She had the perfect story and was certain Tanner would believe it. If God didn't want to help her, so be it. She was only acting in her son's best interests.

Tanner made his way slowly off the plane, searching for Jade, hoping that she'd gotten his letter and the money he'd sent for a plane ticket. He shook his head. What was he worrying about? Of course she'd be there to meet him. He had so much to tell her, so many stories to share.

He scanned the faces of those waiting for passengers and saw his mother's among them. He waved and continued searching until finally he was at his mother's side.

"Hey, Mom, have you seen Jade?"

His mother put her hands on her hips and cocked her head, smiling slightly. "You're gone to Hungary for two months, and the first thing you say to your mother is, *'Hey, Mom, have you seen Jade?'*" She leaned up, pecking him on the cheek and hugging him.

"I'm sorry...." *Where was she? Why wasn't she here?*

His mother searched his eyes and looked him over the way she'd done after football games back when he was a teenager. "So, son, you look like you survived. Did you figure out how to save the world?"

Tanner's eyes roved the perimeter of the airport. *She should be here by now.* Could something have happened to her? A plane delay or something. Ignoring his mother's question, he met her gaze straight on. "I'll tell you about the trip later. But I'm serious about Jade. Have you seen her?"

Tanner watched and thought his mother was acting strangely uncomfortable. She cleared her throat as if she didn't want to speak her next words. "I don't think Jade's coming to Virginia, son."

Tanner felt his insides unwind, and he was flooded with disappointed. He sighed. "I asked her to come."

His mother raised an eyebrow. "You...you talked to Jade?"

What was that in his mother's eyes? If Tanner hadn't known better, he'd think it was fear, but that was impossible. His mother had never been afraid of anything. "Of course not. I couldn't make calls from Hungary, Mother. You know that."

Doris uttered what sounded like a forced laugh. "I know, dear. It's just that you said you told her..."

"I wrote to her. Many times. And I figured based on my last letter that she'd be here."

His mother sighed and stared sadly at her hands. It was a dramatic pose, one she often assumed when she was about to be the bearer of bad news. Seeing his mother that way sent a shiver of terror down Tanner's spine. "What is it, Mother?" He knew he sounded impatient and he felt bad. He'd only been off the plane a few minutes, and already his mother had him on edge.

Doris linked elbows with him and gently led him toward the baggage pickup area. "Son, I'm afraid we have a lot to talk about." She hesitated and Tanner saw contempt in her eyes. "Jade wasn't the person you thought she was."

Tanner stopped in his tracks, forcing his mother to stop as well. "What's that supposed to mean?"

Doris looked uncomfortably at the passersby, some of whom were forced to walk around them. "This isn't the time, dear. I'll tell you everything when we get home. Besides, I have a nice lasagn—"

"I want to know now, Mother." A building panic was causing his head to swim. *What does she mean Jade isn't the person I thought? And where is she, anyway? Why isn't she here so she can help me make sense of this craziness?* He ushered his mother to the nearest seating area and directed her to a seat. He took one next to her and stared at her. "Talk to me, Mother."

She licked her lips nervously, and the sense of panic began

to spread to the pit of his stomach. "I said, *talk* to me, Mother. What's going on?"

"You're yelling." His mother clasped her fingers together tightly and did her best to look proper.

Tanner lowered his voice, but the anger remained. "I'm waiting. Now, tell me."

"I really don't think this is the place to have such conversations, son."

"Mother—"

"All right, all right." She put a hand on Tanner's knee and tilted her nose a degree higher. "I'm sorry to have to tell you this. Especially now...here." She looked around as though she were afraid someone might be listening. "Jade got married while you were gone."

For the briefest moment, he wanted to slap his mother for saying something so cruel. Jade? His Jade? Of course she hadn't gotten married. Whatever his mother had heard was a big mistake. "Mother, are you trying to say Jade Conner married someone else while I was in Hungary?"

Doris nodded, her chin tilted, nose higher still. "She was a two-timer. A loose girl, Tanner. She was only after your name...our money."

A hundred voices were shouting in Tanner's head. It was impossible. Jade loved him fully. She had never loved anyone, never kissed anyone before him. His mother must be losing her mind. "Listen, I don't know where you heard this, Mother, but you're wrong. Jade's going to marry me."

His mother's face grew several shades paler. "Well...I had no idea, Tanner...."

"We were going to tell you together. This week, now that I'm home. I haven't even bought her a ring yet."

Gradually his mother's color returned. "Well...it seems it's best you saved your money." She looked sadly into his eyes. "It's true, Tanner. She married someone else."

Tanner's heart was racing, and he tried to think of a way he could stop this nonsense. He stood, pulled out his billfold, and began searching for his phone card.

"What are you doing? Sit down and let me finish." His mother remained seated, her voice ripe with chastisement.

"I'm going to call her. Right now. Before you say another word." He took his mother gently by the shoulders. "Jade Conner is in love with me. There's no way in the world she would have married someone else."

At his insistence, his mother stood with an exaggerated sigh. "Very well. Where's the telephone?"

"What are you doing?" Tanner felt another wave of fear. If his mother was willing to let him make a phone call…

"I'm coming, too. I want to be there when you see for yourself. Everything I've told you is true, Tanner."

A volcano of anger erupted in Tanner's heart, and he silently fumed. He would not let his mother get the better of him. She was mistaken somehow, and he would prove it. He turned without saying another word and made his way to a row of pay telephones. Swiping his card through, he did what he'd longed to do for two months.

He dialed Jade's number.

His mother stood beside him, watching him, studying him confidently, making him feel five years old again. The phone rang three times, and Tanner glanced at his watch. It was Saturday, ten o'clock in the morning in Kelso. Someone should be home.

The phone rang three more times, and finally Tanner hung up. "No one's home." He did not look at his mother, didn't want to see her smug expression, the surety in her eyes. She would owe him an apology when he got to the truth of the matter. He stared at the phone and racked his brain, thinking who would know where he could find Jade.

The hospital. Of course. He dialed information and got the number for Kelso General.

His mother tapped her foot impatiently. "Now who're you calling?"

Tanner glared at her but didn't answer. The phone was ringing at the hospital.

"Kelso General, how may I direct your call?"

"Children's unit, please." Tanner's heart was racing faster now. *Come on, please. Someone pick up.*

"Children's unit."

"Yes, I'm...may I speak to Jade Conner, please."

The woman hesitated. "She doesn't work here anymore."

Tanner's panic increased and he struggled to speak. "Do...you know where I can reach her?"

"Who is this, please?"

Tanner gulped. *What is this? Why is everyone acting so strange?* "I'm a friend."

"Oh. Well, I'm sorry I can't help you. Jade got married about a month ago. We haven't heard from her since then."

The air around him turned to quicksand, and Tanner felt himself being sucked into a cavernous abyss. *My God, why? What's happened? I loved her, Lord. I thought she wanted to marry me.*

He felt as though his heart might explode. He heard himself thank the girl and watched his hand slowly hang up the phone. His mother's expression was the picture of arrogance and pity, and Tanner walked past her to the nearest chair. There he sat down, dropped his belongings, planted his elbows on his knees, and hung his head in his hands.

"I'm sorry, Tanner. I tried to tell you.... Her father doesn't know where she's living now. No one does."

Tanner wasn't ready to talk, didn't want to look at his mother. *How had this happened? What had Jade been thinking?* As one minute and then two passed, tears filled Tanner's eyes and began dropping to the floor.

Why would she marry someone else? Who would she marry? Tanner felt as if he'd been run over by a 747, and though the tears came more quickly, he had only one answer: His mother was wrong. Jade was not a two-timer; she had not been seeing someone else while they were together that past summer. And she definitely was not after his name or their family money.

Somehow, something had gone terribly wrong, and she had married someone else. Tanner would have to find a way to accept the truth. But he had not been wrong about who Jade was. He knew that much.

His mother's voice interrupted his thoughts. "Come on, son. We need to get home." Doris patted his knee, and Tanner knew she was unaware of his tears. She had never seen him cry and wouldn't think it a sign of strength. But he didn't care. Jade had taught him to be his own person, and now she was gone.

He stood like a man who had aged forty years in a single instant, and he realized a part of him had died with the news about Jade. *So, Lord, this is what it feels like to have a broken heart. A broken life.*

As he and his mother left the airport, he remembered something he'd said as a young boy the first time Jade had disappeared from his life. The words were as true now as they had been back then. He and Jade would be together again one day—even if for only a moment so she could explain what had happened. He would find her. Even if he had to search the world over.

With that thought firmly in place, he collected his things

and took the first step toward a future that was suddenly darker than the winter skies in Kelso.

Part II

"You will seek me and find me when you
seek me with all your heart.
I will be found by you," declares the Lord,
"and will bring you back from captivity."

Jeremiah 29:13–14a

Nineteen

Eleven years later

THE RAIN HAD BEEN RELENTLESS, AND WEDNESDAY, FEBRUARY 9 was no different from a dozen previous Wednesdays. At nine that morning, the women from the Bible study group shed raincoats, umbrellas, and muddy shoes at the door and filed into Jade Rudolph's living room, where the atmosphere was considerably warmer and brighter. Coffee and fresh-baked brownies filled the table, and a glowing fire crackled in the brick fireplace.

The women took their seats, and Jade poured coffee as several moms set their toddlers in the next room with a variety of toys. Jade loved the sounds of the little ones. It made her remember when Ty was a baby.

The Bible study, made up entirely of mothers, had been meeting at Jade's house for the past year, and she'd gotten close to many of the women. They had students of all ages who attended Portland public schools—specifically three schools on the city's northeastern boundary: Shamrock Elementary, Woodbridge Junior High, and Riverview High School.

They met each week and discussed education-related issues, keeping each other apprised about problems that might affect their children. For the most part, they spent the hour in prayer. Deep, heartfelt, fervent prayer. Public schools had taken a violent beating over the past few years. If there was one thing their children needed, it was prayer.

Jackie Conley was among the women in the group. Her husband was a teacher alongside Jade's husband, Jim, at Woodbridge Junior and the two women had become friends when Ty was a baby. Jackie had invited her to a Bible study, and by the end of the eight-week session, Jade's strained relationship with the Lord had been restored.

She thanked God daily for Jackie and trusted her like a sister.

The current discussion involved an issue at Woodbridge. The junior high had adapted as part of its curriculum a government-sponsored program called Channel One. Jackie's husband had expressed concern over the programming content, and Jackie and Jade agreed to research the matter.

The women were alarmed at what they learned. The program provided public classrooms with free televisions along with considerable grant money in exchange for a commitment from the administration: Each day students would watch a fifteen-minute program titled "Channel One." Jade and Jackie had chosen this morning to inform the Bible study group of their findings.

"Explain the problem again...." Susan looked confused. Her daughter was in kindergarten, and she'd told the group that free televisions in every classroom seemed like a good idea. Kids might learn something from the documentaries.

Jade understood. At first glance it sounded like a situation where everyone might win.

"The televisions come with strings attached." Jade fidgeted with her fingernails and thought about how to say it simply. "The school gets the televisions and money as long as the kids watch the Channel One program."

The other women sipped coffee and looked concerned. If Jade and Jackie were bothered, there was probably trouble brewing. Susan shook her head and looked from one woman to the next. "I'm still not seeing the problem."

Jade drew a deep breath. *Help me explain this, God. Please.* "The problem is Channel One has questionable content. Unchecked news programs, two-minute documentaries on the proper use of condoms, open discussions of sex, and at least four minutes each day of advertising."

Susan's eyes were wide, and Jade felt a wave of relief. Channel One was a big mistake, and she was glad the group was finally seeing the problem.

"And they show it every day?" Susan sounded angry.

"Yes. Every day. Classrooms give up fifteen minutes of instruction in exchange for the Channel One time."

Jackie leaned forward and checked her notes. "The corporate sponsors—fast food restaurants, clothing companies—support the programming with commercial money—part of which goes back to the U.S. Department of Education."

Susan tapped her pencil on her paper. "So what you're saying is, the U.S. Department of Education is making a profit on televised commercials being shown to our children each day while they're supposed to be learning at school." She paused. "And our schools have agreed to this garbage because they want free televisions?"

"And grant money." Jade searched the faces in the group. "The government makes the package attractive so the schools buy in on the idea."

Jackie nodded. "Not only are the kids subjected to commercials when they should be learning, but they're exposed to whatever programming the government agrees to. Generally, that can be a fairly liberal, slanted dose of documentaries. Politically correct items about alternative lifestyles and insensitive religious right-wingers along with stories—like Jade said—about the importance of condom distribution in schools."

The women were stunned, and Jade knew they finally understood.

Susan spoke first. "We need to get those televisions out."

Jade nodded. "That's the first thing we want to pray about today." She looked at Jackie. "As some of you know, I've spoken to the school board about this already, and they'll be discussing it at a public forum in a few weeks. Apparently, they're not convinced that commercials and provocative programming warrants the removal of the TVs. So I've done a little digging and found something else…."

Jade explained how she'd seen a Web site advertised continuously at the bottom of the screen throughout the Channel One programming.

"Last week Jackie and I looked into the site and found an entire Channel One menu. Among other things, it had a chat room where people who I presume were junior high and high school students—although they could have been forty-year-old predators—were discussing sex in vulgar and explicit language." She hesitated. "We also found links to documentaries already featured on Channel One."

Jackie sorted through a stack of papers until she found a wrinkled page of hand-written notes. "Many of the programs have been objectionable, but one was a special on a rock singer we've talked about before. He is a favorite among hate groups and has songs with lyrics instructing kids to kill and commit suicide. He is openly, violently hateful toward God and things of God. Once when an interviewer asked him how he pictured his own funeral, this singer said he wanted everyone he ever knew and anyone who had ever attended any of his concerts in attendance. Then, when they were all assembled, bombs would go off and kill everyone."

"That's terrible!" Susan's face was red. "I guess my kids are too young to know about that stuff.... Thank God.... I can't believe anyone that awful would get air time in our public schools!"

"I agree." Jade sighed. "Remember that high school in Denver where the boys killed a dozen classmates and a teacher and hurt about twenty other kids?"

Faces grew troubled as everyone nodded, thinking back on the tragedy. Jackie drew a deep breath. "Those trench-coat gothic kids listened to this singer constantly, quoted from his songs, and apparently bought into his message." She paused. "And Channel One carried a special on the guy that ran into the classrooms of every school that has made free televisions and grant money more important than our children."

"The televisions need to go. Immediately." Susan looked at the other moms for approval, and Jade was glad when she saw them nodding in agreement.

"What's your husband think about this, Jade?" It was Beth, a quiet mother with twin daughters at the junior high. The women knew each other well enough to know that Jade's husband was not a Christian. More, that he was adamantly against Jade interfering with the ways of the school.

"Jim and I are struggling, Beth...." Jade was pierced with sadness. The issue had been a thorn in their marriage for the past month. Not that their marriage had been without thorns prior to Channel One.

There had been numerous issues over the years, times when Jim disagreed with her. Still, Jade had been wrong about what she was capable of feeling for him. Jim proved kinder than she'd thought possible, a good provider and often fun to be with. Although they never connected the way she and Tanner had, she grew to love him in her own way. For a while, she even considered having more children—laughing, sweet faces to fill the house and be brothers or sisters for Ty. But for all the attention Jim gave Jade, he was often disinterested in their son and expressed no interest in having another child.

Three years after Ty's birth, Jim had pulled her aside one evening and shared his feelings about parenthood. "The truth is, I never pictured myself as a father, Jade." His shoulders sagged and his expression was defeated. "All I ever wanted was you and me. Together. Kids…well, they were never part of the picture, you know?"

Jade knew only too well. Nothing about her life was how she had pictured it.

"What I'm trying to say," Jim had continued, "is…I want a vasectomy, just so we don't take any chances."

Jade had been sad at first, but she eventually agreed. She could lavish all the love bottled up in her heart on Ty. She had no need for other children, especially when Jim had no interest in being a father.

He'd gotten the vasectomy weeks later, but in the years since, Jade always thought Jim had been lying about the surgery somehow. Since then on several occasions she'd been plagued with questions. Why hadn't she gotten pregnant in the years after having Ty, especially since they hadn't used birth control? If Jim was so set against having more children, why hadn't he insisted on the vasectomy sooner? And how come there hadn't been any downtime associated with his surgery? The procedure was done in the afternoon, and Jim was back to work the next day without taking so much as a single aspirin.

Somehow there seemed to be a missing piece to the story, and occasionally—when she would note the lack of bonding between Ty and Jim—she would wonder if Jim had been sterile all along. And because of that, perhaps even known the truth.

That Ty wasn't really his son.

There had been other issues over the years, and once, after a particularly rough evening, Jim shouted at her in frustration. "What do I have to do to win your love, Jade? All my life I've loved you, whether I wanted to or not. It's like you're some kind of…of disease that worked its way into my blood." He waved his hand toward Ty's room. "I've seen you love *him.* You love that boy more than anything, but what about me, huh? What sort of curse am I under, driven to love you when all your life you've never, not once, loved me back?"

Jade could still feel how her face had flushed from Jim's accusation. She had never meant to hurt him, but clearly he had been suffering. Her heart had softened as she crossed the room toward him. "That's not true, Jim…. I love you. I've said it a—"

"Stop!" He held up his hand, preventing her from coming closer. "I understand…." His body had been trembling, and he struggled to regain control. "You love me in your own way, on your terms. But I don't care what you say, Jade. This relationship has always been one-sided, and there's nothing either of us can do to change that." He let his arm drop and disappeared up the stairs into their bedroom.

Jade remembered the outburst like it was yesterday.

Jim had been right then, and he was right now. But through the years they had stayed together longer than many of their friends, and Jade knew she would never leave him. God wanted her where she was. And maybe, if she prayed diligently, one day she could love Jim the way she knew he longed to be loved.

Lately, their biggest disagreements came whenever she took a stand on issues that affected Woodbridge. For the past two years, when Jade was busy fighting the school board on whatever issue she was involved in, Jim would grow distant and spend his evenings meeting with colleagues or having drinks with friends. There were times when Jade wondered if maybe he was trying to distance himself from her, finally rid her from his system. When she felt that way, she tried harder to pay him attention, listen to him, be available for him. But she could not stop herself from being involved at Woodbridge and no matter how hard she tried, she felt Jim growing away from her.

Especially now. Her attack on Channel One seemed to make him angrier than all the other issues combined.

She exhaled slowly, and her thoughts returned to the Bible study group and the meeting they were having. "Jim's upset about my involvement, no question about it. He wants the televisions to stay. He says the school gets precious little grant money at Woodbridge, and the kids need the funds."

"What's he think about the government using the kids to make money on those commercials?" Susan raised an eyebrow. "Doesn't that bother him?"

They don't know the half of it. Lord, help me be careful how I talk about Jim. "Truthfully...Channel One doesn't bother him nearly as much as I do, Susan." Jade hung her head. "You can pray about that, too.... Sometimes I don't know if my marriage can take it."

A knowing look crossed Jackie's face. "Jade, we need to talk. Later, okay?"

A ripple of alarm disturbed the waters of Jade's mind. Scott and Jim talked at work, and there were times when Jackie knew what was troubling Jim long before Jade. She nodded to her friend. "Okay, later. Let's pray now."

The women near Jade reached toward her, placing their hands on her shoulders and gripping her knees. While their toddlers continued playing unaware, the group of moms bowed their heads and prayed that Channel One be taken out of Woodbridge Junior High.

And that Jade's marriage might have the strength to withstand the fight.

Meat loaf simmered in the oven, and Jade busied herself with a broom, sweeping the kitchen floor and in general tidying the place before Jim arrived. If there was one thing that upset him, it was coming home to a messy house.

At times like this Jade was thankful she'd stayed in shape and in general had the same strength and energy she'd had ten years earlier. Otherwise she would have been too tired to balance her schedule. When she thought about all she managed to do in a day, the sum of it was almost dizzying.

She had finished her nursing training when Ty started kindergarten and now was one of the most requested nurses with Portland Home Health Care. She worked four to six hours each day traveling from house to house caring for homebound patients. She loved her job and had no complaints about her schedule. As long as she was home when Ty got home.

Ty was in fifth grade—one year away from attending Woodbridge. Twice a week she made time in her schedule to volunteer in his classroom, helping students learn word processing. Ty was proud of her, and she wouldn't have missed the opportunity for the world.

"You're the prettiest mom at school," he'd told her the day before. It was something he mentioned often. "All the guys say so."

"Is that right?"

"Yep. Jack says you're a babe."

Jade had smiled and tickled Ty in the ribs. "This babe wants you to get your homework done, okay?"

They shared the relationship Jade had always dreamed of

sharing with her child. The boy was lanky with an easy smile, gifted both athletically and academically. People liked to say he must have gotten these gifts from her since Jim had long since lost his football physique and allowed himself to grow soft.

But Jade knew the truth.

Ty was exactly like his father.

She swept the floor and mentally calculated that by this hour of the evening Ty would be finished with basketball practice. Jim would be picking him up, and the two of them would be home in fifteen minutes. That was another area of concern. Jim thought they were babying Ty by giving him rides home from school.

"He's a big boy, Jade. He can walk home."

"It's not safe. A boy that young shouldn't have to walk a mile in the dark."

"Sure he should. It'll make him tough."

Jade could have picked him up, of course. She would have walked barefoot in the snow to greet her son after basketball practice. But then she wouldn't be home to have the house clean and dinner on the table. And there was something to be said for keeping peace in their home. Besides, the ride home was the only time Ty and Jim had alone together. Especially now that Jim preferred coming home, eating dinner, and then going back out again.

"It's stressful teaching kids that age." He complained whenever she balked at his evening ritual. "Teachers need to spend time together after school. Deal with it, Jade."

Deal with it, Jade.

His words ran through her mind again and again. Until two years ago, Jim never would have spoken to her that way. He might not have appreciated her viewpoint, but he never mocked her. Not until lately.

She sighed and ran a dishrag once more over the kitchen counter. She had the uneasy feeling that their marriage was falling apart. *Help me, Lord. What can I do to make things better?*

As far as it depends on you, live at peace with one another....

It was the same Scripture that came to mind whenever she doubted her marriage. But there were times when she wished for more than peace. Times when she wanted only to be loved the way she'd felt loved that summer with Tanner. No matter how she prayed and tried to see Jim in a different light, she was never physically attracted to him. She tolerated him and allowed him to have his way whenever he felt the need, but their unions were brief and filled with a sense of hurried desperation. Jim did not concern himself with whether she enjoyed their time together. In that sense, things hadn't changed much since high school. Jim was too concerned with himself. Even in his kindest moments, he genuinely believed Jade was lucky to be married to him, and he reminded her of the fact regularly—especially at night, after they'd been together.

Jade knew it was wrong to compare him to Tanner. But their marriage had never been anything like the magic she'd felt with Tanner that summer. She and Tanner had been wrong their last night together at his apartment, and they would spend their lives dealing with the consequences. But her heart and body had never felt so right. Not before or since.

She wrung out the dishrag and draped it over the faucet. *Tanner.* The memory of him still caused an ache in her heart. It had been many years since she'd seen him, but she thought of him every day, wondering if he'd married or if he was still getting girls into trouble.

Even now, with all the time that had passed and all the miles between them, she struggled with the image of a conniving, womanizing Tanner. Maybe because Ty was so like Tanner had been at that age, or maybe because her son's gentle heart reminded her so much of how Tanner had been that summer. Either way, when she remembered Tanner, it wasn't as an evil, self-centered monster. Rather she thought of him as she would always think of him: pure and wonderful and kind. The only man she had ever truly loved.

Except for Ty, of course.

Jade thought about how fast his childhood had gone and how even now he was like a brilliant comet arcing his way out of her life and into that of his own. She had not pigeonholed him into a career like Tanner's mother had done to her son. Nor had she considered deserting him like her mother had done to her. Rather she treasured every moment, knowing time was both precious and fleeting.

She surveyed the clean kitchen and thought about the mom's support group. Jackie had wanted to talk to her about something, but they'd never connected after the meeting. She crossed the kitchen and reached for the telephone just as the door opened. *Jackie would have to wait.* Jade put away the broom and headed for the front door.

"Mom! You won't believe what happened!" Ty was all legs and wide-eyed excitement as he tossed his gym bag on the recliner and wrapped his arms around her in a hug.

"Tell me." She smoothed back a lock of sweaty hair from his forehead and wrinkled her nose. "Hmm. Shower time right after dinner."

Ty laughed. "Pretty slimy, huh?"

"I'd say." She laughed, too, as she wiped her hand on her jeans.

Ty flopped to the ground and ripped off his shoes and ankle braces, scattering them about on the floor. As he did, Jim rounded the corner, briefcase in hand, and stopped, taking in the mess. A scowl spread across his face.

"Haven't I told you not to throw your stuff around the minute you get in?" His voice was loud. Not angry, like Jade had heard it get lately, but heading that way fast.

Ty's smile fell, and immediately he jumped up and collected his things. "Sorry."

Jim turned and began stomping up the stairs. "You're always sorry. Let's see some action behind it."

"Yes, Dad."

Jade craned her neck and saw that Jim was out of earshot. Then she pulled Ty close again and rubbed a hand over his damp back. "Don't let him get you down, buddy. He's just had a hard day."

Ty nodded and Jade saw the sadness in his eyes. "He always has a hard day."

"I know. But give him a few minutes, and he'll come around."

"Okay." Ty carried his shoes and bag toward the stairs.

"Wait a minute." Jade was careful to keep her voice low so Jim wouldn't think she was contradicting him. "Tell me what happened first."

Her son's eyes filled with adoration, and Jade knew that whatever else she had to do, whatever sacrifices she had to make, they paled in comparison with the joy this boy brought her. Theirs was a good life, and maybe one day things between her and Jim would change, and they could have the marriage she longed for. Until then, she would never go to sleep feeling sorry for herself. She had Ty and a precious relationship with God. In all the ways that mattered, it was more than Jade had ever hoped for.

Ty talked fast when he was excited, and he was reeling off sentences one after another. Whatever had happened it was important to Ty, and Jade listened intently, keeping her eyes glued to his.

"And so I made five rebounds and six inside shots, and no one on the team's ever done that in practice, and Coach Benson said I'd be starting forward at the next game, and—" he took a breath—"next year I know I'll be a starter at Woodbridge and then for Riverview. We're gonna be state champs, and then I'll go to Arizona or Kansas or Duke, and after that probably fourth, maybe fifth round in the draft, and then…"

Ty was breathless from the story and Jade smiled. *He's so full of life, so like his—*

"The draft?" She was playing with him.

"Come on, Mom, you know. *The draft.* The NBA draft. As in pros…professional basketball…" Ty rolled his eyes and flashed a heart-rending grin at her. He headed toward the stairs again and shrugged. "Girls! What do *they* know. But I still love you, Mom."

"Love you more." She watched him disappear and uttered a silent prayer that Jim's recent moodiness wouldn't harm her son.

Ty was upstairs changing when Jim came down. Something about his clean jeans, new navy pullover, and the fresh splash of cologne he wore caused a tremor of anxiety that shook Jade's soul. He came to her, looking up and down her body but never once making eye contact. Then he pulled her to him, nuzzling her neck with his mouth. As he did, he grabbed her bottom and worked his hands up.

"Jim!" Jade pulled away and turned to stir the vegetables on the stovetop. "Ty's on his way down."

"So. When's that ever stopped me?"

What was wrong with him? Was Channel One really the only problem they were facing?

She pushed away her thoughts as he came up behind her, moving his hands wherever he wished. Jade kept her eyes on the dinner and hoped Jim would lose interest. She wasn't worried about what Ty thought. He'd seen his parents kiss before, and certainly Jim could move his hands in an instant if they heard Ty on the stairs. But something had changed in Jim, and she was almost afraid to find out what.

"Feeling prudish, are we?" Jim sneered at her and grabbed a pop from the refrigerator.

Jade could feel her cheeks growing hot. *Lord, why can't he ask me about my day like he used to?* "No, it's just that..."

Jim narrowed his eyes at her. "It's a real shame, Jade. Such a waste." Jim walked away and popped the top on the can.

She glanced at him over her shoulder and opened the oven to check on the meat loaf. "What?"

"God gives you the body of a goddess—" he took a swig of the drink—"and all the desire of a cold fish."

Desire wasn't a problem when Tanner and I—

Immediately Jade banished the thought. *I'm sorry, Lord. That wasn't right. But I won't have Jim talk to me that way, not now or ever.* She pulled the meat loaf from the oven, set it on the stove, and spun around to face her husband.

"What's with you lately? It's like..." she struggled to contain her frustration. "It's like you've turned into someone else."

They locked eyes, and his were filled with meanness. He shrugged. "Maybe I'm finally letting you see the real me, Jade. Or maybe I'm tired of playing games for your attention." He tossed her a sarcastic glance. "Besides, it's your loss."

"I've never been cold to you and you know it." Jade didn't want to fight, but Jim's comment wasn't fair. She made herself available as often as Jim wished. But here, now, in the kitchen while she was cooking dinner, she wanted to be treated with respect. *Help me, God. Is that too much to ask? What's happening to us?*

As far as it depends on you live at peace with everyone....

The Scripture came to mind again and Jade mentally agreed. She moved closer to Jim, put her arms around his neck and kissed him long and slow, desperate to make things right between them again. "Is that better?"

Jim smiled at her and studied her a moment. "Much better." He kissed her back and his voice softened. "You're so beautiful, Jade. I'm sorry.... I know I haven't been myself lately."

Jade nodded and silently thanked God for the guidance he'd given her.

"Hey..." Jim nuzzled her neck more gently. "How 'bout a quickie before we eat? The bathroom, maybe, or the hall closet?"

She heard Ty galloping down the stairs, and Jade raised an eyebrow as she wriggled from Jim's grasp. "How 'bout we eat while the dinner's still hot."

Jim pulled away, took another swig of his drink and made his way to the table. "Don't run on the stairs, Ty. I've told you that before."

Ty rounded the corner, slowed to a screeching halt and walked to the table. "Sorry, Dad."

"'*Sorry, Dad*,'" Jim mimicked. "'*Sorry, Dad...sorry, Dad.*' Is that all you can say? You need to remember the rules, boy, is that clear?"

Ty took his spot at the table, and Jade's heart broke for him. He was probably dying to talk about basketball, and he was just a boy, after all. He'd been so excited he probably could have flown down the stairs and not realized it.

Dinner was strained despite Jim's earlier apology, and Jade prayed her husband would lighten up so the evening wouldn't be completely ruined. Times like this she wondered what deep thoughts Jim was thinking. Why hadn't she gotten pregnant those early years of marriage? And could he possibly know Ty wasn't his....

No, it wasn't possible. Jim would never have kept that kind of suspicion from her. He would have found some way to use it against her. Jade stared at her plate. The meat loaf was dry, and she chewed a piece until it felt like rubber in her mouth. The meal passed without a question or comment from Jim to Ty, and Jade silently grieved for her son. She knew he craved his father's attention, but there was nothing she could do to change Jim's shortcomings as a father.

For the most part, it was the same way Jim treated her or anyone in his life for that matter. The problem was simple: No one was as important to Jim Rudolph as he was to himself. Especially lately.

When Jim was finished, he pushed his plate back and exhaled loudly. "Best meat loaf in town." He patted his stomach and smiled at Jade. "Hey, how did your meeting go today?"

She shifted and moved her food around on her plate with her fork. He seemed so content right now, she hated to answer him. She was sure he wasn't going to like what she had to say. "It was fine. We talked and we prayed."

His smile faded a notch. "Well, you always do that, right? What did you ladies talk abo—" His smile disappeared. "Jade? What was your meeting about today?"

Lord, help me say this right. She looked up and met his gaze, knowing she couldn't lie. "Channel One."

She saw how hard he was working to stay neutral. He didn't seem to want to fight any more than she did. With a sigh, he looked down at the table. "Who brought that up?"

"Well, Jackie..."

His eyes came back to meet hers. "And you?"

She didn't answer. Instead she begged him silently to let it drop, to try to understand....

"So you joined the discussion."

She nodded at the flat statement.

"And I'm guessing you didn't stick up for Channel One."

Swallowing hard, she fingered her fork. "No."

The disappointment in his eyes pierced her. "Jade, I thought we talked about this. I thought you were going to drop it like I asked you to?"

Jade stared at her nearly full plate and remembered several times in the past month when Jim had made a point of asking her to stay out of the Channel One situation. "No...we've, uh, done a lot of research...." She looked up, willing him to understand, to hear her out. "It's not a good thing, Jim. I could tell you—"

He cut her off when he slowly pushed his chair back from the table. His tone was low—and full of hurt—when he spoke. "Do you know what's happening at work? The teachers are practically plotting your downfall. And they keep asking me what's wrong with you, why you're so focused on destroying education in our community."

"I'm not—"

He shook his head, stopping her. "You know what I keep asking myself, Jade?"

She sat in troubled silence, staring down at her clenched hands in her lap. Finally she shook her head and whispered, "What?"

"Why you're so focused on destroying me."

Before she could reply, he stood and moved across the dining room. Grabbing his keys from the countertop, he glanced back at her. "I haven't asked that much of you, Jade. Just that you support me, as my wife. That you show me I'm as important to you as one of your little crusades. That's all." His face twitched, and she had the horrible feeling that he was fighting tears. But that was ridiculous. Jim didn't cry. He never cried.

He gave a heavy sigh, his fingers clenching and unclenching on his keys waving his hand at her. "Instead, you seem determined to humiliate me. To make me look like a fool."

Jade glanced at Ty. The boy hung his head and kept his eyes trained on his plate as he dragged his fork back and forth through his vegetables. *Protect him, Lord. Don't let him be the victim in this.* "I'm sorry, Jim. It isn't about you or your job at Woodridge. It's about keeping our kids safe."

"Safe! Fifteen minutes of television each day isn't going to harm those kids. They watch five hours at home. What's the difference?"

Jade was desperate to diffuse the situation.

"Let's not talk about it right now, okay?" She met his eyes and then glanced toward Ty. The boy seemed to understand his mother's unspoken message, and he excused himself from the table. When they heard him close his bedroom door, Jim leaned back against the counter.

"How do you think it makes me feel, Jade? I spend my day defending evolution and teaching kids to think for themselves, and the other teachers snicker because they think I'm married to the most extreme religious fanatic this side of the Columbia River."

"I'm sorry, okay. I'll see what I can do." Jade forced a smile, anything to keep their argument from escalating. Lately when Jim got angry, she sensed a near violence beneath the surface. As though he wanted to throw something or smash his fist into a wall. The anger was further proof that something was very wrong with Jim.

Is he sick, Lord? Frightened? Or is it me? Have I really humiliated him? I never meant to….

Whatever was happening with Jim, it scared Ty, and Jade knew later that night she would need to console the boy before he would feel secure enough to get to sleep.

Jim stared at her, and she saw something in his face she couldn't ever remember seeing there before: hopelessness. "You'll *see* what you can do?" He shook his head. "Don't make empty promises, Jade. I think you've given me enough of those, don't you? We both know what you'll do. You'll get your oh-so-righteous and oh-so-worried group together and get Channel One removed from the school. You have a way with these things, Jade. But this time you're going too far. I'm warning you…"

Jade wasn't worried about his threat; she was worried about their marriage. Her fight against Channel One came from deep inside her. Something in her soul would shrivel and die if she were to pull out of the battle now. She was driven to be involved, make a difference. It had been the same way anytime she witnessed an injustice. She thought of Shaunie and Kelso General Hospital and how her passionate plea had saved the children's wing.

If only her husband could understand what moved her….

Tanner would have understood perfectly. He'd have been fighting alongside her. Just like he'd wanted to fight for religious freedom back when…

Jade shook her head to clear her mind. *Where were all the memories of Tanner coming from, and why now?* With all that was happening between Jim and her, the last person in the world she should be thinking of was Tanner. She said nothing as Jim flung his jacket over his shoulders.

"I'll be late."

"Where are you going?" For the first time, Jade didn't care what his answer was. If Jim was determined to keep leaving like this, then she would spend a quiet evening alone with Ty. But the pattern stirred an anxiety that had been building in Jade for weeks.

"The Sports Page…that okay with you? Maybe you'd like to start a sidewalk boycott against the place. They serve alcohol, you know."

Jim's tone was still angry, but he had lost interest in arguing with her. Now it was obvious all he wanted was to leave.

Warning bells rang in Jade's mind. *What if he isn't meeting teacher friends? What if the signs have been there all along and I've refused to see them?* "Meeting anyone special?" She tried to keep her voice casual, but inside she felt another stab of fear.

Jim smiled sarcastically at her, and Jade's heart grew heavier. *This isn't how you want our marriage, Lord. Loveless, faithless…. I'm losing him, Father. Help me, please.*

"Why on earth would I want to meet anyone *special* when I have such a loving, tender wife at home?" He uttered a short, harsh laugh, and the sound of it made Jade feel sick to her stomach. "You're such a good little Christian wife. Don't you worry about a thing, Jade; I'll come home tonight like I'm supposed to."

With that, he disappeared out the front door.

When the sound of his car grew faint, Jade picked up the phone and dialed Jackie Conley. "Hi. I only have a minute…" Jade kept her voice low. She didn't want Ty to hear her conversation. "About what you said earlier…what did you want to tell me?"

Jade heard Jackie sigh on the other end. "This isn't easy, Jade. But I think you should know."

The fear in Jade's gut grew. "What? Is it about Jim?"

"Yes." Jackie hesitated. "Scott thinks he may know why Jim's taking this Channel One thing so hard."

"I'm listening." Jade began clearing the dinner dishes, hoping they would cover up the sound of her voice since Ty was still in the next room.

Jackie hesitated. "Jade…I wish I could be there to tell you in person…." She paused again. "Scott says Jim's been spending a lot of time with Kathy Wittenberg. She's new on staff—assistant administrator and part-time health teacher."

Relief made its way over Jade. "That's nothing new, Jackie. Jim spends time with a lot of teachers."

There was a moment of silence, and instantly Jade had the feeling there was more to the story. Jackie drew a deep breath. "Kathy's the one who wrote the grant for Channel One. It was her idea, her project from the get-go."

A clearer picture was taking shape in Jade's mind. "So Scott thinks Jim could be trying to discourage me from getting in Kathy's way."

"Well, there's something else…."

"What?"

"Kathy and Jim are on a committee—not sponsored by the school, mind you—whose primary goal is to stomp out the voice of the religious right in our schools. They literally earmark parents like you and me and do their best to thwart our efforts."

Jade thought of the time her husband had been spending away. "Does the committee meet after hours?"

"Yes."

A cloud of desperation descended on her, and she made her way to the nearest chair. Nausea rose up in her stomach as she considered Jackie's words. *A committee designed to stomp out the voice of the religious right in public schools?* It sounded like something from a science fiction novel or a third-world country. *And Jim is involved?*

"Jade, one more thing..."

"I'm listening." Jade was leaning over the table, struggling to regain her bearings.

"When I say Jim's spending a lot of time with Kathy, I mean a *lot* of time. An awful lot of time."

Another realization came over Jade. "You don't think..."

"Well, Scott didn't come out and say they were having an affair, but..."

"Kathy's married, isn't she?" Jade pictured the blond at Jim's office. She was intelligent and sophisticated, a bit hard around the edges. Not pretty enough for Jim. Jade couldn't picture her husband falling for her.

"They split up two months ago. The divorce is in process."

Jade felt her heart plummet. "So you think there's something going on?"

Jackie paused. "Well, Jade, let's just say the signs are all there." She exhaled slowly. "I thought you should know."

No, Lord, don't let it be true!

Jade's mind raced. Kathy Wittenberg had brought in Channel One and found her primary support in Jim. The two had hit it off and joined a committee to eliminate the Christian influence that classrooms were feeling from certain parents in the district. More time together meant more time for indiscretion. It made perfect sense, and Jade could feel the ground beneath her feet beginning to shift.

"Listen, Jackie, I have to go. Ty's waiting for me."

"I'm sorry, Jade.... I didn't want to tell you."

"No, don't be. I needed to know." Jade closed her eyes. *Give me wisdom, God. Please.* "Pray for me, will you?"

"Always."

Jade closed her eyes. She knew Jackie would keep her word, and she was thankful again for her friendship. "I want God to show me the truth…so I don't have to go out looking for it."

"I will."

Jade's heart was racing, and she felt herself being buried beneath an avalanche of panic. "Jackie…I'm not feeling right…."

"Remember what you always say, Jade. God must have a plan in all this."

Yes, that was it. There must be a reason this was happening. "Could…could you do me a favor?"

"Anything."

"Please, Jackie, pray I'll know the reason soon."

Twenty

TANNER EASTMAN HAD FIFTEEN MINUTES BEFORE MEETING WITH his next client, and he intended to use the time to clear his desk. Neatness was not his strong suit. Generally there were a dozen things that seemed more important than tidying his work space, but if he didn't spend some time organizing soon, Tanner knew he'd have to start over with a second desk.

Office upkeep had been easier back when all he had was a ten-by-ten, rented space with nothing but his name on the door to prove he'd arrived. Now he had ten attorneys working for him, all dedicated to preserving religious freedom. Center for the Preservation of Religious Rights, he called his firm, and it had taken on the moniker CPRR.

As he had been shown during his days in Hungary, God was using him in a mighty way to preserve freedom in the United States. When citizens found themselves in a fight with the ACLU over religious rights, the first group they called was Tanner's. It was no accident that the two groups' initials were so closely linked. Tanner liked it that way. The battle had been one-sided until the CPRR came along, and now Tanner felt confident they had successfully slowed the erosion of rights taking place across America. In many instances they had actually restored them.

He collected two files spread across his workspace and placed them back in his cabinet. As he did, his eyes fell on the elegantly framed picture adorning his desk. *Leslie Barlow. Daughter of California Supreme Court Justice Ben Barlow.*

Graduated Harvard, 1997. Accomplished pianist. Mean tennis player. And about to become Tanner's wife in July—just five months away.

Tanner tried to smile at the thought but felt strangely overwhelmed instead. Which made no sense. Leslie was beautiful and cultured and the perfect adornment for the arm of any prestigious man. His mother had reminded him often how blessed he was that Leslie had come into his life.

Tanner chuckled. His mother used words like *blessed* for his benefit. Regardless of his devotion to God, she had grown increasingly far from things of the Lord. Tanner knew she only tolerated his choice to start the CPRR and defend cases where people were persecuted for their faith. But she hadn't approved of it until he became a household name.

Tanner would never forget the incident that put his firm on the legal map.

School officials at Jefferson High, south of Salem, Oregon, had asked a girl to sing for graduation ceremonies and merely to inform them of the artist and song ahead of time. The girl chose a song by Christian artist Steven Curtis Chapman. When the officials realized the song contained Christian lyrics, they cancelled her performance.

The girl's father was a reporter at the local newspaper, and almost overnight the story took on national public interest. Tanner represented the girl in a lawsuit against the school, and three days before graduation he won the case. The girl was allowed to maintain both her freedom of speech and freedom of religion. In the end a host of reporters covered the ceremony, and the girl sang the song she'd chosen—not just for those in attendance but for a television audience of more than a million.

The aftermath of media attention was both positive and overwhelming.

The program *20/20* did a special on Tanner's law firm—which at the time included him and a part-time paralegal and operated heavily on donations from churches. Next came *60 Minutes*, then *Larry King Live*. Everyone wanted to know why Tanner Eastman—a brilliant young attorney—had devoted his life to fighting for religious freedom.

The attention drew dozens of cases and then hundreds. Tanner began receiving tremendous donations from mainstream churches and organizations. Many times checks were accompanied by notes of encouragement.

"We've allowed the ACLU to tell us their definition of separation of church and state for too long. We'll support you each month. Godspeed and keep up the good work."

"I had begun to fear for my safety each time I prayed before lunch," one high school student wrote. *"Thank you and know that now I pray without fear. And when I do pray, I remember you and your law firm."*

Within the month, Tanner was overwhelmed with business. He had to hire a staff of attorneys and move to new offices, which he did in the San Fernando Valley on one of the top floors of a high rise located in the prestigious Warner Center Business Park.

Meeting Leslie was a direct result of his success. They had been introduced two years ago when he gave a presentation to the California Supreme Court. When the session ended, Justice Barlow and his daughter engaged Tanner in conversation. Leslie was stunning, and that night she suggested Tanner take her out to dinner. He gladly obliged, and they had dated ever since.

Tanner's mother had been thrilled to learn her son was dating the daughter of Ben Barlow. In fact, everyone seemed to agree that she was perfect for Tanner.

On the whole, Tanner agreed with them. He enjoyed himself with Leslie and figured they would be happy together. Only one thing troubled Tanner. Leslie wasn't a Christian, not in the sold-out sense of the word. She claimed a knowledge of Jesus Christ, but she wasn't a strong believer.

And she wasn't Jade Conner.

Tanner sighed as he straightened Leslie's picture. He had done what he could to find Jade and had turned up nothing. Not that it mattered. She was married and obviously not interested in finding him. Certainly at some time in the past five years she had heard his name mentioned, knew of his organization, perhaps read something in the paper about him.

But not once had she called or made contact.

He ran a hand over his desk, scattering a fine layer of dust. He could hear footsteps in the hall, and he knew his next client had arrived. But before he switched gears, before he devoted his entire attention to the next pressing legal matter, Tanner allowed himself to miss her one more time.

Where is she, God? And how long will I ache for her?

Twenty-one

THE MEETING WAS UNDERWAY, AND BY THE MIXED LOOKS ON THE faces of the school board members, it was going to be a night to remember. Jade ran through her notes one more time. *God, help me make sense. Help them understand what children are exposed to because of this program.*

Jackie leaned over and squeezed her arm. "No sign of Jim yet."

Jade felt somewhat relieved. They had argued again before she left. He told her he was staying home, and if she cared at all about what was good for them, she'd forget the meeting. Jade told him she was sorry. Some things simply had to be done and this was one of them. She had taken Ty with her and dropped him off at a baby-sitter's house.

School board president Bo Hepler began the meeting and summarized the argument from Jade's Bible study group. Parents were concerned that the programming on Channel One was questionable and exposed children to subject matter that needed parental approval, at best. Then there was the question of the Web site. By following the directions at the bottom of the Channel One screen, children could tap into a world with meeting places that, according to the moms in Jade's group, would appall most parents in the room. Including those on the school board.

"At this point we'll open the floor to anyone who'd like to comment on Channel One." Mr. Hepler scanned the room.

Jade sat near the front of the auditorium and turned and looked over the audience. Her Bible study was there in full force. Joining them this night were more than a hundred members of the PTSA. Jade and Jackie had made a presentation to the group on Monday, imploring them to take an active interest at Wednesday's meeting. The turnout was more than Jade had hoped for.

Five parents, including an attorney, took turns debating the issue while Jade sat tight, her stack of notes ready for the moment they might be needed. Three of the parents were in favor of pulling the televisions and canceling Channel One. The attorney wanted to keep it.

"Program content should not be an issue where our children are concerned." He slipped a hand in his coat pocket and strolled in front of the school board. Jade wanted to remind him this wasn't a trial, but she sat tight.

Tell me when, God. I'm ready if you'll only give me the words.

The attorney continued about freedom of speech and freedom of opinion and how it did children no good to live sheltered lives when real life was so hard these days.

"Wait a minute...." One of the parents stopped him with her comment. Jade recognized her from the PTSA meeting. "You're saying it's okay to watch a government-sponsored program that—at least once—featured a rock singer whose hate lyrics may have inspired two teenagers to open fire on their classmates in Colorado? You're saying that kind of person ought to hold our children captive for the first fifteen minutes of a school day?"

"I have a document right here wherein the U.S. Department of Education promises not to feature that singer again. It was an oversight."

"And what about documentaries where students learn the

proper way to use a condom? Was that an oversight also? I send my child to school for an education, not to be spoon-fed whatever material the government determines politically correct. Don't you think I have a right as a parent to decide what television programming my child watches?"

The debate grew more heated until finally Jade felt it was time. She stood up and waited to be recognized.

"…and as for the Internet problem. I've logged onto that Web site and never seen anything remotely objectionable."

Jade's hand was up. "Excuse me." The attention of the board and everyone else in the room was directed to her. She held up her notes. "I have a copy of several items I've pulled off that site. I can pass them out if you'd like to see for yourself the types of information our kids are being exposed to.

Mr. Hepler nodded and leaned toward the microphone. "Yes, Mrs. Rudolph. Why don't you hand them out to the board members." He looked to the audience. "If there aren't enough, please share with your neighbor."

Jade did as he asked and then began reading through a few of the most shocking items. In one case a chat conversation included dialogue between two people who called themselves students and members of a neo-Nazi group. Their discussion, caught in print and now in the hands of most of the people in the room, involved advice on how to make bombs and stockpile ammunition so one of the students could "take care of business" at his local school. There were several exchanges that contained blatantly graphic sexual material.

As she was finishing, there was a sound near the back door. Jade turned and saw Jim walk in. She paused midsentence and—along with everyone in the room—watched him walk past her without so much as a glance and take a seat next to Kathy Wittenberg.

Jade felt her face grow hot. Jim had never ignored her in public before. A ruffling of whispers began to build until Mr. Hepler leaned into the microphone and said, "Go ahead, Ms. Rudolph." The school board president seemed flustered, though whether by the interruption or by Jim's choice of seats, Jade wasn't sure. Either way Mr. Hepler was obviously determined to keep the meeting on track.

Jade's knees knocked and she felt her convictions waver. Was anything worth the humiliation she was enduring over Channel One? The answer was swift: *If I don't step up, who's going to fight for freedom in this country once our rights get taken from us?*

They were Tanner's words, and Jade felt a rush of strength at their memory. Tanner had been right. She would fight this battle no matter the cost.

Consider it pure joy whenever you face trials of many kinds, for you know that the testing of your faith...

The Scripture filled her mind and gave her something concrete to stand on. *Okay, Lord, but you'll have to hold me up.* She drew a deep breath and faced the board squarely. "That's all. I thought you'd like to know the full extent of Channel One before we make a decision on whether to keep it." Jade nodded to them and took her seat.

"Are there any other comments?" Mr. Hepler looked directly at Jade's husband, and she watched Kathy squeeze Jim's arm. They exchanged a glance, and he rose slowly.

"Just a few, if it's all right." Jim's tone was friendly and appealing, and Jade was taken aback. This was the Jim she had married, the one she hadn't seen at home for months.

"Go ahead." Mr. Hepler sat back, and Jade had the feeling he sided with her and the Bible study group. *Please, Lord, let justice prevail.*

Jim turned to face the crowd. "I'm sorry for interrupting the meeting." He smiled and Jade saw him for the first time through the eyes of strangers. Jim Rudolph could be charming and persuasive, everyone's favorite teacher. The boy voted most popular at Kelso High so many years ago. "I wanted to go on record as saying that I am in favor of keeping Channel One." A few people shot backward glances at Jade.

"And one more thing. Many of the moms in favor of pulling Channel One aren't here tonight for the kids, folks. They're here with their own political agenda. The agenda of the religious right."

Jade's embarrassment evaporated, and she fumed silently, hoping the school board would remember the documents they'd just seen.

Jim went on. "I think it's time we stop listening to these radical parents and remember the importance of separation of church and state. There's no place in our schools for religious fanaticism, whether it's teachers who lead prayer groups during class or parents—" he looked pointedly at Jade—"who think they can force their religion on everyone else."

He held up a copy of the note Jade had passed out earlier. What? Had he gotten into her file and taken it when she wasn't looking? Why hadn't he asked her for a copy? Jade felt a wave of dizziness wash over her. What was he trying to do?

Jim pointed to the notes. "You'll notice a list of links the Bible study group finds objectionable. These in particular: 'Why prayer must stay out of the schools.' And 'Celebration of Evolution' along with 'Abortion, Every Woman's Choice.' Look past the righteous indignation here, folks, and see that these women are simply trying to stop schools from teaching truth to our kids. If it goes against their religious viewpoint, these mothers don't want it."

Jade glanced around the room and saw several members of the audience nodding and exchanging whispered conversations....

"I, for one, say we can't do that. Not today when we are finally understanding the issue of separation of church and state. Let our children decide. Let them have the benefit of a television set in every classroom. And if parents object, let them sign a note that forbids their student from watching."

Jim looked at Jade once more, and she wished she could stand and fight him face to face on the issue. But she feared she would sound like a fanatic pitted against him. Besides, he was her husband, and a public debate with him would have the entire room gossiping about their private life for weeks to come.

Her conversation with Jackie two weeks earlier came to mind. Was Jim so invested in Channel One because of his friendship with Kathy? She glanced again at the woman sitting beside her husband. Kathy was barely containing a smile, beaming her support for Jim and everything he was saying. The woman had an unmistakable glow about her, and Jade felt a gut instinct, a woman's intuition.

Kathy was in love with her husband. She watched Jim make eye contact with Kathy and wink.

This can't be happening, Lord. Is he really having an affair?

She thought of how Jim had been gone four of the last five nights, and the reality of what was probably happening was finally clear. She could no longer hide from the facts.

Her husband was having an affair with Kathy Wittenberg.

The audience had their eyes glued on Jim as he finished. "Please let our children keep their televisions and the grant money. We have plans to use that money to buy a dozen new computers for the library. Our children deserve the very best in education today. Not a handful of right-wing adults censoring their every thought." He looked at Mr. Hepler. "Thank you."

Jade studied the audience and guessed there were probably twenty-five teachers in attendance. When Jim was finished speaking, Kathy rose to her feet in applause, and a majority of the teachers joined her.

As the applause increased, several members of the PTSA—parents who hadn't been at Monday's meeting—joined in. Jade knew there were at least twenty PTSA members who supported her, friends and acquaintances who were most definitely appalled by Jim's statements and behavior that night. Jade watched as many of them began talking amongst each other so that finally Mr. Hepler had to rap his microphone to regain order.

"That will be all. We'll postpone making a decision on this issue until the board has had time to consider both sides. Thank you."

With that Mr. Hepler moved on to other matters. Jade watched as Jim patted Kathy's knee, whispered something in her ear, and then stood and left the room.

Jade waited a moment so she wouldn't make a scene, and then quietly, she rose and followed him out the same door. Jim was waiting for her, and when she was outside, he turned on her, his voice an angry hiss.

"I warned you, Jade. I will not let you make a mockery of this school's decision to have Channel One or any other program." He motioned toward the still-full auditorium. "They knew what I was saying made sense." His face was inches from hers. "Back off, Jade. You and your friends, back off. Keep it up and you'll really be sorry."

"What's that supposed to mean?" Was he this defensive because Channel One was Kathy's project? Or because he and Kathy had an agenda?

He pulled away and took two steps back toward his car.

"One of these days you just might find out."

Jade was tired of being patient with him, tired of walking on eggshells to keep him from being angry with her. "Is that a threat?"

"Listen, Jade, I don't have time for your games." A couple exited the auditorium, and Jim lowered his voice. "I'm leaving town this weekend, going camping with a few teachers. You need some time to think about what you're doing."

A weekend camping trip with a few teachers? She crossed her arms. "What's wrong with you, Jim? You acted like you didn't even know me in there. Now you're going camping without me and Ty?" She knew she was pushing him, but she wanted him to admit the truth. "Why don't you take us with you? Make it a family trip. Give us a chance to figure things out."

Jim stared at her, his eyes cold. "You've always had some sort of twisted hold on me, Jade, but you know what? Not anymore. I'm finally feeling free from you...and I like what I'm feeling."

She studied his eyes and was shocked to find hatred there.

"You can't come on the trip. I don't want you there. Besides, you wouldn't be interested. Someone might have a drink or say something unkind about your God. Believe me, you wouldn't fit in."

Jade felt the sting of his comments. *What do I do, God? Help me.*

As far as it depends on you, live at peace with everyone....

She drew a deep breath and resisted making a comment about Kathy. "All right. You go. But when you get back, we need to talk. I'm not fighting Channel One as some kind of attack on you and the teachers at Woodbridge. You've got to know that, Jim."

"Right. Neither was the abortion protest you and your group staged at the Women's Care Clinic."

Jade was stunned. *The abortion protest? Had that bothered him, too?* "What do you mean? That wasn't—"

"Don't waste your time, Jade. Or mine." He glanced over his shoulder, watching carefully as people left the meeting. "You know the students at Woodbridge and Riverview use that clinic. You might as well have targeted my students. You can't begin to know the heat I took for that one. *'Hey, Jim, how's your preacher wife?'* I get things like that all day long, and I'm fed up to here with it." He made a cutting motion against the top of his forehead. "And what about the Wal-Mart thing? You and that busybody group of yours getting magazines you don't like pulled from the shelves? Like Portland needs that type of censorship."

"Those magazines were—"

"Spare me your religious drivel, Jade. I've heard it all. You're the pushiest religious do-gooder in the community, and I've tried to be tolerant with you. But now...now you're moving in on my territory."

"As long as Ty is in the public school system, it's my territory, too." She was shaking, not sure what was going to happen next but certain her life was falling apart quickly.

Jim turned and walked toward his car. Before climbing in, he called back, "Don't wait up. I'll be late."

A lump formed in Jade's throat as she watched him leave. Was this what their years of marriage had come to? Fighting and cheating and being angry with each other? Kathy Wittenberg exited the auditorium, glanced at Jade with a look that shouted disapproval, and then headed for her car. She left the parking lot, driving away in the same direction as Jim.

Jade stood alone in the damp, wet night, darkness surrounding her, and all she could hear was Tanner's voice. Soothing, calm, confident as the summer sun. Full of what she had once thought was love.

Remember, Jade, God has a plan for your life. Jeremiah 29:11…"I know the plans I have for you…plans to prosper you and not harm you, plans to give you hope and a future."

She closed her eyes and felt two tears trickle down her cheeks. Then, like all the plans and hopes that had ever mattered, Tanner's voice faded into the darkness.

Twenty-two

THE PHONE RANG AT THREE-FIFTEEN SUNDAY MORNING, AND JADE sat up in bed, alarmed and bewildered. She made a mental checklist and knew that Ty was safe in bed, Jim out with his friends camping. Who would be calling at this hour?

The room was pitch dark as she reached for the phone, knocking over a glass of water in the process. She brushed the water off the dresser and grabbed the receiver on the third ring. "Hello?" Her heart pounded in her ears.

"Mrs. Rudolph?"

"Yes, who is this?" She was trying to clear her head, and she leaned over and flipped on the light.

"This is Dr. Bryce Cleary at Emmanuel Hospital. Your husband's been in an accident."

Jade's eyes were still trying to adjust to the light, and she shook her head. Jim? In an accident? *Please, God, let him be okay. Please.* She felt her fingers beginning to tremble. "Is he…is he all right."

"He's suffered a spinal injury. I'm afraid he's in pretty bad shape. The girl was luckier; she has a broken leg but she'll be fine."

For an instant, Jade wasn't sure how to place that last comment. *What girl? Jim had been with a girl?* "I'm not sure I understand." She wondered if the doctor knew he was revealing something unknown to her.

"Your husband was riding an ATV in the off-road area of the

Columbia Gorge. He had a girl with him, a twenty-nine-year-old woman named Kathy. We think they must have been drinking, and your husband lost control of the ATV. They hit a tree." The doctor paused. "They're both lucky to be alive."

Jade's head was swimming. Kathy Wittenberg had been with Jim on the back of an ATV? Drinking?

Nausea swept her and clutched her stomach. This couldn't be happening. Not again. Not with Jim, too. It had been enough that Tanner was a liar and a cheat. She had married Jim to give her child security. She had tolerated his latest behavior because it seemed best for her son, the godly thing to do. Jim had never wanted anyone but her, and back when they got married Jade had been sure he'd be faithful.

But now...now he'd been caught with another woman. Jade felt as though her worst fears were coming true.

She exhaled slowly and heard the doctor clear his throat. "The woman also suffered a concussion. She's still pretty groggy." He hesitated. "Is she a friend of yours? A family member?"

Jade released a short laugh. "No...she works with my husband."

Dr. Cleary paused. "I'm sorry, Mrs. Rudolph. You might want to come down to the hospital. They're still checking to make sure your husband has mobility. There's a possibility..."

No, not Jim. "You mean he could be paralyzed?" Jade shuddered with alarm. Would God really ask her to care for an unfaithful man who didn't love her? Were these the plans he had for her? Tears filled her eyes. *Surely not, Lord.*

"We won't know for a day or so. But there is a chance. Like I said...he's pretty banged up. Lacerations and lots of stitches. He's semiconscious so he hasn't been able to help us much. We found your phone number in his personal belongings."

Jade sighed. "I'll be there. Thank you, Doctor."

"Mrs. Rudolph...I'm sorry about all this. I'll be here through the night if you have any questions."

She thanked him and hung up. She wanted to creep into Ty's room, curl up next to him, fall asleep, and forget the phone had ever rung. But that wasn't possible. No amount of pretending would erase the truth: Jim was having an affair and he'd been caught. For that matter, he might be paralyzed.

She bowed her head and clenched her fists. After learning the truth about Tanner ten years ago, Jade had nearly suffocated from grief and anger and loss. This time with Jim she was frightened about how she and Ty would get by. But she'd seen it coming, and somehow she knew they would survive. Even if she and Ty had to live alone the rest of their lives.

Whatever else happened, she was not turning her back on the Lord. Not this time. *Lord, I want to do your will. Give me the words to say, the way to act so that I can glorify you in this. Help me know how to cross this great ocean of anger and fear inside me. You know me, Lord. I'll sink if I try to swim it alone.*

She started crying as she telephoned Jackie Conley. Between sobs she explained the situation.

"I'm so sorry, Jade." Jackie offered to watch Ty, and in ten minutes she pulled into the drive. The women hugged, and again Jade was thankful for her friendship. At least the Lord had given her that.

"I'll be okay. Pray for me. For God's will, whatever that is."

They held hands and prayed in quiet whispers. Thirty minutes later she was sitting in a cold chair adjacent to Jim's hospital bed. Dr. Cleary had been right. Jim's face was swollen, his eyes black and blue. His right hand was in a cast, and there were bandages covering numerous leg wounds which Jade presumed had required stitches.

She prayed over him, prayed that perhaps this would be a

turning point in his life, a chance to give his heart to the Lord and come clean with his past.

Sometime before six that morning she fell asleep, still praying over him. She stayed that way until she heard voices. Her eyes opened and she found Jim sitting up in bed, sipping orange juice. Relief swept over her. He wasn't paralyzed, at least not in his upper body. She sat up straighter, and her movement caught his attention.

"You didn't have to come." Jim didn't make eye contact. He reached for a piece of dry toast and gingerly took a bite.

Jade had no idea what to say. She leaned back in the chair and pulled a blanket around her shoulder. Someone must have covered her up after she fell asleep. She watched her husband, wondering how he could eat when their marriage was falling apart.

"Why don't you go home and get some sleep." Still no eye contact.

"Can you move your legs?" Jade's voice was void of emotion. It seemed important that they get past that issue before talking about anything else.

Jim moved the bed sheet with his toes and winced. "I'm fine."

He was nearly paralyzed, nearly killed, and he acts like nothing's happened. Had they told him about the severity of the accident? Did he know how his poor decision to lie and drink and cheat had nearly cost him and Kathy their lives? Jade studied him and saw no signs of remorse.

"I guess they told you what happened." Jim's voice was gruff and his hand trembled as he lifted a bite of scrambled eggs to his mouth.

"About Kathy, you mean?"

Jim showed no reaction. "So you know?"

"I'm not a fool, Jim." Jade could hear the resignation in her voice, and she made an effort not to cry. "I've known for a while now."

He released an exaggerated sigh. "Here we go."

He's become a complete stranger. The man before her was her husband, the one she'd shared the last ten years with. But he had been unfaithful for who knew how long, and now he had the nerve to sound angry about being caught. Her eyes were dry. She had cried enough last night. It was time to face the truth about their future.

"How long has it been going on?"

For the first time, he looked up and stared at her. His eyes held no fear, no anger. Just cold, calculated emptiness. "I won't lie to you anymore." His voice was as cold as his eyes. "Things...well, they haven't been good between us for a long time. You know that."

Her heart responded by skipping a beat, but she said nothing.

"Jade...I want a divorce."

Her fingers wrapped tightly around the arms of the chair, and she steadied herself. This couldn't be happening. He had no intention of working things out. She would be alone again, she and Ty. The thought of it terrified her.

"Because of her? Is that what this is all about?" Jade forced herself to sound calm. Jim hated when she got upset.

"Yes...no...I don't know. It just isn't working between us anymore."

No, this can't be happening.... He's already made up his mind. "People make mistakes, Jim. We can get past this...make it work. People do it all the time."

Jade's heart pounded erratically. She hated having to beg Jim, but how could she support Ty on her own? And Ty needed a father, didn't he? Jim might not have been the most responsive and loving dad, but he was still a real presence in her child's life. Ty's world would be set upside down if they divorced now. Just like hers had been when her mother—

"Jade, I've made up my mind. I don't want a sermon." He spat the words, and with his bruised and battered face she almost didn't recognize him. *He really is a stranger. I don't even know him anymore.* Jim interrupted her thoughts. "I'm in love with Kathy. I want out."

Jade felt the sting of tears. "What about Ty? Have you thought about him."

Jim was silent. He focused on his breakfast again.

"Are you listening to me?" Jade raised her voice and moved to the edge of her chair.

Jim slammed his toast back to his plate and glared at her. "To tell you the truth, I'm worried about the boy."

"Meaning what?"

"Meaning what chance does he have growing up with a mother who's a religious fanatic? You're brainwashing him, Jade. A little more every day." He paused and Jade's heartbeat quickened. *What was he talking about?* "I've hired an attorney."

"When? The accident just happened."

"Nothing just happened, Jade. Who are you kidding?" Jim looked at her like she was a dimwitted child. "I was going to tell you later this week."

"You're serious? You really want a divorce?" Jade felt her foundations shake, and she prayed God would give her the strength to stand. *You are my rock, my God, my strong tower—*

"I want more than the divorce." Jim leveled his gaze at her, and Jade felt a chill run down her arms. "I want Ty, too."

"Joint custody?" Maybe she was in a nightmare? Maybe the whole thing—starting with the phone call—was only a bad dream.

Wake up! she told herself. *Wake up, now!*

"No, Jade. Full-time, permanent custody." He pushed away his tray. "I want the boy. My attorney thinks I can get him."

Jade had the impulse to run from the room, find Ty, and escape with him to some remote Swiss mountaintop. He was *her* child, not Jim's! Besides, why would Jim want him? He had provided for Ty, but certainly he had never shown any fatherly interest. Why would he fight her for permanent custody of a son he'd never cared to get to know? She closed her eyes for a moment and decided he must be playing with her. *This can't be happening.... Help me, Lord.* "You're not serious."

Jim leaned back against the hospital pillows. "Yes, in fact, I am. Dead serious." His eyes were like daggers, slicing to the core of her heart and that place where everything safe and secure had lived until now. "I told you, Jade. I've had it with your religious craziness. I don't want my son raised in that kind of environment. You'll turn him against me, against any hope of free thinking. Personally, I think Kathy and I could do a better job. We don't want to share him with you. Or your extreme beliefs."

Jade uttered an astonished laugh. "*We?* Kathy Wittenberg has no claim on my son." She realized she was on her feet. "You don't have a chance of winning full custody of Ty. No judge in America would grant that."

"You'd be surprised." Jim's hand was steadier as he took another bite of eggs. "Courts aren't happy with people like you, people who tell their kids what to think and who to agree with and how they should act."

"You're crazy if you—"

"No, Jade, you're crazy. Crazy like a fool. I'm telling you, no son of mine—"

She took a step toward him, her voice raising. "He's not

your—"

Her hand flew to her mouth and she stopped herself. *Dear God, help me get a grip here.* Her heart raced and she felt perspiration gathering on her forehead. *What if he's right? He and Kathy will try to make an example of me and then...Could it actually happen? Could a court actually take Ty away from me because of my faith?*

Jim leveled his gaze at her, and again Jade wondered if he knew the truth about Ty. "He's not my what?" Jade saw the accusation in Jim's eyes. *He couldn't know. The dates had lined up perfectly.* He could never have known what led her to his doorstep that day so many years ago.

She thought quickly. "He's not your responsibility. I'm there when he gets home, when he goes to school. I volunteer in his classroom. He needs *me*, Jim, not you. You don't even like giving him a ride home after practice. Why would you want custody of him now?"

"To save him from a wretch like you!" Jim spat the words and then waved his hand at her. "Get out of my room, Jade. You make me sick."

Jade stood up and realized she was light-headed. She braced herself on the arm of the chair and stared at Jim. *Who was this man? What had happened to the Jim I'd longed to love, the man I'd hoped would one day share my heart?* She'd heard enough. Maybe Jim was out of his mind, under the effects of medication or a concussion. Her heart raced and her hands trembled. She needed to get home and check on Ty.

Jade made her way out of the hospital and into the parking lot. *He can't be serious, God. He wouldn't want custody of Ty. And if he did, there's no way he could win. Right, Lord? Please tell me I'm right.*

Trust in me and lean not on your own understanding....

The verse brought a rush of peace and Jade exhaled slowly. As she did, her hands stopped shaking so she could unlock her car door. There was no way he would fight her for full custody. And if he did, there was no way he'd win.

It was impossible.

But as Jade drove home, the trembling returned and she was consumed by fear. She prayed with the intensity of someone clinging to life, and that night in church she held Ty's hand tightly.

This can't be real, Lord. It can't be. Tell me there's nothing to worry about, that I don't have to fear losing Ty to Jim because of my faith. Please, God.

In this world you will have tribulation, but be of good cheer...I have overcome the world.

What did that mean? Why had that Scripture come to mind now? She closed her eyes and knew she was on the verge of crying. Ty squeezed her hand and leaned near. "What's wrong, Mom?"

She opened her eyes and smiled at him. "Nothing, honey, Mommy's just praying."

"About Dad?" Ty knew his father had been in an accident, but that was all. She would spare him the other details until later.

"Yes, dear. I'm praying for Daddy."

A calm came over Ty's face, as if all was right with the world. He wrapped his arms around Jade and held her tight while she fought off a torrent of tears.

The fear didn't return until the next day. At just after four, Jade saw a sheriff's deputy pull up in front of her house and make his way up her sidewalk. She felt her heart stop, and then tumble into an erratic beat as she wiped her hands and opened the door. "Yes?"

"Mrs. Rudolph?"

"That's me."

"I've got a summons for you. I need you to sign here." He pointed to the piece of paper in his hand and held it up for her to read. The document stated that she was acknowledging receipt of divorce papers. She was officially being served. Jade felt a crushing fear, one that wove itself between her ribs and permeated her lung tissue. Her breathing grew labored as she moved the pen across the page.

The deputy turned to leave, taking his portion of the document and leaving Jade standing in the doorway, her eyes frozen on the papers in her hands. She moved slowly into the house, closed the door, and sat at the foot of the stairs where she began sifting through the pages, occasionally reminding herself to exhale.

They were divorce papers, all right, requesting her presence at a hearing set for mid-March.

Their marriage had begun in a small courtroom, and now it would end that way. Jade closed her eyes. *God, I know you hate divorce.... I'm so sorry. Please don't let it happen, Lord.*

In that instant, Jade knew she would have done whatever she could to reconcile with her husband, but she also knew Jim was beyond that point. With her eyes still closed, she reminded herself that with God all things were possible. Jim could wake up tomorrow, repent of his arrogance and pride, and turn his life to the Lord. She could apologize for letting her fight against Channel One take precedence over her marriage. And with God's help she could take him back and somehow save their marriage. With God it was all possible.

Two tears slipped out from the corners of Jade's eyes, but still she kept her eyes shut, not willing to look at the destructive papers in her hands. "Forgive me for my part in this, Lord. I'll pray for Jim every day." She whispered the promise out loud but heard no response. Minutes passed while terrifying thoughts made their way across the canvas of Jade's mind. Eventually she opened her eyes and stared at the documents in her hands.

It must be here somewhere. She began flipping through the pages looking for the section that dealt with custody. Jim had made threats in the hospital, but certainly he didn't really want full custody. The documents were loaded with legalese, but Jade quickly found the area marked "custody." She scanned the words and felt herself grow faint.

"Mr. Rudolph seeks permanent, full-time custody of minor child, Ty Robert Rudolph. Mr. Rudolph cites that Mrs. Rudolph is guilty of mental abuse and brainwashing where the minor child is concerned. He also states that Mrs. Rudolph's views are highly unstable and extremely intolerant. She is mean-spirited, overbearing, and completely lacking in judgment according to Mr. Rudolph."

Jade read the words again. *Highly unstable...extremely intolerant.* Jim's attorney was trying to make her look crazy. As if it had nothing to do with her faith in God. *Mean-spirited, overbearing, and completely lacking in judgment.*

It was the most inaccurate thing anyone could have said about her, and after she'd read it three times through, Jade dropped to her knees.

"No, God! Can't you hear me? Can't you help me? Ty is *my* son, not his." Jade knew she would not survive if she lost custody of Ty. "Help me, Lord. I don't know what to do!"

In this world you will have tribulation, but be of good cheer...I have overcome the—

"No!" She didn't want to suffer tribulation or trials or any such thing where Ty was concerned. "I can't."

You can do all things through Christ.

Jade caught her breath and closed her eyes. Her body shook

from the sobs that wracked her soul. It dawned on her that Kathy—and not Jim—was probably behind this. Kathy had no children and had mentioned on occasion at staff parties that she and her husband were trying to have a family. Now that she was making plans to be with Jim, she apparently thought she could gain a son and save a child from religious fanaticism all in one move.

No, Jim was not using this issue as a weapon against Jade. He was using it to win over Kathy Wittenberg. For that reason, he had made up his mind to make an example out of Jade. He wanted her to look like a freak, someone who was crazy and could certainly not maintain custody of her child.

"Why, Lord?" She cried until her tears became sobs and still she remained on the floor, hunched over her knees, begging God for help and understanding.

Once more the feeling came over her that she needed to get Ty and run away with him, to never look back even if it meant living undercover the rest of her life. Why had she trusted her son to a man like Jim Rudolph in the first place? Certainly welfare and food stamps would have been better for Ty than a father who never loved him and now wanted to use him to make an example of her.

She was not going to let it happen. The date of their hearing had been somewhere in the court papers, and Jade sorted through them frantically. There it was. Mid-March. Ten days away.

Jade leaned against the wall. Her mind raced, thinking of a solution, a way out. First she needed an attorney, someone who understood the nature of custody battles, someone who knew the importance of religious values and freedom of religion....

One name came to mind, and Jade caught her breath. *No,*

Lord, not him. He'd take one look at Ty and know for sure the boy was his. Please!

Once several years earlier Jade had been washing dishes while Jim flipped through the channels. He settled on one station long enough for her to hear Tanner's name. Her heart beat wildly as she set down the soapy dish, wiped her hands on her jeans, and joined Jim in the TV room.

There was Tanner, and Jade remembered how she drank in the sight of him for the first time in too many years.

He'd been more handsome than ever, confident, and genuine as a summer breeze. Jade had watched for several minutes, making herself appear busy so Jim wouldn't be suspicious. He had never known about her relationship with Tanner, but she didn't want to make him curious.

As Tanner spoke that day, she found herself carried back in time. Apparently, Mrs. Eastman had been wrong. Tanner hadn't wanted to be a politician, after all. Instead he had followed his dream and become a fighter for religious freedom. He had a firm called the CPRR with a number of attorneys working for him. Despite her bitterness toward the man, she couldn't help but feel proud of him.

She could still picture his face on her television screen. Jade's heart stopped racing and slowed to a steady thump. She could try to prove Tanner was Ty's father, but she might lose the child for good. Any mention to Tanner or anyone else that Ty was his son would mean Doris Eastman might make good on her promise. She could still hear the woman's hateful words that awful day: *I will hire a batch of attorneys to sue you for defamation. And I will get custody of that child, mark my words. Girls like you would never win a court battle against the Eastman estate.*

Jade sighed and knew she would have to keep Tanner's

place in Ty's life a secret until the day she died. Otherwise it would cause too much public attention, and Ty would be the loser. Tanner hadn't wanted his son, anyway. Just as he hadn't wanted his other two children.

She rose up off the floor, straightened the papers, and set them on her desk. If Jim planned to sue her for full custody of Ty, if he intended to punish her for her beliefs, then she was faced with one undeniable fact: In all the world, only one man could help her now; the one man she must never contact again.

Call him, my daughter.

Jade heard the voice and hesitated. What could possibly come from it?

Call him.

There had been few moments since Jade had become a Christian that she had willfully gone against the still small voice of God. She drew a steadying breath. This was not going to be one of those times.

Walking across the room, she picked up the telephone and began to dial.

Twenty-three

One of the benefits of working in the Los Angeles area was the number of cases that crossed the desks of the CPRR. Of course, they could also be a curse. Tanner studied the mass of humanity seated around him at Tony Roma's. Most of them were blissfully unaware of the desperate battle waged by the CPRR to preserve freedoms long taken for granted by many in the United States.

For all the time and energy he and his staff had put into the battle, Tanner had the sense lately that things were not getting better. If anything, they were heating up. Many times instead of gaining ground, they seemed to be treading water: clinging to basic freedoms while watching others erode with case precedence.

He took a swig of water and glanced at the restaurant's entrance. Matt Bronzan would be there in five minutes. He'd told Tanner he had an urgent issue to discuss. Something about a case that needed their immediate attention.

The cases they handled now would have been unthinkable five years ago. Churches whose tax-exempt status was being called into question, private business owners forbidden by city council from bearing a Christian fish on their store sign, teachers fired on the spot for mentioning God in a public classroom.

The CPRR won nearly all their cases, but not before much money and time was devoted to the matter. Tanner ran his fingers over the water drops on the side of his glass. Fired for mentioning God? He still couldn't believe the case had actually made it to court. Tanner and Matt had won the decision, but barely. How far had they come from the days when teachers were directed to lead prayer in school, how far from the days of even setting aside a moment of silence?

He sighed and stared through his water to the blurry images on the other side. The problem was public opinion. More often than not, his cases made their way into national headlines leaving people with the impression that—in the case of the dry cleaner operator—a Christian fish symbol was somehow illegal. Regardless of the fact that they'd won the case.

The attack by the liberal left and the ACLU was relentless and had served to erode the way the public viewed religious freedom as a whole. Anymore, churches felt thankful that they still had the privilege to meet on Sundays. Forget the freedoms they'd lost in the process.

Tanner spotted Matt heading for the table. At least he had this one friend. Matt had been with him since their first big case—the one with the student who wanted to sing at graduation. A former district attorney, Matt had once prosecuted mainly drunk-driving cases.

Then he met a widow, a Christian woman named Hannah Ryan, whose husband and daughter were killed by a man driving under the influence. Matt took the case and wound up winning a first-degree murder conviction. The drunk driver was given twenty-five to life, and Matt earned national attention overnight.

But something else happened.

Matt fell in love with Hannah. One year after the case was resolved—two years after the accident—the couple married. They had one daughter, Jenny, a sixteen-year-old who was the only survivor from the accident. Shortly after the wedding,

Matt decided he'd spent enough of his life convicting drunk drivers. It was time to branch out. He had heard of Tanner's law firm and contacted him, looking to help.

Tanner liked him immediately. Matt was sharp and sincere and devoted to the Lord. He had won numerous cases since joining forces with Tanner and was, without a doubt, as great a fighter in the cause as anyone at the firm. Occasionally, Leslie and Tanner shared dinner with the Bronzans, and Tanner had always been impressed with Hannah's quiet strength. Whatever nightmare she'd been through, she'd made it to the other side by God's grace. Clearly she and Matt shared a bond that spoke volumes.

The kind of bond he couldn't imagine sharing with Leslie, no matter how wonderful she was. The kind of bond he once thought he'd share with—

"Hey, did you order?" Matt was breathless. He'd probably kept four appointments back-to-back before arriving at the restaurant.

Tanner shook his head. "Just the loaf." Once a month he and Matt met at Tony Roma's for lunch, and the onion loaf was a given. The men were both in exceptional physical shape and knew their monthly indulgence would not make a difference. "How'd the meeting with Swires go?"

"Good." Matt gulped down half his glass of water. "I think I convinced him to give up. Showed him documentation, precedence."

"Good. We might live in a tolerant town, but even Los Angeles isn't ready for the 'Mother God Transvestite Club' to march in the Boy Scouts' Easter Parade."

Matt set his water down. "I told him they didn't stand a chance. Even if they *did* wear merit badges on their dresses."

Tanner laughed. Matt was the only one at the firm he could

lighten up with. They played basketball at Racquetball World and on Saturdays met at seven in the morning for tennis. Time had earned them the right to joke with each other, even when the matters were utterly serious and close to their heart. "Is it just me, or is it getting crazier all the time out there?"

Matt rested his forearms on the table and leaned forward. "That reminds me."

Tanner rocked back in his chair. "The case you mentioned earlier?"

"Right. It's a doozy. Don't know if it's legit, but it has the earmark of a national headline grabber. And then some."

They were all worthy of such attention, but Matt had always had a keen sense for knowing when a case had the potential to shake Americans.

The waitress appeared with the onion loaf, took their order, and made a hasty exit.

"Gotta love these onions." Matt dug his fork into the loaf as Tanner raked a section onto his plate.

After a few bites, Tanner wiped his mouth and exhaled loudly. "Okay, I'm listening. Tell me about this case of the century you've discovered."

"Might be nothing." Matt shrugged. "But if it's true..." He took two more forkfuls of onion rings and then leaned back in his chair. "It's a custody case."

"Custody? As in divorce?" Tanner had handled only a few cases that involved divorce. Usually battles over which church a child would attend or whether the mother or father could force attendance if the child wasn't interested. That kind of thing. "How'd you hear about it again?"

"I got a call yesterday afternoon." Matt hesitated. "Anyway it's this woman, and she's terribly nervous. Says she doesn't want to give her name, but her husband is divorcing her and suing her for complete custody of their son."

Tanner finished the plate of onions and cocked his head. "Where do we fit in?"

Matt wiped his mouth. "He wants custody because he thinks she's an unfit mother."

"Unfit because...?" Tanner was struggling to see the connection.

"Because she's a Christian."

Tanner felt the winds of outrage blow against him. "Are you kidding? He wants custody because of his wife's faith?"

"I'm serious. She told me her husband hasn't been involved in their son's life. The marriage fell apart when she discovered her husband was having an affair. Apparently there's more to it. The caller said she's fairly vocal on the school board or something. Hasn't kept her beliefs a secret."

Tanner was beginning to see the picture. "Now her husband wants to make an example of her...."

Matt raised an eyebrow. "According to the divorce papers, he's out to prove the woman brainwashed the boy into believing and that she's an unfit mother because of her extreme religious beliefs."

Tanner anchored his elbows on the table and brought his fists together. He had feared it would come to this one day but never dreamed with the ushering in of a new century that they were there. If the man were to win this case, parents across the country would have to fear losing their children because of their faith. "What's her name?"

Matt sighed. "That's just it. She wouldn't give it to me."

"Why not?" Tanner was suspicious of people who called anonymously. If they needed help, if the situation was what they said it was, why not be honest about the facts. Including revealing their identity?

"Didn't say. Apparently she called for advice."

"What did you tell her?"

"The truth. No one could take her son away from her because of her faith. I asked her if she wanted someone from our office to help her, maybe represent her at the hearing."

"And…"

"She said no. Real adamant about it, too."

"Is it a financial concern?" Tanner thought it strange the woman would call but then refuse help.

"I told her there was financial assistance available, but she said she wasn't interested. Just wanted our advice."

Tanner sighed. "Strange. How did you leave it with her?"

"She said she'd get an attorney right away and she thanked me. I think she was relieved when I said her husband didn't stand a chance."

"Hmm. When's the hearing?"

"A week or so, apparently."

Tanner thought about the missing details. "We might never hear from her again, but you never know. Did she tell you where she lived."

"Yeah, I got that much. She lives in Portland."

"Why don't you put someone on it. Have them scan *The Oregonian* for the next few weeks, see if anything comes up. If she loses custody of the boy at the hearing, the paper will definitely cover it."

They changed the subject then, but Tanner's mind was stuck on the strange case Matt had shared. His heart ached for the woman—whoever she was—who was living in terror somewhere for fear that she would lose custody of her son.

All because she had chosen to identify herself with Jesus Christ.

Twenty-four

THE NORTH ANNEX OF THE CLACKAMAS COUNTY COURTHOUSE was not an impressive structure. It consisted of a single hallway with various offices and courtrooms on either side. Jade arrived thirty minutes early so she could read the Bible. Matthew, chapters 5 and 6 and part of 7. Jesus' Sermon on the Mount always soothed her fears, no matter what she was facing.

She had read it by herself in a hotel room on the Oregon coast more than a decade ago, and again while waiting for Jim to regain consciousness after his accident.

And she read it now, as the hearing to decide whether she would lose custody of Ty was about to begin.

If ever there was a time she needed a reminder from Jesus it was now.

Therefore I tell you, do not worry about your life....

Jade stopped reading and closed her eyes. *I'm trying not to worry, Lord. Help me believe what that man from Tanner's office said. No way can they take Ty because of my faith. Please, Lord, help me trust you.*

She had survived the previous weeks by telling herself there was nothing to worry about. It was craziness. Pure craziness. No judge in his right mind would penalize a parent for her faith. She was sure of it. The man from Tanner's office had made her confident of the fact.

The day after Jade received the divorce papers, Jim had moved out. He and Kathy shared an apartment now, unabashedly driving to school together. From what she'd heard, Jim was still treated with utmost respect, though several staff members apparently didn't approve of his leaving his wife and moving in with another woman. But then, Kathy was one of them. And she wasn't a religious fanatic.

In the wake of Jim's decision to sue for complete custody, he had become the devoted father. He was suddenly attentive to Ty's needs, showing up on weekends to take him out for ice cream, engaging him in conversations about basketball and evolution, the professional football draft and alternative lifestyles. Kathy was often present.

Almost daily Jade found herself putting out fires Jim had started in the child's mind.

One night after spending an evening with Jim and Kathy, Ty had come home and approached her curiously. "Mom, did you know scientists have found the missing links that prove evolution is true?"

She had taken Ty in her arms and held him tight. "Honey, where'd you hear that? There's a lot about evolution that has never been proven. A lot of very smart scientists have actually stopped believing in it altogether."

Ty scrunched his handsome face sadly. "Dad and Kathy said you'd say that...."

There had been several similar incidents, and Jade wished she could forbid Ty from leaving the house with Jim. But her attorney had advised her to cooperate. Otherwise she would only support Jim's accusations and come across fearful and fanatical. Jim's discussions about evolution and other hot topics were probably only intended to bait her.

"Do whatever you can to get along." Her attorney had repeated that just last week, and Jade knew she had no choice.

Jim's relentless attention toward Ty continued, and Jade was helpless to do anything to stop it. Clearly her son was torn by the situation and had been moody and sensitive as a result. Jade understood. Ty wanted to maintain his fierce loyalty to Jade, but there was no denying how much he enjoyed his father's sudden attention.

Jade glanced at her watch. Fifteen minutes had passed. She heard voices from the other end of the courthouse, and she stared down the hall. Nothing. No one headed her way. Jade twisted her fingers nervously. Her attorney should have been there by now. He hadn't been good about returning phone calls, and Jade feared he might show up late.

Her thoughts drifted back to Ty. Most recently, over the weekend, Ty came home from Jim's almost belligerent toward her.

"Daddy and Kathy say you're intolerant of people, is that right, Mom?" They had been to the Oregon Museum of Science and Industry, and Jade wondered how such a discussion could possibly have related to their visit.

"What people?"

Ty shrugged. "Different people. Like when two guys fall in love and get married."

Jade had to lean back against the kitchen counter for support. Why was Jim doing this? The boy was too young for such discussions. "Well, sweetheart, it's not that I have anything against those people. But God has something against the way they act."

"You mean God doesn't like it when two men fall in love?" Ty seemed genuinely confused, and Jade was sick about it. Jim was turning the child into a pawn for his own interests.

"Right, dear. God says it's a sin."

Ty studied her. "Daddy and Kathy said you'd say that."

Jade struggled to maintain her composure. "Daddy and

Kathy aren't Christians, Ty." Jade had pulled her son close and hugged him. "We still love people who live like that, and we pray for them. But it isn't something God likes, and that's the truth, Ty."

"Daddy says truth is different for different people."

The comments continued until Jade practically looked forward to the hearing. At least then they could come to some kind of agreement and move on. Her attorney was hoping to win 80 percent custody for Jade.

Once he lost his battle for full custody, Jade was sure Jim would give up.

Unless Kathy had convinced him she wanted to be Ty's second mother. Jade's stomach hurt at the thought. *Please, no, Lord.*

Until her attorney arrived—just three minutes before the hearing—Jade remained alone, silent, absorbed in an urgent conversation with the only One who could set her son free.

The hearing was underway, and the Honorable Judge Arthur Goldberg presided. So far Jade was having trouble keeping up. Issues of material goods and financial support and joint bank accounts were discussed and considered. Generally, their possessions were split down the middle, and the attorneys handled the details. Meanwhile, Jade sat on one side of the courtroom; Jim, the other.

Occasionally, she would glance in his direction and wonder again why she had married him. Why hadn't she trusted God to give her the strength to be a single mother? Jim kept his gaze straight ahead and seemed almost unaware that she was in the room.

Judge Goldberg was speaking. "And now, we will decide the

custody matter. First we will hear from the plaintiff."

Jim made his way to the witness stand, and Jade watched him smile warmly at the judge.

"Mr. Rudolph, this court understands you are seeking full and permanent custody of your minor child, Ty Robert Rudolph, is that correct?"

"Yes, your honor." Jim looked the picture of professionalism. Only someone like Jade, someone who knew him well, could detect the steel-hard hatred that lurked deep in his dark eyes. "That is correct."

"Would you please explain to the court your reason for this?"

Jim drew a deep breath and began. He talked about Jade's determination to convert everyone to her way of thinking. It was enough that Jade did this with strangers and merchants and school board members, he said. But now she was doing it with their son. One by one, he rattled off detailed accounts of the battles she'd fought, battles to maintain religious values and overt parental control in areas that concerned her son.

Jade's hands began to tremble as Jim continued. She clasped them tightly and worked to draw a deep breath.

Do not be anxious about anything....

Somehow, when Jim was finished speaking, Jade realized her efforts didn't seem altruistic. They seemed extreme and paranoid and one-sided, a distraction to the job of raising a child. *What's happening here, God? It isn't supposed to be like this.* Jade struggled to breathe under the weight of her fear.

By the time she was allowed to speak, Jade had trouble keeping her head up. She felt like a terrible mother, a criminal almost, and she struggled to make eye contact with the judge.

"Is it true you told your son it was wrong for two men to love each other?" Judge Goldberg's question caught Jade off guard. *What? How did the judge know that? Ty must have innocently passed her comments onto Jim and...*

"Yes, your honor. But only because that's what God's Word teaches." Jade studied the judge's face and saw that clearly he did not approve of this.

"So you're raising your son by the standard of the Bible, is that right?" The judge said the word Bible like it shouldn't be spoken in public places, and Jade looked to her attorney for help. He was sorting through a stack of documents and seemed unconcerned with the dialogue taking place.

Jade continued to answer questions until finally the judge called for a brief recess. Five minutes later he was back with his decision.

"This court finds Mr. Rudolph to be of sound mind and accurate opinion when he states his concern for his son. Indeed, the boy is at great risk for being converted to his mother's way of thinking. I believe he is being forced to adapt her views of intolerance at an age that is too young to make those types of decisions. Intolerant children will only spread hate in our world, and when presented this type of opportunity, I must act the way few judges have acted before."

Jade shot a desperate look toward her attorney, but again he was preoccupied with paperwork and seemed unaware of the proceedings taking place. What did the judge mean that he must "act the way few judges have acted before"? What was happening here? Where had this judge come from anyway? Didn't her attorney know the judge and what his opinions would be about the case?

Judge Goldberg glanced at Jim, and then Jade. "For that reason, I do hereby award full custody of minor child, Ty Robert Rudolph, to Mr. Jim Rudolph. Supervised visits for Mrs. Jade Rudolph will begin one week after the custody exchange takes place."

Jade stared at the judge and blinked. It was impossible. This couldn't be happening. A cold clamminess came over her, and spots danced wildly before her eyes. This wasn't Judge Goldberg's decision to make. It couldn't be. She was Ty's mother, after all, and Jim...he wasn't even...

"Wait a minute!" She was on her feet, her voice ringing through the courtroom. "You can't do this. My son needs me; we need each other."

The judge looked at her over the rim of his glasses. "You had your chance, Mrs. Rudolph. Even over the past few weeks you've been given an opportunity to soften your views. But you've insisted on leaning so far to the religious right that this court no longer feels you to be a safe and responsible parent for your son."

"But you can't!"

"Order!" Judge Goldberg rose from his chair, his face twisted in a scowl as he banged his gavel twice. "If you speak again, I will hold you in contempt of court. Is that understood?"

Jade sat weakly down in her chair and felt the tears begin to flow. *Why, God? What can I do to stop this?* She looked at Jim and saw he was smiling and whispering with his attorney. Jade felt as if her heart had been ripped out and thrown on the floor for everyone to step on and laugh at.

Jim and his attorney had actually done it. They'd won Ty because they had the correct viewpoint and she did not. *I'll get him back; I have to. But until then...Oh, God, please help me.... How will I live without him?*

"Mrs. Rudolph, you will have forty-eight hours. At that point a deputy will arrive at your door, along with Mr. Rudolph and his attorney, and custody will be handed over. If you do not cooperate or do not make yourself available for the transfer, you will be in contempt of court, and a warrant will be issued for your arrest. Is that understood?"

Jade had to force herself to respond. "Yes, your honor." She looked at her attorney once more, but still he seemed like an indifferent bystander watching the proceedings without a single interjection or show of concern.

Feeling helpless, Jade spoke out. "Please make a note that I will be finding a new attorney...." Her lawyer cast her a look and then shrugged. The man didn't care about her pain or whether she won the case. He was merely going through the motions, earning a paycheck. Jade struggled to remain standing and thought she might faint or die from heart failure. Her chest ached from the blow of the judge's decision. She cleared her throat. "And please make a note that I will be appealing this decision."

The judge looked at her, and Jade had the feeling he was mocking her. "That will be noted. You have sixty days to file an appeal, or the decision will stand."

Jade did not talk to anyone, including the reporter from *The Oregonian* who sat in the back row. Why bother? He had a story that would, Jade guessed, make the front page. She needed a new attorney, needed a plan. But right now none of it mattered. As she stumbled to her car, weak from shock and pain, terrified about the future, there was only one thing she wanted: to get home and explain the situation to Ty, help him understand that for a little while—and only a little while—they would have to be separated.

Then she would spend the next forty-eight hours telling him good-bye.

Twenty-five

THE WEDDING PLANS WERE FAR MORE EXTRAVAGANT THAN Tanner had pictured, and by the third week of March they were becoming overwhelming. Leslie showed amazing attention to detail, and Tanner was growing increasingly tired of her twice daily calls updating him on the progress.

He had her on the phone now, and Tanner tapped his pencil against the edge of his desk as he listened to the latest bit of wedding information. Leslie's voice sounded shrill and demanding. Funny how it hadn't seemed that way at first. *What's wrong with me, Lord? I should be thrilled to marry a woman like Leslie….*

Do not be unequally yoked, my son.

The verse caught Tanner square in his gut. Leslie continued to ramble, but he wasn't listening. If God hadn't wanted him to be unequally yoked, why hadn't he pointed it out earlier?

Tanner thought of the Bible, and a sinking feeling settled in his heart. He had known from the beginning that Leslie wasn't a strong believer. In fact, there had been many times when the fact had haunted him late into the night. God had indeed pointed it out earlier. *But she does believe, Lord.*

I know the plans I have for you….

There it was, that Jeremiah verse again. Ever since Jade had married someone else, Tanner had been unsure about the plans God had for him. Leslie had brought him new perspective. She might not have been a dynamic believer, but she had potential.

Certainly she was the plan God had intended for him, wasn't she? Doubts nibbled at him like so many bats in a dark cave.

Tanner forced himself to concentrate on what Leslie was saying.

"There is simply no way we can sign the current caterer. Mother checked his background, and he's only had three years of professional experience. Ours would be the largest wedding he's serviced, and that won't do. We need someone with experience; there's no other way around it."

Tanner stared at the crystal blue sky and wished for a moment he was outside walking somewhere. Between Leslie's wedding plans and the workload he was facing that day, he needed a moment by himself to clear his thoughts. Or maybe his workload had nothing to do with it. Maybe it was the wedding itself making his thoughts foggy. *What am I feeling, Lord? Why am I confused?* He loved Leslie, didn't he? Of course he did. He was only tired of the details. Color schemes, bridesmaids' dresses, tuxedos, flowers.

Leslie was still stuck on the caterer. He tuned back in and tried to feel interested.

"Anyway, Mother says she knows someone in the Bay Area who could fly in, but then I thought we should check into that famous chef, what's his name? The one who creates meals for the stars?"

Stars. For an instant he thought of a night long ago when he and Jade sat alongside the Cowlitz River and counted the constellations. He had seen more stars that night than at any time before or since. Or was that just the way Jade made him feel? Tanner drew a deep breath.

Fine time to be thinking of Jade.

"...of fish and veal, and anyway, it's got to be the right man, don't you agree, Tanner?"

He felt a rush of panic. He had no idea what Leslie was talking about. "Right. Definitely. The right man."

"Tanner!" Leslie's voice was half whine, half reprimand. "You're not listening are you? You never listen when we talk about the wedding. I hope you're planning to show up."

Tanner forced a laugh, but it sounded hollow even to him. "Honey, it's just that you're so much better at making these decisions than I am. I'll be happy with whatever you choose. Really."

"It would be nice if you were interested, even just a little bit." For a woman with a Harvard English degree and a resume littered with accomplishments, Leslie sometimes acted like a child demanding attention. Tanner shook his head and tried again to clear his thoughts.

Leslie's wonderful. Why am I sabotaging my feelings toward the woman I'm about to marry? The woman I'll spend the rest of my life with?

"I'm listening and I'm interested. I'm sorry, honey, go ahead. Have you called anyone about the catering."

Leslie released an exaggerated sigh. "I already told you, I called him yesterday. I'm waiting to hear back later today whether..."

Matt Bronzan entered his office. He held a newspaper clipping, and he looked stricken. Tanner raised his eyebrows in response, and Matt mouthed the word, "Emergency."

Tanner motioned for Matt to sit down and he pointed at the phone, signaling that he would be off in a moment. He waited for Leslie to take a breath. "Honey, something's come up. I gotta run." He hesitated. Why was he feeling so uncomfortable with her? Maybe they needed a day away, time to talk about something other than the wedding.

"As usual. Something always comes up. I'll figure it out by

myself." She was gifted at playing the role of persecuted martyr. "I'll let you know what time to be at the church."

"I'm sorry, Leslie. I'll call you back.... I love you." But the words sounded forced. He did, didn't he? If he didn't love her, what was he doing marrying her? And where were these feelings of doubt coming from? He tried to remember all the reasons he'd asked her to marry him in the first place.

Be careful, my son. Fools rush in where angels fear to tread.

The warning flashed through his mind and hit him like a physical blow. First the verse about being unequally yoked and now this. Was the Lord trying to warn him? He stored the possibility in the back pocket of his mind and turned his attention to Matt. "What's up?"

Matt set the news clipping on the desk and turned it so it faced Tanner. He glanced at the headline. "Woman Loses Custody of Son Because of Religious Fanaticism."

Tanner's eyes grew wide. It was the case Matt had told him about. It had really happened. The woman had been genuine, and now she had lost possession of her son. "Is it her?"

Matt nodded. "Definitely. Portland. Press makes her out to be a freak, just like the guy's attorney and the judge. One of those cases where everything lined up against her."

"Have you read it?"

"Yep. Woman says she's going to appeal, says she's going to need a new attorney."

"Yeah, I guess." How could her first attorney have blown such an obvious case? Religious freedom was a protection guaranteed by the Constitution, pure and simple. Was the entire country losing its collective mind? He reached for the article and scanned the first few paragraphs while Matt waited.

"A Portland woman lost custody of her only son today because of her extreme religious views in what will no doubt become a landmark case. Municipal Court Judge Arthur Goldberg made his decision based on the complaint by the woman's husband. His complaint stated that their son was being forced to believe the same way as his mother. Goldberg cited the boy's age as a leading factor in his decision against the child's mother, Jade Rudolph, 31, of north Portland."

Tanner's eyes froze on the woman's name. *Jade Rudolph. Age thirty-one. No, it wasn't possible.* There had to be other women named Jade living in the Northwest. Besides, his Jade could have moved anywhere by now. It couldn't be her. Not after all these years.

"You with me, Tanner? You look like you saw a burning bush or something." Matt lowered his face and tried to make eye contact with Tanner. "Did I miss something?"

Tanner shook his head slowly. "It's just the..." He met Matt's questioning stare. "I knew a girl named Jade once."

Matt's expression went blank. "How 'bout that. Me, too. In first grade, I think."

"No..." He didn't expect Matt to understand. He'd never told Matt or anyone else about Jade and their summer and all she had meant to him. All she still meant to him. "I...I loved a girl named Jade once."

"Oh." Matt tried to look sympathetic, but it was obvious he wanted to return to the matter at hand. "You never mentioned her before."

"It was a long time ago. I was going to marry her, but then..." Tanner gazed back at the article, at the woman's name. "She married someone else."

Matt leaned back in his chair, eyebrows raised. "You think it's her?"

Tanner shrugged. "Could be, I suppose. It'd be a long shot." He had never learned her married name. "I'm sure it's not her.

She's probably back living on the East Coast by now."

Matt hesitated. "Anyway, we need to get on this right away. It's the biggest issue this country's faced yet. A mother losing custody of her child because of her religious beliefs."

Tanner tried desperately to put thoughts of Jade out of his head. "Right. We need to contact her." He thought about his schedule over the coming week. "Why don't you see if she's free this Thursday? I have appointments Wednesday and Friday, but if she's all right with it, arrange to meet her. We'll fly up Wednesday evening and meet with her Thursday morning."

Matt nodded. "Done. I'll go track her down." He made his way toward the door. "I'll let you know what I find, whether she's open or not and if she's interested in meeting. Last time I talked to her, she didn't want our help."

Tanner's heart felt heavy as he considered the woman's situation. "She's lost her son, Matt." He took the news clipping and folded it, tucking it into a fresh folder. "She'll want our help now."

There was no point sending Ty to school, not with deputies about to arrive at her house and escort her son away. She had explained it several times, but still Ty had spent much of the past thirty-six hours crying.

"Why, Mom? I don't want to live with him and Kathy." Ty had finished breakfast and was sitting across the table from her, desperate to understand why his world had just been turned upside down. "Tell them I don't want to do it, Mommy, please."

Jade leaned toward her son, pulling him close. Tears filled her eyes, but she held them back. She didn't want Ty to see her crying. There would be time for that later.

"I'm sorry, honey. I'm trying hard as I can to change this. We need to pray, okay? God will help us be together again."

Jade believed it with every fiber in her being. If she had doubted it for a moment, she would collapse with grief. Instead, she viewed this as a stunning mistake, an oversight that would be corrected soon. It had to be. A person didn't lose custody of her child because of her faith. Not in the United States.

She ran her hand over Ty's back and felt him shaking. "It's okay, honey. Mommy's going to pray, okay?"

Ty nodded, sobbing quietly against her sweater. Jade closed her eyes and lowered her voice so that it sounded soothing, even to her. "Dear Jesus, we are so sad at what's happened. Please help me get Ty back soon, and please be with him as he goes to live with his dad for a while. Amen."

Ty pulled away and studied her. "How come God let this happen to me, Mom?"

Jade had no answers. She smoothed a lock of hair off Ty's forehead and kissed his cheek. "God has a plan in this, Ty. Things are going to work out. I promise."

For a moment she could picture Tanner whispering those same words to her so long ago. Things hadn't worked out then. Jade sighed. *Help me, Lord. My faith is so weak.*

Her prayer was interrupted by a phone call. "I'll be right back, sweetheart." She tousled Ty's hair, moved into the kitchen, and answered the phone. "Hello?"

"Mrs. Rudolph?"

Jade recognized the voice on the other end, but she wasn't sure from where. "Yes. This is she."

The man sighed in what sounded like relief. "I found you. This is Matt Bronzan with CPRR, the Center for Preserving Religious Rights. I believe we spoke last week, am I right?"

Panic coursed through Jade. "Uh, yes. I called about my divorce."

"Mrs. Rudolph, I saw the article in *The Oregonian.* You lost custody of your son two days ago, is that right?"

Jade struggled to speak past the lump in her throat. If this man knew who she was and the problem she was facing, did Tanner know, too? And if he knew, was it possible he realized who she was? "I…yes, at the…"

The man seemed to understand her sorrow. "It's all right. Take your time." He hesitated. "We'd like to represent you, Mrs. Rudolph. If that would work for you. We feel confident we can win back your custody rights."

Tears streamed down Jade's face, and a sob made its way to the surface. "I'm sorry. This is…very hard."

"I understand." The man paused. "Have you heard of our firm, Mrs. Rudolph?"

Jade's crying subsided and she uttered a shaky sigh. "Yes."

"Then you've heard of Tanner Eastman, the man who founded it."

Heard of him? There was no way to hide from him. Jade remembered that day at Doris Eastman's house, the day she learned the truth about Tanner. She had intended to leave everything about him behind her. She had taken complicated detours in life and done her best to lose track of him. Instead, his was the first face she saw every night while she slept. And in the morning, he was sitting at her breakfast table, smiling at her through the eyes of the little boy that meant everything to her.

"Yes, I've heard of him."

Matt Bronzan sounded relieved. "He's the best in cases like this. He and I would like to handle it together." He paused, and Jade wondered if she could stand the shock of seeing Tanner again. Certainly his mother had kept her promise and told him nothing of her pregnancy. He would never guess that Ty was his son. Or would he?

"I'm not sure..." Her head was swimming. If Tanner found out, would he seek custody rights, too? Would he refuse to represent her case because the child was really his? Would he bring out a team of lawyers to sue her for defamation?

"Mrs. Rudolph," the man's voice was suddenly filled with concern. "It is not easy to overturn a decision. Especially one such as this. I think you should consider—"

"I'm sorry." Jade interrupted. What was she thinking? So what if Tanner found out the truth? If he could help her win back custody of Ty, however that might happen, then she needed to agree. There was no other choice. "Please forgive me, Mr. Bronzan. Yes...I'd like your help very much."

For a moment she considered telling this man that she knew Tanner. That way there would be no surprises. But she couldn't bring herself to say the words. It had been too many years.

"We'd like to fly up and meet with you Thursday if possible. That way we can get to know you and the case a bit better."

Jade managed a short laugh. "You mean see if I'm really a religious fanatic, like the paper says?"

The man did not laugh in response. "After our talk the other day, I'm confident you're not a fanatic or a freak. But still, we need to talk."

Jade squeezed her eyes shut. "Okay. Thursday is fine." How could this be happening? After all these years she would actually see Tanner face to face in just a few days. What would she say to him? Would she hate him for pretending to love her all those years ago?

They finished making plans, and Jade hung up the phone. Her heart raced for fear of the future—especially the immediate future when she would turn her son over to deputies. But somehow, as she made her way back to Ty, she found the courage to believe God was working.

And that seeing Tanner again might actually be part of the solution.

Four hours passed while Jade and Ty sat curled on the sofa, taking turns reading aloud from Michael Jordan's biography. Two suitcases sat nearby, packed with her son's favorite clothes and books and his basketball. When they grew tired of reading, they talked about his season and how quickly the years would pass before he'd play ball in high school.

"You're still going to come to my games, right, Mom?" Ty's eyes were dry and Jade was thankful. She'd prayed constantly throughout the afternoon, aware that her darkest moment was approaching. She owed it to Ty to be strong, and she was pleased to see he was not as frightened as he had been earlier.

"I wouldn't miss 'em." She kissed the top of his forehead. "I'm your biggest fan."

"Do the police have to be there?"

Jade felt her heart sink. "No, Ty, why would you think that?"

"They have to be there when we spend time together, right?"

She felt her shoulders slump, and regardless of her resolve, her eyes grew wet again. "Yes." She hugged him close. "But only for a while."

"But why, Mom? You didn't do anything wrong."

"I know, sweetheart, but the courts are afraid I might take you and run away with you."

Ty's eyes lit up. "Hey, that's a great idea! We could pack our bags and head for the woods or something. Kinda like a movie. The Wilderness Family, maybe."

Jade studied her son, and her heart swelled with love for him. "Does sound sort of fun, doesn't it?"

"I'm serious!" Ty was on his feet. "My stuff's ready. We could have yours packed in a few minutes and be gone before the police get here." He started for the stairs, but she took his hand gently in hers and pulled him back.

"Sweetie, it wouldn't work. God wouldn't want us running away like that." She framed his small face with her fingers. "We just need to believe, Ty. God's in control, and he'll help us through this. In the meantime, I'm here. Any time you want to call me, just ask your dad. The judge said phone calls were okay whenever you wanted. Even if..."

Their conversation was interrupted by a sharp knock at the door. *The police.* Jade's breathing came in short, desperate gasps. *This isn't happening. It isn't possible.* How long could she keep up the front for Ty? Jade forced herself to speak. "Come on, buddy, time to go."

Ty hung his head and clutched her sweater as she lifted the suitcases and carried them to the door. They heard a second knock, and Jade caught the fearful look in her son's eyes. She stooped down and met him at his level. Her throat was swollen with emotion and her voice was barely audible. "It's okay. You'll be back before you know it."

She stood and forced herself to open the door. Two somber deputies stood there, and beyond them Jade could see Jim and his attorney waiting near Jim's vehicle. None of this made sense. Why didn't they trust her? She would have handed Ty over to Jim without the presence of officers and attorneys. Did Jim honestly think a police force was necessary to be sure she complied with court orders?

"Mrs. Rudolph, we've come for the boy." The larger of the two officers stepped forward, and Jade wanted to push him off her porch. She felt like a criminal, and she could see Ty was starting to cry as he hovered beside her.

"If you don't mind waiting down the walk a bit." Jade studied the man through her tears. "I need to say good-bye."

The deputies nodded, took Ty's suitcases, and retreated ten paces. When they were out of earshot, Jade stooped once more to Ty's level. He flung his arms around her neck and spoke in a muffled voice Jade knew she'd remember forever. "I love you."

Jade swallowed hard. "Love you more." She stroked the back of his head, clinging to him as if by doing so she could make the deputies outside disappear, make everything right, the way it had been before. "Ty, whatever happens, however long this takes, you know that Mommy loves you, right?"

Ty nodded. She could see he was trying to be strong. His cheeks were wet with tears, but he stood proudly, his back tall.

"Okay, then, come here." Jade pulled her son close and held him, soaked in the warmth of his little body, and tried to memorize the feeling. She would miss him so much she wondered if she'd survive. The part of her that was moving and breathing and making decisions knew that through Christ she could do all things.

But right now she felt like a blind person balancing on a tightrope strung a thousand feet above shark-infested waters.

"I don't want to go." Ty's voice broke, and it brought another wave of tears in Jade.

"Honey..." She looked at him, searching his eyes, willing him to understand.

His gaze fell and he nodded. "Okay. Bye..."

"Bye, honey. Call me." She pulled him close once more. "And pray. We have to pray for each other, okay?"

One of the deputies shifted positions. "Ma'am, we need to take custody now. Your husband is waiting."

Jade wanted to scream at the officer. Let Jim wait. Let him watch how Ty clung to her and hated to say good-bye. Let him see that he was using this child as a pawn and very nearly destroying him in the process.

She closed her eyes and willed the entire scene to disappear. *Why, Lord? Why are you letting this happen?*

Trust in the Lord with all your heart and lean not on your own understanding.

The Scripture flooded her with enough strength to open her eyes, to let her precious son go. She glanced at the officer. "He's coming."

She rested her hands on Ty's shoulders and smiled through her tears. "You gotta go, Ty. I love you."

"I love you, Mom." Ty hung his head and pulled away. The separation was as painful as if someone had sliced her arms off. She stayed stooped down, sobbing quietly, watching as Ty walked four steps and then five. Then as one of the officers held out his hand, her son stopped and spun around.

"*No!* I won't go!" He raced back to her and flung his arms around her neck. Jade clutched him and covered the back of his head with her open hand, stroking his hair, holding him close as he sobbed out loud. Ty had never cried like this before, and for a moment, Jade wished she had acted on her earlier impulse to run away with him. She should have taken him to Canada or Mexico. Some place where she could love the Lord and not lose her son because of it. At least then she could have spared him this pain. Spared them both.

At least until they were caught. And then she'd never have seen him again.

She sighed. No, this was the only option. She would work with Tanner and his law firm, and they would win Ty back. It had to happen. She held her son and let him cry until he had calmed down. "Honey, you have to go. I'm sorry, baby."

Ty nodded. "I'll be back, right? Soon?" His eyes were filled with uncertainty, his face red and puffy, streaked from so many tears.

"Soon. I promise."

Ty swallowed hard, kissed her on the cheek once more, and then turned and walked to the waiting officer. He kept his gaze downward as the officers handed him over to Jim. He would go, but not gently, not willingly. Jade wondered if the officers could see how ludicrous the situation was.

Ty climbed into Jim's backseat and turned to face her. She kept her eyes locked on his and saw that he was crying hard again. Sobbing. Probably out loud. *Why, God? What good can come from this?* The last thing she saw before Jim and his attorney drove out of sight was the tormented face of her only son, his hand up against the glass of the rear window, and the single word he repeated over and over again: "Mom!"

With visions of him threatening to suffocate her, Jade limped inside, grabbed a jacket Ty had forgotten, and collapsed on the tiled floor. She lay there, sobbing and clutching the jacket, savoring the smell of her little boy until she had no more tears left to cry. Finally, when she could find the strength, she pulled herself up and forced herself toward the bedroom.

With Ty gone she was empty, dead inside. Everything hurt and nothing mattered. That night as she tossed on her bed, God made one thing painfully clear:

Whatever it might cost her personally, she was ready to face Tanner.

Twenty-six

TANNER ARRANGED FOR THE MEETING TO TAKE PLACE IN AN empty classroom at a large church in downtown Portland. According to Matt, the woman hadn't wanted to meet at her house, and certainly a diner would be too distracting. The classroom would be quiet and neutral, and hopefully set the woman at ease so they could get to know her and the story behind her loss of custody. He and Matt arrived at nine-thirty, half an hour early. They spread an assortment of briefs over the table and studied them one last time.

Over the past week they had requested the help of nearly everyone in the office, making certain every case regarding parental custody and issues of faith was researched and summarized. The summaries were contained in the briefs that now filled the table.

"There's enough precedence here to win an appeal without even making an appearance." Matt tossed the last of the cases on the table, folded his arms, and stared at Tanner. "I still can't believe we're doing this."

"Believe it."

"I mean, who'd have thought it?"

Tanner remembered Peter and the people of Hungary. "I have a feeling it'll get worse before it gets better." He ran his fingers over the assorted documents, recalling the highlights of each case. "Bottom line is Jade Rudolph. What kind of mother is she?"

Matt shrugged. "Hard to tell from our conversations."

"But she's not a cult member draped in white linen refusing her son medical treatment and encouraging him to drink cyanide Kool-Aid. We know that much."

"She's definitely not that."

Tanner straightened the documents and pulled out a single sheet, a retainer that the woman needed to sign if she wanted the CPRR to represent her appeal. "The only problem here is the local judges."

"A bit liberal?" A grin spread across Matt's face.

"They define the word."

"Still, it's crazy. We'll win the appeal hands down."

"I'm worried about it."

"Why?"

"Because these days certain judges enjoy going against precedence. Charting their own course in history."

Matt grew pensive. "I hadn't thought of that."

"Before too long, everyone in America will know about this case. Last week it was played on wire stories across the country. Soon the talking heads will get hold of it, and long before the appeal, public opinion will be set—or at least the media's view of public opinion. Jade Rudolph will be dragged through the gutter before this is said and done. She'll be accused of being intolerant, hateful, extreme…."

"Taking Jade Rudolph's son from her is hardly a way of eliminating hate."

Tanner nodded slowly. "You and I know that. But the media wields a fickle finger at times. When I first took on religious freedom cases, they applauded me as a hero, a voice where once there had only been silence. My practice exploded overnight because of the media's positive attention…. But Jade's story is something else entirely."

"The Channel One thing?"

"The media has long supported Channel One as an educational tool. By taking a stand against it, Jade's put herself in a tough spot."

"So you think public opinion could hurt the case?" Matt shifted positions and eyed Tanner curiously.

"It could. In some ways the timing is perfect for a precedent case that would send a message to everyone: Watch yourself. Too much faith might be a bad thing."

"You really think so?"

Tanner remembered the feelings he'd had recently, warnings, almost as if God was trying to tell him something about this case. He had long since dismissed the idea that this woman could be his Jade. But still he felt for her. "All we can do is feed the public a vivid picture of the kind of mother Jade Rudolph really is. Then we cite our case precedence and, of course, the protection offered by the constitution."

Matt glanced at his watch. "She should be here soon. You have the tape recorder ready?"

Tanner tapped his briefcase. "I'm not bringing it out unless she's willing to give me a deposition today, and even then—" There was a knock. Tanner glanced across the room. "I'll get it."

He stood, reached for the door, and pulled it open. As he did, the woman came into view—and the shock was like a sucker punch to his gut, leaving him struggling for breath....

God, Father, it's her.

He stood frozen in place. It was like seeing a ghost, an image lifted from some long ago memory. How long had he searched for her? How many times had he imagined this, wondered what he would say, how he would react?

"Jade..." It came out low and ragged.

"Hello, Tanner." She wasn't surprised. She had known he'd

be here. The truth of that hit, and it was like a physical blow. She'd known he would be here, and still she hadn't called him.

He composed himself and stilled his trembling hands. "Why didn't you tell me?" His voice was a whisper, and he felt tears in his eyes. It didn't matter that she didn't love him anymore, maybe never had. She was here, inches from him, and no matter what had gone wrong so many years ago, she was still the only woman he had ever truly loved.

"I couldn't." She looked the same. Her face was unlined and, though he wouldn't have believed it were possible, even more beautiful. But something was different about her eyes. They were still green, but they didn't sparkle. Instead they held a dense layer of fog, a cloak protecting her from anyone who might try and see into her soul.

Whatever life had dealt Jade, it had left her unwilling to share it with anyone. Especially him. Tanner guessed the barrier harbored an ocean of sadness. *What are you thinking, Jade? What happened a decade ago that drove you into another man's arms?*

He was trapped in her gaze, studying her, a million questions fighting for position when he heard Matt laugh behind him. "Aren't you going to let her in?"

Tanner broke the lock he held on Jade's eyes and stepped aside. "I'm sorry. Come in, Jade."

Matt looked from Tanner to Jade and back. "Did I miss something?"

Tanner searched Jade's face again and shivered. She was cold as ice. "Uh…Jade and I were friends. A long time ago."

A knowing look crossed Matt's face as Jade took a seat next to him and clutched her purse tightly in her lap.

She hates me, Lord. What did I ever do to her?

He cleared his throat. The last thing he wanted to do was

talk about Jade's custody battle. He wanted to excuse Matt and not let her out of the room until she told him what happened.

"Do you still think you can win my son back for me?" As cold as she was toward Tanner, her eyes were filled with hope, and he remembered a conversation they'd shared over pizza once during that long ago summer. If there had been one thing Jade was determined to do in life, it was to stand by her child. She'd been so determined, that she'd told him she'd rather not have children at all if she couldn't offer them a stable home. Again Tanner wondered what went wrong.

"It isn't a clear-cut case. We've done some research on custody cases involving issues of faith. On the surface..."

The words faded to a halt. Tanner couldn't think, let alone talk. He couldn't make sense if he tried. Not with Jade Conner in the same room and a lifetime of unanswered questions dying on the table between them.

He shot a look at his partner and Matt cut in. "On the surface your case looks like an easy win. There's no way a mother should lose custody of her child because of her belief in God. But what we're seeing lately is a shift in public opinion. It's okay to believe in God. Not okay to take a public stand on issues of faith, on areas where morality might be perceived as intolerance."

Jade drew a shaky breath and stared at Matt. "If there's some kind of law these days stating that *I* have to be tolerant of their views, don't they also have to be tolerant of *mine?*"

Matt cocked his head. "Depends. Tolerance is a one-way street. The social definition is to have a viewpoint that is politically, morally correct. The courts and government and media tell us we should accept all faiths, all lifestyles. What you've done is crossed a line. You've taken a stand against Channel One and apparently several other issues that the mainstream is choosing to accept."

"Isn't that my choice?" Jade's voice rose.

Tanner leaned back in his chair and watched her. So some things hadn't changed. She was still a fighter.

"Yes and no. If you were a single parent, no one would have a problem with your decisions to defend your faith. But…"

Jade's face fell and Tanner could see the regret. "Since I'm married it's different, right?"

"Right." Matt crossed his arms. "Now two parents are involved. Your husband was able to convince the judge that his tolerant, accepting mind-set made him a better parent than you."

"So why not force us to split custody? Why take him away from me?"

Tanner stepped back into the conversation. "Because parents like you have become a danger to the system. You teach your child biblical truths and clear-cut lessons on right and wrong, and suddenly, in their eyes, you've brought up a clone, another voter among the masses who isn't politically correct." He rested his elbows on the table and looked at Jade. He'd had time to catch his breath. They could talk about their past later. "At the same time, you deny your husband the chance to raise the boy with a liberal mind-set."

Jade shifted her gaze back to Matt's. "Why is his way better than mine?"

Tanner answered, forcing Jade to look at him again. "Because, like Matt said, public opinion has it that people strong in faith are dangerous, that we're hateful."

Jade's eyes locked on his. *"We're?"*

Tanner felt as if he'd been slapped by the challenge in her tone. "Yes. You and Matt and I. Everyone at the CPRR has a deep and devoted faith."

Her gaze fell to her hands. "I wasn't sure."

What is she saying, Lord? What's happened to her?

Trust in the Lord with all your heart and lean not on your own understanding....

Tanner felt himself relax. Jade obviously had something against him, but there would be time later to talk about that. Now they needed to get through the interview.

The look in Tanner's eyes told Jade he was upset, and she found that disturbing. He hadn't cared for her anymore than he cared for the other women he'd been with. Why had he looked so pained since she opened the door?

He was asking her questions about Ty, about their relationship and daily routine. "How old did you say he was?"

Jade felt her heart rate double. Clearly Doris Eastman had kept her promise and told Tanner nothing about her pregnancy. Still, the answers to these questions were bound to make him wonder. "Ty's nine. He'll be ten in a few months."

Tanner started writing down the information, then his pen slowed. Stopped. He looked up at her, his gaze intent. "When's his birthday?"

Jade knew he was looking for more than a date. He wanted to know when she got pregnant. She considered making up her answer, but the dates had always convinced Jim. No point in lying about a detail that would eventually come out in court. "June 14. Almost nine months after Jim and I married." She hesitated, hating the look in Tanner's eyes. What right did he have to look so upset? It was his fault, after all. He was the one who had used her and lied to her. "Ty was three weeks early."

For a moment Tanner stared at her, and Jade could see the questions in his eyes. She could almost hear him asking her why, what had happened. If only he knew that his mother had told Jade everything about his sordid past and the children he cared nothing for. Tanner's heart was cold as stone, and Jade shivered at his nearness.

Tanner broke the lock they held on each other and scribbled something on the paper. *What was he doing? Calculating dates? Does he know, Lord?* She studied him, looking for any hint that he might doubt her story and think he was the child's father.

"Why don't you tell us about your community involvement. Start with the Channel One thing, since that's been most recent."

At Tanner's change of subject, Jade was caught off guard. So, he believed her. For some reason she felt herself growing angry with him. Did he really think she could leave his arms and so quickly sleep with another man if she hadn't been absolutely desperate? Didn't he for even a moment think Ty might be his son?

She could come up with just one answer: Tanner truly didn't care.

At the end of two hours, Matt suggested they break for lunch. "We can share the case precedents with you after we eat." He stood up and stretched.

Tanner looked at his calendar. "We need to schedule a press conference as soon as possible. The buzz in legal circles is that Judge Susan Wilder might hear the case."

"Is that good or bad?" Despite the emotional strain of being near Tanner, Jade was thankful for him and his staff. She would never have been able to fight this battle without them.

"Very bad. She's a blatantly liberal judge who enjoys making examples out of conservative Christians. I'll tell you more about her later, but pray we get someone else. In the meantime, like I said, we need a press conference so we can give the media a chance to hear your side."

"The press?" Jade felt a wave of alarm. What if they hated her? What if they found out the truth about Ty?

Tanner rocked back in his chair. "They already know about the story. If we ignore them, they'll assume you have deep, dark secrets in your closet."

Oh, Tanner, if you only knew....

Matt was talking now. "Since you don't have anything to hide, this case is a prime example of religious persecution. If we want the media on our side, we need a press conference." Jade watched as Matt looked to Tanner, and she realized how highly Tanner's associate regarded him. Tanner took the cue. "We have to fly home tonight, but I could be back Monday."

"Monday's booked for me." Matt tilted his head thoughtfully. "But I could help from Los Angeles. Work the fax machines, send out data to the media, that kind of thing."

Tanner nodded and looked at Jade with a lopsided grin that caused her heart to skip a beat. The resemblance between Tanner and his son was uncanny, and Jade looked down nervously at her ringless fingers. "Well, Jade, it's up to you. We could set it for Monday afternoon. Then we'd have the morning to go over the questions you'll get that day. Does that work for you?"

It sounded like a nightmare. A picture formed in Jade's mind...Ty weeping and calling for her from the back of Jim's car, reaching for her as the car drove away. She gulped twice and the image disappeared. "Yes," she said quietly. "It works for me."

Tanner stood and straightened his things. "Okay, then, let's head for lunch."

They worked through the meal and late into the afternoon until Tanner and Matt had to leave for the airport. As the hours passed, Jade had the increasing feeling Tanner wanted to talk to her alone. By the day's end, Matt must have picked up on it, too. When they were finished, he excused himself. "We have about five minutes, Tanner. I'll be out in the car."

There was no wink or grin, nothing inappropriate. But clearly he was giving them time alone together. Jade and Tanner stood uncomfortably near the door, their arms crossed.

God, help me. What will I say to him? How can I face him alone after so many years, so many of his lies?

Tanner spoke first. "It's been a long time, Jade." His eyes searched hers, and she looked away again.

"Yes."

"Are you well, other than the obvious trouble?"

"I'm fine." She looked at him quickly. "You?"

"Good. Lots of work, doing what I love." He hesitated. "I'm getting married this summer."

Something like an arrow pierced her heart and stuck there. Her gaze dropped briefly as she struggled for the right words. *Why, Lord? Why does he affect me like this after all he did to me?* She steadied herself. "I'm…happy for you, Tanner. Really." She glanced at him but refused to maintain eye contact.

Jade had taken a dozen detours on the path of life where Tanner was concerned so that he might never find her and Ty. But the path went both ways. Now, looking at him, she knew that even if for some reason she wanted to find a way back to him, she couldn't have. Not then, when they were living on opposite sides of the country, and not now, with him inches from her. She had driven out his memory, and she had no intention of allowing it to haunt her again.

Tanner studied her and for a moment he was silent. "Why'd you do it, Jade?" When he spoke, there was something different in his voice, something that made her hurt inside despite her convictions. Tanner reached out and gently lifted her chin so she had no choice but to look in his eyes.

Tears stung at hers and she felt a lump gathering in her throat. How could any man be such a good liar? Even now he refused to be honest with her. Clearly he did not think she knew about his past, the children he'd fathered and the others he'd helped get rid of.

"Answer me, Jade. Why?"

"It's a long story."

Tanner's eyes shone, and Jade wasn't sure if he was about to cry or to yell at her. "I was coming back for you. Didn't you believe me?"

Jade had the impulse to lean over and slap him. Didn't she *believe* him? If only he knew. She didn't believe anything he said. "I guess not."

"By the time I got home you were gone." Tanner exhaled slowly. "I looked, called around. But no one had any idea who you'd married. Your father wouldn't tell me a thing."

Jade's head was spinning. What was he talking about? Her father had never mentioned Tanner's phone call. She had always believed he'd never tried to find her, all of which had only verified everything his mother had told her in the first place. They had slept together and so he was through with her. He hadn't called once since he returned to the United States. At least that's what she'd always thought. "My dad never told me...."

Tanner raked his fingers through his hair, his eyes angrier than she'd ever seen them before. "You could have called *me,* Jade, told me what happened. You knew where to find me."

"But..." Jade felt her resolve melting, and she steeled herself against him. She would not tell him. There was no point telling him the truth—that she knew about the other women. What would it prove now? They had their own lives, and this meeting was about her son, not the relationship they shared that long ago summer.

"But what?" Tanner took a step closer, and Jade saw how desperately he wanted answers.

"Nothing. You need to go. Matt'll be waiting."

Tanner's eyes were damp, searching hers, and for a moment Jade thought he might break down and cry. Instead he turned and collected his things. Before walking out of the room, he stopped and studied her one last time. "We'll be spending a lot of time together on this case, and I don't want our past to get in the way."

Jade shook her head, again unable to meet his gaze.

"But sometime, when you're ready…I want to know what happened. You owe me at least that much."

She hung her head and said nothing.

"Hey…" Tanner's tone was softer and she finally met his gaze. "I'm sorry about all this. I'm going to do whatever I can to get your little boy back for you."

"I know." She whispered the words and stared at Tanner a moment longer. "Thanks."

"Monday?"

Jade nodded. Tanner reached out and gently squeezed her arm. A show of support, the same one he'd given her the day before he left, just before they started kissing and…

She forced her mind to stop. He was not the person he seemed to be. He never had been. Besides, he was engaged to someone else now. Whoever the woman was, let her deal with his past.

His hand remained on her arm, and she felt herself stiffen under his touch. He seemed to notice and let go, taking one step backward, then heading for the door. "Bye…"

"Bye."

She stood there long after she heard his car pull away, paralyzed by the nearness of him, furious and flustered all at the same time. Saturday would be her first supervised visit with Ty, and if she found a way to get through that, she would have Monday to deal with. First, a private meeting with Tanner, and then a press conference to show the nation that despite previous reports she really was a fit mother. Even if she was a Christian.

Help me, Lord. Help me.

In that moment she was overwhelmed by the sum of it, and slowly, like a sandcastle giving way to one relentless wave after another, she sank to the floor. When her body was little more than a heap of broken dreams, gasping for direction in a world that had gone utterly dark, she did the only thing she could do. The only thing she had left.

She prayed.

Twenty-seven

THE TORTILLAS WERE WARM AND MOIST, THE CHICKEN TENDER, and the strolling mariachi singers brought a festive atmosphere to the dining room. Clearly the women in Tanner's life were having a wonderful time, running over details of the coming wedding and predicting the number of guests who would attend.

Invitations were set to go out in two months.

Tanner bit into a rolled up fajita and wondered why—if everything were so wonderful—he was unable to get Jade's face from his mind. Why he had been unable to pay attention to the conversation?

"Are you listening, Tanner? Your mother wondered if you were going to invite any friends from law school." Leslie set her fork down and stared at him. She was the only person he knew whose lipstick could withstand Mexican food. Her expression was quizzical. "You're not listening, are you?"

Tanner wiped his mouth with a linen napkin. "I'm sorry. I have a lot on my mind."

Leslie rolled her eyes. "What else is new?"

Tanner's mother clucked her tongue. "What could be more important than the concerns of your beautiful fiancée?" She smiled at Leslie, and Tanner was struck again by how quickly they'd become friends. "Men can be so dense sometimes."

Leslie laughed, but Tanner could see she didn't think his lack of attention was funny. She directed her gaze at Tanner.

"Really, don't you think you could listen for just a few minutes? Are your cases so important that you can't give me that?"

Images of Jade crowded his mind, and he blinked them back. "I said I'm sorry." Tanner reached for Leslie's hand and squeezed it. "Go easy on me, huh? I'll try to listen."

Both women looked at him, and eventually Leslie's expression softened. "Okay. Maybe it's my fault. I haven't asked you about your trip to Portland. Did you meet with the woman?"

Tanner's mother frowned. "What woman?"

"Jade Rudolph. She's the woman being sued for complete custody of her child. All because of her faith."

"Jade Rudolph?" Tanner watched his mother's color change and noticed her weathered hands begin to tremble. "You mean Jade Conner? From our old neighborhood?"

Tanner was confused. "Wait a minute...how did you know?" Back when he had first returned from Hungary his mother had sworn she did not know who Jade married or her new last name.

Leslie crossed her legs impatiently. "What girl from the old neighborhood?"

Tanner held up a hand to Leslie. "Hold on." He turned to his mother. "Answer me. How did you know her last name?"

His mother gave a small shrug and took a small bite of salad. When she had finished chewing, she set down her fork and spoke in a calm voice. "You can't expect me to remember that, Tanner. I have no idea. Someone must have told me." She paused. The color was returning to her face. "I do keep in touch with people in Virginia, you know."

Tanner shot his mother a look that said they would discuss the matter later. She had known how desperately he wanted to find Jade. She should have told him the moment she knew. He glanced at his fiancée and saw she was still waiting for an explanation. "Jade was a friend of mine growing up. We...spent time together one summer about ten years ago."

Leslie raised one perfectly arched eyebrow. "What exactly does that mean."

"Nothing." His mother waved her hand as if she was shoeing away a fly. "The girl up and married someone else the minute Tanner left. They were just friends."

Tanner felt his blood beginning to boil. He did not need his mother answering for him. He leveled his gaze at her, hoping she could read the message in his eyes. "If you don't mind, mother, I'll explain the situation."

"There was no situation—"

"Mother!" The musicians strolled past their table singing a cheery rendition of "La Bamba."

"Fine. You tell it." His mother cast a glance at Leslie and returned to her salad.

Tanner looked at Leslie. How could he explain Jade to a woman he wasn't even sure he loved? How could she possibly understand what had happened that summer between him and Jade when he didn't understand it himself. "Jade and I were very close that summer."

Leslie's other eyebrow lifted in surprise. "Is that right? And she's the woman you're representing in this big Portland case?"

"Her husband is suing her for complete custody of their child. It's a national case, bound to set precedence for years to come. Yes, she's the woman being sued."

"That's nice." Leslie tried to keep her tone light, but Tanner could see the concern in her eyes. "I'm here making wedding plans while you'll be running back and forth to some old girlfriend. Does she know you're engaged?"

Tanner met Leslie's stare straight on. "I told her about us, and don't worry. Jade is not interested in me. If she were, she would have called me years ago. She knew where to find me."

His mother had finished her salad. She pushed her bowl carefully to the side. "How many children does Jade have these days?"

Tanner thought the question strange. "One. Why?"

Again his mother's color paled considerably. "How old?"

Why was she suddenly interested in Jade? Just moments ago she was busy convincing Leslie that he and Jade had never been more than friends. "She has a boy. He's going to be ten this year."

His mother coughed hard and was forced to take a drink of water to settle her throat. "Ten?"

"Yes, Mother. Why do you ask?"

His mother took another sip of water, and her nerves seemed to settle considerably. "Seems a child that old should be able to decide for himself which parent he wants to live with."

"That's not the way the courts see it."

Leslie sighed impatiently. "Can we stop talking about Miss Portland and get back to the planning? Neither of you seems to have any idea how much goes into a wedding. We're only a few months away here and still we haven't..."

Jade and her son and whatever importance the case held in his life were forgotten as the two women in his life resumed chattering about florists and videographers and the correct layout of the ballroom where the reception would be held. Tanner watched Leslie, the way she appeared to be including him and his mother in the discussion when in truth she was *telling* them the plans. Her plans.

But that wasn't unusual. Leslie usually found a way to get what she wanted.

He remembered the early days of their relationship. Leslie was funny and charming and witty. She understood his place in the public eye and would work to enhance his image at every turn. Tanner was sure she was a believer, even if he wasn't completely convinced of her commitment to God. His feelings for her weren't what they had been for Jade, but then nothing would ever feel like that. He was older now, and the timing was right. Leslie had his best interest at heart. That was enough, wasn't it?

Tanner thought back to the night they'd gotten engaged. Hadn't that been Leslie's doing, also? He remembered driving her to dinner at the Charthouse in Malibu and thinking that one day, perhaps, he'd like to marry her. Not that night; not anytime soon. But someday. Somehow, though, through the course of conversation at dinner, they'd wound up engaged. In the hours afterward he hadn't been sure exactly how it had happened. They had started talking about the future, and before the conversation was finished, they were engaged.

Tanner had been happy enough about the arrangement. It was what he wanted, too. At least that's what he'd told himself a hundred times since.

But watching Leslie now he realized she had probably come to the Charthouse that night determined to advance their relationship. In many ways Leslie didn't need him. She would host the reception, welcome the guests. Of all the roles she played, she was most excited about being Mrs. Tanner Eastman. That was good, wasn't it? A woman should be proud of the man she was about to marry.

Tanner stared at his plate, pushed his fork around in his fajita and drifted back in time. He couldn't get Jade's face out of his mind, the distance in her eyes and the way she had avoided making eye contact with him. What had he done to make her hate him so?

As the women continued their discussion, agreeing on elements of the wedding that Tanner wasn't even aware of, he was lost in a sea of memories. He and Jade finding each other again at the supervisor's meeting, he and Jade walking along the Cowlitz River, he and Jade sitting on the edge of his bed…

A strange sensation coursed through his veins, and he felt his face grow hot. His heart remembered, but that wasn't all. Clearly his body remembered, also.

Lord, I need your help here. Make me forget her. What we did was wrong. She's changed, moved on. Help me love the woman before me, the woman you've given me.

Tanner said the prayer silently, but his tone was desperate all the same.

Because no matter what Leslie said, no matter how many plans were decided, regardless of how soon the wedding was, there was one undeniable fact.

He was still in love with Jade.

Doris Eastman had no trouble doing two things at once. And so she continued her conversation with Leslie, agreeing and keeping in step as Tanner's gorgeous fiancée chattered on about the wedding. But at the same time—without anyone at the table realizing it—she watched her son.

He was with them in body only. His mind, his heart were three-thousand miles away in Portland, Oregon. Just as they'd been for years after Jade got married.

How was it possible? How had the Conner girl found a way back into his life after so many years? And the child…?

Doris had been having chest pains lately, and though she hadn't told anyone, she had a feeling they were brought on by stress. She wanted Tanner's wedding to be perfect. Fitting for a man of his public stature. Naturally, the preparations could be stressful, especially when they were already so short of time.

Doris had grown accustomed to dismissing the pains. Stress was curable. A little change of diet would work wonders.

But the news Tanner had just revealed brought new meaning to the word stress. The moment Tanner mentioned Jade Rudolph, Doris's heart responded by seizing. She'd almost blown it by giving away the fact that she knew Jade's married name. Her father had known that much, and the second time she called him she caught him sober. Doris knew Jade was married to a man named Jim Rudolph, a school teacher in Portland, Oregon.

But she'd never let the fact slip until tonight.

Nitroglycerin. That was all she needed. A little medicine for the heart pains.

Remember the height from which you have fallen. Repent! Or I will come and remove your lampstand....

Doris massaged her eyebrows. There it was again. Another strange verse from the Bible resounding in her mind for no apparent reason at all. Verses like that had been assaulting her with almost the same regularity as the chest pains. Verses about getting right with God and repenting and asking God to give her a clean heart.

Doris was sick of such verses. Nothing but hogwash! She had no need of repentance. The lies she'd told Jade and Tanner she'd told for their own good. They didn't belong together. Certainly God didn't want her to repent of looking out for her son. And what if God *did* want that? Doris had always done things her own way. Including the manner in which she exercised her faith.

God would simply have to understand.

She forced herself to listen to Leslie's ramblings, tried to appear interested. But her chest was so tight she could barely catch her breath. Rays of pain radiated up her neck into the fleshy underneath portion of her jaw. *Calm down. Get ahold of yourself.*

The mandate did not work. Her heart began racing, and she felt a thin layer of perspiration break out on her forehead. She could pretend all evening, but the truth demanded her attention like a relentless, barking dog.

Jade had one child—a boy, ten years old. Tanner's son. Apparently she had kept her promise and told Tanner nothing about the boy's identity. Doris could hardly believe it had come to this. Tanner was representing Jade in a custody battle wherein Jade's husband wanted full custody because of Jade's faith. And all along the child wasn't even related to Jade's husband.

The child was Tanner's.

She studied her son and saw he was distraught. Oh, he put on a good face, and he knew how to respond to Leslie in a way that kept her from noticing. But Doris knew. Tanner was thinking about Jade, wondering why she'd never called. Doris would have done anything to take the pain from her son's eyes. If only he could get through this dreadful case and forget about her. Didn't he understand how much better his life was without her, how good Leslie was for him?

Doris held her breath and willed the chest pains away. What if Tanner asked Jade the next time they were together? What if they compared stories?

She could barely tolerate the thought. Again the chest pains increased, and Doris understood why. Despite her son's deep faith and strong convictions, if Tanner found out the truth about what had happened ten years ago, he might never forgive her.

In fact, he might actually hate her.

Twenty-eight

JADE SPENT SATURDAY MORNING READING THE FIRST CHAPTER OF James from the Bible, verses about considering it joy when facing trials and how the testing of one's faith develops perseverance. She knew the Scriptures were true. They had pulled her through when she and Jim first married.

For much of the past decade she had tried to forget what had happened when she showed up on Jim Rudolph's doorstep that day. But now, with her life falling apart and her husband living with another woman, Jade wanted to remember. As though recalling her every move might help her realize where she'd gone wrong.

Every part of her body had been shaking while she waited for Jim to answer the door that day. His shock lasted only a moment before a lazy grin spread across his face. "I always knew you'd come to your senses one day, Jade Conner.... Tell me, have you changed your mind about my offer?"

Jade could still hear his words echoing in the hallways of her mind. Going against everything she knew to be true and right and good, she entered Jim's house that day. He didn't ask for an explanation; didn't seem to want one. He'd been eating a tuna fish sandwich, and his breath was heavy but that didn't stop him. The moment the door shut behind them, he pulled Jade close and kissed her. It was a kiss that brought tears to Jade's eyes for want of Tanner and his kisses. But Tanner had lied to her; Jim was all she had left.

"You're not kissing me back." Jim had stared at her. "Why'd you come if you weren't sure about me, Jade?"

She remembered nearly every detail of that first afternoon. She had apologized and forced herself to return his kiss. Jim did most of the talking after that. Jade recognized his desire, and when he suggested a quick wedding, she agreed.

On her honeymoon night, as Jim undressed her, Jade had felt disgusted, worthless, a shell of the woman she'd been only a week earlier. Jim had whispered, "You're so beautiful, Jade, I can't believe you're finally mine." And while he spoke, Jade packed what was left of her heart and hid it away so that all Jim took from her that night was her body.

When they were finished, he turned to her and studied her. "I always knew you'd come to me one day, Jade. I've wanted you since the first day I saw you, and deep down I know you've always felt the same way." He kissed her again. "I promise to make you happy."

There were other times in their marriage when Jim uttered similar promises to her, and Jade believed he had intended to keep them. But she'd never been comforted by his words. She remembered being overwhelmed by the deepest sense of grief. Almost as if someone had died....

Only now did the feeling make sense. The death had been her own.

Jade drew a deep breath and remembered that though she'd been suffering morning sickness the day after her wedding, she had managed to hide it from her new husband. After that, they settled into a routine. He worked; she looked for a job, and when she didn't greet him with a smile or seem to enjoy their time in bed, he would look at her, an odd sadness in his eyes.

So Jade worked harder. After a month, she was so good at acting, Jim seemed to believe her when she told him she was happy. About that time, she broke the news about being pregnant.

A strange look had crossed Jim's face, something hard and a bit frightening. For a moment, Jade was sure he knew the truth. Instead he just smiled. "Any baby of yours is bound to be beautiful, Jade. Let's make sure we keep an eye on your weight."

The subtle attacks on her faith began about a month later.

She could see him still, shaking his head at her for reading her Bible.

"Myths and fables, Jade. Surely you know that…." He put his hands on her shoulders, massaging them. "Of course, some of it makes sense. Doesn't the Bible say something about the wife's body belonging to her husband?"

She didn't think Jim meant harm with his comments. Not really. Faith in God was simply foreign to him. Since she didn't want to argue, Jade had never known what to say, how to answer him. Usually he didn't give her enough time anyway. He'd tug the Bible from her hands, smiling at her. "How about focusing less time on this little book and more on your husband?"

She grew frustrated with herself at the memory. Why had she rushed into marriage in the first place? So that Ty would have a father, a real home with two parents, and dinner that wasn't provided by the government? In light of the crisis she was facing now, the reasons seemed ridiculously unimportant.

Why was I so dense, Lord? Why didn't I see how poorly matched we were. How far apart we were? And how much those differences would hurt us? She stretched her legs across her bed and eased down into the pillows. There was no denying what had happened. She had known Jim wasn't right for her, recognized it all along. That's why she turned down Jim's proposal. But when

Tanner betrayed her, she listened to her own reasoning rather than listening to the Lord. In the process, she had hurried into the marriage with Jim. *Why didn't I wait on you, God?*

She felt tears form as the question hung in her mind. There were other times, moments that made being married to Jim tolerable. They had quiet nights with rented movies and popcorn and conversations about his students. Those had ended in the last few years…a fact Jade hadn't understood until now.

One thing she did know; God hated divorce. It was his will that they remain married and that somehow, through some miracle, Jim might turn his heart to God and change his ways.

Even now Jade desperately wished Jim would hear God's voice and change his mind. The Lord could breathe man into existence. Surely, he could heal her hurt and Jim's betrayal and change him into a believing, godly husband.

Jade set her Bible down and slipped her hands behind her head. Now that she'd had time to think about it, Jade realized he'd probably been having an affair with Kathy for more than a year. Before that, she was sure he'd been faithful. Whatever the reason, she'd held some sort of spell over Jim since their teenage days.

"Sometimes I hate your faith, Jade," he told her once. "But there's something about you, something I've always wanted to call my own. And now that I have you, I won't let you go. Not ever."

It was Kathy Wittenberg who'd put him over the edge. Whatever he felt for Kathy had served to break the spell. In that woman's company, Jim had begun seeing Jade's community involvement as more than an annoyance.

She wanted to believe there was still hope for their marriage. But lately, especially during her quiet times with God, Jade had begun to accept her situation for what it was. Jim wasn't coming back; and if she didn't get significant help from Tanner and the CPRR, Jim and Kathy could wind up with Ty.

Jade turned and gazed out her bedroom window. The pain she felt wasn't about Jim; it was about missing Ty, missing the stable life she had always wanted for him. Jim's affair hadn't hurt her the way it might have. After all, he had never owned even a small piece of her heart, and he couldn't break what he didn't have.

Not like Tanner had.

She pulled on a pair of new jeans, a white turtleneck, and a sweatshirt with the words Shamrock Elementary printed on the front. Jim had taken an apartment across town near the high school. Ty had called each night during the past week and informed her that he had his own bedroom and spent much of his time there.

"Dad's girlfriend is here all the time. They sit on the couch and do all this mushy stuff, so I just go to my bedroom every night and read and talk to you. Mom, I hate this so much."

In many ways, Jade felt like they were both in prison, unable to be together, at the mercy of a man who did not love Ty and a legal system that no longer valued faith. A system that, in fact, rebelled against it. Jade sprayed her favorite perfume and ran a brush through her hair. She always took care of herself, and today would be no exception. Even if her world was crashing in all around her.

She was tired of thinking about Jim and what had gone wrong in their marriage. With an hour left before her scheduled visit, she curled up in a comfortable chair nestled in the corner of her bedroom and gazed out the window. The tulips were making their way out of the ground, and in a few weeks they would dot the Northwest with a brilliance that seemed almost artificial.

The landscape faded, and suddenly Jade's mind drifted back

to the classroom, remembering Tanner the way he'd looked a few days earlier. Why had he acted so strangely? He was the one who'd lied, the one who'd gotten other women pregnant and shunned his responsibility as a father. How could he question the fact that she hadn't called him?

She sighed and watched a hawk drift over the makeshift baseball field across the street. His flight lasted less than a minute before he swept down, grabbed a mouse in his talons, and soared back to his perch in the trees.

That was her. The helpless field mouse. There for the taking for whatever hawk might choose to sweep overhead. Last week the hawk had been Jim and his attorney, then the judge, and now Tanner. It didn't really matter. Now that she'd lost Ty, Jade would gladly take a ride in the talons of any bird of prey. If it meant getting Ty back, she'd do whatever God asked of her. Even spending time with Tanner.

Lord, if only you'll help me survive it all.

There was only silence.

Are you there, God? Jade closed her eyes and tried to hear his voice. Finally, faintly a single Scripture ran through her mind: *I know the plans I have for you...plans to give you hope and a future.* Jade sighed and felt her eyes fill with tears. That wasn't the voice of God. It was memories of her past. Seeing Tanner had brought them to mind again, but clearly they did not apply to her situation now. Her future plans had evaporated like rain on an August afternoon. Life was nothing without Ty.

Jade stood and wiped her eyes dry. It was time. She was about to spend an hour with her son, and at that moment she didn't care that it would be in the presence of deputies. Before now, she and Ty had never been apart longer than a night, and no matter the circumstances all she wanted was to hold him and feel him in her arms again.

She made the drive quickly and saw that the officers were waiting. One of them rolled down the squad car window and motioned for her to join them. She parked and did as they asked.

"We don't think the boy's in any danger, ma'am." The older deputy did the talking. "Crazy case, if you ask me."

Jade shifted positions. "What are you saying? Can I visit with him alone?"

The deputy shook his head. "Nope. 'Fraid not. But how about we wait right here? Catch up on our paperwork. You and the boy can sit in your car or on the grass here. Wherever you like. We'll stay out of your way."

Jade's heart swelled. These men were on her side. They saw how ridiculous the situation was. She smiled at them through eyes clouded with tears. "Thank you."

The older officer tipped his head and leaned back in his seat, directing his attention to the paperwork on his lap. Drawing a deep breath, Jade turned, walked up to the apartment, and rang the doorbell. It took Ty just seconds to fling the door open and run into Jade's arms.

"Mom!" Her son's arms flew around her neck.

"Oh, honey, I've missed you so much." She forced herself not to cry. Ty was so happy to see her she didn't want to give him a reason to be sad.

They sat together on the porch step, Jade with her arm around Ty as he told her about school and basketball and his father's girlfriend. "She's not even pretty, Mom."

"Is that right?" Jade grinned at her son.

"Oh, man, you should see her. Big nose. Big teeth. I think she teaches biology or something. Probably spends her days mopping up frog guts."

Jade laughed. It felt so good to be with Ty again, and it made her more determined than ever. She would work with

Tanner, and very soon she would regain custody of her son. For now, Jim was paying the mortgage and sending her enough money to survive. But eventually—after she won the case—she and Ty would move to another state, and she would have to get a job. That way she wouldn't have to rely on Jim, and after a year or two he was bound to give up the custody issue. Then she could have Ty all to herself.

The hour flew by, and long before she was ready to leave, Jim poked his head out. "Time's up."

Jade wanted to ask him when he'd become such an attentive father that he might actually miss an hour of Ty's time. She wanted to shout a dozen retorts at him and kick the door shut. Instead, she just nodded.

Give me the right words, Lord. Everything I say he'll write down and pass along to his attorney. Help me, please.

She felt a peace wash over her. "Thank you, Jim." She smiled at her husband and turned to Ty. "I'm sorry, honey, what were you saying?"

Her composure seemed to irritate Jim, and he raised his voice. "I said time's up. Now get out of here before I have the deputies haul you out in handcuffs."

Ty began crying, and he stood up, facing Jim. His fists were clenched, and his face was red with anger. "Leave her alone!"

Jim opened the door wider and raised his hand threateningly over Ty. Just as he was about to strike the boy, he realized the deputies were watching him. Easing back into the house, Jim hissed at Ty from a place just out of view of the patrol car. "Don't you sass off to me, boy, you hear?"

Ty was sobbing harder, and he said nothing as Jim disappeared back into the house. Instead, he turned to Jade and wrapped his arms around her neck. "Don't leave me here, please, Mom."

Jade tried to speak, but a lump had formed in her throat.

She blinked back tears and struggled to find her voice. "It's okay, honey." She ran a hand over his back and thought about the last time they'd said good-bye. Was this how it was going to be every Saturday until she got him back? And what if Tanner couldn't make it happen? What if she didn't get her son back? She closed her eyes tightly and held him close. "You can come home soon, Ty. I promise."

The boy was still crying, but he pulled away, his eyes pleading with her. "Dad said I can't ever go home. He said he was going to take you apart for the whole world to see."

A flicker of anger became a hot, burning flame in Jade's heart. "He has no right telling you that, honey. It isn't true."

Ty hung his head. "He says a lot of bad things about you, Mom."

Jade felt like she was suffocating. *Help me, God. This is your problem, not mine. I can't deal with it alone.* She drew a deep breath. "I'm sorry he's doing that. But you know the truth, right?"

Ty wiped his eyes and seemed to catch his breath. "Don't worry, Mom. I know you a lot better than that."

"Okay. Let's pray before I go, huh?"

Ty sat beside her again and held her hand as Jade led them in prayer, begging God to end their separation and to let the truth be known. When they were finished, Ty hugged her, kissed her, and promised to call each night.

"Hurry, Mom, please. I want to come home."

Ty kissed her one last time and then vanished behind the apartment door. Jade walked back to her car, waved to the officers, and slipped behind the wheel. There, safely away from Jim and Kathy and Ty and the deputies, Jade cried as if her heart would break.

Ty's pained expression and the way he'd begged her not to

leave haunted her as she drove home. If Jim wanted to fight, then she was going to have to be a worthy opponent. Especially when the stakes were so high. As she parked the car and went inside she begged God to give her a way out, show her a way in which she might be more effective.

Pray, my daughter. Bring it to me in prayer.

Of course. Jade pulled out her Bible study list and began making phone calls. They would have to meet the following evening because Jade would be busy the rest of the week. Any other time they might have postponed the gathering altogether. But the group hadn't met since she'd lost custody of Ty. These were faithful women, friends who would jump to her assistance and pray without ceasing until the matter was resolved and Ty was home where he belonged. If ever she needed the prayers of her friends, it was now.

One by one the women in the Bible study group arrived at her house until finally Jade was ready to begin. When they were all arranged in a circle, she drew a shallow breath and began speaking. "You've all seen the newspapers?" She looked at the faces around her and saw compassion there.

"So it's all true…?" Susan leaned forward, her elbows on her knees. "They took Ty because you're a Christian?"

"That's not what they're saying. The judge said my extreme views were unhealthy for a young child and that he'd be safer with his father."

Jackie sat across from Jade, and tears filled her eyes. "That means they took Ty because of your faith. It's the same thing. What they're basically saying is that the courts feel it's okay to take our children away if we choose to stand up for what we believe in."

Jade nodded. "That's right."

"Are you doing okay financially?" Jackie hadn't asked before, but Jade didn't mind discussing the issue with these women.

"I'm fine. Jim's paying the mortgage and sending me enough money to survive. Maybe just to make himself look good, but at least I'm okay that way." She wanted to ask them to pray about the situation with Tanner, but she wasn't sure what to say. None of the women knew about Tanner and the role he'd played in her life ten years ago. Still, she needed their prayers on every side, and she thought quickly how best to ask.

"There's going to be a press conference tomorrow, is that right?" Jackie's face was tear streaked, masked with concern.

"Right. And there's something else. The man who's going to represent me is Tanner Eastman."

Lydia perked up. "I've heard of him. He's perfect for this kind of case."

Jackie nodded. "A Christian man, brilliant and full of integrity. Sounds like an answer to prayer."

"He's the perfect guy if you ask me." Susan smiled. She was a single mother and often commented on how few unmarried Christian men there were. "Single, gorgeous, and sold out to God. Maybe you could introduce me."

Jade knew Susan was joking, but she couldn't bring herself to laugh. If only they knew the truth.... "Tanner and I were friends a long time ago, and, well, just pray about that, too. That I'll have the strength to get through it."

Susan squirmed uncomfortably in her chair and seemed to be fighting herself to keep from asking a question. In a matter of seconds she lost the battle and spoke out. "Were you and Tanner...you know...did you date him?"

Jade shook her head quickly. "Nothing like that. But there were some hard feelings. I don't want what happened in the past to play a part in this situation." She hung her head, and tears spilled from her eyes onto the legs of her jeans. "The only thing that matters is Ty. That's what the press conference is all about."

Jade saw that Susan wasn't convinced about the role Tanner had played in her life. Either way the discussion about Tanner was closed. Jade shifted her gaze to the other women and reached for a tissue from a nearby endtable. "Also please pray I say the right things in front of the cameras tomorrow. I need to maintain my stance on morality and faith and somehow avoid coming across as weird or different because of it."

The ladies nodded, and after a brief discussion they bowed their heads, joined hands, and prayed for Jade. That she would have comfort in the temporary loss of Ty, wisdom to speak with the reporters the next day, and strength to face Tanner.

They prayed for nearly an hour, and then the women went home, leaving Jade alone with her thoughts. In twelve hours she and Tanner would be together again, and she realized there was one thing the women hadn't prayed for that night. Because in light of everything that was happening so quickly around her, there was no way she could ask the Bible study group to pray for something she shouldn't have been struggling with in the first place....

The feelings she still had for Tanner Eastman.

Twenty-nine

TANNER CALLED THAT MORNING, AND THEY AGREED TO MEET AT Starbucks at Jantzen Beach—an outdoor shopping mall in northwest Portland along the Columbia River. Jade wasn't hungry, and Starbucks had quiet tables so that she and Tanner could talk without being interrupted.

Jade arrived first and ordered a decaffeinated latte. Her heart was racing badly enough without adding caffeine to the mix. She chose a table situated in a windowless corner of the café. Starbucks was adjacent to a large bookstore, and customers were encouraged to browse through the shelves while sipping their coffee. Jade was certain no one would bother them there. The few customers who sat at tables generally stayed near the windows.

She took a sip of her coffee and stared at the front door. All morning she'd been plagued by a sense of impending doom. Several times an hour this feeling had driven her to pray, seeking God's protection in whatever the day would bring. Still, she was tempted with the notion of finding Ty at school and heading for the Canadian border.

It was raining steadily outside, and Tanner swept into the coffeehouse wearing a business suit and a long, sleek raincoat. The girl behind the counter watched him and nudged her coworker. Jade rolled her eyes. Yes, Tanner still turned heads. Was he carrying on with a handful of women despite his engagement, or had he finally learned to be faithful? Either way she pitied his fiancée. If Tanner could abandon his own children, he was bound to bring her nothing but heartache.

Tanner spotted her and quickly ordered a coffee. When he had his drink, he joined her at the table. Again his eyes looked troubled.

"Hi."

"Hi." Jade glanced at her coffee and felt her stomach begin to churn.

"How'd the visit with Ty go?"

Jade felt a stab of fear at the sound of Ty's name on Tanner's lips. *Get me through this, God, please.* "It was okay. Too fast. Too impersonal…deputies watching us the whole time."

Tanner sighed. "Did you write down anything Ty said?"

Jade pulled a typed sheet of notes from her purse. "Right here."

A smile lit Tanner's face, and Jade's heart skipped a beat. Why did he still have that affect on her? "That was fast."

"My son's at stake. It's not like I have anything else to do."

Tanner stared at her solemnly. "We'll do everything we can to get it admitted during the hearing." He reached across the table to take the notes from her. As he did, their fingers brushed against each other, and Jade jerked back, dropping the paper on the table. Tanner studied her for a moment, and then reached for the paper, opening it and reading slowly. When he was finished he said, "This is great, Jade. Pray they'll let us use it."

She hung her head. *He's reading things his own son said. This is too close, Lord. Help me.*

When Jade said nothing, Tanner moved the paper to his pocket. "I have good news and bad news."

Jade sat up straighter. "I can't take any more bad news. Give me the bad news first."

Tanner frowned. "I found out this morning. Judge Susan Wilder has been assigned the case. It's a done deal."

Jade felt the sting of fresh tears. "Great. What else can go wrong?"

Tanner nodded. "She's not good for the case, but you've got to remember, Jade, God is in control here, not Judge Wilder."

Oh, please, Tanner, stop the hypocritical religious drivel. Jade was irritated with him. A man who'd abandoned his own children had little room to talk about God being in control. "What's the good news?"

"The press conference is set. CNN's covering the whole thing. All the networks, too."

Jade looked up and felt her pulse quicken. "It's that big?"

Tanner slid his chair in closer and leaned his elbows on the table. "Jade, this is national news. A mother's never lost custody of her child because of her faith."

"What are they going to ask me?"

"They know about your involvement in community and school issues. How you had magazines removed from store shelves and books eliminated from the library."

"The magazines had pictures of some evil guy sacrificing animals on stage."

"I know."

"And the books had story lines about kids killing their teachers and classmates." Jade had done the right thing by taking on those battles, and she would do it again if the opportunity arose. If someone didn't take a stand, the children would pay the price. Jade wasn't about to let that happen.

Tanner's expression softened. "I know all that, Jade. I'm just telling you the media knows, too." He hesitated. "I might think you're a hero for doing those things. But for the most part, the media thinks in terms of freedoms. Freedom of speech, freedom of expression, that kind of thing. They see pulling magazines and books off shelves as censorship."

Jade sighed. "And that makes me look extreme."

"Right."

"So what do I do?"

Tanner leaned back in his chair and sipped his coffee. "You remain calm and pleasant. Discuss everything from the perspective of Ty and your intention to protect him. We want the press to see you as a concerned mother, one who cares deeply for her son. Not some angry radical Christian who next week might organize a hit on an abortion clinic."

Jade stirred her coffee. The only thing that angered her was losing Ty. Certainly she could do what Tanner asked, remain calm and pleasant and avoid sounding defensive. "What if they try to trick me?"

Tanner uttered a laugh. "You can count on that much. They're looking for a snappy sound bite they can play and replay on the news tonight. Something where you fly off the handle and declare them all ACLU-card-carrying liberals bent on the destruction of family values and churches in general."

Jade couldn't help but smile at his example. "So whatever I do, don't get angry."

"Whatever you do, don't say something that could be taken out of context. No long pauses or lengthy explanations. They'll cut what you say and use it to fit their storyboard."

Jade wondered if she could remember it all. "Nothing extreme; no lengthy pauses."

"Exactly."

"What about my faith? If they ask me, should I quote the Bible, or is that off limits?"

"Everyone knows you're a Christian. The story has been discussed and replayed in newspapers across the country all week. There's no point in backing down now." He paused. "Besides, I don't think that would please the Lord."

Jade wanted to laugh at him. Here was a man whose children were growing up without their father. Who was he to remind her of what it meant to please the Lord? She forced herself to remember that whatever Tanner's personal shortcomings, he was the expert when it came to these types of legal matters. "I never intended to back down." She met his gaze straight on. "I only wanted to know if there were things I should avoid saying."

Tanner studied her and set down his coffee. "Jade, can I ask you something?"

For the first time since seeing Tanner again she didn't want to run from him. She wanted to take him on face to face and find out why he had lied to her all those years ago. "Anything."

"Why are you angry with me?"

She set her drink down and crossed her arms. "I'm struggling with a lot of things, here, Tanner." *Don't cry. Whatever you do, don't cry.*

He sighed and raked his fingers through his hair, a gesture he'd done since he was a boy back in Williamsburg.

"What did I ever do to you?" He sounded sad, and he kept his eyes locked on hers. When she could stand it no longer, she looked away.

"I don't want to talk about it."

"I loved you, Jade. I wanted to marry you. I go off to Hungary for a few months, and when I come home my mother tells me you married someone else. And now *you're* mad at *me?*"

"I said I don't want to talk about it." If he pushed much more, she would tell him the truth: that she knew everything there was to know about his past.

"I don't care what you want, Jade. We need to talk." Tanner set his cup down hard, and Jade looked up at him. "I got off the plane from Hungary, and you know what I did?"

Jade waited.

"I looked all over that airport for you. I sent you a ticket, and I thought you'd be there."

More lies. "There was no ticket, Tanner. My father would have told me."

"Oh sure, just like he told you about my phone calls."

Jade considered that. "Why would you send me a ticket? You hadn't written the whole time you were there. You expected me to look for a ticket in the mail when I hadn't heard from you in two months?"

Tanner's face twisted. "I wrote you. Every other day I mailed off another letter to you."

"And I'm supposed to believe they all got lost in the mail?"

"No, try asking your father. Maybe he never gave them to you."

A strange sensation began working its way from the back of Jade's head down her spine. *It doesn't matter if he wrote, he still lied to me about his past.* "That's not the point."

"What's that supposed to mean? I'm there at the airport, looking for you, expecting you to be there, and all I see is my mother. She tells me she has bad news. I was wrong about you, she says; you've married someone else."

Tears flooded Jade's vision, and she shaded her eyes with one hand.

"Do you know something, Jade; I didn't believe her. I had to call Kelso General to see if she was telling the truth. I didn't believe it until I talked to one of your coworkers, and she told me it was true; you'd married someone in Portland."

"That's my business, Tanner." Jade uncovered her eyes, her voice little more than a whisper.

His eyes blazed with angry frustration. "Okay, so it's your business, but couldn't you have called me, told me what happened? I thought you loved me, Jade. I'm gone three weeks, and you marry someone else? I didn't understand it then, and I still don't."

"Can we talk about something else?" Jade wiped her eyes and searched Tanner's face. She didn't want to tell him why she'd left. There was no point going back to that time in her life and risking the relationship she and Ty shared. If he ever found out about Ty, she'd be the loser. Mrs. Eastman had made that more than clear.

Tanner exhaled slowly and massaged his eyebrows. "Fine. But give me this."

"What?"

"After the press conference let me take you back to your house."

Jade took another sip of her coffee and noticed her hands were trembling. She didn't want to spend more time suffering in Tanner's presence than necessary. "What for?"

"So we can talk. I want to know what happened, Jade. I'm going on with my life, getting married, putting you behind me. But it's taken a long time, and I think you owe me an explanation. At least that much."

Jade sighed. Maybe if she could tell him the truth about what she knew, without telling him why she was at Doris Eastman's that afternoon in the first place. Maybe then he'd come clean about his past, never make the connection about Ty being his son, and leave her alone. "Fine. What time do you fly out?"

"Not till midnight. I'm taking the redeye back to Los Angeles."

Jade nodded. "Okay. But let's get through the press conference first."

They finished their cold coffees in silence and headed for the door. The media was set to meet them in the lobby of the Clackamas County Courthouse in two hours.

Forty-five members of the press showed up for the conference, and Tanner wished he could watch from a distance. He couldn't stop thinking about Jade and his hunch that there was something she wasn't telling him. Whatever it was it would have to wait. The media event was crucial to their case, and Tanner would have to maintain his concentration.

Tanner took his spot in front of the podium. He thanked them for coming and introduced the case by comparing it to conditions in the former Soviet Union.

"People in this country have never had to fear the government because of their faith. Religious freedom is something guaranteed each of us in the constitution. But here in Portland, in this very courthouse, a woman dedicated to her son has been stripped of her rights as a parent because of her faith."

Tanner made eye contact with each of the reporters, careful to keep his face at just the right distance from the dozen microphones taped to the podium. He still thrived in public situations, and he felt confident as he continued. "If we allow this case to stand, then I'll tell you where we're headed. Ten years from now this kind of custody arrangement will be commonplace, and the people who make up the backbone of this great nation will find themselves being rounded up and arrested for attending church on Sunday."

He paused and saw that eight national news cameras were focused on him. "We are here today to tell the people of this country that we will not stand by idly and watch our rights be stripped away. Mrs. Rudolph will win back custody of her son, and men and women who make up the heart of our nation will be able to sleep better at night. We will fight to maintain the rights promised us by our forefathers. And we will pray, as they did, that the United States courts wake up and recognize the error of their ways."

Tanner finished his opening comments and introduced Jade. He stepped away from the podium and watched her take his place. She looked innocent and utterly beautiful. But most of all she looked sincere. Tanner knew it wasn't an act. Jade—the Jade he remembered—was the genuine article.

He studied her and watched her make a few opening remarks, informing the press that she had gotten involved in community affairs as a way of protecting her son. She hit on each of the issues upon which she'd taken a public stand and explained simply that if she hadn't acted, the problem of immorality and violence among teenagers would only increase. Finally she showed them a few snapshots of her and Ty on various outings, sailing boats in a pond, singing together around a campfire.

The photos were something she hadn't showed Tanner, and he watched her in amazement. First the detailed notes, now the photos. He should have realized she'd do everything she could to help her case. He fought for religious freedom on a national level, but in many ways she'd been doing the same thing in her community.

When she finished speaking, the press pounced with questions about her beliefs and about whether she was in favor of censorship.

"Sometimes censorship is necessary...."

From his position several feet away, Tanner cringed. She had done the very thing he had warned her not to do. *Sometimes censorship is necessary....* He could hear the line played over the networks later that evening, and he wanted nothing more than to stop the cameras and give Jade a chance to answer the question again.

Her comment certainly wouldn't make many people sympathetic.

"But that doesn't mean I'm in favor of censorship across the board. Americans must maintain our right to free speech if we are to remain a strong nation. We wouldn't have Bibles if it weren't for freedom of speech." Jade was calm, but passionate at the same time. Tanner studied the reporters and saw they were still suspicious of her. Tanner wondered if they would get past her remark about censorship being necessary sometimes. By the hard looks on their faces, he doubted it.

"However, when magazines release unfit material on our children for their own financial gain, someone needs to stand up and fight against them. We must care more about our kids than to let them fall prey to the whims of consumerism masking itself in freedom of speech."

Tanner was awestruck. Jade's understanding of religious freedom was strong enough that she could easily take her place alongside him at the CPRR offices. *Way to go, Jade.* If only she hadn't slipped up that one time early on.

The press conference wound down, and when the last reporter left, Jade turned to Tanner. She was flushed and breathless. "Well?"

"You did great."

A look of panic flashed in her eyes. "How come you sound worried?"

Nearly everything Jade said had been brilliant. But that one line, the comment Jade had made about censorship, gnawed at Tanner's confidence.

"I sound worried because I am."

Thirty

They stopped for pizza, and Jade waited in the car while Tanner picked up their order. The evening was beginning to feel too familiar, too much like it had felt when she and Tanner were together that summer. She wanted to be alone, turn on the television, see how the media would play up her interview.

But she figured she owed Tanner this one night to explain herself. Then he could admit his lies, make his apologies, and go back to Los Angeles where his fiancée waited. After that, they would have an easier time remaining on business terms throughout the proceedings, and Tanner wouldn't feel compelled to ask questions about their past.

He returned with the pizza, and Jade didn't have to ask what kind it was. It would be Hawaiian with olives. Just like the pizzas back in Kelso that summer. She stared out the passenger window and remained silent as they drove to Jantzen Beach where her car was still parked.

"I get the feeling you don't want me coming over." Tanner turned toward her and shut off his engine.

Jade shrugged and opened the car door. "We might as well get it over with."

"Look, if you don't want to—"

"No, I'm sorry." They'd come this far. Now she almost wanted to tell him the truth about what she knew. "I have a lot on my mind, but you're right. I think we should talk."

Tanner shrugged and started his engine again. "Okay. I'll follow you."

She climbed out, shut the door, and headed for her car. Fifteen minutes later they pulled up outside her home in Clackamas, a suburb in southeast Portland. They entered the house in silence.

"Nice." Tanner was making small talk, and Jade could tell he was uncomfortable. It was just before six, and Jade had no interest in making him feel at home. The news was about to come on.

"Thanks." She set out paper plates and napkins and moved into the TV room. "The news should be on in a minute."

Tanner helped himself to pizza and joined her. "Try ABC first."

She turned the channel until she found it. A serious-looking anchor told viewers that there was more trouble in Yugoslavia. "But first, we'll update you on a story that is sweeping the nation. Last week Jade Rudolph lost custody of her only son because a Portland judge deemed her viewpoints too religious, too narrow and possibly damaging to the boy. Today, Ms. Rudolph staged a press conference in the Portland Municipal Court Building alongside her attorney, religious rights fighter Tanner Eastman."

The network cut to a live shot of Tanner and his opening remarks. While a reporter shared the voice-over summary, cameras moved on to a shot of Jade responding to the question about censorship.

"Sometimes censorship is necessary...." They cut Jade's remarks there, and Tanner groaned. The reporter picked up with narrative that explained some of Jade's attempts to censor local markets and libraries. The anchor bridged to the next story by telling viewers that maybe the time had come to consider this type of thinking dangerous. Especially where children were concerned.

Jade felt her face grow hot. "How could she? They took that completely out of context."

Tanner sighed and situated himself so he could see her better. "I was afraid they'd do that. The minute you said it, I wanted to jump in and tell them what you meant."

"I told them what I meant." Jade didn't need Tanner explaining her to the press.

"Okay, but you paused." Tanner set his pizza down. "Pauses are deadly in this type situation because it gives them the perfect opportunity to cut."

The television remote shook in Jade's hand, and she flicked the channel. There she was, saying the same thing on the competing network. Only CNN included several of her statements as well as her comment on censorship. But even they were quick to say that this case might have enough merit to stand an appeal.

Why, God? Why, when you've always been so faithful to me?

She felt sick to her stomach as she prayed. Another flip through the channels showed that the other networks presented similar stories. By six-thirty, Jade flicked off the television.

For a moment there was silence. Waves of nausea battered Jade's insides, and she felt dizzy. "Well?"

"It's not good. But I don't think it'll hurt us too badly."

Jade stood up and paced away from Tanner. "What do you mean, you don't think it'll hurt us *too* badly? They made me look like a fundamentalist freak! Of *course* that'll hurt us." She whirled around and stared at him.

"Public opinion is a tricky thing, Jade. Some people might side with you because...well, because you're beautiful. No matter what you said."

He still thinks I'm—

Jade felt her face growing hot, and she was silently thankful he couldn't read her mind. "But they'll probably turn against me because of what I said, isn't that what's worrying you?"

"People might watch and think if you're pro-censorship, then maybe you *are* too extreme to raise a little boy."

Jade sat back down again, dropped her head in her hands and massaged her temples with her thumbs. "This whole thing is crazy!"

"You and I know that, but not the viewing audience." She felt Tanner's hand on her arm, and she changed positions so that it fell to his side once more. Tanner hesitated, and Jade wondered if he was going to say something about her moving away. Instead he sighed and said, "They only get what they see. And what they hear."

Jade tried not to think about what she had said, the line that had made her look like a fanatic. "So we've already lost." She could feel herself beginning to shake. She'd had one chance to face the public and tell them something that would help win back Ty. And now she'd blown it. If she didn't get him back, it would be her own fault.

"No, there's still time. Like I said, it's possible some of the people will agree with you. There's an undercurrent of thinking among many circles that perhaps our country has too much freedom of speech."

"What good will that do?" Jade hugged herself, willing her body to stop trembling.

"It depends. The judge will be swayed by public opinion. Whether that's in our favor or not will make all the difference in the world."

"So what can we do?"

Tanner leaned over his knees and met her eyes so intently Jade felt forced to look away. "Pray that people see it your way."

Jade fell back into the sofa and hung her head as tears fell to her knees. From the corner of her eye she saw Tanner move toward her and then hesitate, as if he'd changed his mind. Three feet separated them, and Jade saw pride in his eyes as he studied her. "Who cares what people think. You did great, Jade. Look at the bright side.... When you get Ty back you can come work for me."

Jade glanced up, and through her tears she felt herself smile. From somewhere deep in her heart a warning sounded: *Don't let him charm you again.* "What's that supposed to mean?"

"I could use an attorney like you. Get your law degree, and who knows." Tanner grinned, but Jade could see sadness in his eyes.

Jade was no longer smiling. *Come on, Tanner, don't play with me. Not after all we've been through, all the lies you've told me.* She crossed her arms and waited for him to be serious again.

In the wake of Jade's silence, Tanner shifted uncomfortably and changed the subject. "Really, Jade, you did great. That press conference was amazing."

Jade relaxed her shoulders and felt her defenses drop. There were still tears in her eyes, and she said, "I'm so worried about it. You do think we'll get Ty back still, don't you?"

Tanner's face clouded. "It all depends on the judge."

Jade thought about losing Ty for several months, even years, and she felt herself grow faint. It was impossible. Ty wanted to be with her; didn't that count for something?

"Lawyers, people in legal circles, they talk about this kind of case." He hesitated. "There are a few judges who might handle the hearing, but like I said before, word is we'll get Judge Wilder. If that's the case, it could mean serious trouble. She doesn't exactly broadcast her opinions, but people in the business know how she thinks. I'm afraid she might want to make an example out of this case."

"What?" Jade felt the room closing in on her. "She can't do

that."

Again Tanner started to move closer and changed his mind. "If she's the judge, she can do whatever she wants. I could ask for a different judge, but like I said, she doesn't make her opinions public. Technically there wouldn't be any grounds to grant a change."

Jade's throat was suddenly dry. "I can't believe this is happening."

"There's still a chance we'll get someone else." Tanner's gaze fell to his hands, and he sighed.

More warnings sounded on the panel in Jade's heart. Judge Wilder would take Ty away forever and then—*God, why aren't you helping us?* "Isn't there anything we can do?"

Tanner nodded and met her eyes once more. "Yes. That's why we needed this press conference."

Jade hadn't expected Tanner to have any doubts. But with Judge Wilder...Her body trembled with panic. "If we lose the hearing, then what happens?"

"We appeal it again. All the way to the Supreme Court if we have to."

Jade let her head fall back against the sofa. "That could take a year. Two years, even. Maybe three." She thought of Ty and the way he'd begged her to take him home. "I don't have three years."

Moving slowly, cautiously, Tanner made his way closer to Jade and gently squeezed her knee. "I know that, Jade. Pray for a different judge. If we get Wilder, I'll do everything I can. I'm just trying to be honest with you."

Don't touch me. Jade adjusted herself once more so Tanner's hand fell away again.

"I guess that brings us—" Tanner took in the distance between them and drew a deep breath—"to the reason we're here tonight."

Jade sat up straight and turned so she could see him. "I guess."

"You're angry with me, aren't you?"

Jade remembered how it felt when Doris Eastman told her about Tanner's children—little Amy and Justin. She thought about how Tanner had left her alone and how he'd lied to her that summer. "Yeah, I guess you could say that."

Tanner seemed to struggle for a moment, as if his own anger were bubbling just beneath the surface. She waited. The house was silent except for the subtle whirring of the refrigerator and the persistent ticking of Jade's grandfather clock in the next room. Tanner trained his eyes on hers and appeared to search for the right words. Finally he drew a deep breath.

"All day I've been thinking about this moment, wondering why in the world you'd be mad at me. And I have to tell you, Jade, I'm still in the dark."

"Come on, Tanner...." Jade was tired of playing games.

"I'm serious. I come back from Hungary, and you've married someone else." His eyes flashed, and Jade wondered how he could maintain his act so well. Did he really think he could keep the truth about his past a secret from her? "I'm sure you must have had your reasons, but really...I think you owe me an explanation, and whatever it is, I don't think it gives you the right to be mad."

That was it. Jade had heard all she could take. "Is that right?"

"Yes. You hurt me, Jade. I still don't know why you did it."

Jade cocked her head and leveled her gaze at him. "Do the names Amy and Justin mean anything to you, Tanner?"

Tanner thought a moment and his brow creased. "Yes...so? What do they have to do with us?"

She wanted to slap him. "They have *everything* to do with us. Did you really think I could go on with my plans to marry you after I found out about them?"

Tanner released a frustrated sigh and leaned closer to Jade, his face a web of confusion. "You're losing me, here. Who told you about Amy and Justin?"

"Your mother." Jade had to force herself to lower her voice. *How could he sit there and—*

"My mother? When did you talk to her?" Tanner leaned forward and dug his elbows into his thighs. His face was contorted in what seemed like genuine and utter confusion

At that instant a thought dawned on Jade, a thought so terrible it caused a churning terror deep in her gut. What if Doris Eastman had lied? What if that was why Tanner was so calm about her knowledge of Amy and Justin? After all, the truth was out, and still Tanner showed no signs of remorse, no shame. "I met with your mother a week after you left for Hungary. I wanted to talk to her about..." *Careful, Jade. Careful.* She heeded her own warning and her earlier fears. "We...agreed to meet for tea one afternoon."

Tanner looked puzzled. "And she told you about Amy and Justin?"

"Yes!" Jade felt tears burning her eyes. "How *could* you, Tanner? How could you lie to me all summer long? And how could you turn your back on those children?"

Tanner drew a deep breath and stood up. He paced the floor from the sofa to the kitchen and back. Finally he sat down and turned once more to Jade. "First of all, I never lied to you." He struggled to maintain his composure.

"How can you say that?" He had lied a dozen times, and now he was lying again. Wasn't he? Everything Doris told her was true, wasn't it? Jade had a strange feeling about the entire conversation and tears of anger and confusion streamed down her face.

"The question I have for you is this: Why do you care about my brother's children? What in the world do they have to do with you and me?"

Tanner's words settled around her like a series of hand grenades. She sat motionless for a beat, unable to move or think. Unable even to breathe. "Your brother's children?" Flashes of light began exploding in Jade's mind. *It couldn't be true.... It wasn't possible....* "Amy and Justin are...Your mother ...she said they were..."

The emotions tore through Tanner's features until his face was a study of controlled fury. He came closer and took Jade's hands in his. "What did she say, Jade?"

"Amy...and Justin...she said..." *No, God, it can't be....*

"My brother Harry is ten years older. He has two children, Amy and Justin. Now what did my mother say?"

One by one Tanner's words exploded in her heart until Jade's breathing came faster and her heart raced with uncertainty. *How could she have*—"What are you talking about? Your mother said..."

"My mother said what?" Tanner held her hands more tightly now, and Jade could see the anger building in his eyes.

"Your mother said you'd...you'd had lots of women." Jade felt as though she were free-falling through space, as if their conversation were something from a disjointed dream. In that instant she hated herself. *You idiot! You believed that old woman and now—*

Tanner squeezed her hands. "What else, Jade? What did she say?"

Jade's breathing was quicker now, jerky, a desperate gasping. She was hyperventilating, and black spots danced before her eyes. *Calm down. You have to get through this. Help me, God. Please.* "She said they were your children, and...and you didn't care about them. You were...you'd been with many women and paid for their...abortions."

Tanner burst to his feet, and his voice boomed through the house. "What? She said that Amy and Justin were *my* children?"

There was nothing Jade could do. Everything about her entire existence was being sucked from her so quickly she was convinced she would die from the shock. Her teeth were chattering so that she could barely speak. "Y-y-yes."

Hot, burning rage filled Tanner's eyes, and he stared at Jade. "She told you that and...and you *believed* her?" He spun around and kept his back to her for what seemed like an eternity.

Jade struggled to breathe. *Calm...be calm. This can't be happening.* Her heart raced faster in response. How could she have believed...? The woman was an evil, treacherous monster. Jade closed her eyes. No matter how hateful Mrs. Eastman had been, Jade knew she was worse.

She had believed the old woman instead of believing Tanner.

Jade heard him sigh, and she opened her eyes. He turned toward her and fell to one knee like a man who'd just been shot through the heart. His eyes looked like two open wounds. In a voice broken beyond description, he whispered the words again. "Jade? You believed her?"

Jade couldn't bear to see his pain any longer, and she closed her eyes again. *Dear God, what have I done? Why? Why did I believe Doris Eastman so quickly?* Then she remembered the faces of Amy and Justin, suddenly as fresh in her mind as the day Tanner's mother had shown them to her. Her eyes shot open and met his, imploring him to understand. "Pictures...She had snapshots. One of each of the children. She said they were yours...and...and they looked...just like you."

This time Tanner closed his eyes, and when he opened them his face was filled with regret. "Of course she had pictures. Harry moved to Montana the year you and your dad left for Kelso. He got married three years later and bought a ranch. He's lived there ever since." Tanner paused. "Harry sends pictures once a year."

Jade searched her mind but found no memories of Harry. Had she ever known about him? Even when they were kids? No wonder his mother knew the pictures would work. Jade's mind raced once more, desperate for an explanation. "Why didn't...why didn't you talk about him?"

"He's ten years older than I am. I guess he never came up."

This couldn't be happening. A lifetime of devastating choices couldn't possibly have been based on a pack of lies whispered on a quiet afternoon ten years ago.

"Did I ever meet him?"

Tanner wrung his hands and stared at the floor. "Probably not. He left home when he was eighteen. A year before you and I met."

Jade did the math in her head. Her teeth were still chattering, and she had the sense she might faint at any moment. "S-so that summer he would have been...in his early thirties."

Tanner nodded and glanced up at her. "Amy was about four then, Justin two."

"Why didn't you tell me about the kids? They're your niece and nephew." Jade was grasping at straws, still reeling from the shock.

Tanner shrugged and moved back up on the sofa next to Jade, his eyes glistening with unshed tears. "You never asked."

Jade was surprised she was sill conscious. *What have I done, Lord? How can this be happening?* She felt suspended in midair, as though there were nothing solid to stand on or cling to. She knew in that instant that Tanner was being completely honest with her—that he'd always been honest with her and that there had been no other women, no paid abortions. He had been truthful all along, and Jade thought surely the realization would kill her.

To think that every bad thing she'd believed about Tanner had been a lie…a lie concocted by a vindictive old woman whose heart pumped pure venom. And now he was marrying someone—

"I can't believe she'd tell you that…and you'd believe her." Tanner buried his face in his hands and when he looked up at Jade again, his voice was angry but quieter than before. "I thought…I thought you knew me better than that."

She had no response. She had been intentionally tricked, but she was without excuse.

Tanner met her gaze and held it. He softened his voice. "There was no one before you…no one since."

Jade's heart felt like a lead weight in her chest. All those years of misunderstanding. And now there was Ty to consider. No, she couldn't tell Tanner now. He would never forgive her. Besides, he was about to be married; his life was finally coming together. She would keep her promise to Doris Eastman and not tell Tanner about the child he'd fathered. Not now when it would only complicate matters and possibly put her relationship with Ty in further jeopardy.

"You…haven't slept with your fiancée?"

Tanner shook his head. "God's always given me control in that area. Leslie's been with two men before me—both boyfriends she dated for several years. But I told her how I felt.

God couldn't honor our relationship unless we stayed pure."

Jade hung her head. She'd heard those words before. "You said the same thing to me, but…"

Her words drifted in the space between them until Tanner finished her sentence. "With you, Jade—" he placed his finger under her chin and lifted her head so she had no choice but to look at him—"with you I had no self-control. I'm sorry now just as I was then. Somehow it changed everything."

Jade nodded and thought of Ty. Tanner had no idea how right he was. A pang of fear coursed through her. He had explained his part; now it was her turn. There was only one place their conversation could go, and she wasn't sure she was up to the explanation. Especially a dishonest one.

Tanner drew a deep breath and stood up. He rubbed his neck and wandered through the room looking at Jade's family pictures. He focused on a snapshot of Jade and Jim and Ty, taken when Ty was three years old. They were smiling in the photo and looked like an all-American family. Tanner kept his eyes on the picture as he spoke. "My mother lied to you. And you believed her."

Jade wanted desperately to go to him, hold him, and tell him how sorry she was. But somehow it didn't seem right. Not now that he was engaged to someone else. "I'm sorry, Tanner. I don't know what to say." Jade remained on the sofa, her eyes trained on Tanner's back. He was crying. She could tell because his shoulders shook slightly, and for several minutes he said nothing.

Oh, God, what have I done? Why did I believe her without talking to Tanner first?

Finally Tanner drew a deep breath and turned to her. She saw his tear-streaked face then and wondered how much pain her heart could take in one night. "You believed her and…so you married someone else." Tanner's eyes narrowed and his voice grew hard. "I can understand that, Jade. After spending a summer with me, after sharing your conversion with me, after we bared our souls and...and everything else...I have no choice but to understand that somehow you believed my mother's lies and decided to marry someone else."

He searched her face, and when he spoke again his voice was choked with another wave of tears. "But three weeks after I left? Three weeks, Jade?"

A single sob escaped from Jade's throat, and she buried her head in her hands. How could she respond? How could she make him understand without telling him about Ty. *Help me, God. I'm falling apart. Please help me.* She expected Tanner to come to her side, reach out and put an arm around her. But he remained on the other side of the room, his feet firmly planted, his back to the series of photographs that had caught his attention earlier.

Tanner waited, and when her crying quieted, he asked again. "Help me understand, Jade. Three weeks? What happened after I left?"

Jade wanted to be anywhere at that moment other than alone in her house facing Tanner and the truth about the past ten years. But she had no choice and she drew a deep breath. "Jim was...always around."

"You never mentioned him."

Jade could be honest with this much. "He wasn't worth mentioning. He was just...always around."

Tanner huffed. "Yeah, Jade, lots of guys hang around girls like you. You're gorgeous. That doesn't mean you marry the guy. Three weeks after..." He didn't finish the sentence.

Jade shook her head. "No, there were never lots of guys. Just Jim. Everyone at school wanted to date him. Big man on campus, that kind of thing."

"And he wanted the only girl he couldn't get." Tanner leaned back against the wall, avoiding the photographs.

"Right." Jade hated herself for having married Jim. But she wanted Tanner to understand. *I never stopped loving you, Tanner.* The words stayed stuck in her throat. "I, well, I was never interested, until..."

"My mother lied to you." Tanner's voice was calm again as he finished her sentence, his eyes clear. Jade studied them and saw a veil of indifference. As if she had hurt him too badly, and now he was choosing to be vulnerable no longer where she was concerned. Tanner sighed. "Still...three weeks?"

Jade was not proud of what she was about to say, but she needed to say it. "My father always told me I'd wind up with Jim Rudolph. Jim asked me to marry him when I turned eighteen and I refused. Daddy found out and said I was an idiot. After I learned about you, I guess I figured there were no other choices. Your mother told me you wouldn't want me.... She said she knew we'd slept together...."

"*What?*" Tanner raised his voice again. "She told you that?"

Jade felt another pang of regret. *Not that, too, Lord.* She was beginning to understand. Anything Doris Eastman had told her was probably a lie. Including this. "She said she knew, said you told her before you left."

The topic was getting dangerously close to forbidden territory, but Tanner didn't seem the least bit curious. Apparently he believed Ty was Jim's son, and even this discussion about their last night together that summer didn't make him wonder. Tanner rubbed his neck again and stared at the ceiling. "I never told her about us, Jade. I never told anyone."

A new wave of hot tears made their way down Jade's face, but this time she didn't bother trying to hide them. She waited until she had Tanner's attention, and then she continued. "Jim wasn't a Christian. He…loved winning me over…but he never really loved me." She hung her head. "I wanted our marriage to work. For Ty's sake."

Tanner nodded, and when he spoke, Jade could still hear his intentional indifference. "And now?"

"He had an affair. A teacher he works with. Obviously we're not on good terms at this point." Jade was desperate to change the topic. "What about you? Your fiancée must be a wonderful girl."

Tanner exhaled slowly. "Jade, I don't want to talk about her. Not now."

"Okay…I'm sorry."

"No," Tanner sighed. "You're right. I want you to know. It's just…oh, never mind. I met her two years ago. Her name's Leslie and…we're getting married this summer."

Jade wished he would return to the sofa and sit beside her again. He felt so far away, standing across the room, his back stiff. "I'm happy for you, Tanner. Really."

She searched his face, and somehow she wasn't convinced that Tanner loved the woman he was set to marry. But that wasn't her business now. There was nothing she could do about the direction their lives had taken. And she was determined to keep the truth about Ty to herself. It was the safest thing for everyone involved.

Tanner hung his head, and again Jade wanted to go to him. He was a tall, strong, powerful man, an attorney feared by special interest groups across the country. But here in her living room he was broken by the truth of the past. His voice trembled when he spoke. "Why, Jade? Why would she lie to you?"

Jade understood what he was talking about. They'd been so busy unraveling the pieces of what had happened Tanner hadn't had time to analyze the truth about his mother. The woman had lied, and in the process, as she had tried to do so often back then, she had managed to change Tanner's life. "She didn't want me to marry you. It's that simple."

Anger flared in Tanner's eyes. "It wasn't her choice."

"But she lied all the same. And now here we are."

Tanner moved slowly back to the sofa and settled into the spot beside Jade. He turned his body so that his face was near hers. "Was it so easy to marry someone else?"

Jade held his gaze. "No." Fresh tears stung her eyes. "I thought about you every day." Images of Ty came to mind, and she looked away, unable to meet Tanner's gaze. "I think about you still."

Tanner framed her face with his fingertips, desperately searching her eyes and positioning her so that she had no choice but to look into his again. "You did love me, didn't you, Jade?"

She nodded, her words barely audible. "Yes, I loved you, Tanner."

"In all my life..." He moved his face closer to hers, and Jade knew what was coming. She knew but was unable to stop it, didn't want to if she could. "I have never loved anyone...like I loved you, Jade."

He moved his mouth gently over hers and kissed her. It was a moment stolen from days gone by, a kiss that assured Jade had she not believed Doris Eastman's lies she and Tanner would be together still. Together forever. His hands wove their way through her hair as he pulled her close, kissing her like a man might kiss his bride before heading off to war. Desperately, hungrily, with an almost fatalistic certainty that this kiss would be their last.

Jade's hands found Tanner's face, his neck, and shoulders.

No man would ever make her feel the way Tanner did, the way he still did. They kissed again and again, and sometime in the midst of the moment, Jade finally understood the Scripture from Jeremiah.

This man, Tanner Eastman, had been God's plan for her, the future and hope he had prepared for her life. But they had given in to desire, and after that she had chosen to handle the situation on her own—without trusting God's voice or heeding his warnings about not being unequally yoked. She had acted hastily in irrational fear and married a nonbeliever while Tanner was studying religious freedom halfway around the world. The life she had now was the punishment she deserved. Punishment for her many sins.

She had rushed ahead of God, and her sentence would last a lifetime.

Tanner pulled away first, and Jade saw guilt in his eyes. He was, after all, engaged. There was no way they could turn back the clock and pretend ten years hadn't gone by. "I'm sorry, Jade."

She kept her hands on either side of his face, her eyes connected with his. "Don't be. It doesn't change anything. I know that."

"You're right." His face was still inches from hers, and Jade found herself wishing he would embrace her once more. His breathing was raspy, and Jade could feel his body trembling beside hers. "I just wanted you to know the truth...I'll never love anyone the way I loved you, Jade."

The hours had slipped away, and Jade felt like Cinderella. Midnight was approaching, and it was time to return to reality. Time for stolen moments from the past to be put behind them forever.

"We shouldn't have..." Jade couldn't bring herself to voice

the words, but she pulled back and caught her breath.

"I know." He stood up and reached for her hands, pulling her gently off the sofa. When they were both standing, he wrapped her in his arms and held her close. Her body screamed for him, and she was certain he felt the same way. There was something between them, a physical chemistry, an attraction that was stronger than either of them. It was the same feeling that had caused them to veer off God's course in the first place. Now life had moved on without them, and Tanner's plane was set to leave in ninety minutes. "I gotta go."

Jade pulled away from him and crossed her arms in front of her. "Are you going to talk to your mother?"

Again anger flashed in Tanner's eyes. "How can I forgive her for what she did? She made up her mind I wouldn't marry you, and she did everything in her power to devise a plan that would keep us apart. A plan that worked. I'll struggle with that as long as I live."

"But you'll forgive her, Tanner." Jade's voice was gentle. Much as she wished Tanner could hate his mother for what she'd done, Jade knew that was impossible. Tanner loved God too much to hold a grudge of bitterness and hatred. "You'll forgive her. You couldn't live with yourself otherwise."

Tanner sighed. "Being with you tonight has made me doubt a lot of things." His eyes held hers, but she kept her distance. "My ability to forgive is one of them."

Tanner made his way to the front of the house, and Jade trailed close behind. He opened the door and turned to her once more. "We still have a lot to talk about regarding the hearing. It's in a week, and I'll probably be back up here at least once before then."

Jade nodded. "It'll be different."

"Yeah, I suppose it will be."

She looked in his eyes, and though she kept her distance, she allowed her fingers to find his face once more. "I'm sorry, Tanner. I wish…"

His face grew serious, and fresh grief filled his eyes. "If only you'd believed me…"

She blinked and two tears slid down her cheeks. "I'm sorry."

Her apology settled over him, and she could see something change in his eyes. He forgave her. No matter that she'd doubted his intentions and believed horrible things about him. Regardless of the fact that she'd married someone else less than a month after his departure, he forgave her.

"At least we're not enemies anymore." Tanner leaned toward her and kissed her tenderly on the forehead. "Good-bye, Jade."

She pulled away. "Bye."

He left then, and she allowed her eyes to follow his car until it disappeared at the end of the street. Why had she ever doubted him? So what if the pictures had looked like Tanner? Hadn't she known him better than that? Hadn't she believed his love for her?

In that moment, with the damp breeze blowing through her hair and Tanner headed for the airport, she knew that had there been a way to go back, she would have found it. If it meant swimming the ocean for days on end or climbing a hundred mountains; if she had to walk the desert floor ten years straight, she would do it. Whatever it took. If only she could go back a decade in time and live life over again.

If she could, she would question everything Doris Eastman said instead of taking the awful things she'd spoken about Tanner as gospel. She would search out the letters Tanner had written from wherever her father had hidden them. Then she would wait for Tanner the way a drowning man waits for his next breath.

As though nothing in life mattered more.

Thirty-one

DORIS EASTMAN WAS ALONE IN HER CONDOMINIUM, CHASING away invisible monsters in the night and praying for relief. Perched on her lap was an open copy of the Bible. Anxiety had plagued Doris before—terrifying, suffocating anxiety—but it had never driven her to read Scripture. It was the chest pains that had done that. Persistent, relentless stabbings somewhere in the vicinity of her heart. Doris was about to turn sixty-six, and in the past week the thought had dawned on her that perhaps this problem wouldn't be cured with diet and exercise.

Perhaps she was dying.

Doris had never actually considered death. It was an opponent she did not fear because as far back as she could remember she was certain she would live to be a hundred. She wore a seatbelt, had annual checkups, ate well and walked a mile each day. Death didn't happen to people like her. It happened to people like Hap who—cheeseburger after cheeseburger—built a gut around their midsection and refused to see the importance of exercise.

But now, though Doris had taken every precaution, though she was clearly the picture of health for her age, she had the distinct feeling she was no longer bulletproof. The chest pains were a constant reminder.

Doris had been to the doctor, and he'd given her a concerned look. Her blood pressure was high, and she seemed short of breath. He'd scheduled a treadmill test for the following week and sent her home with nitroglycerin tablets and medicine to control her blood pressure. She'd been taking both drugs for three days, but they brought little relief from the pain.

And no relief whatsoever from the fear.

Doris tidied her condominium while voices raged against her peace of mind. *Repent! Remember the height from which you have fallen! Woe to you blind guides....*

Even with classical music blaring through her home and the washing machine running in the next room, Doris could not block out the incessant warnings. *I've done nothing wrong. I'm a Christian woman, for heaven's sake.*

But the silent echoes of Scripture she'd long since forgotten screamed in the foyer of her mind: *Broad is the road that leads to destruction and many find it.... And on that day he will separate the sheep from the goats.... Anyone whose name was not written in the Lamb's book of life was thrown into the lake of fire....*

"Stop!" Doris shouted as she flipped off the bedside stereo. "Enough!"

She clutched at her chest and winced as she made her way across the room to her bathroom sink. She flicked on the light, poured herself a glass of water, and took two sips. Silence; that was what she needed. Time to reflect on the strange Scriptures that played constantly in her head. *What are you trying to tell me, God? I'm not the one you should be hounding. What about Jade? She's the one who tricked Tanner into sleeping with her. I did the only thing I could do under the circumstances.*

Woe to you...remember the height from which you have fallen....

Doris squeezed her eyes shut and sank onto the nearest sofa cushion. From what height had she fallen? *Show me, God.*

A memory began to take shape. Doris was twelve, maybe thirteen years old sitting on the bank of a creek in

Williamsburg, Virginia. Her parents had been churchgoers, but they never actually discussed their faith. And that day Doris had found the family Bible and taken it with her to the quiet spot along the water. For three hours she sat there soaking in Scriptures, seeing her faith in a new light. Making it her own.

Though more than fifty years had passed, she could see herself clearly, hear her sweet, young voice as she prayed aloud asking Jesus to be with her always, to walk with her and talk to her and hold her close. It was that day that Doris realized faith wasn't the picture that had been modeled by her parents. It was a relationship with Christ. There on the creek bank she promised God that a day wouldn't go by without her meeting him the way she had that morning. They would meet together, talk together, and in time she would know the Bible by heart.

Doris blinked and the image disappeared. When had she stopped feeling that way about the Lord? Three years later? four? She was seventeen when she met Hap, and she remembered them discussing the Bible on their dates. But sometime before they married things had changed between her and God. The image of Angela Conner appeared, and she gritted her teeth. Yes, that's when everything had changed. When Hap gave in to Angela Conner.

God had allowed Hap to fall, and Doris must have decided she had no one to lean on but herself. The days of sweet fellowship with the Lord died a quiet death after that.

Doris never stopped claiming an allegiance to Christ. It wasn't that she disbelieved him. But she had never quite forgiven him for letting her down where Hap was concerned. Over the years, her hard feelings toward God grew into a distance that now—even with the chest pains—seemed too vast to cross.

Doris returned to her bedroom, sank into a swivel chair,

and leaned against the backseat. Her chest pains eased. Had she come so far from that day on the creek bank that she had actually stopped listening to God? Stopped loving him? She closed her eyes, and the Scriptures returned.

Anyone whose name was not written in the Lamb's book of life was cast into the lake of…

No! God loved her too much to threaten her with fire. Her name was there in the Lamb's book. Surely it was.

Repent! Repent or I will remove your lampstand….

Another image filled Doris's mind, and this time she stared at it in horror. A cross, anchored on a lonely hill bearing the shadowy figure of a dying Christ.

In that moment a tidal wave of remorse crashed down upon Doris, driving her to her knees. And though her bones ached at the odd position, she hung her head and felt the strangest sensation. Her eyes burned and grew moist, and Doris realized what it was. Tears. She hadn't cried in decades, and now a torrent of tears were fighting their way free from the depth of her heart, where they had been trapped so long they'd nearly dried up.

She had become a hard, ugly old woman. A person who preferred to play God rather than talk to him. A liar, a gossip, a slanderer. In that moment she knew she was without a hope should the chest pains grow worse and demand her life.

No wonder she feared death. She thought of the lake of fire, the eternal lake of fire, and suddenly she was desperate for God's saving grace and mercy. Desperate to know she was free from her calloused past.

"Forgive me!" She cried out the words, begging God to hear her. "I'm sorry. Please change me."

Doris sobbed, remembering the precious child she'd been, repulsed by the monster she'd become. As her tears slowed, she caught her breath and realized something had changed.

The fear was gone.

Confess your sins to one another so that you may be healed....

Confess. Yes, that was it. It wasn't too late after all. She would call Tanner and confess. The realization should have brought her peace, but instead she was seized by a new kind of chest pain. This time it felt like an elephant was sitting on her chest.

Call Tanner, my daughter. Confess....

I'll do it. It's what I need to do. Her breathing had become labored, and she struggled to find the energy to move. What was happening to her? The pains grew worse in response, and suddenly she knew.

She was having a heart attack.

She was going to die without having a chance to tell Tanner. He hadn't called her since his return from Portland, and somehow she was certain he'd found out about her lies. Fading in and out of consciousness, Doris gasped for breath and thought how sad it was that she would die at peace with God and at odds with her favorite son.

If only she could reach the phone and call him, let him know she was sorry. Tell him the truth about Jade's son...his son.

Again the pains grew more intense, and Doris fell back against the sofa. There was nothing to do now but wait. *This is it, the real thing.* Doris closed her eyes and accepted death without a fight.

If the Lord was going to take her home before she had a chance to make things right with Tanner, then she'd have to trust God that somehow, someday, Tanner would know the truth. And that he'd understand how sorry she was for lying in the first place.

"Forgive me…Tanner." Her voice was a frail whisper. "Forgive me…."

A sense of peace washed over her, and she saw another vision: her name written in the Lamb's book. And she knew that despite her faithlessness through the years, despite the horrid thing she'd done to Tanner and Jade, God had been merciful. He had always been merciful. Her body slumped onto the floor, and then the sounds around her faded.

And in that instant, the world around her went dark.

Thirty-two

SINCE RETURNING TO LOS ANGELES, TANNER HAD BUSIED HIMSELF in preparations for the hearing. With the entire nation watching for the verdict, he had spent nearly as much time praying about the case as he'd spent researching it. By Thursday afternoon, Tanner had a peace about the hearing that whatever came of it, God would be glorified in the process. And that was enough for him.

The most difficult aspect of preparing Jade's case was the fact that his personal life was falling apart. He had been avoiding his mother and still had no idea when he would confront her or what he would say when he did so. She had lied to him, done everything in her power to manipulate him. And for that he would always struggle with his feelings of anger toward her and the possibilities of what might have been. In many ways she had ruined his life by sending Jade into the arms of another man while he was too far away to do anything to stop her.

But, Tanner knew he would have to deal with his mother later. First he had to deal with Leslie.

He had lain awake the past few nights imagining life with Leslie, being married to a woman who was not capable of giving her heart and all of who she was to him the way Jade had done. It wasn't fair to either of them that he would constantly compare their relationship with the one he'd shared with Jade. And years from now—even after sharing his life with her day in and day out—there was a certainty in his heart that Leslie would still come up short.

There would be no summer wedding. No wedding at all. As Tanner finished his work for the afternoon, he knew he had to tell her that night, before she made any more plans.

He'd considered whether seeing Jade again, whether learning the truth about their past and kissing her had driven him to this decision. He couldn't deny it: In some ways it had. But he would not attempt to rekindle a relationship with Jade now. She had changed since that summer ten years ago. She'd believed his mother's lies, and though Tanner had forgiven her, he could not imagine opening himself to her again.

No, breaking his engagement with Leslie was simply the right thing to do. He had known love once, a long time ago, and what he felt for Leslie was not love. Unless he loved that way again, Tanner would rather stay single.

The phone rang, and Tanner sighed. He was expecting a call from Jade, but usually she waited until he was back at his townhouse. They had talked about the case every evening that week.

"Hello?"

"Tanner? Good, you're still there." Leslie sounded upbeat, ready with another string of details. "What about meeting tonight for dinner? I wanted to talk about attendants, you know...how many ushers on your side, how many bridesmaids on mine. Besides, you've been so busy with that case you haven't given me the time of day. I'm a pretty fun date, Tanner; you ought to take me out sometime." She was trying to sound coy, and Tanner summoned his resolve. "Anyway, I sure hope things will settle down after we're married, but then I'm sure they will. You've got such a busy—"

"Leslie." Tanner hated to interrupt her, but he was so sure of his decision he could no longer pretend. "We need to talk."

She paused. "I agree. We haven't so much as had a quiet

night alone in I don't know how many—"

"No." His word stopped her cold. "I mean about us. We need to talk tonight."

She uttered a nervous laugh. "You sound so ominous, Tanner. Don't tell me you're getting cold feet?"

Tanner sighed. It wasn't his feet that were cold, it was his heart. And Leslie deserved more than that from a husband. "I'm sorry, Leslie. I've been doing a lot of thinking. Like I said, we need to talk."

"Listen, darling, I'm not one for surprises." The cheeriness had disappeared from her voice. "Why don't you just tell me what's on your mind."

She sounded angry, and Tanner knew she was covering the hurt. The things he needed to tell her would leave her world upside down. But eventually she'd find her way back to the surface, and one day another man would come along. One who would love her completely, the way she deserved to be loved. "I don't want to talk about it now."

"Fine." Leslie's voice was hard. "Where do you want to meet?"

"My place. Six o'clock."

She hesitated. "You're serious, aren't you?"

Tanner sighed. "Yes. I'm sorry, Leslie."

The conversation ended, and Tanner pushed himself away from his desk. A month ago he'd been ready to settle for a life with Leslie. She had been the kind of woman he thought would make him happy. But seeing Jade again, remembering what love felt like when it resided deep in his being…

Tanner knew he couldn't marry Leslie.

He thanked God for letting him see that truth now, before the wedding. And he asked him for strength to get through the evening. Then he packed his things and headed for home.

Thirty minutes later Leslie was at his door.

"Come in." Tanner had changed out of his shirt and tie and was barefoot in a Princeton sweatshirt and faded denim jeans. He stepped aside as Leslie huffed past him and stormed into the living room.

"Okay, I'm here. What's so important that you made me drop what I was doing to come talk to you face to face?"

Tanner studied her, the way she shifted uneasily from one foot to the other, running her tongue nervously along her upper lip. She was frightened. Leslie was a pampered young woman, accustomed to getting her own way. When things didn't go as she planned, she fussed and fumed until they did. But that would not happen tonight, and by the look in her eyes, Leslie knew as much.

"Sit down, Leslie. Please."

Her gaze lingered suspiciously on him, and as she sat on the sofa he moved next to her, taking her hands in his. "I've been doing a lot of thinking lately, and, well...I have some things to tell you."

Leslie squeezed his hands, and a bit of her façade collapsed. "You still love me, right, Tanner?"

He hated what he was about to do, but there was no choice. "I love you, Leslie, but not like I should. Not the way a husband should love his wife."

Raw pain flashed across her face, and her eyes grew damp. She started to pull her hands from his. "You're teasing me, Tanner. Of course you love me that way. We're getting married in—"

"No." Tanner sighed. "We're not. I'm breaking it off, Leslie. I can't do it. It wouldn't be fair to either one of us."

Tears spilled onto Leslie's cheeks, and in seconds they had cut two trails through her perfectly applied foundation. Tanner realized that oddly it was the first time he'd seen her look flawed in any way. Leslie dabbed at her face, then excused herself while she got a tissue. When she returned she nestled against him, but he felt himself stiffen in response.

Her jaw fell and she studied him closely. "Wait a minute. You aren't giving me a chance here, Tanner."

Help me be gentle, Lord. "It's too late for chances. This has nothing to do with you, Leslie. You've done everything right. It's me." He stroked the side of her face in a gesture that was more fatherly than even remotely romantic. "I care about you a great deal, like I said. But I don't love you the way I should."

Leslie covered her face with her hands and cried softly, pressing her eyes with the tissue. She spoke in a muffled voice. "What did I do wrong? I thought everything was so good between us."

"You did nothing. It's all me."

"It's that woman in Portland, isn't it? You're still in love with her...." She stared at the engagement ring on her hand and twisted it until it came loose. "I could tell you were still in love with her the first time you talked about her at dinner that night."

"This isn't about her, either. Like I said, it's about me. You deserve someone who loves you completely."

Leslie sniffed and slipped the ring from her finger. "Here. I don't want it. Not now."

Leslie straightened and stopped crying, and in that moment Tanner felt that perhaps she hadn't loved him the way she should have, either. Maybe all Leslie loved was the idea of being married to a man with Tanner's credentials. After all, she had been groomed to marry correctly since she was a very young girl.

She leaned over and hugged him. "You know, I almost expected this would happen...."

"You did?"

"Well, you haven't been interested in the planning, and it's been months since you've called me just to chat." Leslie kept her hands on Tanner's shoulders. "Do you think there's a chance for us, Tanner…someday?"

He wished he could give her hope, but he had to be honest. "No." He shook his head. "You'll meet someone else, Leslie. Someone better for you than I ever was."

She smiled sadly. "It would have been a beautiful wedding…."

"And you'd have been a beautiful bride." He pulled slowly away. "I'm sorry, Leslie. Can you forgive me?"

She thought a moment. "You know, I think maybe I was feeling the same way you were. Like we were going through the motions, hurtling toward the big wedding day with little thought as to what we shared between us."

"Really?"

She nodded. "Really." Leaning close, she kissed his cheek. "Let's not be strangers, okay?"

Tanner nodded just as the phone rang. He rose from the sofa to answer it. "Hello?"

"Tanner Eastman?" Tanner didn't recognize the voice.

"Yes. Who's this?"

"This is Dr. Jeff Young of St. Vincent Medical Center. We have your mother here…. I'm afraid she's suffered a major heart attack." The doctor paused. "She's in the intensive care unit, Mr. Eastman. You need to hurry."

He hung up the phone slowly, bombarded by a dozen conflicting emotions. He still hadn't talked to his mother about the lies she'd told Jade, hadn't given her the opportunity to fill in the missing pieces. Now he might never get the chance.

His throat tightened at the thought of losing his mother

now, when so much of his life was in turmoil. She had been his greatest fan as far back as he could remember. Pushy, demanding, overbearing...but Tanner never doubted her love for him. Even now that he knew about the lies she'd told Jade. In some strange, twisted sense, that had been her way of loving him. *Help me forgive her, Lord. Don't let her die without giving us a chance to talk. Please.*

But there was something even more troubling now that she lay dying at the nearby hospital. Tanner wasn't sure if his mother was really a believer, whether she was ready to die and face God Almighty.

Leslie's face reflected the alarm she must have seen in Tanner. "What's wrong?" She was at his side, her hand on his arm, and Tanner was suddenly anxious to see her go.

"My mother's had a heart attack." He pulled gently away and reached for his car keys. "I'm sorry, Leslie...I have to go."

She nodded, taking his hand in hers once more. Tenderly she peeled back his fingers and slipped the ring inside. "Take this."

With a small sigh, he pulled her close. "We'll talk more later, okay?"

"Okay...."

But he had the feeling they both knew there would be no reason to talk later. The relationship simply hadn't worked. It was time to move on.

He bid her good-bye, thankful she hadn't wept loudly and carried on, hoping she believed what she'd said about it being for the best. Tanner wasn't sure if she did, but right now it didn't matter.

He had to get to his mother before she died.

Thirty-three

TO THE EXTREME SURPRISE OF HER DOCTORS, DORIS EASTMAN pulled through a rough night in which she suffered two additional heart attacks. During that time doctors determined that though her arteries were severely blocked, she was too weak to undergo major surgery. If she survived the hospital stay, certainly it would not be for long.

Tanner held a bedside vigil throughout the night, alerting doctors when his mother looked pained or when she began gasping strangely. By ten o'clock that morning she was heavily sedated, but her heart was stable. Doctors expected her to regain consciousness before noon.

"Of course, it's possible she'll never come out of it," one of the doctors told Tanner earlier that morning. "Her heart was severely damaged. At best she'll be a cardiac cripple."

"What's that mean?" Tanner still couldn't believe she'd had a heart attack at all. His mother was one of the strongest people he knew and seeing her small frame lost in a sea of hospital sheets and plastic tubing was difficult to accept.

"It means she'll never be the same."

The doctor didn't elaborate, and Tanner was left to wonder how the heart attacks had changed his mother. *Let me talk to her, Lord, please.* He prayed quietly at her side until finally at eleven-thirty, she opened her eyes and blinked slowly.

"Tanner..."

Her voice was scratchy, and Tanner could barely make it

out. "Hey, Mom, how are you feeling?" He stood up and leaned over the bed, taking her now frail hand in his.

She motioned for some water, and he helped her take a sip from a straw, disturbed at what an effort it was for her. The ordeal left her breathless and unable to lift her head. Tanner tried again. "Rough night, huh?"

She made a slight nodding motion. "Have to talk...Tanner."

He weighed his options. He wanted to talk about the lies she'd told Jade, but it was more important that he talk about God. "I'm worried about you."

She frowned and shook her head, and Tanner felt his spirits lift. If his mother was showing her usual spunk hours after suffering three heart attacks, maybe she would survive after all. "Nothing...to worry about."

Her talking was improving now that she was more fully awake. Still she seemed unusually calm, and Tanner figured that was because of the medication. "How are things with you and God, Mom?"

A peaceful expression filled his mother's eyes, one that Tanner knew no medication could produce. "Good. Very good. We...had a talk."

"You and God?"

His mother nodded. "He wants me to...tell you something."

Tanner frowned. Was his mother thinking clearly? He leaned over her, searching her eyes. "Now?"

"Yes." She glanced at the bedside chair. "Sit down."

He did as she asked and waited.

"I want to tell you something...I'm not very proud of." She rested a moment. "Long time ago, when your father and I were engaged, Angela Conner was a waitress at the tavern...."

Tanner was beginning to have his doubts. This couldn't be

good for her, rehashing age-old memories and mistakes hours after the heart attacks. "Mom, you can tell me later if—"

She held up a single, trembling hand. "Now. God wants me to tell you now."

Tanner sighed. "Okay. Take your time."

"One night, your father visited the tavern, and Angela Conner asked for a ride home. Our…wedding was still a year away, and when your father pulled up in front of Angela's house…she asked him in."

What? No one had ever told Tanner this story. Why was his mother telling him now, and what did it have to do with God? He took his mother's hand in his and stroked her pale skin. "I'm listening."

"Your father didn't plan for it to happen, but it did. He went inside and…one thing led to another." She coughed weakly, and Tanner helped her take another sip of water. After a moment she continued. "Your father didn't mean anything by it. He was weak…and later he was paralyzed with guilt. He came directly to my house the next day and…confessed."

"You still married him?" The Doris Eastman Tanner knew would have kicked the wayward Hap out of her house.

His mother inhaled slowly. "We broke it off for six months, but eventually I forgave him. I figured it wasn't as much his fault as it was hers…." She struggled to catch her breath. "From that day on…I vowed never to forgive Angela Conner."

Tanner was confused. "God wanted you to tell me that?"

His mother moved her head in a manner that was barely detectable. "I'm not finished." She sighed. "When Angela married Buddy and moved into our neighborhood, I did everything I could to avoid her. But then they had Jade and…you and Jade were inseparable. There was nothing I could do to stop the two of you from meeting together. Until that summer, when Angela ran off with my best friend's husband."

"The summer Jade and her father moved to Kelso?"

Doris nodded. Tanner could see she was getting tired, and he took her hand in his once more. "You don't have to tell me this now, mother. We can talk about it later."

"No. God…will give me the strength." She moistened her lips and appeared to be concentrating on the right words. "When Jade left I was glad. I could see where things were headed for you two and…I was determined that no daughter of Angela Conner would ever date you."

A heaviness settled over his shoulders. He had wondered why his mother hadn't been friendlier with Jade.

"When they moved to Kelso I thought I was rid of Jade Conner. Then…that summer, the two of you found each other again. I tried everything possible to make you change your mind about taking that internship in Kelso. I figured Jade would be a loose woman like her mother.… And I couldn't stand the thought of her bringing you down." She stared hard at Tanner. "Does that make sense?"

He shrugged. In many ways his mother had tried to play God where he was concerned. The truth hit him hard. "Go ahead, Mother, I'm listening."

She studied him for a moment. "You know about the lies, don't you?"

Tanner nodded. "Since Monday."

"I thought so. But God wanted me…to tell you what happened in my own words." She took a few moments to catch her breath. "Jade came to me that day, and I guessed that you'd been together.…"

Tanner felt like a little boy caught in some dreadful act, and he felt his face grow hot. "What made you think that?"

"If Jade was anything like her mother, then it didn't take

much guesswork…to figure out the two of you had probably slept together."

"But she was nothing like her mother, never has been." Tanner rose quickly to Jade's defense, but his mother only nodded weakly.

"I know that now. God has…made everything clear to me, Tanner. Jade is a sweet, precious child who was…never treated well by anyone. Except you."

Tanner was silent.

"But I thought I was protecting you, so I lied. I told her you had been with many women, you had children you cared nothing for…. I told her you wouldn't care for her, either, now that she'd slept with you."

Tanner still couldn't believe the woman before him had said those things, purposefully destroying the one relationship that mattered to him more than any except the one he shared with God Almighty. "You showed her Amy's and Justin's pictures."

"Yes. I did that. It was the only way I could be sure I'd convince her."

Tanner stroked his mother's hand and allowed himself to grieve silently. If only Jade had stayed away, turned down the invitation to go to his mother's that day…. *God, help me forgive her. Help me forgive them both.*

"You'd better rest now, Mom. You said what you needed to say."

His mother shook her head, more adamantly this time. "No." She coughed several times and was barely able to catch her breath. Tanner helped her with another sip of water and waited. "There's more."

He clenched his fists and noticed his palms were sweaty. "More?"

"What did Jade tell you about her son?"

Tanner's heart lurched. Alarm coursed through him, and he was suddenly unable to draw a deep breath. "What do you mean, Mother?"

Doris's eyes filled with tears, and Tanner was flooded with apprehension. His mother never cried. Not even when his father died. He watched her struggle to speak. "Did she…talk about him, mention him when she told you…about the lies?"

Tanner was terrified of the direction the conversation was headed. He shook his head. "No. She wants him back…that's the whole reason I'm representing her." *God, please, where is this going?*

Doris was silent, her lower lip quivering as she stared at her son. "I'm so…sorry, Tanner."

"Mother, tell me, what do you know about Jade's son?"

Doris swallowed hard, fighting for control. "Promise you won't hate me?"

Tanner was losing patience. He knew his mother's condition was fragile, but nevertheless he could not wait another moment. "I love you, Mom. No matter what you've done to me, regardless of how you've manipulated my life I will always love you. Now tell me what you know."

She nodded, and in that moment Tanner thought she looked like a mournful child, confessing a sin too great for her to bear any longer. "I could be wrong, but I doubt it…."

"Wrong about what? Please, Mom, whatever it is, say it."

"The boy…Ty…"

"Yes, what about him?"

Her lip was trembling badly again. When she spoke, Tanner could barely hear her. "I think he's y-y-your son."

Tanner felt himself spinning out of control, falling wildly into an abyss too dark and deep and narrow to ever climb out of. The child…Jade's son…was *his?* It was impossible, wasn't it? "But Jade's husband thinks…"

Doris shook her head. "He doesn't know. There's…there's more to the story." A teardrop slid down his mother's wrinkled cheek. "When Jade came to me that day…it was because she was pregnant."

"What? She told you that?" Tanner's heart was beating erratically; his world had tilted, and he wasn't sure he could ever right it again.

"I guessed." His mother was breathless but determined to continue. "She wanted an emergency number where she could reach you…. I invited her over to discuss it."

"So she hadn't been with any other man?"

"No, Tanner. She loved you. She told me the two of you…were going to be married."

It was making sense to Tanner, more sense than ever before. "So she came to you for help and you…you lied to her. Is that right?"

His mother nodded, her eyes filled with remorse. "I told her you wouldn't want anything to do with the child…and I gave her a check."

"A check?"

"A cashier's check for ten thousand dollars."

"She took it?" Tanner couldn't imagine the hurt Jade must have felt, trusting his mother with her news, and then learning that the man she thought she loved was a—

His mother coughed loudly and struggled for a breath. "She…she didn't want to. But I convinced her she'd need it for the baby. I made her promise…to never tell anyone you were the father."

The shock was almost too much for Tanner to bear. But he understood now why Jade had married so quickly. He could hear himself asking her about children on that hot August day so long ago, hear her telling him she'd only want a child if she could give him the kind of life she never had. A mother and a father, safety, security. Then he left for Hungary, and she was alone, pregnant with no one to turn to.

And so she had wound up with Jim Rudolph, a man she didn't love, but who would give her the life she wanted for the child she loved more than anything.

Lord, I can't bear the pain. Help me, God. Please.

His mother was studying him, trying to convey her sorrow with her eyes. "Tanner, I saw the boy on TV. He…he looks just like you."

Tanner thought of the boy now, rugged and active, sandy blond hair and eyes the same shade as his. Why hadn't he seen it before? Jade must have thought him a horrible man for not at least wondering about the boy.

"Do you forgive me, Tanner?"

He stared at his mother and felt pity more than forgiveness. She had spent most of her days a hard, manipulative woman bent on controlling his life. Now, when her time was nearly up, she had finally seen the light and come clean. Tanner realized that if his mother had died during the night, he might never have known about Ty. But she had lived, and for that he would always be grateful. "I forgive you, Mother." He smoothed a lock of gray hair from her forehead. "You can rest now."

"Will you go to her?"

"Yes." Tanner had no idea what Jade would say, or whether she'd tell him the truth. After all, she'd had her chance the other night, and she'd said nothing about Ty then. He thought of the child he'd missed, the birthdays and milestones and miracles of his young life, and he wondered if the pain in his gut would kill him. "Pray for me, Mom."

"I will." She blinked and another teardrop fell. "I'll be okay. You go…. Jade needs you."

Tanner bid his mother good-bye, and in four hours he was on a plane back to Portland.

Thirty-four

JADE WAS FINISHED WITH THE DINNER DISHES AND MIDWAY through a conversation with Ty. He called her every night at seven o'clock, and as the hearing drew closer, she could detect a growing sense of hope in his voice.

"I can't wait to get out of here, Mom." Ty spoke in a whisper so Jim wouldn't hear him. "It's going to work out all right, I know it is."

She closed her eyes. "Mr. Eastman is doing his best, Ty."

"I saw him, Mr. Eastman. He was on TV with you."

"You saw us?" A nervousness ran through Jade at the thought of Ty having seen Tanner. She chided herself for it. There was no way the boy would ever know. What harm was there in talking about him now. "He's a nice man. He's done a lot to help us."

"I heard what he said, how he stuck up for you." Ty maintained his whisper. "I like him, Mom. I wanna meet him."

Another wave of anxiety hit, and Jade's knees felt weak. She sank into a chair in the kitchen. "Okay…maybe. Sure."

Eventually their conversation wound down, and Ty grew quiet. Jade knew he was probably crying; he had cried every night lately. "Mom…I miss you."

Make it all be over, God, please. I can't take this…. Jade closed her eyes and struggled to find her voice. "Remember…even now I'm with you. Right there in your heart."

Ty gulped loudly. "Okay." He hesitated. "Bye. I love you."

"Love you more." *Enough to marry Jim Rudolph.* "Good night, honey."

Jade hung up and noticed tears on her cheeks. The house was so empty without Ty. She wandered about, idly straightening framed photographs of Ty and precious homemade trinkets he'd brought home from school over the years. She ran her finger over each one, removing the dust and savoring the memories they evoked. She and Ty would have been fine on their own; it was clear, now. *How could I have married Jim?*

In some ways, she was no better than Doris Eastman, who had lied and manipulated to protect Tanner. Hadn't Jade done the same thing? Promised a lifetime of love to a man she didn't care for, rushed ahead of God and made a miserable choice all to protect Ty.

Both she and Doris Eastman were wrong. And regardless of what hope the future no longer held, Jade knew from this point on, when a decision had to be made, she would seek the Lord's wisdom. She would never again rush ahead of him.

There was a knock at the door and Jade jumped. It was nearly eight o'clock, and her porch light was off. *Too late for advertisers or neighborhood Girl Scouts.* Jade moved cautiously toward the front door and peered through the lace panel covering.

Tanner.

Jade's heart skipped a beat. *What in the world…?*

Jade opened the door, but before she could speak he ushered her inside, took her face in his hands, and studied her eyes. "Jade…Oh, Jade, I'm so sorry…."

"What?" Adrenaline raced through her veins. He must have learned something about the hearing…. She was going to lose custody of Ty after all. She pulled back. "What's wrong? Why're you here?"

Tanner sighed, and Jade thought he looked haggard. Dark

circles stood out underneath his eyes. "My mother had a heart attack."

Her insides knotted up. "Is she okay?"

"She's in bad shape, but that's not why I'm here." Jade watched his eyes fill with regret. "We talked this morning. She had something God wanted her to tell me."

Pulling away from him, Jade moved into the living room, tucking herself in the corner of her sofa, her legs pulled up to her chin. *Doris wouldn't have told him about Ty. Certainly not.* So why was her heart pounding so fiercely? "What...what did she say?"

Tanner followed and knelt before her, his face level with hers. "She told me you were pregnant when you came to her...." His eyes filled with tears. "Is it true, Jade? Is Ty...?"

Jade hung her head. She could not lie any longer. Whatever came from this they would have to deal with. Right now he deserved the truth. "Yes."

Tanner held her with his eyes. "He's my son?"

Jade lifted her head and met his gaze. He looked like he'd been shot through the heart. *Oh, Lord, how could I have hurt him like this? What kind of woman am I?* "Yes, Tanner. He's your son."

Very slowly, as if he'd been mortally wounded and was still fighting the final fall, Tanner bent over his knees and settled in a heap on the floor. His first sob was more of an animal cry, the wail of a tortured beast. There were more that followed, and Jade felt her heart breaking as she watched the man she had always loved grieve for the son he'd never known.

The world was spinning, and Tanner could do nothing to stop it. He had spent the past ten years searching for Jade, thinking of her, wanting her. Wondering how she could marry someone just three weeks after he left town. And now he knew. She'd been pregnant with his child. And when she'd come for help, his mother…

Deep, consuming regret covered him like six feet of cemetery dirt, and he was unable to lift his head.

My God, how could I have been so blind? I'm a father…a father to a boy who doesn't even know me. He thought of Ty and his heart ached with the weight of this new reality. Had he really thought Jade could lie in the arms of another man so quickly after his departure? If only he'd found her back then…. The weight of the lost years was more than he could bear. *Help me, God. I'm dying here, I'm—*

"No! It can't be…." His mother's lies had cost him a relationship with his own son.

He was overcome, and he was suddenly aware of Jade moving. Her arms circled around him from behind, and she lay her head on his upper back. She began stroking his arms, and he could feel her shaking. *She's crying, too. We've both lost so much, God…. How can we go forward after this?*

Finally she spoke, and her voice was a choked whisper. "Tanner…I'm so sorry."

He sat up and pulled Jade to him in an embrace that spoke everything they were too devastated to say. They stayed that way a long time, and when he could finally speak, he pulled back and studied her expression. What he saw there was regret as deeply rooted as his own. He took her hands in his. "Why, Jade? Why didn't you tell me?"

His pain was so deep and raw she had to look away. "I promised your mother I wouldn't tell anyone. Not even you."

Tanner's face twisted and he set his jaw. Jade wondered if he was going to cry out again. "I'm his *father.*" Every word pulsed with emotion, and Jade knew much of the blame was hers. *He'll hate me for the rest of his life for this.* "Didn't you think I had the right to know?"

"Your mother said you wouldn't care. She...she showed me the pictures and..."

"And gave you the check?" Jade could see he wasn't making an accusation, just desperate to understand what had happened that day ten years ago.

"I never touched the money. It's in a trust fund for Ty.... I was planning to use it to send him to college."

Tanner looked away, the muscles in his jaw tightening again. She watched as the emotions played across his anguished face: anger, regret, immeasurable sorrow. All the emotions she'd struggled with for so long. He turned toward her once more. "The other night...when we talked. Why didn't you tell me then?"

"Your mother told me if I ever told anyone, she'd take me to court. She told me with her money she'd win...." Jade sighed. "I was afraid of her, Tanner." She glanced at her hands, still wrapped protectively in his. "Besides, it didn't seem like the right thing for anyone. You have your life; you'll be married this summer, and soon you'll have a family of your own."

Tanner leaned his shoulder into the sofa, and Jade watched him, worried. His jaw was clenched tightly, and he passed a hand over his eyes before looking at her again. "I broke it off with Leslie."

"What?" *Why had he—*

"I didn't love her, Jade. It would have been wrong to marry her."

Her head was swimming.... So much had happened in so short a time. "When was this?"

Tanner thought a moment. "What day is it?"

His question broke the tension, and Jade smiled. "Friday night."

"Then it was yesterday after dinner."

"When did you find out about your mother?" No wonder Tanner looked beat up. First Leslie, then his mother, and finally the truth about Ty. It was enough to push anyone over the edge.

"Leslie was still at my house. She left and I went to the hospital. I was up all night with my mother, and this morning she came to. That's when she told me about Ty."

Jade slipped her arms around Tanner's neck. She didn't blame him if he never forgave her, but she owed him an apology. After all they'd been through, all the poor choices and lies and missed opportunities, she needed to speak her mind before another moment passed. "I'm sorry, Tanner. I should have told you first. I…I was afraid of your mother."

His eyes were still racked with pain, but his expression softened.

"I didn't want you to think I was trying to ruin your wedding plans…. I was trying to do the right thing for everyone."

Tanner pulled away and stood up, pacing her living room floor and raking his fingers through his hair. When he stopped, he leaned against the wall and stared at her. As he did, the anger in his eyes was slowly replaced with a love for her that knew no limits. He reached out his arms. "Come here, Jade. Please…."

She went to him, fitting her body against him, her face inches from his. His voice was a whisper that spoke directly to her soul. "So much has happened between us that I didn't know what I was feeling for you…."

Jade felt tears sting at her eyes. "I'm sorry."

He shook his head and placed a single finger over her lips.

"It's over." He tightened his grip on her waist. "It's behind us, Jade. Now…" He seemed to be reading her eyes, searching her soul. "I want to meet my son. I want to—"

Jade closed her eyes, and for a moment she couldn't hear what he was saying. *I can't believe this is happening.* Tanner was here, he was not marrying someone else, and he wanted to meet Ty. A rush of holy gratitude came over Jade, and she felt the arms of God's presence as if he were standing in the room beside them. How was it that God had taken everything that was so awful and turned it into this?

For I know the plans I have for you…plans to give you hope and a future….

Jade opened her eyes and saw that Tanner was staring at her, his eyes filled with compassion and forgiveness. "So…you're not marrying Leslie?"

Tanner leaned forward and gently kissed Jade's forehead. "Did you really think I could be with you the other night…kissing you, wanting you…and then go back home and marry someone else?"

"I guess I—"

Again Tanner held his finger to her lips. "Shh. I'm here, Jade. I never stopped loving you, and now—" he paused and his expression grew deeply serious—"say the word and I'll never, ever leave you again."

The tears that had been building spilled down Jade's face, and she allowed herself to get lost in Tanner's eyes. "Please, Tanner. Don't ever go away again."

"Are you sure?"

He had suffered much because of her lack of trust, their weakness that summer. Jade felt the corners of her mouth lift slightly, and she buried her head in his chest. "I've been sure since I was a little girl."

Jade lifted her face to him, and their kiss was long and slow.

"I love you, Jade...."

She pulled back slightly, and he kissed her chin, her throat. "I love you, Tanner. I never stopped loving you."

He found her mouth again, and his hands moved along her back, holding her closer still. "Let me go with you tomorrow...so I can meet him?"

Their words were breathless, spoken between kisses that were every bit as spellbinding as they'd been a decade earlier. "Okay." Jade sat up, looking at Tanner, studying his face...the face so like her son's....

"Hey, wait a minute!" Jade's mind suddenly raced with the possibilities.

Tanner pulled back, his fingers tracing her cheekbones. "What?"

"Let's call off the whole thing. Get a DNA test and prove Jim isn't Ty's father! Then we can be done with it once and for all."

Tanner's eyes clouded with concern. "The whole way from Los Angeles to Portland I thought about that, but it's more complicated than it seems."

"How come?" The solution seemed simple to Jade.

"First of all, custody is a tricky thing. Jim's fighting for full custody based on the idea that living with you—a person of strong faith—would be damaging for Ty. If we walk in and present a DNA test, you can be sure everyone involved will be highly suspicious. Second, in many states fatherhood is less a matter of biological factors than it is familiarity. The courts have actually awarded custody to boyfriends on that basis. The question here will be who raised Ty? Who does Ty think of as his father? The answer, obviously, is Jim."

Jade listened intently. She still didn't understand why Tanner couldn't call off the trial now that he knew the truth.

Tanner leaned back into the sofa and stared at the ceiling for a moment before turning his gaze on Jade once more. "It's pretty clear here that Jim's not trying to win custody because of some deep love he has for Ty. My guess is that his reason is simple: He wants to make a point. That your faith is dangerous to your child. And if a judge is willing to give Jim complete custody because of your faith, then why wouldn't my faith be equally problematic? I mean, if you're a religious fanatic, what does that make me?"

"Worse?" Jade was beginning to understand.

"Much worse. And since I don't have a relationship with Ty, it would still be very possible for a judge to grant complete custody to Jim. And we can't have that."

The hope Jade had felt moments earlier was gone. "No, that would be awful."

"So I've decided to go on with the hearing. I think our best shot is to win custody back based on your religious freedom, your constitutional rights. If that happens, my guess is Jim will bow out fairly easily. Like I said, I don't think he's really interested in Ty."

"I get it. But it seems like we're playing games. And what if we lose? It could take months or years, and then—"

"Shh." Tanner cradled her close and stroked her hair, and after a minute he pulled back and kissed her again. "Let me take care of it."

"Even if we win, you can't tell anyone the truth, Tanner. Your career would be ruined."

"I don't care about my career. Jade, I've missed you so much. I can't believe I'm here. I feel like…like I'm dreaming."

His being near her made her body feel like it was on fire. She could feel the length of him and knew neither of them would be willing to let go if they didn't stop soon.

She pulled away first. They'd made this mistake once; she wasn't going to let it happen again. "You need to sleep, have you thought about that?"

"I need you…." He reached for her and she took his hand. "Jade, marry me. When this mess is over and everything's straightened out. Please."

Her heart soared, and tears burned in her eyes. *Lord, is this what you planned? Is this the future you have for me?*

Yes, my daughter. For I know the plans I have for you….

The Scripture sounded clearly in her mind, and she was overcome by God's mercy, his faithfulness. She and Tanner had gone against God's will, and in the wake of that she had chosen to go her own way. But still, through every nightmare in the past ten years, God had been drawing them together.

He was waiting for an answer, and with tears streaming down her face, Jade leaned her head back and laughed. "Yes, Tanner. Yes!"

He caught her by the back of the neck and drew her close once more, kissing her. "Jade, I can't believe you're here. Everything that's happened…."

Flee, my daughter.

The warning was painfully familiar, and Jade knew better than not to heed it. She pulled away and made her arms stiff. "Stay back." Despite her purposefully light tone, clearly Tanner understood.

"You're right." He rattled his car keys. "What would you think about giving me directions to the nearest hotel?" He winked at her. "I've got an important date tomorrow with a very special little boy, and a little sleep wouldn't hurt."

"Motel Six, you mean?" Jade grinned and gave him directions. Suddenly everything in life looked so much brighter. They would get Ty back no matter what. After all, Jim wasn't his real father, and Tanner had promised. Whatever it took.

Tanner moved closer to the door and leaned back, his head resting against the frame. "What if he doesn't like me?" She joined him, and he slipped his arms around her waist.

"He'll like you." She brushed a lock of hair off his forehead and leaned her head against his chest. "He already told me so."

He pulled back a few inches so that their eyes met once more. "He told you that?"

"He said he saw you with me on TV, told me you seemed like a nice guy."

"Really?" Jade's heart melted at the concern in Tanner's eyes. How had she thought she could keep him from his son?

"Really. He told me he wants to meet you."

Tanner closed his eyes for a moment, and then opened them slowly. "You're still here."

"What do you mean?"

He nuzzled her neck. "I mean I can't believe you're here."

Jade leaned into him and savored the feel of his face against hers. "When Jim divorced me, I felt God allowed it to punish me for going against him. It only served me right for deceiving Jim. I knew how much God hates divorce, and I prayed he would heal the break between Jim and me. But Jim wasn't open at all. He'd had enough. Then, when I lost Ty—" Her voice broke and she swallowed hard. "Well, I thought God had forgotten about me. But he didn't." She met his eyes and smiled through the tears. "Despite my weaknesses, he had plans for me, remember our verse?"

"I remember. Jeremiah 29:11."

"Right...." Jade ran her finger along the edge of Tanner's neck. It was hard to believe they were finally together, where their hearts belonged. "God had plans for us, but we went against his will and...I thought he was going to punish me forever."

"Ah, Jade." Tanner kissed her forehead tenderly. "God isn't like that. There's another verse you need to memorize. Romans 8:28: God works all things to the good for those who love him."

"Even this?" She snuggled close to him.

"Even this." Tanner found her face again, and they kissed once more. This time he pulled away. "I better get some sleep." He leaned close once more and kissed her again.

"It's hard to let go...."

He drew in a deep breath and exhaled dramatically. "Tell me about it."

"Good night."

"Wait." The door was open, and the cool night air made her shiver. "There's something we need to do before I go."

"What?" Jade saw the serious look in his eyes, and she moved closer to him, appreciating the way he warmed her. He reached for her hands and folded his fingers over hers.

"Pray with me, Jade. Please. It's been so long."

They came together in prayer like they hadn't since that long ago summer. Only this time they whispered words of thanks and requests for strength in the weeks to come. After several minutes, Tanner ended the prayer.

"Lord, I want to pray for the first time ever...for my son." He squeezed Jade's hands. "Thank you that you have always been with him and thank you for letting me find him now. Please help me build a relationship with him. And with Jade."

He kissed her one last time before leaving. And as Jade fell asleep, she heard Tanner's prayer over and over again. *I want to pray for my son...for my son...for my son.* The nightmare was almost over, and when it was, they would finally be a family—the three of them.

The thought of it made Jade's heart swell to nearly bursting.

Thirty-five

JADE MET TANNER OUTSIDE THE MOTEL THE NEXT MORNING, AND while she drove the five miles to Jim's apartment, Tanner fired one question after another. "What's his favorite sport?"

"Basketball." Jade's tone was light, teasing, but inside she was relieved that Tanner cared so deeply. Her son had craved fatherly love and attention, and Tanner wanted desperately to meet those needs.

"What about baseball?"

"Baseball's okay. Basketball's better."

"Did he play Little League?"

"Little League, flag football, and most of all—"

"Basketball." Tanner's grin lit up the car. "That's my boy."

"Anything else?" Jade glanced at him. He didn't look a day over twenty-seven. He'd matured into a very striking man, and again Jade ached at all the years they'd lost.

"Does he like to talk?"

"Yes." Jade laughed. "He comes by it honestly."

Tanner mouthed, "Me?" and pointed to himself in mock astonishment.

"Yes, you. You haven't stopped asking questions since I picked you up."

He smiled. "My way of reminding myself I'm not dreaming. Every time you answer I'm forced to believe it's true." He stared at her, the smile gone, his eyes glistening with emotion. "You're really here beside me."

Jade reached across the car and wove her fingers through his. "I can't believe it, either."

They pulled up in front of Jim's apartment and parked. The officers were already sitting in their patrol car, and Jade waved casually at them.

"Your monitoring crew?"

Jade uttered a brief laugh. "You guessed it. Just in case I do something really harmful—you know, like wield a Bible at Ty."

"I'm still amazed any judge in his right mind would—"

She put her finger up to his mouth. "Don't. It doesn't matter. Everything's going to work out."

When the engine was off, they faced each other, and Tanner's eyes were filled with love for her. "I still feel like I'm dreaming, Jade."

She felt the hairs on her arms stand up straight. "Don't look at me like that in public."

Tanner motioned to the apartment complex. "Come on. Ty will be waiting."

Jade drew a deep breath and squeezed Tanner's hand. "Okay. Let's go."

The sun was making a rare early spring appearance, and Ty raced out the door in shorts and a sweatshirt as Jade and Tanner made their way up the walk.

"Mom!" Ty raced to Jade but stopped when he saw Tanner trailing behind her. "Wow...I didn't think I'd get to meet him today."

Jade laughed and willed herself not to weep at the significance of the moment. "Ty, I'd like you to meet a friend of mine, Mr. Tanner Eastman."

Ty nodded shyly. "Nice to meet you, sir."

Tanner stooped down to the boy's level and placed his hands on the child's shoulders. "Nice to meet you, too."

Jade saw nothing uncomfortable in Ty's expression as he remained there, facing Tanner, his face cocked curiously to one side. "So you're the guy who's going to get me back home, right?"

"I'm going to do my best, buddy."

Jade saw the glint of tears in Tanner's eyes. In all her life she never imagined a scene like this one. God was good, and certainly he would see them through the hearing. Even if Tanner was worried about the outcome.

They settled onto the front porch steps, Jade on Ty's left and Tanner on his right. She had missed Ty terribly and normally would have been anxious to talk with him. Instead, she said little and allowed Tanner the chance to get to know his son.

"I hear you're a basketball fan." Tanner rested his arms on his knees and turned his head so he and Ty were facing each other.

"Yeah, hoops are the best." Jade savored the enthusiasm in her son's voice. How long had it been since Jim had asked Ty about his hobbies or interests? He probably never had. Yet when the hour was up, they would be forced to leave him completely in Jim's care.

It's not fair, God.

In response she felt a deep-seated peace that caused the clouds of bitterness to dissipate. Somehow, no matter how dismal the current situation, she believed that one day they'd be together as a family. It would not be easy, certainly. If she won Ty back, Jade knew the bond between her son and his father would take time to develop. It would never be what it could have been if she and Tanner had followed God's plan instead of succumbing to their own desires. But if they did get their chance, she felt certain the life they would someday share would be true and real, and that it would last forever.

"Think I could come see you play?" Tanner's enthusiasm was genuine, and from where she sat watching them, Jade smiled.

"League play's over...." Ty thought a moment. "But there's tournaments starting next month on the weekends. You could come then!"

"Deal."

"Hey, what's it like being on TV and stuff?"

Tanner laughed. "I'm only on TV when one of my clients winds up in big trouble." Jade caught the concern in his eyes. "Then it's something you forget about. I'm usually too busy helping my client to think about it."

"Mom's your client, right?"

Tanner's eyes met hers, and Jade felt a shiver pass over her. He had a way of seeing straight through her, down to the deepest part of her soul. "Yes." Tanner reached across Ty and squeezed Jade's hands. "Your mom's a client. And she needs a lot of help right now. Lots of prayers."

Ty frowned. "You mean because of the hearing."

"Right."

"You mean I might not get to come home?" Ty had been so happy, but now doubt clouded his face.

Watching him broke Jade's heart, and she pulled him close. "Mr. Eastman's going to do everything he can, honey." She exchanged a quick glance with Tanner. "One way or another we're going to get you back home. Okay?"

"Okay." Tears filled the corners of Ty's eyes.

"I'm not too worried about it. Best thing I can do is pray for help. When I get up there before the judge, God'll have to give me the words to say." Tanner ran the back of his hand gently over Ty's cheek. "You're praying, too, right?"

Ty ran his fists under his eyes and dried his cheeks. "I wanna go home with my mom."

This time Tanner slipped an arm around the boy and hugged him. "That's what we're going to tell the judge."

The door opened and Jim stood there, glaring at them. "Get your hands off my son!" He stepped out on the porch as if he might push Tanner, and in the distance the officers both turned their attention toward Jim. He noticed them and immediately relaxed his stance. This time he pasted a smile on his face and spoke in a quiet hiss. "I said...get your hands off my son!"

Jade didn't bother to get up. Let Jim look like a hothead in front of the officers. "He's my attorney, Jim. Besides, this is *my* time. Leave us alone."

The plastered smile remained, but Jim shot a vicious glance at Tanner and then turned back to her. "I don't care who he is, I want his hands off my son."

Tanner loosened the hold he had on Ty and leaned back. Jade wished he would say something, threaten a lawsuit, anything. But Tanner remained silent.

Ty glared at Jim and slid closer to Tanner. "I can talk to anyone I want."

Jade caught her son's eyes and gave him a look. *Not now, Ty. Don't be rude now.* Ty slid away from Tanner once more, and Jade was proud of him. The upcoming hearing was too packed with emotions and tensions already. At this point Jade, Tanner, and Ty needed to be agreeable.

"Go in the house, Jim. Everything's under control." Jade stared at him until finally he disappeared back through the front door. How she wished they could stop this nonsense, and that Tanner could look Jim in the eyes and tell him the truth.

But Tanner had already explained that to her. The possibility was too strong that Jim would still win complete custody because he was the man Ty identified as his father, and because he was more tolerant in his views than either Jade or Tanner.

No, their best chance was to fight the case from the angle they'd already planned and hope that she'd win Ty back because of her First Amendment protection, her right to believe in God and teach his truths to her child.

The hour was up, and Jim's appearance had dampened the mood considerably. "Well, buddy, nice talking with you. I'm sure we'll talk again sometime soon." Tanner pulled Ty into a hug, and Jade was grateful. Tanner had his reasons for saying nothing to Jim earlier, but he was obviously not intimidated by him.

"And you'll come to my tournaments, right?" Ty's voice was no longer enthusiastic. It never was when the hour was up and it was time to say good-bye for another week.

"Right."

"Ty, we'll see you Monday at the courthouse. You'll be there in case the judge needs to talk to you. Okay?" Jade held her son's face in her hands and searched his eyes.

"Okay."

They said good-bye, and Jade waited until her back was to Ty before she started crying. Without saying a word, Tanner fell in step beside her and wrapped an arm around her shoulder.

"I don't want *my* boy—" his voice was strained with emotion—"living with that man one more day."

A tense and anxious silence filled the car as Jade drove Tanner back to his motel. It was painful to leave Ty behind, knowing the way Jim felt, his lack of love for her son, his anger for Jade.

Help me, God, I'm so afraid. The prayer passed through her mind, and she knew she wouldn't have survived the past weeks without her faith.

Trust in me with all your heart and lean not on your own understanding.

Jade forced herself to breathe slowly. *I'm trying, Lord. Help me trust you more.*

Whatever the coming days held, the waiting was almost finished. The hearing was less than forty-eight hours away.

Thirty-six

THERE WAS NO MISTAKING SOMETHING OF GREAT IMPORTANCE was happening at the Clackamas County Courthouse that Monday morning. Media vans clogged the parking lot and well-dressed news anchors milled about outside, sipping coffee and bemoaning the dampness of spring in the Northwest.

Jade arrived at the scene alone, thankful Tanner had made prior arrangements. In an agreement with Jim's attorney she would park near the rear of the courthouse and enter through a private door. There she would go to Room 12, where she would meet with Ty in what was scheduled to be a private session.

She eyed the sea of reporters and prayed God would protect her from them. At least right now when she had just five minutes before meeting with her son.

Jade parked her car and thought about Tanner. He had met up with his partner, Matt Bronzan, Saturday night, and the two had taken a hotel room near the courthouse. They ordered in meals and without other interruptions ran through every aspect of research and case history pertaining to the case. She hadn't heard from Tanner until late last night.

"Have you read the newspapers?" Tanner sounded concerned, and Jade felt her anxiety increase.

"No. I try to avoid them these days."

"They've done their homework, Jade. Big piece in *The Oregonian* quotes you as saying U.S. Department of Education should not be allowed to parent our children."

Dread filled her heart. "How'd they get that?"

"I'm guessing you said it during one of your school board meetings, right?"

Jade thought back. "You're right. Three years ago, I think."

"Well, they found it, and you can be sure they'll use it against you."

Jade didn't miss a beat. "It's true. They shouldn't be parenting our kids."

Tanner sighed. "I know that and you know that, but judges are part of the judicial system. And the judicial system is part of the U.S. government."

Jade felt sick to her stomach. "So it's me against them."

"Exactly."

"You're really worried, aren't you?"

Tanner paused. "Maybe because I know he's my son…because I've seen how Jim is around him…I don't know. But it's going to take everything we've got to win this time."

Remembering their conversation, she whispered a brief prayer. Then she checked herself in the rearview mirror and slipped on a wide-brimmed hat and a flouncy scarf, both of which helped hide her face. Her eyes trained on the ground, she climbed out of her car and headed toward the back of the courthouse.

The reporters kept their distance. Apparently they were assuming she would arrive with Tanner, so she made her way inside the building without pause and found Room 12. *Okay, Lord, give me the strength.* If she lost the hearing today, this would be the last time she and Ty would spend together alone for months. Maybe even years.

Tanner and Matt had arrived hours earlier and were going over their case one last time in a private office adjoining the courtroom. As Tanner had predicted early on, the hearing would be heard by Judge Susan Wilder, and that fact alone sent shivers of apprehension through Tanner.

In their research over the past few days the lawyers at CPRR reviewed the cases Judge Wilder had heard. She had ruled that a Portland woman, Anna Jenkins, who'd been injured in an auto accident was entitled to only minimal compensation even though she was not to blame in the collision. In her ruling she stated, "Ms. Jenkins was carrying out a work-related task and therefore should have taken into account the hazards of the job."

Matt had done further research and learned that the Jenkins woman was a volunteer with the local crisis pregnancy center and had been transporting handouts from the printer back to the center.

"In other words," Tanner concluded, "the judgment went against her, at least in part, because of her involvement in the Pro-Life movement."

There were other cases. A teacher at one of the public high schools allowed a Bible study to meet in his classroom before school each Wednesday. Time and again this same teacher was denied the stipend usually allotted to staff members who sponsor extracurricular activities. When the case reached Judge Wilder's courtroom, she ruled in favor of the school district.

"In accordance with separation of church and state, it is my opinion that the school district does not need to compensate this teacher for his involvement in an extracurricular Bible study. Other clubs are supported by the U.S. government as being neutral and in the best interest of the students. Bible study—while not something we can forbid—certainly crosses the line that separates church and state and therefore cannot be supported by the government or the school district."

After reading Judge Wilder's decisions for half the day

Sunday, Tanner had taken to pacing the hotel floor. "The timing is perfect for Jade to lose here, Matt. Are you seeing that?"

Matt sifted through the briefs on the table. "If it could happen anywhere, it could happen here."

"Jade's husband couldn't have picked a better judge if he'd paid for one."

They agreed there was just one way to argue before a jurist with such obvious prejudice. And to that end they had spent the remainder of the day and much of the night preparing.

Now he and Matt were already set up in the courtroom. Tanner rubbed his eyes and knew that God alone had used that final preparation session to provide them the inspiration and ideas they would need to win the hearing. They were about to see if it would be enough to sway Judge Wilder.

An hour passed, and Jade entered the courtroom. She wore black slacks and a soft, blue blouse. Tanner smiled in approval. It would not help her cause to show up in a skirt with her hair in a bun. That was often how women with Jade's convictions were portrayed by the media, but Jade—like most women of faith—wasn't someone who fit stereotypes. It was important for the jury to see that a woman could appear very businesslike and intelligent and still have a deep faith.

The hearing was set to begin in twenty minutes, and when Jade looked at him, Tanner could see she'd been crying. He wanted desperately to go to her, hold her, and tell her everything would work out. But the reporters had begun to take their places, and every eye would be scrutinizing the two of them, looking for a chink in their very public armor of faith. They had dared to stand up for what they believed, and many members of the press would be anxiously looking for them to fall—in whatever way possible. A fall would mean conflict; and conflict made for breaking news.

Tanner understood the press well. He didn't believe they were in a conspiracy against people of faith so much as they held to a standard party line. An unfair portrayal in a handful of newspapers meant other editors would see the stories and run similar layouts. The media seldom seemed to report the truth on any topic. Rather, they gave a series of perceptions commonly held by the handful of people who assumed powerful editorial positions on newspapers and news stations across the country.

He looked at the reporters gathered there and thought about what they would do to him—and to Jade—if they knew he was Ty's father. It was something he would have to face eventually, but not until the time was right.

Jade made her way closer and took the chair next to him. Their backs were to the members of the press, and Jade leaned over and whispered, "I feel like a criminal or something."

Tanner gave a slight nod but kept his distance. "In the eyes of some people here, you are. We both are."

Jim and his attorney appeared and took their seats at the table earmarked for the plaintiff. By the time Judge Wilder entered the courtroom, spectators and reporters packed the seats.

Tanner had long since stopped relying on developing a rapport with the judges who heard his cases. He was openly conservative and an outspoken Christian. In other words, he was a marked man. The cases he won, he did so with the help of God and by leaning heavily on America's founding fathers and the ideas they had expressed when writing the constitution.

Today would be no exception.

For the first hour, they heard testimony in favor of the current custody ruling. Jim's attorney marched a handful of upstanding community members onto the stand, who one by one testified that Jade's views were extreme and bound to have a negative effect on her child.

"Why should a person's religious viewpoint make her an unsuitable mother?" Jim's attorney tossed out the question as if he were genuinely unsure of the answer.

The man on the stand, a long-time member of the local school board, raised his chin and glanced at Jade in disdain. "When a parent teaches a child to steal or kill, we have no trouble recognizing that as abusive parenting, and we do the right thing as a society. We take the child away." He paused and resumed eye contact with Jim's attorney. "Mrs. Rudolph is teaching her son to be insensitive to the diverse nature of our culture. She is teaching him to hate. And that—whether we're ready to recognize it or not—is abusive parenting."

Things couldn't have been going worse.

Matt took notes furiously while Tanner listened and provided cross-examination. As a rule, he stayed away from anything that might appear argumentative. They would not win this case by getting in a fighting match with the plaintiff's witnesses. Rather, they would have to present their facts in a manner both calm and approachable, assuring the judge they had nothing to hide.

Tanner knew too well that when a Christian flew off the handle or yelled out in court or showed up carrying banners with Bible verses, newspapers ran photos of the event across the top of the page. This fed the media perception that believers were extreme fanatics, which in turn fueled public perception. Tanner's job was to show these reporters how different Jade was from the right-wing image they'd bought into over the years.

The last bit of testimony presented in favor of Jim Rudolph was a journal entry written by Jim and dated just three weeks prior.

Jim was called to the stand to read it and verify that it was an accurate portrayal of the events as he understood them.

"Today I took Ty home from school after basketball practice. While we were driving, he asked me if I believed in God." Jim paused and glared at Jade. "I told him I did not believe and that this was my choice. I told him everyone was entitled to his or her different beliefs.

"At that point my son became alarmed and told me I was wrong. He said there was only one way to heaven and that was through Jesus Christ."

Jim practically hissed the last two words, and Tanner felt a stab of sorrow for this man who could so openly defame the one who had created him. At the same time Tanner was fiercely proud of Ty. And of Jade, for teaching him the truth.

Jim took a drink of water and continued reading his journal entry. "I told the child that not everyone needed to believe in Jesus Christ. Some people believe in other gods. Some people believe in themselves. I told him he should be tolerant of what other people believed because that was the best way for them."

Jim's attorney nodded in agreement, and Tanner thought he saw the judge do the same. Clearly this was the accepted doctrine in U.S. courts today. The fact that Jim had tried to correct his son with this modern-day "truth" would make him nothing less than a hero in the eyes of too many government officials.

Jim continued. "But Ty looked at me and told me again that I was wrong. He said he was worried that I would go to hell if I didn't accept Jesus and believe in him. He said he knew Jesus was the only way to heaven because that's—" he paused—"what his mother told him."

An almost imperceptible look of dismay crossed Judge Wilder's face. Tanner held his breath. *Dear God, let her be at least partially open to what I have to say. Please.*

He glanced at Jade, at her eyes filling with tears, and he mouthed a silent exhortation: "Pray."

She nodded and briefly closed her eyes.

The attorney directed Jim to other slips of paper that contained additional journal entries. In each there was a reference to faith and the fact that Ty had credited his mother with teaching him to believe.

When it was time for Tanner to cross-examine Jim, he decided to stick to the journal theme. "You brought lots of journal entries with you today, didn't you Mr. Rudolph?" Tanner forced himself to remain calm, casting a smile in the other man's direction.

"Yes. I've been very careful about taking notes for the past few months."

Tanner nodded. "Very well. Then could you locate the journal entries wherein you record your concern for the boy's safety?"

Jim drew a blank look and turned to the judge for help. "Answer, Mr. Rudolph." Judge Wilder adjusted her robe and crossed her arms firmly in front of her.

"I don't understand the question."

"Very well, let me rephrase it." Tanner wandered closer to Jim. "I assume that you are concerned with the child's safety. That you believe Mrs. Rudolph is a danger to the boy, is that right?"

"Yes. She's a danger to his mental health."

"All right then, did you bring any journal entries that describe episodes where you feared for the boy's safety?"

Jim shook his head.

"Answer out loud for the court, please." Judge Wilder's reminder was pleasant but firm.

"No, I didn't bring any." Jim all but snarled his response.

Tanner let his surprise show on his face. "You didn't bring any…or there aren't any? Which is it, Mr. Rudolph?"

Jim exhaled dramatically. "There aren't any."

"So are you telling this court that you have no record of any incidents wherein your wife mistreated the child in question?" Tanner stopped directly in front of Jim.

"She mistreated him all the time." Jim sneered in Jade's direction. "I just didn't take any notes."

The reporters scribbled furiously, and Tanner stared hard at the man. In that instant he would gladly have pushed Jim Rudolph over a cliff. After how he'd treated Jade and Ty, it was all Tanner could do to continue quizzing the man without losing control.

"Objection. The witness is answering beyond the scope of the question."

Judge Wilder glanced at Jim. "Sustained. Keep your answer specific to the question, Mr. Rudolph."

"No. I didn't keep track in the journal."

"Very well, Mr. Rudolph, since you've chosen to open the topic, please tell this court of any incidents where your wife mistreated or abused the child in question." Tanner couldn't bring himself to refer to the boy as Jim's son. Not now.

Jim squirmed on the witness stand. "Specific events?"

Tanner planted himself in front of Jim. "Yes. Whatever events of mistreatment or abuse you can recall."

Jim paused a moment. "I'm not sure I can recall them at this time."

Again Tanner nodded. "Very well. So is it correct to say that you do not have record of any instance wherein your wife mistreated the child, is that right?"

"Right." Jim mumbled the word.

"Speak up, please."

"Right!" Jim barked the word, his eyebrows angled toward the bridge of his nose. Tanner smiled. *Good. Get mad. Make the judge's decision that much easier.*

"And you also cannot recall any specific instance where your wife abused the child, is that right?"

"Yes."

"Thank you, no further questions, your honor."

Tanner expected Judge Wilder would take a brief break before he began calling witnesses in Jade's defense, but she plowed ahead.

"I am not unaware of the stakes in this case." She motioned toward the back of the courtroom. "Virtually the entire country is holding its collective breath outside those courtroom doors. Therefore there will be no breaks until I have heard all the testimony."

Tanner took his cue and called his first witness, Jackie Conley, Jade's friend from the Bible study group. Jackie had a master's degree in psychology and worked part-time as a counselor in a firm that dealt with high-level management clients. She was articulate and straightforward and delivered a glowing opinion of Jade as if she'd spent hours analyzing her.

Jackie was followed by Barry Burns, manager of a Portland convenience store, who had been thankful when Jade brought to his attention the content of magazines he'd been carrying on his shelves. He confirmed that she was merely looking out for the best interest of the community and especially the children.

"Do you think Jade Rudolph is a wacko, Mr. Burns?" Tanner managed to keep a straight face, but several members of the media snickered.

The old man on the witness stand grinned. "No, sir. She's a hard worker, though. I'll give you that."

Finally, Tanner put Jade on the stand. They had agreed earlier that Ty would remain in another room, spared the events of the hearing and from having to act as a witness. Jade felt it would be too much to put the boy through. Especially when he would soon find out the truth about Tanner.

Much like the press conference, Tanner walked Jade through a series of questions revealing the types of issues she had been involved in and her reasons behind them. Time and again, Jade's answer was the same. "I felt I had no choice but to protect the children involved."

"Has Ty ever said anything to you about where he wants to live, who he feels more comfortable with?" Tanner presented the question as casually as he could. He knew that Jim's attorney would pounce on this, accusing Jade of brainwashing her son, but still he thought the court should hear what Jade had to say on the matter.

She struggled for a moment, and Tanner willed her to be strong. *Help her, Lord. Put your peace in her heart.*

Jade reached into her shirt pocket and took out a folded piece of notebook paper. "I could tell you how Ty feels, the things he's said to me..." She held up the note. "Or I could read you this letter. He wrote it over the weekend and gave it to me this morning." She looked at the judge and the members of the press. "He wanted me to read it to you."

Tanner was speechless. Jade had said nothing about the note until now. A surge of hope welled up inside him, and he turned to Judge Wilder. "Your honor, we'd like to admit the letter from the boy as Exhibit A."

"Very well." Judge Wilder looked bored, as if she'd already made up her mind. Tanner prayed she hadn't.

He turned to Jade. "You may read the letter now."

Jade opened the paper near the microphone and the sound echoed throughout the courtroom. "'Dear Miss Judge...'" Jade swallowed hard. "'I wanted to write you a letter so you would know where I want to live. I want to live with my Mom.'" Again Jade struggled. "'I know that you think she's forcing me to believe in God the way she does, but that isn't so. I will believe no matter where I live. I will believe because the Bible is true more than anything else.'"

Jade wiped a tear as it slid down her cheek. "'I am in fourth grade now, and that's pretty old. I am old enough to know that my dad doesn't really care about me. He talks about the hearing all the time, and he told his girlfriend he wanted me to live with him to prove a point. Also so he wouldn't have to pay child support.'"

"Objection, your honor!" Jim's attorney was on his feet, his face beet red. "The child's letter is hearsay. There's nothing on the record to indicate the plaintiff wishes to discontinue paying child support."

Judge Wilder cast a look of reprimand at Tanner. "Objection sustained." Her eyes moved to Jade, "You may continue, Mrs. Rudolph, but please refrain from reading statements that are based on hearsay."

"Yes, your honor." Jade kept her eyes trained on the letter and exhaled slowly. "'My Dad doesn't ask me about my day. He doesn't go to my games, and he doesn't even know my teacher's name, or that I want to be a missionary when I grow up. After I play college hoops, of course.'"

Tanner felt his heart melt at his son's words. *He wants to be a missionary, Lord.* Tanner watched several members of the media smile at the mention of college hoops. Ty wasn't a brainwashed puppet. He was like any other child in America, with dreams and hopes and a desire for his parents to be interested in him. Tanner couldn't wait to fill the role.

Jade drew a deep breath. "'So, what I'm trying to say is,

please let me go home to my mom. She loves me more than anyone. And if you want to know the truth, I think it's because that's the way God wants her to love me.'" Jade smiled sweetly at the words her son had written. "'Sincerely, Ty Rudolph.'"

There was a lengthy pause while the child's innocent words hit their mark. Tanner turned to the judge. "The defense rests, your honor."

Jim's attorney tapped his pencil on the table and scanned his notes. Jade was certain at any moment he would take to his feet and cross-examine her, tear apart the legitimacy of the letter.

But instead he set his pencil down, rose, and announced that he had no further questions. Jade returned to her place beside Tanner as Jim's attorney presented the court with his closing remarks. He referred to the dangers of intolerance and the frightening place the nation would be if parents like Jade were allowed to continue brainwashing their children. He completely ignored any reference to Ty's letter until the end of his speech.

"Children say a lot of things that don't necessarily make sense to adults." The attorney smiled at Judge Wilder. "If children were able to make these decisions on their own, there would be no need for judges and courts." He hesitated and glanced at Jade. "But in this situation we have Jade Rudolph—a wolf in sheep's clothing. Her teachings and right-wing behavior will color the child's perceptions for decades, perhaps for a lifetime.

"It is at times like this that we need to step in and make the decision that is truly best for the child. Even if it is not a popular decision."

Jim's attorney sat down, and Tanner had to give him credit.

His last line had said it all. Taking a child away from his mother because of her faith would not be a popular decision. But if it meant protecting future generations from the narrow-minded views of radical right-wing Christians, it might be the only choice possible.

Usually by this time in a hearing, Tanner knew which way the decision was going to go. But this case was different, more complicated. And the fact that he was so emotionally involved only complicated things that much more.

As Tanner stood to make his closing argument, he had the sinking suspicion that if he didn't say the right things, Jade would lose this case. And her son. Their son. Matt handed him a brief. He had wanted to wait and see how the case went before deciding whether to use the information he and Matt had studied the day before.

Now he knew. The brief was their last hope.

Tanner addressed the judge and recalled character traits about Jade, elements that certainly seemed to prove she was neither fanatical nor extreme and definitely not given to brainwashing her son. As he spoke, he had the sense that Judge Wilder was barely paying attention. He fell silent and walked back to his spot at the table.

There he picked up a one-dollar bill and held it high for the judge to see. He remained that way for a moment so that everyone in attendance had the opportunity to view it. "This is a one-dollar bill, printed by the U.S. government and recognized worldwide as the national currency of this country."

Tanner approached the judge and saw that she seemed slightly more interested than before. "In many ways, your honor, this dollar bill is what started these proceedings in the first place."

He gestured toward Jade. "My client takes a stand against

violence, gets magazines removed from the store shelves, and someone—" he held up the bill again—"is out some money." He paused. "My client takes a stand against books that preach a doctrine of murder and suicide; books get removed, and again someone is out money.

"But when my client takes a stand against a commercialized program replete with questionable material, a program sponsored by the U.S. Department of Education, then suddenly she's crossed the line."

Tanner turned to face the courtroom. "Why?" He held up the bill again. "Because now the people who are out some money are the very ones who have the power to take away what she cherishes most of all." Tanner's gaze settled on Jade and he saw her trembling. "Her little boy."

Tanner stared at the bill for a moment. "It says here—on this bill printed by our government—'In God we trust.'" He paused again and sought out Judge Wilder's face. "Is that so? Or is that only the way we *used* to feel, back two hundred years ago when it was popular to feel that way, back when our country was first founded?"

He looked at the bill again. "George Washington's picture is on this bill, and I thought it would be interesting if we could put him on the stand, ask him what he thought about a country where a parent could lose custody of her child because of her beliefs."

Tanner scanned the courtroom and saw that the reporters were spellbound. "I'll tell you what…George Washington wouldn't recognize such a country."

He set down the dollar bill and held up Matt's brief. "We can't ask Mr. Washington to testify here today because we no longer have the benefit of his presence among us. However—" Tanner held up the brief—"we have the words he left behind."

Tanner glanced at Jade and saw the surprise in her eyes. She had not known what he and Matt had been working on in their hotel room, but from the gleam in her eyes he could easily see she approved. He positioned the document so he could read it. "In a public address in May, 1789, George Washington stated: 'If I could have entertained the slightest apprehension that the constitution...might possibly endanger the religious rights of any ecclesiastical society, certainly I would never have placed my signature to it.'"

Tanner let the comment settle over the courtroom. "Later that year in another public address he said this: 'The liberty enjoyed by the people of these states of worshipping Almighty God agreeable to their consciences is not only among the choicest of their blessings, but also among their rights.'"

The courtroom was utterly still, and Tanner felt as if the former president actually were on the witness stand. This time when Tanner spoke, he did so slowly and clearly, so that not a person in attendance could miss the message.

"Finally, in another public address in 1792, President Washington said this: 'We have abundant reason to rejoice that in this land, the light of truth and reason has triumphed over the power of bigotry—'" he glanced at Judge Wilder—"'bigotry and superstition. And that every person may here worship God according to the dictates of his own heart.... It is our boast that a man's religious tenets will *not* forfeit for him the protection of the laws, nor deprive him of any right...whatsoever.'"

There was a lengthy pause, and Tanner saw a change in Judge Wilder's expression. There was something humbling about listening to the words of George Washington, something that seemed to bring a measure of perspective to a system gone mad.

"And so your honor, I ask you to take seriously the words of George Washington, a man whose signature is found at the bottom of the constitution. On December 15, 1791, the First Amendment was added to the constitution." Tanner read the Amendment in its entirety. As he let the last words sink in, he nodded slowly, facing the judge. "You will notice that it absolutely forbids the government to pass any law—or make any decision—that would prohibit the free exercise of religion."

He leveled his gaze at Judge Wilder. "It seems to me, your honor, that this court has already done that by taking Jade Rudolph's son from her because of her religious views. I ask you now, on behalf of Jade and the people of this country, to prove to this court and the members of the press that we are not willing to let go of the freedoms guaranteed us in the constitution. Rather, we will fight to the end to preserve them.

"Please, your honor, restore primary custody to my client so that the people of this nation can sleep easier tonight knowing their constitutional freedoms are safe. Thank you."

Judge Wilder called a ten-minute recess and slipped through a door to her chambers. Muffled conversations broke out across the courtroom as reporters compared notes and guessed about the outcome. Tanner noticed them, but only briefly. His attention was on Jade and the paralyzing look of fear in her eyes.

He sat down beside her, blocking her view of the reporters and of Jim and his attorney. He spoke so that his voice was just loud enough for her to hear. "Worried?"

Jade nodded. "I can barely breathe."

"She's in there making her decision. Let's pray."

They were silent a moment, and Tanner brought their collective fears before the Lord, blocking out the voices around him so that finally he heard the one he was listening for.

Well done, my son. All things work to the good for those who love God....

Okay, Lord, but let Jade get Ty back. Please.

There was no response, and moments later Judge Wilder returned. She did not need to ask the court to come to order. Everyone in shouting distance was waiting breathlessly for her decision.

Tanner winked at Jade and mouthed a message to her: "Trust."

Judge Wilder glanced at a sheet of notes and cleared her throat. "You must first know that I felt honored to have this case in my courtroom. On a personal level, I have to tell you I agree with the plaintiff. I believe we've reached a level of saturation as far as religion is concerned in this country. It had a place at one time but today is little more than a veil, a thin veneer intended to disguise the roots of hatred."

She paused, and Tanner felt his heart rate double. Was it possible? Had she really understood the importance of what he'd read in his closing arguments?

Judge Wilder exhaled slowly. "The day will come, mark my words, where a parent will lose custody of his or her child if his beliefs are not in keeping with the nation as a whole. Extreme beliefs are dangerous, pure and simple."

She stared at Jade, and Tanner feared for their system, a system that allowed a judge such obvious bias. "That said, the plaintiff in this case simply did not do a thorough job of showing potential for harm. Ms. Rudolph's views, while extreme in my opinion, have not been proven to be dangerous. She has not staged a sit-in at an abortion clinic, nor does she belong to a cult that requires her to ignore medical treatment. Those are a few of the many circumstances that would have caused me to uphold the lower court ruling.

"In addition, aside from recounting his estranged wife's extreme views, the plaintiff did nothing to prove any harmful behaviors on the part of Ms. Rudolph. For that reason, I have no cause to believe the child would be in danger if he was returned to his mother."

Judge Wilder looked at her notes again, then gazed across the courtroom. "I was intrigued and troubled by the remarks belonging to former President George Washington. Rather than mourn the loss of religion, I treasure such a shift in our understanding and believe we are a better country today because of it. The deciding factor in this case then, was not ancient rhetoric nor the childish plea from the boy. Rather it was the First Amendment itself. Unless a child is truly in danger, this court must uphold the constitution of the United States and allow no ruling or law that would prohibit someone their right to religious freedom."

Jade couldn't breathe.

She sat there, still, her hands clenched together, sure she would shatter into a million pieces if she moved.

A million pieces of pure, unadulterated joy.

When Judge Wilder had started talking about the "deciding factor," Jade had let herself believe for the first time that she'd won. Hope, wild and overwhelming, coursed through her. Tears spilled onto her cheeks, and when Tanner took her hand in his, she could barely contain herself. She focused her attention on the judge once more.

"Therefore, in a ruling that is against my better judgment, I am hereby overturning the decision in the lower court and ordering that custody be returned to Jade Rudolph...."

Jade squeezed Tanner's hand to keep from jumping out of

her chair and shouting her thanks to God. Ty would be hers in a few minutes. Tanner had told her that if she won, the bailiff would escort her to the room where Ty was waiting. The officer would then physically hand him over to Jade. No questions asked.

God...God, thank you! You are faithful beyond words.

The judge was still speaking. "Furthermore, since Ms. Rudolph was the primary parent prior to the divorce petition, she will remain the primary parent of record. I have deemed an eighty-twenty split where custody is concerned so that the plaintiff will have the child every other weekend. Are there any questions from the attorneys?"

Jim's lawyer was on his feet. "We'd like to file a motion for joint custody, a fifty-fifty split."

"Duly noted." The judge wrote something down.

Tanner released Jade's hand, rose from the chair beside her, and nodded to the judge. "Your honor, I'd like to file a motion, but I must warn you it's going to seem very unconventional."

What was this? Jade's eyes followed Tanner as he moved closer to the judge. "Your honor, I'd like to file a motion severing the plaintiff's parental rights in their entirety."

Judge Wilder raised an eyebrow. "Do you intend to explain yourself?"

"Yes, your honor."

Jade's heart was pounding against her chest. What was he doing? Where was he going with this? Had he forgotten who was in the courtroom? Enough media to wipe out his law practice in the space of time it took to call in a headline.

"Go ahead, counselor." Judge Wilder looked frustrated, as though Tanner were ignorant of some unwritten protocol.

"Your honor, I have prepared a brief with various documents proving that the plaintiff should not be entitled to any parental rights because—" he paused long enough to glance at

Jade—"the plaintiff is not the boy's biological father."

"What?" Jim bounded up from his chair and had to be held back by his attorney. "He's crazy! He doesn't know what he's talking about."

Tanner remained calm. He retrieved a brief from Matt Bronzan and handed it to the judge. "Everything's there. A DNA test has been performed, and the results will be available soon. At that time there will be no question as to the validity of this brief."

For the first time that morning, Judge Wilder seemed speechless. Jade didn't care. Her eyes were on Tanner, stunned by his admission and the fact that he'd prepared a brief on the issue. How could she have ever doubted him?

The judge sorted through the brief and then stopped, her eyes trained on an item near the back of the document. She looked up, fixing her gaze on Tanner. "You mean to tell me, *you're* the boy's father, Mr. Eastman?" There was mockery in her voice, and as if by cue, the members of the press moved a step closer.

"Yes, your honor. Ms. Rudolph and I were together that summer and...yes, your honor. There are a lot of circumstances involved, but Ms. Rudolph believed I had abandoned her. As a result, she agreed to a marriage proposal the plaintiff had made a year earlier."

Jim glared at Jade and sank slowly into his chair. Their eyes met, and Jade saw anger and humiliation there. But not surprise. And in that moment it became clear to Jade that her longtime suspicions were probably true—he'd known about Ty all the time.

If that were true—if Jim had known Ty wasn't his biological son—it was no wonder he had treated the boy with such indifference. Suddenly the custody battle made sense. Jim had taken her in, thought she'd come to care for him, only to discover that the woman he'd always longed for had betrayed him. With another man. It must have been abundantly clear to him that she'd come out of need, not out of desire. And that had been her greatest betrayal of all.

This—the hearing, the push to take Ty from her—it was Jim's way of paying her back for lying to him all those years. Jade felt a wave of remorse.

God, forgive me. Forgive me for bringing him such grief, such sorrow. Forgive me for whatever part I played in driving Jim into the arms of another woman with my dishonesty. He deserved a wife who truly loved him, Lord.

Tanner was still speaking. "Either way, the information is all in the brief." He shrugged. "Also for the record, when Ms. Rudolph's divorce is final, I will be marrying her and claiming my rightful place as the boy's father."

Judge Wilder fell back against her chair and threw up her hands. "Why didn't you say so in the *first* place? We could have avoided this hearing altogether."

"Because Ms. Rudolph deserved to win this case as a way of protecting her constitutional freedoms. Now that this court has agreed with her rights, it must also know the truth before an accurate discussion of custody can be made."

The judge's face grew serious, and she sat up in her chair. "My decree regarding custody will stand until I have had time to review this brief and examine results from the DNA test. At that point all parties will be notified, and a permanent arrangement will be determined. Court dismissed."

The judge disappeared, and the courtroom erupted in conversation and a push by the media toward Tanner and Jade. Jim and his attorney stood up and headed for the side door.

"Jim, wait...." Jade worked her way past Tanner until she

was face to face with the man who had been her husband. "I'm sorry. You deserved to hear that from me. Not here, like this."

Jim's eyes were cool, almost indifferent. "I was a fool to love you, Jade. To think you ever cared for me. As for the boy—" he shrugged—"I knew from the beginning he wasn't my son. I had an injury in high school, playoff football game my junior year. Doctor told me I'd never have children."

What? An injury…? "Then why…?"

The smile that tipped his lips was bitter. "You came to me, remember? I thought maybe if I didn't say anything…"

An ache developed in Jade's chest. *Dear God, what have I done to this man? Forgive me, please.* "I wondered if you knew, but I wasn't sure. Not until a few minutes ago. I'm sorry, Jim. I never meant to hurt you."

"You never meant to love me, either. You came to me pregnant, hoping I would give you security and a home for your child. I never knew who you'd been with, only that he was a fool to let you go."

Jade saw the anger cool slightly, and in its place was deep and profound pain. Their marriage had never had a chance. Jade's eyes remained locked on Jim's. "And when you realized why I showed up that day, you determined to keep your distance."

Jim nodded. "We should have split up a long time ago, Jade. Your silence about Ty's father told me that whoever he was, you loved him the way you'd never love me. Problem was, I could never quite make myself stop loving you. But these last few years…well, I found someone who cared about me, and you didn't seem to mind. Most of the time you never asked where I was."

The media was moving closer, and Jade needed to get back to Tanner. He would join the bailiff in walking her to the private room where Ty was waiting for her. "You hate me, don't you, Jim?"

His gaze was unemotional. "I don't care enough about you anymore to hate you. This hearing was about what Kathy wanted. She thought Ty could be the son she never had." He looked away. "The boy mattered more to you than I did. Right from the day he was born. If I got full custody of him, then it served you right."

Jade felt a chill pass down her spine. If this man had won today, Ty would have been little more than a pawn. *Thank you, God....*

"I'm sorry."

Jim's eyes narrowed. "You won. But then, you always do. Ty wasn't my boy; I didn't want him anyway."

Jade nodded. She knew Jim's words were in part to conceal the hurt she'd caused him, but there was truth there, too. "I know."

Jim ran his eyes over the length of her. "I'll never forgive myself for letting you get under my skin, Jade. But don't worry your Christian heart over me. I'll be fine." He smiled through cold eyes. "I got bigger fish to fry now. And don't worry about the judge's decision. I'm tired of fighting with you. You can have your kid back. I want no part of him. Or of you."

She wanted to apologize once more, tell him she never meant to hurt him. But there was no point now. After ten years of marriage they were nothing but strangers. "Good-bye, Jim."

Working her way back to Tanner, Jade saw the concern in his eyes. "What did you say to him?"

She held a finger up to his lips. "Later. Right now we have a little boy to pick up."

Tanner took her hand, and they managed to sneak out a side door without answering a single one of the dozens of questions being hurled at him by the swarming members of the media. A bailiff ushered them down a hallway void of any reporters and into the correct room.

"Mom! Mr. Eastman!" Ty ran to her and jumped in her arms. "Well? Did we win?"

Jade wrapped her arms around her son and snuggled her face against his. "Yes. Your—Mr. Eastman was wonderful."

Ty pulled back enough to grin at Tanner. "No offense, Mr. Eastman, but I knew we were going to win even if you bombed."

Tanner laughed. "How so?"

"Because I was stuck back here by myself, and I was doing a lot of praying. About an hour ago I heard the Lord whispering in my ear."

There was something unquestionably innocent about her son's faith, something that made Jade's heart swell with pride. She linked one arm through Tanner's and drew him into their circle. They were a family now, and even if Ty didn't know about Tanner yet, Jade was convinced everything was going to work out.

She kissed Ty on the top of his head. "And what did the Lord whisper to you?"

"It was really weird, a verse we read once in Sunday school. After that, I knew for sure we were going to win."

Jade exchanged a curious look with Tanner. "What verse?"

Ty stood up straight and recited it perfectly: "I know the plans I have for you…plans to prosper you and not to harm you, plans to give you hope and a future."

Jade and Tanner were silent for a moment, and then their eyes met. Jade could read Tanner's expression, perfectly and she nodded in response. It was finally time. "Ty, honey…"

Ty hugged her close, at peace with his world once again. "Yeah, Mom?"

"Mr. Eastman and I have something to tell you."

Thirty-seven

THE FIRST SATURDAY OF NOVEMBER PRESENTED ITSELF WITH crisp, clear skies and an impending sense that soon—very soon—all would be right with the world. It was the kind of day when Doris Eastman didn't mind her body's weakness or the way her ailing heart slowed every move.

In some ways, she had waited all her life for this day.

She rose from bed and opened her Bible to 1 Corinthians, Chapter 13. Since giving her life back to the Lord, every word in Scripture was vibrantly alive and new. And there could be no better day to remember what God taught about love.

Patient and kind, not keeping a record of wrongs, not easily angered.

It was like a heavenly description of Jade and Tanner. Wherever they were that morning, whatever they were doing at this moment, they, too, had waited all their lives for this day.

Marti appeared with her morning water and pills. "Good morning, Mrs. Eastman." The girl was in her late twenties and had moved to Los Angeles from Italy the year before. After her release from the hospital, Tanner had moved her across country, into a condominium not far from his law office. Marti came recommended by a pastor at Tanner's church, and after a trial period, Doris and Marti became fast friends. The younger woman had moved into the bedroom down the hall from Doris's and worked for her full-time.

"It's the big day." Doris allowed Marti to help her to her feet.

"Yes, ma'am. Mr. Tanner's wedding day. He doesn't know you're coming?"

Doris felt a stab of fear. "No. He…thinks I'm too ill."

"Well, the doctor, he said you should stay in bed as much as possible, Mrs. Eastman." Marti's accent was thick, but Doris no longer had trouble understanding her.

"Not today, Marti. I wouldn't miss this for the world."

"I am glad to go with you today. You will tell me if you get too tired, no?"

"Yes, Marti." Doris appreciated the girl's concern; she would not have been able to attend the wedding without Marti. The water shook in her hand, and Marti helped steady the glass. It was always an effort getting the pills down each morning, but Marti's conversation helped pass the time.

"When did Miss Jade and her boy arrive in town?" Marti slipped Doris's robe off her shoulders and helped her to her feet.

"Her divorce was final two weeks ago. They arrived last weekend."

"They have somewhere to stay, yes?"

"With Tanner's friend, Matt Bronzan." Doris winced. Her bones had been aching more than usual, and she figured it was because she'd gotten so little exercise. It was, in some ways, a no-win situation. She needed to rest to conserve energy and protect her heart, but the more she rested, the weaker she grew. The doctor had told her it wouldn't be long now. She had cheated death once; it wouldn't happen a second time.

"They have a new house for after the wedding, yes?" Marti held Doris's elbow gently and eased her into the bathroom.

"Yes. Tanner told me about it. Four bedrooms, a big backyard. Only twenty minutes from his office." She would love to see it, but that was out of the question. It took all her energy just to visit with Tanner for an hour these days. The wedding would be her first outing since the heart attacks.

Meticulously Marti tucked Doris's hair into a shower cap. She knew the routine well and seemed forever one step ahead of Doris, anticipating her needs and struggles. "Hmm. Four bedrooms?" Marti's eyes twinkled. "They have just one boy, no?"

Doris smiled. "Yes. But not for long if Tanner has anything to say about it." She sucked in her breath as Marti led her to a nearby chair. The process of getting out of bed, of donning her bathrobe and a shower cap, left Doris exhausted. She generally needed a few minutes in the chair before she was ready to bathe. "Tanner and Jade are young. Tanner says they want lots of babies."

"Tanner seems very happy. You must be proud."

Doris thought about the pain she'd put her son and Jade through, the lost years her lies had cost them both. Marti knew none of those details, though, and Doris had no need to share them now. "Yes, Marti. Tanner and Jade are very happy." She hesitated and felt herself getting weepy. "I am very proud of them both."

And terrified at the same time. She remembered Tanner's visit not long after she was settled in her condo. "Call Jade, Mother. She wants to talk to you."

But Doris had used her health as an excuse, both then and again weeks ago when Jade arrived in town. "I'd love to see Jade and Ty," she'd told Tanner. "But dear, I'm simply not up to visitors."

The truth was, she desperately wanted to meet Ty—her son's only child, her grandson. But guilt formed a barrier of shame she couldn't see past, and instead she had written a letter to Jade apologizing for her inexcusable lies, her wicked behavior. In turn, Jade had written back, assuring Doris of her forgiveness. Still, Tanner told her often that she should meet Jade face to face, talk things out and make amends in person.

"Don't run from this," Tanner had begged her. "Jade forgives you, Mother. But you two need to talk, face to face now that she's in Los Angeles. For both your sakes."

A small voice within Doris had told her that was true, but still she held back. What if it didn't go well? She shook her head. No, it wasn't right. She didn't want to do anything to mar this time for either Tanner or Jade. With that in mind, Doris declined her invitation to the wedding. "I'd ruin it for her, Tanner."

"That isn't true. Mother, she wants you there."

Tanner didn't understand. God may have forgiven her, but Jade...How could Doris look the girl in the face and apologize to her? How could Jade ever really forgive an old woman who had cost her ten years of happiness?

And yet, more and more over the last few days, Doris had felt the urging—almost as though someone were giving her a strong nudge in her spirit—to go. Finally, yesterday, she'd given in. She would go, trusting God to work things out.

Marti helped Doris up, carefully removed her nightgown and eased her into the shower. Doris could still bathe herself but the process left her drained and Marti had taken to staying within arm's reach. "You're so wonderful, Marti. What would I do without you?"

"God is good, Mrs. Eastman. Good to both of us."

When she was finished showering, Marti helped her dry off and for a moment Doris remembered how independent she'd been, how proud and hard hearted.

Now she was grateful for having help in and out of the shower. Although she missed her vitality, she knew better than anyone that the true condition of her heart was worlds better than it had been before the heart attacks. And for that she thanked God constantly.

Marti slipped the robe back over Doris's shoulders and eased her into the chair once more. "I'll be all right, Marti. You go ahead and get ready. I need some time with the Lord."

The girl smiled and then dashed out the door down the hall toward her room. When she was gone, Doris closed her eyes and thanked God for his faithfulness. He had brought Tanner and Jade back together, where they had always belonged. He had spared her life long enough to allow her to repent and tell Tanner the truth. And he had done something she still couldn't believe.

He had spared Tanner's career.

From the hospital bed set up in her Los Angeles condominium, Doris Eastman had scrutinized every article and news story she could find about her son. The newspapers had been so shocked by Tanner's revelation that at first their stories seemed almost ambivalent.

What had happened over the next weeks and months had been nothing short of a miracle. Rather than rail against Tanner for his immorality years earlier, the media learned the story behind Tanner and Jade and embraced him as a modern-day hero. A man of faith with whom the people could relate. Not perfect, but perfectly committed to God.

Since August, editorials in the Los Angeles *Times* had described a major groundswell of public support should Tanner Eastman decide to run for state senator. Tanner had talked about it with Doris during one of their visits, and for the first time he thought serving in a public office might actually be the path God was choosing for him.

"Matt's ready to take over the CPRR office." Tanner had

been unable to hide his grin. "Who'd have thought there'd come a day when the idea of public office actually appealed to me."

Doris had enjoyed his easy banter. The two were much closer than they'd been before the heart attacks, giving her yet another reason to be grateful. "I always knew you'd be on the ballot one day. But of course you had to do it your way."

In reality she knew that though she would probably not live to see her son elected to office, or the children he and Jade might have in the future, she was no longer concerned with the choices he made. He had chosen to follow God's path, and from where Doris sat now, she would be eternally grateful.

She thought about the wedding and the fact that sometime later that day she would face Jade. It would be their first meeting since that afternoon in Portland. And then...she would meet her grandson for the first time. *What if Jade hates me? What if she asks me to leave?* Doris wanted nothing more than to make peace with Jade, but in that instant she was struck by a palpable sense of doom.

My precious daughter, remember nothing is impossible with God....

The words filled her mind and brought with them an unearthly peace. Yes, that was it. With the Lord, nothing was impossible.

God had given Tanner the strength to follow him.

Now it was her turn.

The ceremony was to be held west of Los Angeles at Chapel in the Canyon, a stucco building with a Spanish tile roof situated amidst rocks and wild brush. The view from the courtyard was breathtaking, and Jade stood outside savoring a moment of solitude before the wedding began.

In a million years, she would never have dreamed that this was what God had planned for her…that this was the future she—

"Jade."

The voice was weaker than before, but it was distinct all the same. Jade's heart skipped a beat. *No, it can't be…not now…*She spun around, her veil swishing gently behind her. "Mrs. Eastman."

A younger woman waited in the distance as Tanner's mother took slow, shuffling steps toward her. *What was this? She had come after all. Despite her failing health and adamant refusal to receive visitors, Tanner's mother had come.*

"Jade, I know you weren't expecting me today." She was out of breath, and Jade could see something different in her expression, something soft and genuine that had been missing the last time they spoke. Tanner had told her a dozen times how different his mother was, how her faith was new and alive and how everything about her had changed as a result. Now Jade could see that for herself.

Jade's heart pounded, and she struggled for the right words. "No…I mean, yes…we want you here, Mrs. Eastman. I'm so glad you could make it." The woman's eyes told Jade she had nothing to worry about. This was not a trick or a trap like their last meeting. Mrs. Eastman was a changed woman.

Mrs. Eastman moved closer still and placed a hand tenderly on Jade's arm. "You're a beautiful bride, Jade. Tanner is a lucky man."

Jade was speechless, overwhelmed by the power of God's love and forgiveness.

"I'm sorry, Jade." There were tears in Mrs. Eastman's eyes, and Jade began to tremble. "I'm old and worn out, but God has been merciful. He allowed me to be here and tell you to your face. I'm so very, very sorry, Jade. What I did was…it was shameful. There's no other way to say it. I'll be sorry as long as I live."

The confession seemed to add years to Mrs. Eastman's countenance, and her shoulders drooped as she stepped back. "I won't bother you anymore. If you don't mind, I'll go inside and watch."

Too full of emotion to speak, Jade took Doris Eastman's hand in hers and squeezed it gently. "We all paid a price for what happened that summer." Tears sprang to Jade's eyes. "But God, in his mercy, has worked it out for good." Through watery eyes, Jade smiled her forgiveness at the woman. "I told you in my letter that I forgave you, Mrs. Eastman. And I do. The past is over."

She led Tanner's mother to a side door near the back of the church and flagged down Matt Bronzan. "Get Tanner, please." Jade squeezed Mrs. Eastman's hand gently and smiled at her. "Tell him his mother is here."

Jade entered the building on Matt Bronzan's arm, and Tanner had to remind himself he was not dreaming. Jade was stunning in a simple, straight-cut ivory gown, and in her eyes he saw a love for which he'd gladly wait a lifetime. When he thought of Jade now, it wasn't with remorse for the years they'd lost. Rather it was with gratefulness to God for bringing them back together.

The minister was telling their few close friends the importance of keeping God in their marriage, and Tanner exchanged a brief smile with his mother, who was seated in the front row, in the place of honor that was rightfully hers.

"The Lord is more than a wedding guest," the minister was saying. He was a somber man, and his message hit the mark for Tanner. "He wants to be part of the marriage."

He told them that Scripture teaches how a cord of three strands is not easily broken. "With God at the center, you will build a marriage that will be a beautiful thing, a union that will draw people to the Lord." He looked at Jade and Tanner and smiled. "Why? Because the world so desperately wants what you already have."

Ty stood beside Tanner as his best man, and Tanner's heart swelled as he glanced at his son. He had taken Ty fishing and to breakfast and even hiking in the past week. After months of phone conversations and letters, the child willingly accepted Tanner as his father. The road ahead looked promising for all of them.

It was time for the vows, and Jade and Tanner turned to face each other.

They had agreed to say their own vows, rather than repeating something read by the minister. Tanner went first.

"Jade, you are the treasure of my heart, my friend, my lover, my past, my future." Tanner tightened the grip he had on Jade's hands. "I promise before God and our friends, to love you, honor you, cherish you now and forever, no matter what bends appear on the road ahead. God created man with a missing rib, a missing part."

Jade's eyes glistened and she tilted her head, her eyes locked on his.

"You, Jade, are that missing piece, the part I have searched for all of my life. From this day forth I will cling to you and you alone. From this day forth I am whole." He slipped a gold band on her finger and saw tears glistening in her eyes. "With this ring, I, Tanner Eastman, do thee, Jade Conner, wed."

Jade swallowed hard, and Tanner could tell she was struggling to speak. He squeezed her hands gently, encouraging her, and she gave the slightest of nods. Then she stared at him; her eyes lit up from all she was feeling inside.

"You, Tanner Eastman, are the one with whom my soul rejoices. You have given me hope when I had none, life when I was dying, and love when I thought I would never love again. On this day, with God as our witness, I promise to love you, cherish you, honor you, and respect you all the days of my life." Her hands trembled as she slipped the ring on his finger. "With this ring as a token of my promise, a reminder of my unending love, I, Jade Conner, do thee wed."

And in that moment, Tanner knew that whatever else lay ahead, they would never again be alone. Because God had brought them back together, and one day, in the sunset of their lives, God would lead them home.

The reception took place at the Bronzans' house in Malibu, with a view overlooking the Pacific Ocean. A seafood dinner had been catered in for the occasion, and Hannah Bronzan had decorated the house beautifully.

It was three hours into the party, and many of the guests had already left, but still there was no sign of Doris Eastman. Her nursemaid had taken her home moments after the ceremony with promises to bring her back for the reception if she was feeling up to it. Tanner had tried to call her twice, but there had been no answer.

"I'm worried about her." Jade found Tanner in the kitchen and leaned up to kiss him. "She should be here by now."

Tanner shrugged. "I'm not sure she's coming. She wasn't supposed to be at the wedding. Doctor said no outings until she's stronger."

"Well, I want her here. She wasn't in any of the pictures and..."

"And?" Tanner pulled her toward him and kissed her tenderly.

"She didn't get to meet Ty yet." Jade gazed out the window toward the ocean. "I want her to meet him before—"

Tanner held a finger to her lips. "God knows that, Jade. Don't worry about her. She'll probably be here any minute." He kissed her tenderly. "Have I told you lately how beautiful you are, Mrs. Eastman?"

Jade's heart soared and she returned his kiss. The nearness of him made her long for the morning, when they would leave for four days in Cabo San Lucas. Ty would stay with the Bronzans, and after that the three of them would spend a weekend in San Diego, deep-sea fishing off the coast.

"Have I told you how much I'm going to enjoy being Mrs. Eastman?" Jade snuggled closer to him.

"Okay, okay, break it up." Matt bounded into the kitchen with Hannah and Ty in tow. He wore a conspiratorial grin, and Jade couldn't help but smile. The Bronzans had become very dear friends, and she was sure they would only get closer in the years to come.

Matt and Ty squared up a few feet away while Hannah shrugged sweetly in the background. "Now—" Matt poked an elbow at Ty, and the child grinned—"Your son has a special request. Something about checking out the fishing equipment in the garage." Matt held up his hands in mock surrender. "I know it's not appropriate to talk about fishing on your wedding day and all, but..." He grinned at Jade. "If I could borrow Tanner for just a few minutes."

Jade laughed. "Go ahead. Hannah and I will stay here and talk about the joys of cleaning fish."

The last guests had gone home, and only Hannah's daughter, Jenny, remained in the other room studying for a high school English exam. The women watched as the men disappeared into the garage, talking all at once and sounding like three children on the verge of a great discovery.

When they were gone, Hannah leaned against the kitchen counter and smiled at Jade. "Congratulations."

"Thanks. You guys have done so much for us…."

Hannah cocked her head. "You know, in some ways you and Tanner remind me of Matt and me. Love forged out of pain." Hannah hesitated. "Know what I mean?"

Jade knew pieces of Hannah's background, but not the whole story. She nodded. "Yours was much more painful, though. Tanner's told me about what happened. The collision."

There was a long-ago kind of sadness in Hannah's eyes as she gazed at Jade. "My husband and daughter were killed by a drunk driver." She paused, and Jade could see she was at peace with this. But it was painful all the same. "Matt prosecuted the case."

Jade reached out and squeezed Hannah's hand. She had the distinct feeling this woman was going to be a close friend someday. "Tell me about it, okay? When the time's right."

Hannah returned the squeeze and smiled. "It's an amazing story of God's faithfulness."

Jade nodded thoughtfully. "He's definitely that."

The men returned, and Matt carried with him a dusty guitar.

Hannah laughed. "I thought you were looking at fishing poles."

"We were. But we found my old guitar. Isn't that great?"

Hannah exchanged a look with Jade, and both women giggled. "You planning to use it as bait?" Hannah walked to Matt and ran her hand over the neck of the guitar.

Matt looked hurt. "No." He turned to Tanner. "Actually it was Tanner's idea."

"What?" Jade moved between Ty and Tanner and put her arm around them both.

Tanner kissed her cheek. "I thought we could sit on the deck and sing while Matt plays."

Jade smiled. It was a warm evening; the sun was just beginning to set. "Perfect."

Hannah wrinkled her nose. "Matt, I haven't cleaned the chairs out there in weeks."

Jade cut in. "It's okay, Hannah. Really. It'll be the perfect ending to the most perfect day." She smiled at Tanner and then Ty.

"Do I have to sing?" Ty looked worried, and the adults laughed at his sincerity.

"No, son." Tanner tousled Ty's hair, and Jade felt as if her heart would burst. Any concerns she'd had about whether Tanner and Ty would bond had long since dissolved. Tanner led the way outside and the others followed.

When they were seated, Tanner grinned at Ty. "Of course, you haven't heard me sing before. We just might need your help."

The ocean stretched out toward the horizon, gentle swells glimmering under the setting sun. Matt tuned his guitar and then called for requests.

"I have one." Hannah gave Jade a knowing look. "My favorite song."

"Ah, yes…" Matt practiced a few cords. "'Great Is Thy Faithfulness.'" He looked at the others. "You guys know it?"

Jade nodded and wove her fingers through Tanner's hand. It was the perfect song for her. And Jade had the feeling it was equally perfect for Hannah.

It had been a day to remember, but still it had been hectic at times. When Matt began playing the song, the strains carried on the breeze and soothed what remained of the wrinkles in Jade's soul.

"Great is thy faithfulness, Oh, God our Father, there is no shadow of turning with thee. All I have needed thy hands hath provided; Great is thy faithfulness, Lord unto me…."

They had just begun the second chorus when Doris Eastman and her nurse appeared at the foot of the deck. A broad smile filled Tanner's face, and he rose to meet her. While the song played on, he helped his mother up the three wooden steps to a cushioned seat. Doris's nursemaid took the spot beside her, and Tanner returned to Jade's side.

"Great is thy faithfulness, great is thy faithfulness, morning by morning new mercies I see…."

Ty tapped Jade's arm and motioned toward Mrs. Eastman. Jade nodded, and the boy crossed the deck and gently hugged the grandmother he'd never known. She held him close, her frail arms shaking, and then she moved so that he had room to sit down. Smiling innocently at the older woman beside him, Ty took her fragile hand in his and joined in the singing. Somehow the song magnified the beauty of the moment, and Jade's voice grew stronger.

At that moment, Tanner's mother caught Jade's gaze, and her eyes spoke volumes. Jade nodded to Doris and smiled. The old woman wanted to be her friend. Jade could see it clearly, and her heart melted. They were finally, completely at peace with each other, and, God willing, the future would hold many chances to talk.

Jade savored the words to the song, singing them in a prayer to God alone. As she did, Doris closed her eyes and raised an unsteady hand toward heaven, adding her voice to the others. "Great is thy faithfulness, great is thy faithfulness…."

Jade understood. The song belonged to Doris, too. It belonged to all of them. God had kept his promise and given every one of them a hope and a future. All because his mercies truly were new every morning.

Jade clung to Tanner's hand and closed her eyes as the final strains of the song drifted out to sea.

"All I have needed, thy hand hath provided.... Great is thy faithfulness, great is thy faithfulness, great is thy faithfulness, Lord, unto me."

Dear Reader,

First, you must know what a privilege it is to have been handed several hours of your time as you followed the story of Jade and Tanner. I hope you have received much in return as you traveled with them through the abysmal pit of sin and regret to the peace-filled plains of God's mercy and forgiveness.

As with each of my novels, it is my prayer that *A Moment of Weakness* did more than entertain you. I pray it helped you—as it has me—to grasp one of God's many truths. In this case, God's truth about sin.

There are obvious lessons in *A Moment of Weakness* for those tempted by sexual sin. But perhaps you cannot relate to this temptation. Maybe you are one who has—with good intentions—stood in judgment. Someone in your church family or even your immediate family has succumbed to a moment of weakness in his or her own life, and you, like Doris Eastman, have led the contingent in seeing that he or she receives punishment in full.

I remember well the story of a preacher's young daughter who wound up pregnant. She was broken and repentant, still the congregation was split in their reaction. Some hugged her close and promised prayer and support. Others pointed fingers behind her back, whispering mean-spirited words and inciting outrage among that body of believers. The girl was a 4.0 student with a brilliant mind and, before her weakest moment, an equally brilliant future. Though she could have secretly had an abortion and maintained her pure image, she chose to take responsibility for her sin and move forward in God's grace. Today God has blessed her with a godly husband and several beautiful children.

I never feared the repercussions her sin would have on her

own life. Not with her faith so firmly rooted in Christ and his saving grace. Rather I feared for those who considered themselves judge and jury, those who were ashamed of her and held a grudge against her. Scripture teaches us not to judge others or we, ourselves, will be judged. Forgive one another, encourage one another, build one another up. Love one another.

Please learn a lesson from Doris and remember God's grace the next time someone in your circle gives in to sin.

That said, I believe more of us relate to Jade and Tanner. Most people have been or will be tempted by the powerful pull of sexual sin. The Bible is as clear on this issue as it is on any that God feels strongly about. Scripture says flee immorality. Avoid sexual sin. Be pure. Be holy, set apart. Do not commit adultery. As with Tanner and Jade, God does not give these commands to punish us or dampen our pleasure. Rather he provides them so that our joy will be complete. Had Tanner and Jade waited until they were married, they would have been spared a decade of heartache and despair.

God's ways are always more satisfying than acting out what seems or feels right in our own moments of weakness.

Sadly, in America today, sexual sin—including pornography—has been cast into an almost comical light. This despite the fact that it has ruined people of authority and power on both sides of the political spectrum, people in Hollywood, and people in churches across the country. Our society seems to have bought the lie that somehow sexual sin cannot be avoided.

As a nation, we are wrong in this thinking, wrong for encouraging it, and wrong for celebrating sexual sin as a means of entertainment. It is time that you and I and all who would believe take a stand for holiness and purity. If that means turning off the television set or canceling your Internet service to maintain a healthy, holy environment for you and your children, then turn it off and cancel it. Remember, we are to hate what is evil; cling to what is good.

Finally, if you or someone you know is struggling with sexual sin, the time has come to seek godly counsel. There is glorious hope and a bright future for those who will get right with God, who will repent and turn away from this pervasive, addictive sin. Otherwise, there is only dark desperation and the consequences of sin as they are spelled out in Scripture.

In the meantime, I will pray along with you that each of us grows closer to God, his perfect Word, and his perfect plan for our lives.

Jesus Christ wants to be our personal friend and Savior. If you don't have a relationship with him and want to know more about becoming a Christian, making sure your name is written in the Lamb's Book of Life, please connect with someone at a Bible-believing church in your area.

God is there, even now. Waiting, watching. Ready to forgive, ready to make us new creations, to welcome us with open arms into his everlasting presence.

As always, I'd love to hear from you. Write me at:

Multnomah Books
12265 Oracle Boulevard, Suite 200
Colorado Springs, CO 80921
Or e-mail me at: rtnbykk@aol.com

Discussion Questions

1. Read Jeremiah 29:11. How does it make you feel knowing that God has plans for you?
2. Among the characters in *A Moment of Weakness*, can you most relate to Jade, Tanner, or Doris Eastman?
3. Tell about a special childhood friend you had. What do you remember about that time? Have you kept in touch with him or her? Why or why not?
4. During the years Tanner and Jade were apart, how was God working in Tanner's life?
5. How was God working in Jade's life during those years?
6. Why do you think Doris Eastman was a valuable character in this book?
7. How did you first come to have faith in Christ? Was your situation similar to Jade's? If so, explain. If not, tell about someone you know who has doubts about God, the way Jade did.
8. When have you felt a certainty that God was at work, shaping your future?
9. Religious persecution is a common thing today. Discuss examples or times when you have seen Christians persecuted in the modern-day United States.
10. What religious freedoms do you see disappearing in our country? What can you do to help shore up the freedoms promised to all Americans in the U.S. Constitution?

BOOK THREE

FOREVER FAITHFUL

Halfway *to* Forever

Dedicated to...

DONALD, MY KNIGHT in shining armor, my one true love. Can this really be our fourteenth anniversary? Years slip by like hours in a day, but I cherish every one. With you by my side the best keeps getting better, and I thank God that you are such an example to me, to our children, to your students and athletes. Thank you for being my best friend and for believing in forever. Aren't we having a blast? Year after year after year after year… I love you so.

Kelsey, my sweet little "Norm" who has long since shed her little-girl image and traded it in for the look of a young teen on the brink of everything new and wonderful and exciting. You're busy these days, sweetheart, but it does my mother-heart good to know you still remember who you are: a child of God, a daughter, a sister, a student, a friend. I cherish the times we have together even more now that you are in middle school, because in the distant corridors of time I see you, not too very far from here, in a cap and gown. I can't slow the ride, but I can be grateful for every minute, knowing full well that God's plans for you will be nothing less than amazing. I am so proud of you, honey. Always remember that I love you, Kelsey.

Tyler, my handsome, budding young writer. I love when you tell me you're going to act and sing when you grow up—but in your spare time you might write for fun. I guess that's all writing is, after all: fun. The way God intended His gifts to be. I will long remember your "one voice" ringing out across the school's Veteran's Day assembly. May God lead you to always be that one voice ringing out for Him, and may His plans for your life become more evident with each passing year. I love you, Ty.

Austin (or Michael Jordan, depending on the moment). This

past year I have watched you take giant steps away from babyhood and into the strong, strapping young boy you are becoming. I will never forget sitting on the edge of your bed that September evening before your fourth birthday, singing with you, kissing you goodnight, and saying good-bye to my three-year-old. You're not my baby anymore, but you are still my miracle boy. The heart that beats within you is fully devoted—whether slamming a basketball through a net or singing songs for Jesus. Keep that, honey, as God's spectacular plans for your life unfold. Keep it always. I love you, Austin.

EJ, our youngest Haitian son. Adopting you has blessed us beyond words. We have watched you grow from a shy, insecure little boy to a confident, goal-kicking, letter-sounding, smiling child with no limits to your potential. God definitely brought you into our lives for a reason, and I am grateful every day. I can't wait to see what He has planned for you. I love you, EJ.

Sean, our half-angel boy. When we brought you home from Haiti you made an instant place in our hearts for one reason—you were constantly praying to Jesus. Even now, when we give you a present, you drop to your knees and thank God for the giver. When we give you a meal, you won't take a bite—no matter how hungry you are—until proper thanks has been given. And when you finish eating you look to the heavens and say, "Thank you, Jesus." You told me recently that you would grow up and get a good job one day so you could give me and Daddy some money because we'd helped you so much. With teary eyes I told you that wasn't necessary, just love Jesus all your life, Sean. And as God reveals His plan for you, I am convinced that will always be the best advice I could give you. I love you, Sean.

Joshua, chosen by God for our family. When I went to Haiti to adopt your two best friends, I didn't know about you. But you worked your way into my heart in minutes with your sweet songs for Jesus and your sad little smile. How wonderful God is to bring you into our family this past September. You are brilliant at everything you do, from reading, to those soccer foot skills that would make any teenager envious. At six years old you clearly have a great desire to do things right, a determined spirit that will take you far, and a compassion for others that makes you a natural leader. Always remember where your gifts come from...and that God has very special plans for you. I love you, Joshua.

And to God Almighty, my Lord and Savior, the Author of Life, who has—for now—blessed me with these.

Acknowledgments

SO MUCH GOES into the writing of any single book. I couldn't possibly move on to my next project without stopping to thank the people who have made this one possible. First, and foremost, it is my great pleasure to thank God who has given me the gift of writing. I am amazed at the letters pouring in from my readers, letters that prove God is changing lives with the gift of story—just as He did when Jesus walked this Earth. I pray I always use His gift in a way that touches hearts and glorifies God.

Also, thanks to my wonderful husband and children, who understand when life goes on hold because Mommy has a deadline. Donald, you have the most uncanny ability to pick up where I leave off when I need a little extra help. "Thanks" doesn't come close. In addition, thanks to my extended family, many of whom tirelessly continue to spread the word about my novels. I am grateful for each of you.

Beyond family, there are those friends who have prayed for me, supported me, and listened to me discuss story ideas. In that light, a special thanks to Sylvia Wallgren and Ann Hudson, my personal prayer warriors, without whom none of this would ever happen. And to those special friends and sisters in Christ who have made such a faithful impact on my life. You know who you are.

A sincere thanks to Amber Santiago, my dear friend and personal assistant. You have a golden voice, the best I've ever heard. You could be performing for all the world, yet instead you spend each day taking care of my sweet Austin and overseeing dozens of other tasks that make my writing possible. May God bless you for your servant-heart. And to Jenna Hiller who stepped in and helped with our six children during crunch time.

When researching a novel, I often call on experts. For this book and several others I want to thank Bryce Cleary, M.D., and Attorney Stan Kaputska for their valuable insight. Also my father, Ted Kingsbury, who often takes an hour from his morning to brainstorm ideas with me.

Once a novel is written, there are still many people who take it to the next level—the place where you, the reader, receive it. For that reason, a special thanks goes to my agent Greg Johnson and the folks at Alive Communications. I am continually awestruck by your talent, Greg, and humbly blessed that I have the chance to partner with you in bringing these books into being.

Also, thanks to my editor, Karen Ball. Each time you edit a book it's like taking a class from the very best in fiction writing. You are so good at what you do, Karen. Thanks for rubbing a little of your incredible talent on my books. And thanks to Julee Schwarzburg, Chad Hicks, Steve Curley, and Lisa Bowden, who champion my work with the great people at Multnomah Publishers. All of you at Multnomah are like family to me, and always will be. Thanks for taking a chance on me four years ago. In addition, thanks to Joan Westfall, who always does an amazing job on my final edit. I'm blessed to have your help.

A huge thanks to Kirk DouPonce, the brilliantly gifted man who designs my covers. I can only pray that people *do* judge my books by my covers, and that in the end the story measures up. Thank you for offering your best work on behalf of mine.

Finally, thanks to the Skyview Basketball team, you hustling, runnin', gunnin' guys—for giving me a reason to cheer, even on deadline.

One

Hannah Bronzan rarely visited the cemetery.

The grassy knolls and quiet, sad whispers were not necessary for her to remember Tom and Alicia, because they did not live in the confines of a garden of stone, but in Hannah's heart.

Where they would always live.

But on this day, Hannah climbed out of the car, slipped on her sunglasses, and gazed across a sea of cold, gray tombstones. Her heart ached as she drew a slow, shaky breath.

Much as she didn't want to be here, it was time. Despite the emotions warring within her, Hannah knew she had no choice. She needed to come now, just as she'd needed to come two years ago when Matt Bronzan asked her to be his wife.

By then she had grieved the loss of her first husband, and with a strength that was not her own, she'd survived. Enough to tell Matt yes, to believe there was indeed a new life for her and young Jenny on the other side of a darkness and pain that had nearly destroyed them both.

Coming here had been difficult back then too, but it had given her a chance to say good-bye to Tom, to thank him for all they'd shared, and to release him. To let die a flame she thought would burn forever. Hannah set her gaze in the direction of their tombstones and pulled her sweater tighter.

Her eyes welled up. Now it was time to let go of Alicia.

This was a private moment—one she needed to share with

Tom and Alicia alone. Regardless of shaded grounds, the glasses would stay. She walked amidst the markers, her fingers brushing against an occasional cold stone as she made her way across the cemetery to the place where their markers lay, side by side.

Her eyes drifted from one to the other. *Dr. Thomas J. Ryan…Alicia Marie Ryan.* The birth dates were different, but the date of death was the same: *August 28, 1998.*

A lump formed in Hannah's throat, and she swallowed hard as she knelt down, sitting back on her heels. She wiped an errant tear from her cheek… Alicia would have been nineteen, finished with high school and making her way through college. In love, perhaps, or dreaming of a career.

Alicia. I miss you, baby…

It was harder to picture them now, harder to see the crisp definition in her mind's scrapbook…how Tom's eyes sparkled when she was in his arms, or the way Alicia's smile lit up a room…

They'd lost so much in one terrible moment. A drunk driver, an awful collision…and the life she and Tom had spent years building was shattered.

Hannah exhaled, and the sound mingled with the breeze. *You can do this.* She squeezed her eyes shut, searching for the strength to move ahead. She and Matt had worked out the plans for more than a year. It was the right thing, she was sure of that much. Even now, with sadness covering her heart like a blanket, she could feel the excitement welling within her, convincing her that somehow, sometime soon, it would happen.

She would be a mother again.

"Hi…" She set her fingertips on Alicia's tombstone and dusted off a layer of dirt. "I have something to tell you."

A crow sounded in the distance. This visit was for peace of mind and nothing more. Hannah's precious oldest daughter would never have questioned her intentions, never have doubted her place in Hannah's heart. Her fingers stopped moving and settled over Alicia's name.

"Matt and I have decided to…to adopt a little girl." Her voice broke, and from behind her sunglasses tears trickled down her face and dripped off her chin.

She waited until she could find her voice. "After…after the accident I couldn't imagine ever loving another man," Hannah wiped the back of her hand across her wet chin. "Or another daughter." A sound that was part laugh, part sob slipped from her lips. "But here I am, happy, married, and…convinced God has another daughter for me somewhere out there."

The traffic hummed from the road behind her. "You understand, right, Alicia? I'm not trying to…to replace you, honey." She sniffed. "The bond you and I shared, the one you and Jenny shared, that's something none of us will ever have again. Not like it was."

Hannah paused and gazed up, willing herself to see beyond the blue to the place where Tom and Alicia now lived and loved and laughed.

Gradually her eyes shifted back to the tombstones. "I saw a documentary last night about kids in America, kids waiting for someone to love them, and…I don't know…something inside me snapped." She shrugged and managed a smile despite the fresh tears on her cheeks. "I can't have more babies. We've known that since Jenny was born. But adoption?" She sniffed. "I wasn't sure I could do it…until last night. Then, all of a sudden, I knew. I *could* open my heart to another little girl."

The background noise faded. Hannah traced the *A* in Alicia's name, pushing away the dirt that had gathered there. "We'll adopt a toddler, someone who needs a second chance at life." She blinked, and two more tears slid off the tip of her nose onto Alicia's stone. "I don't know where she is…or who she is. But I know she's out there somewhere. And I wanted you to know bec–"

There was a catch in Hannah's voice, and she held the sobs at bay. "Because she'll be your sister."

Hannah closed her eyes again and waited. The image of her oldest daughter grew clear in her mind once more. "Alicia…"

There she was. The smile, the honey blonde hair, the warmth in her eyes…it was all as close and real as if she were standing there in person.

There were no words, but a distinct sense of approval pierced the darkness. The feeling swelled, and Hannah had no doubts. God wanted her to know Alicia would have supported this decision with her whole being.

Hannah ached to reach out and pull the image of her daughter close, but the lines began to blur. As they did, peace oozed between the cracks in Hannah's heart. It was okay to let her daughter's memory fade for now. The visit had reminded her once more that she no longer needed to feel the pain of Alicia's and Tom's deaths with every excruciating breath, but only as a sad truth that simply was and could not be changed.

Hope wrapped its arms around her as she opened her eyes. It was time to go home, time to let Matt and Jenny know what she'd decided. Of course, Jade and Tanner Eastman would want to know, too. The couple had become their best friends these past years. They'd been there while Matt and Hannah walked through a year of collecting documents and filling out adoption forms, gathering letters and completing a dossier.

The Eastmans understood. They were desperate to have a baby, but so far hadn't been able.

Despite Hannah's tears, a smile tugged at her lips. Yes, Jade and Tanner would be thrilled that Hannah was finally ready to move forward.

She let her eyes settle on Tom's tombstone. "Pray for us, Tom." Two tears landed near his name, and she wiped her cheeks with her fingertips. "Pray for the little girl…whoever she is."

Once more she looked back at the stone, at Alicia's name carved in it. "One more thing, honey. When we bring her home and…and people ask me how many girls I have…" Hannah wiped at her tears again. "I'll always tell them three. Two who live here with me…and one who lives in heaven."

Two

The day had been nothing but salty sea breeze and endless blue skies. Matt and Hannah were gathered on the back deck of their beach home, their picnic with the Eastmans in full swing. They sat there, eating, overlooking the surf and a blazing sunset, and Matt reached for Hannah's hand. He set his burger down on the paper plate and looked around the picnic table at the others—their own precious eighteen-year-old Jenny, and Jade and Tanner Eastman and their thirteen-year-old son, Ty.

"We have something to tell you." He smiled at Hannah, and his presence soothed her soul the way it had since the first day they met. She leaned against him. They had already told Jenny their plans, and Hannah thought her response had been positive. Guarded maybe, but good all the same.

Matt went on. "We contacted our social worker yesterday…and gave her the green light."

Jade's eyes lit up and she clasped her hands together as she caught Hannah's gaze. "Are you serious? You've decided to—"

"Yes." Hannah smiled, and the accomplishment in that one single word hung like a gold medal around her neck. How far she'd come since that awful August day four years ago, how greatly God had blessed them. And suddenly—surrounded by the people she loved, enjoying a barbecue on the deck of the beachside home she and Matt and Jenny shared—the sum of all they'd been and all they were…all they were about to be…was almost overwhelming. "Yes," she said again. "We're ready to adopt."

Tanner's face broke into a grin and he reached across the table to shake Matt's hand. "Congratulations."

There was a brief flicker of sadness in Tanner's eyes, and Hannah understood. Tanner and Jade wanted more children, but since marrying more than a year ago, Jade had miscarried once and been unable to get pregnant since then. Hannah's heart went out to her friends, and though neither of them mentioned their own situation, she knew what they had to be feeling.

Tanner swung his arm over Jade's shoulders. "So, the world's best business partner is going to have a little one running around, huh?" He leaned back in his chair. "Okay, don't keep us waiting…" He took a bite of his burger, and a blob of ketchup landed squarely on his khaki button-down shirt. "Give us the—"

Hannah and Jade exchanged a look, and they both giggled.

Tanner finished chewing. "What?" He looked around the table.

Matt smothered a grin with his hand, and Jenny and Ty laughed into their napkins.

Jade was the first to rescue her husband. She pointed to his shirt, and Tanner glanced down. He chuckled and shook his head. "That settles it. Someone else will have to teach the Bronzans' new little girl how to eat."

Hannah and Jade locked eyes again and burst out laughing. How often had their good-looking, powerful husbands spilled a drink or stained a shirt or broken a chair at their legendary get-togethers? Matt and Tanner might run the nation's most powerful religious freedom law firm, but at home they were often little more than oversized boys.

Matt loosed his grip on Hannah's hand, and his dimpled grin lit up Hannah's heart. "Well, Tanner, I, for one, am appalled at your manners."

Tanner nodded, his expression playful. "That's what I get for hanging out with you."

Amid the laughter, Jade dabbed a wet napkin at Tanner's shirt, giggling so hard her shoulders shook.

Hannah studied her friends through smiling eyes. It was good to see Jade laugh. She'd been dragging for several weeks lately, tired, achy. Jade blamed it on a lingering cold, but after all she and Tanner had been through, Hannah hated to see her sick.

The conversation shifted back to Matt and Hannah's adoption plans. As the evening wore on, Jenny took Ty to a movie with her friends, and the men congregated on the deck around Matt's old guitar. Hannah and Jade took a walk down the beach.

It was mid-March, and though the temperatures were cool, there had been no fog for days. As the sun set, the Pacific Ocean stretched out like a blanket of liquid blue beneath a canopy of crimson and gold. A hundred yards down the beach, Hannah stopped and stared out to sea, breathing in the damp, salty air. "I never get tired of it."

Jade drew up beside her. "It's breathtaking."

"Like a living masterpiece direct from God."

The picnic that day was one of their monthly get-togethers, their way of staying connected and supporting each other. Jade and Tanner lived in a spacious house in Thousand Oaks, twenty minutes away, on two acres of rolling hillside. They had four bedrooms and a bonus room, a monument to Jade and Tanner's dream of having a houseful of children one day.

The women started walking again and Hannah turned to Jade. "You look better, not so pale."

Jade nodded and something in her eyes grew distant. "I felt good today, being with you and Tanner, laughing a little."

Something caught in Hannah's heart. "Things are okay at home, right?"

"We're fine." A smile tried to climb up Jade's cheeks, but fell short. "Just wondering about God's plan."

"Babies?"

"Babies." Jade sighed and her eyes grew wet. "We love Ty so much, but he's thirteen. At this rate, he'll be busy with his own life by the time we give him a brother or sister."

Hannah walked a few steps and stopped. "How does Tanner feel?"

"He doesn't get it." Jade brushed her dark bangs off her face and shook her head. "He missed so much of Ty's growing up years...all he wants is a baby in every room, a chance to be the type of father he couldn't be to Ty."

The cool, damp sand filled in the places between Hannah's toes. "Ty was eleven before Tanner found out about him, right?"

"Right." Jade stared at the sun as it dropped below the horizon. "You'd never know it; the two of them are inseparable. Tanner is such a good dad. Still...sometimes I think the whole baby thing is taking a toll."

"Meaning...?" The soothing sound of a lone seagull punctuated their conversation.

"He's been burying himself at work, staying later, going in earlier. There's always a pressing case..." Jade hugged her arms close to her body. "Lately it's like he could work day and night and it wouldn't be enough." She was quiet, but after a moment a soft huff crossed her lips. "No one believes in his cause more than I do... I'm the one who talked him into it fifteen years ago. But sometimes it feels like he's pushing me away, closing down his emotions."

Hannah nodded and fell in step alongside Jade. "Matt gets that way sometimes. There were times when we'd talk about adoption for three weeks straight, until I needed a break. A day or two to sort out my feelings. Those would end up being the same days he'd work late."

Jade bent down and picked up a broken piece of a sand dollar.

"Then there's my health." She brushed a sprinkling of sand off the shell, and Hannah had the clear impression Jade was refusing to make eye contact with her.

A knot formed in Hannah's gut—a knot made from strings of fear she could no longer ignore. Bad things didn't happen just to other people anymore. They happened. It was that simple. She stopped, and Jade turned to look at her. "The headaches?"

Hannah saw a heaviness in Jade's eyes. She was thirty-five and usually looked ten years younger. But the past couple months...

"The headaches only come once in a while. Nothing to worry about." Jade slipped the broken sand dollar into the pocket of her windbreaker and shrugged. "I'm tired all the time. After a shift at the hospital and Ty's baseball game, I'm wiped. No wonder Tanner has his mind on work."

Hannah swallowed and considered her words. Jade was a trained nurse, after all. Surely if she were worried, she'd go in for tests. "Have you thought about seeing a doctor?"

Jade smiled. "Now you sound like Tanner." She faced the ocean and seemed to stare at something unseen and far away. "You know what I think it is?"

"What?" Hannah took a few slow steps back toward the house, and Jade kept up beside her.

"Depression." A sigh slipped from Jade's lips and blended with the ocean breeze. "Isn't that crazy?"

"Of course not." The knot relaxed. Depression was better than other possibilities. "Lots of people get depressed."

"But me?" Jade stretched her hands over her head and took a slow breath. "I wasn't depressed when my life was falling apart. But now that I'm living my dream, married to a man I've loved since I was a little girl...*now* I get depressed? It doesn't make sense."

Hannah remembered the miscarriage Jade had eight months

earlier. "It makes perfect sense. It hasn't even been a year since you lost the baby."

Quiet fell between them, and Jade wiped at a stray tear. "I think about that child every day. Sometimes it seems like everyone else has forgotten there ever was a baby."

"Even Tanner?" Their steps were slow and easy, the beach empty but for the two of them.

Jade shook her head. "No. Tanner talks about her."

"Her?"

"Yes." Jade sniffed and ran her fingers through her hair. "All my life I've wanted a daughter and…yes. The baby was a girl. She'd be two months old if she'd lived."

Hannah gazed across the watery horizon. "Losing a child isn't something that ever goes away, Jade. Whether that child was miscarried—" she thought about her visit to the cemetery the week before—"or killed in a car accident."

Jade's teary eyes locked onto Hannah's. "I don't know how to let her go. I want a baby so badly." Jade hung her head and gentle weeping overtook her.

Hannah pulled her close, hugging her the way a mother hugs her lost child. Hannah knew Jade's story well. Her mother had abandoned her when she was a child and left her to be raised by an alcoholic father. Jade had no siblings, so though Hannah was only four years older, she sometimes was the next best thing to a mother—or maybe an older sister.

"It's okay." She ran her hand along Jade's shoulder. "You should have said something sooner."

Jade nodded and after a while she pulled back. Her face was wet with tears. "I keep telling myself I'm supposed to let it go. People miscarry all the time, right?"

"But it still hurts. If you don't talk about that kind of pain it'll eat you alive, Jade."

Jade sucked in a deep breath and started walking again. "Maybe that explains my health."

"Exactly." Hannah kept her steps slow, giving Jade a chance to sort through her feelings.

They walked in silence until Jade turned, her eyes searching Hannah's as though looking for an unfathomable secret. "How did you do it, Hannah? How did you learn to live again?"

Hannah knew the answer as surely as she knew her name. "God carried me." She slowed her pace, and after a few more steps stopped and faced her friend. "He'll carry you, too."

She nodded, fresh tears in her eyes. "I know. I feel like this…this depression is keeping me from getting pregnant. Like I'm too tense to conceive."

Hannah angled her head and smiled. "You'll have more children one day, Jade. I believe that with all my heart." She sat down on the sand, pulling her knees to her chest, then patted the spot beside her. "Wanna pray?"

Jade dropped beside her, every motion slow and weary, as though she lacked all hope. They bowed their heads, and Hannah prayed for Jade's broken heart and empty arms. She asked that God bring healing and joy and health to Jade and a deeper understanding to Tanner.

"And please, Lord, one day soon…bring Jade another baby."

Matt drew his guitar close and kicked his feet up on the deck railing. "What else?"

Tanner grinned from a nearby lounge chair and stretched out his legs. He hadn't wanted to come tonight, but like always, time with the Bronzans was medicine to his soul. "Eagles. 'Desperado.'"

Matt plucked at a few chords and began to play. The music filled Tanner's senses, and he closed his eyes, singing along despite the fact that neither of them was exactly on key. They sang about losing all their highs and lows, about getting down from the fences before it was too late… The surf provided percussion in the distance.

When the song ended, Matt studied the fingers on his left hand and winced. "They're shot." He set the guitar down beside him. "I need to play more."

"*We* need to play more."

Matt cast him a lazy grin. "We?"

Tanner tossed his hands in the air in mock indignation. "I'm vocals, you're guitar. A few more nights like this, and we can forget about law. Take this act on the road."

They both chuckled at the thought, but as their laughter faded Tanner crooked one elbow behind his head and uttered a sigh that felt like it came from his feet. He stared at the canopy of stars above, then looked at Matt. "I'm worried about Jade."

Matt nodded once, his voice slow, thoughtful. "She looks tired."

He gazed at the sky again. "She's always tired."

"Maybe she should see a doctor."

"Yeah, maybe…" Tanner could hear Jade trying to reassure him. She was a nurse. She knew enough about medicine to know when she needed a doctor, and she didn't think she did. He'd tried to change her mind, but for now it was a closed subject unless some other symptom came up. Tanner let the worry fade. Whatever was wrong with his wife, it wasn't the Bronzans' problem. And tonight was supposed to be a celebration. Matt had been talking about adoption almost from the first day he started working at the firm. It was Hannah who couldn't make up her mind. In fact, just four weeks ago at lunch Matt had been more discouraged than Tanner remembered ever seeing before. He said he didn't think Hannah would ever make a decision and he wanted to prepare himself for the fact that they might never raise a child together.

He looked back at Matt. "What made Hannah decide?"

Matt crossed his arms, his eyebrows lowered. "It was the strangest thing. We were watching this documentary on TV about kids in the social services system—thousands of them waiting for a permanent home. All of a sudden she started to cry."

Tanner leveled his gaze at Matt. "Because of the show?"

"Because one of the kids—a little girl—really touched her." Matt shrugged. "I put my arm around her and asked her if she was okay, but she shook her head like she didn't want to talk. Then she told me she loved me."

Tanner gestured his approval. "That's always a good sign."

"Yeah. Except after a minute she was crying so hard she went upstairs to bed. I thought it was a setback on the whole idea of adoption. But the next morning she woke up and told me she'd made her decision." Matt's eyes sparkled with excitement. "Now it's just a matter of finding our little girl."

"And Jenny?"

"She's been great. Helps us find web sites with kids up for adoption, made copies of the dossier for us. Nothing but happy about it. Besides, she'll be in college in the fall. UCLA."

"Premed, right?"

Matt smiled. "Just like her dad."

Tanner studied his friend, amazed. "Doesn't it ever hurt? How much she still misses him?"

There was a softening in Matt's eyes. "Jenny loves me; I'll never doubt that as long as I live. I'm her protector, provider, confidante, and safe place. But I'm not her daddy." Matt cocked his head. "I'm okay with that."

Tanner stared at Matt for a moment and then back at the moonlit water. He couldn't imagine raising someone else's child.

Watching Matt, seeing his face light up when he talked about adopting… He shook his head. "I don't think I could do it."

Matt picked up his guitar. One string at a time, he strummed a chord that soothed the anxious places in Tanner's soul. "Do what?"

"Adopt. Raise someone else's child." He clenched his fists and relaxed them again. "I missed watching Ty grow up. Doesn't God know we want another baby?"

"I'm sure He does." Matt gazed up at the moon. "More than any of us will ever know."

Tanner exhaled hard. "I know. I hate when I doubt." He uttered a single laugh, one that was more frustration than humor. "Look at me. Fighting religious freedom battles in front of the entire nation and doubting whether God can bring us a child."

Again Matt moved his fingers over the guitar strings. "Doubts are normal. But don't stop praying, Tanner. God has a plan; He always does."

As they fell into silence, Tanner realized how much lighter his heart felt. His problems hadn't been solved. Jade would still be tired when they left the Bronzans' that night, and the empty longing for a baby would still be as real as the air they breathed. But somehow the time spent relaxing with Matt had given him hope again. His friend's enthusiasm about adopting was contagious. It left Tanner believing that one day—maybe one day soon—they'd be celebrating their own good news.

"So, what's the next step?"

Matt let his hands rest on the edge of the guitar, and Tanner was struck by the calm in his friend's face. A calm that was only possible by walking through the fire and coming out refined on the other side. "We've already talked to our social worker and she's looking for an available child."

"A girl, right?"

Matt nodded. "Hannah and I both want a little girl. Three or four years old, doesn't matter what ethnic background. We would have a better choice of children if we were interested in the foster-adopt program. We're licensed for it, but neither of us wants to risk getting a child and having her taken away."

"So you want one who's already legally available?"

"Right. Our social worker doesn't think it'll take long."

Again Tanner was struck by Matt and Hannah's faith. So much could go wrong with a child abandoned to the social services system. Drug abuse, bonding issues, or worse. Watching Hannah and Matt go through the adoption process was like watching a living illustration of faith. "What about that Haitian agency?"

"Heart of God? Great group of people. We filled out the paperwork and paid the program fee, but they didn't know how long it would take until they had a girl that age. Right now, their older children are almost all boys."

"And now Hannah wants to adopt from the U.S.?"

"At first she was afraid to. That's why we looked at Haiti. The statistics are..." Matt's voice drifted and he clenched his jaw. "More than ninety percent of the U.S. kids legally free for adoption have been abused. Some of them so bad it would take a miracle to make a difference."

Tanner narrowed his eyes, barely making out a sailboat on the darkened horizon. "You're taking a big risk."

"Yep." Matt didn't sound worried, only accepting, confident. "There's always a risk."

An easy silence fell between them again, comfortable, meaningful, and Matt moved his fingers over the strings, blending his music with the sounds of the sea.

Muffled voices broke the reverie—Jade and Hannah were back—and Tanner looked at his watch. He swung his legs over the side of the lounge chair and patted Matt on the shoulder.

"Well, friend, I guess we're both in need of the same thing then."

Matt set his guitar down, stood and stretched. "What's that?"

"A miracle. Nothing short of a miracle."

Three

Grace Landers lay in her sleeping bag and trembled. The voices were always loud, but tonight they were too scary to sleep, too scary not to think about.

Besides, the handcuff was hurting her wrist.

The van was small. Grace's sleeping bag was at the very back on the floor, against the double doors. There was barely enough room to sleep there, and she'd had to fold her sleeping bag in half to make it fit.

Mommy slept on the backseat; the front part of the van was where they kept their ice chest. The living room, Mommy called it.

Grace ran her finger over the place where the cold metal scraped against her hand. She would have been a good girl. She tried to tell her mommy, but Mommy wouldn't listen.

"I'm having a man friend over tonight. I don't want you gettin' in the way, ya hear?"

Her mommy locked one part of the handcuff to a pole near the bottom of the backseat and the other part to her wrist. Then mommy made a really mean face and told her to keep quiet or else.

"Not a peep, Grace. If anyone finds out about us living here, the cops will take you away again. This time forever."

Grace was very afraid about that. If the cops took her away, she'd have to live with someone she didn't know. Or maybe even go to jail. That would be scarier than the man her mommy was with tonight.

It was always the same when Mommy had a man friend over.

They'd talk a little and make slurping sounds, like they were drinking pop. Then her mommy's voice would get funny, all tired and slow.

The noises would change after that, almost like Mommy was getting hurt. Then the van would start shaking…that was when Grace closed her eyes and pretended the handcuff was a good thing, that it kept her from being hurt like her mommy. She would lie there in her little bed on the floor at the back of the van and think about something else.

Flowers or butterflies or clouds. Something that helped her fall asleep.

But tonight… It was different.

Mommy's friend yelled a lot, and no matter what Grace tried to think about she couldn't make her arms and legs stop shaking.

"I paid ya for more than that, woman."

There was a sharp sound, like when Mommy spanked her for being bad. Then her mommy started to cry. "You gave me dope, not money, Hank. I need *money.*"

The sharp sound came again. "Dope *is* money, idiot. Now lay down."

The man shouted at her mommy for a long time and used words Grace wasn't allowed to say. Over and over the sharp sound filled the van, and Grace began to cry. *Be quiet*, she told herself, and she held her breath so Mommy and the man wouldn't hear her crying. She couldn't let the cops take her away. Never, never.

If only she could get her hand free. Then she could roll under the backseat and sleep there. Maybe the noises wouldn't be so loud, maybe—

There was a loud smack, and her mommy screamed. The noises grew louder and louder, and Grace was too afraid to breathe.

"Help me," she whispered.

Her mother's screams kept coming, but suddenly they were quieter than before. Grace could feel invisible, warm, Daddy hands soothing out the shakes in her arms and legs and heart, making her feel hugged and happy.

She stared around in the dark, but there was no one there. No one at all.

Then she remembered who it was. It was the invisible Daddy, the one Grandma had told her about before she died. Her mouth formed the word *Hi,* but no sound came out. Still she smiled in the darkness, safe and secure in His presence.

Whoever He was, He'd come to her before.

Whenever she thought she might die from being sad and afraid, He'd come with warm hands and a safe feeling. Almost like a daddy taking care of her, the way she pictured a daddy might if she'd had one. He made her feel safe and sleepy and little. Even littler than four years old. And even though she couldn't see Him, He didn't scare her.

She stopped crying, and her mother and the man grew very quiet. Not far away there were sirens, but even though they got louder and louder, Grace wasn't afraid. *I'm okay... I'm okay...* The handcuff still cut at her wrist, but her hand relaxed and she closed her eyes. In a few minutes she drifted off to sleep.

Thinking about flowers and butterflies and clouds.

And an invisible Daddy who loved her even if no one else did.

Four

The headaches were getting worse.

Jade's hands trembled as she took two painkillers from the bottle in her purse and downed them with a glass of water. As she swallowed she glanced around the hospital cafeteria… The edges of the room were blurred.

She squinted. In fact, the edges of everything were fuzzy. Not enough to trigger panic, but enough to frustrate her. Was this all the faith she could muster? An unshakeable sadness over losing a baby? Discouragement at not being able to get pregnant? Depression strong enough to affect her vision and give her headaches?

She sighed. Not much of an example of faith, especially when she had the miracle of Ty and Tanner at home to remind her daily of God's amazing power.

The medicine started working, and the lines became crisper. Jade took another drink of water, then smoothed out the wrinkles in her nurse's uniform. She walked to the closest table, steadying herself on an occasional chair along the way, and sat down. The nausea was back… Maybe it was from the medication.

Or from the one thing she dared dream.

Either way, in seven hours she'd have the results. Her period hadn't been regular for a while, but the past cycle had been completely absent. Susan at the lab had been more than happy to process the pregnancy test. But Jade needed to work her shift before she might know the answer. No matter how she was feeling.

Help me get through the day, Lord…

Jade stood and glanced at her watch. One o'clock. Time for Brandy Almond's chemotherapy.

Jade's head still pounded with every heartbeat as she made her way down the hallway to the children's cancer ward. There were times when she questioned her sanity… It was one thing to work in the general children's ward as she'd done when she was just out of high school. Kids with kidney problems or bad cases of tonsillitis.

Cancer was something altogether different.

Still, there was nothing more rewarding than giving sick children the gift of hope, and Jade seemed to be able to do that better than anyone at Mount Sinai Children's Hospital. Because every now and then, children survived cancer's attack. They grew stronger and healthier, and their hair grew back.

And once in a while those children would go home to live normal lives.

As far as Jade was concerned, *every* child had a chance to go home. Brandy Almond was no exception.

It was nap time at Mount Sinai, so the hallway was quiet. None of the children were touring the ward in wheelchairs or sitting around the schoolroom table or building castles with wooden blocks in the playroom.

On the nurse's station, there was a tray stenciled with Brandy's name. On it were three pills and a bag of liquid poison that would kill the leukemia cells—along with the cells Brandy needed for eating and breathing and living. Jade took the tray and set her sights on a room four doors down the hall. The girl was a high-school track star and the oldest child in the children's cancer wing, and she regularly complained about the fact.

Without making a sound, Jade let herself into Brandy's room. A rerun of *I Love Lucy* whispered from the television. Brandy looked up, her eyes dark and sunken, then shifted her gaze back to the TV.

"You're supposed to be sleeping." Jade smiled and set the tray down.

"I'm not three."

"No, but you're sick and your body needs rest." The bag hanging over the girl's bed was empty. Jade replaced it with the full one from her tray and crossed her arms. "How are you feeling?"

Brandy's eyes welled up and she looked out the window. "Fine."

Jade's heart went out to her. It was prom week at Thousand Oaks High School where Brandy was a junior. She ran track and had been a state contender with one of the fastest miles of any girl her age.

Then she started bruising.

When she was first diagnosed back in February, dozens of teens from the track team frequented Brandy's hospital room. It was all Jade could do to maneuver her way through the maze of visitors to administer the chemo treatments. But over the weeks, as Brandy's long blonde hair fell out and her muscled legs atrophied beneath the sheets, her friends stopped coming. It was track season after all, and Brandy's teammates were busy.

This week especially.

Before Brandy got sick, there had been a boy—a quiet, dark-haired long jumper on the track team. The two of them had planned since September to attend prom together. He'd come by earlier and hemmed and hawed for fifteen minutes before stating the real reason for his visit.

He was taking someone else. He wanted Brandy to hear it from him first.

Jade prepared a needle with anti-nausea medication and injected it in the least bruised area she could find on the girl's arm.

Then she sat on the edge of Brandy's bed and patted her frail hand. "How are you really?"

Brandy clenched her teeth. "It doesn't matter. The whole year's a waste."

"Okay. So start working toward next year." Jade kept her voice quiet, calm…subdued enough that Brandy took her seriously and upbeat enough to do the one thing she believed in, the thing that kept her working in this department: to infuse hope and life and love right alongside the chemotherapy. Drop for drop.

Tears welled up in Brandy's eyes again and she gazed at Jade. "What if there isn't a next year?"

Jade's heart sank as she layered the girl's hand between her own. "There will be. You need to believe that."

Brandy blinked and tears forged their way down either side of her face. "I don't have faith like you, Jade." Her fragile body heaved twice as a series of sobs broke through. "It's hard…to believe anything good will ever happen again."

The moment called for more than a hand hold, and Jade leaned down and hugged Brandy, letting her sob. "Shhh…it's okay, sweetheart. It's okay."

"I'm…I'm afraid." The girl clung to Jade as though she'd never admitted her fears before. "What if I don't make it?"

"Oh, honey, look at you." Jade smoothed the girl's hair. "You're getting better all the time."

"But…but I'm still here. I'm still sick."

Since the day she was diagnosed, Brandy had acted as though her illness were nothing more than a serious inconvenience, a speed bump in what would otherwise have been a wonderful year. She complained about being in the children's ward, complained about the food, and rolled her eyes when she got word that she needed to stay another week. But never for a moment had she acknowledged any fear about the cancer.

Her parents were no different. They were certain that the cancer would go away and their daughter's hair would grow back in time for her senior portrait. That next year at this time she'd be competing at state.

With all her heart, Jade prayed they were right.

Both Brandy's refusal to talk about her cancer and her parents' eternal optimism were normal, but they'd left Brandy nowhere to voice her questions, no one with whom to share her deepest fears.

Until now.

Jade stayed in Brandy's room for half an hour, simply listening. When she left, she hugged the girl and promised to pray.

Brandy sniffed and wiped the tears from her cheeks. "You really think it'll help?"

"Yes." Jade angled her head and smiled. "In every way that matters."

Brandy nodded, and though she stopped short of agreeing, her expression softened.

Help her, God... She's thinking about You. Maybe for the first time.

Jade remembered something Tanner had told her once, when they first found each other after being separated for so many years: Everything happens in God's timing... It was true. First for her and Tanner.

And now for Brandy.

When Jade left her shift at eight o'clock that night her head still pulsed with an aching that almost never seemed to go away. But because of Brandy's questions, Jade felt the breath of God's presence more tangibly than she had in days.

She walked across the hospital to the lab. No matter what the test results showed, she had more than enough reason to be happy. She was fifteen minutes from home, from seeing Tanner.

And if anything could cure her headache, it was that.

Like every case that ever seemed to matter, this one came in to the Center for the Preservation of Religious Rights (CPRR) by way of an anonymous phone call. Matt and Tanner ran the firm as equal partners, but the caller wanted only to talk to "Mr. Eastman."

Though a dozen situations demanded his attention, Tanner took the call. It was a woman, and Tanner could tell from her broken sentences that she was crying. "They're…They're taking our church from us."

Tanner gazed out his office window. "Who's taking it?" There was a chance she was a nutcase or a prank caller. But something in the woman's voice made him think otherwise.

The woman drew a shaky breath. "The city of Benson, Colorado."

Tanner grabbed a legal pad and sat up straighter. Benson was a suburb of Colorado Springs, the hub for a dozen Christian ministries. Rumor on the religious freedom vine was that Benson was run by a city council hostile to anything remotely Christian.

In the past year Tanner had heard of two situations that very nearly became full-blown national cases, both of which were based in Benson. The first involved a judge who refused to remove from his courtroom wall a plaque bearing the Ten Commandments. The judge took early retirement and the issue was resolved before a case could be filed.

A few months later a public school teacher was told he couldn't sponsor a community betterment club. The reason? His beliefs might bias students toward his faith. Just as the situation was gaining public attention, the Benson City Council ruled that it could no longer be responsible for community betterment groups. The high school club was dropped and the situation became a nonissue.

"Okay." Tanner kept his tone factual and prayed it would have a contagious affect on the woman. "Why don't you tell me what you know?"

Once the woman had control of her emotions, her story was clearer than water. The congregation at First Church of the Valley had a lease arrangement with the city to hold services at City Hall. The woman's husband was Pastor Casey Carson, who headed up the church and had worked out the lease deal himself.

According to the woman, three weeks ago the church leaders were notified by someone on the city council that they were in violation of their lease agreement. They were ordered to stop holding services at the hall. Four days later a Sunday morning class on transcendental meditation began meeting there instead.

The woman released a tired sigh. "Not only did the city council cancel services, they refused to refund the remaining lease money. We paid for a year in advance. That's what they asked for and… We had no options."

Tanner felt his heart engage. "How many months were left?"

"Four."

Four months of rent money? "That would be thousands of dollars."

"Right."

Tanner scribbled as fast as his hand could move. "On what grounds?"

"Violation of contract."

"Violation?" Tanner's enthusiasm fell flat. If the church violated some aspect of the contract there would be no case.

"We read the contract and didn't see it—" The woman was clearly on the edge of tears. "We never imagined that by…"

The woman paused, and Tanner tapped his pencil. "By what?"

"My husband believes there's only one way to heaven, through Jesus. And…and that's why they pulled our lease."

The pencil fell to Tanner's desk. He eased his chair in a half rotation and stared out his window, across Warner Center and over the Los Angeles foothills. *Just when I think I've heard it all…* "They pulled your lease because of the content of your husband's sermons?"

The woman's voice was barely a whisper. "Yes."

Tanner made an appointment with her for the next day and met with Matt in the conference room before leaving that evening. "It could be big."

Matt leaned back and stroked his chin. "Could be a misunderstanding."

There was silence for a moment. "Good point." Tanner slid a copy of his notes from the earlier conversation across the table.

That's why he liked working with Matt Bronzan. Matt's considerable experience as a district attorney tempered his reaction to cases like this one, especially in the early stages.

Tanner considered his partner. Matt liked to say that Tanner was the firm's fiery energy, its passion and heart. Tanner was at his best in closing arguments, spilling his guts without reservation as though the jurors were close friends privy to his deepest, most intimate feelings. Tanner seldom failed to win a jury's empathy—and most often its vote. It was what earned him a reputation as the best religious freedom fighter in the land.

But Tanner knew none of it would have been possible on his own.

Matt was the conduit through which Tanner's energy flowed, a stabilizer with an endless ability to reason and debate prior to trial. He brought to Tanner's fire a wealth of research knowledge and an uncanny talent for finding perfect precedent cases. There was no way Tanner could have run the firm without him, and after three years Matt was more than a brilliant partner.

He was Tanner's best friend.

Aside from Jade, of course. The thought of her sent a shot of anxious adrenaline through his veins. What was wrong with her, anyway? He'd waited all his life to love her, to be her husband and share forever with her. So why the headaches? Could she still be struggling that much over the miscarriage?

In a single motion, Tanner pushed his chair from the table and stood. That had to be it. Because he couldn't begin to imagine the alternatives.

Matt looked up from the notes. "Going home?"

"Yeah." Tanner reached for his leather bag, his shoulders feeling suddenly heavy. "Hey, pray for Jade, will you?"

Concern flooded Matt's expression. "The headaches?"

Tanner nodded and exhaled in a way that filled his cheeks. "She can't get rid of 'em."

The office air conditioning clicked off, and a somber quiet filled the room. Matt studied Tanner, and when he spoke, his voice was soft. "You're really worried, aren't you?"

There was no point hiding the truth from Matt. The two of them had seen enough heartache in their days to know better than to lie to each other. "I am." A strange mix of anger and sorrow seized Tanner's heart, and tears stung his eyes. "She *can't* be sick." He blinked twice and worked the muscles in his jaw. "Not now…after all we've been through."

Matt linked his fingers and stared at the floor. When he looked up, he patted the empty chair beside him. "Why wait." His smile didn't erase the worry from his eyes. "Let's pray."

Tanner's fingers relaxed one by one, and the bag dropped from his hand. With small, slow steps, he made his way around the table and sat across from Matt. Then they did the one thing that set their business relationship apart, the thing that convinced them their friendship would outlast anything they might do in the field of law.

They prayed.

In quiet unison, heads bowed, they lifted Tanner's precious Jade to the very throne room of heaven.

An hour later Tanner was tossing a football with Ty out front when Jade pulled up.

"Hey, Dad..." Ty caught the ball and jogged to Tanner's side. "She looks good."

It was true. The heaviness in her eyes had lifted, and there was a spring in her step as she made her way from the car to the place where the two of them stood.

Jade grinned at Ty and then at Tanner. Tanner felt his pulse pick up when he saw her eyes well with tears, but then a smile broke across her face. She wrapped her arms around both of them, drawing them close.

"Guess what, guys?"

There was joy in her voice, and Tanner held his breath as Jade lay her head on his shoulder. "I'm *pregnant!*"

"You are? Yeah!" Ty let out a whoop and tossed the football high in the air.

Elation and relief coursed through every vein, every inch of Tanner's body. "Thank God!" He cradled Jade's face with his fingertips and kissed her, the same way he'd kissed her that night when they first found each other again. His voice was the happiest whisper. "I love you, Mrs. Eastman."

She giggled and kissed him back. "I love you, too."

"Come on." He took Jade's hand and led her to the house with quick steps. "Let's call the Bronzans."

Jade's quick smile ignited fresh sparkles in her eyes. "Can I call?" She grabbed Ty's hand and they headed inside together. "Hannah has to hear the news first."

Tanner stood back with Ty, watching Jade tap out the

Bronzans' number. His heart soared. How long had it been since he'd felt this good? The corners of his mouth felt like they were permanently fixed halfway up his cheeks.

"Hannah, it's me. I went to the doctor today, and they found out what's wrong. You won't believe it..." She squealed. "I'm *pregnant!*" Pause. "I know. Yes, God is so faithful. Always."

The phone conversation between the women continued and Tanner closed his eyes. He refused to think of the what-ifs. They didn't matter anymore; Jade was pregnant! All their prayers had been answered—his and Jade's, Matt's, and Hannah's. They'd each begged God on Jade's behalf, and now the tiny baby growing inside her was His miraculous reply. Her headaches, the nausea...all of it was for the best reason of all.

Jade was going to have a baby, a brother or sister for Ty. The child they'd dreamed of.

And everything about their lives and the happily-ever-after they were building was going to work out just fine after all.

Five

The phone was ringing as they brought in the groceries. Jenny went back for the rest while Hannah set three bags down on the counter and grabbed the receiver. Her heart still felt light within her. The same way it had felt since hearing Jade's good news the day before.

"Hello?" Hannah leaned against the counter and gazed out at the ocean.

"Mrs. Bronzan?" The caller's voice was familiar, but Hannah couldn't quite place it.

A flock of seagulls filled the sky, standing out against the clear blue. "Yes."

"This is Edna Parsons from Social Services." The woman hesitated and Hannah's heart skipped a beat. "We have a little girl for you."

Hannah's breath caught in her throat and her knees went weak. Was it really possible? Had the social worker found the child they'd been praying for? "You…you do?"

Jenny entered the house with the last of the groceries.

"Your file says you're not interested in the foster-adopt program." A heavy sigh sounded across the phone lines. "But I've worked in this department for twenty-four years. Mrs. Bronzan, there's no way this little girl's going back to her mother."

Anger stirred in Hannah's heart. This wasn't the call they were waiting for. It was some sort of mistake. Why were they calling if the girl wasn't legally free? Hadn't Hannah and Matt made it clear that the last thing they wanted was to fall in love with a child they might wind up losing? *I'll say we're not interested…* Hannah drew a deep breath. "Tell me about her."

Jenny came up beside Hannah and arched an eyebrow. Hannah covered the receiver with her hand and whispered, "Social Services."

Mrs. Parsons continued. "Well…she's a Caucasian child, four years old. Our department took an anonymous call up in the Santa Maria area. The child was living with her mother in the back of a van in an abandoned field. Her mother worked as a prostitute and was part of a drug ring, one that police have been trying to bust for months. The woman's been moved to Los Angeles because of an outstanding warrant here. She's in jail awaiting trial; the little girl is in temporary foster care in the San Fernando Valley." The social worker paused. "This is the third time the woman has been arrested for drug trafficking and prostitution. It was her last chance and she blew it. There's no next of kin. The judge has already started the process of terminating the woman's rights to the child."

Hannah's eyes grew wet. "What… What does that mean?"

"The woman goes to trial in two weeks. At that time if she's sentenced to prison—and she will be—the judge will order the child placed in a foster-adopt home pending termination of the mother's rights. In cases like this, the child should be legally free within six months."

Legally free in six months? The thought danced about the surface of her heart. That wasn't so bad, was it? Hannah pictured the little girl sleeping in the back of a van. If anyone needed a stable family, this child did. Besides, life was full of risks.

And if she said yes…if they were willing to look past the technicalities, she might be a mother again in a matter of days!

Hannah wanted to shout out loud with the possibility, but she bit her lip and locked eyes with Jenny. The mix of emotions in her daughter's face made her reach out and take Jenny's hand. Excitement, fear, sorrow. Feelings they were all bound to have throughout the adoption process.

This was only the beginning.

Hannah closed her eyes and pinched the bridge of her nose. "Why us, Mrs. Parsons? We made it clear we weren't interested in taking a child unless she was legally free for adoption."

"I'm aware of that."

Phones rang in the background in the office of Social Services, and Hannah struggled to concentrate. She was dying to tell the social worker yes...yes, they'd take the little girl and give her a real bed, a real home, and a family who would love her forever.

But what if something happened? What if somehow the mother's rights weren't terminated? How in the world would the child survive then? How would *she* survive?

What am I supposed to do here, God? Give me wisdom...please.

Edna Parsons drew a deep breath. "I've met the girl, Mrs. Bronzan. And, well, she's very special. Other than a very rough first few years, she's in perfect health. She'll be very easy to place. I called you first because I can picture her in your family."

Hannah opened her eyes and felt the familiar sting of tears. A lump in her throat made it impossible to speak. She swallowed hard, already drawn to the lonely little girl sitting in a foster home somewhere.

A little girl whose name God was even now writing on her heart.

Mrs. Parsons interrupted her thoughts. "I can give you a few days to think about it. If you're not interested, I need to look through my other files as soon as possible."

Hannah squeezed Jenny's hand and nodded, finding her voice once more. "That'll be fine. I'll call you tomorrow. Thank you for thinking of us." She almost hung up, but then she stopped. "What's her name?"

She could hear the smile in the social worker's voice. "Grace."

Grace...

The moment the phone was on the hook, Hannah led Jenny to a sofa in the next room. Her heart raced and her hands trembled as she faced her daughter, smiling through eyes clouded with tears. "They have a little girl for us. Mrs. Parsons said she could picture her in our family."

Jenny searched Hannah's face. "But—" her voice was barely audible—"she's a foster child, right? Isn't that what you said?"

Hannah shrugged. She released her hold on Jenny's hands and leaned back. "For now. She'll be free in six months. The mother's in jail, and in a few weeks Grace will be placed in a foster-adopt home."

"Grace?" A flicker of hope danced in Jenny's eyes.

"Yes." Hannah smiled and played the child's name over again in her mind. *Grace*. It was a good name, a good sign. It was God's grace that made the risk worth taking. Somehow the Lord would see them through the adoption process.

Jenny folded her hands, her forehead a mass of wrinkles. "How old is she?"

Hannah reminded herself to breathe. Her mind still spun from the information. The phone call felt like something from a dream, and now that Mrs. Parsons had explained the situation, Hannah could already imagine the girl coming home in a few days. "Four. She's been living in the back of a van."

Jenny's chin quivered. She stared out the window at the gentle surf and breathed out, soft and slow. Hannah's heart ached for her daughter and the emotional roller coaster they'd ridden these past years—as well as the one they'd ride in the coming months if they took this child.

Jenny faced Hannah again. There were tears on her cheeks, and she wiped the wetness with the back of her sleeve as the uncertainty in her eyes fell away. In its place a grin formed, one that convinced Hannah beyond a doubt that they were doing the right thing by adopting. "We're going to take her, right?"

"Well..." Hannah laughed and sobbed at the same time. "When Matt gets home, we'll talk about it."

"What's there to talk about?" Jenny's eyes sparkled and she threw her hands up. "God must want her with us. Otherwise he wouldn't have had the social worker call."

Hannah wrapped her arms around her daughter, taking in the warmth of her, the fresh smell of her shampoo. She silently thanked God for sparing this precious child four years ago. Hannah pulled back and searched Jenny's eyes. "So if we take a vote, yours is yes?"

A smile filled Jenny's face. "Absolutely."

When Matt got home an hour later, the decision was unanimous.

Hannah called Mrs. Parsons the next morning and told her the news. "How soon can we have her?"

The social worker laughed. "Within an hour of her mother's sentencing."

From the moment Hannah hung up the phone she was bathed in reassurance, grateful for the little one God was bringing into their lives. It was a miracle, really. In two weeks she would be a mother again, sharing the joys of parenting a child who desperately needed love and security, a home and a family that would be hers forever. A miracle that never would have happened if they hadn't lost Tom and Alicia.

Further proof that God grew fragrant flowers of hope in the ashes of loss.

The days dragged on. More than once Hannah would be out shopping for a toaster or a purse or groceries, and find herself drawn to little girls' dresses. *No*, she told herself. *Not until the hearing*.

But in further conversations with Mrs. Parsons, the social worker explained that some clothing for Grace was necessary if the child was to be brought to them as soon as the hearing took place.

Hannah and Jenny set out one night intending to buy a single outfit and a pair of pajamas. Instead they came home with leggings and flowered T-shirts, jeans and frilly socks, two dresses with smocking and lace, a floor-length pink nightgown, and a package of multicolored hair bows. Just in case she had long hair.

Matt chuckled at the array of clothing spread across the dining room table that night. "I think Grace is covered for the first few days, anyway." He put his arm around Hannah and kissed her forehead.

"Actually, we held back." Jenny grinned as she ran her fingers over the soft cotton leggings. "My little sister needs nice clothes, you know."

Later, when Jenny was out with friends, Matt and Hannah took a stroll along the beach. The night was warm, signaling the coming summer. Matt wove his fingers between Hannah's, and for a while neither of them spoke. Hannah savored the ocean breeze on her face, the warmth of Matt's strong hand in hers, the way she felt safe and protected in his presence. The way he had always made her feel since the accident.

Never in her wildest dreams could she have imagined a life with anyone but Tom Ryan. But now she was in love with life once more, amazed that God had provided her with not one, but two men capable of capturing her heart.

Matt broke the silence first, his voice as gentle and soothing as the winds from the Pacific. "Are you worried? About the risk?"

It was something they hadn't talked about. Mrs. Parsons didn't expect there to be a problem. If Grace's mother was put in prison, the judge would begin the process of terminating her rights that same day. And only then would Grace be placed in their home. The process seemed safe enough to Hannah.

"Are you?" Hannah had already dismissed the risks associated with adopting Grace. If the child's mother was sent to prison and Grace came to be their daughter, no one could ever take her away. Hannah was sure of it. Imagining risks now made Hannah's future feel no more stable than the sand beneath her feet.

"There's a risk." Matt's steps were slow and thoughtful as he caught her gaze and held it. "No matter how small."

Hannah swallowed. "I can't think that far ahead." She side-stepped a pile of seaweed. "If the judge starts the termination process, then the law's on our side. I have to believe that."

They walked a bit further, and Matt stopped. He reached for a piece of driftwood and flung it out to sea, watching as it disappeared beneath the waves. "The law's a funny thing." He looked at her again. "It won't be final until her mother's rights are legally severed. You need to understand that." He paused. "Just in case."

Hannah shifted her gaze toward the dark ocean and felt the sting of tears. Alicia's face came to mind—beautiful, intelligent, and kind. Alicia's future had been brighter than the sun, but today she lived in heaven. "Nothing's for sure." She faced Matt and placed her hands on his shoulders. Her eyes held his, and she waited for the lump in her throat to subside. "I learned that much four years ago."

"Okay." Matt nodded, love overflowing from his heart to hers. "As long as you understand."

"I don't want to think about it, but I understand."

Matt wove his hands around Hannah's waist and clasped them near the small of her back. The chill from the wet evening air disappeared. "What should she call us? Have you thought of that?"

Hannah smiled. "Mommy and Daddy. Because that's what we'll be."

Matt brushed a lock of her long hair back from her face. "So you're not worried."

She smiled despite the tears that pooled in her eyes. "Worrying doesn't help. I worried all the time before the accident and it didn't make a bit of difference when Tom and Alicia were killed." Her throat was thick with emotion, but a single ripple of laughter made its way up. She rubbed the tip of her nose against Matt's. "If Grace comes to live with us, then she's our little girl." She closed her eyes and she could see Alicia waving good-bye from the backseat of the Bronco that long-ago summer day. "Whether we have her for a day or a lifetime."

The waiting was worse than anything Matt could remember. Especially because there was a chance it was ushering in a season that might end in devastating loss. He tried not to think about the fact, but his legal background told him anything was possible.

One week turned to two, and on May 11, Jade and Tanner came over to see Jenny off for her senior prom.

"Jenny, you're breathtaking. You look just like your mother." Jade hugged her.

"Jade's right, sweetheart." Matt stood nearby, his heart all lit up inside. "You and your mother could be sisters."

"I don't know about that." Hannah giggled from across the room, her eyes shining with pride. "But there's no doubt you'll be the prettiest girl at the dance."

Tanner put an arm around Jenny and squeezed her shoulders.

"Ty's at baseball practice, but he says hi. Oh, and not to worry. He'll miss his game the day of your graduation." He winked at Matt. "Thanks for letting us share your day."

Jenny glowed under the attention and adoration, and Matt couldn't help but feel his heart swell. Some days it seemed like only yesterday when he burst into Jenny's room and found her nearly dead, bottles of pills spilled around the bed from her attempted suicide. Watching her now, tall and lean, with the curves of a young woman, it was hard to believe four years had passed since that awful time.

The distance Jenny had come since then was a race that could only have been run with God, and Matt was most thankful for Jenny's faith. A faith that added an angelic glow to her considerable beauty.

Matt pulled Jenny aside before her date arrived and took her hands. "You'll be the most beautiful girl at the dance." He kissed her cheek. "I want you to know how proud I am of you."

"Thanks." Jenny's eyes were watery and she smiled. There was a gentle silence between them, and Jenny's face grew serious. "A long time ago I asked you whether you loved my mom, remember?"

Matt felt his expression soften. "Yes. Outside the jail. After the verdict against the drunk driver."

"Right." Jenny blinked and two tears left tracks across her made-up cheeks. She dabbed at them and laughed at herself. "I wasn't going to cry."

Matt reached for a tissue and handed it to her. Then he told her the same thing he'd always said when her losses seemed overwhelming, when tears overflowed the walls around her heart: "Tears are okay, Jenny. They mean you're breathing."

She smiled and nodded. "Anyway," her gaze met his, and he could see how much of the little girl had faded from her face these past years. "I'm glad the answer was yes. You've made my mom so happy. And you've made us a family again." She sniffed, her eyes more serious than before. "Maybe...maybe I don't say it enough, but I love you, Matt. You may not be my daddy, but you're my father. I think of you that way more than you know."

Matt hugged her tightly. There would be other times like this...the day he would walk Jenny down the aisle in place of the dad she'd lost, the day she would have her firstborn...

But this day, this moment, would remain in the treasure chest of his memory forever. Her feelings for him were more of a gift than she knew, and it took him a moment to find his voice. "I love you, too, honey. You'll always be my oldest girl."

He wondered about Grace then, about raising a little girl who had suffered so little love in her early years. "I hope Grace grows up to be just like you." He grinned at Jenny and reached for his camera. "Come on. Your mom's waiting. I think she wants about a million pictures."

By the time the hearing for Grace's mother arrived two days later, Hannah had the photographs of Jenny's night developed and in a scrapbook. In fact, she was more organized than she'd been in years. Anything to pass the time.

Matt and Jenny both stayed home with Hannah that morning, each of them silently finding ways to keep busy. Hannah pictured the courtroom somewhere on the other side of the Santa Monica Mountains and imagined what stage the proceedings might be at.

Do any of them know what's at stake?

At eleven o'clock the phone rang. Hannah stared at it while Matt and Jenny hurried in from other parts of the house. Her heart pounded as she reached for the receiver. "Hello?"

"Mrs. Bronzan?"

"Yes?"

"This is Mrs. Parsons from Social Services." She hesitated while Hannah held her breath. "Grace's mother was sentenced to fifteen years. The judge ordered termination of her parental rights to begin as soon as possible."

The tears were instant and Hannah smothered a cry with her hand. She glanced at Matt and Jenny and nodded. "So…so you can bring her here now?"

"Yes." The woman's answer was quick, confident. "Grace is waiting. I'll have her home in time for lunch."

Hannah hung up the phone and hugged Matt and Jenny as tight as she could. "She's ours!" Tears spilled onto her cheeks as she shouted for joy. "Grace is coming home!"

They made lunch together, guessing what type of personality their little girl would have. Would she be shy or silly, withdrawn or affectionate? And what would she look like? Most of all they talked about how right they felt about taking her in.

Fifteen minutes later Mrs. Parsons pulled into the drive. With Matt and Jenny at her side, Hannah saw the little girl for the first time—and her breath caught in her throat.

"Dear God…" She stared at Grace, at the child's creamy complexion and the mass of dark blonde curls that framed her face. "I don't believe it."

"Mom…do you see what I see?" Jenny's eyes were wide.

Matt's face was blank as he looked from Hannah to Jenny and back. "What's wrong?" He stared at the child. "She looks like an angel. So?"

Hannah shook her head, her throat dry. "No…she looks like…" She was too shocked to speak, too caught up in the vision of the child before her. Almost as though she were seeing a ghost.

"She looks—" Jenny took her mother's hand and finished the explanation for Matt—"She looks exactly like Alicia."

Mrs. Parsons and Grace were at the door, and Matt opened it, his eyes dancing. He smiled big. "Hi."

The social worker grinned in return. "We've come to bring Grace home."

Hannah stood two feet behind him, mesmerized by the child. Up close it was clear that though the resemblance to Alicia was uncanny, this little girl was more serious, older than her years. She would be her own person, not a replica of a daughter that was no longer with them.

But that was as it should be.

"Come in." Matt motioned to Mrs. Parsons, stooped down, and placed his hands on his thighs. "Hi there, Grace."

The child leaned into Mrs. Parsons and buried half her face. She barely lifted her hand and wiggled her fingers at Matt, looking at him with one wide eye. Then the part of her mouth that could be seen curved into a shy smile.

Grace and Mrs. Parsons stepped into the house, and Grace raised her eyes up at Hannah. "Hi."

Hannah's heart sang within her and she knelt near Grace. "Hi, honey." She ran her fingers over the child's feather-soft curls. "We're glad you're home."

Grace nodded and looked at something near her feet.

A flock of questions invaded. Did she like them? Would she always be this shy? Hannah struggled to force them from her mind. It was too soon to make judgments about Grace's personality. Of course she was shy! She'd never met them, and now she was being told this was her home, her family.

But even in those early minutes, after being brought to yet another family, Grace's quietness faded when she met Jenny.

Hannah watched her teenage daughter kneel before the little girl.

"Hi, Grace. I'm your sister." There was a mist of tears in Jenny's eyes as she took the child's hand. "My name's Jenny."

Grace blinked and let go of Mrs. Parsons. She came to Jenny and leaned into her arms. Then she said the one thing that convinced Hannah beyond a doubt that Grace was destined to be their daughter. More convincing than Mrs. Parsons' phone call a few weeks ago. Even more convincing than the way Grace looked so much like Alicia.

With eyes hungry for love, Grace smiled at Jenny and said, "I always wanted a big sister."

Edna Parsons spent nearly an hour at the Bronzans, taken by the loving way the family had welcomed the child. As Edna left, she gazed at the ocean and thought of the cozy warmth that made up the Bronzans' home. The family had all the necessary means to give Grace a life she'd only dreamed of.

Edna sighed as she made her way back to the car, seized by a pang of fear. What if Grace's birth mother appealed her case and was set free? What if the termination didn't go through? What if something happened and Grace had to leave this family?

She slid into the driver's seat and shook off the feeling. It wasn't possible. Grace's situation was simply too bad for any solution other than a termination of the mother's rights.

She thought about Grace's file, reports she'd read again just that morning. They'd been no different from hundreds of other files she'd seen in the past year, but something about Grace tugged at Edna's heart. Maybe it was the most recent report, the one detailing the child's removal from her mother's care.

The details were enough to turn Edna's stomach, and though she wasn't a praying woman, she took a moment from her schedule and placed before God two very specific requests. First, that the Bronzans be permitted to adopt Grace.

And second, that they never learn the awful things that nearly transpired the night their new little girl was taken into protective custody.

Six

Something was wrong.

Jade was utterly nauseous, her headaches more severe than before. And on several occasions her vision had doubled. She did everything she could to rationalize the way she felt. Her age must be a factor, she told herself, or her hormones. Maybe the baby was bigger than Ty had been at this point, or possibly the stress of the miscarriage a year ago had strained her system more than she realized.

Maybe she needed glasses.

Jade tried to calmly analyze her symptoms, but each night she lay down in raw, heart-pounding fear, terrified something was wrong with the baby. Sometimes, after Tanner was asleep, she'd sit straight up in bed and stare out the window, willing her heartbeat to slow down, desperate for a grip on her emotions.

Day after day the fear ate at her, but not once did she tell Tanner. Oh, she told him when she didn't feel well or when she had to lie down because her headaches were so bad. But she didn't tell him her deepest fears, that there might be complications with her pregnancy. She barely acknowledged the possibility to herself.

But now, six weeks after learning she was pregnant, Jade was worried about more than the baby's health.

She was worried about her own.

That was why, when she awoke at four in the morning one Monday in June with a splitting headache, she promised herself she'd make the call. Whatever was causing the pain in her head, it had to be checked. She'd start with Dr. Layton, a neurologist friend who worked with her at the children's hospital. He would know what to do.

No matter how great her fear, there was no better time to go in and be seen. Ty had spent the night at a neighbor boy's house, and today he was going to the beach with the boy's family. Jade had no plans whatsoever for the day.

Her head throbbed as she eased herself to a sitting position, careful not to wake Tanner. He would be up in two hours and he needed his sleep. He'd been coming home from the office earlier since Jade's announcement, but he was so excited about the baby that they had talked until after midnight the past few nights.

Despite her pain, the sight of her sleeping husband filled her with joy. There couldn't be anything seriously wrong with her. Not now, not when she had everything she'd ever dreamed of with Tanner.

She brushed a lock of hair off his forehead and admired the angles of his face. He'd been treating her like a China doll since hearing the news, doting on her, bringing her ice water, and encouraging her to rest whenever possible. Because of the severity of her symptoms, he wanted her home from work, and she agreed. Her last day would be at the end of the month. She would reevaluate after summer, since the baby wasn't due until December.

Whenever Tanner worried about her headaches and nausea, Jade would lean close and kiss him into silence. "I'm supposed to be sick. Morning sickness means I'm carrying a healthy baby."

It was enough that she was concerned; there was no point worrying him also. For the most part Tanner was willing to believe her explanations.

She closed her eyes. *Make it go away, Lord, please. Take the pain from my head so I know there's nothing wrong with me.*

Her skull ached in response, and images from the night before filled her mind.

She and Tanner had gone out onto their bedroom balcony to watch the moonlight glistening on the rolling hills behind their home. In the shadows they had spotted a pair of deer making their way to a thicket of oak trees. Tanner came up behind her and slipped his arms around her still-flat mid-section.

"You're beautiful, Jade. More beautiful than anything." He whispered into her ear and she leaned her head back against his chest.

"Mmmm." She closed her eyes. "It feels so good to be with you."

"I'm sorry you're sick." He left a trail of feather-light kisses along her neck. "But I love that you're pregnant. I want to be a part of everything I missed when you had Ty."

Tears had burned in Jade's eyes. "I wish there was a way to get back the years we lost." She drew a deep breath and savored the weight of his body against hers. "Sometimes I still can't believe we're together."

The memory faded, and Jade stared out the window at the still-dark morning sky. Her first pregnancy had been marked by pain and turmoil, all of it orchestrated by Tanner's mother and her web of lies.

Jade thought for a moment of the girl she'd been when she got pregnant with Ty, the way she'd ached for Tanner, yet wound up marrying someone else instead, someone she never loved and shouldn't have married. In the end, it was Doris Eastman's confession that brought her and Tanner together.

It was amazing, really. After marrying Tanner eighteen months ago, Jade had actually come to like Doris. She was a woman changed by Christ's forgiveness during the final days of her life—so much so that Jade grieved alongside Tanner when she died a year ago.

Jade's head pounded harder, and a wave of panic came over her, the same one that seemed to hit with increasing frequency these past months. Against her will, a thought she'd been fighting came back again…

What if the headaches were some sort of punishment? What if God was punishing her for marrying Tanner after being married to Jim Rudolph all those years?

She swallowed hard, reached out, and laid her fingers on Tanner's bare arm. *Were we wrong, God? Were these not the plans You had for us?*

Jade had voiced her fears to Hannah Bronzan before, and each time her friend's answer ran along the same lines: "You did what you could with Jim. You've told the Lord you're sorry for your part in the marriage, but you were never unfaithful, Jade. Jim was. God doesn't hold you guilty for that. Not you or Tanner."

Then Hannah would reiterate what all of them already knew. Jim had moved in with another woman and divorced Jade in a bitter case that nearly cost her full custody of Ty. By the time the divorce was final, Jim had nothing but anger and bitter words for Jade. Three days later he married the woman he'd left Jade for.

Hannah's reassurances came to Jade again: "You made your mistakes, but you didn't cause the divorce. The fact that Tanner entered your life again at that time wasn't some trick by the devil. It was God's way of blessing both of you after a decade of heartache."

Her friend's words sounded right, even now. But still…

There had been women at church who wrinkled their noses at Jade after her decision to marry Tanner, telling her that according to Scripture she was living in adultery.

The idea that what she and Tanner shared might somehow be against God's will was almost more than Jade could take. Especially when she loved him more than life itself. She'd read the

Scripture in Matthew about divorce over and over again. At first she'd been convinced that she was in the right, that God granted exceptions in cases where one spouse had been unfaithful. There was no question that Jim was guilty of marital unfaithfulness. He'd refused to rectify things with her even when she'd wanted to try.

But the stronger her headaches grew, and the weaker and sicker she felt, the more terrified she became that somehow God was angry with her. Her face grew hot and her heart raced wildly. *Don't punish us now, God, please…*

A veil of sweat broke out on her face, and she pushed her fears aside. Nothing good came from worry. She reached for a glass of water and two pain relievers from a bottle on her bedside table. They were a mild, over-the-counter brand—the strongest thing she would consider taking while pregnant. They hadn't worked well in past days, but as she swallowed them she told herself she'd be fine in an hour.

The perspiration on her face was heavier than before. She took her hand from Tanner's arm and ran it across her forehead. As she did, Tanner stirred and blinked a few times before squinting at the clock.

"Jade…it's 4:30, honey." His eyes closed as he snuggled against her and circled his arms around her waist. His voice was thick with sleep. "What're you doing up?"

Her head pounded in response and her mind raced. "I'm hot. I think I'll take a shower."

Tanner tightened his grip on her. "Mmmm, baby, are you sure? Stay here with me."

"I'd like to." Jade ran her fingers through his hair and down the length of his arm. "But the morning sickness is kinda strong."

Tanner opened his eyes again. Even in the dark she could see his growing alarm. "Hey…shouldn't that be over by now? You're what…twelve, thirteen weeks?"

"Yes." Jade forced a smile. Tanner had dozens of briefs he could be studying, but instead she had often found him these past weeks in their office poring over the daily breakdown of what to expect during pregnancy. "You know what it is? This baby of ours is so healthy, my morning sickness might last four months. Who knows, right?"

Tanner thought about that for a moment and the worry left his face. "I love you, Jade." He leaned up and brought his lips to hers.

Their kiss lingered, and for a brief moment Jade forgot about the pain in her head. "I love you, too."

"Go shower." He smiled. "And I'll pray it won't be four months." He settled back into the pillow and closed his eyes once more.

"Okay. Sweet dreams."

Jade studied the image of her husband as she stood and pulled her robe tight. As she headed for the bathroom, his words rang her heart. *I love you, Jade...*

Despite her aching head, the thought of an angry God punishing her for loving Tanner seemed nothing short of outlandish. She knew God better than that.

But five minutes into her shower, her vision doubled and grew so blurry she couldn't see. As she struggled to focus, a piercing pain sliced through her head, and she screamed in agony. "Tanner!" She groped to keep her balance as everything around her began to spin. "Help me!"

His footsteps sounded fast and hard against the floor outside the bathroom, but it was too late. Darkness overtook her as she collapsed on the floor of the shower, unable to move.

"Jade!" Tanner was at her side. "Dear God, help me..."

She could feel his hands on her shoulders, then under her arms as he lifted her from the wet tile, but the sounds around her were fading fast.

And in that moment her symptoms seemed terrifyingly clear. Nausea, morning headaches, double vision. Now this...

How many children had she cared for with similar symptoms? If it was what she feared, then her thoughts hadn't been irrational after all. God must indeed be punishing her. Punishing both of them.

Jade opened her mouth to speak but she no longer could. *No, God...please. Don't let it be...*

She wanted to tell Tanner she was sorry, that she loved him more than words could say, and that he needed to call an ambulance, but she couldn't make her tongue work to form words.

For a while Tanner was gone, and Jade fought to remain conscious. *He's calling for help...everything's going to be fine.* Then he was back and he swept her into his arms again. The last thing she remembered was his breath on her face, his distant voice begging her to hold on, telling her that help was on the way.

And something else...a damp area on her chest. With a jolt she realized Tanner was crying. *Tanner...honey, don't cry. I'll be okay, I promise.*

Then there was nothing but cold, quiet darkness...and the lingering wetness of Tanner's tears.

Tanner could force himself to do only two things as he followed the ambulance in his car: breathe and pray. Neither was easy. The moment he had seen Jade on the floor of the shower, her lips blue, her arms and legs jerking unnaturally, a grenade of raw fear had exploded in his heart.

Over and over he had pictured himself waking to her screams and finding her on the floor. "No, God!" he'd shouted as he stared at her, panic coursing through his veins. He'd had no idea what to do first. Call for an ambulance? Help her stop shaking?

In a split-second decision, he dropped to the floor, took her by the shoulders, and tried to force her body to stop shaking.

When that didn't work he called 9-1-1.

"What's the emergency?" an operator had asked him.

"I don't know…my wife is dying! Come quick. Please!"

In the minutes after that, Tanner hadn't meant to cry, but tears came anyway. Streams of them. As though his heart knew something his mind wasn't ready to grasp. That there was something terribly wrong with the only woman he'd ever loved.

When the paramedics arrived, Tanner told them Jade was pregnant. They noted the information, hooked her up to several monitors, and gave her a shot of something. While they did, Tanner pounded them with as many questions as he dared ask. Was this something they'd seen before? Was she dying? What was the shot for? Could they help her stop shaking?

Two men worked on her, loading her onto a stretcher, and one of them answered Tanner's questions, his tone calm and confident. "It happens often," the man explained while he helped his partner hook an IV line into Jade's arm. "She isn't dying. She's having a seizure. The shot will calm her down."

Seizure? The word screamed in Tanner's mind even now. A seizure? Other people might have seizures, but not his wife. Not his precious Jade.

The memory evaporated in a desert of fear. Tanner swallowed hard and kept his eyes glued on the swirling lights in front of him. He knew nothing about medicine, but he knew this: Seizures were a sign of something bad.

Something very bad.

It was more than Tanner could process, so he continued to pray. Not the conversational prayer he so often shared with God, but a desperate cry for help, for an answer they could live with. One Jade could live with.

At the hospital Tanner tore from his car and raced into the emergency room. Jade was being moved through the lobby toward the back. Tanner was at her side in seconds, his heart racing as he gently leaned over and hugged her close.

"Jade, honey..." He took hold of her hand and walked alongside the stretcher. "How are you?"

She forced a smile, and Tanner tried to keep the fear from showing on his face. She looked small, almost childlike, lost in a sea of sheets and intravenous lines. Her face was pale, her tone groggy. "I have a headache."

"I know. Dr. Layton's on his way."

Her eyelids lowered partway. "I'm tired."

Tanner kept his stride even with the moving stretcher and glanced at the paramedic pushing her. "Is that normal?"

"Yes. It's the medication." The man angled the stretcher around a corner and into a room. He patted Jade on the hand. "Go ahead and sleep. Dr. Layton will be here in a few minutes; he'll take good care of you."

She was asleep before the man left the room, and Tanner stared at her. A chill had worked its way into the marrow of his bones. *What's happening to her, God? She's everything to me.*

Sweat beaded across his brow, and he reached for her hand. She couldn't be sick, couldn't have anything wrong with her. *Please God, not Jade. She and Ty and the baby...they're all I've ever wanted, all I've ever prayed for since–*

A technician entered the room, cutting his thoughts short. "She needs to go to X ray." He positioned himself at the head of Jade's bed and began wheeling her out of the room. "The doctor wants a CAT scan."

Tanner stayed by Jade's side as much as possible, and at eight o'clock that morning, Jade was admitted for observation pending the results. She was still groggy when Dr. Layton entered the room and walked over to her bed. Tanner was glad this doctor was handling the situation. The two men had met on several occasions, and Tanner liked his professionalism. From everything he knew of the doctor, if anyone was up-to-date on current medical breakthroughs, it was Robert Layton.

The man nodded at Tanner, his expression serious. Then he smiled at Jade. "Looks like you're feeling better."

Jade uttered a weak laugh. "Talk about morning sickness, huh?"

Dr. Layton's expression fell and his eyes narrowed. "Jade—" he glanced at Tanner, then back at Jade—"I'm afraid it's more than morning sickness."

Tanner held his breath and tightened his grip on Jade's hand. *No, God...please...* Nothing felt real. The whole scene felt like a poorly scripted TV drama.

The doctor drew a breath and moved a step closer to the bed. "The CAT scan shows a brain tumor, Jade. It's about the size of a walnut." He pursed his lips. "We need to do a needle biopsy."

Even as the doctor spoke, as he delivered the worst verdict of Tanner's life, Jade's expression went unchanged. She nodded and listened the way she might if the doctor were talking about a simple case of the flu or a patient down the hall.

Or one of the kids she worked with.

Tanner wanted to scream at both of them, to shake the doctor and demand to know the odds, the risks. To know if Jade would be okay when the nightmare that had just begun was finally over.

Instead, he struggled to still his spinning thoughts and focus on what Dr. Layton was saying.

"The seizure means that the tumor is growing." He glanced at a clipboard in his hands and then back at Jade. "If it's aggressive, there's no time to waste. Even if it isn't cancerous. You know that, right?"

No time to waste for what? Tanner wanted to scoop Jade into his arms and run from the room, find some way to stop the craziness. Instead he stayed stone-still and felt the slightest trembling in Jade's fingers. He clasped his other hand around hers, and the trembling stilled.

There was a pause, and Tanner cleared his throat. "I don't understand."

Jade turned to him. "If the tumor's growing, they'll want to do brain surgery right away." She hesitated, and for the first time he saw tears in her eyes. "But that puts the baby at risk."

Tanner's heart pounded in his throat. Surgery? Risks to their baby? None of it was possible. He tore his eyes from Jade's and stared at Dr. Layton. "What are the options?" His tone rang with frustration.

The doctor angled his head. "It's too soon to say." He set his hand on Jade's shoulder. "Let's get through the needle biopsy and then we can talk."

The test was set for just after lunch, and neither Jade nor Tanner wanted to talk about the possibilities. Instead, Jade slept, and Tanner held tight to her hand while he called Matt.

"Hey, listen, I'll be out of the office for a few days." He squeezed his eyes shut and pinched the bridge of his nose, holding his tears at bay. His heart thudded hard against his chest. "Jade's—" Fear stopped him from finishing the sentence. He couldn't say it, couldn't admit the truth this soon. His hands trembled and his throat refused to let him speak for several seconds. *Control, Tanner. Come on.* He swallowed hard and cleared his throat. "Something's come up."

Matt paused. "Everything okay?"

"Yeah." Tanner's answer was too fast, but he prayed Matt wouldn't ask any hard questions. He wasn't ready to talk about the doctor's findings. Not yet. Not when he was still desperately trying to catch his breath and believe the news himself. "Jade isn't feeling well."

"Oh. Right." Matt seemed relieved. "Morning sickness?"

"Yep." Tanner closed his eyes briefly as the lie left his lips. *If only it were true…*

"Tomorrow then?"

"Sure."

The phone call ended and tiny sweat drops made their way down Tanner's forehead. He hated lying to Matt, but he couldn't admit the awful truth. Not to Matt or Hannah or the neighbor who was caring for Ty that day.

Not even to himself.

Using his wife's name and the words *brain tumor* in the same sentence was too impossible to imagine. Maybe the tests were wrong. Maybe they'd insert a needle in Jade's skull and find out there wasn't any tumor there at all.

The seizure medication made Jade sleep through the biopsy and into the afternoon. Tanner called about Ty and asked the neighbor if he could spend one more night with them.

"Jade's not feeling well." He glanced at her, at the bandage on the small patch near the front of her head where they'd pulled out a sample of the tumor. Despite his sweatshirt, Tanner began to shiver.

The neighbor agreed and put Ty on the phone. "Hi, Dad, the beach was so cool! Me and Karl bodysurfed three hours straight."

"That's great." Tanner dug deep down and found the courage to continue. "Hey, buddy…uh, your mom's not feeling so well. Karl's mom said you could stay over tonight and she'll bring you home tomorrow before dinner."

"Okay." Ty didn't hesitate, and a small wave of relief splashed against Tanner's taut body. Why tell the boy now, when they didn't know anything about the monster they were about to battle? The bad news could wait until tomorrow. Ty's tone was light. "Give her a kiss for me, all right?"

"All right. Be good."

"Okay, Dad. I love you."

"Love you, too."

When Tanner hung up, he was reminded, as he always was, of how many times he'd missed out on telling his son he loved him. Eleven years. Even now it was impossible to imagine that while he'd spent all those years pining away for Jade, wondering why she'd married someone else, Ty had been growing up without his father. It was a tragedy Tanner could only withstand because of the close bond he and the boy shared now.

In the nearly two years since they'd found each other, Tanner had taught Ty how to throw a spiral using the laces of a football, and how to perform the crossover in basketball. He had pitched him a thousand baseballs in the field across the street from their house, and he jogged with him three times a week.

Despite the constant blur of motion he generally made in their home, Ty had a sweet side as well. That semester at school he befriended Karl, their neighbor. The boy didn't have a father. When Tanner and Ty played catch or hit balls, Ty often asked if Karl could come, too.

"Karl reminds me of me back before I knew you," Ty would say when the two of them were alone. "I wish he had a dad like you. You and Mom are the best parents in the world."

Tanner shuddered again. Telling Ty that his mother was seriously ill was more than he could imagine. And so he focused his gaze on Jade's beautiful face, and sometime around midnight, after the night nurse had made her final rounds, Tanner fell asleep.

At ten o'clock the next morning, Dr. Layton appeared again. He was holding a file, and this time the gravity of the situation was etched in the lines on his forehead.

"It's cancer, Jade. I'm sorry."

Tanner stared at the doctor, his eyes unblinking. What had the man said?

Cancer?

The word screamed at him from every wall in the room. Jade couldn't *possibly* have cancer. It was all a nightmare. He was going to wake up at home in their own bed, Jade beside him, smiling at him, assuring him everything was all right, and promising him that she and their baby were perfectly fine.

No, God, not cancer. Not Jade...

Tanner hung his head for a moment, his hands clenching into fists. Then just as quickly, he realized he hadn't said a word to Jade. Ignoring his pounding heart and uneven breathing, he lifted his chin and reached for her hand. She had been watching him, her eyes filled with too many emotions to sort. Sadness, regret, disbelief. And fear, of course. But...Tanner frowned. He saw guilt, too. As though somehow she felt responsible for the doctor's awful news.

Her eyes welled up. "I'm sorry, Tanner."

"No." He forced a partial smile and uttered a single desperate laugh. "It's not true, Jade. Tests can be wrong." His gaze shifted to Dr. Layton. "Isn't that right? Can't the tests be wrong?"

The doctor's mouth formed a straight line, and he looked from Tanner to Jade and back again. "Not this time."

Tanner stared at the man. He wanted to scream or punch a wall, shout at anyone who would listen, insist the diagnosis wasn't true. His gaze shifted back to Jade and he saw quiet tears streaking down her cheeks. He tightened his grip on her hand. "We'll fight it, Jade. People beat cancer all the time."

She nodded, smiling as her eyes filled again. "We'll beat it." She swallowed a single sob. "God's...not finished with me yet."

Tanner nodded, his mouth dry with the blasting winds of hot, merciless fear. "We'll fight it together." He wove his fingers between Jade's and leaned against her arm as the doctor explained their opponent in detail.

"Jade has a glioblastoma, a fairly common type of brain cancer."

Tanner forced himself to concentrate. He still had hold of Jade's hand. "It's curable, right?"

The doctor leveled his gaze and his voice fell a notch. "Yes. In about half the cases." He hesitated. "It depends on how fast the tumor's growing. Of course, there's no way to tell how long it's been there." Dr. Layton let the file fall to his side. "Jade's pregnancy seems to have compromised her immune system and sparked what looks like aggressive growth."

The words were like something from a nightmare. *Tumor…cancer…aggressive growth.* Tanner massaged his left temple with his free hand. The doctor might as well have been speaking Russian for as much sense as it all made.

"I'm recommending two weeks of intense radiation therapy followed by removal of the tumor. At that point we can implant radioactive pellets and begin chemotherapy until—"

"Stop." Tanner held up his hand, and Jade and the doctor looked at him. "Radiation? Removal of the tumor? That's surgery, right? Brain surgery?" He alternated his gaze from Jade to the doctor.

Dr. Layton sighed. "Yes."

Jade opened her mouth to speak, but Tanner wasn't finished. He let go of Jade's hand, stood, and paced three quick steps toward the door and back. "What's that mean for the baby?"

"I know what it means." Jade's tears spilled onto her cheeks and she turned her attention to Dr. Layton. "I won't terminate."

Terminate? What was she talking about? The baby? *Their*

baby? Tanner tried to breathe but he couldn't. The air around him had turned jagged and sharp, cutting at him as he struggled to drag it into his lungs.

"I'm... I'm lost." Tanner crossed his arms and managed to grab a quick breath. "If someone would clue me in here." He sat back down and leaned over his knees, his eyes locked on Dr. Layton's.

The man uttered a tired sigh. "The treatment I'm recommending would require terminating the pregnancy, Tanner. There's no way a fetus could survive the radiation and chemotherapy. Even the surgery holds considerable risks."

"And if she terminates the baby, you think the treatment will...that she'll be okay?" Tanner's heart skipped a beat. He was wandering toward a cliff he'd never come anywhere near, but what choice was there if it meant Jade's life?

"Yes. I think there's a good chance. But I'd like to begin first thing in the morning. First we would—"

Jade shook her head. "No!"

"Jade..." Dr. Layton hesitated.

"I said *no.*" Jade shot the man a fierce look, ignoring the tears that spilled onto her cheeks.

The doctor gritted his teeth. "I'm recommending you terminate this afternoon. I'm sorry, Jade. I don't see any other option. Right now the tumor—"

"Excuse me." Tanner held up his hand. "Could you give us a half hour, doctor?" His palms were suddenly damp, his heartbeat irregular. "Jade and I need to talk."

Dr. Layton nodded and left the room, closing the door behind him.

The moment they were alone, Jade sat up straighter and cried out in a tone that was both angry and hurt. "What are you *thinking*,

Tanner?" She splayed her fingers across her chest. "We don't need a half hour or five minutes. I wouldn't consider terminating this pregnancy. Not for anything."

Tanner was on his feet again, and as he walked to the window, he felt suddenly twice his age. Frustration became anger and it boiled near the surface of his heart. When he turned back to her, his eyes were damp. "I want this baby more than my next breath." He lowered his voice and took a step closer to her bed. "But if it means losing you…" His words were strangled in emotion. "Maybe it's our only choice."

Jade's eyes grew wider still. "Tanner, I can't believe you mean that."

He blinked, and the fog of confusion cleared just enough for him to see through it. Had he really said that? Really alluded to the possibility that he'd agree to abort their baby? What was he saying?

He fell to his knees and then back on his heels. There he let his head hang forward and allowed the tears to come. Jade was right, of course. He'd made a living defending the religious right, protecting people who protested in front of abortion clinics, people who thwarted the efforts of high school nurses to provide condoms and secret abortions for students.

Wasn't he the one whose closing arguments had once included Dr. Seuss's famous story about Horton the Elephant finding an entire town on a dust speck? *A person's a person, no matter how small.* He could hear the sincerity in his voice even now.

He'd never stood on this side of the great debate over life. But he had to face the truth…without a doubt, if he had to decide this minute whether to save Jade or the baby, there would be no question what he would do. He'd sign the termination papers without hesitating.

And that truth terrified him.

What did it say about everything that defined him? His faith, his passion for the law, his integrity…? Was it all a sham? Just something to use in the courtroom?

The only thing he didn't doubt was his love for Jade. His desperate, lifelong love for a woman with eyes as green as Chesapeake Bay, a woman he'd loved since they were children, back when they skipped rocks and rode bikes and spent endless summers growing up in the same Virginia neighborhood.

A woman who could no more terminate the life of the child she was carrying than she could will herself to stop breathing. Life…the love of life was part of who she was. Part of why he loved her.

"Tanner…"

Her voice pulled him up from the floor. His feet moved like they were stuck in mud as he walked to her bedside.

There was no anger in her eyes now. Only a quiet certainty. She ran her tongue over her bottom lip and shook her head. "I can't…"

A sob slipped from her throat, breaking free a dam of emotion. She reached out her hands, and Tanner laid his upper body across hers, working his hands and arms behind her and clinging to her.

"I know." He brought his mouth close to her ear, his own tears mingling with hers. "I'm sorry…"

Tanner remembered a documentary once about two men and a little boy who got caught in severe rapids while boating on a river. When the vessel overturned, the two men were killed, but by some miracle the child made his way to the distant shore and scrambled up a muddy tree root. He clung to the underneath edge of that cliff until help came, knowing that to let go meant certain death.

For three hours the boy hung there, his fingers bloodied and locked into place by the time rescuers showed up.

Tanner closed his eyes and nestled his face against Jade's. He was that child now, clinging to Jade with all that remained of his hope and courage and belief in forever.

Because to let go, to lose her now, would certainly kill him.

Even if it took a lifetime for his heart to stop beating.

Seven

Dr. Layton would never suggest terminating a pregnancy for anything but the most serious causes. Jade could remember the man arguing with other doctors about taking extreme measures to save not only pregnant patients, but their unborn children as well. He was not a man of faith, but he was one of the kindest doctors Jade had ever worked with.

The fact that he disagreed with Jade and Tanner's resolve to keep the baby could only mean one thing: He feared for Jade's life.

That afternoon, she and Tanner huddled against each other in the hospital room as Dr. Layton detailed his alternate treatment plan, one that would hopefully take Jade and the baby safely through the next several months.

"We'll deliver the baby at thirty-two weeks. Not a minute later." Dr. Layton's sigh rattled Jade's nerves. *Thirty-two weeks? That's too early, God…the baby won't be able to breathe on his own…*

The doctor continued. "In the meantime we'll watch the tumor."

Tanner gripped her hand, his face pale. "What…what should we look for?"

"Seizures are the biggest concern." The doctor frowned. "Jade's tumor is in the frontal lobe of her brain. That means even the smallest growth could trigger more seizures like the one she had yesterday." He looked from Jade to Tanner. "The solution is an anti-seizure drug. It would be the least likely to have an ill effect on the baby."

Jade nodded. She was familiar with the medication, and terrified at the same time. She had been so busy worrying about Tanner and his reaction to the news, so concerned with having a good attitude toward her ability to fight the tumor and God's ability to heal her, that she'd taken almost no time to consider the road ahead.

Especially if it included five months of anti-seizure medication.

She glanced at Tanner. *Please, God...give him strength.*

The doctor drew up a chair and sat down across from Tanner. "Seizures could be nothing more than a painful inconvenience...or they could kill Jade and the baby. We have to prevent them. Let's talk about the anti-seizure medication." He leveled his gaze at Tanner, and Jade held her breath. She knew what was coming. "The drug has side effects. Personality changes, excessive grogginess, slow speech, slow motor skills. Depending on the dosage, it could temporarily appear that Jade has brain damage."

The remaining color drained from Tanner's face. Jade wanted to rip out the IV line, grab Tanner's hand, and run for her life. She'd seen patients on anti-seizure medication, kids with inoperable brain tumors who sometimes didn't recognize their parents after three weeks on the drugs. This was why brain cancer was the most dreaded of all childhood types—the medication and the fact that the prognosis was usually so poor. Jade thought of Brandy Almond... How was the girl doing? Maybe her cancer was in remission by now.

The doctor was telling them that the side effects were often reversible once the tumor was removed. "I'll start you on a low dose, but as the tumor grows, we'll almost certainly have to increase the medication. We'll have to monitor it."

It was almost four o'clock when the doctor left them alone.

Tanner crossed the room and anchored himself at the window, his back to her. "Did you hear that?" He looked over his shoulder at her. "The drug could change your personality."

Jade ached to climb out of bed and hug him, to promise him that no matter what medication found its way into her veins she would never see him differently, treat him differently. But she wouldn't lie to him. She'd seen the effects of the drug too often.

"Okay." She summoned every bit of faith within her and spoke in a voice that barely carried across the room. "We'll have to pray it doesn't."

Tanner shrugged and came to her side once more. "I guess."

There was something numb in Tanner's tone, and it frightened her. Was Tanner doubting the power of prayer? Was he questioning whether God could help them? The possibility scared Jade more than any cancer ever could. *God, give him faith...help him.*

In response a Scripture came to mind. It was their verse. Their life verse: *"For I know the plans I have for you...plans to give you a hope and a future and not to harm you..."*

She folded her arms against her chest and tried to believe it was still true. "You guess? Is that all, Tanner? After all God's brought us through?"

He gripped the side rails of her hospital bed and locked his elbows. "God allowed a brain tumor to grow in your head, okay? I'm still trying to deal with that. You and I—" his jaw tensed—"we love the Lord with all our hearts but because of my mother's wretched lies we lose a decade together. Ten years, Jade." His knuckles turned white as he tightened his grip on the bed rails. "Now this?" He groaned. "I'll pray. Of *course*, I'll pray. But right now I don't know if it'll make a difference."

Tears filled her eyes again. She hadn't cried this much since she walked out of Tanner's mother's house thirteen years ago believing he didn't love her. "Tanner...please."

He was rigid, tense with anger and fear and confusion. But at the sound of his name on her lips, his hands and arms relaxed, and he closed his eyes. When he opened them, Jade saw something that gave her hope again.

Resolve.

She exhaled in relief. This was the Tanner she knew and loved, the one who would fight to the death for what he believed. And certainly now, in the darkest moment of their lives, he would trust God to lead them through. What choice did they have?

"I'm sorry, Jade. Forgive me, okay?"

She nodded and reached toward him, slipping her hand in his.

He brought her fingers to his cheek and searched her eyes, his voice hoarse. "I'm just scared. Scared to death."

"Me, too."

He looked at her for a long while. Then he closed his eyes again and broke the silence between them with the most intense, most heartfelt prayer Jade had ever heard him utter.

When he finished, he opened his eyes and said the thing they must both have been thinking since getting the results that morning. "Let's call Ty."

Jade held her breath while Tanner phoned Karl's mother. He explained that Jade was in the hospital for tests. The woman was more than willing to bring Ty there, and an hour later, Tanner left to meet them in the hospital lobby.

The few minutes alone in her room gave Jade time to soak in the reality of what was happening to her, of the dark path that lay ahead. She thought of Ty, the years they'd shared when she was married to Jim Rudolph, back when the boy received little or no attention from anyone but her. For years she had tried so hard to forget about Tanner, but it had been impossible. Ty was a perfect miniature of him. Through the boy's pale, blue eyes, Tanner had shared breakfast with her each morning and hugged her each night.

Never back then had she thought it possible that Ty and Tanner would meet, or that somehow she and Tanner would find their way back together again. And now…

Will you take me home, God? Will you leave Tanner to raise our little boy? Is that the plan you have for me?

The questions formed a lump in her throat, and when the two men she loved most in life—one a shorter replica of the other—entered her room, it was nearly a minute before she could speak.

"Mom, what's wrong? How come you're here?" Ty wore a stained baseball shirt. His eyes were bright with panic. Jade held her arms out as he ran to her and hugged her for a long while. When he pulled back, he ran his finger over the IV line. "Dad says you're sick."

"Yes." She found her voice and set her hand on his shoulder. "I have cancer, Ty. Brain cancer."

They had decided to tell him the truth. After all, he would be affected by every stage of her treatment. Especially the difficult months when she'd be on the anti-seizure medication.

"Cancer?" Ty's face went white, and he took several steps away from her until he was snug against Tanner's side. "Does that mean…you're gonna die?"

"No, honey." Jade forced a smile, despite her breaking heart. "Cancer can be treated." She closed her eyes for a moment. *Help me say the right words, God.* Ty had to feel her hope now, at this early stage. That way he'd be more likely to stay hopeful when things got worse. "I'll be sick, though, so you and Dad need to stick together."

After a half hour of questions, Ty seemed content to sit in the chair beside Jade and watch baseball on the hospital television. Tanner took the time to call the Bronzans.

"I'm at the hospital, Matt." Jade watched her husband massage his temples and struggle to say the words. "We got some bad news today."

There was a pause, and she saw her husband's eyes well up. "Jade has…Jade has brain cancer. The doctors told us a few hours ago."

Jade couldn't hear their conversation, but she could tell from Tanner's reaction that Matt must have been shocked. Tanner nodded a few times and then choked out a single request before hanging up. A request that frightened Jade because it was so out of character for her self-reliant, fun-loving husband.

"Please come," he said, his voice cracking. "We need you guys."

The Bronzans were there in half an hour. Jenny stayed at home with Grace, since small children weren't allowed in the room.

Matt vowed to contact the firm's mailing list and request prayer support for the weeks and months ahead. Hannah offered to do what she could to help with Ty. Still, despite their words of encouragement, Jade caught them both wiping tears throughout the evening.

For the first time Jade could remember, Matt and Tanner shared not a single one-liner or smile between them. She wanted to shake them both.

I'm not dead yet! Don't give up on me…

But she kept her thoughts to herself. She was too new in her role as cancer victim to know how to act.

When visiting hours were over, the Bronzans offered to take Ty home with them. Jade would be released from the hospital in the morning, sent home with specific instructions and a month's supply of anti-seizure medication. Hannah would take Ty to baseball practice and bring him home after that.

"Thanks," Jade reached out and held Hannah's hand. Tanner, Matt, and Ty were near the door, not listening to their conversation. "You're the best friend I have, Hannah."

"You, too." Tears filled Hannah's eyes and this time she didn't try to hide them. "I learned something after Tom and Alicia were killed."

Jade nodded, her own tears blurring her vision.

Hannah struggled to speak. "I learned that even in the darkest nights, morning eventually comes." She smiled, her lips trembling. "It's God's promise. Fight this, Jade. Fight it with everything you have."

"I will." She blinked back the tears. "If I ever look like I'm giving up, tell me again, okay?"

Hannah nodded, and soon Ty and the Bronzans were gone for the night.

Tanner turned off the light in the room and pulled his chair near her bed again. He planned to sleep at her side as he'd done the night before. "Maybe..." His voice was a quiet whisper. "Maybe you won't have any side effects."

His statement confirmed what she already knew. The thing that weighed most heavily on both their minds here and now, at the starting line of their race against death, was the medication. What if she suffered from it the same way some of her young patients suffered? Would there be a time when she might look into Tanner's loving eyes and not know him? Feel the precious touch of his hand on her skin and be startled, even frightened?

He tried again. "Maybe you'll be the exception."

She consciously raised the corners of her mouth. "Maybe."

The nurse brought in a tray bearing a glass of ice, a pitcher of water, and a straw. There was also a small saucer with two orange capsules. Jade didn't have to ask what they were. She'd given them to her patients too many times for that.

Tanner looked from Jade to the tray and back again as the nurse poured her a glass of water. There was a heaviness in Tanner's eyes that broke Jade's heart. "Is it…?"

She nodded. "Yes." There was no sense in dragging out the moment. She placed the pills on her tongue and took a long swig of water.

And with that, Jade's uncertain journey into darkness began.

Eight

Nearly six weeks had passed since Grace came to live with them, and Hannah was so giddy about life she felt guilty.

What right did the four of them have to be happy when Jade and Tanner were living through the most difficult time in their lives? Of course it wasn't a question that could be answered. Hard times came to everyone who lived long enough, and as Matt had been there for her during her darkest days, so the two of them would be there for Jade and Tanner.

Still, Hannah found herself consumed with warring emotions. Half the time she was elated by the leaps and bounds Grace made each day, but there were moments, hours, when she was drawn to the sad, quiet pondering of Jade's future.

It was the morning of July 3, and Jenny was upstairs helping Grace get dressed. The three of them were going shopping for the big party the following day, the one she and Matt had thrown each Fourth of July since they were married two years ago.

Hannah worked in the kitchen, taking care of the morning dishes and savoring the sound of Grace's laughter upstairs. Had it been nearly two months since that day when Mrs. Parsons brought her home to live with them? The victories they'd notched since then were unbelievable, making up the sweetest bouquet of memories.

The four of them had learned to trust each other. They had shared tenderness and tears, sunshine and silly laughter. Many nights when Grace was tucked in bed, Hannah and Matt marveled at how far she had come.

How very far.

A breeze filtered in through the kitchen window, and Hannah paused, staring at the endless blue beyond the sandy beach. There had been times during those first two weeks when Hannah wondered if Grace would survive the transition.

Times when she wondered if *any* of them would survive it.

The child would wake in the middle of the night, grabbing at her wrist, of all things. Then she'd scream in a way that would bring all of them, even Jenny, running to her bedroom.

Hannah shuddered as she remembered Grace's first night. After Mrs. Parsons left, they showed the child her room and her pretty new clothes. Grace ran her fingers over the delicate pink things and looked at Hannah, her eyes wide. "Who will wear them when I'm gone?"

There was a pause while Hannah, Matt, and Jenny exchanged a look. Finally Hannah knelt down before the girl and stroked her hair. "Grace," Hannah's voice had been a mix of fear and compassion. "We want you to stay here. With us."

Grace shook her head. "I never stay for very long. The police come and take me back to Mommy."

Hannah hadn't known what to say, so Matt set his hand on Grace's shoulder and took over. "Honey, the police won't take you away anymore."

Grace wrinkled her nose and tiny tears filled her eyes. "Mommy said..." She was crying, but in a way that was different from any other child Hannah had seen. Tears streamed down her cheeks and her small shoulders shook, but she made no sound at all. She wiped her face and looked at Matt. "Mommy said if I got took away from her, then the police would put me in jail."

Jenny covered her mouth, stifling a cry.

The horrible picture Grace had painted made Hannah's head reel. She and Matt circled the child in a hug. "No, Grace, that'll never happen." Matt's tone was soothing. "We want you to stay with us forever."

Hannah had expected Grace to stop crying. Instead her little body convulsed. With the three of them watching, Grace climbed onto her bed, curled in a ball, and said just one more thing before falling asleep. "I w-w-want my *mommy.*"

She came to the table for dinner that evening, but ate nothing. Regardless of their attempts to get her to talk, Grace remained silent, wary through her bath and while she was being tucked into bed.

When they were downstairs and out of earshot, Jenny collapsed on the sofa. Her eyes were dry but frustration was written into every crease on her forehead. "She hates us."

Hannah sat beside her daughter, and Matt pulled up a chair nearby. He spoke in a voice that was low and full of compassion. "She's afraid."

"That's right." Hannah slipped her arm around Jenny's shoulder. "Mrs. Parsons said that would happen."

"I know, but still..." Jenny let her head fall against the back cushion. "How long will it take before she trusts us?" She leveled her gaze at Matt. "Before she laughs and plays like a regular little girl?"

Matt reached out and patted Jenny's knee. "With God on our side, my guess is not long."

Grace's first scream pierced the peaceful silence of the Bronzan home at two o'clock the next morning. Matt and Hannah grabbed their robes and raced down the hall just as she released her second scream.

Matt sat her tiny body up and shook her gently. "Grace, honey...it's okay. Wake up."

The child opened her eyes, but didn't make eye contact with either of them. Instead she stared straight ahead and screamed again. Eyes wide, she grabbed at her right wrist, shaking that hand

and slapping it over and over and over.

Finally Matt caught her fingers midair and brought them down. "Grace, it's okay. Wake up."

In response she shook her head faster and faster and screamed again, this time looking from Matt to Hannah and back. "No! No…no…no…*no…!*"

Hannah anchored the child on the other side, and together she and Matt wrapped their arms around her, whispering words of hope and peace until she stopped screaming.

"I want my mommy; I want to go home." Then she hung her head so that the curls made a tent around her face. "Go away. Please go away."

The floor of Hannah's heart fell that night as she drew back and took in the picture Grace made. She was a little girl alone in the world, unable to let go of the nightmares of yesterday long enough to believe in the treasure of today.

And there was nothing she or Matt could do about it.

On her way out of Grace's room, hot tears slid down Hannah's cheeks. *Get us through this, God…please. What have we done?*

It was a prayer she prayed often that first week, and by the ninth day—with Grace barely speaking to any of them and still asking hourly to go home—Hannah considered calling Mrs. Parsons and asking for help.

Jenny handled Grace's reluctant beginning by being gone more than usual.

Hannah had cornered Jenny that week and tried to reason with her. "You'll never connect with her if you're not home."

"I don't know what to say." Jenny shifted her weight to one hip. "Besides, she doesn't care if I'm here or not."

Hannah took hold of Jenny's arm. "That's not true. She told you she wanted a sister that first day. She may not talk to you, but she likes you."

Jenny narrowed her eyes and lowered her voice. "That's not the kind of sister I was expecting."

There was more that Jenny wanted to say; the intensity in her eyes told Hannah that much. Of course Grace wasn't the type of sister Jenny had been expecting. The only sister she'd ever known was Alicia, and the two of them had been inseparable, laughing and playing together. Delighting in the same kinds of games and music and with that uncanny ability to finish each other's sentences.

The way only sisters could.

Even if Jenny hadn't intended to, she clearly had expected Grace to be something of a companion. A little sister to her the way she had once been a little sister to Alicia.

The situation had been heartbreaking, and there was nothing Hannah could do about it.

Before the night was over, Jenny apologized for being impatient. But the entire situation had Hannah at a breaking point.

Midway through the second week, Matt linked his arms through hers and pulled her close. "It takes time, Hannah. I'm not willing to give up."

"Me, either. I just wish I knew what God was doing."

Matt grinned. "Building a bond between us, maybe?"

Hannah's mind went blank. "A bond? By giving us a child who won't talk or smile or respond to us?"

"Ahh, but remember this..." Matt put a finger to Hannah's lips. "One day when she *does* talk or smile or respond, we'll know it's real, won't we?"

Hannah remained doubtful. Would they ever be able to truly reach Grace? That night she and Matt prayed on their knees in the sand outside their house.

"Give us wisdom, God." Matt closed his eyes and directed his face toward the starry sky above. "It's been nine days and she's so quiet, so locked up inside. What can we do different, God? Just show us, please. We love her. We'll wait as long as it takes."

The breakthrough happened the next day.

Matt was at work and Hannah was making oatmeal when Grace entered the room. She came up beside Hannah and tugged on her sleeve. Hannah smiled at her, but before she had time to speak, Grace tucked her hand in Hannah's and said, "I have something to tell you."

Hannah set the spoon down beside the pan and turned to face her. "What, honey?"

"I'm sorry." Grace lowered her chin, but kept her eyes on Hannah. "I haven't been very good. I miss my mommy."

Tears stung at Hannah's eyes, and she blinked them back, stooping to the child's level. "That's okay. You're still getting used to us, Grace. It takes time." She hugged her and kissed her cheek.

Grace ran her thumb over Hannah's hand; her touch was velvet. "Do you like me, Hannah?"

Hannah framed the child's face with her fingers, brushing the curls back and looking deep into her eyes. "I like you very much."

Grace doodled an invisible design with her toe. "I'm scared the police will come and take me to jail...but I'm still here."

Hannah nodded. "I know you miss your mommy, honey. But sometimes God gives little children a new mommy and daddy. Ones that can take care of them better and—" she was treading on slippery ground, but she forged ahead—"And sometimes love them better."

This time Grace bobbed her head up and down, and throughout breakfast she chattered away about the beach and her toys and Hannah and Matt and Jenny.

"You and Matt are Jenny's mommy and daddy, right?" Grace had long since finished eating her cereal and now sat opposite Hannah, her hands folded on the table.

"Right." Hannah wanted to say more. *We're* your *mommy and daddy, too, Grace*. But she held her tongue.

"Hannah?" Grace cocked her head.

"Yes?"

"You have only one girl, just like my mommy, right?"

Hannah wondered whether the sting of that question would ever go away. "Actually..." She allowed herself to pause. "I had two girls. Jenny and Alicia. But Alicia died a few years ago."

"Oh." Grace's nod was matter-of-fact. "She's in heaven with Jesus."

The breath caught in Hannah's throat. Mrs. Parsons hadn't gone into detail about Grace's background, except to say it had been challenging. All they'd been told so far was that Grace was a child with no physical, mental, or emotional disabilities. Whatever that meant.

Still, there'd been no reason to think she adhered to any faith.

"How do you know about Jesus, sweetheart?"

Grace shrugged. "My grandma told me."

Grandma? An alarm sounded in the control center of Hannah's soul. Mrs. Parsons had said there was no extended family, no one who would fight for Grace once her mother's rights were severed. "Grandma?" Hannah tried to smile. "I didn't know you had a grandma."

"I don't anymore. She died at Christmastime." Grace folded her arms and swung her feet. "Grandma loved Jesus very much. She told me Jesus was like an invisible Daddy, and sometimes, when Mommy had a bad night, I knew Grandma was right. I could feel my invisible Daddy hold me and keep me safe."

Hannah fought the urge to let her mouth drop open. The child seated before her—who for more than a week hadn't spoken to them or shown any sign that she was capable of loving or being loved—not only knew about Christ, but had felt his love in her life.

Before Grace went to sleep that night, she smiled at Hannah. "Know what, Hannah?"

Hannah leaned down and kissed the girl on the forehead. The burden of frustration from the past week lifted like fog. She could hardly wait to tell Jenny about the change in the child. Hannah's fingers soothed Grace's brow. "What?"

Grace batted her silky eyelashes. "I like you, too."

Over the next two weeks there were more moments like that.

One afternoon she and Grace took a walk on the beach and found a sandy knoll where they watched seagulls swooping low over the water. "Know what, Mommy?" Grace looked at her, squinting in the sunlight.

"What, honey?"

"We should sing a song."

"We should?" Hannah grinned at Grace and reached for her hand.

"Yes. A happy day needs a happy song."

"Okay." Hannah nodded, biting her lip to keep from giggling. "What should we sing?"

"You teach me a song." Grace shaded her eyes with her hand. "Please, Mommy."

Hannah thought a minute. "Do you know 'Jesus Loves Me'?"

Grace's fair eyebrows came together in deep concentration. "I don't think so."

"Oh, Grace!" Hannah brought her hands together in a series of light claps. "It's the happiest song of all."

There and then, with the seagulls providing backup, Hannah taught Grace the familiar tune. Immediately it became Grace's favorite, and after that they sang it at dinner and every time they walked on the beach.

As Grace opened her heart, every day was more of a blessing

than the day before. Not just to Hannah, but to each of them in different ways.

Two weeks ago Sunday, they'd been coming home from church when Hannah checked the rearview mirror and saw Grace and Jenny holding hands. Three days later she came home from the grocery store and found Grace in Matt's lap. He was reading to her, nuzzling the side of his face against her creamy cheeks and giggling with her at the silly parts.

Hannah froze in the doorway, moving in slow motion as she set the bags at her feet. She remembered thinking that it was finally happening, just as Matt had known all along. Grace was falling in love with them, and they with her. Not because they were just another nice family who took care of her for a few weeks while her mother dealt with the legal system, but because Grace was starting to understand the truth.

This time she wasn't going anywhere. She was home. Forever.

A week after that, Jenny took Grace to a park down the street and then out to lunch. When they came home, they both wore gaudy, blue-beaded bracelets and matching grins. "Grace wanted to go shopping." Jenny laughed and swept the girl up onto her hip. "We bought sister bracelets, right Grace?"

Grace planted a wet kiss on Jenny's cheek. "Right." She slid down and ran to Hannah. "Wanna see?"

Hannah studied the band of beads and saw a silver plate on top that read, "Sisters Always." The words were barely legible through her tears. "That's wonderful." She straightened and grinned at Jenny. "I'm sure Jenny won't take it off for a minute."

In the days since then, Grace had established a nighttime ritual. Hannah and Matt would walk her up to bed and pray with her. Then they'd give her a chance to pray, and almost always her prayer was the same.

"Dear Jesus, thank you for giving me a family. Please don't ever take me away from here because this is my home. And I want to live here forever and ever."

Once in a while, Hannah and Matt exchanged a glance as Grace finished praying. A glance that, in a moment's time, spoke both their greatest fears and their greatest faith that certainly God would grant the child's request. Not once in the past three weeks had they voiced concerns that Grace would be anything other than their forever daughter.

With a sigh, Hannah let the memories fade as she worked the sponge into the countertop. They had heard nothing but good news from Mrs. Parsons. The termination process was on schedule, and within six months Grace would be free for adoption. The path ahead looked smooth and without trouble.

Still…

She paused and stared once more out the window at the sea. It would be good when the process was over. When Grace Bronzan would forevermore and legally be Grace Bronzan, and her little-girl prayers could be about schoolwork and making friends and having a good day. The way other little girls' prayers were.

Then they could get on with life.

The thought sent a piercing reminder through Hannah's heart. Once the adoption was complete, they could indeed move on. But what about Jade and Tanner and Ty? What about their unborn baby?

It was still almost too much to believe. Jade had cancer? How could she? After all she and Tanner had been through? Hannah pictured Jade in the hospital room the other day. If anyone could make it through brain cancer it was Jade. Hannah smiled. Her friend always fought for what was right, whether as a parent volunteer in Ty's classroom or by encouraging Tanner in his legal work.

Certainly she would fight now. After all, there could be nothing more right than seeing Jade well again, seeing her baby safely delivered, seeing the four of them become a family, the way Jade and Tanner had always dreamed they'd be.

She thought of the hundreds of conversations she and Jade had held. Together they had shared their life stories, sometimes in laughter, sometimes in tears. They marveled often at how much they had in common, how God had brought both of them through the flames of loss and heartache.

But this time…the situation was as grim as it had ever been. Hannah's heart skipped a beat as she considered the possibilities. It wasn't right that Jade was sick. Hadn't they had enough grief in their lives already?

Hannah held her breath and then exhaled long and slow. As her anxious thoughts faded, she closed her eyes, and with everything in her, she thanked God for the friend she had in Jade Eastman. A friend she had come to love.

Then she begged God to move mountains and part seas…whatever it took, so that one day very soon Jade would be well again.

Nine

The Fourth of July dawned without a trace of fog and by midmorning Jade had stirred together her famous potato salad. She was ready for taste testers.

It had been a week since her diagnosis, a week since she'd taken her first dose of anti-seizure medication, and so far she was holding her own in the battle. There had been no personality shifts, no changes in her gait or speech. She was tired and less focused, but she was determined not to let Tanner and Ty see even that. It was important that they think she was making progress. Their enthusiasm was bound to make her feel better, which would make the few symptoms she was experiencing all but disappear.

Jade didn't know if it was the holiday or the fact that she was one week closer to a safe delivery for her baby, but she felt particularly upbeat. She expected the picnic at Matt and Hannah's later that day to be a huge success.

Jade took a bite of the potato salad and licked her lips. "Okay guys…" She raised her voice so Tanner and Ty would hear her upstairs. "I need tasters."

A moment later there was a galloping sound above her. "Coming!"

It was Ty. Jade smiled and filled a clean spoon with more of the salad just as he pounded down the stairs and rounded the corner. He took the spoon from her and grinned. "I already know it's good."

Jade lowered her chin and put her hands on her hips. "Humor me, okay." She tousled his hair. "I can never get the spices right till someone else tastes it."

Ty ate the mouthful in one bite. "Tastes great." He hesitated. "Well, maybe a few more spider legs."

He ran from her just as she reached out to paddle him with the spoon. When he was a few feet away, he spun around. "Hey—" his teasing expression faded—"You look great, Mom. I'm praying for you."

Joy filled Jade's heart, and she studied her son as she hadn't in months. He was taller, looking more like his father every day. And he was thirteen. A teenager now, with more maturity and wisdom than most boys his age—maturity and wisdom born of a painful past they'd survived together.

But those days were behind them. They were together now, a family like they always should have been. These were the good days, the times of their lives. Jade clenched her teeth. Nothing would change that, not even her cancer.

"Thanks." She walked the few steps that separated them and set her hands on Ty's shoulders. In a year or so he'd be taller than her. "That means a lot."

Ty winked at her. "I'll be out back."

"Okay." She gave the muscles along his shoulders a couple of quick squeezes and raised her brows. "Impressive. The girls will be lining up at the door."

"Girls can wait." He grinned. "I have hoops to play." He kissed her on the cheek and headed for the backyard and the half-court where he spent much of his time.

"Ty..."

He turned back. "Yeah?"

"Where's your dad?" Jade hadn't seen Tanner since that morning.

"Upstairs. We were playing Nintendo, but I beat him right before you called me."

"Oh." Jade felt her smile fade. Why hadn't he come down with

Ty? Was it her imagination or had he been avoiding her? When they were together, all he wanted to talk about was her health, how she was feeling and what changes she was noticing from the medication.

She hid her frustration. "What's he doing now?"

Ty shrugged. "I think he's working."

Jade nodded and Ty disappeared through the back door. She felt suddenly tired, but made her way up the stairs and found Tanner in his office, writing on a legal pad.

The sound of her footsteps caused him to look up. "Hi."

The tension in Jade's shoulders eased. Tanner's tone was cheery. Maybe she was only imagining the distance she sensed between them. "Hi." She came up behind him and worked her hands along the base of his neck. "I called for testers on my potato salad."

Tanner's muscles stiffened beneath her fingers. "I had to work."

"I know." Jade stooped so their cheeks were touching. She spoke softly, her voice a whisper. "But it's my famous potato salad. It won't be the same without your professional tasting ability."

Tanner stared at his notepad for a moment, then back at her. "How are you feeling?"

"Fine." Jade straightened and walked around his chair. She knelt in front of him and sighed. "But why does it seem like that's the only question you ask me lately?"

For a moment Tanner said nothing, then he set his pencil down and wheeled his chair backward so there was some distance between them. "Is this how it's going to be?"

Jade let her hands hang at her sides. "How what's going to be?"

"You have cancer, Jade. Brain cancer." Tanner crossed one leg over the other and leaned back in his chair. He narrowed his eyes, his voice loud and frustrated. "Last time I checked that was something serious." He gestured toward the door. "But there you are, making potato salad and getting ready for some big Fourth of July picnic like everything's fine."

Jade folded her arms. "What do you want me to do, Tanner? Lie down in bed and wait until I get sicker? Turn out the lights and give up on you and Ty?" She placed one hand over her abdomen. "On our baby?" A huff slipped from her throat. "I'm sorry, honey, but I can't do that. I *won't* do it."

Tanner uncrossed his legs and dug his elbows into his thighs. "That's not what I mean, and you know it."

"What *do* you mean?" Jade threw her hands in the air. "Ever since you heard the c-word you've been different. Like you're afraid to touch me, to love me."

"That's not true." Tanner's tone was softer as he stared at her with helpless eyes. His gaze fell to his feet, and he covered his face with his hands. "Ah, Jade. You have no idea."

Jade's anger cooled and she crawled closer, resting her head on his knee. Of course Tanner wasn't put off by her illness or bent on being negative. He was simply afraid.

Scared to death at the thought of losing her.

She reached up, peeling Tanner's fingers from his face until she could see his eyes. "I'm sorry."

He studied her, his gaze layered in pain and fear. "Don't pretend everything's okay, Jade. Please."

"I'm not pretending." She forced a smile despite the tears that stung her eyes. "I feel good, Tanner. Better than I thought I would."

"But you're sick. You can't act like you're not."

"Yes, I can." She uttered a single laugh. "I can act happy and normal and crazy in love. Don't you see, Tanner? You and Ty and our baby, all of you matter more to me than being sick." She brought her lips to his and kissed him long and slow, working her hands along his sides and dusting his neck with her fingertips. "Ty's outside." Her voice was deep with desire as she rose to her feet.

Taking his hand in hers, she led him out of the office toward their bedroom, where she did everything in her power to make Tanner forget about cancer and surgery and the medication's devastating side effects.

Everything except the way she so desperately loved him.

The picnic was going strong and so far Matt thought it had been a huge success.

Jade and Hannah were inside washing dishes, and Jenny and Ty were on the beach playing Frisbee with Grace. Matt cleaned the barbecue while he watched Tanner run a dishrag over the picnic table. The usual afternoon breeze had kicked up and Matt decided against getting his guitar. They almost always sang after dinner, but he wanted to give Tanner a chance to talk

They finished their jobs, found their sunglasses, and took seats in adjacent beach chairs. For a while they watched the kids as they ran through the surf, chasing the Frisbee and splashing each other.

"Grace looks happy." Tanner kept his gaze on the child.

Matt studied her, amazed at how she'd become part of their family. "She's a special little girl."

"Any word from her birth mother?"

Matt shrugged. "She's in jail. The termination should be finished up in four months."

Tanner shook his head. "Amazing."

They fell silent again, and Matt watched as Jenny swept Grace into her arms and ran from Ty. The boy was a miniature of his father. Strong and agile. Beautiful in motion. He caught the girls in ten strides and the threesome tumbled to the sand, laughing and tickling each other.

There was a full feeling in his heart and Matt realized what it was: He was a father, really and truly. Not just to Jenny, whose heart would always belong in part to another man, but to Grace as well. No longer was the child's presence in their home something of an experiment or a way to help a child in need. She was his daughter, through and through.

She had moved into his heart, where she would always remain, regardless of what the months ahead brought. He no longer had even the slightest emptiness in the father's heart that beat within him. That place was filled with a little girl he loved more with each passing day.

A little girl who—regardless of her biological makeup—was absolutely his own.

The wind stung at Matt's eyes and he shifted his gaze to Jenny. *Good for you, Jenny girl.* She was two months from starting college and could have turned her back on the idea of Matt and Hannah adopting a child. Instead, she'd been determined to be a part of the process from the beginning. And now that Grace was part of their family, Jenny had blossomed in ways Matt had never seen before.

He studied her again. What was it exactly? Something in her carefree expression, or the twinkling in her eyes…

Just then Jenny threw her head back and laughed with abandon as Grace took her by the hand and tried once more to outrun Ty.

That was it. Her laughter. Jenny laughed more easily than before. Suddenly Matt remembered a conversation he and Hannah had shared not long after they were married. They were walking together and Matt had commented that Jenny seemed back to normal, content and happy with life.

But Hannah cast him a sad smile and shook her head.

"She's not the same as before the accident."

They kept walking, and Matt asked Hannah what she meant.

"The way she laughs is different. She doesn't throw her head back and giggle like she used to before Tom and Alicia died." Then Hannah had said something Matt still found utterly sad. "You want the truth?"

"Yes." Matt tightened his grip on Hannah's hand.

"I don't think she'll ever laugh that way again."

The memory faded, and Matt stood to get Hannah. She had to see it, had to watch for herself the fact that Grace had helped Jenny laugh again. But as he turned toward the house, he saw Hannah was already outside, standing a dozen feet behind him, seeing the same thing he'd just seen.

Her hand was over her mouth and tears filled her eyes. "I never thought..."

Matt crossed the deck, slipped his arm around Hannah and held her close. "I was coming to get you."

"It's..." Hannah's voice was raspy with emotion. "It's because of Grace. Jenny has a sister to love again." Hannah focused hard on the smaller girl and shook her head. "The resemblance to Alicia is uncanny, Matt."

Matt nodded and watched the two girls for a long while. "I love her so much it scares me." He looked at Hannah. "Ever feel that way?"

"Yes." Hannah shifted her gaze back to their two daughters. "All the time."

After a minute Hannah went back inside, and Matt returned to his seat beside Tanner.

"Everything okay?"

Matt nodded. "It's Jenny. She's really blossoming as Grace's big sister."

Tanner stroked his chin and studied the children again. "They look alike, have you noticed?"

A smile lifted the corners of Matt's mouth. "Yeah, we noticed." Matt shifted in his chair and searched Tanner's face. "Hey, how are things?"

Tanner filled his cheeks with air. He held his breath, then leaked it out again. "Work's good. I like the Benson, Colorado case. The pastor's wife sent me the contract they had with the city. Came in the mail yesterday." Tanner shrugged. "She's right. Deep into the document there's a clause that says City Hall can't be rented by any group who teaches faith in Jesus Christ as the only way to salvation." He grabbed a quick breath. "It's amazing because even without looking at case precedent, we've got a winner here, and personally, I think it'll be—"

"Tanner." Matt reached out and took hold of his friend's wrist. "I wasn't talking about work." He hesitated. "I was talking about Jade."

"Oh, that." Tanner seemed to shrink an inch as he settled back in his chair. "Jade says she's feeling good."

Matt nodded. "She looks good."

"Right." Tanner waited awhile then leaned forward again. "Anyway, I told the pastor's wife we'd set up a conference call after the holiday. That way we could figure out what to do, whether we file suit now and interview people at the church or fly out for a conversation with…"

Matt let Tanner ramble on about the case, but concern for his friend grew with each passing sentence. Since Jade's diagnosis, Tanner had responded one of two ways whenever the topic came up. Either he was angry and full of questions or he refused to talk about it.

Neither response was a solution in a situation like the one

Jade faced. The one their whole family faced. Because even if she felt good now, there were dark times ahead. The premature delivery of their baby, radiation, chemotherapy, and brain surgery.

So while Tanner droned on about the Colorado case, Matt prayed that his friend would stop avoiding the truth and figure out a way to handle the situation.

Because the hardest days of Jade and Tanner's lives were just around the corner.

By the time the two families lined up their beach chairs on the sand at dusk that evening, Jenny was exhausted. Fireworks shot off the pier in Redondo Beach lit up half the sky. Grace cuddled between Jenny's legs and jumped a time or two when a firework was particularly large or loud.

There was no way to explain the change that had come over Jenny's heart in the past few weeks. At first she had been irritated by Grace's silence, but over the days she'd seen a connection growing. After all, Jenny knew what it was to be withdrawn in the face of loss. Even if Grace's mother had been awful, Grace was bound to feel sad and uncertain over being taken from her.

Jenny figured the connection between her and Grace happened about the time they got their sister bracelets.

But now there was something even deeper, stronger. Something she hadn't felt since before Alicia's death. As the fireworks ended, Grace squirmed around and hugged her. It was then that Jenny understood what she was feeling. It was a sense that she belonged to Grace, and Grace to her—a special feeling that couldn't be replaced, not even with a best friend or a loving parent.

After four long, empty years, Jenny was finally a sister again. And no matter their age difference or the fact that Grace was adopted, Jenny knew something else.

The feeling would last forever.

The group was making their way into the house, folding chairs and commenting on the dazzling display and the fact that another Fourth of July was behind them. Jenny stood and took Grace by the hand. "Come on, sweetie. Let's go inside."

After a cup of milk and two more chocolate chip cookies, Jenny led Grace toward the adults. "Grace and I are tired." She smiled down at her sister. "We're turning in for the night."

There was a round of good nights and Jenny helped Grace up the stairs and into the bathroom where they brushed their teeth. After Grace had her nightgown on, Jenny tucked her under the covers and kissed her forehead. "You wanna pray or want me to?"

Grace grinned. "Let's both pray."

When they were finished, Grace blinked twice. "Can I keep the lights on for a few minutes? I want to look at my Bible."

Jenny smiled and reached for the bright blue children's picture Bible near Grace's bed. "Sure, honey." She pointed to the wall adjacent to the child's bed. "I'll be on the other side of that wall getting ready, okay? I'll check on you in a few minutes."

Grace locked eyes with Jenny and smiled the sweetest smile Jenny had ever seen. "I love you, Jenny."

A rock settled in Jenny's gut, and for a long time she stood there, not sure what to say. She *did* love Grace, didn't she? But those words had never been something Jenny said lightly. In all her years, she'd only said them to four people: her parents, Matt, and Alicia. The people who were permanent in her life, people she could count on. It was her way of maintaining the meaning of the words.

Don't let her notice, Lord. Please. I'm just not ready…

Jenny swallowed quick and smiled as big as she could. "You're my favorite girl, Gracie; you know that, right?"

The corners of Grace's lips fell a bit. "Yep. You're my favorite girl, too."

Jenny clenched her fists as she left Grace's room. *What's wrong with me? I do love her, don't I?*

She wasn't sure and she was too tired to dwell on the issue. Five minutes passed and Jenny was taking out her earrings when it happened. Three soft thuds sounded on the wall between her room and Grace's. Jenny's heart stopped, and her breath caught in her throat. Suddenly she was four years younger, and the girl in the next room was not Grace, but Alicia.

It had been a different house, of course, but a similar wall had separated their rooms, and from an early age they designed a code. One thud meant hello; two meant come quick. And three thuds represented the three words she and Alicia shared every day for as far back as Jenny could remember. The words Jenny reserved for only a select few.

"I love you."

Of course there was no way Grace could have known that, but still, the sound of the thuds had been almost like hearing Alicia's voice again, like having her alive once more and as close as the next room.

Before Jenny could unfreeze her legs, the thuds came again. Once, twice, three times. And in that instant Jenny wanted nothing more than to go to her little sister and hold her, share with her all the love that had been building in her heart for the past few weeks.

Without hesitating, she rounded the corner into Grace's room, sat on the edge of her bed, and took her small hand. "Hi, honey. Did you want something?"

Grace nodded and yawned, setting her Bible back on the nightstand. "I wanted to tell you I love you."

This time a partial cry came from Jenny's mouth before she could silence herself. She leaned over the little girl and held her close, feeling a dam of emotion breaking free within her heart.

"Sweetie, is it okay if I sleep with you tonight?"

Grace grinned. "Like a sleepover?"

"Right." Jenny stroked the child's soft hand.

Grace slid over and made room as Jenny turned off the light, crawled in bed, and cuddled up to Grace. "Can I tell you something?" Jenny whispered.

"Yes." Grace wiggled her nose against Jenny's.

The tears were coming now and Jenny knew she had to say it before she was weeping too hard to speak. "I love you, Grace. You're my sister and I love you."

Grace's smile lit up the dark room. Jenny's words seemed to settle something deep within the little girl's heart. She was asleep in five minutes. The moment she was, Jenny's tears began spilling onto the pillow. *Dear God, I can't believe it. These feelings I have for Grace…it's like what Mom means when she says Your mercies are new every morning…thank You. Thank You.*

Without making a sound, she wept until she could barely breathe, holding tight to Grace and stroking her hair. And for the first time, the tears weren't because she missed Alicia, but because she had a sister again.

A sister she loved with all her heart.

Ten

Only one antidote could dim the fear in Tanner's heart: work.

As far back as he could remember, Tanner had wanted to be a religious freedom fighter, and now that the symptoms of Jade's tumor were being managed by the medication, it was easy to convince himself she would be fine. That this whole episode was merely some wild and crazy speed bump on the road to forever, and that if he buried himself deep enough into his caseload, one day he'd wake up and Jade would be better, the cancer behind them.

With those thoughts holding the reins to his emotions, Tanner flew to Denver, Colorado; rented a car; and drove to Benson to determine exactly what had caused the Benson City Council to pull the permit on the church's contract to meet there.

What he learned proved without a doubt that they had a case.

He visited Pastor Casey Carson at home. The man who headed the First Church of the Valley had eyes that sparkled and a contagious energy. Tanner had a feeling the pastor would be easy to work with.

"Just a minute—" Pastor Carson pulled something from his file cabinet and handed it to Tanner—"Here. It's our lease agreement."

Tanner leaned forward and read it word for word, searching for the place where Carson and his congregation might have violated the lease.

On the eighth page, four paragraphs down, Tanner found what he was looking for. There, listed as a stipulation of the lease was this statement: "City Hall may not be rented by any group who teaches faith in Jesus Christ as the only way to salvation."

Tanner had seen the copy, but now, holding the original, he was speechless. He let the document settle to his lap, and for a moment his mouth hung open. He lifted his eyes toward Pastor Carson and shook his head. "I still don't believe it."

"I didn't notice the clause before we signed the agreement." The pastor's face was relaxed, humble. "I'm no attorney, but even I couldn't believe that was right, that a clause like that was legal in a city-sponsored rental agreement."

"It's not." Tanner was on his feet and he read the clause once more. Suddenly an idea hit him, a simple idea that truly could make the case a national landmark. His insides relaxed. This was going to be fun. He sat down once more, smiled at the pastor, and tapped the contract with his finger. "Here's what we're going to do..."

That meeting led to others with the associate pastor, and then with the elders at the church. All of them said the same thing: one Sunday, several members of the city council visited their church service. That next Monday, the pastor received notice that they could no longer hold Sunday services at City Hall because the church had violated the terms of the rental agreement.

At night Tanner got back to his hotel room and used his laptop to research case precedent. He talked to Matt the second night and shared his idea.

"Brilliant." Matt's tone held awe, and the excitement bubbling in Tanner grew. Maybe this was the case that would sway public opinion away from dismantling the country's religious freedoms. Maybe more people would be willing to fight for the cause if they could see what was happening in local government, the extreme to which elected officials were willing to go to squash Christianity from any place remotely public.

"We'll handle it together." Tanner's mind raced as he imagined the soundness of the argument they'd have to make on behalf of First Church of the Valley. "Clear your caseload and you can start research next week." He rambled through a list of ideas and stopped only to catch his breath. "Sound good?"

On the other end of the line, Matt hesitated. "Okay."

"If you have a minute, I'll go over the interviews with you; that way you'll be—"

"Tanner, stop." Matt's voice was stern. More stern than Tanner ever remembered hearing.

"What?"

"Have you called Jade?"

At the mention of her name, Tanner felt the blood leave his face. "Why? What's wrong?"

Matt huffed. "She has cancer, remember? You leave her alone with Ty to do research in Colorado and you haven't even called her? In two days?"

Tanner's heart resumed a normal beat. "I worked too late last night. Besides, she said she had projects to catch up on before..."

"Before she got sicker?" Matt's voice was quiet but his words brought a sledgehammer down on Tanner's heart. "If she's going to get sicker, then these are the days she needs you most. While she's still well enough to love you."

Tanner let his head fall into his free hand. "How'd you know I hadn't called her?"

"Hannah told me."

"So she's mad at me?"

Matt groaned. "She's not mad; she's hurt." Matt paused and Tanner knew him well enough to know he was searching for the right words. "You're running. It's only going to hurt worse if you don't stop."

Tanner clenched his fists. "I'm not running; I'm working. We own a law firm, remember?"

"Your wife is sick, Tanner. There's no case more important than that."

"Fine." Tanner had heard enough. What did Matt know of having a sick wife? What did he know about Tanner's fear that any day Jade's personality could change or the tumor could grow and before they had time to prepare for any of it both Jade and their unborn baby could be gone? Matt had no right telling Tanner how to handle the situation. If Tanner wanted to devote this time to his work while Jade was still well enough to leave at home, then that's what he'd do.

Regardless of Matt's feelings.

"I'll call her. Then you and Hannah can stop worrying about us."

"Tanner. No one blames you for being afraid. We're all scared." The compassion in Matt's tone made Tanner regret his unkind thoughts. Matt was only being his friend.

"You're right." He leaned back against the hotel wall and massaged the bridge of his nose with his thumb and forefinger. "Sorry for snapping."

"It's okay. Just don't isolate yourself. We're all in this together."

Tanner hesitated. "Right. Thanks."

Matt meant well, but Tanner wanted to disagree, to tell his friend there was no one who could really understand how he felt. Jade was his entire world, the reason he had chosen to follow his dreams, the only woman he'd ever loved. There was no one who could truly understand her place in his heart, no one who could share his pain if he lost her.

He made the call as soon as the conversation with Matt was finished. Although it was after eight o'clock, she sounded upbeat and happy to hear from him. "How's the research going?"

"Great." Had Hannah really heard from Jade? Maybe the Bronzans were only imagining that his silence had hurt Jade. "I can't wait to share it with you."

"Think it'll be big?"

"Truthfully, Jade..." His mind shifted to the legal plan he'd been forming those past two days. "It could be the biggest of all."

"That's great."

There was silence between them then, and Tanner thought her tone was perhaps too upbeat. "Hey, I'm sorry I didn't call yesterday. Time got away from me."

When Jade didn't answer him, he knew Matt had been right. He hunched over his knees and stared at the hotel carpet. Why hadn't he called? Was it like Matt had said? Was he running from her? There was hurt in her voice when she answered him. "Ty wanted to tell you good night. Me, too." She drew a sharp breath and sounded peppy once more. "But that's okay; I know you're busy. At least you called today."

"Yeah, well, I should have called yesterday."

"It's okay, Tanner. Really."

He dug his elbows into his knees and tightened his grip on the receiver. What was wrong with him? Why wasn't he home with her where he belonged? "How are you?"

"Fine. Ty and I went to the zoo. The baby giraffe was on display for the first time."

"That's nice, but it's not what I mean." He swallowed back his frustration. "How are you *feeling* Jade? You."

"I told you, I'm fine. No side effects, no more headaches. Everything's okay."

Her response made him want to hang up the phone and dive back into his research. Maybe this was why he was running. She refused to discuss her illness or any of the symptoms, almost as though she could pretend away something as life-changing as cancer. And as long as she wasn't willing to talk about it, Tanner didn't have anyplace to share his fears. No wonder it was easier to invest his time at work. It was the only way to silence the terrifying questions that Jade didn't want to talk about and no one else could answer.

Jade put Ty on, and the boy shared his latest escapades on the baseball field. "You'll be home for my game Thursday, right Dad?"

"Right. Absolutely." Tanner smiled and realized it was the first time he'd done so that evening. "Listen, Ty, could you do me a favor?"

"Sure." Tanner closed his eyes and he could picture his son as clearly as if he were standing in the same room.

"Make your mom some tea, okay?"

"Okay." Worry crept into Ty's voice. "She's doing good, right?"

"Right. That's what she tells me."

"Sure, I'll make her tea."

"Thatta boy. And give her a kiss for me."

Tanner talked to Jade once more, but when he got off the phone, he couldn't get back into his research. No matter how hard he tried, his mind kept drifting back until all he could think of was the way he felt the first time he lost Jade.

The summer of his twelfth year, the summer Jade and her father moved away.

That year Jade and he were best friends growing up in the same neighborhood, spending endless days racing bikes and playing together. Scandal and hatred and gossip swirled around them like a typhoon, but they were blissfully unaware.

"Jade's family isn't good people, like us," he could hear his mother saying. "Her father's a drunk, and her mother's run off with another man. She's always been a harlot. I have my proof."

Back then he hadn't understood what she meant, not that it mattered. With or without her mother, Jade was moving. She had a day to pack her things and tell Tanner good-bye. He could see her still, those green eyes flashing as they sprawled across his front yard picking single blades of grass and staring at a canopy of blue sky above them.

Tanner hated the idea of Jade leaving. More than once on their last day together, he asked her about when she'd be home again. "You sure you're coming back?"

"Yes, I promise." Her tone had been frustrated. "We'll meet Mama in Kelso and then when Daddy's job is done, we'll come back here."

They'd only been kids back then, but she was the most beautiful girl Tanner had ever seen. When they said good-bye an hour later, it took all Tanner's strength not to cry. It wasn't until two days after that Tanner heard his mother say she was glad Jade's family was gone for good.

"What do you mean?" Tanner remembered being angry at her. He couldn't begin to understand why she didn't like Jade. "They're coming back. Jade told me so."

"They'll never be back." His mother patted his head. "Forget about her, Tanner."

"Yes, they will! She promised me."

But summer turned to fall, and one year led to another without any sign of Jade and her parents. Tanner had no way to look for her, no ability to check her whereabouts. Often in the years that followed, he'd ask his mother about her.

"I have no idea where the girl is!" His mother would huff and busy herself in the kitchen. "Why must you insist on asking about her?"

Tanner's youthful answer was as clear today as it had been all those years ago: "Because I'm going to marry Jade one day, that's why."

Eleven years would pass before he and Jade would find each other again.

Tanner leaned back in his office chair and doodled Jade's name on a notepad, taking special care with each letter. It was a miracle they'd found each other at all that summer. He had long since forgotten where she had moved, and his mother pretended the same. Who would have thought his internship with the Kelso Board of Supervisors would place him in the very town where Jade lived?

A quiet chuckle came from someplace deep inside him. He remembered the first time they saw each other again. Tanner had been asked to suggest at a public meeting that the children's ward be eliminated from the Kelso hospital as a way of saving money.

Jade attended the meeting. Her argument that day caused the board of supervisors to change their mind and opt for different budget cuts.

But not before Jade had a chance to verbally slay Tanner and his ideas.

Tanner laughed again at the memory. Neither of them had recognized the other at first, but when the meeting was over, Tanner realized who she was. He caught her before she left and when the afternoon was over, they were old friends again.

Friends who spent the summer falling in love.

"Ahh, Jade…if only things had been different." Tanner whispered the words as his eyes found their framed wedding picture on his hotel dresser. He never traveled without it, and now as he studied Jade's green eyes a piercing sadness poked pins at his heart. "We lost so much time…"

Tanner remembered hurting when he learned the truth about Jade's teenage years in Kelso. Life had not been easy for Jade since she'd moved from Virginia. By the time Tanner found her again that summer, the walls around her heart were so high and thick, there were times he thought their relationship didn't stand a chance.

But gradually Jade opened up and the walls fell. Not only that, but midway through July, Jade became a believer, a Christian with a deep love for God. With everything in common, Jade and Tanner's time together was magic.

Until then, Tanner had kept himself from intimate situations, determined to wait until marriage before sharing himself with a woman. Jade, too, was a virgin, and early in their dating Tanner couldn't imagine their relationship ever becoming physical.

Tanner bit his lip, his eyes still locked on his wife's framed image. The truth was, they both let walls tumble that summer. By the end of August, the day before he was scheduled to go back to college on the east coast, there was nothing either of them could do to resist the temptation of being together.

And that single night—the decision to give in to a moment of weakness greater than either of them—changed everything about the next decade.

No matter how much time passed, the truth about what happened that fall was still depressing. It made Tanner long for a way to go back and change things so he and Jade could somehow share every one of the days they missed.

After their fateful night together, Tanner left for Europe on a lengthy mission trip. He was there, completely out of communication, when Jade learned she was pregnant. With nowhere else to turn, Jade called Tanner's mother, who told her that Tanner was a liar who randomly slept with women and made them pregnant.

Tanner opened his eyes and exhaled in a way that filled the hotel room with sadness. The fact that Jade had believed his mother was always the hardest part for Tanner. That and what happened next.

Alone and pregnant with nowhere to turn, no one who seemed to care about her, Jade panicked. It was as simple as that.

She married Jim Rudolph, a man who shared nothing of Jade's newfound faith. It was a marriage intended to do one thing: give Jade's baby a chance at a normal life.

Instead, it caused all of them a decade of heartache.

Tanner stood and stared out the window at the distant Colorado mountains. There were no words to describe the pain that had suffocated him when he returned from his mission trip that fall and found out Jade was married. Tanner tried desperately to reach her, but to no avail.

Tanner turned back to the hotel room and glanced at the clock. Matt was right. What good was he doing Jade here in Colorado researching his next case? He could finish his research at home.

He wandered about his room, gathering clothes and tossing them into his suitcase. A heaviness settled over Tanner's heart, and he knew it was from the flood of memories that had carried him through the past hour. The pain of losing Jade all those years ago never dimmed, not even a little.

Maybe that's why he was running so fast these days.

He'd been heartsick watching her move away when he was a boy. Then after they'd found each other again in Kelso, after they'd fallen in love and made promises to marry, Tanner had been devastated by losing her a second time. It had taken years before her face didn't haunt him at night, before her name wasn't fresh on his mind in everything he did.

Now the stakes were higher than ever, and Tanner was sure of this much: If he lost Jade again, it would destroy him.

Eleven

Fear coursed through Patsy Landers' veins as she sat on a stone bench amidst the wild daisies, pink roses, and brash violets that took up most of the courtyard outside her small house in Bartlesville, Oklahoma.

This was her prayer garden, the place she came when she wanted quiet time alone with God. It was a place she'd visited often these past four months while she prayed about the situation with her wayward daughter. And now, as her heart raced within her, she was sure of His answer.

It was time to take action.

Not for Leslie's sake. Unless Leslie gave her life over to Jesus, there was no way the girl was going to change. She was twenty-one, hooked on crack, and determined not to take help from her mother or anyone else. At this point she could be living on the streets or with a band of drug runners. There was no way to tell.

Patsy lifted her chin and let the breeze dry her tears. If Leslie were not a mother, it would be time to let her go. Let her come to the end she seemed desperate to reach.

But Leslie was not alone.

She had little Grace with her, even though Patsy had offered—as she always did—to care for the child herself. Patsy folded her gnarled hands and a small sigh slipped from between her teeth. The loan had been Patsy's last-ditch attempt, the only way she knew to be sure Leslie would stay in Oklahoma. She borrowed against the equity in her Bartlesville home and gave the money to Leslie on one condition: Use it to purchase a house around the corner, a small place where she and Grace could start a normal life, one that didn't involve drugs and strange men and living out of various broken-down vehicles.

It was the money Patsy was going to use to have her hips replaced, an operation doctors assured her would ease her arthritis pain. But the surgery could wait.

If the money would mean getting Leslie and Grace out of California and off the streets, it was worth every penny.

Patsy was certain Leslie was going to cooperate. Together they toured the small house she'd chosen and contacted a realtor. Escrow papers were drawn up, and Leslie seemed excited about her new chance at life.

The day the deal was set to close, mere hours before Leslie was to show up with the cashier's check and take ownership of the house, she fled. She left with Grace and the money, and Patsy hadn't heard a word from them since.

At first Patsy considered calling the police and reporting the money stolen, but that wouldn't have helped. Besides, she'd given the money to Leslie. Yes, they'd had an arrangement as to where the money was supposed to go, but either way, Leslie hadn't stolen it. Not by legal definition.

Next, Patsy thought about getting in her car and heading down the highway toward California, because if she knew one thing about Leslie, it was this: If she was running, she'd eventually wind up in California. Santa Maria, to be specific. That was where her drug base was, the place where she could crash at any of a dozen houses and have people smoke and drink and shoot up with her. People who would watch Grace for days on end if Leslie wound up in a stupor that couldn't be slept off.

Patsy was as sure as winter that Leslie was there.

But she was also sure that this time there was no point chasing her. Leslie would do what she wanted, regardless of Patsy's attempts to stop her. That being the case, Patsy chose to take an hour every day and do the one thing she knew with absolute certainty would make a difference: Pray.

She prayed that somehow Leslie would arrive in California and feel compelled to find a new start, that she wouldn't return to her drugged-out friends, and that she'd realize there would never be another time when she'd have so much cash on hand.

"Help her think clearly," Patsy would pray quietly while she sat in her garden. "Let her use the money for a house or an apartment. Something stable for Grace."

Because really, what it all came down to was the child.

Patsy could release her hold on Leslie. She could shelve her concerns that her only daughter would wind up in a gutter someday, facedown, dead from a drug overdose. If that happened, so be it. There was nothing Patsy could do to stop it.

But Grace deserved better.

Sweet, precious little Grace. Patsy loved the child like she was her own and would gladly have raised her, would have fought Leslie in court for the chance to do so if only it seemed like the right thing. The problem was that Grace loved her mother. Every time Patsy considered using legal means to take the child from Leslie, she was stopped by that single fact. It was a terrible inner conflict. What was best for Grace? Life with Leslie, or life with her grandmother?

Now, in light of Leslie's disappearing with the money and remaining silent these past four months, the answer seemed perfectly clear. Grace was four years old, after all, and there was no telling what horrific things awaited her if she accompanied her mother back to the culture of drug users and criminal types.

Patsy thought back to the time that had passed since Leslie's disappearance. The months had been filled with pain, not just emotionally but physically. Patsy's arthritis was worse than before and even simple activities were almost more than she could bear. The weeks had become months, and still Patsy prayed. But not until this morning, with the rich smell of blossoms hanging in the humid air, was Patsy sure it was time to act. She took slow, painful steps toward the house. Once inside, she began making phone calls.

Two days later she had enough information to string together what had happened to Leslie and Grace since they left Oklahoma. The facts acted like so many spears, impaling Patsy's heart further with each devastating blow.

As Patsy had suspected, Leslie headed for Santa Maria, but instead of using the money to find a safe place for her and Grace, she blew the entire amount on drugs. Neighbors who lived near a house that Leslie frequented were able to tell Patsy how wild things had gotten. So bad, in fact, that they'd taken to watching little Grace so she wouldn't be run down in the driveway by the constant flow of traffic and party-goers.

Something the neighbor said knocked the wind from Patsy.

"Leslie told us you were dead," the neighbor woman said. "She said you were sick and died. That's why they left Oklahoma."

It was a full minute before Patsy could speak. "She had…a lot of money. Did she say anything about that?"

The neighbor was quick to answer. "Yes. She said you left it to her in your will."

When she hung up, Patsy felt numb from her toes to the basement of her heart. So that's how it was. The guilt of what Leslie had done was so great that she'd simply written Patsy off.

The rest of the truth was no less easy to accept.

When the money was gone, Leslie did what she always did when reality crashed in around her. She took Grace and disappeared, this time in an old van. Police records told the story of what happened next. Broke and unable to buy food or water for her and Grace, Leslie took to prostitution, something she'd done before. She operated out of the van, which she parked in an abandoned field outside town.

That's where she was when police found her. Details of those final days were hazy, but one thing was terrifyingly clear. Leslie was in jail and Grace had been taken into foster care. The court intended to terminate Leslie's rights as a mother. And that meant one thing.

Grace was about to be a ward of the court, adopted out to strangers, all because Leslie had been too proud to place a call to Oklahoma and give Patsy the chance to raise the child.

The policeman she'd spoken to had been kind enough to trace Leslie's file and relay the information Patsy needed if she was ever going to find Grace again. Patsy thanked the man and scribbled down the name of a social worker, the woman who had placed Grace in the home of someone named Bronzan.

Patsy's heart sank. What if Grace had already been adopted? What if it was too late?

She closed her eyes and held her breath. *Help me get her back, God. She needs me. Besides, Grace is my little girl, my angel baby. She doesn't belong with strangers.*

Finally Patsy opened her eyes and allowed herself to breathe again. Then, without hesitating, she picked up the phone and dialed the number the policeman had given her. Someone answered on the first ring and Patsy cleared her throat and asked for Edna Parsons, Grace's social worker.

There was a pause and then a woman came on the line. "Yes?"

"Mrs. Parsons?" Patsy winced as her body tensed.

"Yes, how can I help you?"

Patsy drew a deep breath. "I'm Grace Landers's grandmother. I'd like to see about getting permanent custody of her."

Edna Parsons' heart skipped a beat the moment the caller identified herself. She hoped it was a hoax, one of Leslie Landers's friends seeking to disrupt the termination of Leslie's parental rights.

But there was something very real and logical about the woman's story. She knew Grace's full name and birth date and had examples of what the child liked to eat and wear and watch on television. The grandmother lived in Oklahoma and promised to fax in documentation proving she was Leslie Landers's mother and showing that she had the means to permanently care for little Grace.

The woman suffered from arthritis and lived on a disability pension and the retirement funds from her deceased husband. She was slow, but not crippled, she explained. "I can care for Grace, no problem. She's a sweet child; she knows I don't get around very well."

By all preliminary standards, Patsy Landers seemed well enough to be named the child's legal guardian, but that didn't make the situation any easier. After all, Grace was adapting beautifully with the Bronzans. Edna had been by their house a few days earlier and had been moved to tears watching Grace run on the beach with her new sister. Hannah and Matt said the change in their family had been miraculous.

"It's like she's always been our little girl," Hannah told Edna when she gathered her things and left that day.

Edna's throat swelled with sorrow. She'd done everything she could to see that something like this wouldn't happen, but still it had. These sorts of disruptions in foster-adopt homes weren't supposed to happen! Leslie Landers had said her mother was dead, after all. Of course, Edna had realized the woman could be lying, so she had done a national name search on Patsy Landers—just to verify that the woman was indeed dead. When nothing turned up, Edna assumed Leslie was telling the truth—but Patsy was listed under the name of her second husband, a man who had passed away a decade ago.

It didn't matter now. None of that would help the Bronzans once Edna notified them of Grace's grandmother's intentions.

Losing Grace would be overwhelming to people like the Bronzans, people who had suffered so much loss already.

Edna wanted to go home, shut herself in her bedroom, and cry for a week. But she knew there was something she had to do first. Not now, not until she had the proper documentation from the woman in Oklahoma, but as soon as she did there'd be no way around it.

She would have to call the Bronzans and tell them the truth.

Twelve

A month into the medication, Jade was still herself—no personality changes, no shuffling gait, no slurred speech or memory loss.

She felt tired, but nothing worse.

It was the end of July and Tanner had been home from Colorado for nearly a week. He seemed less distant, more willing to share with her, talk to her. Whatever had happened while he was gone, the change had been a good thing. In fact, everything about life seemed better than ever lately, and Jade couldn't help but thank God with every breath she drew.

Not only that, but the tumor seemed to be staying about the same size—something Dr. Layton said was nothing short of miraculous, considering pregnancy was often the worst time for cancer to hit. Meanwhile, her nausea had let up and she was beginning to feel the first fluttering of movement deep within her, movement that meant their baby was alive and well.

The whole of it was enough to make Jade sing her way through the days, sure that somehow when she reached the end of her battle with cancer, she would emerge victorious. She and Tanner and Ty and the baby. All of them together, without fear of anything else happening to them.

Of course, every now and then there were still times when she wondered if the tumor was God's way of punishing her for what happened with her and Jim Rudolph. But most often, she refused to allow those thoughts a chance to develop. Yes, she'd made mistakes in her marriage to Jim, but she'd done everything in her power to rectify them. There was no point wallowing in guilt now.

"You have to stay positive," Hannah told her every time they were together. "Keep believing God will get you through this. That's where your thoughts should be."

And that's exactly where Jade intended to keep them.

She finished her salad, drank a glass of water, and sat herself down at the computer. A friend from the hospital had told her about herbal vitamin tablets she could purchase online. The blend was designed to bolster the immune system of pregnant women who were battling cancer.

Jade found the web site, read up on the tablets, and ordered a three-month supply. Then she checked the mirror and headed for the hospital. It was just after noon, and she had an ultrasound scheduled for two o'clock. An ultrasound that would most likely tell her the information she and Tanner were dying to know—whether the child she was carrying was a girl or a boy.

As she made her way into the hospital parking lot, Jade remembered a conversation she and Tanner had shared the night before.

"It doesn't matter to me; you know that, right?" They were lying on their sides, their faces inches apart, wrapped in each other's arms.

"I know." Jade brushed her lips against his. "But what if I can't have more kids?"

"Well..." Tanner smoothed her hair back from her forehead. "Then I'd say a little boy would have Ty as the best big brother in the world." He hesitated and touched his lips to her brow. "And a little girl would be a priceless gift...priceless beyond anything I could imagine."

His words ran through Jade's mind as she entered the hospital and headed upstairs to the children's ward, where she had worked before taking leave. It had been that long since she'd seen her patients, and there was one in particular she wanted to check on.

Jade made her way off the elevator and greeted her friends at the nurse's station, all of whom were full of compliments and thrilled to see her up and around. After several minutes, Jade motioned down the hall.

"How's Brandy Almond?"

The eyes of several of the nurses lit up. "She's doing better," one of them said. "There's something different about her. Go see for yourself."

Jade grinned and hurried toward the girl's room, knocking on her door before opening it and stepping inside.

"You came!" Brandy was sitting up in bed, her cheeks full and more colorful than they'd been. "They told me you were going to have a baby!"

Jade hesitated for a moment. Was that all they'd told the young girl? That she was having a baby? Nothing about the brain cancer? Jade swallowed and considered her choice of words. "Yes. That's right." She placed her hand over her abdomen. "An active baby, by the way my insides feel."

Brandy's eyes danced. "You'll name her after me if it's a girl, right?"

"Absolutely." Jade laughed and sat on the edge of Brandy's bed. "Enough about me. Look at you, Brandy. You're glowing. Like you're ready to run a race or something."

The girl beamed. "I'm getting better. Just like you prayed."

"What?" Jade raised her eyebrows. "Brandy Almond? Talking about prayer?"

Was she…? Did the girl believe now? Was that the difference?

Tears filled Brandy's eyes. "After our talk I decided to give it a try. I told God I'd believe He was real if He'd send me a sign of some kind. Some way so I'd know it was right to trust Him."

"And…" Jade marveled at the light in Brandy's eyes. It was a light that couldn't be manufactured. Jade could hardly wait to hear what had happened to convince Brandy of the truth.

"The next day one of my teammates came in with a Bible." Brandy smiled. "Can you believe that? Just out of the blue for no reason."

Brandy's energy never waned as she shared the story of what happened. The girl approached Brandy and told her she'd been praying for her every day since she'd gotten sick. But that afternoon, the teammate felt sure God wanted her to bring Brandy a Bible and share the truth of Jesus with her.

"'It doesn't matter so much whether you run again or even if you get better,' she told me. 'But if you miss out on knowing Jesus…that'll be a real tragedy.'"

Brandy took the girl's visit as the sign she'd prayed for. "She told me about Jesus and placing my faith in Him. She said if I trusted Him, I'd go to heaven one day."

"And you agreed?" Jade squirmed in her seat, her heart bursting with joy. She took Brandy's hands in her own and squeezed them.

"Yes! I'd be crazy not to. All of a sudden it was like I got it. This Jesus you always talked about, the one my teammate loved, He was not only real, but He loved me. I didn't want to wait another minute to accept that love and start loving Him back."

"Oh, Brandy, that's wonderful." Jade leaned over and hugged the girl close. "You'll never be sorry. And your health…" Jade stood and checked the chart near Brandy's door. "You look so much better."

A laugh bubbled up from Brandy's throat, and she clasped her hands. "Doctor says if my counts stay good for another week I can go home. I'm in remission, Jade. They thought I was done for, and now I'm in remission. Isn't that, like…so *God?*"

Jade fired a grin at Brandy. "Yes, it's definitely, like, so God!"

The file told the story. Jade read it and shook her head. The girl was right; her blood counts had been excellent for the past three weeks. She returned to Brandy's side, hoping she would never find out about the brain cancer.

The expression on Brandy's face changed. "Now tell me why you took off work so early. Don't most people wait until the baby's about to come?"

Jade's pulse quickened. *Give me the words, God...please.* "Yes." She searched her mind for something to say. "But, uh, my morning sickness was worse than most." She lifted one shoulder. "I was too tired to work."

The answer pacified Brandy, and the two of them talked for another thirty minutes before Jade told the girl good-bye. "I have an ultrasound downstairs." She grinned at Brandy. "In an hour I should know if we're having a girl or a boy."

Brandy waved a finger at Jade, her face masked in mock seriousness. "Don't forget, now. If it's a girl, you name her after me." Her eyes sparkled. "Hey, and you can bring her to one of my track meets next year!"

"We wouldn't miss it." Jade laughed. "Get some rest, Brandy. And if they spring you next week, don't forget to stop by and visit."

Brandy grew quiet and she reached her hand toward Jade once more. "No matter what happens, Jade, I'll never forget you."

Sudden tears burned at Jade's eyes and she took the girl's fingers in her own. "I won't forget you, either."

"You saved my life; you know that, right? I was ready to give up, and you told me to pray. Otherwise..."

"Otherwise someone else would have told you." Jade brushed away a tear, leaned over, and kissed the girl on the cheek.

But Brandy shook her head. "No, otherwise I might already be gone."

There was a lump in Jade's throat, and she couldn't speak. Instead she shrugged and pointed heavenward.

"Have that little baby and hurry back, okay, Jade?" Brandy's voice broke and her eyes grew wet. "The kids here need you."

The conversation with Brandy played again and again in Jade's head as she made her way downstairs toward the ultrasound room. *Thank You, God…thank You for healing her. Thank You for sending her teammate that day…thank You.*

Only one part of what the girl had said didn't sit well with Jade.

The part about hurrying back. It wasn't that Jade didn't want to return to her hospital work. Rather, she had stopped making plans that far in the future. As though to do so might be presuming on God's blessing.

She checked in and was ushered to a changing room where she slipped into the blue and white medical gown. *Let me get through the pregnancy, God. Please. My return to work can come later.*

While Jade waited, she wondered again if the baby within her was a boy or a girl. All her life she had wanted a daughter, a girl of her own to mother the way she herself had never been mothered. Deep in her heart, Jade was sure a daughter would be God's way of smiling through the fog of uncertainty caused by Jade's cancer. It would be His way of telling her everything was going to be okay, that He had heard the desires of her heart and now was granting her those desires, even amidst the fear of the unknown.

Of course, a boy would be wonderful as well, a smaller version of Ty, another son to follow in Tanner's footsteps.

The minutes crawled by, and finally half an hour later the technician was ready for her. The young woman wasn't someone Jade knew, but she was kind and gentle and not overly effusive. Though the technician didn't say anything about the cancer, Jade had a feeling she knew.

While the woman positioned the ultrasound wand over her stomach, Jade remembered how terrifying it had been the first time she was pregnant. She hadn't sought medical care until she was several months along so Jim wouldn't be suspicious.

I never should have married him, Lord. I'm so sorry. If I had it to do over again, I'd wait and talk to Tanner first. I wouldn't have trusted Doris Eastman's story until I had a chance to–

"There's a pretty clear picture." The technician smiled and froze the image.

Jade stared at it, but being a nurse didn't help her much. She wasn't sure what she was seeing. Reading ultrasounds required special training. She grinned at the woman and shrugged her shoulders. "What are we looking at?"

"Well, I'd say she's about as perfect as a baby can be. She looks completely healthy."

"*She?*" Tears nipped at the corners of Jade's eyes. Was it possible? Had God allowed her another chance to mother a little girl?

"I'm sorry." The technician looked surprised. "I thought you knew." She looked back at the screen and pointed to the baby. "There's no doubt about it. You're having a girl, Mrs. Eastman."

Jade blinked back the tears and closed her eyes, allowing herself a moment's privacy. God was going to let her survive after all. Otherwise He wouldn't have blessed her with a little girl; He wouldn't have let the baby live this long, past the point when Jade had miscarried the last time. Happiness shot through her veins, infusing hope to every part of her being. Yes, she was going to survive.

She could hardly wait to tell Tanner.

An hour later she was home, fixing pasta on the stove, when an unspeakable pain shot through her head, dimming her senses and shading her eyes in a cloak of sudden black. She sank to the floor and fought for the strength to shout for help.

"Tanner!" Her voice was weak and fading. "H-elp…"

He should be home any minute, but that wouldn't help her now. Her heartbeats came in short bursts without any sense of pattern, and the pain intensified as she collapsed. The cold tile floor smacked against her arms and face, and she lay there, unable to move.

Terror gripped her heart, her mind. If Tanner didn't get there soon, these might be her last moments alive. Their daughter's last moments. *God, I'm not ready to die! I haven't said good-bye to Tanner or Ty or…*

The pain doubled its intensity and Jade moaned. "Tanner!"

The thought that she might not live through the seizure was sadder than anything Jade could imagine. Not because she had fears about where she'd spend eternity, but because she'd miss out on telling Tanner what was supposed to be the happiest news they'd had in a month.

That the precious child inside her was a little girl.

Even if Tanner arrived in time, the seizure meant everything had changed. She tried to call out again, but it was no use. Her breathing was infrequent and shallow and there was nothing she could do to help herself. Her body was rebelling against an invasion deep in her brain. An invasion that could only mean one thing.

The tumor was growing.

Tanner heard Jade's soft cries the moment he opened the door.

"Jade?" He sprinted for the kitchen. Steam filtered up from the stove where a pot of boiling water spilled onto a flame-red burner. "Jade, where are—"

Something on the floor caught his attention and he stared at her. "Dear God, no…not again."

He raced to her, turning off the stove and reaching for the phone as he fell to his knees beside her. Fear made breathing next to impossible. "Jade, baby, wake up!"

Her eyes were wide open, unblinking, and her arms and fingers were frozen stiff. She was still shaking, her limbs jumping off the floor, and he could do nothing to help her stop. It took less than fifteen seconds to call the ambulance; then he remembered Dr. Layton's advice from last time she had a seizure.

Lay her flat...check her pulse, her inhalations. Don't administer CPR unless she's stopped breathing on her own...

Tanner forced himself to concentrate and follow the doctor's orders. Her heart was still beating, but it was weak and irregular. He lowered his face to hers. "Come on, Jade; fight, baby. Don't leave me." His eyes fell on her upper chest. She was breathing, but only the faintest bit of air passed over her lips. Tanner gripped her shoulders and clung to her. "Stay with me, Jade. Don't leave..."

The seconds slowed to a crawl, and Tanner begged God to help them. His eyes remained locked on Jade, looking for the moment when he might need to start CPR. "Keep breathing, Jade...please keep breathing."

Tanner wasn't sure how much time passed, but he felt a hand on his shoulder and turned to see the paramedics. He scrambled out of the way, his body weak from terror. What if it was too late? What if they couldn't help her? Why was any of it happening to them?

As usual, there were no answers.

The paramedics moved fast and spoke quietly. Before Tanner could glean anything from their conversation, they whisked Jade into an ambulance and off to the hospital.

Again Tanner followed behind, his mind numbed by the nightmare unfolding before them. *What's happening, God? Why this? Why her?*

A Scripture from a sermon they'd heard the week before flashed in Tanner's mind. *"In this world you will have trouble. But take heart! I have overcome the world."*

Tanner steadied his hands and kept his attention on the ambulance in front of him. *Is this the trouble you have for us, Lord? That Jade suffer like this?*

It was more than Tanner could bear. He forced himself to believe it was all a mistake, that the seizure was merely an adverse reaction to Jade's medication or maybe somehow related to her pregnancy and not the cancer at all. He was at her side the moment he saw her inside the emergency room. Though she was conscious, she was too exhausted to speak.

"Hang in there, honey. I'm here."

Dr. Layton met them at the hospital and pumped a megadose of anti-seizure medication into Jade's veins. More tests were performed, and Tanner could do nothing but stay by her side, hold her hand, and pray it was all a bad dream. That somehow they'd wake up and Jade would be the same cheerful person she had been that morning. Back when brain cancer seemed little more than a diversion in what was otherwise a perfectly normal pregnancy.

Two hours later, the prognosis was painfully clear. The tumor had grown, and Dr. Layton ordered an immediate increase in Jade's anti-seizure medication.

"At this point, Jade's in a race against her biological clock." The doctor stood close to Tanner, his hand resting on Jade's bed. "And there's something else. The tumor isn't growing neatly like we'd hoped. It's starting to grow tentacles. The more that happens, the less likely we'll be able to operate when the baby's born. I thought you should know."

The information settled like a dense cloud of poisonous smoke over Tanner's consciousness as he struggled to make sense of the doctor's words. The tumor had tentacles? Seizure medication—though replete with side effects—could prevent further attacks. But if the tumor continued to grow, it could cause a stroke or sudden death. The baby was still eleven weeks away from the set delivery date.

"If things get bad enough, we'll have to take the baby and hope for the best." Dr. Layton bit his lip. Jade's eyes were closed, and Tanner doubted that she either heard or understood any of the information the doctor had just shared.

Tanner nodded. "What's the soonest the baby could live?"

"We've saved them as early as twenty-five, twenty-six weeks. Jade's just about twenty-one weeks along now." The man hesitated. "Jade's wishes are clear about keeping the baby. We'll only deliver that early if we have no other choice."

There was no way Tanner could think that far in the future. He smoothed the hair off Jade's forehead and thanked the doctor. "I think we need to be alone, if that's all right with you."

Dr. Layton's shoulders slumped and he nodded. "I'm sorry." He raised the file he had in his hand. "The nurses will explain the increase in medication. I'm afraid…" Tanner understood the pause. The doctor knew all too well that there was only so much bad news a person could handle. Finally he went on. "I'm afraid the extra medication is bound to cause the more serious side effects we discussed earlier."

Tanner clenched his teeth and waited for the doctor to leave. He wanted to scream at him that none of the news they'd received that day was right or fair or even remotely possible. Jade's tumor was growing tentacles? Sudden death was a possibility? None of it seemed real, and suddenly Tanner couldn't sit by his sick wife another moment.

He stood in a burst of motion and strode to the window, staring outside as a rush of tears blurred his vision. Memories from days gone by danced on the screen of his mind. He and Jade finding each other again that summer in Kelso, walking along the Cowlitz River and holding hands in the park while they caught up on the first decade lost.

Jade…I need you. Don't leave me again.

He squeezed his eyes shut and another image appeared.

It was Jade two years ago, the afternoon they found each other again. She was crying and telling him that yes, Ty was his son. Her words echoed in his heart. *"I love you, Tanner…I never stopped loving you…"*

He could hear her voice, feel the touch of her fingers against his face as they realized the devastation caused by his mother's web of lies.

Dozens of memories flashed before Tanner's eyes, a tapestry of happy moments they'd shared in the two years since they'd been back together. He gripped the windowsill as despair worked its way through his veins. He didn't have one single happy memory without Jade. He stared out the window at the sunset over Thousand Oaks, silent tears sliding down the sides of his face.

God, what am I going to do if she dies? Please…don't take her. Please, God…

"Tanner?"

Her weak voice made him spin around. He wiped his hands across his cheeks, determined she wouldn't see him cry. "I'm here, baby." He was at her side again in three quick steps. "How're you feeling?"

The corners of her mouth struggled into a smile. "Did…did the doctor tell you the news?"

Tanner's heart pounded within him. *How do I tell her the truth, God…give me the words.* "Yes. He told me."

Jade's eyes sparkled despite her exhaustion. "You don't look excited."

What? Was the medication messing with her already? He tried to keep his voice even. "Excited?"

"Tanner, it's the best news we've had in a month." She held out her hand and he took it, weaving his fingers between hers.

"Jade…I don't understand…" He bit his lip and shook his head. "What news?"

Her half-closed eyelids opened wider than before. "Then you don't know." A slow chuckle came from her throat. "Fine. Let me be the first to tell you." She brought their hands to her lips and kissed his fingers. "Congratulations, Mr. Eastman. You're going to have a daughter."

Thirteen

The girls were at the grocery store and Hannah was folding laundry in Grace's room when the phone rang. She straightened a rag doll on Grace's pink ruffled pillow and answered the phone in the office down the hall. "Hello?"

There was a pause on the other end and Hannah rolled her eyes. Salesmen. They never came right out and gave you their pitch anymore. Instead there was an annoying three-second computerized delay. Hannah was about to hang up when she heard Edna Parsons' voice.

"I need to speak to you. Can I come by, or would you rather talk now, on the phone?"

Inch by inch, Hannah sank into the chair near the phone. Her heart was in her throat. "Now's fine."

The social worker sighed. "I hate to tell you this..."

Hannah's pulse quickened, and she struggled to breathe. What was this? It couldn't be about Grace. Her mother was in jail, after all. They were just a few months from finalizing the adoption. "Just tell me. Please."

Again Mrs. Parsons hesitated. "I've been in conversation this week with Grace's maternal grandmother."

Hannah's stomach dropped. This wasn't happening; it was impossible. Grace didn't have a grandm—

"It seems...well, she isn't dead after all."

Hannah was falling into a dark and endless pit. She knew what was coming and there was nothing she could do to stop it.

Her grip on the phone tightened. "How…how do you know she's telling the truth?"

"The woman provided us with documentation proving she's Leslie Landers's mother. Apparently she gave Leslie a great deal of money and tried to help her purchase a house in Oklahoma."

Oklahoma? The woman lived in Oklahoma? Did that mean… Hannah squeezed her eyes shut and tried to focus on the social worker's explanation.

"Instead Leslie took the money and ran to California. She blew it on drugs and told everyone, including Grace, that Grandma Landers was dead."

Hannah swallowed. "What does the woman want?"

Another sigh filled the phone, this one heavier than before. "She wants Grace. She says she's been like a mother to the child since she was born. The only stability Grace has ever known."

Until now, Hannah wanted to say. *Until she came to live with us!* The technicality of their situation didn't matter; Grace was *their* daughter. Even if the adoption wasn't finalized. "Don't…don't we have some say in this? Grace belongs to us now."

"Grace belongs to the state. She's a foster child, a ward of the court." Mrs. Parsons paused. "I had no idea this would happen. I feel terrible, Mrs. Bronzan."

Hannah's mind raced for a solution. There had to be a way out. Maybe she and Matt and Jenny and Grace could pile in the car and head for Mexico. Maybe she could hang up and the entire phone call would be nothing but an unthinkable nightmare. Hannah rubbed her forehead and stared at the floor. Her heartbeat was so loud she was sure the social worker could hear it. "Does…does the woman know how happy Grace is? Does she understand?"

"She wants her granddaughter, and according to California

law she has the right to take custody of her as long as she's fit. We checked her out and she's a fine woman, Mrs. Bronzan. She's flying here today from Oklahoma to take Grace home."

To take Grace home? There was a searing pain in Hannah's heart. So that was it? Grace's grandmother figured out where she was and now Grace would have to leave? As though she and Matt and Jenny had never been a part of her life at all? Tears spilled from Hannah's eyes and she struggled to find her voice. "You're taking her today?"

"No." There was a shuffling sound of papers in the background. "We'll come for her tomorrow morning. Say ten o'clock. Her grandmother wants to come, too. She…she wants to thank you for helping Grace these past three months."

"Yes…I see…" Hannah mumbled a good-bye and hung up the phone. As she did, her eyes fell on a framed photograph of Grace and Jenny, their arms slung across each other's shoulders; grins spread across their faces. Her face contorted as the sobs came. "No!" She shouted the word so it sounded throughout the empty house. "No, God! Don't take her away!"

Hannah reached for the picture and clutched it to her chest, weeping over the thought of telling Grace good-bye in the morning. There would be no time to prepare, no time to let her know how much they loved her. Not only that, but after tomorrow she'd be living in Oklahoma.

How would they survive? Any of them? The child had worked her way into the very fiber of their family, into the deepest crevices of their hearts. It would be like losing…

Hannah couldn't finish the thought. Her weeping grew louder, more desperate, and she collapsed over her knees, still holding the photograph. *No, God…not again.*

The pain that wracked her body was as gut-wrenching as it was familiar. Hannah knew all too well what it was to lose a daughter, to receive the kind of news that destroyed a family in an instant.

Her tears were not only for Grace and what tomorrow's loss would mean. They were for Alicia and Tom and everything about that awful day when Hannah first understood how life could change forever in the course of a few minutes.

The last day of summer. Four years ago, almost exactly.

The events of that day were etched in a part of her brain where they would remain for moments like this, moments when drifting back was simply inevitable. And so, still clutching the picture of Grace and Jenny, Hannah was sucked back in time, back to a golden afternoon, the last day of summer vacation, 1998.

She had busied herself that day readying for her family's return from what had become an annual summer's end camping trip. She remembered sneaking a look out the window every ten minutes or so as evening drew closer, impatient for their return.

But time slipped away until they were thirty minutes late, and then an hour. Hannah was still staring out the kitchen window when the police car pulled up that evening.

His exact message was jumbled in her mind, but key words stood out still. There'd been an accident, serious injuries, Tom and the girls were at the hospital.

It was the beginning of a time when Hannah felt like she was walking underwater, as though everything she heard or saw was somehow muffled by a dense layer of pain unlike anything she'd ever experienced.

At the hospital Hannah was ushered into a small room where a doctor used kind, careful words to tell her the news. Jenny had injuries, but she'd be okay. The others weren't so fortunate. Rescue workers had made a gallant effort, but both Tom and Alicia had died at the scene.

Before the night was through she followed the doctor to a room where Tom's and Alicia's bodies lay, and at a time when they should have been laughing and sharing stories over dinner, Hannah bid each of them a final good-bye.

Next she learned that the driver of the other car had been drunk. In fact, he'd been convicted of drunk driving several times before hitting her family.

The news—all of it—turned Hannah overnight into someone even she didn't recognize, someone angry at God and bitter with life, determined to make the drunk driver pay. Someone oblivious to the cost her revenge was exacting on Jenny.

The memory faded and Hannah sat straighter in her chair. She looked once more at the photograph of Jenny and Grace, and though fresh tears swam in her eyes, she knew somehow she'd survive. The Lord would see her through. After all, He'd given her Matt, and with Matt by her side Hannah could survive just about anything.

She thought about her tall dark husband and the way he'd made her life beautiful these past years. Matt, who had walked her through the year-long court battle against Brian Wesley, the drunk driver. Matt, who had represented the spirit of Christ at every turn, seeking not revenge but justice. Matt, who had been Hannah's constant friend and supporter.

It was no surprise, really, that she'd fallen in love with him.

Not that the process had been quick.

It started more than a year after the accident, when Hannah acted on Tom's dying wish. That day she walked into a prison meeting room, sat across from Brian Wesley, and forgave him.

Afterward, when Hannah joined Matt and Jenny outside, something had changed. Hannah couldn't place it at first, but in time she realized that forgiving Brian Wesley had removed ice from around her heart. With the cold gone, she was able to see

Matt in a way she hadn't before. In fact, for the first time since the collision she was able to imagine her future, to admit she still had one.

For a long while she and Matt hid their feelings, each not sure the other was ready for romance. Hannah remembered the turning point.

It was a few months later in late February and Matt had spent the day with her and Jenny. Though the sun was out, a cool breeze filled the air, and the three of them flew kites at a local park. When the sun set, they returned to Hannah's house and Matt barbecued steaks.

As soon as dinner was over, Jenny announced she had plans with a friend. Half an hour later she was gone for the evening, and Matt and Hannah had the house to themselves. They spent the first hour walking to the local high school and circling the track. For the first time none of their conversation centered around Tom's and Alicia's absence. Rather they talked about his dream of joining a law firm that fought for religious freedom and spending the next part of his career upholding rights that too many people took for granted.

"I'm finished with drunk drivers," he told her. Their steps were unhurried and every now and then their arms brushed against each other.

"You met your goal. A drunk driver was convicted of murder one." Hannah gazed at the treetops beyond the school. "I don't blame you for wanting something new."

Matt shook his head. "It isn't that. Murder one was the right conviction for Brian Wesley. But even that won't keep it from happening again. Tonight, tomorrow...every night after that...someone will drink too much and climb behind the wheel. They'll break laws and drive without licenses and kill people like Tom and Alicia and my friends."

Hannah angled her head, curious in a sad sort of way. "So, we should give up?"

"No." Matt slipped his hands in his pockets as they kept walking. "You should keep working for victim rights as long as you feel God wants you to. I think that kind of thing helps, especially with teenagers. There you are talking about your losses, showing pictures of Tom and Alicia. That kind of message is bound to stop some of them from drinking."

He paused for a moment and Hannah savored the peace that resonated in her soul when she was with him. He continued, his tone thoughtful. "But *prosecuting* drunk drivers doesn't keep anyone from drinking and driving."

"It made Brian stop." Hannah wasn't being argumentative. She only wanted Matt to know how important his role was in seeing Brian sent to prison for what he did. Yes, she forgave him. But after numerous drunk driving accidents and convictions, after killing two people, Brian belonged in prison.

It was the only way he wouldn't kill again.

"For now." Matt shrugged. "But Brian won't serve his whole term. And then we'd better pray he finds healing from his alcoholism. Otherwise, it could happen again. You and I both know that."

Hannah didn't respond. The thought of Brian Wesley back on the street, possibly drinking and driving again, was too depressing to imagine. She waited for Matt to continue.

"I'd like to invest my time where I could shape American law, set precedent for generations to come. Cases that would preserve freedoms for millions of Americans."

Hannah remembered her heart swelling with pride as Matt shared his hopes with her that evening. Their conversation shifted to his basketball days in college and she found herself wishing she'd known him then.

"If you played with as much passion as you practice law, you must have been very good." She smiled up at him. The sky was growing darker and without saying a word they shifted direction and headed back to Hannah's house.

Once inside, Hannah made coffee, and they continued their conversation over a board game Matt had given her. He was winning handily when he tapped her foot under the table and flashed her his cards, alerting her to the fact that he'd been cheating.

"Matt Bronzan!" Hannah's laughter rang like wind chimes in springtime. "Here I thought you were a man of honor."

"Well, let's see…" He looked at the ceiling, pretending to be deep in thought while he calculated something. "You've beaten me the last five games. I'd say even men of honor have to resort to drastic measures now and then."

But as he finished his sentence, his elbow bumped the playing board, messing up the meticulously placed chips and putting an immediate end to the contest. "Aha!" Hannah snatched his cards from his hand. "Justice, again!"

In his attempt to grab the cards back, Matt missed and took hold of her hand instead. The air between them changed, and their eyes locked. Both their smiles faded. Time ceased to exist as they stayed that way, his hand clutching hers, while they searched each other's eyes and tried to think of something to say.

He made the first move. Clearing his throat, Matt removed his hand, took hold of his coffee mug, and finished what was left of his drink. "I should be going."

Hannah was confused as much by his reaction as her own. Why was he upset with himself for holding her hand? Didn't he have feelings for her? And what was this sudden ache in her heart? It was only eighteen months since losing Tom… Had she been so quick to fall in love with another man?

She had no answers as she followed Matt to the front door.

Though she planned to merely thank him for a fun day and bid him good-bye, she couldn't stop herself from asking the question. The one that burned stronger in her with each passing day.

"Why, Matt?" They were standing face-to-face near the open door, him filling the doorframe and her leaning against the wall as she studied his eyes for answers.

He cocked his head, his tone soft. "Why, what?"

"Why are you here with me? You could be dating a dozen different women, getting on with your life." She hesitated and she could hear her heart beating hard within her.

For a moment she thought Matt might laugh or launch into an explanation, the kind he was expert at giving. Instead, he moved closer and cradled her chin in his fingertips. Then he brought his lips to hers and kissed her.

When he drew back, his eyes were glistening. "Because..." He kissed her again, his touch gentle and sweet, but burning with a thinly veiled desire. "Because I love you, Hannah."

The explosion of emotions within her that night was more than she could bear. Tears spilled from her eyes and she was speechless. She was in love with Matt Bronzan, and that meant she was healing. Though she had never expected to love any man other than Tom Ryan, here she was, kissing Matt and savoring the sensation of falling once more.

Matt's expression filled with subtle alarm when he saw her tears. He brushed them from her cheeks as his eyes clouded over. "I'm sorry, Hannah. It's too soon. I just...I had to tell you." He glanced at his feet and back at her. "I'm sorry."

A sound that was more laugh than sob came from Hannah and she wrapped her arms around his neck. When the hug ended, she found his lips again and kissed him the way she'd wanted to for months.

The days after that were a blissful bouquet of moments that

were almost impossible to believe. By the end of the week, Jenny caught on to what was happening between them. One night she was on her way out with friends when she winked at Hannah. "Tell your boyfriend hi for me."

Alarm sliced through Hannah's happy heart and she held her breath. "Boyfriend?"

"Yes, *boyfriend.*" Jenny laughed and Hannah's body went limp with relief. "I kept wondering what was taking you guys so long. I figured this would happen months ago."

After that Matt and Hannah were inseparable, and on Easter Sunday he took her and Jenny to brunch and asked Jenny's permission to marry Hannah. Jenny was so thrilled she clapped her hands like a little girl. "Yes! We're going to be a family."

As the summer wedding date drew near, there were many conversations between Hannah and Jenny and Matt, acknowledgments that Matt could never replace Tom, but that what they shared would be every bit as rich. Maybe richer, since great love was often born of great loss.

Though she would never forget Tom and the love they shared and the family they raised, Matt was her closest friend now. The bond they forged in Hannah's time of grief was stronger than anything she'd ever experienced. She loved Matt with a strength that surprised her and made her grateful for every new morning in his arms.

The memories grew distant, and Hannah wiped her tears. She stared at the photo in her hand. Matt had helped her survive the loss of a daughter once before. He would help her again, wouldn't he?

Hannah considered the strength of Matt's love for Grace, the way the child ran to him each evening when he came home from work. Hannah gritted her teeth. How could she call him now and tell him it was all over? That their time with little Grace had ended before it even had time to really begin?

Matt had helped Hannah cope with Alicia's loss, but Alicia hadn't been his daughter. He'd never even met her.

It occurred to Hannah that this loss would be a different matter altogether. Grace wasn't merely a sweet girl whose absence was bound to break Hannah's heart. She was their daughter. Matt's daughter.

Help me be strong for him, Lord, the way he was strong for me. Help us survive...

She prayed until there was nothing left to do but call Matt and tell him. As she dialed his office, her heartache grew. The news about Grace was bound to break off a piece of Matt's heart, a piece that would be gone forever. And so Hannah prayed once more that somehow she'd have the strength to help him survive.

The same way he'd helped her survive four years earlier.

Fourteen

Matt knocked on Tanner's office door and let himself in before his partner could respond. "Got a minute?"

Tanner looked up and nodded to a chair on the other side of his desk. "Sure." He let his eyes fall back to the file in front of him. "What's up?"

Matt wasn't sure how to begin. Tanner hadn't said more than a few words about Jade's condition since her last seizure. He spent hours at the office, working well past his usual six o'clock, and seemed entirely focused on the Colorado case.

Normally that might be fine. That kind of devotion happened once in a while at the offices of CPRR. But not now, not with Jade so sick her life was at stake. Matt sank into the high-backed leather chair across from Tanner and stroked his chin.

It was best to start on safe ground. "How's the case?"

Tanner looked up, a brief smile lifting the corners of his mouth. "Good. We'll file suit against the city tomorrow. I'll need to be there a few days each week for the next month."

"Still going for the sneak attack?" Matt studied Tanner. The man was brilliant when it came to strategy, and the solution he'd mapped out for this case was no exception. In fact, if it went the way Tanner expected it to, the case could serve as a major precedent for a decade to come. Still, with Jade sick, there had to be a better answer than Tanner flying to Colorado.

Tanner laughed. "It'll surprise 'em, that's for sure." He tapped the file on his desk. "It'll be heard in Colorado Springs. You knew that, right?"

"No." Matt raised an eyebrow. "You got the change of venue."

"Last week. I thought I told you." Tanner's gaze fell for a moment. "The judge thought we needed a jury outside of Benson for a fair trial."

"Pretty big news to keep to yourself."

"Yeah." Tanner looked up again, his eyes narrowed as though his heart was a million miles away. "I've had a lot on my mind."

There was a moment of silence between them and in the distant background they heard the ringing of the office phone. Matt softened his tone. "How's it going, really?"

"Good." Tanner shrugged. "I'm praying we get the right verdict the first time around. Maybe we can skip the appeals process if I can make a strong enough argument."

"Tanner." Matt blinked. "I'm not talking about the case." He hesitated. "How are things with Jade? You never talk about her. Hannah and I are desperate to help, but we don't know how."

Tanner pushed back from his desk and leaned deep into his chair. "She's fine. The doctor increased her medication, and she has a full-time nurse in case she has another seizure."

Matt's mind raced, trying to make sense of everything his friend was saying. "The tumor's grown, is that what happened? That's why they had to increase her medication?"

"Yes." The look on Tanner's face was almost angry. "It's growing, okay. But we're handling it just fine. Jade's nurse is taking care of everything."

"Okay…" Frustration built in Matt and he leaned forward, resting his forearms on Tanner's desk. He'd never seen his friend so cold and shallow. It was like someone else had taken over Tanner Eastman's body. "So bite my head off, why don't you?"

For a moment Tanner looked like he might snap back, but instead he exhaled long and slow, his shoulders slumping in the process. "I'm sorry." He rotated his chair so he faced the window, his back to Matt. His voice was hard to hear over the traffic nine stories down. "You don't deserve that."

Matt sat straight again and studied his friend's back. "No. And you don't deserve a sick wife, but that's where you're at. All I'm saying is, Hannah and I want to help."

Tanner was motionless for a while. Then without turning around he began to speak, his voice quiet and broken. "It's hard for her to have visitors. She's...she's slower than before. Her speech, the way she walks...."

Matt's heart broke as Tanner turned around once more and their eyes connected. Tanner's were dry, but only because the fear in his face was stronger than the pain. Matt clenched his jaw and shook his head. "I'm sorry."

Tanner nodded. "The doctor says she should be back to normal once the baby's born and they can remove the tumor. But for now..."

Their eyes held for a moment, and Matt didn't know what to say. No wonder he didn't talk about it much. He was too terrified to voice his concerns. "I can't imagine."

"It's like..." Tanner lifted his hands and let them drop. "It's like I lose her a little more each day." He planted his elbows on his desk and hung his head, his shoulders trembling. There was an ocean of sadness in his voice. "I'm so scared."

There was nothing left for Matt to say. He stood and circled the desk, stopping behind Tanner and placing a hand on his shoulder. "Let Hannah and me come over tonight and pray with you. Please."

Tanner wiped the back of his hand beneath his eyes. "I'm not sure Jade would be up to it."

Matt's heart sank. "Then let us bring you dinner. If she's feeling good enough, we'll stay for a while."

Tanner lifted his head and looked about to protest when

Matt's secretary poked her head in. "Matt, line two. It's Hannah."

Normally Matt would have taken the call there, in Tanner's office, but something told him Tanner needed to be alone. He followed the woman, glancing back at his friend. "Be right back."

Matt's office was next door. He dropped to the chair behind his desk, picked up the receiver and punched the flashing button. "Hannah?"

Her breathing was rough, and Matt heard the muffled sound of sniffling. "Hi. Sorry to call you at work."

There was no question about it. She was crying. A surge of adrenaline coursed through Matt's veins. "Honey, what's wrong? You sound terrible."

"Mrs. Parsons called." Hannah struggled with each word. "Grace's grandmother is alive. The judge is ordering that Grace live with her."

The words hit him like so many bricks. "What?" Matt's reply came out as more of a gasp, as he hunched over his knees and dug his elbows into his thighs. "That's impossible."

Hannah sniffed again. "It's true." She hesitated. "Grace leaves tomorrow."

Not Grace! Matt screamed the thought silently, the pain so deep, so great, it was impossible to voice. There didn't seem to be enough oxygen in the room, no way to take a deep breath. Every thought in Matt's head spun wildly out of control. "They can't do that."

"Well, they are." A small sob made its way across the phone lines. "Come home, Matt. Please."

"Okay." He didn't recognize his own voice. "I'm on my way."

He hung up the phone and stared at his hands, willing himself to deny the fact that Hannah had called, or that the social worker had delivered the news. Wanting to disbelieve all of it. How could their social worker have missed the fact that Grace had a grandmother? And why weren't they told of the judge's decision sooner?

Matt clenched his fists. If only he'd had an hour before the judge. Surely he could have convinced the man that Grace was better off in a family, with a mother and father and sister who loved her. Matt would have argued that the grandmother could have visitation rights, but full custody? To a woman Grace didn't even know was alive?

The effort of standing took everything that remained of Matt's strength. Like a man moving through water, he made his way back to Tanner's office, walked inside, and closed the door.

The moment Tanner saw Matt, his expression filled with alarm. "What is it? What's wrong?"

Matt realized Tanner thought the call had been about Jade, that perhaps the news—whatever it was—was so bad it couldn't come directly to Tanner.

Matt shook his head. "Nothing about Jade."

There was a subtle easing in the lines on Tanner's face. "Hannah, then?"

For a moment Matt did nothing but hold his breath, his eyes locked on those of his friend. Then he shrugged his shoulders, feeling the sting of tears. "They're taking Grace from us tomorrow."

Tanner stared while the news sank in. Then he let his head drop as though the news was more than he could bear. When he looked up he had just one word. "Why?"

Matt worked the muscles in his jaw. "Her grandmother came looking for her. The judge decided—"

"No!" Tanner slammed his fist onto his desk, his voice filling the room. "Why is this happening to us?" He stood and stared outside, gripping the windowsill. His knuckles were white; his back trembled. "It isn't supposed to be like this. We're on God's

team, you and me. We fight heaven's battles, and in return we're supposed to get a break, isn't that right?"

Matt let his gaze fall to the floor for a moment. The pain in his heart was crippling; there was no way he could respond.

Tanner exhaled and the noise filled the room. He spun around. "You know what's eating at me?" His voice was saturated in bitterness. "When was the last time He helped either one of us?"

Matt was conditioned to have the list on hand: his health, his marriage, his job, his home, the familiar accounting of God's numerous blessings. But all he could think about was Grace, her apple-cheeked smile, her twinkling eyes and curly hair. And the way it would decimate his family when she said good-bye. "I don't know what to say."

"Me neither." Tanner laced his hands behind his head, clenched his teeth and moaned. "I don't know how much we're supposed to take."

There was nothing Matt could do but agree. He closed his eyes. *Give me strength, God; get me through this.* As he prayed, an anchor appeared before his eyes. It came in the form of a Bible verse he'd memorized as a college senior. Without thinking, the words were on his lips. "'In this world you will have trouble…'" His tone was calm, belying the condition of his heart. "'But take heart! I have overcome the world.'"

"I know." Tanner's shoulders slumped and he leaned against his desk. "It's just…"

The heartache ripping through Matt was getting worse. He had to get home to Hannah, had to see if there was anything they could do to stop the madness that had come upon them. "I need to go."

Tanner drew a deep breath and crossed the room, hugging Matt with the crook of his arm the way he might hug a close brother. "Call me."

"I will."

Moving in a fog of fear and uncertainty, Matt grabbed his things and headed for the car. There was roadwork on Malibu Canyon and the ride home would likely take twice as long as normal. That was fine. Matt needed the time to think.

He stared at the brake lights in front of him and then gazed up.

A blue sky stretched from one mountain range to the other, and the sun overhead sent rays of light along the narrow canyon road. Warmth filled the car, numbing his fear, and Matt shifted his attention to the wheat-colored rolling hills in the distance.

As he did, he was drawn toward the tunnels of time.

It was the pain, of course. The pain reminded him of meeting Hannah for the first time, of looking into the eyes of a woman who had just lost her husband and child.

He remembered the first time he and Hannah met in court, before one of the hearings. He'd never seen so haunting a face before. Hannah was equal parts devastated, determined, and defiant. And more beautiful than any woman he'd ever seen.

With the Pacific Ocean just ahead, Matt gripped the steering wheel with both hands and remembered the depth of despair she had carried that first year of their friendship, the year he spent prosecuting Brian Wesley.

Everywhere she went back then, Hannah wore a pin with the photos of Tom and Alicia. As he worked the case, Matt often relived his own grief from years before, when his best friend in college was killed by a drunk driver. But over the months of working with Hannah, he came to realize no matter how strong his pain had been at losing his friend, it paled in comparison to losing a spouse.

Or a child.

"It's a kind of pain you can't know until you feel it yourself," Hannah had told him.

Memories of her voice faded as Matt reached Pacific Coast Highway. He was five minutes from home. Was it really happening? Would he walk inside and find Hannah crying? And what about Jenny? She'd already lost one sister, and that had just about done her in.

How would she handle losing Grace?

He remembered the night before when he sat on the edge of Grace's bed, holding her hand and reading her a nighttime story.

"Daddy?" She looked at him from a nest of soft blankets and lacy pillows and batted her eyelashes. "Will you always read me stories?"

Matt grinned at this little one who'd so captured his heart. "Forever and ever, Gracie."

"Even when I'm big?"

A lump formed in Matt's throat, a combination of gratefulness and sadness. Grateful because this precious child was his daughter, and sadness because one day she'd grow up and leave them. "Yes," he said when he found his voice. "Even when you're big."

The image disappeared as Matt pulled into the driveway and climbed out of the car. Now there would be no lifetime of storytelling, no growing up together, no little girl to call his own.

And in that moment, Matt knew Hannah was right. Losing a child created a kind of heartache that could only be understood through experience. Because the hurt that weighed on him now was greater than any Matt had ever felt.

He steadied himself before opening the front door. *Carry me, Lord…*

Be still and know that I am God…

The flash of words in his mind was so strong, Matt knew they'd come straight from heaven. Still, the pain remained. And Matt knew that whatever happened next, Hannah would show him the way through it. She knew what to do, how to act, how to grieve. How to survive this kind of loss.

After all, she had lost a child before.

Now it was his turn.

Fifteen

Grace's grandmother didn't look like a monster.

Quite the opposite, in fact. Sitting across from Hannah and Matt in the Bronzans' living room the next morning, Patsy Landers looked nothing short of genteel. She was petite, with fashionably cropped gray hair, compassionate eyes, and a pleasant smile. A strand of elegant pearls lay over her beige cashmere sweater, and despite her considerable limp, she had the polished mannerisms of a cultured woman.

But Hannah couldn't help think it all a clever disguise. After all, she was here for one reason only: to tear their family apart.

Of course the woman claimed to love Grace and want the best for her. But why take her from the only stable home she'd ever known? What kind of love was that? Hannah kept her feelings about Patsy to herself. There wasn't time for ill will toward the older woman. Not now, when they had less than an hour left with a child they had come to love as their own.

Hannah and Matt sat huddled on one sofa, Grace squeezed between them, Jenny close against Hannah's other side. Mrs. Parsons had given them their explanations and made it clear their legal options were reduced to none.

It was time to say good-bye.

Hannah wiped the tears from her cheeks and looked at the two older women sitting across from them. "Would you mind if we had a few minutes alone with Grace?"

The social worker gave a quick nod. "Take your time." She stood and motioned for Patsy Landers to follow. "We'll walk on the beach. Thirty minutes sound okay?"

Hannah nodded and hung her head.

Her life since Mrs. Parsons's phone call the day before seemed like something from a nightmare. Matt had gotten home just after one o'clock and spent the next two hours talking with various officials at Social Services.

He had started with Mrs. Parsons. The questions sounded like something from one of Matt's famous cross-examinations, and Hannah sat cross-legged nearby, staring at the floor, listening to Matt's end of the conversation.

"What if the woman isn't mentally sound?" Pause. "Have you checked her financial records?" Another pause. "Does she have the space to raise a child? The energy?"

When he had exhausted all avenues with Mrs. Parsons, Matt asked to speak to her superior. Again Hannah listened.

"I understand that, but the judge has already given her permanent placement in our house." Silence. "I realize that, but any psychologist would tell you that once a child has bonded to parental figures, it's more traumatic to separate that bond than it is to work within it." More silence. "Maybe you're not hearing me. I said we'd be happy to work out visitation rights with the child's grandmother...Yes, I know she lives in Oklahoma, but right now we're Grace's parents and that's how it should stay even if..."

Matt's efforts went on that way until Jenny and Grace spilled through the front door, giggling and grinning from their day together. Jenny saw Hannah sitting on the floor crying and Matt on the phone.

The smile faded from her face and her eyes grew wide.

Matt got off the phone and they all listened as Grace rattled on in a happy singsong voice about the lunch out with Jenny, the shopping, and the fun time they had playing at a local park.

Hannah had wiped her tears and smiled at Grace. "Sweetheart, why don't you go to your room for a little bit and play with your baby doll. Mommy has to talk to Jenny."

Grace was oblivious to the mood in the room and she skipped off, blowing Hannah and Matt a kiss on her way. Before she left, she ran up to Jenny and kissed her on the cheek. "Can I tell you something, Jenny?"

Jenny's voice was pinched, and Hannah had the feeling her daughter somehow knew what was about to happen. "Sure, sweetie. Anything."

"You're the best sister in the world." Grace smiled big at her and threw her arms around Jenny's neck. "I love you for always and always."

When Grace was out of earshot, Hannah stood and held open her arms. Jenny came to her, hugging her close while Matt stood beside them. "Honey, I'm so sorry to tell you this."

Hannah could feel the heavy thud of Jenny's heartbeat and a wave of nausea swept over her. The entire scene reminded her of that awful day in the hospital room when Jenny regained consciousness after the accident. The day Hannah had to tell Jenny that she'd lost both her father and her older sister. This was different, of course…but it was every bit as painful and just as final.

Jenny had pulled back, searching Hannah's face. "What happened?"

Normally Matt would have stepped up, put his hand on Jenny's shoulder—something that would come across as a show of support…but he was drowning in his own pain. He said nothing as Hannah tried to explain.

"Grace's grandmother has turned up. The judge says Grace has to live with her. In Oklahoma."

Jenny stepped back, her face knotted in angry confusion. "*What?* They can't do that! She belongs to *us*."

Hannah took careful hold of Jenny's arm, bridging the distance between them. "She's here on the foster-adopt program."

Hannah's voice broke. "We all knew that."

Jenny backed out of Hannah's grip. "But Mrs. Parsons said there were no doubts! Nothing that would stop her from being ours. She said the foster-adopt thing was a technicality, remember?"

Neither Hannah nor Matt spoke.

Jenny struggled to keep from yelling. "Can't Matt do something about it? He's a lawyer; they'll listen to him."

"I tried." Matt took a step closer to Jenny. "Grace's grandma is fit enough to care for her. That's all the courts care about. The law is clear. If an existing relative is suitable for guardianship, then that relative gets the child. There are no gray areas, Jenny. I've tried everything."

Jenny leaned forward and spread her fingers across her chest. "How can God let this happen to us twice?" She hesitated and Hannah could see tears on Jenny's cheeks. *"Twice?"*

Hannah blinked back a lake of tears. "God brought her to us, Jenny. He'll get us through." It was true—Hannah knew it with every fiber of her heart—but in that moment the words sounded trite and pat.

Jenny's mouth hung open and Hannah wasn't sure if she was going to cry or scream. Instead she turned and ran to her bedroom.

Hannah started after her, but stopped near the stairs. "Jenny…"

The girl stopped and looked back at Hannah. "What?"

"Don't stay up there too long; Grace leaves tomorrow."

The evening had been an emotional roller coaster, one like Hannah had never experienced before. When Tom and Alicia died, none of them had seen it coming. There were no final meals or final bedtime talks or final goodnight kisses.

That wasn't the case this time, and as evening came, the finality was almost more than Hannah could bear. Hannah and Matt decided to wait until after dinner to tell Grace about her impending move to Oklahoma. And since Grace liked the beach better than any place at all, the three of them prepared a picnic dinner they could eat near the water. Before dinner Jenny joined them, and they filled the next two hours with as much joy and love and happiness as they possibly could.

They ate Grace's favorite meal—peanut butter sandwiches with raspberry jam, and chocolate chip cookies. Then they built a sandcastle on the shore and watched as the waves came closer and closer. A minute later they jumped back when a big wave came and washed the castle into the sea. Only Grace clapped with delight as it disappeared.

It was all Hannah could do not to break down right there. The castle seemed to represent everything about their time with Grace. All that they'd spent months building. When Grace was gone, there would be nothing more to show for their time together than a hole in their hearts where once stood a beautiful castle.

They held hands—all four of them—as they walked back home, and after Grace's bath they gathered in her room and told her the devastating news.

Hannah had agreed to do the talking. Matt and Jenny would stay close by, helping Grace know that this decision was not one they agreed with. That no matter what happened she would always be their little girl.

"Grace?" Hannah sat on the child's bed, her heart pounding in her throat. "We have something to tell you."

Grace was lying flat on her back and a quick smile came over her face. "You mean like a story?"

Hannah's eyes filled, blurring the image of Grace. "No, honey. Stories aren't real. The thing I have to tell you now is real."

"Okay, what?" Grace's fingers gripped the satin edge of her

blanket on either side of her chin. "Tell me."

A light-headed feeling came over Hannah and she begged God for strength. *And the right words, God...please. Something that will make the transition easier for Grace.* She managed to grab a mouthful of air, and decided to start with the good news.

"Grace, they found your grandma. She isn't dead; she's alive."

Grace scrunched up her face. "Mommy said she was dead."

Hannah cast a desperate glance at Matt and then turned her attention back to Grace. "Your mommy was wrong. Your grandma is alive and she's coming to see you tomorrow."

Grace sat straight up and stared at Hannah. "My grandma's coming tomorrow?"

"Yes." Hannah took hold of Grace's hand. "In the morning."

"From Oklahoma?"

Hannah had nodded, and her throat grew thick again. Grace was very bright for a four-year-old. She seemed to know more, retain more information than most children. Then again, Grace hadn't ever had a childhood.

At least not until she lived with them.

Hannah steadied herself. "There's something else." She paused. "Your grandma wants you to go back to Oklahoma. She wants you to live with her."

Grace's blonde eyebrows settled lower on her face. "You mean for a bacation?"

"No, honey..." Behind her, Hannah could hear the sound of Jenny stifling her tears, and Matt came alongside her, slipping his arm over her shoulder. She focused on Grace once more. "I mean forever. Your grandma wants you to be *her* little girl."

Tears flooded Grace's eyes. "In Oklahoma?"

"Yes, baby. You'll be moving to Oklahoma with her tomorrow."

"But..." The tears spilled onto her velvet-soft cheeks. "But will you come with me?"

The child's words sliced Hannah's heart to ribbons. She had thought nothing could be more painful than Mrs. Parsons's call earlier that day. She was wrong.

Will you come with me…?

Hannah bit her lower lip and found the strength to speak.

"We can't, honey. Our house is here. Your house will be in Oklahoma." Hannah imagined how her answer must have sounded to Grace and she cringed. "Your grandma wants you all to herself." Tears were tumbling down Grace's cheeks, and Hannah cocked her head, desperate to ease the child's sadness. "You love your grandma, right?"

"Yes." Grace's chin quivered, and two soft sobs came from her throat. "But you're my mommy and daddy and Jenny." She looked around. "This is my room. And if my room is here then this is where I live. I wanna stay, Mommy. *Please…*"

They were all crying now, tears coursing down Hannah's, Matt's, and Jenny's faces alike. Hannah pulled Grace close and smoothed her hand over the child's silky hair, hair that was so like Alicia's at that age. Jenny crawled under the covers on the other side of Grace and Matt knelt up against the bed. They formed a group hug, each of them crying in soft whispers, desperately hanging on to the moment.

Hannah could almost feel herself pushing against the hands of time, begging God for more hours, days. Whatever He might give them. As though by staying there at her side they might somehow avoid the good-bye ahead.

But long after Grace had cried herself to sleep, time marched on, and that morning when the doorbell rang, her two large suitcases were packed and ready to go.

Hannah had imagined Patsy Landers to be an older version of Grace's mother, hard and mean, tarnished from years of drug abuse. The real Patsy couldn't have been more different.

Mrs. Parsons made the introductions. Jenny had taken Grace outside until the given signal, allowing the adults to discuss the matter away from her at first.

When they were seated, Patsy turned to Hannah and spoke in a voice that trembled with emotion. "You have no idea how sorry I am about this." She turned to Matt. "I had no idea Grace had been placed in foster care. I'm afraid..." Her gaze fell to her lap for a moment. "I'm afraid my daughter told her I was dead."

The entire story spilled out, and by the time it was finished, Hannah knew that despite her limp, the woman was obviously capable of caring for Grace. Clearly she had wanted custody of the child long before this, but time and again had been refused by her daughter. What's more, it seemed the woman was a believer, just as Grace had told them from the beginning. Hannah and Matt need not worry; this woman would keep Grace grounded in her faith.

But the most obvious truth was this: Patsy Landers loved Grace with all her heart. And so there was no doubt in Hannah's mind that the child's move to Oklahoma was not only final, it was the right thing. Maybe not now, maybe not in the short term, while Grace was bound to miss them. But in the bigger picture. Grace would not know the love of parents the way she would have if she'd been allowed to stay, but she would have a woman who had known her all her life and loved her since birth. A woman who, like all of them, had been a victim of Leslie Landers's drug addiction.

When their discussion was over, Patsy thanked Hannah and Matt and promised to pray that God would bring another child into their lives soon. Jenny led Grace into the room after that, and now here they were. After months of learning to love a little girl they'd never known before, months of breaking through her silence and isolation and hurt, months of caring for her as though they'd have forever together, it was time to say good-bye.

Patsy and Edna left through the back of the house and closed the door behind them. Hannah summoned all her strength to lift her head and kiss Grace on the forehead. "Your grandma is a very nice lady, Grace."

Jenny bit her lip, and Hannah knew she was trying to stop the tears that flowed from the corners of her eyes. Matt was utterly still, his chin resting on Grace's head. Grace realized the finality of the moment and she, too, started to cry. "Come with me, Mommy, please…" Grace looked up and pressed her cheek against Hannah's. "I don't want to live in Oklahoma."

"But you love your grandma, Grace." Hannah squeezed her eyes shut, wanting more than anything to tell the child she could stay. "This is the best plan for you now. Everyone thinks so."

"But I love *you*. You're…you're…" Hannah opened her eyes. Grace's sobs were becoming too great for her to speak. She struggled for a long moment while Hannah and Matt stroked her back. "You're my…*family*."

Jenny moved off the sofa and fell to her knees in front of Grace. "We'll always be your family, honey. Always. Anytime you think of us, we'll be right there."

Mrs. Parsons had advised that in situations where foster-adopt placements were disrupted, it was best not to maintain contact between the child and the foster parents. "Too much pain for everyone involved," the social worker explained. "Complete severance will give Grace the best chance for a healthy adjustment."

Now Hannah wanted nothing more than to add to what Jenny was saying, to promise letters and pictures and phone calls. But she held her tongue, knowing that somehow Mrs. Parsons was right.

Matt cleared his throat and tightened his grip on Grace's slim shoulders. "In my heart, Grace, you'll always be my little girl." Hannah glanced at him through her tears and saw that he was silently weeping, crying as she'd never seen him cry before. He swallowed hard. "Will you remember that?"

Grace clung to Matt and nodded her head against his chest. "Yes, Daddy. I'll remember for always."

Matt pulled a delicate golden locket from his pocket and Hannah blinked so she could see. She had wondered when Matt was going to give Grace the present they picked out for her. "Here." Matt opened the clasp and fitted it gently around Grace's neck. He opened the locket and exposed a small picture of the four of them—Matt, Hannah, Jenny, and Grace. Matt cleared his throat. "This is for you. So you don't forget."

Grace's eyes grew wide and she stared at the picture. "Oh, thank you Daddy. I never had a necklace of my very own." She looked at Hannah and Jenny. "I'll wear it every day forever and ever."

Their thirty minutes passed in a blur, and the women returned. Mrs. Parsons cast a sad, questioning look at Hannah. "Ready?"

Ready? Hannah almost laughed out loud. How would they ever be ready to tell Grace good-bye? To watch her walk out of their home and their hearts forever? Hannah shook her head and shrugged. "I guess."

Mrs. Parsons explained that she would carry Grace's bags to the car and then they'd need to leave. Grace and her grandmother had a flight to catch. Once she was gone with the suitcases, the rest of them followed and stood near the car. Matt swept Grace onto his hip and wiggled his nose against hers. "Don't forget us, okay?"

Grace tilted her face so her eyebrows met up with Matt's. "Okay."

Matt handed her to Hannah then, and though she tried to be

strong, a sob sounded from her throat. "Oh, Gracie, I love you, honey. I love you."

While she was in Hannah's arms, Jenny snuggled her face against Grace's and kissed her cheek. The words she whispered were for Grace's ears alone, but Hannah heard them. "I never had a little sister before. And you'll always be mine."

Huge tears swam in Grace's eyes again and she whispered in a choked voice, "Me, too."

Finally, Patsy came forward. "Thank you." She put her arms around the group of them. "I'll always be grateful for everything you've done for Grace. And like I said, I'll pray that God fills your home quickly."

Hannah and Matt and Jenny clung to each other as Patsy took Grace and walked her to the car where Mrs. Parsons was waiting. They said one last good-bye while Grace sobbed, begging them to come. The three of them stood there, linked together long after the car had driven out of sight.

The pain was crippling, and Hannah could tell from the steady flow of tears that it was the same for Matt and Jenny. For a long while none of them spoke; then in a voice quiet and strong, despite his wet face and the depth of sadness in his eyes, Matt began to sing.

"Jesus loves me! This I know, for the Bible tells me so…."

Hannah closed her eyes and let the words wash over her. Grace's favorite song…the one Hannah had taught her on their walks along the beach. The one Matt had hummed along with her when they cuddled at night.

Despite the vast desert of hurt in her heart, Hannah couldn't help but feel comforted by the very real presence of God; she felt it hovering over them as they stood together there in the driveway. And before Hannah could find the strength to sing, the Lord gave her one more reason to believe they'd survive.

Jenny was singing, too.

Her voice joined Matt's as the quiet song built among them. When they reached the part about God being strong even when children were small and weak, Hannah's throat grew thick. It was true, and Hannah pulled in tighter to the two people she loved most in life. If it was true when times were good, when life was easy and unfettered, it was true now when the darkness seemed blacker than night. Hannah opened her mouth and somehow, despite the emotions lodged in her throat, the words began to flow, the sound of her voice mixing with the others.

Yes, Jesus loved them. He loved them and He loved Grace. If the Bible told them anything, it told them that. Hannah could feel herself growing stronger as the song continued. "Yes, Jesus loves me... Yes, Jesus loves me... Yes, Jesus loves me...the Bible tells me so."

When they were finished singing, Matt prayed. "Lord, only You could fathom the ache in our hearts this morning, the greatness of loss over saying good-bye..." His voice cracked and again they pulled closer to each other. "Saying good-bye to Grace. But Lord, give us open hearts and open minds. Though we cannot imagine a different little girl in our lives, if there be one out there who needs us, bring her our way. Please, Lord." He hesitated then, and Hannah knew he was trying to compose himself. "And please take good care of our little Gracie."

It wasn't until they were back in the house that Jenny turned to them, her eyes intent, serious. "I know what Grace's grandmother meant, and I understand your prayer, Matt." She looked at Hannah. "But I want you to know something. You can bring another little girl into this house and raise her. But that's the last time I let myself fall in love with a sister." Fresh tears fell from her eyes. "Losing one sister was hard enough. Now..." She shook her head. "I'm sorry, I...I won't do it again. Not unless God answers my questions."

Hannah and Matt watched her go; then they came together, embracing each other like two children who'd long since lost their way and had no idea where to turn next.

Though the song they'd sung minutes earlier still rang in Hannah's heart, though she knew God's promises were true and that somehow they'd survive, she couldn't help but ask herself the same question that had to be troubling Jenny.

Why, after all they'd been through, had God let such loss happen again?

Sixteen

Tanner was gone. Again.

He would have a good excuse. He always did. Over the past few weeks he'd given her dozens of excuses, but the bottom line Jade knew was this: If she was dying of cancer, he didn't want to be around to see it happen. The whole thing was too much for him; the wasting away of her energy and health and even her life was too difficult to watch. And so he had tuned out in every way that mattered.

Emotionally, spiritually, and most of all physically.

He hadn't meant to hurt her; Jade believed that with all her heart. But it hurt all the same, there was no denying the fact. His absence had pockmarked Jade's heart with a loneliness and sorrow she hadn't imagined possible.

After taking the trip to Colorado, Tanner had made a brief effort to spend more time with her. But now Jade hardly ever saw him. She was lonely and afraid and she ached for him whenever she was awake. She missed him more than at any other time in her life, even the years when they'd been apart.

His absence was putting a distance between them that scared her and left her with no one to talk to, no place to vent her fears. During their few minutes together, Jade refused to share her true feelings with him. If fear was what kept him away, she was determined not to give him more reason to be gone.

Especially now, when she needed him so badly.

Because the truth, regardless of what she wanted to tell Tanner, was obvious: The medication was changing her.

She began to notice the changes two days after the second seizure, when Dr. Layton increased her dosage and assigned her Helen, a full-time home nurse.

Jade was more tired than she imagined possible, and no amount of sleep made her feel better. Though her brain might intend to spew out three quick sentences, her mouth would only respond with one. One very slow, very deliberate string of words that sounded monotone and robotic, even to Jade. About the same time walking became difficult. Every step required thought and planning, and so her pace was half her usual quick-footed gait.

Then there was her lack of balance. The medication—or the tumor itself—was affecting her equilibrium. There were times, even when she otherwise felt good, when the room seemed to slant so drastically she would fall to her knees if not for the help of someone at her side—usually Helen or Ty, since Tanner never seemed to be home until after she was in bed.

At first it was easy to pass the symptoms off as coincidence, signs that she needed more rest. But after two days of sleeping practically around the clock, Jade could no longer lie to herself.

These thoughts simmered in Jade's mind while she lay stretched out on the sofa in their den. The den was just off the kitchen and for the past two weeks, since Helen had come to live with them, it was the place where Jade spent most of her time.

She reached for the water bottle on the end table and took a long, slow sip. Her Bible was on the floor beside her, but Jade couldn't remember why. Had she read it? Was she intending to read it? The water slid down her throat, soothing the parched feeling that was almost constant these days.

The sun was making its way toward the western ridge of mountains behind their house, so it had to be afternoon. But was it Tuesday? Wednesday? And where was Ty? She lifted her wrist, struggling to steady her hand in front of her. The numbers on her watch came into focus. Three-thirty. Ty would be home in ten minutes unless he had practice or a game. Jade had no idea what his schedule was. For that matter she had no idea about Tanner's schedule, either.

Helen took care of everything now. The woman was kind and orderly, a believer in her late fifties with no family. She was conscientious about her work and took little time for small talk.

Jade wondered how the woman was with Ty. When she took him to his baseball games, did she cheer for him? Ask him how he made a tough catch?

Tears poked pins at Jade's eyes. Before getting sick, she had never missed her son's games. *Help him understand, God...help me get better so I can be there for him.*

The baby shifted position, and Jade's eyes fell to her swollen abdomen. *Hold on, baby girl. You can make it. Just a few more weeks.*

The number became a giant in her mind, stomping out every other thought she'd been thinking. Three weeks? She had to exist this way, like a rotting vegetable, for three more weeks? The idea seemed as impossible as scaling Mount Everest.

Jade's eyelids grew heavier. If there was a silver lining in the fog of medication within which she existed, it was this: She had no trouble sleeping. When she couldn't remember what day it was or where Ty was supposed to be or whether he had a game or what time Tanner was supposed to be home, she could close her eyes and let all of life slip away.

She drew a slow, steady breath and smoothed her hand over her abdomen. The road ahead was long and dark, wrought with terrible possibilities. What if the tumor grew again before the baby was born? What if it killed her? Would the doctors find a way to save their tiny daughter or would she die, too? And what if they both survived until October 7, the date doctors had set for her C-section?

Instead of relishing the birth of her daughter, she would be faced with two weeks of intense chemotherapy and radiation. And after that there would be surgery—an operation that carried with it dire risks in the best of circumstances.

A sad, shaky sigh leaked from Jade's throat and two tears trickled down her cheeks. *How will I survive, God? I need Tanner…*

Do not be afraid…

The words echoed in her heart, and Jade wondered if she was imagining them. It was terrifying to live with a brain that no longer responded the way she expected. *God? Can you hear me? I'm scared.*

Do not be afraid, daughter…I am with you.

A subtle reassurance settled over Jade, and she knew the still small voice in her soul was nothing less than God's own comfort. She closed her eyes, grateful that He still had His hand on her, still loved her and stayed by her even though she was sick.

Especially because she was sick.

Am I dying, Lord? Are You taking me away from Tanner? Away from Ty and our baby girl?

In response, Jade remembered the verse that had been on her heart constantly the summer she and Tanner found each other again. The words soothed her soul and she played them over in her mind again and again.

"I know the plans I have for you…plans to give you a hope and a future and not to harm you…"

A door slammed in the distance and Jade's eyes opened. "Ty?"

"Hey, Mom."

She heard him trudge inside, toss his backpack in the corner, and fling his baseball cap on the nearby chair. His footsteps grew closer, then his warm face was up against hers, kissing her cheek and stroking her hair.

"Hi." He sat back on his heels. "You look tired."

Jade managed a grin. "Thanks, buddy."

"Sorry." Ty must have caught her hint of sarcasm. "I didn't mean it like that. You look great, really."

She messed her fingers through his wheat-colored hair. Tanner's hair. "That's okay; I know what you mean. I *am* tired. Too tired lately."

"You're not worse, are you?" Concern flashed in Ty's expression.

"No." Jade reached for his hand. "I'm fine."

"Do you need anything? A cookie or juice or something?"

"No, champ, that's okay." Jade struggled to sit up and swing her legs over the side of the sofa. "Let's get a snack together. We can eat out on the patio."

Helen walked past and stopped at the sight of Jade working herself up onto her feet. "I can get the chair…"

The chair. Jade appreciated the way Helen didn't call it a wheelchair, but that's what it was. A wheelchair in case she wanted to get out or be pushed around the block. Dr. Layton had said she would only need it until the baby was born. Between now and then, too much walking could stimulate tumor growth and more seizures.

"No, thanks." Jade smiled at the older woman. "I'm not going far." She held her elbow out toward Ty, and he took it in a way he'd long since perfected.

When he wasn't at school or busy with sports, Ty was constantly at Jade's side, checking on her needs and offering to help her walk from one spot to another when she felt unsteady. This was one of those times.

Arm in arm, she and Ty moved into the kitchen. Jade sat on a stool while Ty put together a tray of apples, crackers, and cheese. He carried the tray outside, placed it on the patio table, and poured two glasses of orange juice. When the snack was set up, he led Jade across the kitchen and through the back door.

"Sort of a preview, huh, Ty?" Jade's head was spinning and the room tilted. She clung to her son's arm, determined to make the walk without falling. She managed a chuckle. "What life'll be like when your mom's an old lady, right?"

"Nah." Ty led her to a patio chair and helped her sit. "You'll never be old."

Once they were situated, Ty filled a small plate for each of them. Jade reached for an apple slice and took a bite.

"Mom…" Ty wrinkled his brow. "Aren't we going to pray?"

"Oh, sorry." Jade set the apple down. "Go ahead."

Ty bowed and paused a moment before starting. "Dear Lord, thank You for this snack, thank You that Mom feels good enough to eat it with me, thank You that she's not getting worse. And please God, make her better soon." He opened his eyes and grinned. "Now we can eat. I'm starved."

Jade's heart swelled. Ty had always been that way. Even when he was a small boy, he would catch Jade starting a meal before praying. It didn't matter if it was Sunday dinner or a midday snack, her son's dependence on God was as natural as breathing.

"You won't believe it." Ty grabbed three crackers from his plate and shoved them into his mouth. "Guess who quit the baseball team?"

Jade pulled one foot up onto the chair and rested her chin on her knee, pretending to think hard on the question. "Carl the Mugster?"

"No…" Ty made a face and chomped on an apple slice. "The Mugster wouldn't quit. He might be having a bad year, but still." Ty's eyes grew wide. "Really, Mom, guess who quit? You won't believe it!"

The apple tasted like metal and Jade ran the napkin over her mouth, spitting the pulp into the paper and wadding it up in her hands so Ty wouldn't know. "I give up; tell me."

"Okay. It's a long story, but it started last week after we lost to the Reds, remember?"

Jade nodded, doing her best to keep a serious face.

"Well…after the game the other team's pitcher came over to our dugout and…"

The rays of sunshine warmed Jade's shoulders, and listening to Ty and his stories made her dizziness less severe. She couldn't bring herself to eat, but that was okay. Helen was bringing her protein drinks three times a day, so even if food didn't look good, at least she and the baby were getting the nutrients they needed.

The smell of jasmine, rich and sweet, filtered up from the landscaped grounds, and a light breeze stirred up a handful of puffy clouds against the deep blue sky.

Jade breathed it in. She loved this time of the year, the way the heat eased up and the Santa Ana winds cleared away the smog. Would she be alive next year at this time? Or was this her last Southern California fall?

"Mom, are you listening?"

At the frustration in Ty's voice, Jade was pierced with guilt. "You were telling me who quit the team, right?"

Ty huffed and fell back against his chair. "I finished that story. Now I'm telling you why Miss McMacken doesn't like my math work."

Jade shook off thoughts of everything but her son. "I'm sorry. Tell me again."

"Okay." He smiled his forgiveness. "But listen this time."

He was just about to move on to another topic when Helen poked her head out the doorway and held up the cordless phone. "Mr. Eastman, for you."

A current of electricity ran through her heart, the same as it always did whenever she heard Tanner's name. Even now there were times when her life felt like a dream, when she feared she might wake and find Tanner was nothing more than the stranger he'd been for ten years after Ty was conceived.

She reached for the phone. "Thank you, Helen."

"Tell him I got an *A* on my history quiz." Ty helped himself to another handful of crackers. "But don't talk long. My game's in an hour."

Jade nodded and held the receiver to her ear. "Hello?"

"Hey..." Tanner sounded close enough to be next to her. "How're you feeling?"

"Fine." Disappointment blew through the hallways of her heart. If only he'd start the conversation some other way. *Jade, I love you*...or *Jade, I miss you*. The dizziness was back, and she closed her eyes. "How 'bout you?"

He sighed. "Busy."

Jade could almost see him, elbow planted on his desk while he sorted through a file. "Looks like it'll be another late one."

Her eyes welled up, and for a moment her throat was too thick to speak.

"Are you there?"

"Yes." She coughed. "Ty wants me to tell you he aced his history quiz. And he has a game in an hour."

"Good." Tanner's answer was quick. "Tell him I'm proud of him and I wish I could be there. Maybe next time."

Jade wanted to scream. What was so important that he couldn't come home at a decent hour? And why weren't Ty's games a priority any more? Tanner ran the office; he could take the time if he wanted to. But she had neither the energy nor the desire to fight with Tanner now.

Instead she brushed the sleeve of her sweatshirt beneath both eyes so Ty wouldn't see her tears. "Fine."

"Fine?" Tanner sounded irritated. "What's *that* supposed to mean?"

"Never mind."

"That isn't fair. Don't tell me you're mad again. Look, Jade, the cases I'm working are demanding, okay? Maybe it isn't good timing, but what can I do? The office needs me."

She shifted her gaze to the passing clouds, her voice quiet, sad. "We need you, too."

"This isn't the time." Tanner exhaled hard. "We'll talk later. I love you, Jade."

"Okay." Jade pulled the phone from the side of her face and ended the call. *Okay*? Jade had always been quick to confirm Tanner's declarations of love with one of her own. But this time the words simply wouldn't come.

Ty finished his story and brushed the crumbs from his hands. If he noticed the fact that the phone call had upset Jade, he didn't say. Instead, he kissed the top of her head and darted toward the door. "Gotta get dressed. Helen's taking me to the game." He paused before going inside. "I'll hit a home run for you, Mom. That'll make you feel better."

She gave him a thumbs-up, touched by his tender heart. "Can't wait to hear about it."

Jade stayed outside, staring at the hills behind their house. If she focused hard on one thing—a tree trunk or a cloud—her sense of balance seemed almost normal. She stayed that way for a long while, refusing to think of anything but the beauty around her. Eventually she heard the front door open and minutes later the sound of the car pulling away.

Certain that she was alone, Jade let her mind drift back to the conversation with Tanner. It was wrong for him to spend so much time at work. Couldn't he see how badly she wanted him home? Did he think a nurse could replace having him at her side?

Betrayal and anger rocked her soul. There were no answers, at least none she cared to think about. Jade pushed her plate back and stared at her wedding ring. An ocean of tears spilled from her heart and down her face.

She missed Tanner so much she could barely stand it.

What if she died? Tonight even? Was this how she and Tanner would spend their last days, distant and frustrated and rarely together?

"God..." Sobs tore at her, and the sound carried on the breeze. "I'm so scared and alone. I need him. Why doesn't he want to be home? What have I done to push him away?"

Since her diagnosis, life had become a nightmare of second-guessing and doubts.

Sweet Hannah, her dependable friend, had begged Jade not to blame herself for what was happening, but it was impossible not to. If only she hadn't called Tanner three years ago when she needed legal help. If only she'd been a quiet wife for Jim, maybe he never would have left her.

Maybe then she wouldn't be sick.

Jade leaned her head back and lowered her eyebrows. What was she thinking? God wasn't using her cancer to punish her for what happened with Jim. Besides, Jim had tried to take Ty away from her! She'd had no choice but to call Tanner. Ty was his son, after all. And Jim would still have divorced her whether she'd called Tanner or not.

And if she hadn't called, Jim would have taken Ty with him.

Still...

The pendulum of her emotions swung back the other way. Enough people had pointed a finger at Jade since her divorce that sometimes she wondered. Was God angry at her for marrying Tanner? Certainly there were reasons for the hard times they were facing, but was her cancer His way of punishing her? At least in part?

The idea flew in the face of everything she knew about the Lord.

Jade had studied Scripture on the matter and realized there were two schools of thought. The first read that anyone who divorced, except for reasons of marital unfaithfulness, and then married another was guilty of adultery. The second group tended to look past the exception and see only the last part of the verse. Marriage after divorce was adultery, pure and simple.

Most of the time Jade sided with the first group. The idea that God would be merciful to a person whose spouse had chosen to take up with another seemed more like God than the second viewpoint.

But sometimes… Jade wondered. What other reason was there for the trial they were suffering if God wasn't angry with her? With both of them? Her sobs returned with a vengeance.

She didn't know how long she stayed there, silently begging God to forgive her, but after a while, the back door opened and Helen appeared. "Ty's going home with his friend. He'll be spending the night there if that's okay."

"It's fine." Jade hung her head. "Thanks."

Jade couldn't take another evening inside waiting for Tanner's return, trying to stay awake long enough to exchange a few shallow sentences. Her head hurt worse than it had in weeks and she couldn't keep her fingers from trembling. Maybe death was right around the corner; maybe the Lord would come for her tonight.

Her tears came harder. "Helen, I need…to get out of here." She turned so she could see the older woman, and the effort was exhausting.

"Well, I don't know…" Helen was at her side, concern etched between the wrinkles on her forehead. "Maybe you should sleep first."

"No!" The tears made it almost impossible to talk. Jade held her breath and shook her head. *Calm down*, she ordered herself, but her heart raced in response. If this was her last night alive, there was no way she would spend it sleeping. When she could speak, she looked at Helen. "I have someplace to go. I'll need my chair."

Helen helped her into the house and, with a shaky hand, she scribbled a note for Tanner.

I can't take it anymore, Tanner…I'll be out late. Don't wait up. I love you more than you know.

Jade

She studied it through a fresh layer of tears. So what if Tanner didn't know where she was? He hadn't been home enough to notice how bad she'd gotten; hadn't spent time with her and Ty the way he might have. Jade hesitated.

It was fear; it had to be.

Tanner cared, of course—he loved her more than his own life—but whatever had come over him since her last seizure, his absence was more than Jade could stand. Especially now, with death breathing down her neck. All of life had become a race for survival. A race in which she was losing Tanner.

Whether she lived or died, she was losing him.

There were a dozen things Jade was desperate to bring before the Lord—her health, her baby's chances of survival. Her life. But before she left that night, Jade uttered the only plea that really mattered.

God, bring Tanner back to me. Please. Before it's too late.

Seventeen

There was no point trying to concentrate.

Tanner planted his elbows in the open file on his desk and pressed his fingers against his tired, aching eyes. How could he work, when all he could think about was Jade, the hurt in her voice as they'd talked…?

He gave a hoarse laugh. Talked? Who was he kidding? They hadn't talked in days, not really.

His late hours were frustrating her; that much was clear. But what was he supposed to do? The case needed him. Desperately. Every hour at work meant a greater chance for success at the trial. Victory wouldn't come unless he stayed devoted.

Right?

Tanner tapped his pencil on his desk as a dagger of guilt sliced through his heart. The arguments he had created to justify his time away from Jade suddenly collapsed like a house of cards. He covered his face with his hands and tried to settle his nerves. *What is it, God? What's wrong with me? My wife's home dying, and I'm here at work.*

He peered through the spaces in his fingers, and his gaze settled on a plaque near the edge of his desk. Jade had given it to him on the one-year anniversary of his helping her win back custody of Ty. A Scripture that was one of their favorites was carved in the middle…

Be still and know that I am God.

The words played again and again in Tanner's mind, but they seemed to have no relevance to any of the troubles burying him at the moment. He let his hands fall to the desk and stared at the outline for what could be his biggest case yet.

Tanner's research had been exhaustive. He had reams of information he could hardly wait to share with a jury. He imagined their reaction when he revealed his favorite little-known facts. He glanced at his notes. For instance, separation of church and state, the idea most people attributed to the Constitution, was actually not in the Constitution at all.

The First Amendment said only this: "Congress shall make no law respecting an establishment of religion, or prohibiting the free exercise thereof."

His eyes moved down the page.

The idea of separation of church and state came from a letter Thomas Jefferson wrote to a group of Baptists, assuring them that no act of government would infringe on their right to believe. Why? According to Jefferson's letter, because that clause in the Constitution provided a wall separating church and state.

A wall that separated the *church* from the *state,* not the state from the church. The state was the power that threatened the church, not the other way around as was so often interpreted today.

Every case Tanner and Matt had ever fought had somehow been birthed out of that single letter from Jefferson, but never had Tanner turned the tables and used the same argument in favor of a client.

Until now.

His approach would surprise not only the attorneys representing the city of Benson, but in time it would surprise the entire nation. The case could be that big. The reason it was taking so much time, though, was that while Tanner's premise was simple, proving it would be something entirely different.

But if Tanner thought building a precedent-setting case

against a hostile city council was difficult, it was nothing compared to the effort of concentrating on work while Jade was wasting away at home.

He clenched his teeth and turned his chair toward the window. The sun was setting, leaving a trail of pinks and oranges that was characteristic of the Southern California evening sky. Who was he trying to fool? He should be home with Jade, caring for her, waiting on her, loving her.

But watching her waste away was more than he could bear. Even if he couldn't think straight, he was better off at the office, doing his best to push the hands of time to a place where the nightmare they were living might be over.

Besides, Jade didn't miss him. She slept most of the time and when she was awake…

Tanner's eyes burned with the onset of tears. When she was awake, she could hardly carry on a conversation. The medication had affected her that much. Snapshots from the past few weeks flashed in the photo album of his mind. Jade trying to climb out of bed and falling to her knees; Jade picking at a plateful of food, unable to eat.

But worst of all were their conversations. Moments like the one that had taken place the night before. He'd come home late again and found Ty and Helen watching *I Love Lucy* reruns. He kissed Ty and asked about his baseball practice. After a few minutes he looked around. "Is Jade in bed?"

"She wanted to stay awake until you got home." Helen cast him a disapproving look. "But she was too tired."

Tanner ignored the unspoken accusations. "Oh." He looked at Ty. "I'll be back in a minute."

Upstairs he found Jade asleep, propped against a stack of pillows. He took quiet steps toward her and sat on the edge of their bed. "Jade…"

She moaned and moved her head an inch in either direction.

Tanner angled his head, his heart breaking at the sight of her, weak and frighteningly thin despite her pregnant belly. "Jade, I love you."

"Hmmm." She blinked several times, squinting at the light and then recognizing Tanner. "Oh…hi. You're home."

Her words were slow, measured. Tanner steadied himself. "How're you feeling?"

She raised one shoulder, and her eyes struggled to stay open. "Okay. The same."

They looked at each other for a moment, and Tanner searched for the words that might help. There was only one thing that really mattered—whether Jade was feeling worse, experiencing new symptoms. But clearly she didn't want to discuss herself.

He spread his palm out on the bedspread and leaned back. "I'm using the separation of church and state ruling in the case against Benson."

For a moment, Jade's eyes were blank. Then gradually they narrowed as though she were concentrating on something intensely serious. "Sepa…sepra…seprish…" She clenched her fists and uttered a frustrated groan. "Help me say it, Tanner!"

"Hey—" he sat straight up, his stomach churning—"Take it easy. You're tired, that's all." What was wrong with her? Was the medication taking her ability to talk, or was the tumor growing into the part of her brain that controlled speech? Her words were not only slow they were slurred, so either option was equally possible.

And equally terrifying.

He swallowed. "I said I'm using the separation of church and state ruling in the case against Benson."

Jade bit her lip and tried again. "Separsh…sepa…"

That was all. She hung her head, and tears fell on the bedspread. "I can't...say it. The letters get all mixed up."

There was nothing he could do, nothing at all. So he turned off the light, stroked her forehead, and waited until she fell asleep before joining Ty and Helen downstairs.

The memory cleared and he looked once more at the plaque on his desk.

Be still, and know that I am God.

He had no doubt about the last part. God existed as surely as the sun and moon. Tanner might not understand what God was doing in their lives, why after so many years apart Jade had to get sick, but his faith remained.

No it wasn't the belief-in-God part of the plaque that troubled Tanner. It was the being still part. How could he be still? The pain of watching Jade fade away was never more intense than when he stopped moving, stopped thinking about work or Ty or the problems other people faced. People like Matt and Hannah.

He read the verse again...and was struck by a thought. He *had* to keep working. Only by staying busy would the days pass and lead him to the place where their baby girl was home and Jade was healthy. But staying busy was also keeping him from Jade...from the woman he loved with all his heart, the woman who needed him.

Tanner stared at the Benson file and slowly closed it. His head ached and his heart hurt. Even if Jade was sleeping, even if the medication was sapping the life from her, he needed to be home. Maybe that's why the plaque on his desk had shouted at him for the past hour. Maybe God wanted him home with Jade, even if seeing her slow and sick and tired was the hardest thing in his life.

He drew a steadying breath and exhaled through clenched teeth. "Okay, God, I'll go."

Thirty-five minutes later, Tanner walked through the front door and stopped short. The lights were off. It looked like even Helen wasn't home. "Hello?" His voice echoed through the foyer, but otherwise the silence remained.

Typically Helen would have cooked something for dinner, but there was only the faint smell of vanilla, Jade's favorite fragrance, mostly likely left over from a candle she'd burned that morning. "Jade? Ty?"

When there was no response, Tanner's heart skipped a beat and he rushed into the kitchen, flipping on a light switch. There on the island countertop was a note. Tanner pictured Jade seizing again, falling to the floor…Helen calling an ambulance. What if this time it was worse than before? What if…?

He reached for the slip of paper, his voice quiet and unsteady. "No, Jade…not again…"

His eyes raced over the page.

I can't take it anymore, Tanner…I'll be out late. Don't wait up. I love you more than you know.

Jade

At the bottom, in Helen's handwriting, were a few sentences that must have been written to keep Tanner from worrying: *Ty's spending the night at a friend's house. Jade and I are at church.*

Tanner read the note three more times, grabbed his car keys, and headed back outside. As he drove to church, he realized that everything he'd gone through in his life before this—the hurt of losing Jade as a boy and again as a young man, the ache of knowing that he had missed out on raising Ty all those years, even the devastation of Jade's illness—all of it paled in comparison to this pain, this terrible ache that never went away.

Because always before the hurt was someone else's fault. Never had either of them acted willfully against the other. But now, as the words of her note took root in his soul, he knew that only one person was responsible for making Jade feel lonely and let-down in her greatest hour of need.

That person was him.

Pastor Steve was still in his office when Jade and Helen entered the sanctuary. The man—a kind preacher in his forties—heard them enter, and when he saw Jade in her wheelchair he came to her. Both the Bronzans and the Eastmans attended Los Robles Community Church and took turns doing the puppets for children at second service. All of them considered Pastor Steve and his wife friends.

Jade raised her hand in the pastor's direction. She hated the fact that she was crying, and that being pushed down the center aisle in a wheelchair was obvious proof she was not doing well. She wiped at her tears and nodded to the man. "Hi, Pastor."

"Jade..." He put his hand on her shoulder. "What's wrong, dear?"

There were so many things to say, so many questions to ask, that Jade didn't know where to begin. But the relief of knowing someone was willing to listen brought on another wave of tears. "I...I'm sorry." Her voice cracked. "I need to talk."

Pastor Steve glanced at Helen. "I have time. Would you like me to take her home?"

"Yes." Jade nodded before Helen could answer. "Why don't I do that, Helen? That way Tanner won't worry. Besides—" she looked back at Pastor Steve—"I might be here awhile."

"That's fine. This is my late night. Normally I have counseling appointments but no one showed up." He gave her a smile. "I'll be happy to drive you home."

Helen left, and once they were alone, he took a seat on the edge of one of the pews and faced Jade. "I see a dozen emotions on your face, as clearly as if they were written there."

Jade's gaze fell, and she tightened her grip on the arms of the wheelchair. "At least a dozen."

"Like I said, I have time." The man's voice was patient and

filled with kindness. "Why don't you start by telling me why you're here?"

The memories that had troubled her for so long came to mind again, and Jade leaned back in her chair. She looked at Pastor Steve's face and saw nothing but understanding. Then, with only a few tears here and there, she told him everything. She talked about finding Tanner that summer in Kelso and getting pregnant the day before he left for a six-week mission trip. And she explained the mistake she made in marrying Jim Rudolph, and every sad milestone from that point until their divorce. She told him how, after marrying Tanner, some people condemned her for committing adultery.

"And now I have to wonder..." Jade's heart beat stronger than before. Though she was still weak, telling the story to Pastor Steve infused her with a strength she'd been missing for days.

The pastor leaned forward a bit. "About what?"

Jade crossed her arms in front of her and gripped her elbows. "About whether God is using cancer to punish me. You know, for committing adultery."

"Oh, Jade, no..." Pastor Steve shook his head. "You can't think that."

"But...why else would God allow this?"

The pastor leaned back and crossed one leg over the other. "First, let's talk about illness." His eyes softened. "Bad things happen to God's people, Jade. That's always been true. This is a fallen world, and life here is not the ultimate goal. Heaven is."

Jade had heard the explanation before, but it always fell flat. God was a miraculous God. Certainly he could have healed Jade by now, or better yet, prevented the cancer from growing in the first place. The idea that she was being punished seemed far more likely. "But it feels like God's mad at me."

For the next half hour the pastor reminded her of Bible verses, sharing example after example of something bad happening to someone who loved God. When he was finished, he shared a final verse from the Book of John, "'In this world you will have trouble. But take heart! I have overcome the world.'"

The words soothed the raw places in Jade's soul. She had read the verse dozens of times over the years, but now it was as though she were hearing it for the first time...understanding a truth she'd always missed. The Lord hadn't only overcome the world's trouble, He had overcome *hers*. Personally.

Tears swam in her eyes and she studied Pastor Steve's face. "I never thought of it that way." She reached for a tissue in the pocket of her wheelchair. "Like God had already—" she looked down at her chair and back at the pastor—"overcome this."

Pastor Steve hesitated. "There's more. Let's talk about marriage and divorce. I've been asked about this so often that one day I wrote a brief explanation. It's something I printed up for people like you, people with these questions and concerns." He stood and headed for his office, which adjoined the front of the sanctuary. "I'll be right back."

Seconds later he returned with a preprinted card. The front read, "In case you wonder..."

Jade opened it and began to read:

> Dear friend, I appreciate your questions about God's view on marriage and divorce. While I do not have the definitive answer in this matter, I have searched the Scriptures on the issue. In that light, I would like to give you my understanding of Christ's position, as I see it in the Bible.
>
> Each of the Gospels talks about divorce to some degree. However, the text in Matthew 19:9 says, "I tell you

that anyone who divorces his wife, except for marital unfaithfulness, and marries another woman commits adultery."

I've thought and thought on this verse, and in trying to understand it I've used the word replacement method. In the following examples I've replaced the key words from that verse, but kept the sentence structure the same. Here goes:

Anyone who eats pizza, except for cheese pizza, will get heartburn.

Who doesn't get heartburn? The person who eats cheese pizza. Let's try another:

Anyone who lies in the sun, except for the one who wears sunscreen, will get burned.

Who doesn't get burned? The one who wears sunscreen. Or this one:

Anyone who misses school, except for illness, will receive a fail.

Who doesn't receive the fail? The one who misses school because he's sick.

Many people will argue that once a married person is divorced, they must never remarry because to do so would result in adultery. Yes, there are verses that say this, but there is also Matthew 19:9.

Now if God said it, I believe it. In this case, the words are God's, not mine. We are left to stand back and look at the larger picture, the picture of Christ as our merciful God and Savior. Why would He say, "Except for marital unfaithfulness?" I have to believe it's for this reason: When a person's spouse is unfaithful—physically or otherwise—and has a hard heart toward reconciliation, God does not seem to condemn the faithful spouse to a life of isolation.

Therefore, though the Lord hates divorce, the faithful spouse who remarries is not guilty of adultery. That's how I read it, anyway. If you have any questions, contact me at the church office.

Sincerely, Pastor Steve

With each clear-cut sentence, a river of peace flowed more freely in Jade's heart. She blinked twice so she could see through her tears. "But I was at fault, too. I lied to Jim about Ty from the beginning."

The pastor bit his lower lip. "Well, Jade, you shouldn't have lied, but the test God gives us isn't one of perfection, it's one of intent." He studied her. "Did you intend to see your marriage end in divorce? Even at the end?"

Jade shook her head. "No, even after I found Tanner again I wanted to make things work with Jim. *He* was my husband. But by then Jim had made up his mind."

There was silence between them for a moment, and Jade remembered her feelings from earlier that afternoon. "I guess there's only one other thing." Her eyes settled on her hands and she noticed they were trembling. "I feel like I'm dying. Maybe even tonight."

At that moment, a door opened in the back of the church, and Jade turned just as Tanner rushed in. When he saw her, he stopped, his eyes locked on hers. Even from a hundred feet away, Jade could feel his apology, read it in his face and hear it in his unspoken words.

Her heart filled with a joy so strong it nearly eclipsed her fears. She soundlessly mouthed the only thing that came to mind, a truth that started her crying in earnest and made her ache for his touch: "You came."

Pastor Steve nodded toward Tanner, cleared his throat, and patted Jade on the knee. "I'll be in my office if either of you need me."

When he was gone, Tanner came to her, lifted her from the chair, and cradled her close to his body as though she were a small child. His tears mingled with hers as he brushed his cheek against her face. "Jade. I'm so sorry, baby."

With every ounce of her remaining strength, she held on to him, breathing in the smell of him, savoring his heartbeat against her chest. Careful not to bump her arms or legs, he sat down in the wheelchair, still holding her close.

She wrapped her arms around his neck and buried her face in his shoulder. "Don't let go of me, Tanner, please." Two quick sobs slipped from her throat. "I'm so afraid."

"Of what, sweetie?" He drew back enough to see her face. His voice was like a caress. "Tell me."

"Of dying." She sniffed. "I think I might die tonight."

"Tonight?" Tanner's eyes grew wide and his expression softened even more. "Honey, don't say that."

"But I'm so scared..."

"You?" He looked genuinely puzzled. "I thought you were...you always say everything is fine." He nuzzled his face against hers. "Baby, how long have you felt this way?"

Jade swallowed back several small sobs. "Since...since the day we found out."

His body responded to her words, tensing and flexing beneath her. When he spoke, his voice was choked with sorrow. "All this time I thought I was the only one who was afraid." He tightened his hold on her. "I didn't know, Jade. I'm so sorry, baby. So sorry. You said you were okay."

"I *wanted* to be." Her forehead fell against his shoulder. "I thought if I got scared everything would spin out of control."

"No, honey, that wouldn't happen. It's okay to be scared."

Suddenly Jade's fear of dying that night faded like a winter sunset. Tanner stroked her hair and continued. "It kills me to see you like this...hurting, unable to walk." He paused and touched his lips to hers. "And when you pretended it didn't matter..."

She lifted her shoulders. "I knew you were scared, Tanner. I thought if I told you the truth you'd...you'd be gone more." She clutched his shirt and drank in his sweet breath near her face. "I love you, Tanner. I need you more than ever."

He placed his hands on either side of her face and positioned her so he could see straight into her soul. "What do you need from me, Jade? Whatever it is, I'll do it."

She didn't take even a moment's consideration. Blinking back an onset of fresh tears, she kissed him as she hadn't in weeks. When she pulled away, she studied his face, praying that this would be a turning point, because the battle she was fighting could not be won without him. She knew that now. "Are you serious?"

Tanner's eyes glistened and he nodded. "As serious as I've ever been. What do you need from me?"

"Okay." She drew a steadying breath. "I'll tell you."

And for the next hour, with Tanner hanging on her every word, Jade did exactly that.

Eighteen

Each time the dream was the same, and that September night was no different.

Jenny stood in front of her house, her mom and Matt on either side, and together they waved to Grace. The car Grace and her grandmother left in was maroon, and Jenny watched it back out of the driveway, stop and shift gears, then take off down the street.

The whole time, Grace's face was up against the window, tears running down her cheeks, her hand pressed against the glass as she said her final good-byes.

Two seconds passed, three, four…

Then the car glided into an intersection, and suddenly from out of nowhere a giant white pickup came from the side and there was a horrendous crash. Jenny's senses filled with the assault of grinding metal, shattering glass, screeching tires, and flying debris.

"*No!* Not Grace. Not her, too."

She raced as fast as she could toward the accident scene. But when she came upon the spot where the collision occurred, there was nothing but pieces of the car. Small, maroon pieces. Tires and car doors and engine parts. The giant white truck had continued on its way and was long gone.

There were no seats, no floorboards, and no sign of Grace or her grandmother. Only Mrs. Parsons stood there in the midst of the mess, her body intact and free from injury.

Jenny ran to her and grabbed her by the shoulders. "Where is she? Where's Grace?"

"I don't know." Mrs. Parsons' expression was unsympathetic. "I guess I lost her."

"No! You can't lose her. She's my sister! We have to find her!"

Then Mrs. Parsons disappeared.

"Grace!" Jenny darted from one piece of the broken car to another, lifting it and looking for Grace's small body. "Honey, I'm here." She yelled the words, still frantically searching the intersection. "I love you, Grace. Where are you? I need to find you and–"

There was the sound of screeching tires and the roar of a powerful engine. Jenny looked up and gasped. Something terrifying was hurtling toward her. There was no way out, no way to avoid being run down, and in that instant she screamed in terror.

Because the thing coming at her was the giant white truck...

Her eyes flew open and she jumped out of bed, the scream still coming from deep within her. Her heart pounded in her throat, her face damp with sweat and tears.

"Jenny!" Her mother tore into her room, eyes wide with fear. "What is it?"

It didn't matter how often she woke up this way. Each time the sound of her frightened scream terrified both of them. They stared at each other for a beat and then Jenny shuffled across the room and into her mother's arms.

"I'm sorry." She let her head fall against her mother's shoulder and tried to stop sobbing. "I dreamed it again."

The two of them were quiet, but Jenny knew what her mother was thinking. At first, after the accident four years ago, Jenny only dreamed about the happy times, the days when Alicia was still alive. But two years later, Jenny began having horrifying dreams about a giant white truck.

Brian Wesley, the drunk driver, had been driving a white pickup when he hit them.

After a month of nightmares, Hannah and Jenny both agreed

she needed counseling, needed to talk through the feelings she bottled up back when the accident happened. Twelve weeks of regular sessions with a Christian therapist seemed to be just what Jenny needed. The nightmares stopped and never came back.

Until now.

"Honey." Her mother was calmer now. "We can take you back to the counselor if you think it would help."

Jenny eased out of her mother's arms. The terror of the dream took minutes to pass and even now her entire body shook. She ran her fingers through her hair and dried her face with the sleeve of her nightgown. "No. I'm okay. I just…" A lump in her throat kept her from speaking.

Her mother pulled her close once more and stroked her back. "I know honey, I miss her, too."

Jenny swallowed and found her voice, new tears spilling onto her face. "I want her back with us, Mom. She's my sister; nothing can change that."

They were silent for a while; then her mom drew back and kissed her cheek. "Let's talk about it in the morning."

Jenny nodded. "I'm sorry."

"Don't be sorry. We all want her back."

"It's not just Grace." Jenny's voice was the softest whisper. "I miss Alicia, too. Losing Grace makes everything worse."

"I know. It's the same for me."

Jenny studied her mother in the moonlit room as the sobs came once more. There had been a time when Jenny doubted her mother would ever understand. But in the past three years they'd become incredibly close. Jenny was grateful. "I love you, Mom."

"Love you, too." Her mother took hold of Jenny's hands. "Let's pray."

They whispered in the darkness, begging God to bring them both peace in light of Grace's absence. And Alicia's. And to help

Jenny's nightmares go away. When they were done, her mom blew her a kiss and headed for the bedroom door. "See you in the morning."

They returned to their separate beds, and Jenny glanced at the clock. It was just after three in the morning. Though she was tired, Jenny lay awake, staring at the ceiling and thinking about the dream. The counselor had told her that the giant white pickup seemed symbolic, because Jenny had never wanted to hate Brian Wesley over what happened.

Even that first year after the accident, when her mother was determined to see the man locked up for life for what he'd done, Jenny couldn't hate him. She'd never hated anyone in her life and feelings that strong scared her. The pain in her heart was great enough simply dealing with the loss of her dad and Alicia without adding hatred to the mix.

But since she refused to hate the drunk driver, her fear and anger about what happened somehow focused on the white pickup Brian Wesley was driving. After all, that was the only thing Jenny remembered about the accident. One minute she was talking to Alicia about school starting the next day and what teachers they hoped to have and which boys might have changed over the summer.

The next minute she saw a white pickup barreling down on them.

Then there was nothing but darkness.

Jenny rolled over in bed and curled up as small as she could. It was a good thing she had no memory of what happened next. She'd heard the entire story, and that was all the information she needed. If she'd been conscious she didn't think she would have survived.

The idea of seeing Alicia dead at the scene from head injuries and her dad trapped in the car while firemen used torches to cut through their car and get him out was more than she could take in. To hear him gasp for breath, knowing that the paramedics were frantically trying to save his life…

She thanked God she'd seen none of it.

Her injuries had been minor—a concussion and a broken arm. And the next day when she woke in a hospital bed, her mother was at her side. It was then that she found out what had happened. Since the last thing she remembered was the white pickup truck headed straight for them, it was no wonder that was the source of her nightmares.

"Daddy, I miss you…" Fresh tears rolled across the bridge of her nose and onto her pillow. "Give Alicia a hug for me."

Her whispered words faded into the night and Jenny drifted back to their last camping trip. Everything about that weekend was still as clear and vivid as if it had happened days and not years ago.

She and Alicia had been inseparable, despite the fact that they were so different. Alicia was pretty and popular, a cheerleader with more friends than any girl at West Hills High School. Jenny was nearly two years younger and had none of her older sister's charisma and confidence. She was shy and awkward, with a secret desire that one day she might grow up to be like Alicia.

But despite her busy social schedule and the attention she received from her peers, Alicia preferred spending her free time with Jenny. After school—even up until the day she was killed—she and Alicia would listen to music, or take a walk, or ride bikes together.

They were more than sisters; they were best friends.

And the campout with their dad had long been the highlight of every summer vacation. That year they camped at Cachuma Lake, a place known for its fishing spots. The Ryan father-daughter campouts were always marked by lots of time fishing. Fishing and talking.

Jenny saw that now. Back then she and Alicia would roll their eyes and slip into their old jeans and sweatshirts before the sun came up, complaining about the cold or the early morning hour. "Do we have to fish today?" they'd whine.

He always acted shocked by their question. He'd silently mouth the question back at them as though nothing could be more outrageous than to wonder about such a thing. "Of course we're going fishing! Ryans fish; it's what we do."

Jenny blinked away the tears and her sniffle broke the dark silence that surrounded her.

That last day, the day of the accident, had been just like that. They'd gotten up early and fished by flashlight until the sun came up. When it was time to go, she had the most fish. They were making their way up the shore, Alicia in the lead, teasing Jenny about her catch and how maybe fishing was her talent, when Jenny spotted a coiled rattlesnake and screamed.

They all froze, which prevented Alicia from stepping squarely on the snake. Their dad, a doctor when he wasn't fishing, spoke in a voice Jenny remembered still. In his most serious tone, calm and even, he directed Alicia to back away from the rattler one step at a time. Seconds later she was out of danger and the snake slid away.

For months after the accident Jenny remembered the close encounter with the snake. She couldn't help think that if she hadn't screamed, Alicia would have stepped on the snake and been bitten. Though that would have been bad, it would have meant leaving the campsite immediately, before packing up. That way they wouldn't have passed through the intersection of Fallbrook and Ventura Boulevard at the same exact instant as Brian Wesley.

And they would have been alive today.

If only Jenny hadn't screamed.

She knew thoughts like that were crazy, but they came anyway. Now that Grace was gone, it made her wonder what she could have done to prevent *that* from happening. Maybe if she hadn't given her heart over so quickly, so completely…maybe if she'd allowed the precious girl to be nothing more than a welcomed guest…maybe then Grace's grandmother never would have come looking for her and today she'd still be living with them.

Jenny dried her face with the edge of the sheet and turned onto her other side. This time she kept her words silent, allowing them to echo only in the most private places of her heart.

Lord, I know You can hear me. I have a favor to ask. Please, God, when You see my dad and Alicia today, could You tell them to pray? Have them pray for Grace. Because I don't believe she's better off in Oklahoma; I believe she needs to be here with us. And right now I need my dad and my best friend to pray for me. But You see, God, I can't ask them, because they live in heaven with You. So please, God…ask them for me, okay? And when You do, tell them I miss them. Tell them I always will.

The idea that she could ask God to give her dad and Alicia messages was one that always brought peace to Jenny's soul. Despite nightmares about giant white pickup trucks or a little sister she might never see again living a thousand miles away, Jenny drifted off to sleep, resting in the arms of the only One who could keep her dad and Alicia—and now little Grace—alive in her heart.

The only One who could make them feel close enough to touch.

Nineteen

The next morning, nothing felt right to Hannah. She waited until Matt and Jenny were gone for the day, poured herself a cup of coffee, and curled up in a deck chair outside. The fog had settled in overnight, and the damp gray of the sea and sky fit Hannah's mood.

When Grace was taken from them, she made a decision to handle it well, to show the world and her family how much she'd changed since losing Tom and Alicia four years ago. Losing Grace would not set her back a year, wouldn't make her turn against God or renounce her faith. It would be painful, but she would survive.

At least that was the plan.

Instead she'd been short with Matt, distant from the Lord, and several times she'd canceled her volunteer work at the hospital so she could stay home and clean the house or take walks along the beach. Of course, she always wound up in Grace's room, straightening her pillow and dusting her shelves. Jenny was the only one who understood. Poor precious Jenny was suffering at least as badly as Hannah.

The hot steam from her coffee warded off the chill in the morning air, and Hannah held the mug closer to her face. She took a careful sip, wishing the hot liquid could somehow burn away the anger and doubt and bitterness that had crept back into her heart.

She gazed across the water and bit hard on her lip.

Why?

Why did God bring Grace into their lives in the first place? And why had they agreed to take her? She was a foster-adopt child, after all. A child with risks she and Matt had agreed up front not to take. The reason was easy enough. Mrs. Parsons had convinced them. She had told them the chances were basically nonexistent that anything would disrupt Grace's adoption. And so they'd agreed.

Many times in the past three weeks, she'd mentioned to Matt that someone ought to do something about the social worker, file a complaint against her or notify her superiors that she'd reneged on a promise. How dare the woman bring Grace into their home and give them time to fall in love with her unless she was absolutely certain that nothing would stop the adoption.

And what about Patsy Landers? How could the woman call herself a Christian, then without the slightest hesitation take Grace from the most stable home she'd ever had? How could she deny the girl a lifetime of love from two parents who cherished her?

Hannah's eyes welled up. She wasn't sorry they'd taken Grace in. The little girl had been worth every minute. The memory of watching her blossom into a talkative, confident little girl in the months they had her was something all of them would cherish forever.

But still it didn't seem right. Mrs. Parsons should have checked Grace's background better, researched to see if Grace's mother was telling the truth about the grandmother in Oklahoma.

Hannah took another sip of coffee just as the door opened. Matt stepped outside and sauntered over, taking the seat beside her. "Hey."

Immediately a ray of sunshine pierced the darkness around Hannah's heart. "Hi." Matt rarely came home in the middle of the day, and almost never in the morning. She situated herself so she could see him. "Did you get fired?"

"Nope." His eyes twinkled. He leaned back in the chair and lifted his chin, letting the ocean breeze wash over his face. "I'm home for two reasons."

"One..."

He reached for her hand and wove his fingers between hers. "One, I had something profound to tell you."

She raised her brows, hearing the teasing tone in his voice. "Two?"

The corners of his mouth rose a notch. "Two...I forgot a file I need for a meeting this afternoon."

"I knew there had to be a catch." She dusted her thumb over the palm of his hand. "Okay, what's so profound?"

Matt's expression grew serious. He shifted his weight forward and met her gaze. "We need to talk."

Hannah's stomach tightened. "You sound serious."

"I am." With the fingers of his free hand, Matt traced her cheek. In his eyes she saw love, but something else. Concern, maybe. Or disappointment. "You're doing it again, Hannah."

His words hung together and formed something she didn't recognize. "Doing what?"

"I know you don't mean it—" he rested his forearms on his knees and studied her— "but ever since Grace left..." He met her eyes. "You're angry again. Like you were after Tom and Alicia died."

The hairs on the back of Hannah's neck rose as quickly as her temper. How *dare* he accuse her of being angry! Who did he think he was, telling her how to feel? "I have a right to be mad."

"Okay." Matt leaned back in his chair. "At who?"

"At Mrs. Parsons...at Patsy Landers." Hannah balled her hands into tight fists. "At myself for agreeing to take Grace in the first place. At you for not stopping me. I don't know." She released a loud huff. "I'm just mad! It wasn't right what happened with

Grace. She was our *daughter,* Matt."

Something about the calm in his eyes made Hannah even angrier. She raised her voice, her tone harder than she intended. "That was the profound thing you wanted to tell me?"

"Yes." Matt shrugged. "And that I found something in the Bible today that might help you."

His suggestion felt like a slap in the face. "My faith is fine, thank you."

He studied her as though weighing what he was about to say. "You wasted a year hating Brian Wesley, Hannah. Where did it get you?"

She narrowed her eyes. "Don't throw that at me, Matt. I had a right, and you know it."

"Hey..." He reached for her hand, but she jerked it back. He hesitated, and she knew he was trying to maintain his cool. "You gave up your rights when you agreed to be a Christian, remember? The only real right you have now is to ask God for help in forgiving your enemies. Whoever they are." He softened his tone. "Isn't that what Tom's last words were all about?"

The reminder tightened like a noose around her neck. Frustration multiplied within her, and she hissed her response. "That isn't fair." She stood and glared at him. "I don't need Scripture or a lecture or a reminder about Tom's dying words, okay?"

Matt cocked his head, his expression harder than before. "What do you need, Hannah?"

"I need Grace, okay? And I need you to leave me alone." Before he could say another word, she stormed inside, through the kitchen and upstairs to their bedroom. There she slammed the door and flopped on the bed.

Fifteen minutes passed, and she heard Matt leave. She sat up and watched through the bedroom window as his car pulled away, and regret welled up within her. She balled her hands into fists. Why was she taking it out on Matt? He'd coddled her fragile emotions since Grace left; it wasn't his fault. Hannah exhaled through clenched teeth.

Still she was angry. Even at him.

Matt's words came back to her.

You're doing it again...being angry only hurts you more...

Was it true? Was this the same way she responded four years ago after losing Tom and Alicia? Memories moved across the screen of Hannah's mind. The times when she shut everything from her mind except her desire to see Brian Wesley pay for what he'd done. Times when she asked Matt to stop praying for her, stop mentioning God, stop making references to Scripture.

She had been too angry to hear any of it.

Hannah crossed her legs and dropped her head in her hand. Since Grace left, she'd told herself that she was handling it better than before, especially when it came to her faith.

I still believe in You, God, don't I? I haven't turned my back on You.

There was no response, no whispers of holy assurance...and Hannah realized it had been days since she'd prayed. She stared at the pattern on their bedspread. Maybe she wasn't openly against God like before, but she certainly hadn't gone to Him for help.

Tears spilled onto her ankles, and a mountain of discouragement settled on her shoulders. She hadn't learned a thing about forgiveness. She was right back where she'd started all those years ago, back when she and Tom were kids growing up in the same neighborhood.

Hannah pictured the basketball game when Tom first noticed her problem. A boy from two streets over had beaten her at a game in Tom's driveway. Afterward he turned to her and told her, "You play basketball like a girl."

The comment infuriated her. Years later the same boy was in a class with Tom and Hannah, and she constantly fired rude comments at him.

"What's your problem," the boy shot back at her one afternoon.

Even now Hannah could feel the way her eyes narrowed at the boy. "I play basketball like a girl, remember?"

Tom had witnessed the exchange, and later that day he shoved her playfully in the shoulder. "When you're mad you never let up, do you?"

Hannah remembered feeling somewhat embarrassed, but her ability to hold a grudge came up a handful of times in the years that followed.

Especially the year Tom began dating a girl at Oregon State University while he was playing baseball there. Some of the biting comments Hannah made about the girl were legendary even a decade later. Comments they laughed about, but comments that were wrong all the same.

At least for someone who professed faith in Christ.

Hannah had studied the Scriptures over the years and read verses about mercy being better than judgment and how anyone who judged another would also be judged. She read about forgiving a brother not once or seven times, but seventy times that. And still she struggled.

Of course the ultimate battle was really more of a war, one that had been waged against Brian Wesley, the drunk driver who killed Tom and Alicia. For an entire year Hannah could barely think about anything but her determination to see Brian Wesley punished. In the end it hadn't been a conviction or a Bible verse or anything Matt said that helped her live again.

Rather, it had been Tom's dying words.

She leaned over her legs and dried her cheeks on her jeans. It had been three years since Hannah had looked through Tom's Bible, the place where she kept the letter containing his last message to her. There had been no reason to dig it out during that time. And now…now that there was reason, she wasn't sure she wanted to.

She stared out the opposite window at the still foggy coastline, trying to convince herself she didn't need the painful reminder of Tom's last bit of wisdom to help her let go of Grace. But the more time that passed, the more she knew she was wrong. Hadn't she kept the letter for this very purpose?

She moved from the bed into the hall closet and there, on the top shelf, pushed toward the back wall, was the leather-bound, cracked blue Bible that once had been Tom's daily morning companion. Hannah took it down and stared at it a moment. *Thomas Ryan* was engraved in the lower right corner on the cover. She ran her fingertips over the name and hurt with a sadness that hadn't crossed her heart in months.

Regardless of how happy and in love she was with Matt, a part of her would always miss Tom, the man she'd fallen in love with as a girl, the one she'd fully expected to share her life with. She pushed those thoughts away and carried the Bible back to her bedroom, holding it the way she might hold a bouquet of dried flowers. This time she found a chair and once she was settled, she took a slow breath and opened it to the page, halfway through the book of Proverbs, where the letter lay tucked inside.

Her name was scrawled on the envelope, but it was neither Tom's paper nor his handwriting. He'd spoken those final words to a police officer at the scene of the accident, a man who failed to pass them on for more than a year because he didn't think them logical.

Hannah took it from the envelope and remembered how the flood of emotion had been unleashed in her soul the first time she read it. She opened it, and with eyes blurred by tears, she read it once more.

> Dear Mrs. Ryan,
>
> My name is Sgt. John Miller. I worked the accident scene the day your husband and daughter were killed. I came to your house with the news that day, and later I talked with you at the hospital. You may not remember me, but I remember you. For the past several months I've been thinking about the accident, almost as if God wanted me to remember something.
>
> This morning I remembered what it was. I was with your husband in the minutes before he died, and he wanted me to give you a message. He wanted you to know he loved you and the girls, but there was something else. And that's what I finally remembered this morning. At the time it didn't make sense, and I figured he must have been hallucinating or suffering the effects of blood loss. But now I am convinced that I need to deliver his message to you in its entirety.
>
> Tom told me to tell you to forgive, Mrs. Ryan. He wanted you to forgive.

Even now it was amazing to imagine Tom, trapped in the twisted remains of their car, yet having the wherewithal to know exactly what Hannah needed to hear. *Tell Hannah I love her…and tell her to forgive. Tell her to please forgive.*

But here, now? Did Tom's words apply to this situation also? To the hurt she'd harbored since losing Grace?

Hannah read the letter once more, and one by one the walls around her heart began to collapse. *Tell Hannah to forgive…*

Yes, the words applied as much today as they had three years ago.

She pictured Edna Parsons and Grace's grandmother and even Matt. She'd been angry with all of them and for what reason? Mrs. Parsons hadn't meant to cause them pain; she truly believed Grace's adoption would go through. Otherwise she never would have called in the first place.

Patsy Landers was only doing what *any* grandmother would do in her situation. Certainly if Jenny were jailed and left a baby to the care of the social services system, Hannah would search the country looking to care for that child.

She couldn't be angry at them or unforgiving, not when neither of them was guilty.

And Matt…

Hannah's stomach churned as she folded the letter, placed it back in the envelope, and returned it to its place in Tom's Bible. Then she spent the rest of the day waiting for Matt to come home, praying he'd forgive her.

She went to him the minute he walked through the door. When he saw her, he set his briefcase down in the entryway, and his eyes told her she had nothing to worry about. He forgave her even before she asked. That was the kind of man he was.

"I'm sorry." Hannah took his hands in hers and stood so their toes were touching. Her voice was thick with pain over what she'd done. "I've…I've been awful."

His arms intertwined with hers and he hugged her for a long while. "It's no one's fault, Hannah." His words were a sad whisper, and he pulled back so he could see her face. "Anger is contagious." He lowered his chin, their eyes locked. "When I left here earlier, I felt just like you. Mad at the state, mad at Grace's grandmother." He gave her a sad smile. "Mad at you for being mad at me."

Hannah's insides melted. How could she have been angry at

Matt? When all he'd ever done was try to help her? She bit the inside of her lower lip, then let her mouth hang open for a moment, searching for the words. "I took your advice."

He raised an eyebrow, and she giggled, breaking the tension of the moment. "You…Hannah Bronzan…took *my* advice? Should I call the press?"

She spread her hand on his chest and pushed him with her fingertips. "Stop. I'm serious."

"Okay." His smile faded, but the light in his eyes remained. "What advice?"

"I found Tom's Bible and read the letter, the one from Sgt. Miller."

"With Tom's message, right?" Matt's voice lacked any element of smugness. "About forgiveness?"

"Right." She hung her head for a minute and then looked at him again. "You were right about all of it. There's no one to be mad at, just a—" tears burned at the corners of her eyes—"Just a great big hole where that little girl still lives." She nuzzled her face against his neck. "I miss her so much, Matt."

"I know." He worked his fingers into her back and stroked his hand over her hair. "We all miss her."

Hannah sniffed and a single chuckle came from her throat. "I'm tired of crying all the time."

Matt shifted his head and brought his lips to hers. "I'm tired of it, too."

She kissed him then, savoring the feel of his body against hers. She hadn't felt this alive since the day Grace left. When the kiss ended, Hannah whispered against Matt's cheek. "What are we supposed to do? Where do we go from here?"

Their noses brushed against each other and Matt caught her gaze once more, his face masked in peace. "We take Tom's advice. We forgive and we move on."

"So, you forgive me?"

"Forgiven." Matt kissed her once more and afterward his expression changed. "I had an interesting day."

"Interesting?" Hannah lowered her brow.

Matt grabbed his briefcase, slipped it into the closet, and led the way into the living room. When they were seated side by side on the sofa, he laced his fingers behind his head and exhaled long and slow. "We had a good-bye lunch for one of the guys at the firm."

Confusion roused Hannah's curiosity. "Who's leaving, one of the interns?"

"Not an intern."

Hannah folded her arms. "Okay, I give up. Who?"

Matt settled back into the cushion and angled his head, his eyes locked on hers. "Tanner Eastman. Today was his last day."

Twenty

Grace's smile was missing.

Patsy Landers looked out the back window of her Bartlesville home and realized that was what was different. Outside, Grace sat in the swing, still and alone, staring at the sky. Her expression was wistful, far away. It wasn't that she was sad, exactly. The past three weeks had gone better than Patsy expected. Sure, Grace had cried some and asked about the Bronzans, but that was to be expected. But by all standards—her sleep patterns, her personality, her behavior—she was adjusting.

She just wasn't smiling.

Patsy had enrolled her in preschool, and three days a week a van with cartoon characters painted on the side picked her up at eight and dropped her back at home at three. Grace brought home artwork, sheets of carefully printed letters, and tales of playground antics.

Patsy studied the child through the window once more. It wasn't what she brought home that troubled Patsy.

It was what she didn't bring—the ear-to-ear smile that had always been a part of Grace even when life was at its worst.

"What's wrong, honey?" Patsy would ask. "Is someone making you sad at school?"

Grace would shrug her thin shoulders, barely lifting the corners of her mouth. "No, Grandma. School's fine."

Patsy watched her now as the child shuffled her feet in the dirt beneath the swing. Maybe that was it. Everything was fine, but nothing was good.

A sigh filtered through Patsy's lips as she limped across the floor to the dining room table. They'd gone to the library earlier in the day, and Grace had picked out two Dr. Seuss books. Patsy chose something more practical. She stared at the book on the table and ran her hand over the cover. *101 Things to Do with Your Kids.*

The book was full of activities for parents and their children. If even ten of them brought a spark of life to Grace's disposition, it would be worth the time spent reading. Besides, there was no time like the present to invest in Grace. Patsy hadn't done enough of that with Leslie. And look how she had turned out.

If there was one thing Patsy was determined to do, it was prevent Grace from going the way of her mother. The idea that she had a second chance to raise a little girl, another opportunity to rectify the mistakes she had made, to make up for the things she had missed out on the first time around...it made Patsy's heart swell. And it made losing Leslie almost bearable.

Patsy opened the cover of the book and gazed at the table of contents. *Take an Adventure Walk...Build a Birdhouse...Knit a Scarf...Jump Rope Games...Learn a Song...*

The suggestions seemed endless, and just reading them lightened the load on Patsy's heart. She might be slow with her cane, but she could take an adventure walk if she saved up her energy. And knitting scarves was something she'd done back when Leslie was a small girl. Certainly Grace would have fun doing those things.

If they spent that kind of quality time together, Grace was bound to be happy. And maybe then she'd find something more than good times together.

Maybe she'd find her precious granddaughter's smile, as well.

Twenty-one

Tanner clicked the remote control and a sports program filled the television screen.

"ESPN?" Jade moaned.

"Sports are good medicine."

She giggled. "Okay, but my movie's on in fifteen, deal?"

"Deal."

Tanner wrapped his arms around Jade, savoring the way she snuggled in close to him on the sofa. Her hair smelled like fresh soap. He closed his eyes and rested his cheek against the top of her head. He could have stayed that way forever. Jade cradled against him, Ty asleep upstairs, happy and content and unaware of the impending danger his mother faced.

It was one week until Jade's early due date, the day that would give both her and the baby the best chance at surviving. Since the day he'd walked out of the office for the last time—hours after his talk with Jade in the church that night—Tanner had spent nearly every waking moment at her side.

Briefs and case precedents and troubled files meant nothing to him. Not anymore. Instead his days were filled with everything about her—the way her eyelashes looked when she slept, the sound of her voice over morning coffee, the brush of her skin against his. He'd fallen in love with her all over again, and no matter how much time they spent together, it wasn't enough. Tanner cherished every moment, even the difficult ones.

In the process, something amazing had happened. Jade's speech was still slow, but no longer slurred. And though she shuffled her feet, she got around most of the time without the wheelchair.

"I don't get it," Tanner had told Dr. Layton at Jade's last visit. "What's the difference?"

Jade had smiled at him. "I already told you."

Tanner gave her a skeptical look and then leveled his gaze at the doctor. "Jade thinks it's because I'm around more, but that wouldn't change someone's physical condition. Maybe the tumor's shrinking."

Dr. Layton glanced at Jade's file on his desk and stroked his chin. "It isn't growing, but it isn't shrinking, either." He looked at them. "I think Jade may have a point."

Tanner remembered thinking he hadn't heard the doctor right. "Meaning what?"

"There's a growing body of research showing that love—the physical touch and closeness of someone we care for—has a positive influence on the body's immune system. Some studies say it's more powerful than diet, weight, fitness, and heredity combined."

Jade had smiled at him. "See?" She squeezed his hand. "*You're* why I feel better."

After hearing Dr. Layton's information, Tanner wanted to cry for a week. If his nearness to Jade had helped her improve in so short a time, imagine what it could have done if he'd been there since the beginning, since she was first diagnosed.

The memory faded and Tanner was glad. There was no point beating himself up over what he hadn't done. He was here now and there was no place he'd rather be. Matt called every few days and gave him updates on what was happening at the office. But only updates.

Tanner had made his departure clear to all of them. He was taking an indefinite leave of absence. Whether that would be three months or a year or even two, he had no idea. Until he returned,

Matt was in charge. All questions would go to Matt and occasionally, a few times a week, Matt would call Tanner and keep him posted on the current caseload.

"I want to know what we're taking on," he told Matt after the good-bye lunch. "But stop me if I get specific. Strategies, case precedents, meetings with opposing attorneys. None of it. I need to be completely focused on Jade and Ty."

"You're sure about this?"

Tanner had looked straight at Matt and given him a sad smile. "Right now I'm not sure if Jade will live to see tomorrow. I'm not sure I'll ever see our baby girl, and if I do, I'm not sure she'll survive her first month. I have no idea how Ty and I will go on if we lose Jade, but leaving work?" He patted Matt on the shoulder. "I'm absolutely sure about that."

"Good." Matt's eyes were thoughtful. "It's just what you need. Time together."

Tanner gazed at the ceiling for a moment and shook his head as his eyes found Matt's again. "Why'd it take me so long to see it?"

"Life's like that sometimes." Matt hesitated. "Was this time off...did Jade ask you to do it?"

"Not in so many words." Tanner's eyes grew wet. "She told me she needed me. That she'd take as many minutes as I could give." He blinked back the tears. "In that moment, everything here paled in comparison to spending even one more minute with Jade."

"If I was in your shoes, I'd do the same thing." Matt slipped his hands in his pockets. "Exactly."

"Probably sooner."

Matt grinned. "I wasn't going to mention that, but..."

Tanner reached for a thick file on his desk and handed it to Matt. "I'm giving you the Benson, Colorado, case." He hesitated. "My strategy is outlined in the first document. After that you'll find my interview notes, case precedent research, and copies of the lease contract that started the whole thing."

Matt thumbed through the file and then looked at Tanner again. "This case meant a lot to you."

A lump formed in Tanner's throat as he leveled his gaze at Matt. "Jade means a whole lot more."

Matt held the file up. "I'll give it my best." As he left Tanner's office, Matt pointed heavenward. "I won't be working alone."

Tanner grinned. "I have no doubts."

The memory faded again and ESPN went to a commercial.

"Time for my movie." She batted her eyes, and for a moment Tanner was lost in them. Whether she was sick or not, Jade's eyes were a gorgeous green, green as the water in Chesapeake Bay.

He sighed in mock frustration. "You sure you don't want another half hour of SportsCenter?"

"Positive."

This time he sighed long and hard. "Okay…what's the movie."

She grinned, and for an instant looked like the little girl he'd befriended back in Virginia. "*The Way We Were.* Channel Eight."

He silently mouthed the title. "Chick flick, right? Tearjerker?"

Jade nestled in closer to his side. "Yes, but you'll like it. I promise."

Tanner groaned. "And if you're wrong?" He kissed the top of her head.

"We can watch war movies for a week." She giggled hard at the thought, and the sound was like nourishment for his soul.

How would he survive without the melody of her laugh, the feel of her body against his? He forced the question from his mind. "Okay. Channel Eight it is."

For the next two hours, they watched Barbra Streisand and Robert Redford fall in and out of love until finally, at the end, they went their separate ways. Through the last fifteen minutes, Jade dabbed at an occasional tear and sniffled without being loud. When it was over, Tanner flicked off the television and turned down the light.

"See?" He twirled a lock of her hair between his fingers. "I told you it was sad."

"It reminds me of us. Before we found each other again."

Tanner thought about that, how empty life had been when they'd been tricked into going their separate ways. "Yeah." He danced his fingers down the length of her arm. "But our story..." He stopped himself.

"Our story what?"

He wanted to say their story would have a happy ending, that there would be no final parting for the two of them...but there was no way he could finish that sentence. Not yet, anyway. Not while Jade was fighting for her life. "Nothing. Hey, what should we do tomorrow?"

Jade let the issue pass. Instead, she gazed up at him and traced his lips with a trembling finger. "Have I told you how much I love you, Tanner Eastman?"

Her question made his knees weak, and though he never would have dreamed it possible, the feelings he held for her were stronger than they'd been that summer in Kelso, the summer they first fell in love. Stronger than they'd ever been before. He kissed the tip of her finger. "You don't have to tell me."

"Yes, I do." Her eyes glistened. "I never asked you to walk away from the office, but here you are. The past two weeks I've hardly thought about being sick."

"Good."

"Remember that night at church, when I told you I thought I might die before morning?"

A lump formed in Tanner's stomach. "Too well."

"I never feel like that anymore." She laid her head on his chest and sighed out loud, the same way she did when she eased herself into a hot bath. As though being beside him was the greatest feeling in the world. "It was my fault you kept your distance before. I should have told you how I felt."

"I should have asked."

"It's over; we both learned something." She took his hand and set it on her pregnant belly. "Can you believe she'll be here in a week?"

The lump in Tanner's gut twisted into a knot. "Thirty-two weeks. How early is that?"

She sat up a bit, staring at her swollen abdomen. "It's early, but her lungs should be developed. It could take a month before she can go home, but maybe not. It depends on her weight."

Tanner ran his hand over her stomach and hesitated. As he did, the baby pushed against his palm. "Ohhh. So you're a fighter, little girl." He grinned at Jade and pretended to whisper, "Just like her mother."

A dreamy look filled Jade's expression. "I feel like you're closer to her lately."

"Yeah—" Tanner moved his hand and the baby kicked him again—"Me, too."

They watched the baby moving beneath her maternity shirt and laughed. "She's rowdy tonight."

Tanner's heart was filled with awe. "It's all so amazing. How could anyone question whether God created life?"

"Especially when you know what's happening inside me, how a real person is being knit together. It's the most beautiful miracle of all."

Sorrow streaked the moment. "I wish I'd been there when Ty was born. All the time I missed…it still kills me."

Jade shifted onto her side and wrapped her arms around Tanner's waist. "You've more than made up for it." She hesitated.

"If something happens to me, I know you'd be okay. The three of you."

Tanner's back stiffened. "Don't say that."

"I'm sorry." Jade was quiet. "I just want you to know I trust you, Tanner. You're a wonderful dad. With or without me."

"You aren't going anywhere. God and I already talked about it."

"I know. But just if…if God takes me home, you and the kids will be fine. You're wonderful with Ty and you'll be amazing with our daughter."

"Daughter…" Tanner let the word dangle in the air like a delicate wind chime. "Are we ever going to name her?"

"Last time we talked about it you wanted to wait. At least until we got this far."

"That was before I left work."

"True." She gripped his shirt and clung to him tighter than before. "We weren't talking about a lot of things back then."

"Well…I think it's time." He brushed his thumb along the side of her arm. "What names do you like?"

"The same ones we talked about before, I guess. The names we would have called our last little girl."

Tanner worked the muscles in his jaw. "How old would she be now?"

Jade did not hesitate. "Seven months."

"You always know, don't you?" A pang of guilt struck him and he paused a moment. "I miss her, too. I just…I don't know. What am I supposed to say about her? 'She would have been beautiful? Precious? She still lives in my heart? We'll see her one day in heaven?' Anything I say won't bring her back." He leaned to the side and met Jade's eyes. "You know?"

"I know. But Tanner, do me a favor." Her eyes traveled a path deep into his heart. "When you're feeling those things, say them. It's all right to talk about her."

"Okay." He looked into her soul. "You know what I think?"

"What?"

"I think we should name her, before we name this little girl. So we're not always talking about her like she was only an idea."

Tears filled Jade's eyes as a smile filled her face. "Okay."

"So let's name her."

They thought for a moment and Jade wiped at a single tear. "I have an idea." She tilted her head and her eyes grew cloudy, as though she was remembering something from a long time ago. "Back when I was a girl, after we left Virginia and I thought I'd never see you again, everything about my life was lonely. My mother was gone forever, Dad drank every night, and, well... You know the things he said to me when he was drunk. He forbade me to go out or have friends in, not that I would've brought anyone home." She hesitated. "Know how I survived that time in my life?"

Tanner hadn't heard this part of her story before. "How?"

"I had an imaginary friend." Jade's smile softened. "She would sit with me on the front porch and read with me in my bedroom. I could tell her my secrets and she would laugh at my silly stories. Best of all, she looked just like me."

An understanding dawned in Tanner's mind. "What was her name?"

Jade lowered her chin. "Jenna."

"Jenna..." Tanner let the word play on his tongue for a moment. "I like it. So that's what you want to name her?"

Jade nodded. "Jenna Eastman."

"Our first daughter. The daughter who lives in heaven."

Jade's eyes grew wet again. "Let's not tell anyone about her name. Let's make it our secret, just the two of us." Her words were slower, and Tanner knew she was getting tired.

He looked at her, curious. "Why?"

Jade lifted one shoulder. "I don't know. That way, whenever we're thinking about her or wondering how old she'd be, we can talk about it together. Alone. Besides, when you miscarry, most people don't think of it as losing a child. We're the only ones who miss her."

Tanner's heart swelled. How good God was to give him Jade, this woman who cared so deeply and loved him so much. "Okay. Jenna's our secret."

Jade tapped her fingers on her stomach. "I'm kinda tired. Can we talk about this one tomorrow?"

Tomorrow. A shadow fell over the moment. "You have an appointment at the hospital tomorrow, remember?"

Peace masked Jade's face. Peace and acceptance. "Yes, to check the tumor growth."

Tanner pictured Jade sliding slowly, steadily, through the MRI tube, motionless and pale under the fluorescent hospital lights, her pregnant belly protruding through the hospital sheets, a stark contrast of life in the shadows of death.

"I hate those tests."

"It'll be okay. The tumor hasn't grown; I'd know if it had." Jade's face lit up. "Besides, if we use the waiting time to talk about names, I won't be so nervous."

"Okay." He relaxed some. "Sounds like a plan."

They were quiet a moment; then Jade leaned against him again. "Did you ever love someone so much it hurt?"

Tanner cradled her body against his and closed his eyes. Again he longed to stay that way, holding her, breathing the same air.

"Yes, Jade, I've loved someone that much... Every day; every hour. Every minute."

Twenty-two

Jade and Tanner arrived at the hospital at nine the next morning and were ushered into a private waiting room. Everything about the place was familiar since the facility was adjacent to the children's hospital where Jade had worked these past years.

The test was not particularly grueling—there were no strange liquids to drink or painful positions to maintain—but Jade felt as uneasy about it as Tanner.

Lying on a flat tray, being moved through the white cylinder one inch at a time and then back through it again set her nerves on edge. Only by praying constantly—for Tanner and Ty and their unborn daughter, for Matt and Hannah and Jenny, and anyone else that came to mind—was she able to keep her thoughts from the place where they were tempted to be.

On the fact that her brain was being examined by microscopic rays that would determine the course of her life. And even whether she would live at all.

Ty was staying at his friend's house, which meant Jade and Tanner could spend most of the day at the hospital. In addition to the MRI, Jade was scheduled for an ultrasound and appointments with both Dr. Layton and her obstetrician. The team of doctors was working together to make sure the baby's birth would come at a time when Jade's brain tumor seemed stable.

The day was bound to wear on her, so Jade had allowed Tanner to bring the wheelchair. Before they left the car, they held hands and prayed about the hours ahead. Now that they were in the waiting room, Tanner eased her from the wheelchair onto a vinyl sofa next to him.

She eyed the chair and tried not to hate it. It represented such failure and desperation, such proof of her illness. *It's temporary*, she told herself. Then she turned to Tanner. "Okay, I guess it's time."

"Time?" Tanner's blank expression made her laugh.

She pointed to her belly. "Time to figure out a name for little Miss Eastman here."

A knowing look filled Tanner's eyes and he slipped his arm around her. "Oh, that. Right."

For the next half hour they talked about a dozen different names, but finally they settled on Madison. Jade remembered that she had jokingly promised to name her daughter after Brandy Almond, her teenage patient at the children's hospital. But Brandy would understand. Besides, Madison was the name of Tanner's grandmother, a woman who had been rock-solid in her faith and drove Tanner to church long after his own parents stopped attending. Years after her death, her favorite Scriptures played in Tanner's mind and often helped shape the strength of his views.

"Besides that, she was beautiful."

"Of course." Jade smiled and traced her finger along Tanner's cheekbone. "She was related to you, wasn't she?"

"So, you like it?"

"I like it a lot. I only wish I'd known your grandmother."

Tanner kissed the tip of her nose. "She would have loved you."

Jade leaned her head back and stared at an aquarium in the corner of the waiting room. She pictured heaven and having the chance to meet the elderly Madison Eastman, and Jenna, and Hannah's Tom and Alicia. Calm reigned in her soul, and her heart felt full to bursting. "Sometimes I can't wait to get to heaven." A smile played on her lips. "All of us and Jenna. Together forever…"

Concern flashed in Tanner's eyes. "Don't say that, Jade, please."

"I'm not ready to go today." She eased his face nearer and kissed his cheek. "Sorry."

She could feel the muscles in Tanner's arms relax. "It'll be great—in another sixty years or so."

Jade smiled. "Madison what? What's her middle name?"

"Well…" Tanner's eyes twinkled. "Let's make her middle name after this woman I know who loves God and would go any distance to take a stand for her beliefs. If I could only remember her name…" He stroked his chin and stared at the ceiling as though he were trying to conjure up the woman's memory. "Hmmm. She's gorgeous beyond words, dark hair and eyes as green as Chesapeake Bay…"

Jade rolled her eyes and giggled. "Gorgeous?"

A mock indignation filled Tanner's expression and he flashed her a sharp look. "Absolutely!" He returned his gaze to the ceiling and then suddenly snapped his fingers and stared at her. "I remember, now. Jade. Her name is Jade Eastman."

She laughed harder. "You're crazy."

Tanner pointed at himself and mouthed the word, "Me?"

"Yes, you." Her laughter faded. "Come on, Tanner. I'm serious. She needs a middle name."

"I *am* serious." He took her hands in his and studied her eyes. When he spoke again, his voice was softer, more serious. "Madison Jade Eastman. I love it."

Lately it seemed Jade was constantly discovering new depths to the love she and Tanner had for each other. This was one of those times. "You really mean it?"

"Yes." He leaned in and kissed her lips, in a way that took her breath. He drew back only an inch or so, his whispered voice racked with sincerity. "Please."

Jade blinked back tears, and a sound that was more laugh than sob came from her throat. Tanner was right. The names sounded beautiful together. And there was something neither of them was saying. Jade's name would live on, even if somehow the cancer…

She squeezed her eyes shut and let her head drop for a moment. She wouldn't think that way, not now. Not when their baby was about to be born. She had to believe there was life ahead for them. For both of them. When she looked up, she found Tanner's eyes again and smiled. "I like it."

He kissed her, and his face lit up. "It's perfect."

They were talking about nicknames for Madison when the technician entered the room and motioned for them to follow. As Tanner was helping her into the wheelchair, Jade had an idea.

"Don't I have an hour between tests?"

Tanner glanced at his watch as he eased her into the chair. "You do."

"Let's go see Brandy."

"Who?" Tanner was behind her now, easing the chair through the doorway and following the technician down a long hallway.

"Brandy Almond, the high school track star with leukemia. Actually she should be home by now, but I want to try, just in case she's here. Besides, I'd like to see the nurses. It's been a while."

Tanner nodded. "It's a plan."

The test was tiring but uneventful. When it was over and Jade was back in the wheelchair, the technician found them in the waiting room. She handed them a folder. "I'm not supposed to give you results," she said, grinning at Jade. "But you're a nurse."

Jade waited, her heart in her throat.

The technician continued. "I compared these results with the last ones, and there hasn't been any growth. If anything, the tumor's smaller than before." She winked at the two of them. "But you didn't hear that from me."

The woman left, and the moment she was gone, Tanner took

hold of Jade's shoulders and lowered his face next to hers. "I *knew* God would get you through this."

Jade reached up and took hold of his hands. She closed her eyes and a single happy sob came from somewhere deep within her. "Thank you, Jesus. Thank you."

Their moods were higher than they'd been in months as they followed a long corridor into the adjoining children's hospital and made their way to the cancer ward. At the front desk, Jade's former coworkers fussed over her and agreed that she was looking wonderful.

They talked about the department and the victories that had taken place in the time since she'd been gone. Finally everyone drifted back to her work except Linda, the head nurse. She looked from Jade to Tanner then back again. "So what do the tests show?"

Jade's heart soared. "I get the results later today." It was wonderful to have hope again. "But it looks good. I'm going to make it, Linda. I really think so."

Linda brought her hands together and lowered her voice. "We're praying for you Jade. All of us."

Jade reached for Linda's hand and squeezed it. "Thanks."

Linda was a new believer, one of the many people Jade knew who became a Christian after terrorists attacked the United States a year earlier. Across the country, in the aftermath of that tragedy, there were barely enough seats in churches for all the people looking for answers, looking for peace and hope and stability in a world gone mad.

And many of them had found the answers they needed in the One who so clearly was watching over Jade and her baby. Without saying a word, Jade raised her hand and, from where he stood behind her wheelchair, Tanner took hold of it.

It was time to find Brandy.

Jade gazed down the familiar blue-carpeted hallway, which

led to a dozen hospital rooms...places where Jade had administered medicine and held the hands of crying children and parents. Places where children had been healed.

Places where they had died.

She looked back at Linda. "I came to see Brandy." She smiled, anxious for the visit. "Tell me she's gone home."

Linda's smile faded. "Oh, Jade..." Tears welled in her eyes and her chin quivered. For a moment the woman couldn't seem to speak. "You didn't hear."

"Hear what?" Alarms sounded in the sanctuary of Jade's soul. What had happened? Was she sicker? Had she slipped out of remission? Whatever it was, there was still hope. Jade and Tanner would spend the hour at her side, cheering her up and praying with her. But even as those thoughts flitted through her mind, the next question stuck in Jade's throat.

"Last time I was here she looked great." Jade's voice sounded hollow. From behind her, Tanner tightened his hold on her hand. "She was...she was in remission. I kind of hoped she might be back at school by now."

Linda shook her head. "I'm sorry, Jade. I know she was special to you." The woman moved closer to the wheelchair and placed her hand on Jade's shoulder, the way nurses do when they're about to deliver bad news.

Jade's head began to spin, and she had the urge to leap from the wheelchair and run out of the building. What had Linda said? Had she used the dreaded past tense? *I'm sorry, Jade...I know she* was *special to you...*

No! Jade wanted to scream. *Not Brandy. Not when she was doing so well. This was her year, the year she was going to run again and win the track meet. Please, God, no.*

Tanner must have known how she was feeling, that she could hardly breathe, let alone speak. He cleared his throat and voiced the very thing Jade wanted to ask. "Is she sick again?"

Two tears spilled onto Linda's cheeks and she brought her hand to her mouth. "A week after your visit, Brandy got pneumonia." Linda looked from Tanner to Jade. "She was very sick. A week later…the leukemia came back full force." The woman paused. "She never recovered, Jade. We lost her three weeks ago."

Three weeks ago?

How come no one had called her? Jade's heart ached. She would have wanted to be at the funeral. At least then she could have comforted Brandy's parents or known the peace of telling Brandy's friends that she was in heaven with Jesus. That somewhere Brandy Almond was running again, her long beautiful hair blowing in the breeze of heaven's wind. Running faster and freer than at any other time in her life.

Anger mingled with excruciating feelings of loss, and Jade forced herself to speak. "How come…no one told me?"

Linda's gaze fell to the ground for a moment before finding Jade's once more. "We didn't want to upset you." Linda released the hold she had on Jade's shoulder and folded her arms. "We figured you had enough to deal with."

"Well…" Jade's heart pounded in her throat. "I appreciate that. But you figured wrong." She splayed her fingers against her chest. "I loved that girl…very much."

"I'm sorry." Linda shook her head and wiped at another tear. "We didn't know what to do."

Jade hung her head, and Tanner squeezed her hand, silently assuring her that he shared her grief. Every bit of it. Tears flooded Jade's eyes and spilled onto her stretch pants. She wanted to fall to the floor, crawl to Brandy's room, and climb up in her bed. She wanted to weep and wail and demand that God tell her why. Why He would take one so young and precious and new in her faith, one who would have had such an impact on her friends if she'd lived.

Jade lifted her head and noticed that it took most of her strength. *God, get me through this…*

I am your refuge and your strength, an ever-present help in times of trouble…

The Scripture from Psalms worked its way through her being and she drew a steadying breath. When she lifted her head, she looked at Linda and nodded twice. "It's not your fault. You did what you thought was best."

Linda squirmed, clearly anxious to get back to work. "Her friend—the one who told her about God—comes in once in a while and brings toys for the sick kids. I could give her your number if you want."

Jade managed a smile. "I'd like that. Thanks." She tightened her grip on Tanner's hand. "I have an appointment next door in a few minutes. Tell everyone I said good-bye."

They were halfway down the corridor toward the other building when Tanner pushed her into a quiet waiting area where they could be alone. He came around the front of her chair, knelt by her feet, and hugged her knees to his chest. "I'm sorry, Jade."

Tears, hot and steady, streamed down Jade's face. Yes, death was a reality, especially in a children's cancer ward. Illness was always a threat when a person's immune system was unstable. But Brandy had looked so good the last time they were together…

Jade squeezed her eyes shut and took quick breaths through her nose, trying to slow the sobs that sought to overtake her. "I can't…believe…she's gone."

Tanner laid his head in her lap and clung to her. "She's with Jesus; we both know that."

A thread of terror stitched its way across Jade's heart. "Is that what people will say about me a month from now? 'She's with Jesus?'"

Tanner lifted his head and stared at her, his eyes stark with pain and fear. "Don't say that! What happened to Brandy has nothing to do with you."

She sniffed and grabbed two more quick breaths. She didn't want to attract attention so she kept her tone low. "You...you say that, but actually it does." She tossed her hands in the air. "We get a good report so we think, great, maybe I'm going to get through this thing. But the truth is cancer can turn on you like that." She snapped her fingers. "One week you can be heading toward your senior year in high school, hoping to break a state record in track and field, and the next week you're gone."

Tanner studied her, his eyes helpless and desperate. "Just because Brandy lost her battle doesn't mean you'll lose yours. You can't think that way." He leaned in closer to her. "I need you, Jade."

"I know." She released another series of quiet sobs. "I'm sorry. I'll get a grip." She looked at her watch. "We need to go."

The rest of the day was filled with nothing but positive reports. The baby was perfect, healthy and big enough for the scheduled C-section next week. Dr. Layton examined the results from the MRI and confirmed the technician's assessment. The tumor had stopped growing and perhaps had even shrunk some.

They left with plans for Jade to see her obstetrician once more that week. If everything looked fine, he would do a C-section on Jade Monday, October 7.

It was an evening when Jade should have been walking on air, convinced that God was working miracles both in her body and that of her baby. Instead, she and Tanner spent the evening at Ty's football game, huddled together despite the fact that temperatures were still in the high eighties.

There were no words. When it came to feeling optimistic about cancer, Brandy's death had said it all.

Twenty-three

The sound of screeching tires out in front of Los Robles Medical Center snapped Hannah to attention and brought her to her feet. She searched for the admitting clerk. "Tina! Quick!"

The tall, graying woman hurried around the corner, back to her spot behind the counter. "Patient?"

"Yes." Hannah pointed outside. "Look."

It had been a slow morning, the type that made Hannah wonder if they really needed her volunteer services. Lately she'd been thinking about helping at the children's hospital instead, in the ward where Jade used to work.

Either way, at least she was back in a regular schedule. Reading the note from Tom's Bible and talking to Matt that evening had helped her hear God's voice in her life once more. Despite the pain of losing Grace, Hannah could feel His merciful hand of healing upon her broken heart. They would survive, even if no other children came their way.

Hannah was convinced of that much.

Now she and Tina stared out the double glass doors as a beat-up Lincoln lurched to a stop in front of the emergency room entrance. The driver's door inched open, and a rail-thin woman spilled out, struggling to stay on her feet. She was holding something, a rag or a blanket. Hannah couldn't quite—

Something moved, and Hannah gasped. "Dear God..." There was a baby in the woman's arms, an infant no more than a few months old. "Tina, call someone!"

Tina didn't wait. She shouted over her shoulder, her eyes still on the woman and baby outdoors. "We need a doctor outside. *Stat!*"

Down the hallway, a doctor and two interns dropped the charts they were working on, grabbed a wheelchair, and ran through the waiting room toward the woman outside. One of them took the baby; the other two helped the woman into the chair. Hannah couldn't hear the doctors, but their expressions were dark and troubled. They raced the woman through the double doors and back into one of the rooms. Tina followed, and Hannah knew she needed to make a chart on the woman.

On his way past, the third doctor handed the baby to Hannah. "Can you hold him? I'll check his vitals in a minute, but he looks okay."

Hannah cradled the baby against her chest and looked at the doctor. "What happened?"

The doctor's mouth formed a straight line and his eyes narrowed. "Drugs." He spat the word as though it tasted bad. "The woman can barely breathe."

A gust of anger blew against Hannah's soul. *Barely breathing?* She let her eyes fall to the woman's baby, snuggled in her arms. He was dressed in a tattered blue sleeper and he was wet through his blanket.

Barely breathing? How dare that woman drive in that condition, drugged and half-dead? What if she'd killed this precious child? Or hit someone else—a family, or a father and his daughters coming home from a fishing trip? The baby wasn't crying, but he was waving his hands and working his mouth.

"There, baby." Hannah kissed the infant's forehead. "It's okay, honey; I'll take care of you."

She clenched her teeth and stared down the hallway toward the room where the woman was being worked on. Holding the baby close to her chest, Hannah walked to the nurses station and nodded to a supply of diapers behind the counter. "He needs changing and a fresh blanket."

An older woman sat behind the desk. "Poor little tyke. I sure hope his mama makes it."

Hannah ignored the comment. People who drove drunk or drugged didn't deserve children. They deserved jail. Even when she was feeling compassionate and forgiving, even in light of Tom's dying words, that much was true. "Call up to labor and delivery and see if they'll bring me a few bottles of formula, will you?"

"Sure."

Hannah took the diaper and found a gurney just outside the drugged woman's room. While she changed the baby's diaper, the woman began thrashing about the bed, screaming and flailing at the doctors around her. "Stop it! You're killing me! Where's my baby?"

A nurse came up beside her and gave her a shot of something, and in less than a minute, the woman calmed down. Doctors took her pulse and checked her heart, rattling off numbers as they worked. "Ma'am, what did you take this morning?"

Hannah wrapped the baby in the clean blanket and held him against her heart. Then she positioned herself so she could see the woman. Hannah's stomach turned at the way the woman's bones stuck out, as though they were trying to break free from her skin. Hannah had never seen anyone so thin.

"I...didn't take nothin' until...until after the baby was b-b-born." She was shaking now, her limbs lurching beneath the sheets. "Don't let me d-d-die...I didn't mean to do it. Please! Don't let me die."

A doctor moved, and Hannah got a better look at the woman's face. What she saw made her breath catch in her throat. It wasn't a woman at all, but a girl. A young girl no more than sixteen, seventeen years old. She was so frail and damaged by whatever drugs she'd been taking that her posture, her eyes looked forty years old. But there was no mistaking the youthful skin and hair.

The doctor leaned over her and yelled near her face. "Ma'am, we need to know what you took! Tell us what you took this morning." The girl's eyes were still open, but she didn't respond. Gradually her legs and arms lay still.

"We've lost her pulse!" A doctor on the other side of the bed tore back the sheet and began performing CPR.

Hannah's eyes filled, and the infant in her arms began to squirm and cry. Soundlessly Hannah swayed the baby back and forth and cuddled her face against his.

Meanwhile, another doctor slapped paddles on the girl's chest and gave a signal. Her body convulsed grotesquely up and off the bed and then settled back down in what looked like a heap of brittle bones. "It's not working!" The doctor's voice was grim. "Again!"

Hannah's heart raced and she shook her head, backing away from the room with quick steps. The baby's mother was dying before her eyes. She had to get out of there before she was sick to her stomach. She hurried to the nurses station, and the woman behind the desk handed Hannah a bottle. "Poor little guy," the woman whispered.

There was nothing Hannah could say. She took the bottle, carried the baby down the hall into a private examination room, and closed the door. In the quiet of the small room, for the first time, Hannah studied the baby's face. He was beautiful. Big blue eyes, and lips that formed a perfect rosebud mouth. He sucked his fingers, hungry and threatening to cry again.

"There, baby, it's okay." Hannah put the bottle near his mouth and he found it, latching on with practiced skill. "You're all right, honey. You're safe now."

He stretched his baby hand out and Hannah placed her finger against one of his palms. With a strength that took her by surprise, the baby gripped her finger and held on.

In all her days volunteering at the hospital, she'd never done this, never held a baby while his mother clung to life in the next room. Her pulse quickened, her thoughts anxious and scattered. *How should I pray for him, God? He made it here safe this time, but if his mother lives…*

Hannah knew only too well the risks the baby would face if his mother took drugs and drove with him again.

Be still, and know that I am God.…

The verse filled her heart, and she realized she'd been holding her breath. She breathed out and kissed the baby's velvety cheek. *Be still, and know that I am God.*

It was the Scripture Jade had given Tanner for their first anniversary. Hannah had been with her when they picked it out. "When life gets tough," Jade had said, "that verse is a hiding place."

It was always true at the CPRR law firm, and it was true now. Hannah brought the baby's face against hers again and prayed for his mother. She prayed the girl would live and find help in recovering from her drug problems. And she prayed the girl would never again drive intoxicated.

Then she placed her hand on the baby's head, his finger still gripping hers. *Sweet baby, if only I could protect you from everything happening down the hall.* Hannah took a slow breath, her heart breaking for the child in her arms. "Jesus, I bring You this little one, this nameless boy who You created, and I ask You to bless him. Make his home a safe one and let his mother love him all the days of her life. Let him know the touch of a father's hand and the peace of Your salvation. And bless him to be the young man You would have him be. Keep your Spirit on him, Lord…" Hannah hesitated. "Even now, when his future seems so uncertain. In Jesus' name, amen."

It was the same type of blessing she had prayed over Jenny and Alicia when they were born.

The baby's eyes had grown heavy, and his milk was almost gone. When he stopped sucking, Hannah set the bottle on the floor. Then in a way that felt as familiar as it had eighteen years ago with her own children, she held the baby up against her shoulder and patted his back, cooing at him the whole time. "It's okay, sweetie, Jesus loves you. It's okay."

When she was sure he had no air bubbles in his tummy, Hannah cradled him again. The chair she sat in was rigid and hard, but she rocked him gently, singing songs she'd sung to her own babies.

Including Grace's favorite.

"Jesus loves you! This I know, for the Bible tells me so. Little ones to Him belong; they are weak but He is strong." Hannah nuzzled her face against his, her voice soft and low. "Yes, Jesus loves you... Yes, Jesus loves you... Yes, Jesus loves you.... the Bible tells me so."

He fell asleep in her arms, but still she sang, studying him, mesmerized by his beauty. After nearly an hour there was a knock at the door. She answered as quietly as she could so the baby wouldn't wake. "Come in."

It was one of the doctors who'd been working on the baby's mother. He stepped inside and closed the door behind him. Then he studied the baby with heavy eyes. As he did, he breathed out, discouragement written across his face. "There was nothing we could do."

Fresh tears stung Hannah's eyes and her heart filled with a sudden, overwhelming sense of protection for the infant. "She's dead?"

The doctor nodded. "Traced her to a women's shelter. Seventeen-year-old runaway, clean her entire pregnancy. Got hooked up with one wrong guy and overdosed in a single hour." He ran his thumb over the baby's forehead. "It's a miracle they got here alive. The baby rode in on his mother's lap." He lifted his eyes to Hannah's. "If she'd had even a fender bender he could have been killed."

Hannah's throat was thick with sadness. She stared at the baby, ignoring the tears that fell on his blanket. "What happens now?"

"Police will be here any minute. They'll take the baby to a short-term foster home until Social Services can determine the next of kin."

Hannah nodded and swallowed hard so she could speak. "Poor baby."

And poor family who would care for him over the next few weeks. She couldn't imagine having this precious boy for even a day and then letting him go. Even now, after their short hour together, there was no question about it. Hannah had bonded with him. It made sense. In his mother's dying hour, Hannah had been the one to love him, feed him. Pray for him. Of course she was connected to the baby.

The doctor studied him once more. "He looks like an angel."

Hannah nodded and smiled through her tears. "I hope he gets to live like one."

Edna Parsons got the call just after noon that a healthy baby boy needed short-term foster care. Her job was to find next of kin—a task she took far more seriously since the incident with the Bronzans. If there was a grandparent or aunt or uncle or father somewhere in the world capable of raising the child, Edna would find out.

She met the police at the house where the baby would live for the next few days. Once he was safely placed, Edna visited St. Anne's Shelter, where the baby's mother had been living until her drug overdose.

Edna met with a pleasant woman who ran the shelter. There were Scripture verses stuck to various places on her office wall.

"Milly Wheeler was the mother's name." The woman bit her lip and brushed at the corners of her eyes. "She was seventeen, a runaway."

"I see." Edna scribbled the details on her notepad.

"We do drug testing here." The woman lifted one shoulder. "Milly was clean through her pregnancy. She attended Bible studies twice a day." The woman's voice caught. "I…I really thought she was going to make it."

The woman explained that in the course of their Bible studies, Milly had shared much about her life and background.

"I've got it all right here." The woman handed a folder to Edna. "It's Milly's file."

Edna opened it and the story began to unfold. Milly's mother was a drug addict, a street person in San Francisco, who died three years ago from an overdose. At first Milly tried to live on her own, scrounging food from other street people and digging through trash bins behind restaurants when all else failed.

"She was determined not to follow her mother's footsteps, to stay away from drugs." The woman frowned. "She kept that determination until she turned fifteen."

At that point, Milly apparently assessed her options and decided there was only one way she could make enough money to survive: prostitution.

"The trouble was, with every trick she turned, Milly saw another piece of her soul fade away." The woman crossed her arms. "Finally she could only describe herself as dead. Breathing, moving, existing...but dead all the same."

Edna glanced at the notations in the file. "And that's when she took her first hit of speed."

"Right."

Edna shook her head, her heart heavy for the girl whose story was so familiar, so like that of dozens of girls she'd worked with or taken children from over the years. Drugs were a wicked, evil prison, and once a person willingly walked through the doors, there was seldom any easy way out. "And then...?" Edna scanned the file once more.

"She stayed in San Francisco, turning tricks and taking speed until she got pregnant. The minute she knew for sure, she took a bus to Los Angeles and came here. Her withdrawals were so bad we thought she'd lose the baby. But we got her help and she never took another hit." The woman paused. "Until last night, I guess."

"Yes. She had enough crack in her blood to kill a horse."

Edna closed Milly's file. Across from her, the woman's eyes grew wet again. "She wanted her baby to be a preacher or a writer, someone who would help people be strong in God." She lifted her hands off the desk and let them fall again. "I don't know what happened. She didn't come home last night. I guess she went with one of the guys who hang around here. Even with her faith, Milly was very lonely."

"So you think the baby's clean?"

The woman nodded. "Definitely. Milly was clean through her pregnancy right up until two days ago. Clean and determined to give her baby a life different from that of hers and her mother's."

Edna made several notations on her clipboard. "What about the father?"

"Milly was a prostitute, Mrs. Parsons. The baby's father lived in San Francisco and could be any one of a hundred different men."

"What about AIDS?"

"She tested negative for HIV. Almost a miracle really, coming from San Francisco."

Edna had all the information she needed. She'd still run a name check in the San Francisco area, but Milly's story—the way she'd told it to the people at the shelter, anyway—seemed very plausible.

The women stood and shook hands. Before she left, Edna hesitated. "Is there any way we can prove that her mother's really dead?"

The woman reached for Milly's file once more and thumbed through it. Seconds later she handed Edna a photograph. "This is pretty good proof if you ask me."

Edna took it. "You're right." It was a picture of a small gravestone carved with the name Henrietta Mae Wheeler. The dates of birth and death made the buried woman the right age to be Milly's mother.

The photo was worn on the edges and peeling at the corner. Edna gave it back to the woman, her heart heavy for the tragedy young Milly had suffered. "Why would she keep a photo like this?"

"As a reminder to stay away from drugs." The woman reached for a tissue and held it beneath her right eye. "She didn't want to leave her baby orphaned, the way her mother left her."

If nothing showed up on the name check, Milly's baby boy would be a ward of the court, legally free for adoption. Suddenly a flashlight of hope shone on the day's dismal events. "Do you mind if I take Milly's file?"

"Not at all." The woman handed it to Edna. "Is Kody okay?"

"Kody?" Edna's heart beat faster as a plan took shape.

"Kody Matthew. That's what Milly named him."

Kody *Matthew*? Edna nodded. The irony was almost too

much. "Kody's fine. He's a beautiful baby."

The woman nodded. "I hope you find him a good home."

"Yes." Edna smiled and realized it was the first time she'd done so since hearing about Milly's death. "I think I know just the place for him."

Twenty-four

Leslie Landers hated prison.

A door slammed in the cell next to hers, and the sound echoed through the unit. There was no way to escape the stench of body odor and bacon grease that filled the air. Leslie huffed in disgust. Even her senses were behind bars.

In prison, every single sound echoed. Every scream and cry and loud burst of laughter. Every slamming door and slamming fist. Twenty-four-seven, the place was a madhouse of animalistic behavior, loud voices, and violent actions. A place where the outside world all but ceased to exist.

Prison proved that at least one thing her mother said was true. Hell was real. No question about it, because she was now a resident. Wore her residency numbers on the pocket of her shirt.

But at least her residency was temporary.

None of this lifer stuff for Leslie, no sir. Not like the women on either side of her, women who had killed parents or husbands or strangers and didn't mind saying so. Leslie was different from them. She would bide her time, put in her hours and days and weeks, and one day—before a year was up, if her attorney was right—she'd walk out of here and never go back again.

Even if it meant dying instead.

The minute she was out, she knew just what she'd do. She'd take the pittance of money they give to parolees and buy a bus ticket to Bartlesville, Oklahoma. Then she would take Grace, and this time the two of them would disappear for good.

Leslie grabbed hold of two bars and pressed her nose in the

space between. She'd never been claustrophobic before, but now… There were times when the urge to break free of her cell was so strong she thought she could bend the bars in two. Times when she tried, even. But never when the guards were looking.

Good behavior was the only way she'd get out again, the only way she'd save Grace from a lifetime of preaching and Bible verses and suffocating control by Leslie's mother.

Leslie remembered hearing from her attorney that Grace's adoption had fallen through. She spun around and threw herself on her bunk. Good thing. Strangers shouldn't be raising her kid.

Still, Leslie had been confused until the attorney mentioned her mother. "Apparently Social Services thought your mother was dead." Her attorney shrugged. "Once they found out about her existence and her desire to adopt Grace, they pulled her from the foster-adopt home immediately."

There was no information about which foster home or who was going to adopt Grace before her mother intervened. Not that it mattered. Those people were out of the picture. And now that Grace was in Bartlesville, she'd be easy to find. Probably being spoiled rotten, poisoned with lies about the mistakes her terrible mother had made.

The whole situation made Leslie want to puke. Grace was already spoiled enough. Imagine what living with her mother for a year would do to her?

No, Leslie couldn't let Grace stay in Bartlesville. That wasn't the type of life she should have. She wasn't a Bible kid, a Christian kid. Grace was *her* kid. Leslie Landers's kid. And that meant that, yes, sometimes she'd have to hang around while Leslie made a little money in the sack. And sometimes the kid would have to sit loose while Leslie partied with the guys in Santa Maria, guys who would want to see her when she returned.

But that was no reason to take Grace away and put her up for adoption. The street life that Leslie could give Grace was a good thing. It toughened kids, made them wise to the world and ready for whatever the future held.

Whatever Grace's future held, it didn't involve Leslie's mother or some family of strangers taking over as Grace's parents. Leslie was doing just fine, thank you. The problem was, they needed more money. Which meant Grace needed to pull her weight.

The idea hadn't occurred to her until that last night, the night the cops busted her. The guy she'd been with that night roughed her up pretty good, and in the process he knelt on the seat and spotted Grace on the floor.

She could still hear his words, still feel the way they spawned the idea that just might save them. "You didn't tell me you had a little beauty hiding in the back."

Leslie had been angry with the man. Angry and high. At first she didn't understand what he meant. Before they could talk about it, the police showed up. And only in the days since she'd been in prison had she considered exactly what he was saying. Grace *was* pretty. Pretty enough that if their money started running low, Leslie could put her to work. Films or short projects. Whatever. Nothing dangerous, just something to help them survive.

Besides, it was time Grace made herself useful. Leslie had catered to her long enough, busting her own tail to make sure their cooler was full of milk and cookies and sometimes bananas. It was only fair. Grace needed to make money, too.

And if they worked together, maybe…just maybe, they'd find a way to survive. Then they could set up an apartment somewhere and go about the business of living. Of course, Leslie shared none of this with her attorney. But she did tell him one of her intentions.

"I want Grace back. The minute I'm out of here."

The attorney, an older man who worked for the state, looked

concerned by Leslie's request. "It's possible. With good behavior and a series of letters, maybe."

"Letters?"

"To your mother, sent to my office. I'll make copies and send them on. That's the only way you'll be able to prove how much you miss your daughter."

Leslie wasn't excited about the idea of writing letters, but if that's what it took, she would do it. Her mother probably loved the fact that she had Grace now. Probably figured she was being given another chance at raising a child, since she'd blown it so completely with Leslie.

She grabbed a piece of paper from a pile beneath her bunk. Her mother had been a terrible excuse for a parent. Busy all the time and spewing Bible verses as though they might make up for the lack of time they had together.

Leslie gritted her teeth and stared at the blank sheet of paper. No wonder she'd turned to drugs. At least those friends wanted to spend time with her. She grabbed a pencil from beneath her foam mattress and began to write.

> Dear Mother,
>
> Things are going good here. My attorney says I will be out in less than a year. At that time I will come to Bartlesville and take over custody of Grace. I know you think she belongs with you, but my attorney says that isn't true. She's my daughter; I can raise her.

Leslie tapped the pencil on the paper and thought about what else to say. She put her pencil to the paper again.

> Please let Grace know about my choice. I'll be out very soon.

Leslie hesitated for a minute and smiled, her heart pinched with hate.

Besides, I've thought of a way we can make enough money to survive. I know we'll never go hungry. Kiss her for me. Leslie.

Twenty-five

The moment had finally arrived, and Jade was neither anxious nor afraid.

A strong Santa Ana wind rattled through the canyons, and before daybreak, Jade and Tanner gathered in Ty's bedroom and prayed. Jenny Bronzan was meeting them at the hospital, where she would spend the day hanging out with Ty.

Jade settled on the edge of Ty's bed and watched him slip a sweatshirt over his head. "Now remember, the whole time you're having little Maddie—" Ty's voice was muffled until his head poked through the hole—"I'll be praying for you. The whole time."

"Okay." A surreal calm had come over Jade days ago and now, on October 7, it was still in place. "I'll remember."

"And the minute she's born, you'll tell her what I told you, right?"

Jade stared up at the ceiling and rattled off the words she'd long since memorized. "'Welcome to our family, Maddie. You have the best big brother in the world.'"

"Yes!" Ty pumped his fist. "I can't *wait* to be a big brother."

Tanner poked Ty in the ribs and gave him a partial grin. "It won't happen unless we take this show down to the hospital."

The three of them formed a circle, Jade still sitting on the bed. Tanner drew a steadying breath and began to speak. "Lord, this is it, the day we've been waiting for. Father, You know all things, even down to the timing of Madison's birth." He paused, and Jade could hear the concern in his voice. "Please, God, keep Your hand on Jade and Maddie. Help them come through the operation healthy and strong, and please, Lord, bring them both home soon. We trust You...we thank You ahead of time."

The sun was just peeking over the horizon as they gathered Jade's things and loaded the car. They needed to be at the hospital by seven o'clock, and Jade knew Tanner didn't want to be late. In the myriad of emotions they'd experienced in the months since Jade's diagnosis, they'd done a role reversal once again.

There was no question that, at first, the news of Brandy's death set Jade back, set her and Tanner both back. But after a few days of deep prayer, times when only clinging to Scriptures pulled her through, she had somehow emerged clothed in peace.

Tanner was the anxious one now, but this time he shared his feelings with her. Even last night, hours before they would leave for the hospital, he admitted the depth of his fear.

They'd been in bed, and Jade was quiet, praying silently as she fell asleep. Next to her, Tanner was a study in motion. He tossed and turned from his left side to his right and back again. Finally, Jade leaned up on one elbow and whispered in his direction. "What's wrong, Tanner? Talk to me."

He rolled onto his back and an anxious sigh slipped through his lips. "I'm sorry, Jade. I didn't mean to keep you up."

She laid her head down on his bare chest. "Talk to me. What's on your heart?"

For the first time in an hour, Tanner was still. He pounded his fist into the mattress between them and groaned. "I want to grab the alarm clock and smash it against the wall. Every time the hands move, I feel that much closer to tomorrow."

Jade touched his face. "Is that a bad thing?" She was careful not to sound condescending or unnaturally optimistic. "Our baby's going to be born tomorrow."

"But there are risks, Jade. You and I both know it." His body relaxed beside her. "Assuming you get through the delivery okay, there's the baby to worry about. She's still so small."

"I know."

"And then we'll have maybe a day before they assault your body with the worst kind of chemicals known to man. The thought of it kills me, Jade. It kills me."

She leaned over and kissed him, silencing his fears and smoothing her thumb along his eyebrows. "You're beautiful, do you know that?"

"What if..." His whispered voice was choked with concern. "What if something happens?" He hesitated, searching her face. "I couldn't live without you."

She prayed for the right words. "Remember a long time ago in Kelso, when I didn't think God would ever love me, didn't feel I belonged in a church? Remember the Scripture you gave me back then?"

The anxiety in Tanner's expression eased some. "Yes."

"'"I know the plans I have for you," declares the Lord, "plans to prosper you and not to harm you, plans to give you hope and a future."'"

"Right."

She searched his eyes. "Believe it, Tanner. Believe it now just like you believed it then. God has a plan for us. For me and little Madison and you and Ty. His plans are perfect." She kissed him again. "You don't have to be afraid."

A single tear slid down his face and he nodded, easing her head back down to his chest. "Don't leave me, Jade."

"Never, Tanner. Never ever."

After that they slept...but now that they were driving to the hospital, Jade could see the tension in the flex of her husband's jaw, feel it in his lack of conversation. He believed, of course. God had brought them back together, after all. But they both knew there were no guarantees that this time God's plans would be the ones they hoped for.

They met Jenny at the hospital, and she produced a bag holding milk and a muffin for Ty. "Looks like we get a day together, huh?"

Ty nodded. He wasn't as chipper as he'd been earlier that morning—probably because of the tension he sensed from Tanner—but so far he hadn't cried, and Jade was glad. Glad that he'd been busy in this season of her illness, glad that he didn't fully comprehend the risks or the hard road that lay ahead.

Jade was in her wheelchair, but she hugged Jenny around her waist. "Thanks for being here."

Jenny gave a half smile and squeezed her hand. "Mom and Matt will be here later. Before the baby's born."

"I can't believe it's already time."

"Mrs. Eastman—" Jenny met her gaze, and Jade saw that the girl's eyes were wet—"We're all praying for you. All of us."

"I know." Jade pulled away and reached up for Tanner's hand. "We feel it."

They followed Jade to a private room where she could wait with them until it was time for the delivery. Tanner would stay with Jade in the operating room, but Ty and Jenny would have to wait down the hall.

After a while a nurse came in and announced it was time. Jenny left the rest of them alone, and Ty came to Jade's side. "I love you, Mom."

"Love you, too, buddy."

"Talk to you in a little while, okay?"

"Okay."

She kissed him on the cheek and smiled, determined not to cry, determined that this would be a happy moment for their family. God knew there would be plenty of harder moments ahead.

Ty left, and the nurse wheeled Jade down the hall with Tanner at her side. They situated Jade on an operating table and gave her an epidural, all the while watching her vital signs, looking hard for clues that her body might be shutting down or seizing.

Jade felt only an occasional prod and poke until, at 7:23 that morning, the doctor lifted Madison Jade Eastman for Jade and Tanner to see. "Congratulations!" The doctor beamed. "She's a beauty."

Through teary eyes, Jade stared at their tiny, fighting-mad daughter, and then at Tanner. "She's *here.*" A relieved ripple of laughter came from her throat. "Can you *believe* it?"

Tanner was crying without any sound, as though a leak had sprung on either side of his face. He smiled bigger than she'd seen in months; then he turned to Madison, her arms flailing as she spouted soft baby cries of protest. "It's unbelievable, Jade. I can't believe this feeling." He raised both fists and stared toward heaven. "I have a daughter!"

Madison's cries grew more lusty in response, and Tanner laughed. "Her lungs are healthy." He grinned at Jade, and she tried to imagine which was better—seeing Madison for the first time, or seeing Tanner so happy. He lowered his voice and stared at their newborn daughter, his eyes dancing. "She's perfect, Jade. Absolutely perfect."

Tanner hovered near the doctor as Madison was passed to a nurse, cleaned up, weighed, and wrapped in a blanket. "Four pounds, two ounces," the doctor announced. "Bigger than we expected."

Jade closed her eyes for the briefest moment, overwhelmed with gratitude. *Thank You, God. Whatever happens after this, thank You...* She opened her eyes in time to see the nurse hand Madison to Tanner.

"Okay, little girl, go to Daddy."

Tanner took her in his arms, holding her like a priceless piece of china. The minute his arms were around her, Madison stopped crying and squinted at the fluorescent lights. "That's right, sweetheart. No more tears. You're with Daddy now." He cooed at her. "You're the most beautiful baby in the world, little Maddie."

"I knew it!" Jade giggled. "A true daddy's girl; love at first sight." She was tired, and her words slurred, but nothing could have dimmed the happiness bursting within her.

Jade studied her husband and daughter, and for the flash of an instant she wondered if she would live long enough for their baby girl to know her. The thought didn't dredge up sorrow in her as it might have a week ago. Because Jade knew that if all Maddie had was the love of a father like Tanner, she'd never want for anything.

Fresh tears came, but Jade blinked them back. She didn't want anything to blur the image of Tanner and their newborn daughter. Madison looked lost in Tanner's muscled arms as he cradled her against his body and carried her to Jade. He leaned down and nuzzled his face near hers, with Madison snuggled between them.

"Everything's going to be okay, Jade," he whispered. "I can feel it."

She wanted to say something, but her throat was too thick for words to pass. Instead, she nodded and ran her finger lightly over Madison's silky dark hair.

"Time for the incubator." A nurse came up behind Tanner and held out her hands. "We don't want her to get too cold."

Reluctantly, Tanner eased their daughter into the nurse's arms. When she was gone, Tanner spoke in a soft voice near Jade's ear. "You see it, don't you?"

"What?" She brushed her cheek against his.

"She looks just like you."

Jade smiled and settled back against the operating table. She had been thinking the same thing. There were few pictures of her as a child, but the box of belongings she took from her father's house included one baby photo. There was no question that Madison looked like a small version of her. "I think you're right."

"I know so." He kissed her cheek. "She'll be a knockout."

Jade was quiet for a moment. There was something she'd wanted to tell Tanner, but the timing had never been good, especially this past week when Tanner had been so fearful of the looming delivery date. "You brought the video camera, right?"

"Right. I'll take pictures when I visit her down the hall."

"Keep it here, okay? In the room. I have something I want you to do tomorrow."

Tanner didn't seem concerned with her request. He was too taken with the giddy reality of witnessing Madison's birth and the fact that Jade had come through the surgery so well. "Whatever you want, honey. I have everything I've ever wanted. I can't think of anything I wouldn't do for you."

Jade was still strapped to the operating table, the doctor working to stitch her closed. Despite the IV tubing, she managed to drape her arm around his neck. "There's only one thing I really want."

He brought his face up against hers. "The video camera?"

She shook her head.

"Pickles and ice cream?"

Her laughter rang through the room. He'd teased her throughout her pregnancy about the fact that she never had cravings. "No, silly. Not that."

His face grew serious and he framed her cheeks with his fingertips, kissing her in a way that needed no words. "What then? Anything…"

"You, Tanner." She whispered her answer straight to his heart. "Always only you."

It had been four days, but still Hannah thought of the baby boy with every passing hour. Where was he and who would raise him? Would they teach him to love Jesus? God had heard the prayers she'd prayed over him, that much was certain. Even if they were the only prayers ever said for the boy, somehow she knew God would answer.

But still she wondered. Because in their short time together, the baby had left an indelible mark on her heart. She'd told Matt about him over dinner that night, how he'd looked into her eyes and how she'd fed him and sang to him, prayed over him for more than an hour.

"If I could have, I would have brought him home then and there, Matt. I'm sure of it. He felt like my child."

"I wish I could have seen him."

"So you'd be okay with a boy? One day down the road, I mean?"

"I only want a child, Hannah. Whatever child the Lord gives us." Matt cocked his head. "What happens to the baby now?"

"He's in short-term care until his relatives can be notified. I'm sure someone in his family will take him."

In the days since then, Hannah had tried to push thoughts of the boy aside. She even wondered if she was dwelling on him as a way of letting go of Grace. Whatever it was, the feel of him in her arms, cradled against her chest, was not something that was fading with time.

Now it was Monday morning, and she and Matt had planned to be at the hospital by seven. Instead, she'd burned the oatmeal, and by the time the two of them had cleaned the mess, they were running late. Hannah was sitting at the kitchen table putting on lipstick and Matt was washing the breakfast dishes when the phone rang.

He dried his hands on his jeans and grabbed the receiver. "Hello?" He cradled it against his shoulder as Hannah threw him a dish towel from the table. "Okay." Matt winked at her. "Just a minute."

"Salesman..." He mouthed the word and handed her the phone.

"Thanks." Hannah pointed to the clock. She kept her hand over the mouthpiece. "We have a baby to meet."

"Sorry." Matt shrugged and chuckled. "They asked for you."

Hannah brought the phone to her ear and dropped the whisper. "Hello?"

"Mrs. Bronzan, I'm sorry to call so early. This is Edna Parsons at Social Services."

The floor fell away beneath her. Why on earth was the woman calling now? To give them an update on a little girl they'd never see again? To offer more false promises? Hannah clenched her teeth. It did no good to be bitter now. "Yes, Mrs. Parsons." She motioned for Matt to join her. "What can we do for you?"

Hannah heard the woman draw a deep breath. "First, I want you to know that what happened with Grace was...well, it was devastating for me." She hesitated. "It was the first time in my career that anything like that took place, where a birth mother lied about her existing family members. It's changed the way I handle cases."

Matt pulled up a chair and sat across from Hannah, his eyebrows lowered. A streak of regret pierced the walls around Hannah's heart. Maybe her thoughts about the social worker had been too harsh. "It was hard for all of us."

"Anyway, that's not why I called."

"Okay, what's up?" A part of her didn't want to know, didn't want to hear about another child who would almost certainly, positively, practically, for sure be theirs if only they were willing to ride out the process. She held her breath and waited.

"We have a healthy baby boy, an infant. He's been cleared for adoption, Mrs. Bronzan. No foster care involved. You're the first person I've called."

Hannah could feel the blood draining from her face. A healthy baby boy? Could it be…

It wasn't possible.

The woman couldn't be talking about the baby from the hospital the other day, the little boy who had grabbed so tightly hold of her heart and held it every day since?

Hannah closed her eyes and reached for Matt's hand, her grip on the phone tighter than before. There was no way it could be the same child. Thousand Oaks had become a big city, and besides, Mrs. Parsons worked with families from all over Ventura County.

She blinked back tears and ordered herself to be calm. Mrs. Parsons was waiting for an answer. "What…what do you know about him?"

"Well…he's six weeks old and very healthy. His mother's name was Milly Wheeler; she was a teenage runaway from San Francisco…"

Hannah squeezed Matt's hand while Mrs. Parsons continued. "Apparently the mother was a drug addict. She stayed clean through the pregnancy, but took an overdose of drugs early one morning last week. On Thursday morning she showed up at Los Robles Medical Center, barely alive. Her baby was on her lap and—"

"Dear God, it can't be…" Hannah's hand flew to her mouth and she hung her head, her mind spinning. It was a dream; it had to be. The baby, the one she'd loved through the most defining moment of his life, couldn't possibly be the one Mrs. Parsons was talking about.

Could it?

"I'm...I'm not sure I follow you, Mrs. Bronzan."

"Thursday morning? At Los Robles Medical Center?"

"Yes. His mother died in the emergency room. He's been in foster care ever since. I've checked out his background, and he has no one. Late Friday afternoon, the judge made him a ward of the court and cleared him for adoption."

Matt leaned back, searching Hannah's face for clues. She held up a single finger and closed her eyes. She had to hear it for herself before she could tell Matt. "He...he was wet. He needed a diaper and a blanket and a bottle."

Mrs. Parsons paused. "Who?"

"The baby. I was there that day. I held him while his mother died in the next room. I prayed for him and sang to him and told him everything would be okay. I wanted to take him home and never let him have another day like that again in his life."

There was a long pause, and when the social worker spoke, Hannah could hear the tears in her voice. "Then I guess God really does answer prayers. Yours and Milly Wheeler's."

Hannah moved her chair beside Matt's and rested her forehead on his shoulder as her tears soaked through his shirt. "What did Milly Wheeler pray?"

Mrs. Parsons cleared her throat. "She prayed her son would grow up to love the Lord and one day tell people about His miracles." She paused. "And what did you pray, Mrs. Bronzan?"

"That God would make his home a safe one...that his mother would love him all ...all the days of her life." She brushed her face against Matt's. "That he would know the touch of a father's hand and the peace of Christ's salvation."

There was silence for a moment, and Hannah knew they were both soaking in the impossibility of what had happened. The social worker broke the silence first. "Does this mean you're interested?" Her tone was light and happy, and clearly she was sure of Hannah's answer before it was spoken.

Hannah locked eyes with Matt and remembered what he'd told her four days ago over dinner. Whatever child God blessed them with would be fine. She smiled through her tears and spoke her answer clearly. "Yes, Mrs. Parsons. We're interested. How soon can you bring him home?"

They worked out the details, and at the end of the conversation Mrs. Parsons told Hannah the baby's name. When Hannah hung up, she was at a loss for words. Matt searched her face and chuckled, his eyes brimming with tears. "Why do I have the feeling our life just changed?"

"Remember how I said we had to hurry? Because we needed to meet a baby?"

Matt nodded and wove his fingers between hers.

"Well, we do. But not Jade and Tanner's baby." She kissed him, pulling back only enough to study his eyes. "Our baby, Matt. The little boy I prayed for, remember?"

"The one whose mother died..."

"Yes." She struggled to find her voice. "He's ours, Matt. And get this...his name is Kody *Matthew.*" She uttered a single laugh and ran her fingers through her hair. "Can you believe it? I feel like I'm dreaming, but it's true! Mrs. Parsons is bringing him home this afternoon. I prayed that he'd have a safe home, that he'd know his mother's love and his father's touch—and the whole time I was praying for— " Her breath caught on a sob.

Matt wrapped her into a hug and held her close. "You were praying for us."

In the hallways of Hannah's heart, she could still hear Grace's little-girl laughter, the laughter of a child they would never know again, a child they would miss forever. But in that moment, she knew again the truths she learned four years ago. Nighttime might be long and dark, but eventually morning would come, because that was God's way. His mercies were new every morning.

Just when it seemed like the darkness would last forever, morning would come. Hannah and Matt were living proof of that. In the end, even the bleakest night would always pass away.

Just like God said it would.

Twenty-six

Hannah and Matt had less than eight hours to prepare a nursery.

But before they could do anything, they needed to go to the hospital. Jenny had called immediately after Mrs. Parsons to say that Jade and Madison were both doing well. Hannah kept the phone call short and exchanged a knowing glance with Matt. This was not the time to tell her about her new brother.

They arrived at the hospital half an hour later and found Jenny and Ty in the waiting room watching television. Jenny grinned at them. "Nice of you guys to show up."

Hannah was bursting with the chance to talk to Jenny, but she played along. "You know how I am in the kitchen..."

Jenny laughed and stood to hug them. "Tanner says the baby's beautiful. Looks just like Jade."

"You haven't seen her?"

Jenny tapped Ty's tennis shoe with her own. "Ty has, lucky guy. Got to wear a gown and a mask and scrub up like he hasn't done for a year or more."

Ty chuckled, and Hannah thought he looked tired. He'd probably been more worried about Jade than anyone knew. Hannah smiled at him. "What's she look like?"

"She's so tiny."

Matt patted Ty's back. "She'll grow. How's your mom?"

"Good. I got to see her, too. She told me she feels a lot better now that Madison's out."

They all laughed, and when the room grew quiet, Hannah

motioned to Jenny. "Can we talk to you a minute? Out in the hallway?"

The slightest sense of alarm filled Jenny's eyes. "Everything okay?"

"Yes." Hannah glanced at Matt. "We want to tell you about a phone call that came this morning."

Jenny's expression went blank, but she followed them to a quiet place in the hallway. "What phone call?"

"Mrs. Parsons called…"

The expectancy in Hannah's voice caused a knowing look to cross Jenny's face. "No, Mom. No more sisters. I told you, it's too hard."

"Hold on." Matt placed his hand on Jenny's shoulder. Hannah's insides melted at the compassion in his eyes. "Not a sister…a brother. A baby brother."

"What? You're serious?" Jenny's face went pale. "I'm going to have a brother?"

Hannah reached for Jenny and pulled her close so the three of them were huddled together, much as they'd been that awful morning when they said good-bye to Grace. "Remember the baby I told you about, the little boy at the hospital whose mother died?"

"You prayed for him and held him while the doctors tried to save her."

"Right. Mrs. Parsons ran the check on him, and he's legally free for adoption. Today! She's bringing him home this afternoon."

Jenny looked from Hannah to Matt and back to Hannah again. She let loose the sweetest ripple of laughter. "Wow, I don't know what to say. You guys and the Eastmans having babies on the same day? Isn't that kind of like a miracle?"

Hannah laughed. "I hadn't thought of that." She looked at Matt. "We need to tell Tanner."

At that moment they spotted him trudging down the hallway,

still wearing the scrubs he'd worn for the delivery. He saw them and waved, his face taken up with an enormous smile. Relief washed over Hannah. A smile that size could only mean one thing: Jade and the baby were doing well.

Hannah crooked her arm around Tanner's neck and hugged him. "Jenny told us she's beautiful. Looks just like Jade."

Tanner nodded and shifted to hug Matt as well. "They're both fine." The smile remained, but from this close, Hannah could see the concern in his eyes. "Jade's tired. Ever since the baby was born, all she wants to do is sleep."

"That's normal." Hannah squeezed Tanner's hand. "Having babies is hard work."

Tanner relaxed a bit. "She got through the surgery without any seizures. The doctors were worried about that."

"Fantastic." Matt looked at Hannah and winked. "Looks like October 7 will be a day we'll all remember."

Tanner looked from Hannah to Matt and finally to Jenny. He grinned at her as he elbowed Matt. "What're your parents up to now?"

Jenny ran her fingers through her bangs and shook her head. "You'll have to ask them about this one."

Hannah giggled. She knew how overwhelmed Jenny must feel. The day had been nothing but a series of life-changing announcements. The sum of them was draining, and she and Matt still had to set up a nursery.

"I give up." Tanner scratched his head. "Someone tell me what's going on."

"Okay." Matt tried to hide his smile. "Hannah and I are going to be parents."

Tanner studied Matt's face. "Seriously?"

"Seriously. The social worker called this morning. She has a healthy baby boy for us. Six weeks old. His name is Kody

Matthew, and she's bringing him home tonight." Matt tousled Jenny's hair. "So—" he checked his watch—"in six hours, Jenny's going to have a baby brother."

Tanner raised a fist in the air and hooted out loud. "Is God good or what? That's awesome." He hugged the three of them, and then he took Matt's shoulder and looked him straight in the face. "We can draw up the papers next week."

Now it was Matt's turn to be confused. "Papers?"

Tanner tried to look indignant. "Of course, papers. Madison Jade will need a fine upstanding husband one day, right?"

"And...?" Clearly Matt didn't see the connection, but Hannah did and she laughed out loud.

Tanner anchored his hands on his hips. "If we're going to arrange the marriage now we'd better draw up papers next week. That way there'll be no question about it. No dating until she's twenty-two and out of college, at which point she will be free to marry Mr. Kody Matthew Bronzan. Sounds good to me."

They all laughed, and Hannah was glad to see Tanner so happy. When the laughter died, she asked about Jade. "Should we wait and see her tomorrow?"

"I think she'd like that." The teasing left Tanner's eyes and his face was filled with gratitude. "I'll tell her you were here. It'll mean the world to her."

They said good-bye and made plans for Jenny to meet them at home early that afternoon, before the baby arrived. A neighbor friend of Jade's would take over with Ty at the hospital and watch him overnight. Then they would all meet at the hospital again tomorrow to visit Jade and see her baby.

Before they left, Tanner thanked them again for coming. "And give my future son-in-law a big kiss, will you?"

It was a happy moment, and as Hannah and Matt left the hospital, she prayed that memories of this day would stay with

Tanner for weeks to come. Because there was no question about one thing: The hardest days for Jade and Tanner were right around the corner.

The next twenty-four hours passed in a blur for Tanner.

Hannah and Matt brought their new baby boy to the hospital and gave Tanner a chance to hold him. It was strange, really. Here he was at the hospital having his own child, but the baby he got to spend more time holding was Matt and Hannah's.

The constant twist of events was enough to make him dizzy.

Jade seemed to know what was going on around her, but she was tired most of the time and that worried Tanner. She passed her congratulations on to the Bronzans, and after Matt and Hannah got a chance to see Madison through the window of the neonatal intensive care unit, they did the same. It was a giddy time—a time when doctors assured them Madison was thriving, given the timing of her birth. She had no lung problems, no cerebral palsy, and no serious dangers. They would keep her in the hospital only as a precaution until she reached five pounds. Then she could go home.

Jade's situation was another story.

Though she had survived the surgery without seizure or signs of trouble, her white count was high. Dr. Layton explained that was because she was fighting an infection somewhere. Maybe at the site of her C-section, maybe in her brain. It was hard to tell.

Either way, an MRI done late the previous evening showed that the tumor had grown a fraction of an inch in the past week. Enough to cause Dr. Layton to worry. Treatment couldn't wait any longer, and the doctor detailed the plan they would follow.

"First of all, we're keeping Jade in the hospital." He directed his comments to Tanner, because even now, with so serious a discussion going on, Jade could hardly stay awake. "We'll start massive chemotherapy and radiation tomorrow and administer treatment for two weeks." He paused. "I'd hoped for three. But I think it's more important to get the tumor out. A woman's hormones change radically after a baby's delivered. Sometimes that can cause a stable tumor to double in size overnight, which in this case would have grave consequences for Jade. Other times it can cause the tumor to send tentacles into the brain. In which case the tumor would become inoperable."

He went on to say that they'd do an MRI each day to monitor the tumor's behavior throughout the two-week treatment phase. "By then the most we can hope for is that the tumor will have shrunk and stayed intact."

Tanner stared at the doctor, speechless. Sometime around the point where Dr. Layton started describing treatment, the floor had shifted. Since then, he'd had the constant feeling that he was falling.

Why hadn't the doctor explained these things before? The tumor could double in size? With grave consequences? What was *that* supposed to mean? Tanner grabbed hold of the nearest chair to steady himself. And what would happen if the tumor grew tentacles…? Tanner was too terrified to ask. He forced himself to slip into lawyer mode, so he could ask questions without allowing his emotions to get in the way. "What are her chances?"

"If the tumor does what I want it to, I think they're good. There are risks of course, but we can talk about those later."

It was after three o'clock on Tuesday afternoon, and Tanner was exhausted. He'd stayed in a vinyl reclining chair, which the nurses set up adjacent to Jade's bed. Though he was comfortable enough, Tanner couldn't bring himself to sleep. Instead he watched the monitors flashing Jade's vital signs. And when he grew restless, he would visit the neonatal intensive care. They'd told him he could come any hour of the day or night to see Madison, and even though he could only stroke her tiny arm through the holes in the incubator, he wanted to spend as much time with her as possible.

Now that everyone was gone, Tanner leaned back in the chair and took Jade's hand in his. Maybe he could grab an hour's sleep before dinner was delivered. He studied Jade and thought it strange that her stomach was so flat. Overnight she looked as though she'd never carried Madison.

Something sank in Tanner's gut as the reason dawned on him. Her lack of excess weight was because of the cancer. She'd barely gained ten pounds. No wonder her stomach was flat. In fact, if anything she looked thinner than before she got pregnant. Too thin.

He sighed out loud. One more thing to worry about. His eyes closed and he turned his thoughts toward God. *How do I get through it, Lord? It feels like we're walking through a minefield and everywhere we turn there's danger.*

In response, he pictured the plaque on his desk, and the inscribed words filled his mind: *Be still, and know that I am God...*

The words soothed his heart and shone a ray of light through the dark tunnel they were traveling. That was it, really. The answer to life's most difficult moments. Life was full of craziness, chaos and inexplicable tragedy. Like the tragedy a year ago of the fallen Twin Towers in New York City or the damaged Pentagon in Washington, D.C.

What sense did life make at all if not for that one single verse.

He could almost hear the Lord whispering the words directly to his soul.

Be still, Tanner, My son. Be still, and know that I am God.

The words calmed him and lulled him to sleep. Two hours later he felt something on his arm and he was instantly awake.

"What is it?" He looked around and found Jade studying him from her hospital bed.

She giggled at him. "Sorry. I didn't want to wake you."

He sat straight up and moved to the edge of the chair, searching her face for signs of weakness or trouble or any one of the myriad of troubles Dr. Layton said might come to pass. "How are you?"

"Fine." A smile filled her face. "How's Maddie?"

The tension left Tanner's neck and shoulders. "She's beautiful. No problems, just a bit small. The doctor said she can go home as soon as she hits five pounds."

Jade's face glowed in response. "God's so good to us, Tanner."

Dr. Layton's warnings from earlier that morning ran through Tanner's mind, but he pushed them back. "Yes." He took Jade's hand in his and ran his finger over the bruise marks where the IV had been for her C-section. "God is very good."

They were quiet for a moment. "I know what you're thinking." Jade's eyes were brighter than they'd been since the surgery, and Tanner was flooded with relief. Maybe Hannah was right. Maybe Jade was only tired because of the delivery, like any other woman.

"What?"

"You want to know how I'm feeling, right?"

Tanner grew serious. "Always."

"I feel good, Tanner. I was half-asleep but I heard Dr. Layton. The tumor isn't going to double overnight...it isn't going to grow tentacles into my brain. God wouldn't bring us this far only to let that happen."

"But you said yourself sometimes God's plans aren't ours."

"I know. But right now, right here, I don't feel like a cancer patient. I feel like a new mother, alive and awake and anxious to hold her baby. Thrilled beyond words to be married to the man of my dreams and certain I'll be around..." Jade paused as tears glistened in her eyes. "Long enough to see that man walk our little girl down the aisle someday."

Tanner's throat was so thick he couldn't speak. Instead, he lifted Jade's hand to his mouth and kissed it, soft and tender, as though it might break.

"But just in case...I have a favor to ask."

He looked up and coughed, still struggling to speak. "Favor?"

"Yes. Remember? I told you I needed the video camera for something today?"

Tanner nodded. "Vaguely." He cast her a silly smile. "I was a little distracted yesterday."

"Well, it's time. Now. Before dinner."

He had no idea what she was leading to, but he reached for the camera and took off the lens cover. "Okay, what am I shooting?"

"Me." She pointed to the closet. "I had the nurse set a bag in there. Inside is a pink journal. Could you get it for me?" She cast him a sweet but tired smile. "Please."

Tanner knit his eyebrows together. He had no idea where this was going but he did as she asked. The journal was where she said it would be, and he gave it to her without pausing to see what it contained. Then he returned to his seat, positioned the video camera, and saluted her. "Tanner, the cameraman, at your service."

Jade sat up a bit straighter, wincing. "They don't tell you how sore your stomach'll be." She smiled and straightened first her bathrobe, then her hair. "Okay, I'm ready."

A strange, uneasy feeling made Tanner lower the camera. His teasing tone was gone. "Wait a minute. What's going on?"

Jade leveled her gaze at him, her face every bit as peaceful as before. "I have something to tell Maddie, something I want her to have when she's older."

Tanner's heart raced and he shook his head. "You just got done telling me you feel fine, that you know you're going to make it and everything's going to work out."

"Yes..."

"So, I don't get it—" He stopped, aware his voice was louder than before and bordered on angry. He started again. "Are you saying you want me to tape some...some sort of good-bye message to Madison?" He paused and glanced about the room, searching for the words. Finally his eyes found Jade's again. "I can't do it, Jade. Ask the nurse, ask Hannah. But I can't sit here and watch you say good-bye through the lens of a video camera."

She waited until he was finished. "It doesn't have to be a good-bye video, Tanner. It's simply a message from me to her. And I want you to tape it." Her eyes grew more intense than before. "Please."

A light huff slipped from his lips. His gaze fell to his lap and the camera lying there. He wanted to do this for her, but how? Tanner thought back over the months, how he hadn't been there for Jade after her diagnosis...

If she was brave enough to speak a message to Maddie from the bed of her hospital room, looking into their family video camera, then in God's strength alone he would be strong enough to film her.

He looked up and his eyes met hers. "I'm sorry." He held the camera up and flipped the screen on the side. "Of course I'll film it."

Jade cleared her throat and nodded to Tanner. At her signal, he began filming and she smiled into the camera. "Hi, Maddie. I'm here in the hospital room the day after you were born, and—" she held up the pink journal—"I wanted to share a few things with you."

Tanner did his best to keep the camera still.

"This is a gift for you, Maddie. Something I've worked on for a long time. It's a book of letters from me to you." She smiled and opened the journal, pointing to the pages inside. "Each letter is sort of a talk, really. Something I might tell you when you take your first steps or say your first words. The encouragement I'd give you on the first day of kindergarten or the first day of middle school."

The book was full, front to back, with handwritten letters. Tanner could see the tears in Jade's eyes, but only if he looked hard. His own silent tears blurred the image of Jade, and he blinked, fighting for the strength to continue as Jade kept talking. "One letter tells you how I like to apply mascara and the best way to blend foundation. Another tells you what to look for in a friend and what kind of boy to stay away from."

Jade flipped through the pages. "I wrote you a letter for the day you get your first kiss and the day you leave for college. And I wrote you a letter for the day you get married, sweetheart." She closed the journal and held it close to her heart. "Those and lots more, honey. They're all here."

She hesitated and her smile faded just a bit. Tanner blinked back another wave of tears and tried not to sniff. He didn't want anything to ruin the miracle he was capturing on tape. Jade swallowed hard. Her eyes narrowed as though she could see the face of their daughter in the camera lens. "My prayer, honey, is that you and I are watching this together. That we get the chance to watch it together lots of times and even share it with your children one day." Jade plucked at her terry cloth bathrobe. "We can laugh at how silly I look and talk about how much time has passed and how quickly. But whether I'm there or not, you'll know that at this time in my life, I got sick. Very sick."

Tears slid from Jade's eyes and she wiped them with her fingertips. Tanner wanted to rescue her, help her through the moment, but there was nothing he could do except keep the camera rolling.

Her voice trembled as she continued. "Tomorrow I'll start treatment, medicine and radiation that the doctors hope will make me better. Then in two weeks I'll have an operation. One that we all believe will save my life."

Jade steadied herself. "Your father and I have prayed about it very much, and we believe God's word is true. He has a plan for me, for you. For all of us. A plan to give us hope and a future and not to harm us."

Her composure broke then. She brought her hand to her face and for several seconds she hung her head, staving off the sobs Tanner knew were just beneath the surface. When she looked up, she bit her lip and smiled through her tears. "But sometimes, honey, God's plans are not our own. Even if that means I don't make it through this, I want you to know how great God has been to our family. Your dad will tell you the stories, but…but I wanted you to hear it from me. If I'm not there beside you, Maddie, I'm in heaven with Jesus."

Tanner's tears were coming in streams, and it took everything in him to keep the camera in place. Jade shook her head. "Don't ever blame Jesus for the things that don't go as we plan, sweetheart. He's the only One who always knows what's best. Even if it isn't what we want."

Jade paused, drawing in a deep breath. "Whew." She stuck out her lower lip and blew her bangs off her forehead. "This is harder than I thought." She smiled and ran her fingers beneath her eyes again. "There are a few things I don't ever want you to forget." She tightened her grip on the journal. "They're in here, written in the front of the book, but I wanted you to hear them from me. Just in case I don't get another chance to tell you."

Tanner held his breath, his heart breaking.

"I want you to know I love you more than you could ever imagine. I dreamed about you for two years before you were born, and now I feel like God's granted me the sweetest miracle by giving you to me and your dad and Ty."

Her smile faded. "I also want you to know how much I love your father. He is the greatest man I've ever known, and no matter what happens, I pray you and Ty will follow his example as long as you live. He is my strength, my song, my protector. Ever since I've known him, he's led me to Christ again and again. And Christ is the only One who could give me the peace that's in my heart right now. Your father will lead you there, too, if you let him." Jade's voice broke again. "So let him, baby. Please let him lead you to Jesus."

Jade kept her gaze straight at the camera lens. "Finally, I want you to love your brother. He's older than you, yes, but he loves you so much. And he's very, very special to me. A time may come when he wonders about life and God and why I had to get sick. If that happens, be there for him, Maddie. Be his friend. Be the one he talks to…especially if I can't be there."

Tears streamed down Jade's cheeks again and she shrugged. A smile filled her face and a sound, more laugh than sob, came from her throat. "I guess that's all. I hope you like the book, honey. I'll love you forever and no matter what happens, I'll see you at home."

Jade lifted her eyes to Tanner's and he turned the camera off. Moving like a man who had aged twenty years in fifteen minutes, Tanner set the camera on the floor, stood, and embraced Jade across the bars of the hospital bed.

They stayed that way a long time, weeping without a sound as they lay on each other's shoulders. No words were needed. Regardless of what Jade had said about the video, its message had only one purpose.

When she could speak, Jade whispered against his face. "The hardest thing…is to think of leaving her…the way my mother left me."

Tanner's eyes were swollen, his nose completely stuffed from crying. Still he found his voice and spoke it into her hair, the hair that would be gone in a matter of weeks. "It would never be like that, Jade. Your mother left you on purpose."

"I know." She muffled a sob in his shoulder. "But I still missed her. I wondered what she'd tell me on the first day of middle school, or when I came home in love with you after our first night out in Kelso." She took three quick breaths. "I don't ever want Maddie to wonder. I want her to feel me there with her even if it's only my words."

Despite the depth of his pain and fear, Tanner couldn't have been more proud of her. "When did you have time to write that?" He drew back, his voice still a whisper. "And how come you didn't tell me?"

"I wrote it when you were still working. I kept looking for the right time to tell you, but finally I decided this would be the best way. Besides, I wanted to make sure she was here and…and healthy before I did the video."

"What about Ty?"

Jade smiled. "I wrote him one, too. I'll give it to him before my surgery. But I already videotaped my message for him. It's in my top drawer in the bedroom."

Tanner's mouth hung open. "I had no idea…"

"I used the automatic setting." She angled her face. "It worked fine."

There was a knock at the door and a nurse entered with two trays of food. Tanner returned to his seat, and they ate their meal side by side with few words.

Jade was tired after making the video and needed sleep. The next morning treatment would begin, and she had to be strong if her system was going to handle the strain of both chemotherapy and radiation, especially while she was still recovering from the C-section.

The only bright spot was that Dr. Layton had promised her a visit to the nursery in the morning so she could spend an hour with Madison before starting treatment. Tanner knew the entire next day—the next two weeks, in fact—would be the hardest in his life. But that night he was determined to be upbeat. For Jade.

They laughed about some of the silly things Ty had said in the past, and then Tanner read Psalms 23 and 91 to her. When he was finished, she yawned and held out her arms. He leaned over the hospital bed bars and kissed her. "I love you, Jade."

She smiled, and though her eyes glistened, she didn't cry. "No matter what happens tomorrow, no matter how bad it gets, I'd do it all again to be with you, Tanner. No one will ever love you like I do."

Fifteen minutes later she was asleep, and though he'd ordered himself to be strong, Tanner was helpless to stop the tears. Dr. Layton had said her hair would most likely be the first thing to go once the chemotherapy began. He gulped back a sob and wove his fingers through her hair. It looked thick and shiny dark against her pink robe. She'd never worn it long, but in light of the impending cancer treatment, she'd grown it out.

Jade had made light of it. "I'll be bald soon enough anyway."

But Tanner couldn't imagine Jade without hair, couldn't picture her silky dark head bald and cut open.

The room was so quiet he could hear his heartbeat, and he wrapped a thick strand of her hair around his finger and held it that way. He stared at her, studying her, watching her breathe through most of the night. Terrified that if he fell asleep, Jade—the Jade he knew and loved and cherished—would disappear from his life.

Not just for a day or a week or a season.

But forever.

Twenty-seven

Grace's absence and Jade's illness were the only marks on an otherwise perfect time for the Bronzans.

During the next two weeks, Hannah prayed daily about both situations.

Grace's curly hair and contagious smile still flashed in Hannah's mind every morning, and occasionally—although less often than before—it took several minutes to remember that she was no longer their daughter, no longer living in the frilly bedroom down the hall.

They had talked about converting the room into Kody's nursery, but there was a small room across the hall that Hannah had used for odds and ends that worked just as well. Besides, she and Matt still believed that somehow, sometime, God would bless them with another daughter.

Becoming parents to a son, however, was nothing less than an act of God. A complete surprise that none of them would have sought out and that had made their home a place of hope and miracles. Overnight Jenny had taken to spending long hours rocking Kody and cooing at him. They marveled at his glowing skin and clear bright eyes, at the fact that a runaway teenage girl had managed to care for her baby so well, and herself so poorly.

Long before Kody awoke each morning, Hannah would find herself restless, missing the weight of him in her arms and wanting to hold him, feed him, sing over him as she'd done that first time in the hospital room. More often than not, she would tiptoe into his nursery, sit in the rocking chair next to his crib, and stare at him, awed by God's hand in her life.

Hannah Bronzan? The mother of a son? It was something she had never imagined, something she had even avoided when they first entered the world of adoption. All she'd ever known were girls. But now, holding Kody, she could sense a difference in the strength of his fist around her finger, the lust of his cry. He was a good-natured baby, yes, but he was all boy. A fighter with strong will and determination that overshadowed anything she'd seen in her girls at this age.

Hannah often sat in the dawning shadows of morning and studied his face through the crib bars, imagining what great thing God had planned for him. Maybe he'd be a preacher, like poor Milly had prayed. Or the faithful president of a company, leading his employees by example. Or maybe a teacher, a coach. A freedom fighter like Matt, or a doctor like Tom.

It didn't matter really. Whatever Kody was, he'd always be a miracle first. A boy whom God had handpicked for their home, their arms. Their family.

That was something else. After Grace was taken from them, Hannah doubted the entire idea of adoption. It was too painful. Besides, other families could take in hurting children. She wondered if perhaps she had only agreed to adopt in an attempt to re-create what she'd lost that awful day four years ago. Not that she could ever replace Alicia, but maybe she could re-create the busy family atmosphere that had marked her life before the accident. Hannah had desperately missed that.

Grace's presence had restored a sense of that, but not really. She was so mistrusting at first, so delicate. They had only just begun to feel like a real family, to sense the balance and laughter and safety a family represents, when she was taken away.

But now, since the moment Mrs. Parsons brought Kody Matthew home, everything about their home seemed different, warmer. More focused on love and life and faith.

Hannah spent hours pondering the change Kody had brought to their family, and she figured it was because Jenny was practically grown up and gone. Before adopting, their family hadn't spent great amounts of time together. Rather Hannah and Matt lived like newlyweds, learning what it was to share a bathroom and a bedroom and a kitchen.

Jenny was a part of it all, of course. But she was gone much of the time, busy with friends and football games and study groups at school. Now Jenny made a point of being home. She and Hannah and Matt spent most evenings circled around the living room, cuddling with each other and taking turns holding Kody.

They talked more and laughed more and somehow, in the process, they loved more.

The sum of it made Hannah's heart swell, and on Sunday, at the end of the first whole week with Kody, she stood at the front door and told Matt as much. The next day would be the first in the trial against the Benson City Council, and he had plans to be there most of the week.

It was six-thirty, and upstairs Kody and Jenny were still asleep. Hannah rose up on her tiptoes and circled her arms around Matt's neck. "Be careful." It wasn't something she used to think about, but after losing Tom and Alicia, and after that fateful day last September, it was impossible not to. Yes, there were more security measures in place, but there were also more angry terrorists. Not that fear had kept them from flying, but Hannah made a point of telling Matt how she loved him before he left for an airport.

Just in case she never got another chance.

He smiled at her and brushed back her bangs with his fingertips. "I will." He kissed her. "Take care of Kody. He'll probably cry more with me gone."

Hannah giggled. "He might need therapy when he's older."

"Actually," Matt pretended to look hurt. "I think you're right. He's very bonded with me."

They both laughed, and Hannah straightened the collar on his suit coat. "Knock 'em dead, will ya? Tanner could use something positive right now."

Matt's eyes narrowed. "I care about every case. Pray about it, search the Bible for help." He shook his head. "But this one's more important than anything I've done in a long time."

"Because of Tanner?"

"Yes." Matt's expression was pensive. "Tanner has such passion, Hannah. Such heart for what we do at the firm. This case mattered a lot to him; it's precedent-setting stuff."

Hannah bit her lip, her heart heavy. "And he gave it up for Jade."

"That's just a glimpse of how much Tanner loves that woman." Matt looked at the ceiling as though he was searching for the right words, words that might come close to describing the relationship between Jade and Tanner. "He's loved her since he was a boy."

Hannah nodded and tears welled in her eyes. "I know."

Matt narrowed his eyes, his jaw clenched, and stared at her a long moment. "What'll he do if something happens to her?"

"No." Hannah shook her head. "We can't think that way."

"I know." He hesitated. "I'll be home before Monday. I promised Tanner."

Hannah stared at her slippers. "Next Sunday night, before the surgery, let's pray around her hospital bed."

"Definitely." He studied Hannah's face. "God's in control. Nothing will happen to Jade that isn't somehow part of His plan."

Tears threatened to spill onto her face and Hannah bit her lip to keep from crying. "I feel so helpless." She let her head fall against his chest. "Pray that God gives me a way to help her this week, okay?"

Matt nodded. "I will." He glanced at his watch. "I've gotta run. Keep me posted on how she's doing."

"I will." Hannah opened his suit coat and slipped her arms around him, hugging him long and close, relishing the feel of his strong, warm body against hers. Since the day they met, Matt had made her feel safe and protected. And lately—as they shared the role of parenting Kody—she was falling more in love with him every day. "I love you."

Matt drew back, his hands still locked near the small of her back. "I may not have known you since I was a boy, Hannah, but I've waited a lifetime for you. And now…I can't help but know that God had me wait because He knew. He knew one day a beautiful woman with a broken heart would come into my life."

He brought his lips to hers and kissed her in a way she would remember all week long. His voice was thick with emotion when he continued.

"And He knew that only together would either of us find the strength to love like this."

Twenty-eight

From the moment he stepped foot in the courtroom, everything that could go wrong for Matt did.

More than half the jurors were single women in their late thirties and forties. Two jurors were high school teachers, one a college professor, and two were entertainers—young men who had, respectively, a pierced eyebrow and tongue, and a full-neck tattoo.

Usually, in the cases he and Tanner handled, it was best to stay away from anyone too liberal or artsy, anyone in entertainment or academia. Those types of people often, though not always, made jurors who already had their minds set against anything remotely involving God. Some of them would have bought completely into the current-day separation of church and state mind-set. There was a chance these people walked through life believing even the mention of God was illegal.

Matt remembered attending a book conference once in which he and Tanner were promoting a title, *Stand up for Freedom*, that had come out of their early work at the CPRR. The book was intended to appeal primarily to Christians, but the publisher had seen its crossover potential for the general market and asked them to attend the conference.

Midway through the morning, a woman approached Matt and Tanner and looked at their book. Then, as though she were a covert operative in an underworld spy game, she leaned close and asked, "Is this book...you know—" she looked both ways—"religious?"

Matt remembered Tanner's grin. He leaned close in turn, looked both ways as she had done, and whispered, "Yes! It's about religious freedom." He dropped the whisper and stood tall. "The good news is in America you don't have to whisper about religion. It's your right to talk about it." He glanced around the room—a place where every topic from mysticism to magic arts to a dozen Middle Eastern practices was highlighted in dozens of books. "In fact, you can even talk about it right here." He handed her the book. "Read it and see for yourself."

Monday morning, Matt assessed the jurors and wondered what Tanner would have done about it. Thanked God, probably. Assumed there was a reason and moved ahead. So even though the jury selection was grim at best, Matt committed the case to the Lord and carried on.

The premise of Tanner's case, which he'd built long before Matt took over, was simple. After interviewing everyone involved, after studying the contract signed by the Benson City Council and Pastor Casey Carson of the First Church of the Valley, Tanner had thought of something new, something he'd never considered before.

If the Benson City Council was requiring First Church of the Valley to refrain from teaching that Jesus Christ is the only way to salvation, then, in a sense, a local public governing body was defining religion.

Maybe not defining it for the entire state of Colorado, or even the town of Benson, but in drawing up a contract that allowed any group to use City Hall except those who preach the Gospel of Christ, they were, without a doubt, defining religion.

Tanner's tactic, therefore, was this: The city of Benson was in violation of the Constitution, wherein no law should be made "respecting an establishment of religion or *prohibiting the free exercise thereof.*"

In other words, for the first time since religious freedom cases had become necessary, Tanner intended to use the very argument his opponents had used for years. Instead of spending an entire case trying to prove his client had not violated the separation of church and state clause, he would turn the tables and accuse the defendant of that very thing.

So Matt's task was twofold.

First, he would have to depict the First Church of the Valley as a law-abiding organization with as much right to rent City Hall as any other group. Then he would present the biased contract and accuse the Benson City Council of making a law that established a Christ-less religion and prohibited Pastor Carson's church from the free exercise of their faith.

Matt had never prided himself in his opening or closing arguments. He preferred the behind-the-scenes research and examination phases of a case. But now, with Tanner holding a bedside vigil at Jade's side, counting down the days until her brain surgery, Matt had more righteous fire stirring within him than at any time in the past few years.

Because their side had filed the suit, Matt presented his arguments first. He stood and made his way toward the jurors, meeting each of their gazes with a warmth usually reserved for church friends and business associates. "Good morning," he said, nodding in their direction. "Thank you for being here today, for believing that in this courtroom over the next few days there might be something more important happening than your routine schedules. Something in which each of you obviously believes."

Matt glanced at the notepad in his hands and his confidence grew. Tanner had to be praying for him; the words coming from his mouth sounded so much like Tanner it was uncanny.

Thank You, God; give me the words…

Be strong and bold, for I am with you.

The answer resonated in his soul and came straight from the Scripture he'd read that morning. A sense of peace and sureness filled his senses as he began explaining his case for the jury in clear and passionate detail.

He told them that the First Amendment to the Constitution involved a safeguard for people like Pastor Casey Carson. "People whom the founders of this great nation wanted to protect." Matt stopped, slid his left hand into his pants pocket and moved his gaze from one juror to the next. "Do you know why? Because they were familiar with religious persecution. It was something that troubled them enough to leave the comforts of England, their homeland, and venture into a new world, a new life."

Matt's tone grew stronger. "No one would tell them whom to worship and how. No, in America a person would be free to worship as they chose, and the government—no matter how many generations would pass—would never, ever establish a law prohibiting the freedom of religion."

Out of the corner of his eye, Matt saw the attorneys for the City of Benson conferring in silent whispers. Tanner was right! They were surprised by this argument. No doubt they had planned to take the very same approach, accusing Pastor Carson and the First Church of the Valley of crossing the line that separated church and state by daring to preach the name of Christ in a public building.

But now, just minutes into the trial's first day, partway through Matt's opening arguments, there was a current of electricity running through the courtroom that Matt was sure everyone could feel. The church hadn't crossed a line, the Benson City Council had.

Matt took three sure steps over to the plaintiff's table and pulled the lease agreement from a file. When he was back in front of the jury, he held it up. "I hold a lease agreement written and agreed upon by the Benson City Council." He paused and paced a few steps. "Now keep in mind, when the founders of the Constitution referred to Congress, they meant *any* public governing body. Therefore, the First Amendment applies to the Benson City Council as strongly as it applies to the president of the United States."

He raised the lease agreement higher and uttered a single, humorless chuckle. "I'm about to read you a clause in this lease agreement that will astonish you. It will make you wonder how it is that the U.S. Constitution has come to be taken so lightly by people like the Benson City Council members."

Matt could almost picture Tanner in the corner of the room giving him a thumbs-up. Encouraged by a strength that could only have been from God, Matt continued. "At first this...lease agreement...looks like the ordinary sort. It includes the names of the lessor—in this case, the City of Benson—and the lessee—in this case, First Church of the Valley. It requires that a specific amount of rent be paid on time each month and that the facility is cared for in a specific manner."

He flipped the page. "It details how the building may be set up for community events and how it must be cleaned after each use." He pointed to a section highlighted in yellow near the bottom of the second page. "The part you won't believe is down here."

There were still a few feet separating him from the jury box, and now Matt took a step closer, leaning on the railing and angling his back slightly toward the jury. That way when he held up the lease agreement, most of them in the middle section could read the words over his shoulder. "Right here, on line forty-three, item seventeen, is a stipulation to the agreement that reads: 'City Hall may not be rented by any group who teaches faith in Jesus Christ as the only way to salvation.'"

Matt turned and faced the jury again. The outrage he'd felt upon first reading the clause was fresh within him, and Matt let it show in his eyes. "Give yourself a minute to let that sink in. City Hall, a place that may be rented by any group willing to pay and follow a lease, may *not* be rented by a group who teaches faith in Jesus Christ…as the only way to salvation."

He paused and leaked the air from his lungs, giving his expression time to relax. "There's a name for people who teach that type of doctrine. In this country, we call them Christians." At this point Matt returned to the table and exchanged the lease for a hardback copy of the Bible, paper-clipped at a verse in the book of John.

Matt opened it and stood squarely before the jurors. "Many of you may not read the Bible; you may not even like the Bible." He leveled his gaze at them. "But you are Americans, and for that reason you must hear what I'm about to read. He'd memorized the verse decades ago, but he read it from the Bible now, so the jury would have no doubts about the teaching and where it came from. Matt cleared his throat. "In the book of John, chapter fourteen, verse six, the Bible quotes Jesus as saying, 'I am the way and the truth and the life. No one comes to the Father except through me.'"

There was utter silence in the courtroom as Matt closed the Bible and met the faces—some curious, some troubled—of each and every juror. Matt's voice was so quiet they had to strain forward to hear him. "Jesus told the people that he was the only road to heaven. And that, friends, is the very belief banned by the Benson City Council."

Matt set the Bible back on the table, selected another document, and tossed his hands in the air, his voice loud once more. "Sure, you can rent the City Hall in Benson if you believe in voodoo or witchcraft. You can preach a doctrine of multiple gods or no God at all." He raised a single finger. "Ah...but preach the Christian doctrine, the one established by Jesus, and here's what will happen."

The jurors were clearly spellbound. Across the room Matt saw the opposing attorneys scribbling furiously on their legal pads. He leaned against the jury box and positioned the document in his hands so the jury could see it. "This is a letter Pastor Carson received from the Benson City Council eight months after he and the First Church of the Valley—a Christian congregation—began renting out the Benson City Hall."

He glanced at the document, holding it in the air just in front of his face so he had no trouble reading it. "'Dear Mr. Carson, this is to inform you that your right to meet at the Benson City Hall has hereby been reneged due to a lease violation by you and your group.'" Matt raised an eyebrow at the jury and then returned his attention to the letter. "'Our records show that because of this violation, the city of Benson owes you and your organization no money in refunded lease payments. This enforcement goes into effect immediately, as your time slot at City Hall will be filled by another organization this coming Sunday. Sincerely, the Benson City Council.'"

Matt went on to explain how the letter took the First Church of the Valley by surprise.

"See—" he gazed at the jurors—"the church leaders had missed the clause at the end of the lease agreement. They had no idea why they were in violation of the lease." Matt paced several steps back and forth, making eye contact with each of the jurors. Any doubts they may have had about him and his argument were dissolving like sugar in water.

The church, Matt told them, had paid one year's rent up front—seven hundred dollars per month for a total of $8,400. "In addition to kicking the church out of their rented facility with virtually no warning because of a lease clause that clearly violates the U.S. Constitution—" he paused for effect—"the Benson City Council made the poor decision to keep thousands of dollars in lease money. Even though the building was no longer available to the church."

For the next twenty minutes Matt gave the jury the gist of the story, the fact that Pastor Carson contacted the City Council and talked to a secretary who told him about the overlooked clause in the lease and then added, "Your church's name convinced us you wouldn't be in violation."

Matt allowed his tone to grow incensed for a moment, and he could read the same emotion in the eyes of several jurors. "The church's *name?*" He shook his head. "In other words, since the name Christ or Jesus wasn't in the name of Pastor Carson's church, the Benson City Council thought they were safe. Safe enough that they didn't need to check what doctrine was being preached each Sunday." He shifted his weight and cocked his head. "But then someone told someone, and they told someone else, and the Sunday before Pastor Carson's church lost their lease, three members of the Benson City Council showed up at the Sunday service."

Matt prayed his closing words would leave an impression. "This was a case, ladies and gentlemen, that *had* to be brought to trial. Because the Benson City Council had the audacity to make a law prohibiting the free exercise of religion—in this case, the Christian religion. An action that flies in the face of our Constitution and everything this country stands for. An action our founding fathers hoped to avert when they wrote the First Amendment."

He paced to the far end of the jury and noticed that each pair of eyes followed him. "We cannot allow that, friends. Not here, not in Benson. Not anywhere in the United States. Because once we let our government decide what's acceptable in church meetings taking place in City Halls, we're only a short jump to letting them decide what's acceptable in churches." Matt's voice rang with sincerity. "And that would mean everything our forefathers stood for, every battle fought in the name of freedom, would be for nothing."

Matt shrugged one shoulder. "And so, honestly, ladies and gentlemen, this is not a case about separation of church and state. It's a case about standing up for freedom. My freedom, your freedom." He pointed to the front row of spectators where Pastor Carson was seated next to his wife among fifty people from First Church of the Valley. "Their freedom. On that note, we are not only asking that this church be allowed to maintain their lease with the Benson City Hall. We're asking for damages. Certainly the money kept by the city these past months, when Pastor Carson's church has had to meet in various less desirable facilities. But also punitive damages."

He glanced at the attorneys for the city of Benson and several City Council members seated behind them. "Because what the Benson City Council did in this matter is inexcusable and deserves some type of punishment. That way word will get out: We're serious about freedom in America. Dead serious." He gripped the jury box and looked at them with a heart full of compassion. "You can't write laws that fly in the face of the Constitution and expect that act of defiance to go unpunished." There was a beat. "Each of you is here today to carry on where Thomas Jefferson and his peers first began. Protecting freedom for this generation and every generation after it." Matt nodded. "Thank you."

The lead attorney for the City of Benson was an older, distinguished man whose tone was irritating and who focused on the appearance of things. Leasing City Hall to a Christian church would give the appearance of state-sponsored religion; allowing

First Church of the Valley to preach Jesus Christ as the only way to salvation would give an appearance of narrow-mindedness, a lack of political tolerance. The entire matter gave the public the appearance that the Benson City Council had crossed the line between church and state. The attorney barely brushed over the fact that Pastor Carson had signed the lease agreement, binding him to whatever stipulations it contained. If a clause in the contract violated the U.S. Constitution—as Matt was suggesting—the fact that the pastor signed it would be of no significance.

Matt took notes and knew exactly how he'd play out the examination phase. His witnesses were simple, trusting people. People like Pastor Carson, who had never intended to rile up a case that was drawing sparks of national attention; and the church secretary, who kept the books and related in chilling detail the fact that the Benson City Council had no intention of refunding the church's lease money or restoring its lease unless, "You people stop talking about Jesus Christ."

Throughout his examination, Matt inserted questions involving the appearance of things. "So did the Benson City Council give you the appearance of not returning your lease money?"

"No. They actually didn't return it. They kept it even though we'd done everything right. Everything except preach the doctrine they wanted us to preach."

And to Pastor Carson, "Once the clause about doctrine was pointed out to you, did you feel it gave the appearance of discriminating against your group because of your religious views?"

Two people in the jury box stifled a giggle, and Matt knew they understood the point he was trying to make. Pastor Casey twisted his forehead into a grid of lines. "The appearance? I'd say it was more like the left foot of fellowship. We were kicked out of that building because of what we believed. Appearances had nothing to do with it."

Halfway through the first day, Matt had no doubts whatsoever that he would win the case. The jurors were bored and often hostile to the cross-examinations of the Benson attorneys. Every question they asked just looked like another attack on what the people at First Church of the Valley believed, and though the jurors may not have believed the same way, they had clearly caught Tanner's vision about standing up for freedom of choice. Whether that choice involved believing in Jesus Christ or not.

Attorneys for the Benson City Council brought very few witnesses, none of whom were effective. Matt tried to keep a straight face while the examination took place, and rarely bothered to add anything on the cross-examination. There was no point. With each passing hour the jurors were looking at their watches, appearing bored.

Each night back at his hotel room, Matt would call Hannah and give her the report. "You can't believe how well it's going." His heart soared with the way the case was progressing. "There were a dozen newspapers there today, and tomorrow we're expecting at least one national news show."

"That's wonderful."

"Usually they'd be coming to watch us lose, to witness another church group take a fall. But this time they're on our side. Can you believe it? We're not defending religion this time around; we're defending America. The word's getting out, and everyone wants a piece of the story."

He could hear Hannah clap her hands in the background. "Oh, Matt, it's just like Tanner dreamed it would be."

"Have you told him?"

"Every day when I go to the hospital." Her tone grew more somber. "I think it's helping him get through the week."

Matt leaned back on his hotel pillow and kicked his feet up. "You must have everyone we know praying."

The trial wrapped up late Thursday and deliberations began Friday morning. One of the jurors wore a T-shirt that bore the American flag and the words, "United We Stand." Matt took it as a good sign.

The judge informed the jury that First Church of the Valley was seeking fifty thousand dollars punitive damages, but that it was up to the jury to decide the actual amount—higher or lower.

Tanner had called Matt the night before after seeing a segment about the case on the evening's national news. "Hey, I heard the highlights of your closing arguments on CBS." Tanner sounded tired, but there was no denying his enthusiasm. "You're brilliant, buddy. I could never have pulled it off so well."

"That's where you're wrong." Matt grinned into the phone. "I'm only imitating everything I've ever seen or heard from you." Matt hesitated, his voice softer. "Hey, how's Jade?"

Tanner paused and Matt figured he was struggling to speak. "She's...she's very sick, Matt. The treatment is tearing her up. Hurry home, will ya?"

"You tell her to hang in there. I'll be there the minute I'm done."

Throughout deliberations, Matt interviewed with thirteen local and national news anchors and a handful of print reporters. He answered questions about expectations and the Constitution and national freedom, but he refrained from predicting a certain victory. His experience had been that no matter how sure the win, the jury should break the news first.

Finally, at just after four o'clock, the jury foreman notified the court clerk that they'd reached a decision. Matt was almost always anxious at this point in a trial. Bird-sized butterflies would attack his gut the same way they'd done before every basketball game he ever played in. This time, though, the butterflies were still.

In their place was the familiar calm that had comforted him all week. Matt knew it was because people were praying: Hannah and Tanner and the staff at the firm. Even Jade, sicker than she'd ever been, had sought God's divine help for this trial. And only God could have pulled off the type of trial and the accompanying media interest that had taken place that week.

Matt took his seat at the plaintiff's table and watched the jury file in. Several of them cast confident glances in Matt's direction. The clerk took the decision from the jury foreman and handed it to the judge. With little fanfare, he revealed the outcome.

"We, the jury, find in favor of the plaintiff. In doing so we agreed that the defendant must award the plaintiff—" The judge paused and appeared to study the number. Matt's eyes were glued to the man, urging him to continue. The judge cleared his throat and looked at Benson's attorneys. "Five hundred thousand dollars...half to be paid up front, and thereafter five years of fifty-thousand-dollar payments until the judgment is paid in full."

The moment the judge spoke the words *five hundred thousand dollars,* Matt let his held breath out and thanked God. Thanked Him because this case would have a ripple effect that would be unprecedented in the fight for religious freedom. And a half-million dollar judgment? It would put every civil rights group and governing body in the country on alert that the time had come to back off. Americans had the right to practice their religious freedom. In a church...in a school...in a public building. Even in a rented City Hall.

Matt could hardly wait to tell Tanner.

Interviews with reporters took place immediately after the verdict, and time and again Matt gave credit to God and Tanner.

"No one understands the severity and importance of our battle to maintain religious freedom in this country like Tanner

Eastman." Matt looked straight at the cameras, believing every word. "This was his strategy, his victory. I'm glad for the chance to carry it out."

The media circus over what had happened took three hours to die down. Of course, it all paled in comparison to the vigil being held at Jade's bedside several states away. Back at his hotel room later that evening, Matt tossed his things in his suitcase and took a shuttle to the airport.

By ten o'clock he was on a flight home.

Twenty-nine

Hannah's desire to help Jade had been there long before Matt left for Colorado.

Despite the joy of having Kody as their son, Hannah's heart ached almost constantly for Jade. Yet until Matt returned from Colorado, Hannah couldn't think of anything tangible she could do. In fact, if anything, she felt more disconnected than ever. Here it was, the most trying, painful time in Jade's life, and Hannah was busy buying blue bedding and baby bottles.

And with Matt gone, she'd had no time to do anything but care for Kody.

Now that he was home, she had an idea, something she could do that just might make all the difference for Jade. That Sunday morning, the day before Jade's surgery, Hannah called Pastor Steve at church and told him her plan.

"I want to form a prayer chain for Jade Eastman. Different from any prayer chain ever done before."

During announcements that morning, Pastor Steve explained the plan to the congregation. Hannah listened, praying they would catch her vision.

"You've heard of prayer chains before," the pastor told them. "Well, Hannah Bronzan has put together something a little different. It's called the Jade Chain."

Hannah sat between Matt and Jenny, and without hesitating she took their hands. She looked around and saw that people were listening, some of them nodding, eyes teary. Nearly everyone knew the battle Jade was facing and the very real possibility that she wouldn't survive.

The pastor continued. "Most of you know that Jade is battling brain cancer and that even now—days after delivering their baby daughter—she is undergoing severe treatment. Tomorrow morning doctors will perform a delicate brain surgery on Jade, and truthfully, her chances are not good. She could lose her memory, her personality…her life." He gave Hannah a sad smile. "Hannah's idea is this: Anyone wishing to participate will sign up for a half-hour block of prayer time, starting with midnight tonight. During that block, you will pray for Jade. Pray for her newborn daughter, her husband, and her son. Pray that God heals her and that nothing happens during the surgery to rob her of the person she is, of the dynamic personality she's been blessed with."

He searched the faces of the five hundred people in attendance. When he spoke, Hannah could hear the ache in his voice and she wasn't surprised. "I guess what I'm asking is that you'd sign up. Please. And pray for a miracle for Jade Eastman."

After the service Matt and Jenny went to get Kody from the nursery, and Hannah found the pastor. "Thank you." She blinked back tears. "I'll call you tomorrow as soon as we hear anything."

"No need." The pastor took Hannah's hand, his expression more serious than she'd seen before. "I'll be there first thing in the morning. I'm planning to stay all day."

Hannah hugged him, losing the battle with her tears in the process. There was no question that Pastor Steve understood how ill Jade really was. She thanked him again, then hurried off to the foyer to check on the Jade Chain sign-up sheet.

What she saw stopped her in her tracks. What was this? Why were so many people bottlenecked in the church foyer?

Then it hit her, and her hand flew to her mouth. *Father, I don't believe it…You're so good, Lord.*

She stared, open-mouthed. The scene before her was the most amazing, breathtaking picture of a church family she'd ever seen or imagined in her life.

Snaking in a line up and down the length of the foyer were easily two hundred people.

Men, women, children…baseball players from the local high school, elderly men with canes and wobbly knees, a diabetic woman in a wheelchair. People Hannah knew well and others she wouldn't have recognized if she'd met them on the street. All of them waiting in line to put their name on the sign-up sheet.

Each of them as desperate as Hannah to find a way to help Jade Eastman.

Patsy Landers stared at two handwritten letters spread out on her kitchen table and considered her options.

At first, the activities she and Grace had been doing seemed like they might be enough. Taking a walk, building a birdhouse, singing a song. Each had been fun, and once in a while Grace would even seem happy. Patsy knew this because every now and then Grace would smile.

But it was never her old smile, the one that used to light up a room.

Concerned that something might be seriously wrong with Grace, Patsy took her to see a counselor, a Christian woman whose office was across the street from Patsy's church. For two days, the woman spent an hour with Grace, talking to her, asking her questions. Listening. At the end of the second session, the woman pulled Patsy aside.

"I'll be candid with you; Grace shows all the signs of post-traumatic stress disorder."

Patsy blinked. "Post what?"

Grace was sitting ten feet away. The woman glanced at her, and lowered her voice. "Mrs. Landers, the events that have taken place recently in your granddaughter's life are affecting her deeply. In my opinion, she's suffering from depression."

Depression.

The word was like a tourniquet around Patsy's heart even now. Depression? How was it possible? Yes, the child was bound to miss the Bronzans, but certainly she'd get over it. After all, Patsy had loved Grace since she was an infant. There were times in Grace's four short years when she stayed with Patsy for months on end before Leslie would come around and whisk her away somewhere.

Patsy had been a rock for Grace.

So why now, when Grace knew she would never have to leave, was she struggling with depression?

Patsy sighed. As if those troubles weren't enough, ten days ago she received the first letter in the mail. She stared at the letters again. The first was from Leslie; the second, from a woman who claimed to have a cell next to Leslie's in prison.

Leslie's letter was written in pencil. Patsy picked it up, feeling the same queasy feeling she'd felt the first time she saw it. Leslie's attorney's name and address were on the return corner of the envelope, and the moment Patsy received it she knew there had either been a problem or a miracle.

Leslie simply wouldn't have written otherwise.

The letter took up less than a page, and Patsy studied it once more. Leslie had written it for one reason: to inform Patsy that the minute prison officials released her, she'd be back for Grace. Not only that, but apparently she'd dreamed up some way to make a living.

Patsy's eyes ran over the strange last line in the letter: *Besides, I've thought of a way we can make enough money to survive. I know we'll never go hungry. Kiss her for me. Leslie.*

We? Who was we? Leslie and Grace? What possible way could Leslie and Grace make money? Patsy had studied the line for a long time and decided Leslie must have been referring to a boyfriend, someone she planned to live with once she was out.

However Leslie intended to make money, Patsy doubted her methods would be legal. That afternoon, when Patsy finished reading the letter, she was on the phone with Edna Parsons. "She can't take Grace, can she?"

When Edna hesitated, panic raced through Patsy. "Well, that's tricky. If Grace were adopted to another family, the answer would be no. But since you're her mother, the courts see it as a gray area."

The social worker went on to explain that if Patsy welcomed her daughter into her home and allowed her to visit with Grace, it would be very possible that one day Leslie would be given custody again.

"Besides, you haven't actually adopted Grace yet. You're her legal guardian, but even that becomes open to interpretation once the courts deem Leslie has paid her debt to society."

"You mean she could hire an attorney and fight me for custody?"

Mrs. Parsons let loose a small huff. "If you welcome Leslie into your home, she could leave with Grace, and unless she breaks a law, no agency in the country would consider it a kidnapping." She paused. "The alternative is to get a restraining order on her as soon as you know she's out of prison, but even then you'd have to give cause."

The conversation had played in Patsy's mind a dozen times since then. Especially after she received the second letter. Three days after opening the first, Patsy found a letter in her postbox addressed to Mrs. Landers. The handwriting was unfamiliar.

Patsy set down Leslie's letter and picked up the other one. The message was brief and to the point.

Dear Mrs. Landers,

My cell is next to your daughter's. I heard her talking the other day about making money with her little girl. Grace, I think it was. She was talking about some pretty bad stuff and it made me remember my little girl. Bad stuff happened to her, too. But I ain't never tried to make money off her. I hope you understand what I'm telling you. I don't want any more little girls hurt that way. I got your address from Leslie's notebook when she was on duty.

Candi

Patsy tried every way she could to read something other than the obvious into Candi's note. It wasn't possible. Leslie wanted to make money with Grace? In a way that someone sitting in prison thought was "pretty bad stuff"?

Horror filled Patsy as the possibilities slammed against her mind. Leslie had done some awful things in her life, made some terrible choices…but making money off Grace? The idea and all it entailed was more than Patsy could bear.

Again she called Grace's social worker, Edna Parsons, and read her the note over the phone.

"Sounds like Leslie's made some dangerous connections in prison." Mrs. Parsons's tone was troubled. "Save the note. It might help you get a restraining order."

"But…do you think she's talking about…" Patsy couldn't bring herself to finish the sentence.

"Pornography or prostitution." The words were hand grenades in Patsy's heart. "I'd say it was one or the other. There's an entire network of children Grace's age trapped in that underworld. Police are constantly working to arrest the adults behind it, but it happens. I won't lie to you."

"And you really think Leslie could…could do that?"

The social worker sounded tired. "Mrs. Landers, I haven't told you this information before, but maybe now it's time you hear. The scene at that deserted field, when police found Leslie and Grace, was a grim one."

The things Edna Parsons told Patsy then left her weak and in tears. Her stomach hurt, and she covered her eyes, confused about one thing. "But she asked for her mother for weeks after going to live with the Bronzans."

"That's normal. At that point she could transfer all blame for her situation on to the bad guys her mother spent time with. After spending time with the Bronzans she knew differently." Mrs. Parsons drew a quiet breath. "I saw how Grace changed with that family. For the first time she knew what a real mommy was supposed to be like."

The picture was becoming clearer. "That whole time she thought I was dead."

"Right."

Patsy's tears felt hot on her weathered cheeks. "She must have believed she'd been given a new life, a chance to have a family who would never leave her. Never hurt her."

"Exactly."

The despair in Patsy's soul was worse than anything she'd suffered in all the years of disappointments with Leslie. "What am I supposed to do, then? How can I make Grace feel secure?"

"It takes time."

"And what about Leslie's threats. She'll take Grace whether it's legal or not, by the sounds of it." Patsy's voice trembled and she felt utterly weak.

"First, you should get an attorney and see about officially adopting Grace. Second, I'd follow through with the restraining order. And you might want to consider moving, as well."

Attorney? Restraining order? Moving? Patsy's head swam and she could barely find the strength to speak. "In other words, I'd never see Leslie again."

The social worker's answer rang with finality. "Quite possibly. But then, she considered you dead before any of this ever happened."

Memories of the conversation faded.

Patsy reached for a manila envelope on her lap and tucked the letters inside. She craned her neck and saw that Grace was still on the recliner where she'd been an hour earlier, watching television with the same dazed look she'd had since she'd arrived in Oklahoma.

God, what am I supposed to do?

There was no loud answer, no letters from heaven giving her step-by-step directions on how to raise little Grace. Patsy shifted her gaze forward once more and stared at her hands. Her shoulders shook and tears formed a logjam in her throat.

For years she'd prayed daily for Leslie, begging God to change her heart and bring her closer to Him. Now, in some ways, Patsy was being asked to choose. Give Grace the home and safety she deserved, but eliminate Leslie from her life entirely. It was the most gut-wrenching thing Patsy had ever been asked to do.

She closed her eyes, folded her hands, and brought them to her face. *Please, God, give me wisdom. I feel like I'm going to lose no matter what I do.*

Ask and you will receive...seek and you will find...for the LORD gives wisdom.

The Scriptures soaked through her frightened soul as though God Himself were writing them there.

Bit by bit, an idea began to form in Patsy's head. One she would never have considered if not for Leslie's threats and Candi's warnings—and most of all her own conversations with Mrs. Parsons.

Ever since receiving Leslie's letters, she'd seen only one way of carrying on, a way that grew darker and bleaker with every passing day. But now…in light of God's gentle whispers…she saw a way she'd never considered before. It wouldn't be easy or pain-free, but suddenly it loomed as the answer to her prayers.

The idea grew and took root and by that evening, Patsy was sure it was the best answer. A way that, in the end, would not involve losing, but winning. Not just for Patsy and Leslie and Grace.

But for the Bronzans as well.

Thirty

Only Tanner knew exactly how hard the treatment had been on Jade.

In two weeks she had lost fifteen pounds and most of her hair. She vomited several times a day and was often too exhausted to do anything more than make a short trip to the nursery to see Madison.

Ty visited every afternoon, and Jade made sure she had a scarf around her head before he came. He had a hard enough time understanding her cancer without watching her hair fall out. Finally he'd brought her his Los Angeles Lakers baseball cap.

"Here, Mom." He helped position it over her balding head, pulling the sides down carefully over her ears. "This way you'll have a part of me with you even when you sleep."

Jade had worn the hat every day since, even when the convulsions in her stomach left her doubled over a bedpan for nearly an hour.

They had arranged with their neighbor to watch Ty any time that Tanner wasn't home. And since the second day of Jade's treatment, that had been almost constantly. He came home to sleep and spend time with Ty, but only when Jade insisted. At least four times he'd stayed the night, holding her hand and pulling back the thin clumps of hair that remained on her head so they wouldn't fall in the bedpan.

For all the ways Jade loved Tanner, the time they spent together those two weeks raised her feelings to another level. By letting him see her now, when death was pulling at her from every side, she had shown him everything there was to see, allowed him into every closet in her heart.

Tanner had seen her collapsed on the bathroom floor, clinging to the toilet, and he'd wiped vomit from her mouth when she was too exhausted to move. He'd applied ointment to her C-section incision and spoon-fed her when she was too weak to lift her hands. When she needed to soothe the radiation burns on her face and neck, Tanner worked tirelessly to keep her washcloth cool.

He'd done all that, seen her at her worst and weakest, yet Jade could tell by his touch that he had never loved her more.

The days passed in a slow, sickening blur. Rarely did they talk about the impending surgery when it was all they could do to survive each day. The news was both good and bad. While the tumor hadn't grown tentacles—which would have made it very difficult if not impossible to remove surgically—it had not shrunk nearly as much as Dr. Layton hoped.

Because of that, and because the treatment was taking such a toll on Jade, Dr. Layton decided to go ahead with the scheduled surgery date of October 21. Two weeks after she'd given birth to Madison.

"There's no point waiting," the doctor had told them after one week of chemotherapy and radiation. "Not since we're not seeing a dramatic response to the treatment."

Finally, mercifully, it was Sunday evening.

Dr. Layton had spent an hour with her and Tanner that afternoon, explaining once more the benefits and risks of brain surgery.

"First of all, it's the only way to rid Jade of the cancer." He looked from Tanner to Jade and back again. "Otherwise her condition would be terminal."

He detailed that if all went well, they would remove the entire tumor without disturbing the surrounding brain tissue. If the margins around the tumor tested clean, there was a very good chance Jade would be cured, and that five years from now, if she had no recurrence of cancer she could be given a clean bill of health. Her battle with cancer would be over forever.

If not…

Jade had barely been able to tolerate hearing the list of things that could go wrong. First, they might not get the entire tumor. In that case, if the margins around the tumor showed remaining cancer cells, Jade could easily face a second brain tumor down the road or cancer in another part of her body—most likely her lungs.

Even if they managed to remove every cancer cell, there was a possibility that Jade's brain would be permanently altered in the process.

"That's the part I'm a little foggy on." Tanner leaned forward, holding tight to Jade's hand with one hand and resting his chin in the palm of his other.

Dr. Layton studied the floor for a moment and then looked at Tanner once more. "It means she could lose her memory or suffer a change in personality. When we remove a tumor this size, we try to leave the brain undisturbed. But some tissue is bound to be lost in the process."

Jade watched the blood drain from Tanner's face. These details had always been clear to her, but apparently Tanner had not fully understood until now. "How…how will you know?"

Dr. Layton folded his hands, his brow lowered, eyes dark with the severity of the situation. "We won't know until she regains consciousness. After the surgery."

When the doctor finally left, Tanner hung his head and cried.

Jade wanted desperately to crawl out of bed and go to him, to sit on his knee, wrap her arms around his neck, and promise him none of those terrible things would happen. That tomorrow at this time she'd still be with him and that everything was going to be okay.

Instead she ran her fingers through his hair, praying that her touch would be enough to help him through. "He has to tell us that, Tanner. We can't be blind to the risks."

Tanner shook his head and wiped the sleeve of his shirt across his eyes. "I'm sorry." She saw raw fear in his eyes. "I want to wake up at home with you beside me, with Maddie and Ty down the hall, and know that every bit of this was just some awful dream."

A nurse came then and brought Jade her last meal before the surgery. Now it was six o'clock, and before they could talk about what the morning might bring, there was a knock on the door.

Tanner looked up. "Come in."

The door opened and the Bronzans filed through. First Matt, then Hannah.

"Hey, guys!" Jade smiled at them and pushed a button on the remote control, raising the back of her bed several degrees. "Where's Jenny?"

Matt gave her a partial grin that didn't quite reach his eyes. "Downstairs with Kody."

Jade nodded. She had seen their baby once earlier that week and marveled at the grace of God, the perfection of his timing and design in bringing them this child. Especially while the pain of losing Grace was still so real.

Matt and Hannah crossed the room toward her bed. Hannah carried a large envelope and already Jade could see tears in her eyes.

"How are you?" Hannah took hold of Jade's hand, her face intent.

Jade's throat was suddenly thick with emotion and she could only nod.

Tanner stood, and he and Matt hugged. They'd talked at

length the day before so Matt could fill Tanner in about the trial and the judgment and how all of it had been more than they could ask or imagine.

There were no words between them now, though.

Everyone in the room knew why they were there. They'd come to say good-bye.

Hannah moved close to Jade's side and held up the envelope. "We have something we'd like to hang over your bed."

Jade smiled and adjusted her baseball cap. "Not a Lakers poster, right? Ty already tried that. The head nurse is from Portland. A Blazers fan." She glanced at Matt. "It's all she can do to let me wear the hat."

"No…" The tears in Hannah's eyes spilled onto her cheeks. She managed a sad smile as she took Jade's hand. "It's not a Lakers poster."

Hannah pulled out a small stack of notebook paper. "It's a prayer chain, Jade." Hannah's smile faded and she leaned closer. "Pastor Steve agreed to ask the congregation for forty-eight volunteers." Hannah passed the stack to Jade. "But 240 people signed up."

Tanner positioned himself on the other side of the bed and stared at the pieces of paper. "Are you serious?"

Jade stared, speechless, at the names listed before her.

Hannah Bronzan, midnight; Amy Hannan, 12:30; Adam Sonney, 1:00 A.M.; Ben Bailey, 1:30…

The list of names flowed the length of the sheet and continued to the next page and the next. Ten pages of names. People whose children she had taught in Sunday School or women she'd sat next to in church. Girls in the high school youth group and boys barely old enough to drive.

Names jumped at her from the page: *Brandon Daves, 5:00 P.M.; Ann Hudson, 5:30; Sylvia Wallgren, 6:00 P.M.; Landon Heidenreich, 6:30…*

It was overwhelming.

Her hand began to shake and she let the stack fall to her lap. Her hands fluttered to her throat and she worked to find her voice. "I…I don't know what to say."

There were tears on all their faces now as Hannah took the list and pulled a roll of tape from the envelope. With Matt's help, they taped each sheet above Jade's bed, and finally they placed a small banner over the list of names that read simply: "The Jade Chain."

Jade craned around to see the list as two quiet sobs shook her body. All this time she'd wondered if her church family really liked her or not. The comments about her being an adulterer had only come from two older women, but still, Jade had wondered.

Until now.

When she needed them most, they had stepped up and agreed to pray for her every hour of the day until she was no longer in danger. Jade buried her face in her hands. They loved her… They loved her after all.

She steadied herself and let her hands fall to her lap while Matt and Hannah finished with the wall. "I can't believe it…" Jade looked at Hannah. "Thank you so much, Hannah. I've never…never had a friend like you."

Hannah leaned over and hugged Jade, and the two stayed that way for a long while, holding on to the moment, weeping from someplace deep inside them at the thought of what would come next.

When Hannah straightened again, Matt put his arm around her and patted Jade's knee. "We wanted to pray with you and let you know we'll be here all day tomorrow, helping with Ty and checking on Madison so you and Tanner can be alone."

Jade's heart hurt, swollen with equal parts grief and joy. How blessed she was to count the Bronzans as family, to know that if anything happened to her, Tanner and Ty and Madison would always have friends who understood. Friends who had been there since the beginning and would be there to the end.

Whenever that might be.

Jade tightened her grip on Hannah's hand and searched her eyes. Matt cleared his throat, and Jade shifted her gaze to him. "We love you, Jade. We'll always love you." Matt's voice broke. "We're here for you and Tanner and the kids whenever you need us. Whatever you need."

Matt reached out and took hold of Tanner's hand so the circle was complete. "Can we pray for you?"

"Yes." Jade choked back a sob. "Please."

Jade watched the others close their eyes and bow their heads, and she did the same. Matt spoke in a shaky voice. "Lord, the time has come to place our friend, Jade, in Your arms. We trust You, God, that whatever happens tomorrow will be perfectly part of Your will, Your plan. But we beg You..."

When he halted, Jade knew he was crying.

"We beg You to heal her. Guide the surgeons' hands and give them Your eyes, Lord. To take out every bit of the cancer. Please let the time pass quickly and...and bring Jade back to us very soon. In Jesus' name, amen."

If the good-bye with the Bronzans wasn't painful enough, an hour later their neighbor brought Ty up and turned him over to Tanner. The surgical procedures would start too early in the morning for Ty or anyone else to see Jade. Only Tanner was allowed in her room until she was taken into surgery, and that would happen sometime around six the next morning.

Beside her on the bed was the journal Jade had written for Ty. Tanner had wrapped it a week earlier. Jade held her hand out and studied her son. "Come here, buddy."

He still hadn't cried, not once since Jade's diagnosis. But now, as he shuffled across the slick hospital floor toward her bed, she could see his nose was red and his eyes were puffy. When he was next to her, he scrunched his face into a mass of wrinkles and gripped his temples with his thumb and forefinger.

Tanner stood at his side, his hand on Ty's shoulder, too distraught to speak.

Jade swallowed hard and somehow found her voice. "Ahh, buddy, it's okay." Jade released the bed rail and pulled him close, hugging him and stroking his back while he sobbed in grunts and small gasps as only a thirteen-year-old boy can. The sound of it broke what was left of Jade's heart, and she realized how hard he'd worked to mask his fears before this.

"I...I don't want them to hurt you." He clung to her as he hadn't done since he was a small boy, as he hadn't done since sheriff's deputies showed up at their door to take him away that awful morning three years ago. The week after Jim had won full custody of him.

"Ty, it's okay, honey." Jade whispered the words close to his ear. "The doctors aren't going to hurt me; they're going to help me. So I can get out of here and come home with you and Daddy and Maddie."

"I'm...I'm so scared, Mom. I need you." He pulled back, and she saw terror in his eyes. "What if something happens?"

"God's in control, Ty. You believe that, right?" Jade ignored her own tears and wiped her thumb across Ty's wet cheeks.

He nodded and sniffed hard. "It's just that...well, other than Dad..." He glanced at Tanner and back to her. "Other than Dad, you're my best friend. You *have* to be okay."

Jade pulled his head to her chest once more and let him cry. There was no way she could give him the journal now, not with him worrying about whether she'd survive. Without letting Ty see what she was doing, Jade moved the package beneath her sheets. She would give it to him later, when she was on the other side of this nightmare.

And if not…

Jade squeezed her eyes shut and refused to let her thoughts go that way. Tanner moved in closer, sheltering the two of them with his body, lending his strength whatever way he could.

After a while, Ty pulled back, reached for a tissue, and blew his nose. "I'm sorry for crying. I—" he blew his nose again—"I wanted to be strong for you, Mom."

Jade caught his hand in hers once more. "Never be afraid to cry, son. It means you have a heart."

"Yeah…I guess." Ty tried to grin, his eyes nearly swollen shut. "I love you."

"I love you, Ty." She wanted to tell him something positive, something reassuring. A promise he could hang on to no matter what happened in the morning. She settled on something truthful. Whatever the outcome might be. Their eyes locked and she directed her words straight to his soul. "We'll be home together soon, okay?"

He nodded, missing the double meaning, and this time his smile came more easily. "Okay. Be safe."

Be safe…

The words washed over Jade, and she steeled herself against another wave of tears. They were the words she'd told him since he was small, words she said whenever it was time to say goodbye. She answered him with the words that were his typical response. "Always."

Tanner put his arm around Ty, and together they turned for the door. Before they walked out, Ty turned once more and looked at her. The tears were back in his eyes and hers. Jade managed a smile and raised her hand—her two middle fingers tucked in close to her palm: sign language for, "I love you."

He did the same, and then together he and Tanner left, shutting the door behind them.

Only when they were gone did Jade give in to the tears and heartache that had been building inside her since Ty arrived. *God, help me...I want to see him again. I want to see him grow up...*

I am here, daughter...I know the plans I have for you.

The answer was as real as if God had announced it over the hospital PA system. Jade's body relaxed some, though her sobs continued. She was still crying when Tanner returned.

"He's going home with Matt and Hannah."

Jade nodded and grabbed four quick breaths. In every way that mattered, she was exhausted, but she had to get through this. In the past few hours, she'd had to say good-bye to everyone that mattered to her.

Everyone but Tanner.

And now, before she fell asleep, she would have to do that, too.

Without saying a word, Tanner flipped off the overhead light. The glow from the monitors lit his way as he walked toward her bed. Careful not to bump the machines or disturb the tubing that bound her to them, he climbed onto the mattress and lay beside her on the starchy sheets. The smell of sterilized hospital bedding mingled with his subtle cologne and filled her senses.

I'll remember this smell as long as I live...

He held his face against hers, letting their tears mix and fall to the pillow together...inseparable. Just as she and Tanner were inseparable.

He ran his fingers along her arm and the sides of her face, and Jade savored the feel of his body against hers. For a long while, neither of them spoke. Then, Tanner leaned up on one elbow and studied her face.

His voice was a caress. "When I was in college, I hated English Literature."

The corners of Jade's mouth raised a bit. Even now, at the saddest moment in their lives, Tanner could make her smile. "I didn't know that."

"I did." He ran his thumb along her cheekbone. "I couldn't understand why reading William Shakespeare would ever help me in life."

Jade had no idea where he was going with this, but the diversion felt wonderful. Though her voice was scratchy and weak, for the first time that day it held a trace of humor. "I can see that."

"But yesterday I remembered a quote from Shakespeare."

Jade lifted her eyebrows. "'Wherefore art thou Romeo?'"

"No." Tanner smiled, though the sadness in his eyes remained. His voice grew more tender, if that were possible. "'Give sorrow words: the grief that does not speak whispers the o'er-fraught heart and bids it break.'"

The quote played over again in Jade's mind. This was so like Tanner. Whether he was in front of a jury or sitting beside her on their back deck, his thoughts were always profound. Still, there was no way she could give her sorrow words. Not now, with a thousand yesterdays blocking her ability to speak.

Fresh tears spilled onto Tanner's cheeks and rolled off the end of his chin. "And so I have to speak, Jade. Otherwise…otherwise my heart will break."

She nodded and tried to lift her head from the pillow. When her body wouldn't cooperate, Tanner lowered his face to hers and kissed her—not the passionate kiss of two lovers, but a kiss of longing and sorrow and grief. It was Tanner's attempt to express the depth of what he was feeling.

When he pulled back, he shifted to his elbow again. "I love you, Jade. In all my life I've only loved you."

She forced back the lump in her throat. "I love you, too, Tanner."

"I keep asking myself, what if you don't know me when you wake up? What if you don't remember Virginia or Kelso or Ty or Maddie? And if something happens, how long before I'll see you and Jenna in heaven...what if..."

Then, despite his obvious desire to say something eloquent and memorable in these, her last hours before surgery, he hung his head and wept. Taking great care, he positioned his face over hers and wrapped his arms beneath her, much as Ty had done earlier. "Don't go, Jade..." His voice was racked with torment. "Don't leave me. Please... Come back to me, baby."

"I will..." She kissed his neck, clinging to him. "I will, Tanner. I will..."

Jade wasn't sure how long they stayed that way, but at some point they fell asleep, side by side. As though they might be back at home, holding each other through just one more happy night instead of clinging to their final moments before Jade's surgery.

At five the next morning, a nurse woke them. "They're ready for you, Mrs. Eastman."

Jade squinted at the machines surrounding her and tried to remember what was happening. Then it all came flooding back. It was the morning of the surgery. Her surgery. And after today...

Tanner coughed and eased himself from the bed. Jade could see that he wanted to ask the nurse to leave the room, give them another few minutes alone. But it was too late. Preparations for the surgery were already in motion.

Minutes later two technicians and Dr. Layton entered the room. "Good morning, Jade." He smiled and she appreciated his upbeat manner. He would be assisting in the surgery, after all, and she needed him and the other doctors to be positive.

"Good morning."

The doctor looked from Jade to Tanner and back again. "Well, Jade, this is the first day of the rest of your life."

Jade nodded and glanced at Tanner. He was whiter than the sheets, and his expression was a contrast of trust and sheer terror. She leveled her gaze at Dr. Layton. "I'm ready."

Tanner stood back while they lifted her from the bed to the gurney. She winced as they gave her the first in a series of shots that would knock her out for the operation. Before they took her away, Tanner came alongside her and whispered, "I love you, Jade. Come back to me, okay?"

A warm sensation made its way through Jade's veins and her eyelids grew heavy. "I will, you'll see."

"I'll be praying."

"Thanks…" Her words were slurred, and everything faded around her.

The last thing she saw as she was wheeled from the room, as the medication took her under, was Tanner's face. After that she closed her eyes.

Somewhere she'd read that the last image a person saw before brain surgery would be the first they'd remember when they regained consciousness. If that was true, only one image could help her brain survive the coming hours, help preserve her personality and memory and everything else she held dear.

The precious image of Tanner Eastman's face.

She fought the medication's pull, doing everything in her power to hold Tanner's image there, but no matter how hard she held on, the crispness of his face began to blur and fade until finally the image disappeared entirely.

Then there was nothing but darkness…and the strangest sense that she was being carried. Not by human arms, but holy ones. The sensation grew stronger until finally, despite the total darkness, Jade fell into the deepest, most peaceful sleep she'd ever known.

Six hours later, Tanner was sitting in the waiting room with his loved ones when Dr. Layton came up to them. Tanner was immediately on his feet, his heart soaring over this one fact:

Dr. Layton was smiling.

"Well…?" Tanner's heart raced and he struggled to breathe. "How is she?"

"The surgery went beautifully. We're almost positive we got all the cancer."

A chorus of, "Thank You, God" and "Thank You, Jesus" came from Matt and Hannah and Pastor Steve.

Ty ran across the room and hugged Tanner. "I *knew* she'd make it, Dad. I knew it."

Tanner's knees trembled. She was alive! Thank God, she was alive. He closed his eyes and clenched his fists, his voice merely a whisper. "Thank You…thank You…" Almost at the same moment, he shifted his attention back to Dr. Layton. "Can I talk to her?"

"Not exactly." A shadow fell across the doctor's face. "You can sit with her, but she's unconscious, remember? That's what we expected. We'd like to see her come around in the next few hours." He hesitated. "The longer she stays in a coma, the more likely she'll have some memory loss or personality changes."

"Personality changes?" Ty looked up at Tanner, his eyes wide with new concern. "What's that mean, Dad?"

Tanner narrowed his eyes and tried to keep from collapsing. He was riding the wildest roller coaster of his life. After hitting the highest high in the past six months, he was right back where he'd been all that morning. Begging God to heal his wife and bring her back to him, where she belonged.

Where she had always belonged.

"Well..." Tanner tightened his grip on Ty and spoke with as much strength as he could muster. "It means we keep praying, son. We just keep on praying."

Thirty-one

At eight o'clock that night in the hospital waiting room, Matt was talking in quiet whispers with Pastor Steve when his cell phone rang. He cringed, realizing he'd forgotten to turn it off when he arrived at the hospital. He snatched it up and headed for the door, shrugging when Hannah cast him a curious glance. He stepped outside and took the call.

"Hello?"

"Mr. Bronzan?"

The connection wasn't very strong, and Matt plugged his other ear so he could hear the woman. "Yes?"

"I'm sorry to call you so late, but Edna Parsons gave me your number." The woman hesitated. "This is Patsy Landers, Grace's grandmother."

Matt's heart skipped a beat. "Uh…hello, Mrs. Landers." Matt ached at the sound of Grace's name. He still missed her more than he talked about, more than he admitted even to himself. "How is she?"

"Well…" The woman's tone grew higher-pitched, as though she were upset. "She's been having some trouble."

Matt closed his eyes, overcome with sorrow. If only there were a way to hold Grace right here, right now, he would rock her and soothe away the pain. Whatever had caused it. "Is she okay?"

"She's healthy, if that's what you mean. But she's…she's not happy, and I think I finally understand why."

Confusion rang through Matt's mind. Why was she calling him about Grace? The child was no longer a part of their lives. It killed him to think of her troubled or sad, but there was nothing he could do about it.

Nothing at all.

Matt inhaled, waiting until his lungs were full before speaking. "Mrs. Landers, if you'll excuse me, I'm not sure I understand why you're calling."

"Because…" The woman on the other end was quiet for a moment. "Because I have an idea and…well…I'd like to share it with you."

"Yes…" An idea? About Grace's happiness? Her future? Matt's heart began to pound. "I'd like to hear it."

The days blended one into the other, and still Jade remained in a coma.

Whenever he met with Tanner, Dr. Layton's voice was somber and he frowned often. Clearly the man was discouraged, though Tanner thought he tried to hide the fact. Either way there was no dancing around the obvious. Every hour, every day that passed, the chances of Jade making a full recovery grew more and more slim.

Tanner existed in a fog of prayer and encouragement from Matt and Hannah and the others. At least once a day Ty was allowed in the room, and that was usually when Tanner was at his best. He would encourage Ty to talk to Jade, to touch her. And in the process he would find himself believing she could really hear them.

It was strange how his fears had changed time and again since Jade's diagnosis. Before her surgery, Tanner was most afraid that somehow she'd wake up a different person, no longer knowing him or loving him.

Now, though, at dawn of the fourth day since her operation,

Tanner only hoped she'd wake up at all.

He studied her face, serene and still, and glanced at the prayer chart above Jade's bed. It was still happening. Somewhere in the city of Thousand Oaks someone was praying for Jade's recovery. Tanner was grateful. There were hours when he couldn't find the strength to form another prayer, times when the knowledge of the Jade Chain was all that pulled him through.

His eyes fell back to Jade. The medication had made her face look full again, like it had been before she'd lost so much weight. Her head was still swathed in bandages, but otherwise she looked better than she had in months.

He took her limp hand in his and massaged his thumb over her wedding ring. "Jade, baby, good morning." Tanner cooed the words, inches from her ear. "Today's the day you wake up, honey, okay?"

It was the same thing he said to her every morning. And every time, when she failed to respond, he would start telling her stories. Dr. Layton had told him that conversation was one of the greatest ways to rouse a person from a coma. Memories were another.

That being the case, Tanner had decided to talk about the past. Every day, every hour if necessary. As much as was humanly possible.

"Remember that trust game we used to play when we were kids?" He searched her face for signs of a response. When there was none, he continued. "You'd close your eyes, and I'd lead you around the backyard. Remember? And when the weather was good, remember how we'd ride bikes around the neighborhood?" He relaxed back into the chair, his fingers still clutching hers. "Back then my favorite times were when we'd race. Really, Jade, I used to let you win. I mean, I wouldn't tell you back then, of course, but I loved the way your eyes sparkled when you'd win. It was worth losing just for that."

He took a sip of water and continued, sharing stories about her leaving for Kelso and him promising anyone who would listen that one day—no matter how long it took—he would marry her. Even if he had to search the whole country to find her again.

Tanner tried to sound upbeat. "It worked. I'm here, aren't I?"

Story after story spilled from him, even the sad ones, and in Jade and Tanner's years apart there had been plenty of those. He talked about finding her in Kelso that summer and how attracted he'd been to her, how difficult it was to keep his distance. He celebrated again the choice she'd made that summer to become a Christian and the strength she'd roused in him by challenging his intention to be a politician.

"I would have hated that lifestyle. I can never thank you enough, Jade, for helping me follow my dreams."

His voice grew somber. "After I came back from that trip and found you gone, married to someone else, I thought I'd die from grief. It was all I could do to—"

Tanner froze.

Had it been his imagination or had Jade moved her foot? He leaned forward and stayed utterly still, silent. Then he remembered Dr. Layton's advice:

It's especially important that you talk to her as she's waking up. Help her find her place again. But don't overwhelm her. Take it slow.

Tanner gulped hard and searched for the right words. "Jade, baby?" He waited. "Can you hear me?"

There it was again. Only this time, she moved the fingers on her right hand, too. She was coming out of it! *Please, God, let her come back all the way...please...*

Jade's head moved back and forth, and she moaned like a toddler waking from a long nap.

Tanner was on his feet, his eyes burning with unshed tears. "Jade, baby, it's me, Tanner. You're okay, honey. The surgery was a success." His eyes scanned her body and there was no question about it. She was moving the toes on both feet! Suddenly her hand wriggled against his, then gripped it with the faintest movement.

"Jade, wake up, honey. I'm here with you. Me, Tanner. Can you hear me, honey?"

Her eyelids began to flutter, and in seconds she opened them, squinting from the light. At first she looked around the room and Tanner held his breath.

Please, God...let her know me.

A heartbeat later, she turned her eyes on him...and the corners of her mouth lifted a fraction of an inch. Her voice was slow and croaky. "Hey..."

Tanner's heart jumped. She *knew* him! Jade knew who he was! He grabbed a quick breath and tried to keep from shouting out loud. *Calm. Stay calm.* "Hi."

This time there was no question, she was trying to smile. "Is your...o'er-fraught heart still in one piece?"

Tanner tried not to react, but a flash of concern set him back in his chair. "What?"

"Can I..." She sounded like she'd been sleeping with cotton in her mouth. "Can I have water?"

Water! Tanner grabbed the plastic pitcher at her bedside and poured a cup. "Here." She lifted a shaky hand and took the cup. There were a million things he wanted to ask her, tell her, but Dr. Layton wanted her to lead the conversation once she was awake.

Tanner tried to help her out. "What...what were you asking about?"

Jade's face filled with exhaustion as she raised her head several inches and took a sip. Her head fell back against the pillow, but when she looked at him, Tanner saw her eyes sparkling. "I'm guessing that your...o'er-fraught heart...is still in one piece."

"Because?"

"Because..." She grinned this time, and he could see a familiar teasing in her eyes. His heart soared as she continued. "I heard *everything* you said for the past two hours and...you, my dear attorney husband...have definitely given your sorrow words."

"Yes!" He shouted the word again and flew to his feet. She was back!

Only Jade, his Jade, would have used humor in a moment like this. Now there was nothing anyone could do to keep him quiet. "Thank You, God!" He raised his hands to heaven, staring through the ceiling at a God who was not only his Savior and Lord, but his deliverer. Because only a deliverer could have walked them through the valley of the shadow of death and brought them to this point.

He stared at Jade, wonder seeping into his every pore. "You're back. You're okay!" He wanted to swing her out of bed and into his arms, but he settled for leaning his upper body along hers, careful not to disturb the bandages on her head or put pressure on her. He wove his hands beneath her shoulders and hugged her close. "Thank God you're back. I was so afraid I'd lost you."

"How long have I been out?"

"Four days, Jade. Four of the longest days of my life." He drew back and searched her eyes. "We thought...Dr. Layton said we had to prepare for the worst."

"And the surgery...you said it went well."

There were questions in her eyes, and Tanner wanted to allay her fears before any more time passed. "Tests on the margins came back negative. There's no sign of cancer cells anywhere. They got it all, Jade."

"What about Maddie?" Jade's eyes were heavy again. "I missed you all so much, Tanner."

"Maddie's perfect. She's gaining weight. Her doctor said she might be able to go home in three weeks."

"I knew it." A look of peace filled Jade's face and her eyes closed for a moment. "God is so good."

"What do you remember about the surgery? Anything?"

Jade smiled. "Two things." She took another sip of water. "Your face." She moved her free hand up and traced his jawline with her forefinger. "And the strangest sensation."

Tanner studied her face. No matter how long he lived, he would never get enough of her. "What?"

"Right from the moment I went under I felt the Lord pick me up and hold me, like I was lying in Jesus' arms from then…until now. Isn't that something?"

Tears burned in the corners of Tanner's eyes. "Maybe that's what happens when people are praying for you around-the-clock."

"Maybe. I just know I felt it. As real as if you'd picked me up yourself." Her hand was trembling and she let it fall back beside her. "I'm tired, Tanner."

"I know."

"But before I sleep…I want to see Ty. He needs to know that I'm okay."

Tanner nodded. He didn't want to exhaust her on her first day, not with days of tough recovery ahead. His eyes fell to her hands and arms. The coma had atrophied what little muscle remained on her thin frame. Dr. Layton said she'd need another week of radiation, just as a precaution.

But the days would go by quickly…and very soon they would walk out of the hospital, a family again.

He was reaching for the phone to call Ty when it rang. Surprised, he hesitated a moment before answering it. "Hello?"

"How's she doing?"

It was Matt.

Tanner beamed, the joy of what had happened that past half hour still bursting in his heart. "I have her back! She came to thirty minutes ago." His tone was filled with disbelief. "Can you believe it, Matt? I have her *back.*"

"She knows you? Everything's the same?"

Tanner grinned at Jade. "She's as ornery as ever."

"Thank God…" Matt paused and coughed a few times. When he spoke again it was with tears in his voice. "Tell her we love her… We can't wait to see her." He uttered a single laugh, one that sounded like part cry. "Tell her it's going to be a miracle day for *both* of us."

Tanner lowered his brow. "Both of us?"

"Hi, Matt, it's Hannah on the other line."

"Hi." Jade was watching him, and he mouthed the fact that Hannah was on the phone also. "Okay, so our miracle is obvious. What's yours?" At this point Tanner figured anything was possible. After all, miracles had been sprouting like springtime tulips since Maddie was born.

Hannah did the talking. "We've been in conversation with Grace's grandmother these past few days. At first we weren't sure where it was headed, but yesterday afternoon our social worker called us. Grace's grandmother wants to give her back to us, Tanner. She wants to visit once a year, but that's all. She told us God had showed her it was the best thing for Grace." Hannah's voice broke. "She'll be here this afternoon."

"That's not all." Matt sounded happier than Tanner could ever remember, and the combination of his friend's joy with his own was enough to make his heart burst. "We found out that Grace's mother's rights have been permanently severed. Our Grace is free for adoption. We'll start the process Monday."

"That's wonderful. I never stopped thinking of her as your daughter."

"Jenny's beside herself." Hannah sounded like she was ready to burst. "She slept in Grace's bed last night, thanking God."

They talked a few more minutes before Tanner explained he had to go. They hadn't called Ty yet and needed to do that as soon as possible. When they were off the phone, he explained the situation to Jade.

She smiled, and for the first time since she'd come to, her eyes filled with tears. "Hannah loves that little girl so much." She shook her head, searching for the words. "What can I say? God is so good."

Tanner was about to dial the neighbor's house where Ty was staying when a thought occurred to him.

He glanced up at the Jade Chain still taped to the wall above the hospital bed. Then he checked his watch. Just after eight o'clock. He calculated back. That meant Jade had come out of her coma at 7:15.

Narrowing his eyes, he leaned closer to the prayer chart and used his finger to follow the list. "I wonder who was praying for us at—"

Jade rolled onto her side, craning her neck to see what Tanner saw. "What?"

Tanner could only stare at her, his mouth open. "People have been praying for you around the clock, right?"

"Right…" Jade looked confused.

Tanner studied the chart again and huffed. Chills ran down his arms and legs and he turned back to Jade. "Guess who was praying for you from seven to seven-thirty this morning? When you came out of the coma?"

"Who?"

Tanner checked the name once more and then leveled his gaze at Jade. "Ty Eastman."

Jade's eyes widened and she gasped. Before either of them

could say another word, the phone rang.

Tanner answered it on the first ring. "Hello?"

"Hi, Dad, it's Ty." He waited a beat. "Can I talk to Mom?"

"Wait a minute..." There was laughter in Tanner's voice, laughter and an unrestrained joy that hadn't been there for a very long time. "How did you know she was awake?"

"You mean she really is?" He hooted loud enough for Jade to hear. "I *knew* it!"

Tanner's head was spinning. "You knew what?"

"When everyone was signing up to pray for her, I got in line and signed up, too. 'Course I've been praying every day and stuff. But this morning when I was praying I felt like the Lord touched me on the shoulder. That ever happen to you, Dad?"

"Yeah...sure."

"For a minute it was like He was sitting beside me, and you know what He said?"

It took a while for Tanner to find his voice. The entire morning had been nothing less miraculous than the parting of the Red Sea. "What, buddy?"

"He told me Mom was awake and she was going to be fine."

"Is that right?" Tanner reached for Jade's hand and held it against his heart. "What else did He say?"

"He told me Mom was never in any danger."

"No?"

"No." Ty took a quick breath. "Because Jesus was holding her in His arms the whole time."

There was a knock at the door and Hannah's breath caught in her throat. "She's here." Her voice rang through the house. "Come on."

From different corners of the house, Matt and Jenny bounded into the foyer. Matt took a single step forward, grinned back at them and then opened the door.

There stood Edna Parsons and Patsy Landers, her eyes brimming with unshed tears. And beside her, the child whose face had haunted Hannah every day since she was taken from them.

Their precious little Grace.

"Mommy! Daddy! Jenny...I'm *home!*" She squealed, hands clasped, eyes shining. Then she ran into their arms and clung to the three of them. The locket on her neck bounced with every step. "I'm back. I'm back forever and ever!"

There were murmurings of welcome home and declarations of love between the four of them, and after a moment Hannah fell to her knees. There, with the rest of them gathered around, she held her youngest daughter close to her heart. *Tell me I'm not dreaming, God. Please...*

So often after losing Tom and Alicia she had longed for one more day, one more chance to hold them or talk to them or tell them she loved them. Then after losing Grace, she'd felt the same way, longing for the chance to somehow, somewhere see her again.

But she had never dreamed of this.

Jenny and Matt dropped to their knees, and the four of them formed a huddle. Hannah could only imagine the sacrifice it had taken for Patsy Landers to bring Grace back, to admit that this sweet child was better off living with strangers who loved her than in a home where her birth mother might one day harm her again.

From her place on the floor, Hannah locked eyes with Patsy Landers. Then silently, in a moment meant for the two of them alone, she muttered the only words she could think to say. "Thank you, Mrs. Landers. Thank you."

The older woman nodded, her cheeks wet, chin quivering. When she answered, it was loud enough for all of them to hear. "Grace is home now." She bit her lip to keep from crying. "She has a wonderful family and she has something else. Something she hasn't had since I took her from you."

The rest of them stood and faced Mrs. Landers, their arms around each other. Grace snuggled in the center, smiling from ear to ear.

Matt gazed at Grace, then back at her grandmother. "What's that?"

Mrs. Landers took Grace's hands, her wise, old eyes brimming with love and tears. "Her smile." She looked at each of them. "She has her smile back."

With that, Hannah's heart soared, despite her tears. They would never have to wonder about this little lost daughter, where she was living, how she was doing, who she was with.

Or whether she was still singing "Jesus Loves Me."

Grace was theirs for good now.

They were a family, without any missing pieces, whole and complete, back together as only God could have fixed them.

Thirty-two

The breeze from the Pacific Ocean was warmer than usual for April, and Jade was grateful. The sun warmed her face and filled her heart as she gazed at the blue sky. It was the only appropriate backdrop for the party that afternoon.

It had been six months since she woke from the coma, six months since little Grace had come home to be with the Bronzans forever. There was no place any of them wanted to be but there at the beach, together. The way they always wound up eventually.

Jade drew a cleansing breath and smiled at the scene below her on the beach. Matt and Tanner, tossing a Frisbee down on the shoreline. Not far from them, Jenny, Ty, and Grace worked diligently on a sand castle that already boasted turrets and tunnels and intricate shellwork.

She shifted her gaze to the stroller beside her. Inside, Maddie was sleeping, her face washed in peace. Jade touched her daughter's fingers and marveled at her tiny perfection. Maddie had come home the day before Thanksgiving, and though she was small, she'd thrived every day since.

The door opened behind her, and Jade turned. Hannah came out, Kody on her hip. He was eight months now, six weeks older than Maddie and twice her size. Hannah sat down, cradled Kody in her arms, and put a full bottle in his mouth. "Feeding time."

Jade laughed. "When isn't it?"

The sound of their families playing and laughing mingled with the pounding of the surf, and Hannah eased her head back. "I never get tired of the miracles around us these days."

"It's amazing." Jade turned toward Hannah. "Did I tell you about my doctor appointment?"

Hannah shook her head and grinned. "Good?"

"Better than good. They took pictures of my brain again, and there are no detectable signs a tumor was ever there."

"Oh, Jade…" Hannah's eyes danced. "That's wonderful."

"You know…" Jade shifted her gaze back to their families. "There was a time when I wondered what God was doing to us." She paused, breathing in the sweet, salty ocean air. "I mean, here we were, all of us, halfway to forever, and suddenly everything that could go wrong, did."

Hannah looked at Grace and nodded. "You're right."

"But you know what?"

Hannah adjusted Kody's bottle so she could see Jade better. "What?"

"I realized something that will stay with me forever, something I needed to learn."

There was a peaceful silence while Hannah waited.

"When I first became a Christian, the only truth God wanted me to know was that He loved me and had plans for me, good plans." Jade smiled. "That was enough back then." She paused and a seagull cried out in the distance. A familiar peace came over her. "Now I understand that even when life is going along perfectly, trouble will come. As long as we're breathing, it will come."

Hannah sighed, and her sad smile told Jade she understood. She, better than any woman Jade knew, understood how swiftly trouble could come. Hannah gazed at Jenny and Grace as they carried a bucket of water from the ocean to the castle. "It's so easy to take the good times for granted."

Jade nodded, feeling wiser than her years. "But we can't afford to, can we?"

"Never. Every day is a gift all by itself."

The afternoon slipped away in a blur of play and laughter, and after dinner they all gathered on the deck except the babies, who were asleep inside. Jade cozied up against Tanner, with Ty on her other side. There was a chill in the air, but the warmth of Tanner's body made it disappear.

Across from them, Matt moved his fingers over the strings of his guitar. "Tanner and I have a musical announcement to make."

Jade shifted and raised her eyebrows at her husband.

Next to Matt, Hannah grinned. "Sounds important."

Grace was sitting in Jenny's lap nearby, and both girls giggled at Hannah's tone. Jenny looked at Hannah. "This should be good."

"We—" Matt kept his face serious and nodded in Tanner's direction—"have decided to give up law for one year and hit the road."

"Hit the road?" Ty wrinkled his nose and stifled a laugh. "With what, a hammer?"

Tanner poked Ty in the ribs as he stifled a grin. "Come on now, we're serious. Let the man finish."

Matt tipped his head at Tanner. "Thank you." He winked at Ty and glanced at the group. "As I was saying, we feel the many evenings spent singing here, for all of you, have prepared us for a career as professional musicians." He looked at Tanner for support. "Isn't that right?"

Tanner gave a firm nod. "Absolutely."

Matt gave a formal plucking of his guitar strings. "On that note, we thought we'd share our opening song with you. The one that will—what can we say—" he cocked his head slightly and tossed his hands in the air—"bring down the house."

"Not while we're in it, okay?" Jade whispered the comment to Tanner but made sure it was loud enough for everyone to hear.

Giggles came from everyone but the men, and Jade brought

her hands to her face, trying to keep from laughing out loud. This was what she loved about the Bronzans. Not only were they the type of friends who stood by when troubles came—even terrifying trouble—they were friends who laughed and loved life.

Friends who made life fun.

There was a twinkle in Matt's eyes when he continued. "Fine." He shrugged in Tanner's direction. "Partner, it looks like the only way to silence our critics is to sing."

Tanner cleared his throat and leaned forward, his expression as serious as he could manage. "Hit it."

Matt began strumming the tune to the Eagles' "Desperado," and Hannah bit her lip to keep from laughing as she rolled her eyes at Jade. The music filled the deck, and Jade giggled in Hannah's direction.

Four times the guys forgot the words, and three times Tanner was noticeably off-key. Jade listened, covering her mouth whenever she was tempted to laugh.

When it was over there was silence. Jade looked around and saw Hannah run her tongue along the inside of her lip.

"So…" Hannah used her hands to show she was doing her best to understand. "Your act will be sort of an offbeat, off-tune, missing-word impression of the Eagles? For all the hip concertgoers craving that type of music, is that it?"

Matt grinned and pretended to hit her with the backside of his guitar. "I told you, Tanner…"

"You did." Tanner lifted one shoulder.

"True artists get no respect."

Jenny laughed out loud, and the sound snapped what remained of Jade and Hannah's restraint. Soon even Matt and Tanner joined in, and when the laughter died down, Tanner leaned closer to Jade once more. "Fine. We'll keep our day jobs."

"I was going to say…" Hannah bit her lip. "Good thing."

Matt shook his head in mock disdain. "If we're not ready for the road, at least we can take requests." He tapped Grace's knee. "Okay, sweetheart, what do you want me to sing?"

Grace lowered her chin, and batted her eyelashes at Matt. "'Old McDommer's Farm,' Daddy. Pleeeease!"

Jade's heart swelled as she watched the scene. Grace had come so far since her return to the Bronzans' home. Patsy Landers had been out for a visit already, and there was even talk of her moving to California to be closer to Grace. But never, no matter what, would she ever tell her troubled daughter about Grace's whereabouts.

It was part of the deal they'd made six months earlier.

Matt made a sweeping bow at Grace. "Your wish is my command."

Hannah chuckled and leaned into the circle, pretending to share private information with the rest of them. "That's for sure…"

"'Old McDonald' it is!" The melody sprang from Matt's guitar as he worked his fingers over the strings.

When they were done, they did "Jesus Loves Me" for Grace's second request, and a silly camp song for Ty. When the children were finished making requests, Matt angled his head toward Jade, his eyes more serious than before.

"Okay, Jade, you're the reason we're all celebrating." He gave her a gentle, knowing smile. "How about you?"

Tanner took her hand, and she leaned her head back, staring at the starry sky and trying to imagine what song summed up the wealth of love and hope and joy in her heart.

Then she knew exactly what she wanted to sing "I've got it." She grinned at Matt. "'Great is Thy Faithfulness.'"

"Ahhh." Hannah nestled closer to Matt and gazed at him for a long moment. "Our favorite song."

The air between them filled with a sense of quiet holiness as

Matt began to play. The music mixed with the sound of the distant surf and Jade closed her eyes as they started to sing.

"'Great is Thy faithfulness, O God my Father; there is no shadow of turning with Thee.'" Their voices joined together, and Jade savored the sound, every word a prayer to heaven. To think she'd believed her cancer a punishment from that same faithful God seemed almost ludicrous now.

She'd learned that, too, these past months.

A smile filled Jade's face as the song built. "'Thou changest not, Thy compassions, they fail not; as Thou hast been, Thou forever will be.'"

Jade opened her eyes and looked at the people around her, people who, just six months ago, she thought she might never see again. Hannah, whose passions were so like her own, but who had been more like a sister these past months; Matt, who had helped Tanner be strong when he had no strength of his own; Jenny, whose sweet heart had been broken far too many times, but who now seemed happier than she had in years; and Grace and Kody and Maddie, who would be a part of all of them forever.

The song played on and Jade shifted her gaze to Ty on her left side, strong in character and handsome like his father, but still so much a boy. He grinned at her and she hugged him.

Then she turned to Tanner. Their eyes met and held, the words to the song dancing on both their lips. She studied the shape of his chin, his jaw, and cheekbones. Everything about him was written on her heart, and she realized that she could read his thoughts more easily since the cancer. Although there were no words spoken between them, his voice played in her heart, telling her he had never been happier, that he needed her more than air.

She leaned into him again, and turned her attention once more to Matt.

He was starting the third verse, one that Jade was not familiar with. Only Matt and Hannah knew this part of the song, and Jade listened, hanging on every word.

"'Pardon for sin and a peace that endureth, Thine own dear presence to cheer and to guide; strength for today and bright hope for tomorrow, blessings all mine, with ten thousand beside!'"

Jade could hardly believe it.

Every word was as though Jade had written it herself. It was the story of her life. God had pardoned her sin and brought her peace. He'd cheered her on through the darkest days of her life and given her an inhuman strength to carry on. She thought of her verse from Jeremiah, about the plans God had for her. There was no question that her tomorrows were filled with hope.

Hope brighter than the sun.

Gratitude flooded her heart to overflowing. Ten thousand blessings, indeed! All of them had so much to be thankful for. Suddenly Jade had a vision of their two families gathered together this way, singing this song, ten years from now…twenty. Thirty.

Tears filled her eyes as one final time they joined their voices for the chorus.

"'Great is thy faithfulness! Great is thy faithfulness! Morning by morning new mercies I see. All I have needed Thy hand hath provided; great is Thy faithfulness, Lord, unto me!'"

Dear Reader Friends,

First, I must share with you how hard it was to let go of the characters in this book. Matt and Hannah and Jade and Tanner have become like close friends, and as I neared the end of *Halfway to Forever* the impending good-bye was almost painful. Of course, my husband thinks I'm delusional. Crying over stories I made up, missing people that don't exist. He says I'll make an interesting old woman one day, when I start wondering why it's been so long since Jade and Tanner have visited.

But for now he humors me.

Halfway to Forever has been close to my heart for a long time. I got the idea for the book on a cross-country flight, thirty thousand feet closer to heaven—the source of all my ideas. Thoughts began to come, and before long I was jotting down plotlines as quickly as I could write. Within an hour I was dabbing at tears. It was the first time I've ever cried when outlining a book.

The thing that struck me most about *Halfway to Forever* was the truth that trouble comes…even for us who believe. I've heard it said that we are either leaving a crisis, entering one, or smack in the middle of one.

It's true, isn't it?

The tragedy of September 11 told us as much. We can make our plans and determine our paths but only to a small degree. So much of life is out of our control. Disease comes, jobs go, children move away. Plans dissolve with a single phone call or newsflash. What seemed so strong and certain today can be reduced to nothing but ash tomorrow. We know that; we've seen it happen. Not just on television and in New York City or Washington, D.C., but in our own lives as well. We all have "twin towers" we hold dear, things or people that seem indestructible until one fateful moment.

The good news is no matter what happens, there is One who

ultimately is in control. He has promised us that if we love Him, He will work all things out for good. All things. Think about that for a minute.

Of course, that doesn't mean every burning building or flash of fear on the landscape of your life will turn out the way you'd hoped. That's not how God works. Rather, He sees the bigger picture. We have the comfort, the peace, of knowing that we can rest in His hands because He will take care of everything. Whatever the trouble is.

As many of you know, my husband and I have six children—three by birth, three from Haiti by means of adoption. When we're taking a long road trip, we often hear multiple voices asking,

"Are we almost there?"

"Where are we going?"

"Why don't we stop here?"

"How come we didn't take that road?"

"I'm tired of this trip."

We try to answer the questions patiently, but the bottom line is we *know* where we're going. We wouldn't take the trip if we didn't think it was going to be good for all of us in some way. Still, children often don't understand and so they question.

Aren't we the same way with God?

There is much we want to know about our journey through life, and God tries to meet our needs by way of His Word and others in the body of Christ who comfort us. But sometimes there are no answers except one: He is God.

He is in control; He will lead us safely home in His timing.

The other day we took our four-year-old to his first professional basketball game. This is the same blonde, blue-eyed boy who tells people his name is Michael Jordan; the boy who plays basketball two hours every day—rain or shine—and can't get enough of the round, leather ball. We thought he'd be thrilled about going to a Portland Trail Blazers game. The problem was he had to leave a birthday party early to go. His sad little pout made for a quiet ride to the stadium.

It wasn't until we got to the game and took our seats that everything changed. His eyes grew wide as saucers, and he sat on the edge of his seat throughout the entire contest, cheering and shouting and raising his chubby fist in the air. It was the time of his life.

The analogy was striking for my husband and me.

In the here and now, we are having fun at the birthday party, but ultimately God wants to take us somewhere else, to a heavenly place where we'll have the time of our lives. The wonderful place where young Brandy Almond went in *Halfway to Forever.*

Yes, we will question. But only God holds the answers, and many of them won't be clear until we get to the Big Game.

While writing *Halfway to Forever,* I was reminded of the Israelites wandering in the desert for forty years. God's provision for them was daily. He never gave them more than enough to get through one, single day. That's how it was for the Bronzans and Eastmans. Yes, there was crisis. Yes, troubles came. But God provided enough grace and strength for each sunup, one day at a time. At first their situations felt overwhelming, as though God had abandoned them.

But that is never the case, is it? Not for these characters, and not for us in real life. If there was anything Hannah and Matt learned, it was that through the darkest night, morning would always come. If there was anything Jade and Tanner learned, it was that God's plans were always good, no matter how they seemed at first.

Just like our son's trip to the Blazers game.

I pray that in journeying with me through the pages of *Halfway to Forever,* you've been reminded of these truths as well.

No matter what, God is in control. He loves you and He'll never let you go.

On a personal note, our family is adjusting beautifully to the adoption of our three new little boys. Sean, EJ, and Joshua are in first grade, learning to read, and loving American sports, American customs, and most of all American food. They pray often and know the One from whom our blessings come. All the terrifying possibilities we imagined and sometimes entertained in the days leading up to their adoption never materialized. Not one.

Our children love each other and are living testimonies to the power of prayer. Our prayer and yours. Thank you for being a part of the miracle of their lives. Your continued prayers are so appreciated.

Until we're together again, I pray God will bless you and yours and leave you with a deeper understanding of his Holy provision.

Day by day by day.

As always, I'd love to hear from you. You can reach me through my Web site at www.karenkingsbury.com or at my e-mail address, rtnbykk@aol.com.

Love and grace in Christ,

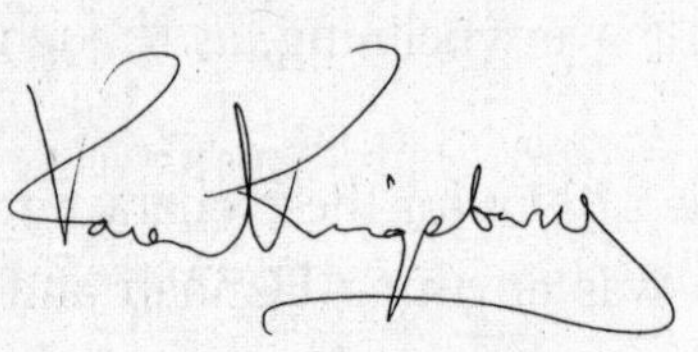

Readers Guide

1. The strength of Jade and Tanner, Matt and Hannah, was their friendship. Why is friendship important to us all? How is it specifically important to you?
2. Explain how friendship is a tool God uses to bring us closer to Him.
3. We meet up with these characters during a season in their lives when they are all undergoing hardship. Explain those hardships and how they are different from each other.
4. Are you more like Jade, Tanner, Matt, or Hannah when it comes to handling the troubles life sometimes brings? How so?
5. Think of a time when you and a friend shared a difficult season. Describe that time and tell how friendship made a difference.
6. Sometimes when we come against hard times, we're tempted to compromise. Discuss the compromise Tanner considered when Jade's brain tumor was threatening her life. What was his final choice, and why?
7. How did Tanner's determination to stay the course contribute to the way this story played out?

8. In *Halfway to Forever,* Matt was torn between two struggles. Have you ever felt caught up in a fight for your faith? If so, discuss that time and what you learned from it.
9. Jenny goes through a transformation in this book. Explain that, and share about a time when God allowed circumstances to transform you.
10. Describe the miracle that occurs with Hannah toward the end of this book. Name a time when God worked a miracle in your life. How are the situations similar?

Other Novels by Karen Kingsbury

Where Yesterday Lives
978-1-59052-753-5
In the wake of her father's sudden death, Ellen Barrett must journey back to the small town where she grew up and spend a week with antagonistic siblings. In the process, she must reckon with a man who once meant everything to her.

When Joy Came to Stay
978-1-59052-751-1
Maggie Stovall is trapped inside a person she's spent years carefully crafting. Now the truth about who she is—and what she's done—is revealed, sending Maggie into a spiral of despair. Will Maggie walk away from her marriage and her foster child in her desperation to escape the mantle of depression cloaking her? Or will she allow God to take her to a place of ultimate honesty before it's too late?

On Every Side
978-1-59052-752-8
Jordan Riley, an embittered lawyer, sues his hometown to have a public statue of Jesus removed. The conflict causes him to cross paths with a spirited young newscaster named Faith, who opposes Jordan's suit in surprising ways. Perhaps most amazing of all is how Faith begins to disassemble the walls around Jordan's heart. Will love be enough when the battle rages on every side?

Visit www.WaterBrookMultnomah.com for chapter excerpts and more!

What People Are Saying about

KAREN KINGSBURY Fiction...

"Karen Kingsbury has been such a godsend. Her books have brought me to God and have motivated my husband and me to remarry after a bad divorce. After not being able to have kids, we now have an adopted boy and are trying to adopt another. Your books show faith, love, and tenderness, and I love them."

—KATHY, Rancho Santa Margarita, CA

"Karen Kingsbury's fiction has changed my life by reminding me that there is hope amid seemingly hopeless circumstances and that faith in God's redemptive plan is the anchor I can hold on to when life's compasses fail."—AMY, Lawrenceville, GA

"Karen Kingsbury is our book club's favorite author. We often discuss how each of her books not only entertains us, but inspires us to live out our faith in a real, everyday, every-moment way. Thanks for your stories, which challenge us to be better disciples of our precious Lord Jesus."—LYNDA, Covington, WA

"Karen Kingsbury's books have touched my life in many different ways, but *Where Yesterday Lives* really helped me in the death of my father-in-law... Thank you for the great stories."—CHRIS, Zeeland, MI

"I have read every book Karen Kingsbury has written. Each book has brought me to a place of repentance and helped me to forgive myself for things I've confessed to no one but God. Her books have given me hope for the future, the assurance of forgiveness, and the strength to look forward to what the Lord would have me do and that I can accomplish it in His strength! Thank you."—KAREN, Campbell, CA

"The Lord prompted me to find a Christian author I enjoyed, and I found Karen Kingsbury. I have struggled with depression to a certain degree all my life, but when I read her book, I was at the bottom. This was the beginning of a wonderful journey to recovery for me."—DANNELL, Brawley, CA

"A dear friend handed me *A Time to Dance,* and it was the beginning of some much needed deep healing in my marriage. Just knowing that others could walk through muddy waters and make it through to the other side gave me hope and a sense of relief that maybe, just maybe, I too could be okay again. Thank you, Karen Kingsbury!"—JO ANN, Dickinson, ND

"Karen Kingsbury's work always reminds me of God's grace in my own life, especially the times I really didn't deserve it! After each book, my faith is stronger, and I can't wait for the next book to come out!"—NANCY, Salem, IL

"I just love all of Karen Kingsbury's books. Every one has touched me in a very deep way, relating to one or another 'storm' I have gone through and yet giving me hope that God is always there, carrying us when we don't care anymore whether we live or die. I have been to that place, and God did lift me up from the depths of sorrow and pain! Thank you so much!"—HENRIETTA, British Columbia, Canada

"Karen Kingsbury's books never cease to amaze me. When I finish reading one, I not only feel connected to the characters and the events; I feel that I have walked in the presence of Christ and that He has spoken mightily to me. I always cry when I finish one of her books...tears to say good-bye to the friends I've come to know and love and tears of thankfulness to my heavenly Father. I can't wait to read the next one!"—LINDA, Batavia, IL

"My grandmother has been diagnosed with dementia... Right after her diagnosis, she asked me to bring her some books. I took her everything I own by Karen Kingsbury, which is about ten books. She devoured them! They encouraged her and gave her hope."—DONNA I.

"A friend recommended *A Moment of Weakness*. I gave it to my teenage daughter at the time and she read it as well. It opened up a chance to discuss remaining pure until marriage. She is now twenty-two and married a few months ago as a virgin. We had many other discussions, but your book hit home where my lecturing may not have. God has given you a very special talent, and I am sure He is smiling at your use of it. Thank you!"—KATHY, Livonia, NY

"Karen Kingsbury's novels have not just touched my heart but also my soul. When things go topsy-turvy in my daily life (as with four children they sometimes do), I often think of the Scriptures I've read in your books. Your books have not only kept me up at night anxiously waiting for what is going to happen next, but more important, they have helped me in my walk with the Lord."—STEPHANIE H.

"As a biblical counselor, I have used several of Karen Kingsbury's books to reach the hearts of many of my clients. They have been most helpful in this respect, but I also admire Karen's courage in speaking out on tough issues within our Christian culture."—SANDY K.

"The greatest impact Karen Kingsbury's works have had on my life was to help me with forgiveness. Not just to say the words, for that's what's expected of me, but to actually feel it in my heart... I marvel at how God has used you to work in my life and the lives of countless others."—HARRIETTE, Durham, NC

"I've read several of Karen Kingsbury's books, and after finishing them, I was challenged about the depth of my surrender to whatever the Lord allows in my life. Thank you for taking me to another deep place with my Father."—PAULA M.

"From Karen Kingsbury's very first book to her most recent, she has inspired me to be a better person, have a stronger faith in God, and to question how I am raising my family in a world filled with hate and evil."—PATTIE, Oceanside, CA

"When I went off to college, I fell into a dark depression but convinced myself that Christians not only don't suffer depression, but that it is inherently un-Christian to be depressed... I bought *When Joy Came to Stay* and read it in one sitting... I was able to receive treatment for my illness and work on dealing with events and behaviors that led to this depression. The book made it easier for me to see that God can use even dark times to bless us and help us grow."—DEIDRE E.

"Karen Kingsbury's fiction has helped me with my family problems. Karen's books have taught me how to stick together with my family through thick and thin. They have taught me that even when your family may be having a tough time, never give up."—ASHLEIGH, Fairfield, CA

"I can't tell you how much Karen Kingsbury's books have blessed my life. The novels make me think seriously about what commitment means, sticking it out even when all seems gloomy, and understanding the covenant of marriage."

—NATA, Nigeria

"Karen Kingsbury's fiction is so easy to identify with. These books have been a source of refuge in my emotional struggles after going through marital difficulty and divorce. It helps to know that someone understands what people like me go through!"—MELISSA, Bethel Springs, TN

KAREN KINGSBURY

AND PRISM COFOUNDER TONI VOGT

THE PRISM WEIGHT LOSS PROGRAM

The PRISM® Weight Loss Program, founded in 1990, has helped more than 60,000 people transform their eating behaviors with a sensible, lifestyle-change approach. Now available in The Prism Weight Loss Program by bestselling author Karen Kingsbury and PRISM cofounder Toni Vogt, the book shows readers how to not just "tame the monster" of food addiction, but destroy it through simple eating strategies and biblical principles. It includes testimonials, descriptions of the authors' personal struggles with food addiction, details of the program, and a fabulous recipe section that will help readers become the fit people God created them to be.

ISBN 978-1-59052-846-4